I0660515

THE
PHILIP
JOSÉ
FARMER
CENTENNIAL
COLLECTION

THE PHILIP JOSÉ FARMER CENTENNIAL COLLECTION

Edited by Michael Croteau

Introduction by Joe R. Lansdale

Foreword by Tracy Knight

Meteor House

The Philip José Farmer Centennial Collection

Edited by Michael Croteau

Meteor House and the editor would like to give special thanks to Danny Adams, Christopher Paul Carey, Win Scott Eckert, Keith Howell, Tracy Knight, Joe R. Lansdale, Zacharias L.A. Nuninga, Paul Spiteri, Howard Waldrop, and Mark Wheatley for their invaluable contributions to this collection.

Meteor House

ISBN 978-1-945427-11-4
First Trade Paperback Edition

Dedicated in loving memory to Bette Farmer. As Phil wrote many times, she was the driving force in their family, the dedicated woman behind the successful man. She urged him to go back to college, supported him, and encouraged him to write. If not for her, much of this book—perhaps all of it—would not exist.

Table of Contents

Introduction

Joe R. Lansdale

Philip José Farmer is my favorite science fiction writer, but to brand him with that moniker would eliminate so many things that he wrote that weren't truly science fiction. Still, in Phil's case, I think calling him a science fiction writer, and seeing him as one of its true geniuses, is not altogether incorrect. He worked best with those tools.

His mind practically crackled with energy. He could generate more unique notions in one page than most writers could in a series of novels written over a lifetime. He once told me that the only way to write was to climb out on a literary limb and saw it off, and sometimes with you sitting on the wrong end of the limb. That's a lesson any good writer should learn. Even an interesting failure is better than a bland success.

When he was growing up, Phil read Edgar Rice Burroughs, and his fiction, his inventiveness, excited him and made him want to write, and the influence he had on Phil never went away.

Phil loved Burroughs, but as he grew older, he began to think of how one might look at Burroughs' work with an adult's view-point, because over time Burroughs' work aged, creaked, and even embarrassed, something I think is dynamically obvious these days.

Phil spun off Burroughs' ideas and inventiveness, and eventually jumped way out beyond adventure fiction, and into psychology and sociology, and the examination of myth without becoming mired in navel gazing. Burroughs was in many ways a Farmer springboard, as were the pulps. Phil could do pulp with the best of them, but he was at his personal best when he disassembled it, looked beyond its shiny parts, and down into the steamy, sexual, violent engine of the machine.

Part of what made Phil so good, besides his brilliant mind, was the fact that he was not only well read in science fiction, and all its classics, he was well read in literary fiction and its classics. Everything from Jack London to Dostoevsky to Henry Miller to Hemingway to Jack Kerouac to William Burroughs, not to mention pretty much everything in between and lurking on the outskirts of that fictitious village. He disassembled all of that as well, and during that dissection, he let the hot creative oil of those arts bleed into the oil of the pulp creations he had dissected.

The combination was brilliant.

That's why this book is so important, and why Phil should become a household name, in the manner Philip K. Dick has, though they are considerably different sorts of writers.

But they both transcended the markets they sold to. One line I remember from Phil, and I paraphrase, but he said he was so busy being a science fiction writer that he didn't always have time to be a writer. Meaning, as it was with Philip K. Dick, he had to turn out so much material merely to keep his head above water, he didn't always have the time to explore ideas the way he might have wanted to.

This book will let you see what he was like when he was exploring. There is fiction and non-fiction, some speeches he gave. But the only thing that really matters, is all of it was written by Philip José Farmer, and he wrote to set his brain and yours on fire.

Foreword

Tracy Knight

In early 2008, shortly before Philip José Farmer's 90th birthday, I sent him a note that included a few quotes I thought he would enjoy and/or relate to. The first was from William James: "Common sense and a sense of humor are the same thing, moving at different speeds. A sense of humor is just common sense, dancing." Throughout his life and his writing, Phil demonstrated that principle in spades, a clear-eyed, jubilant rhumba throughout his earthly years, in both his writing and his life, and you'll find his complexity and his joy in full display between the covers of this impressive collection.

Although he possessed a supreme intellect—always eager to discuss a staggering range of topics from philosophy to anthropology to theology to name-your-favorite-ology—Phil never lost his ability to perceive the sheer basics of existence with an empathic eye, prodding our human foibles, appreciating the absurdity of the universe we share. Even when writing his most serious works, one can always sense a wry smile and knowing nod regarding the characters into which he breathed life and the worlds they struggled to navigate. Through this empathy, Phil was able to truly value virtually all of his fellow humans, being equally gratified by Richard Francis Burton, Jesus, and Moe Howard.

The second quote I shared with Phil was written by Rumi: "Sell your cleverness and buy bewilderment." Phil possessed and shared an omnivorous mind that went far beyond intellect; his senses of wonder and curiosity were as acute as any I've witnessed, and propelled his fiction into remarkable realms as he roamed the implications of new imaginings, caressing their textures, exploring their dimensions, combing for distinctive angles and fresh perspectives. Even more impressive to me is that in Phil's best works, the reader can directly detect and experience Phil's wonder as the stories unfolded before his eyes. Often, his tales were not the product of precise, mechanical design and outline; they were active excursions into Phil's search for meaning and patterns. They were, and are, alive.

Indeed, the serene yet powerful way that Phil approached living was emblematic of the last quote I offered on his 90th birthday, the observation by James Bugental: "We hold our life in our hands and we jump into the dark." If one appreciates the contours of Phil's life and his writing, one recognizes how frequently he exhibited the noble and quiet courage Bugental suggests.

As a human specimen, Phil was among the most splendid mélange of traits I've encountered, including the desirable ability to playfully find the potential for humor in any situation. One day near his 90th birthday, I picked Bette up to go visit Phil, who had been hospitalized. When we arrived, Phil was receiving occupational therapy, sitting in a chair and performing repetitive arm exercises with some of the equipment. After acknowledging us, Phil grumbled quietly about being imprisoned in this boring activity. Bette said, "Phil, get serious and just do it! My goodness, look at that man over there!" She gestured toward a gentleman across the room who was holding tightly to parallel bars, being assisted by an aide as he walked on his new prosthetic leg. Phil looked at me and shrugged. "There's always a show-off," he said.

Now, ten years later, I continue to physically feel Phil's absence, as do his many friends and admirers. We miss Phil not only for his presence, his complexity and intelligence, but perhaps even more so for his common sense, dancing. Yes. And now, through this collection, we are once again able to experience his dance, his journey, his grand adventure.

And ours.

The 1940s

Philip José Farmer was born January 26th, 1918, in Terre Haute Indiana. In 1923 his family moved to Peoria, Illinois, where he would spend most of his life. When he was only six years old, playing outside one day, he looked up and saw a silvery dirigible flying west. This was the moment he became interested in lighter-than-air craft, something he would incorporate into his writing many times over his career.

As a young man he read everything, from mythologies to the classics to pulps, his favorites being Baum, Burroughs, Doyle, Carroll, Cervantes, Chesterton, Cooper, Defoe, Dickens, Dumas, Haggard, Homer, London, Shaw, Stevenson, Swift, Thackeray, Twain, Verne, and Wells. He was also very athletic, earning the nickname "Tarzan" for his tree climbing abilities.

When Phil was in the fifth grade, his classmates wrote letters to the Peoria County Tuberculosis Association about their Christmas Seal program and their fight against TB. A ten-year-old Phil however, wrote a short story, which they published in their "Open Air Crusader" newsletter:

Christmas Seal's Fight
Crash, bang, "I got you in the ribs. Ho, ho," laughed Mr. Christmas Seal.

"Ouch," yelled Mr. Germ. "Just wait until I stick you."

Mr. Christmas Seal and Mr. Germ were fighting for their lives. Mr. Seal was trying to put Mr. T. B. germ in jail, as he had been making children sick. He was the leader of a notorious gang of germs who are responsible for so much unhappiness among the children. Mr. T. B. greatly resented Mr. Seal's interference, and so they had come to blows.

Just as Mr. Seal was about to win the battle, a number of T. B.'s gang appeared, and they all jumped on Mr. Seal. Mr. Seal had barely time to blow his whistle, and call Mr. Milk, Mr. Vegetable, Mr. Fresh Air, and Mr. Sunshine. They pressed around the germs, and soon killed them.

—Philip Farmer, Grade 5, Columbia School

A gifted student athlete who ran track and played football, Phil graduated from Peoria Central High School in 1936, and was one of only five lettermen elected to the National Senior Honor Society. In the fall he entered the University of Missouri to study Journalism, but in the first of many professional setbacks, he had to drop out after his freshman year. His father had invested money in a business that failed. Phil worked on a line crew for Illinois Power and Light from July 1937 through February 1939 to help his father repay his debts, and to save money so he could return to college.

When he did return to college, he transferred to Bradley Polytechnical Institute in Peoria, and switched his major to English Literature with a minor in Philosophy. He even won a creative writing scholarship, but when he discovered that being on the football and track teams had something to do with his winning, he quit the football team.

Conductor Fred Waring had a popular radio show at this time and was hired to write the fight song for the Bradley Braves. Because of his Cherokee blood, Phil was chosen to fly to New York

Picture from the *Bradley Tech* of Phil presenting Fred Waring
with a headdress in New York, October 1940.

as an ambassador of the school and present Mr. Waring with a headdress. Phil's account of this trip, "Bradley Brave Sees New York,"
was published in *The Bradley Tech* school paper.

While attending Bradley, Phil met Elizabeth Virginia Andre,
a musical scholarship student, and his future wife. They were
secretly wed in May 1941. That summer, Phil joined the Army
Air Force, and while in preflight school at Kelly Field in Texas,
Japan attacked Pearl Harbor. However, Phil, an erratic pilot,
washed out of flight training and asked to be discharged. They
returned to Peoria and he took a job with the Keystone Steel &
Wire Company. It was only supposed to be temporary, but he
stayed there eleven-and-a-half years. During this time, they had a
son, Philip, and a daughter, Kristan. And Phil began writing.

He would eventually use his experiences at Keystone in two
works, the mainstream novel *Fire and the Night* and the short story,
"Keep Your Mouth Shut," in *Farmerphile* #6, October 2006.

19

He also made his first professional sale. "O'Brien and Obrenov" was accepted by the *Saturday Evening Post*, on the condition that he cut out a drunken scene that he felt was too important to the story. He decided not to make the cut and the story was sold to the lower-paying *Adventure* magazine, appearing in the March 1946 issue.

Phil finished the 1940s working full time, attending college part time, and writing when he could. He also published two poems, "Good But Not Good Enough" in the *Bradley Quarterly*, and "Imagination" in *American Sings an Anthology of College Poetry*.

Bradley Brave Sees New York

Highlights of my trip to New York: Being forced down by the increasing fog at the Holy Name Aeronautical School and having to hire a student there to drive me to the Metropolitan Airport, about twenty miles away . . . the blue light in the stewardess' eyes, and her smile, too ravishing to let one completely relax . . . watching the popeyes of the passengers as they saw the huge Stratoliner whiz by at 284 m.p.h. gait as if we were anchored to a cloud . . . And, climax of climaxes, dancing out upon the stage, uttering warwhoops and chasing Chief Waring around the stage . . . Anti-climax was having my turkey-gooble crack in the middle of a note and climb far above high C . . . very embarrassing . . .

Waring Looks Older

Big Chief Waring is a brave Bradley should be very proud of having initiated into its ranks . . . His physical appearance is too well known to enlarge upon, except I might say that his greying hair and somewhat tired eyes belie the youthful look he has in the photos the public usually sees. However, this maturity gives him a dignity that becomes him on the stage and off. During the 35 minute show after the radio broadcast, he plays the dignified leader of a bunch of monkeys. While he is attempting to make some announcement to the audience, his band's antics keep everybody frantic. An intentional and mental uproar rock the theater every second.

Offstage he is very gracious, anxious to please, and rather quiet. Rehearsal just before the broadcast was going none too good, but Waring refrained from ranting. His gentle but firm handling of his men (and women) showed none of the temperament that one might expect from a great band leader.

His wit is neither the belittling kind nor the straining-after-laughter sort. While I was presenting the headdress, he did make some remark about my knees shaking, which was too, too true. But his very observance of the fact steadied the clicking bones. He could not attend the banquet given by the New York Alumni after the show, but his public relations man, Mr. Stromberg, was pleased to come. Waring, of course, had to relax between broadcasts. He did so by playing ping-pong.

None Smoked

Important observations: Donna Day, Waring's blonde songstress, is a dream. She has to be touched to be believed . . . neither Waring nor Mr. Hatch, the alumni president nor myself smoke, yet all three took a stab at smoking the peace pipe. Our efforts almost resulting in strangling. Incidentally, the peace pipe was taken from the walls of the Wigwam . . . New York is a wonderful place, out after eight hours of steady walking, one begins to wonder it, after all, it is the proper place for a new pair of shoes . . . my neck still aches, but only part of the soreness came from looking up at the tall buildings. One can come awfully close to unsocketing one's neck if one wishes to watch the American Airline's stewardess walk up and down the aisle. And this one did . . . A walk up and down Broadway and through Central Park convinces one that New York City is 80 percent non-Aryan—a sort of Hitler's nightmare.

Manhattan, a treasure of towers in day and an explosion of neon at night, the greatest city in the world, is a tribute to our jewish population. They are shaping mankind's greatest works there; Hitler is raping all that they and civilization are doing to lift mankind up . . . Please excuse this digression, but one's thoughts can't be helped . . . Bob Armstrong, Waring's publicity relations man and Dave Owen once worked together in Wisconsin in their younger days . . . Brainard Hatch deserves the thanks of Bradley for his unceasing efforts to carry out the eastern end of the deal . . . And the livewire campaign of Dave's cannot be appreciated enough. Both Stromberg and Waring felt that Bradley had a real gem in its possession of Dave . . . Nor must the student body be forgotten. When all's said and done, it was their wampum that sent me to New York . . . I wish to thank them all and to state they should all be proud of having put over a great stunt.

O'BRIEN AND OBRENOV

Colonel O'Brien, of the Umpteenth Infantry Regiment, was about to step into a tub. There was a reason for this—the colonel stank. But the goatish odor was about to be washed away and replaced by the colonel's normal stench, one of soap and cologne. Remembering it was his first bath in eight weeks, he shivered with ecstasy and stuck a testing toe in the hot water.

The tub had once belonged to Herr Gruenz, ex-mayor of the town of Mautz. Herr Gruenz must have been fond of his enormous tub, modeled after Goering's famous one. It was while floating in warm water and black market soap suds that the mayor had decided to slash open his wrist-veins and die as pleasant a death as was possible under the circumstances. His decision was hastened by the news that the Americans from the west and the Russians from the east would soon meet in his town. He had reasons to believe it would be better to take a chance on his reception in the next world than to wait for a certain one in this.

In fact, the mayor's oyster-like lips had no sooner blubbered out his last breath than Colonel O'Brien skidded his jeep to a halt before the house, jumped out, kicked open the door, and strode in. The colonel was looking not so much for the mayor as he was for his famous bath-tub. He found both. It was an indication of his stubbornness that, having sworn to bathe in Herr Gruenz's tub, he wasn't balked by the mess that greeted him.

He ordered the ex-mayor to be buried in Potter's Field and the tub cleaned. The scouring of the tub was done by two of Herr Gruenz's cronies. They protested. The MP guarding them pulled out his pistol and remarked it was getting rusty from disuse. They got the idea, and began cleaning vigorously.

Glowing with happiness at the thought of the coming bath, O'Brien then drove to the town square where he met Colonel Obrenov of the Russian forces that were occupying the eastern half of Mautz. They talked under the shadow of the famed "Spirit of German Wrath" statue. It was a bronze figure of Goethe, dating from the last century, that had been set up by the burgomasters of Mautz to commemorate the fact he'd once lived here—perhaps a week or two. With the Nazis' rise, Goethe's stock had gone down. They couldn't stand that great artist's internationalism and broad-mindedness. An order was issued to tear down the statue, but the penny-pinching citizens of Mautz had what they thought was a brilliant idea. The bronze plate on which was inscribed the dates of Goethe's brief stay at Mautz had been ripped off and a new plaque titled "Spirit of German Wrath" had been installed at the pedestal's base.

More important, the iron pen in Goethe's right hand was removed to make place for a gigantic sword. The result was disconcerting. The cumbersome sword, besides being almost as long as the statue itself, that is, eight feet, was held in an unnatural position. Its edge was hard against the great man's face. Anybody but the fat-brained citizens of Mautz and Germany could have seen that the "Spirit" was engaged in a struggle, not to ward off the Reich's enemies, but to keep from cutting off its own nose.

The deep-graven lines of his forehead and mouth, once intended to portray the agonies of his soul while writing *Faust*, were now supposed to portray a bloodlust in battle. Nobody but an Aryan's Aryan would have thought so, or been able to overlook the fact that the former Goethe's eyes, instead of staring ahead at his foes, were cross-eyed, looking at the hand that once had held a pen.

The reconverted statue was grotesque enough to cause comment even from two men as ignorant of art as the Colonels

O'Brien and Obrenov. What fixed the statue in O'Brien's mind, however, was the discussion he'd had with the Russian about removing it.

Shortly before the two armies had met in Mautz, the mayor, under pressure from the Nazi bigwigs, had ordered the statue pulled down as a contribution to the latest scrap drive. Halfway through its uprooting, the laborers, alarmed at the closeness of the Allies, had abandoned their work. The "Spirit of German Wrath" was left leaning forward to the south at a 110-degree angle.

The colonels agreed it was a public menace. O'Brien suggested his men pull it down, but Obrenov demurred; he wanted his soldiers to haul it away. The "Spirit" was a symbol; he liked knocking down Germans, whether they were actual or symbolic.

Finally it was agreed that both sides would pull it down at some future time.

After the colonels had drawn a chalk line down the exact middle of the town square, and set up guards on each side of the line, and made arrangements for a get-together that night, and decided the Americans would bring Scotch and the Russians vodka, O'Brien had gone back to his headquarters. He found his bath ready.

Now the colonel sat naked on the edge of the tub, a short, thin man of forty-two with close-cut, wiry, carroty hair, a snub nose and a long upper lip. He was preparing to slide into the warm water and finish the bath Herr Gruenz hadn't been able to live through.

O'Brien was thinking what a queer fish Colonel Obrenov was. A stickler—a stiff-backed, long-faced stickler. First, there'd been his insistence on having the honor of demolishing the statue. Second, he had demanded that one of his engineers survey the exact half of Mautz. He wanted no complications, no mistakes. And he'd invited O'Brien to check the line with an American engineer. Courteously, O'Brien had said he would trust Obrenov. The Russian had urged he check.

Annoyed, O'Brien had delegated the task to Major Razzuti of the Engineers. Razzuti had gone through the farce with a straight face, announced the line was correct, and congratulated Major Krassovsky, the Russian engineer, on his achievement. Krassovsky, who understood little English, had smiled and shaken Razzuti's hand.

Then the Yanks and the Russians had saluted each other and gone back to their respective headquarters with everything happily settled. O'Brien was now poised on the tub's marble brink for a descent into paradise.

At that moment a knock sounded at the bathroom door. The colonel, as was the way of soldiers, cursed at the interruption.

"It's me, Lieutenant Tarpitch." Tarpitch sounded miserable.

"Anything you can't handle, Tarpitch?" O'Brien snapped.

"Yes sir. The colonel'd better speak to Sergeant Krautzenfelser. He's the one that wants the colonel. It's urgent, He says we got Schutzmiller."

There was a pause. Tarpitch coughed. "He also says we have not got Schutzmiller."

The colonel forgot about his bath. "What d'you mean—have and haven't?" he growled.

"I don't know, sir. Better speak to the sergeant."

The door swung open. Sergeant Krautzenfelser stuck his dark Choctaw face in.

"Close the door. What do I have to be to get any privacy—a four-star general?"

"Guess so, sir," grinned the sergeant. "Better hurry, sir. Urgent. Can't handle it. International complications."

"Well, what is it?"

"Can't say. See for the colonel's self. On the spot. Schutzmiller."

O'Brien coughed with exasperation, not for the first time during his three years' experience with the Indian. Mule-headed as he knew himself to be, he had met in Krautzenfelser an inflexible stubbornness that far surpassed his own. Krautzenfelser had inherited the German name from a Prussian grandfather who'd settled in Oklahoma shortly after the Civil War, but he was three-fourths Choctaw, and he showed it clearly.

He was a college graduate and had been, before volunteering

for the Army, a professor of art at Kansoka University. In fact, he was now thriftily combining his wartime experiences with his profession by writing in his leisure hours, which were few, a monograph "On the Effects of the Fumes of Explosives on the Artistic Creativeness in the Period 1450–1920 A.D." The sergeant condescended at times to explain his thesis to the colonel. It irked O'Brien that he didn't know what Krautzenfelser was talking about.

Despite the Indian's brilliance, he had never been recommended by O'Brien for officer's training. "The first time he got mule-headed and did things his own way, instead of the Army's, he'd have his bars yanked off, or, worse, get shot. He'll be better off under my wing," the colonel had commented to his brother officers.

Still, he was a good man, intelligent enough not to burst in on the colonel unless the situation was too tough for anybody else to handle. He'd better haul hind-end—and fast. O'Brien gave up trying to dig a clear statement out of the sergeant. After one fond look at the tub he dressed quickly.

Schutzmiller! When you thought of atrocities, you thought of Schutzmiller. He was the SS colonel-general wanted badly by every one of the Allies. His name wasn't far below Hitler's on the War Criminal List.

As far as the Umpteenth Infantry Regiment was concerned, he was at the top of the list. They had been looking for him since the Battle of the Bulge, where, before his cold black eyes, over a hundred freshly-captured Americans had been lined up and machine-gunned. Half of them had been O'Brien's men.

When the sergeant spoke of Schutzmiller, he invoked the one name that had power to tear O'Brien away from his long-anticipated bath. As the colonel buckled on his pistol, he thought of this man to whom slaughter, rape, and torture were all in a day's work. Yet Schutzmiller raised love-birds and canaries, had once shot a man for kicking a dog, and was reputed to be a kind and loving husband and father.

Probably, thought the colonel, the dog had been Schutzmiller's personal property. The man he'd shot had been scheduled to be killed, and the dog was an excuse. Still, that didn't argue away the love-birds or the kids who thought their old man was the best in the world. Queer people, these Germans.

The colonel's jeep sped over to the town square. Krautzen-felser, who was driving, said, "See what I mean, sir?"

O'Brien saw. In the middle of the square was a knot of soldiers. They were pulling on something that was poised above the chalk-line dividing the square. That something was SS Colonel-General Schutzmiller.

When he was closer, O'Brien saw that two of his sergeants had a tight grip on the German's right hand and leg. Holding fast with an equally tight clutch on his left hand and leg were two Russian non-coms. The four were engaged in a tug-of-war with Schutzmiller's body as a rope.

His head was thrown back. His huge nose was pointed straight up; the bushy black eyebrows, supposedly the thickest in Europe, were writhing in agony. His mouth was as wide open as the beak of a worm-swallowing baby bird. Out of it streamed a gabble of curses and high-pitched commands to be let loose.

The sergeant said, "That's what I meant, sir. Those two and I were searching the houses. Our side of the square. We scared out this kraut. There."

He pointed to a hotel which dominated the south side of the square. "He bolted. Into the square. We knew it was Schutzmiller. We tried to take him alive.

"Those Russians. They spotted him. The kraut ran down the chalk-line. He tripped. We all piled on top of him. And the Russians wouldn't let go."

Colonel O'Brien threw his helmet off onto the cobbles. It bounced, landed on its rim, and rolled away. The colonel's orderly ran after it, not for the first time in his career as the colonel's orderly. The junior officers froze; the colonel was ready to blow his top.

Only Krautzenfelser ignored the colonel's anger. He grinned. "Well, sir. International complications. And on the first day here."

"Quiet, Sergeant! When I want your opinion, I'll ask for it." O'Brien's face was as red as his hair. What a thing to happen! On the surface of it, a comic-opera situation, something that could only happen on the stage.

But the complications! If he ordered his men to turn Schutzmiller over to the Russians, he would lose face both with his own men and with the Russians. Worse, there would be questions from GHQ, maybe from Washington. The brass hats would want to know why in thunder, why in the blankety-blank this and that, he allowed himself to get into such a predicament. And, secondly, once on it, why he hadn't immediately pulled himself out of it.

Worse and worse, Senator Applebroom, who was making a tour of Europe, would fly into Mautz tomorrow. There'd be senatorial fulminations, denunciations, philippics, cries for action, yelps to uphold the honor of the American public. The congressman would swing every ounce of his political weight in an effort to grab all the publicity he could. A spasm of disgust shook O'Brien. The fat Applebroom didn't like military men, and he would delight in spattering his muck on O'Brien; he would make him look like a fool and a heel.

The Colonel thought fast, but not fast enough. There was a screech of brakes as Colonel Obrenov's jeep shot into the square and came to a halt a few feet from Schutzmiller. Obrenov shouted at his chauffeur.

Tarpitch, standing at O'Brien's shoulder, translated. "He's cussing out his driver, a certain Sergeant Kublitch, for not running over Schutzmiller, purely by accident, of course, and solving the dilemma. He says Kublitch would have got a medal out of it. He says a Tartar never did have any brains. Kublitch is saying nothing."

"I don't need an interpreter to tell me when a man says nothing," snapped O'Brien. He looked at Obrenov's face, so startlingly like his own with its bright red hair, snub nose, and long upper lip. It was, as usual, grave.

O'Brien decided to waste no time. He stepped up to the line and said, with Tarpitch translating into Russian, "I say, Colonel, shall we settle this thing at once before our respective headquarters hear about it? It'll save our countries a great deal of embarrassment, not to mention ourselves."

Obrenov, instead of listening to Tarpitch, spoke to his own interpreter, who, in turn, spoke English, but addressed himself to Tarpitch, not O'Brien.

"The colonel would like to settle first which interpreter we're going to use. The colonel says that at our last meeting the American lieutenant translated. The colonel says that this time it is consonant with Russian dignity and might, not to mention fairness, that the Russian lieutenant, myself, interpret. The colonel insists."

O'Brien was for a second taken aback at the irrelevancy of the request. Then he saw that Obrenov was fighting for time. His brain, like O'Brien's, was spinning as rapidly as a cyclone and, like that greedy storm, seizing on everything he possibly could.

O'Brien said, "Tell the colonel the colonel may use the Russian interpreter, yourself, all the time. I don't care."

Tarpitch translated O'Brien's English into Russian, the Russian lieutenant listened gravely, then told Colonel Obrenov. He shrugged his shoulders, waved his hands, and borrowed a cigarette from one of his officers. While lighting it, his keen hazel eyes flickered a curse at Schutzmiller.

The German had ceased his ravings to listen to them, and he suddenly cried in English, "I surrender, I surrender, but to the Americans, not the Russians. Take me. This is no way to treat a colonel-general."

The Russian interpreter, Lieutenant Aramajian, quickly spoke to Obrenov. The colonel's body stiffened. His officers bridled and shot hostile glances across the border.

O'Brien said to Tarpitch, "Tell Schutzmiller he'll have to surrender to the Russians at the same time. According to treaty, we're bound to make no separate peaces."

Tarpitch spoke in German. The Russians, who understood it, unbent. Obrenov smiled, and said, Aramajian translating, "Now that that is understood, let us arrive swiftly at a solution. Apparently Schutzmiller is equally divided between the Americans and us. Apparently. But it may be he is a quarter of an inch more or less to one side. I suggest that we survey him, and whichever side has the most, gets him. That seems to be the only fair solution to an awkward situation, and that way, neither Moscow nor Washington will have a kick coming."

Aramajian smiled and dropped his role of interpreter for a moment. "A kick coming. Is not that a correct colloquialism?"

Tarpitch assured him it was.

O'Brien was astonished at Obrenov's proposal, simple enough to come from an imbecile, yet savoring of genius. He recovered quickly and agreed.

Razzuti and Krassovsky surveyed the prisoner. They turned long faces on their commanding officers. Razzuti said, "Major Krassovsky and I agree that the line splits him into two equal parts. Neither side has the advantage."

O'Brien suppressed a groan and suggested to Aramajian, "Tell the colonel that in America we often flip coins to decide issues."

Aramajian replied for Obrenov. "The colonel thanks the colonel for his suggestion and his cooperation, but the colonel doesn't think it would be consonant with the dignity and might of the Russian nation to settle issues in so flippant a manner."

Aramajian said, "Flippant, is that not good? It is a pun, is it not?"

Tarpitch congratulated him on his achievement.

Obrenov, who must have been aware by Aramajian's manner that he was ad libbing, pulled him up sharply. The lieutenant lost his grin.

Schutzmiller screamed, "This is no way to treat a German officer. It is not honorable."

Obrenov looked at Schutzmiller. The sight of the cruel hawk's face must have given him an idea. He produced a paper, scanned it, then spoke.

Aramajian said, "The colonel says the colonel has here a paper on which are enumerated in detail the crimes for which Schutzmiller is wanted by the Russian government. The colonel suggests the Russian and American list be compared. Whichever list is highest wins."

Schutzmiller screamed, "Let me up! Am I to have no chance to defend myself? Is this honorable? In front of these enlisted men, too. Is this honorable?"

O'Brien snorted, "Honorable? Where'd you get that word?" To Aramajian he said, "Tell the colonel, O.K." To himself he muttered, "Anything will do."

Lieutenant MacAngus, a giant with a red mustache and an even redder face, a lawyer in civilian life, compared his list with the one held by Captain Schmidt, the Russian representative. They stood at Schutzmiller's head, and the German threw his head back to stare up at them.

Fear now replaced arrogance on his face as the two read out his crimes.

"My colleague, Captain Schmidt and I," reported MacAngus, "find that whereas we, that is, the Americans, British, and French, I say we, that is Captain Schmidt and I, find that whereas we, that is, the Allies, and not Captain Schmidt and I—"

"We know," said O'Brien. "Come on, Mac, the facts."

"We find the allies have 1,002 known executions of prisoners-of-war, 5,012 known starved prisoners-of-war, 300 known civilians tortured to death, 1,003 civilian hostages executed, all at Schutzmiller's orders. And 10 known women raped by Schutzmiller personally. The total on the Allied side is 7,327.

"On the other, the Russian, hand, we find they have 2,003 known executions of prisoners-of-war, 3,002 known starved prisoners-of-war, 1,102 known civilians tortured to death, 1,210 civilian hostages executed, and 11 known women raped by Schutzmiller personally. The Russian total is 7,328. They beat us by one.

"At first glance that would give the German to the Russians. But one of the raped women's names, Anna Pavlovna Krylov, appears twice. Either there are two Anna Pavlovnas or, more likely, she was raped twice. My colleague admits the truth cannot be ascertained immediately.

"Therefore, we have agreed that, for the time being, and until the affair of Anna Pavlovna is cleared up, the lists are to be considered equal."

O'Brien and Obrenov

O'Brien and Obrenov shrugged their shoulders and looked at each other. From the first they'd sized each other up and come to the conclusion it would do no good to pull any rough stuff. Both were stubborn, and eager to advance the interests of their countries, but they were equally anxious to thread their way out of the labyrinth into which the capture of Schutzmiller had thrown them. Not only was it a problem which might easily lead to strained, if not snapped, relations, it was a problem which might cost O'Brien his hide and Obrenov his head.

"Tell the colonel," said O'Brien, "that we seem to be stymied, but I have an idea. The colonel has refused a coin-flipping contest, and I think the colonel is correct—it leaves too much to chance and is undignified. But if the colonel will step to one side, I think I have a contest of another kind to interest him, one which should appeal to the sporting blood I know runs in Russian veins."

Obrenov hesitated and glanced at his fellow officers, doubtless wondering if a tête-à-tête with an American would be reported to his discredit back in Moscow.

O'Brien said, "Tell the colonel he may report what I say later on. There are those here, however, who shouldn't hear." He glanced meaningly at the enlisted men.

Obrenov blushed at the reference to his fear of being turned in, but stepped off to one side. Aramajian followed. O'Brien whispered hurriedly, Aramajian whispered to Obrenov, Obrenov whispered back to Aramajian, who whispered to O'Brien. At the conclusion of the low-toned conference, Obrenov grinned and shook O'Brien's hand. Then they saluted each other and left.

Before going back to HQ, O'Brien put Sergeant Krautzenfelser in charge of the detail holding Schutzmiller's right arm and leg.

The sergeant protested, "Sir, couldn't we drive stakes between the cobblestones? Handcuff him to them? Hard on the men—squatting here, holding him."

"No. We're not allowed to manacle our prisoners."

"That's what those Russians are doing."

He pointed at Sergeant Kublitch, who was approaching with a pick, a hammer, stakes, and chains.

"I can't help that," replied the colonel testily. "Russia didn't sign the convention."

"But—"

"But, hell! Sergeant, you're presuming on our long and close acquaintanceship."

"Yes, sir." The Choctaw saluted.

"Oh, yes, Sergeant, it looks like rain. You'd better draw slickers for your squad."

O'Brien went back to the ex-mayor's house to resume his bath. While he undressed, the water was re-warmed. Just as he sat on the edge of the tub and stuck in his toe with a shudder of anticipatory ecstasy, he was disturbed by a knock on the bathroom door.

"Tarpitch, sir. It's about Schutzmiller's food."

"Give him what we eat. Do you think I'm a dietician?"

"No, sir!" Tarpitch was emphatic. "Schutzmiller won't eat Russian food, says it might be poisoned. And when we started to feed him, the Russians objected on the ground that he's half their prisoner, and they're entitled to give him half his food. They won't let us feed him unless we go halves, and the German won't touch their stuff."

O'Brien looked for his helmet to throw. Fortunately for Tarpitch, it hung on the outside of the door.

"Let him starve," he growled. "Tell him any time he wants food, he can have it, provided he'll eat half-Russian food."

"Yes, sir. Only he's making trouble by telling the Russians of alleged American atrocities and telling us of things the Russians have done to our boys."

"Now I know he won't eat! Tell him he either shuts up or starves. Personally, I hope he does."

"Yes, sir."

O'Brien listened to Tarpitch's departing footsteps. He sighed and slid into the water. He closed his eyes and let everything go. Ah, heavenly! The hot water was dissolving the sweat, dirt, and stink of eight weeks' accumulation. And unwinding a little the bow-string of tension that had drawn tighter and tighter since D-Day.

It must have been ten minutes later, though it seemed a

second, that he was roused from his half-stupor by a knock on the door. He opened his eyes.

"Tarpitch, sir. It's raining."

"Good God, man. Do you think I can order it to stop?"

"No, sir. But Schutzmiller's hollering for shelter. He says we got to give it to him or else betray the Geneva Convention."

"Doesn't he know we can't move him?"

"Yes, sir. I've taken steps. We've put up a pup tent over him."

"Doesn't that satisfy him?"

"No, sir. The tent doesn't go any farther than the border, sir. And the Russ refuse to put one up on their side—they say they've got no orders about sheltering half-prisoners, just whole ones. The rain's coming in from the east side. Our tent is doing no good. He's drenched."

O'Brien grunted, "Too bad. My heart bleeds . . . Well, we've done what we could. You go and get ready for the party, Tarpitch, and don't bother me until it's time to go."

The colonel closed his eyes again. Was the world always to clamor at his bathroom door? A fist banging was his answer.

The colonel reached for a pistol that wasn't there. "You're lucky, Krautzenfelser," he cried, "if I don't have you shot at sunrise. What is it? And what're you doing away from your post?"

He knew it was the sergeant. Only one man had temerity enough to beat the colonel's door as if it were a gong.

"Sorry, sir," said the sergeant with no trace of sorrow, "Lieutenant Tarpitch sent me. It's the statue. It's going."

"Going?" repeated O'Brien testily. "Going? Where's it going? Since when does bronze walk?"

"Don't get me wrong, sir. It's falling, not running. When those heinies pulled it over, they loosened the bands that clamp it on its pedestal."

"Let it fall."

"It might hit Schutzmiller, sir."

O'Brien gave a chuckle which rumbled in the huge bathtub and echoed to the sergeant's ear like a ghoul slavering at the bottom of a meaty grave.

"Hagh! Hagh! Sergeant, when you have any tales of beauty and promise like that to tell, I'll forgive your bursting in on the sanctity of my bath. It's wonderful. Now, go. And don't come back unless Schutzmiller's dead."

"Yes, sir."

"Stop! Sergeant, does Schutzmiller know the 'Spirit' is coming down?"

"He's facing south, sir. But he heard it shift. By throwing his head back, he can see it. He knows it might fall on him."

"Agh, hagh! Sergeant, weren't some of your buddies lined up and shot by Schutzmiller's men?"

"Yes, sir."

"Sergeant, if you were Satan, and Schutzmiller had died and come under your jurisdiction, what torture would you think most appropriate?"

"Sir, I'd stretch him out on the ground, put over him a slowly toppling figure that might, or might not, dash out his brains. Then I'd let him sweat it out."

"Sergeant, you are a clever fiend."

"Yes, sir."

"Dismissed."

That evening, at 1900 hours, a group of American officers, guests of Colonel Obrenov, selected for a certain capability, got into their jeeps and drove off. O'Brien, in the lead car, stopped at the Russian border in the square. Krautzenfelser's big form strode through the heavy rain up to the colonel. He saluted.

Though he could see well enough for himself, O'Brien asked, "How's Schutzmiller taking it?"

"Sir, that kraut is tough. Here he is, drenched. Freezing. Maybe pneumonia coming on. And all he does is complain. Says it's an insult. To be guarded by a Jew."

The colonel blinked. "What Jew?"

"Me, sir. He thinks I'm a Jew. May I tell him, sir, I'm three-fourths Choctaw? Then maybe he'll shut up."

"Let him think you're a Jew. What do you care?" The colonel

was enjoying the sergeant's discomfiture. "Isn't he scared of the 'Spirit' any more?"

Krautzenfelser looked downcast. "No, sir. It's falling slower than my arches, sir. I think it's gone as far as it's going to."

He jerked his thumb to indicate the "Spirit." The Germans had torn up the cobblestones and dug a pit on the south side down to the bottom of the slender marble pedestal. The cement ball which had anchored its end had been chipped away and thrown out. Ropes, attached to its neck and waist, had been used to jerk over the statue and the base, which wasn't much thicker than the figure, at the same time. The intention had been to drag it out in one piece.

But the work had been stopped halfway, and now the "Spirit" leaned forward, poised for a nose dive, deterred only by the bronze clamps which passed through its feet and curved tightly over the top of the pedestal. Half-broken through, the clamps still looked enough to hold for a few more decades. Schutzmiller seemed safe, and the hopes the colonel had pinned on its falling were blown away.

"Do you think he'll catch pneumonia, Sergeant?"

"He's too mean to die that way."

"If he does, give him prompt medical attention. No matter what our feelings, we've got to be humane."

"Yes, sir. But we can only treat half of him. Besides, sir, is it humane to leave him in the rain? With that statue hanging over him?"

"We can't move him unless the Russians consent. That's what tonight's conference is about. Besides, if we do let him die, though it wouldn't be humane, it would be humanitarian."

"I see what the colonel means."

Krautzenfelser suddenly leaned over and stared hard into O'Brien's eyes. He winked, and winked again.

"Sir, could I have the colonel's permission to measure the 'Spirit's' dimensions? Necessary information for my monograph 'On the Effects of the Fumes of Explosives'."

"Measure it? Monograph? Sergeant, how often do I have to

tell you not to bother me with that stuff? This is war, man. Forget you were once a professor of art—and stay down off that statue."

Krautzenfelser shot O'Brien an indecipherable look. It made him feel the sergeant had been trying to tell him something without actually saying it, and that he had missed the train.

Then the sergeant grunted and twitched his shoulders as if he were shrugging off a disappointment. His face hardened into a mold the colonel had seen before; the times the sergeant had decided to bull along in his own way and to hell with the Army's!

It dwindled subtly into his usual happy grin. He smiled at the tarpaulin-concealed cases of Scotch on the jeep's back floor.

"Yes, sir. Happy conference, sir."

The colonel veiled his eyes and ordered Tarpitch to drive on.

The sergeant's buddy slouched up through the rain.

"The Old Man sure likes to gab with you, Krautzy, even if he does have to put you in your place now and then."

"Yeah," the sergeant grunted. He pointed at Schutzmiller. "What'll we do with that Thing? Do you realize the implications? He could be the cause of a serious quarrel. Between the Allies."

"Too bad we can't plug him and claim it was an accident."

"Thought of it. 'Twouldn't work. Courtmartial. Guess I'll go talk to that Kublitch. Looks like he's got Indian blood in him. Might not be a bad guy."

He walked to the chalk-line and spoke in German. The Tartar answered in the same language.

Did Kublitch know the brass hats were beating out their brains over Schutzmiller? . . . He did? Good . . . And did he know they hadn't come to a solution? . . . And that only a couple of good enlisted men, such as Kublitch and himself—used to simple ways—could cut the Gordian knot? . . . He did? . . . Well, here's what he thought ought to be done. He explained . . . Schutzmiller, who had been listening, screamed a protest.

Colonel Obrenov, welcoming his guests, seemed no longer the stiff and stubborn character he'd been on the chalk-border. His face, so much like O'Brien's except for the dignified, mournful lines into which it was usually cast, was now smiling. If it hadn't been for his uniform, he would have been indistinguishable from the American.

He shook hands with the Yanks and said, through Aramajian, "Welcome, friends, I have good news for you. In the cellar of this house, which you no doubt know once belonged to the late Baron Pfugelkluckensheimer, we have discovered an enormous amount of wine bottles, all, luckily, filled to the full with wine of rare vintage. I suggest we down those first, and then, if we're still thirsty, we can start in on the whiskey. It is a go, no?"

"It's a go, yes!" enthused the Americans.

Two high stools, much like those on which the umpires of a tennis match sit, were brought in and placed one on each side of the banquet table. Captain Pichegru, representing the Yanks, mounted one; Captain Ivantchenko, of the Russians, the other.

"Now, gentlemen," said Obrenov, "the ostensible purpose of this meeting is to break the Schutzmiller case. It is best, for all concerned, to find a way out before dawn. At that time a Senator Applebroom will land to make a tour of inspection on the American side. Undoubtedly, if he finds the German spread-eagled on the border, he will raise hell.

"To make it worse, a political commissar from Moscow is flying in tomorrow to investigate. I need not remind the Russian officers here that Moscow does not like unpleasant situations and often passes the buck with lead. In other words, painful words, the firing squad might remove us because we haven't removed Schutzmiller. We had hoped the 'Spirit' would fall and obliterate the kraut. But it isn't going to accommodate us.

"Colonel O'Brien and I have talked ways and means, but ended up stuck in the mud. So, we decided to hold a contest, a drinking race. Whichever country ends up at dawn with the most men on their feet gets the German. The rules are: Colonel O'Brien and I will start the toasting. If we fall silent, whoever has a good toast on his mind, let him stand up and get it off his chest. Should any officer feel full to the gills and turn down a toast, he is to be disqualified by the umpires. Is it clear as mud, gentlemen?"

The gentlemen agreed it was. Obrenov raised his glass.

"One moment, please," interrupted O'Brien. "Are the poor judges to go thirsty?"

A storm of protest broke out. Bottles were offered to the unreluctant Pichegru and Ivantchenko.

"A toast. To America!" cried Obrenov.

"A toast. To Russia!" proposed O'Brien.

"To the President . . . To Stalin . . . To Eisenhower . . . To Zhukov . . . To O'Brien . . . To Obrenov . . . To victory . . . To success . . . To the men of Rooshia . . . To the men of the U.S. . . . To the women of Rooshia . . . To the women of America . . . To the women of the world . . ."

Toast followed toast so rapidly there was little chance to grab a bite between. No sooner had one torn off a strip of the delicious chicken or roast beef, mouth watering in anticipation, than one was forced to gulp a glass of wine. The system had an advantage; in a short time one felt lightning flashing through one's veins, not to mention the arteries, one felt glorious and dizzy, one ceased to remember that one had a belly crying for food. One lifted one's glass, emptied it down one's palpitating throat, and hurled it at the fireplace. One drank and drank.

"To the melting-pot of the nations, America," said O'Brien.

"This melting-pot, what means it?" asked Obrenov, through Aramajian.

"The U.S. is famed as a melting-pot, a mixture of different bloods, the sum total of which adds up to strength. For instance," O'Brien pointed down his side of the table at which sat his officers placed according to seniority, "there's Lieutenant Colonel Obisto, Major Razzuti, Captain Schmidt, and Lieutenants Tarpitch, Smith and MacAngus—all of widely different nationalities and creeds."

"Ah, yes," nodded Obrenov, "this Tarpitch is of Russian descent, no?"

"No, he is of English."

"But Tarpitch is a Russian name."

"Only seems to be. It is not derived from Tarpavitch, son of Tarpa. It is made up of tar, which means pitch, and pitch, which means tar."

"Ah, I see," said Obrenov with a puzzled expression. "This Smith, is of English descent, too?"

"No, he is of Hungarian. His parents, on coming to America, changed their name from Kovac, which means Smith, to Smith."

"Ah, I see. But your Captain Schmidt, like our Captain Schmidt—odd coincidence—is of German descent, no?"

"No, he is of Russian. Though if you were to go far enough back, you would find a kraut hanging from his ancestral tree."

Obrenov's expression became desperate. "But surely this MacAngus, he is Greek, yes? I say Greek because his name ends with a *u* and an *s*."

"No, MacAngus is an old and widespread Scotch name."

"Ah, but surely this Obisto is of Spanish descent, yes?"

"No, he is a Jew whose ancestors came from Portugal."

Obrenov sucked in his breath and blurted, "I will make one more guess. This Razzuti, he is of Italian descent, yes?"

"Yes."

"Ah, ha!" Obrenov was pleased. "Well, it is puzzling. One must get mixed up in your country. But so is Russia perplexing—we, too, are a big nation, a melting-pot. Lieutenant Colonel Efimitch is of Tartar origin, Major Krassovsky is a Jew, Captain Schmidt, of German ancestry, Lieutenants Riezun, Aramajian, and Stadquist of Ukrainian, Armenian and Swedish-Finnish grandparents, respectively."

He rose to his feet. "Gentlemen, to our ancestors, who—"

The rest of his speech was lost to the Americans, for at that moment Aramajian slid off his seat and disappeared under the table. He went early. But as the night thickened with darkness, so did tongues thicken and stumble, and other men, too, followed in Aramajian's footsteps.

These men who had all suffered and bled for their countries were now getting patriotically drunk. They gave their all. Some grew white as paper and dashed outside for air; the umpires disqualified them. Some laid down and quietly gave up the ghost of their reputations as topers; others were more noisy, but they, too, went the way of supersoaked flesh.

The umpires checked them off. Came the time when the umpires had deserted their posts. Pichegru had stumbled outside mumbling a sentence the words of which were too blurred for understanding, but the urgency of which impressed the officers. He didn't come back. Ivantchenko put too much trust in his equilibrium and crashed off his high stool on to the table. He made no effort to get up, at least none that could be seen; merely blinked at the chandelier's brightness a while, then, smiling happily, dozed off.

Obrenov and Riezun were left for the Russians; O'Brien, Tarpitch, and MacAngus for the Yanks. Even while O'Brien was counting his men he had to strike his interpreter off the list.

The survivors were degraded to speaking German, a language they had difficulty in understanding when sober.

"To the best man!" toasted O'Brien. They drank; Riezun accomplished the impossible feat of staggering while sitting down. O'Brien compared Riezun's condition with MacAngus's and smiled. He had faith in the big fellow's alcoholic impregnability. Mac came from a long line of whiskey-saturated ancestors; his corpuscles were Scotch in more ways than one.

Two more toasts, and Riezun foundered. Obrenov was left, as he muttered in thick German, left alone to bear on his shoulders the dignity, might, and honor of the Russian nation.

"To the bearer-er—gulp!—to the man who carries the honor of Rooshia," MacAngus managed to propose.

They hurled their glasses at the fireplace. During the course of the evening the empty goblets, which had at first unerringly crashed against the iron grates, had taken a tendency to wander far and wide. Many landed on the mantel or sailed through the open window by the fireplace.

O'Brien noticed that his and Obrenov's shattered close enough to count as near-hits, but Mac's wobbled off to one side, struck a portrait of the late Baron Pflugelkluckensheimer, and bounced back on the thick carpet, upright and unbroken.

"Come on, Mac, get up," croaked the colonel. "Don't leave me alone."

"Gawd, I can't!" groaned MacAngus. "So long, Colonel, I'm going. Dammit, I can outdrink anybody in whiskey—but not in that gawdforsaken wine. Who woulda thought it, an Irishman and a Rooshian, old buzzards at that, drinking me, a MacAngus, under the table? Da— sz, sz . . ."

The two stared at each other, reluctant to propose another toast. Slowly, O'Brien stood up.

"T' you and me. Two old buzzards, And t' whoever gets Schutzmiller."

They drank and stood, swaying, refusing to sit down for fear they might not be able to get up again. O'Brien suddenly felt sick, not from the wine, but from the realization he was a fool. Here was Schutzmiller breeding division between two great countries, a problem which needed unaddled wits and swift, firm hands, and here were two old drunken fools childishly engaged in a contest that was supposed to prove which was the better man. Yet, at the moment he'd proposed the toasting spree, he'd thought it was a good idea. His fantastic Irish imagination sometimes got the better of him. This was one of those times. Tears oozed from his eyes.

Obrenov was crying, too. "Instead of standing uselessly here, like a couple of stuffed owls, let's go down to the square and take things in our own hands. To hell with the consequences."

Arms around each other's shoulders they lurched outside. The heavy rain had been followed by a light drizzle; the north wind was blowing strong, strong enough to cool their superheated brains and sting some wits into them.

They passed through the dark streets. Now and then Obrenov barked the counterword to a challenging sentry. Presently they came to the edge of the square and paused to reconnoiter.

Searchlights, centering on the sprawled-out figure of Schutzmiller, were slowly weakening. Dawn was leadening the black clouds of the horizon.

O'Brien peered with bloodshot eyes. "What's Krautzenfelser doing on that statue?" he asked.

"I don't know. What's Kublitch up to?"

The Choctaw was hanging in the air with one arm wrapped around the "Spirit's" neck. With his free hand he held a tape-measure which he apparently was using to estimate the sword's length. His position was precarious; his legs dangled four or five feet above the cobblestones.

"Is that fool trying to break his neck?" muttered Obrenov.

"Why, I told him to stay off that thing. But no, the mule-headed ass has to go ahead and mix his artistic nonsense with business. Who cares what size that monstrosity is? I'll slap him in the jug. Where's an MP?"

He stepped out into the square. "You, Krautzenfelser! Get down! Consider yourself under arrest! You, Krautzy!"

He stopped. He ground his teeth in a convulsion of fear. The statue had suddenly shifted downward. The clamps around its feet, partially broken, were giving way under the sergeant's two hundred and thirty pounds.

"Hey, Krautzy! You'll break your fool neck!"

His voice wasn't heard. Schutzmiller, who'd been looking backwards with such wide eyes that even O'Brien could see the whites, began screaming, "Nein! Nein! Nein!"

The clamps squealed again. The statue lurched downwards an inch. Krautzenfelser lost his hold and fell backwards. He landed close to the German's head, and one of his buddies, seeing he was too hurt to get up, jumped forward and pulled him to one side.

He was in no danger—the "Spirit" had halted. It was suspended, sword in hand, giving birth in the bystanders' minds to the inevitable phrase—"like an avenging angel."

Schutzmiller must have thought so. He kept yelling his useless "Neins" until he saw the statue wasn't going to fall. His screams choked into a sob of relief.

O'Brien stood for a moment. Then he shrugged his shoulders. "There goes our last hope," he said to Obrenov. "Krautzy was trying to pull the 'Spirit' over on Schutzmiller under the guise of measuring it. It was a noble effort. I'll have to sentence him to a few days in jail for disobeying orders, but he'll eat caviar and drink champagne behind the bars. Too bad. Oh, well."

He walked up to the sergeant. He said, "Sprained your ankle disobeying orders, eh? Serves you right, Krautzenfelser."

The sergeant said, "I wouldn't mind the ankle if I'd succeeded in getting the measurements, sir. Anything in the cause of art, sir."

His eyes widened. He pointed up. O'Brien followed his finger and saw that the sword, slanting down in the statue's fist, was shaking.

The quivering ceased. The sword slipped out of the "Spirit's" loose grasp.

Schutzmiller gave a final scream. The tip of the sword halved his brains, and the left side of his head flopped neatly over the Russian border, while the right side of his head flopped neatly over the American border.

It was Obrenov who, in his simple Slavic way, pointed out what was obvious, but what he wanted to make sure all would see. "If it had been a pen in the 'Spirit's' hand, instead of a sword, it would have missed Schutzmiller."

Imagination

Can imagination act
Perpendicular to fact?
Can it be a kite that flies
Till the Earth, umbrella-wise,
Folds and drops away from sight?

Miles above the Earth we know,
Fancy's rocket roars. Below,
Here and Now are needles which
Sew a pattern black as pitch,
Waiting for the rocket's light.

Poet, steer your rocket down.
Lights are useless, though they crown
Half of space with glory, yet
Leave this hard old globe in jet.
Earth's the start, the end of flight.

THE 1950S

Philip José Farmer began the 1950s graduating from Bradley University with a B.A. in English. He had written and sent out many stories over the last several years, mostly to mainstream publications, but had not sold any since 1946. Although he had been a fan of the science fiction pulps growing up, he didn't try to sell any science fiction stories until 1952. His first story in the genre, "The Lovers," appeared in the August 1952 issue of *Startling Stories*, and made a huge impression on the field. Phil and Bette attended WorldCon 10 in Chicago in September just as buzz about the story was heating up.

While the editors had expected the story to make a stir because of its sexual content, letters about it poured into the magazine and were published regularly over the following two years. Most of the feedback was positive and included letters from luminaires of the day such as Forrest J. Ackerman, Ray Nelson, Jim Harmon, Henry Moskowitz, John Brunner, Poul Anderson, Marion Zimmer Bradley, Alfred Bester, Richard E. Geis, Theodore Sturgeon, and Sherwood Springer.

Phil quickly followed "The Lovers" with "Sail On! Sail On!" It was one of his most reprinted stories. Next came "The Biological Revolt," "Mother," a story that goes into great detail about alien biology, and "Moth and Rust," a sequel to "The Lovers." At

WorldCon 11, held in Philadelphia, PA, September, 1953, Phil was awarded the first annual Achievement Award (later named the Hugo Award) as the "Most Promising New Talent." This was Phil's third convention in his first year in the science fiction community, as he and Bette also attended MidwestCon 4 in Russel

Phil holding his award for "Most Promising New Talent," at WorldCon 11, in Philadelphia, September 1953.

Point, OH, in May. They would also attend WorldCon 12 in New York the following year.

Fresh off that win, Phil decided at the last minute to enter a $4,000 science fiction novel contest sponsored by Shasta Publishers and Pocket Books. Shasta, a specialty science fiction house, would publish the hardcover, and Pocket Books would bring out the paperback. It would also be Pocket's first science fiction novel. Phil wrote *Owe for the Flesh* in less than a month and mailed the manuscript on the very last day.

In December 1953, it was announced that *Owe for the Flesh* had won the contest. Phil, buoyed by this success, quit his job to become a full time writer. However, after traveling to Chicago to meet with Shasta, he was told Pocket Books would not release the prize money until he made some changes to the book. Thus, Shasta strung Phil along, asking for multiple revisions until he hired an agent who contacted Pocket Books about the matter. Pocket had long ago paid Shasta their portion of the money and never asked for any revisions. Shasta had diverted the funds into a different book, one they believed would be a surefire best seller, but it bombed. By the time this all came to light, Phil had lost his house and had to take a job as a laborer in a dairy to make ends meet. Pocket Books washed their hands of the affair, the book was not published, and worse yet, the original manuscript was lost.

Phil also occasionally wrote articles for some of the science fiction fanzines. "Lovers and Otherwise" for *Fantastic Worlds* gave a firsthand history of the difficulties he encountered getting "The Lovers" published. "The Tin Woodman Slams the Door" for *Destiny* is about his love for the Oz books. "White Whales, Raintrees, Flying Saucers" first appeared in the digest *Fantastic Universe*, but a revised and expanded version appeared in *Skyhook* along with a follow-up letter "by Tim Howller" about whether or not science fiction can be good literature. "The Golden Age and the Brass" was his first article for the *Burroughs Bulletin*, in which he described his attempts to get his son to read Tarzan novels instead of comic books.

A lover of all types of literature, Phil also published several more poems: "Sestina of the Space Rocket" in *Startling Stories*;

"The Pterodactyl" and "Black Squirrel on Cottonwood Limb's Tip" in the fanzine *Skyhook*; and "Beauty in This Iron Age" and "In Common" in *Starlanes,* a fanzine exclusively for science fiction poetry.

But of course his main focus was writing science fiction stories which were sold to a wide variety of magazines: "Attitudes," the first Father Carmody story appeared in the *The Magazine of Fantasy & Science Fiction (F&SF)*; "Strange Compulsion" was his second and final sale to *Science Fiction Plus*; and "They Twinkled Like Jewels," "Rastignac the Devil," and "The Celestial Blueprint," all sold to *Fantastic Universe.* "Daughter," a sequel to "Mother," was his final sale to *Thrilling Wonder Stories.* He sold "Queen of the Deep" to the men's adventure magazine, *Argosy;* "The God Business" to the short-lived *Beyond Fantasy Fiction*, and several more stories to *F&SF*: "Totem and Taboo," "Father," and "Night of Light," the third and most important Father Carmody story that would later be expanded into a novel, as well as "The Alley Man," which was nominated for a Hugo Award.

He also wrote a novel titled *A Beast of the Fields* that was to be serialized in *Startling Stories,* but the magazine folded in 1955 before the novel ran. It was eventually published as *Dare* in 1965.

In 1956, the Farmer family moved to Syracuse, New York, and Phil began his career as a technical writer for General Electric. In 1958, they moved to Scottsdale, Arizona, when Phil took a job as a technical writer for Motorola's military electronics division,

He did finally publish his first novel, *The Green Odyssey*, in 1957. It was released by Ballantine in hardcover and paperback simultaneously. Most of the hardcovers were sent to libraries; to this day non-library copies of the hardcover first edition are his most valuable book amongst book collectors. He never did write his proposed sequel, *The Greeniad.*

Phil's literary output in the 1950s was remarkable when one considers that he finished college, worked full time through almost the entire decade, and dealt with the setback of losing his house because of a shady publisher.

The Lovers

FOREWORD

During the day, the dreadnaught *Gabriel* squatted in a park in the center of the city of Siddo, on the planet Ozagen. From sunrise to sunset the *Gabriel*'s personnel ventured out among the Ozagenians—or wogglebugs, as they were familiarly and contemptuously called—learning all they could of Ozagen's history, customs, language and other things.

The "other things," though the Earthmen did not mention this to the wogglebugs, were Ozagen's technologies. As far as could be seen, the wogs had progressed, roughly speaking, to the level of Earth's early 20th-century science. Logically, there should be nothing to fear from them. But the men of Earth's Haijac Union trusted no one. What if the wogs were hiding terrible weapons, waiting to catch the men unawares?

At nightfall, the spaceship rose to a height of fifty feet and poised there until the sun rose again. Then it sank back into the deep depression made by its own weight. Always a radar gig hovered in the stratosphere and probed for other spacecraft. Presumably, neither Earth's Israeli Republics nor its Bantu-Malay Federation knew of Ozagen . . . but if they found out!

Meanwhile the Terrans searched, studied, prowled and planned.

Before they attacked the natives, before they began their decimation project to make room for the hordes that would follow, they must learn the wogs' potentialities.

And so it was that, a month after the appearance of the *Gabriel* above Siddo, two presumably friendly (to wogs) Terrans set out with two presumably friendly (to Terrans) wogglebugs on a trip. They were going to investigate the ruins of a city left by a dead humanoid race. They rode a vehicle fantastic to the men . . .

✐ ONE ✐

The motor hiccoughed and jerked. The Ozagenian sitting on the right side of the rear seat leaned over and shouted something. Hal Yarrow twisted his head and yelled, "Quoi?"

Fobo, sitting directly behind Hal, stuck his mouth against the Earthman's ear. He translated the gibberish into French:

"Zugu says and emphasizes that you should pump the throttle. That little rod to your right. It gives the carburetor more alcohol. Ou quelque chose."

Fobo's antennae tickled Hal's ears. Hal said, "Merci," and worked the throttle. To do so, he had to lean across the gapt, sitting at his right. "Pardonnez-moi, monsieur Pornsen!" he bellowed.

The gapt did not look at Yarrow; his hands, lying on his lap, were locked together. The knuckles showed white. Like his ward, he was having his first experience with an internal combustion. motor. Unlike Hal, he was scared by the loud noise, the fumes, the bumps and bangs, and just the idea of riding in a manually controlled vehicle.

Hal grinned. He loved this quaint car, so reminiscent of Earth's early twentieth-century autos. It thrilled him to be able to twist the stiff-acting wheel and feel the heavy body obey his muscles. The four cylinders banging and the alcohol's reek excited him. As for the bouncing, that was fun. It was romantic, like putting out to sea in a sailboat—something else he hoped to do before they left Ozagen.

Also, anything that scared his gapt pleased Yarrow.

His pleasure ended. The cylinders popped, off-key. The car jerked and then rolled to a stop. At once, the two wogglebugs hopped over the side and raised the hood. Hal followed. Pornsen sat. He pulled a package of Merciful Seraphim from his uniform pocket, took one out and lit up.

He noted that it was the fourth he'd seen Pornsen smoking since morning prayers. If Pornsen wasn't careful, he'd be going over his quota. That meant that the next time Hal got in trouble, he could blackmail the gapt into helping him. Judging by his troubles so far on this expedition, it wouldn't be long before he would have to.

Hal bent over the motor and watched. Zugu seemed to know what the matter was. He should, since he was the inventor and builder of the only—as far as the Terrans knew—native-made self-propelling vehicle on this planet.

Zugu used a wrench to unscrew a long narrow pipe from a round glass case. Yarrow remembered that this was a gravity feed system. The fuel ran from the tank into the glass case, which was a sediment chamber. From there it ran into the feed pipe, which in turn passed to the carburetor.

Pornsen called harshly, "Well, Yarrow, are we going to be stuck here all day?"

Though he still wore the hood and goggles the Ozagenians had equipped him with as windbreaks, the gapt's expression was clear enough. He would take out his annoyance in a report that would not be favorable to Hal. Unless, that is, his ward came across something so important in the humanoid ruins that it would justify this long trip.

The gapt—G.A.P.T., or Guardian Angel Pro Tempore—had wanted to wait the two days that would be needed until they could get a gig. The trip to the ruins could then have been made in fifteen minutes, a soundless and comfortable ride through the air. But Hal had argued that driving through the countryside would be as valuable—if not more so, in detecting any hidden large industries—as reconnoitering by air. That his superiors had agreed was another thing that had exasperated Pornsen. Where his ward went, he had to go. So he had sulked all day while the young Terran, coached by Zugu, wheeled the jalopy down the forest roads. The only times the gapt spoke was to remind Hal of the sacredness of the human self by telling him to slow down. Hal would nod and would ease his foot off the accelerator. But after a while he would roar and leap down the dirt road.

Zugu unscrewed both ends of the pipe, stuck one in his V-shaped mouth, and blew. Nothing came out the other end. Zugu shut his big blue eyes and blew again. Nothing happened, except that his already green-tinged face turned a dark green. Then he rapped the copper tubing against the hood and blew once more. No reaction.

Fobo reached into a large leather pouch slung from a belt around his big belly. His finger and thumb came out holding a tiny blue insect. Gently, he pushed the creature into one end of the pipe. In about five seconds a small red insect dropped out of the other end. Behind it, evidently in pursuit, came the blue. Fobo picked up his pet and put it back in the pouch. Zugu squashed the red thing beneath his bare heel.

"Voilà. C'est un mangeur de l'alcool, monsieur," said Fobo. "It lives in the tank and imbibes freely and unmolested. It extracts the carbohydrates therein. A swimmer upon the golden seas of alcohol. What a life! But now and then it goes into the sediment chamber, eats and devours the filter, and passes into the feedpipe. Voyez! Zugu is even now replacing the filter. In a moment we will be on our way and road."

Fobo's breath had a strange and sickening odor. Hal wondered if the wog had been drinking liquor. He had never smelled alcohol on anybody's breath before, so he had no experience to go on. But even the thought of it made Hal nervous. If his gapt knew a bottle was being passed back and forth in the rear seat, he would not for a minute let Hal out of his sight.

The wogs climbed into the back seat. "Allons!"

Pornsen pursed his thin lips. He had meant to ask Zugu to drive, but he realized the wogs might think he lacked confidence in Yarrow. He did, but he could not admit that in front of an Ozagenian.

Though Hall started slowly enough, he soon found his foot heavy. The trees began whizzing by. He glanced at Pornsen. The gapt's rigid back and set teeth showed that he was thinking of the report he would make to the chief Uzzite back in the spaceship. He looked mad enough to demand the 'Meter for his ward.

Yarrow breathed deeply the wind battering his face-mask. To H with Pornsen! To H with the 'Meter! The blood lurched in his veins. This planet's air was not stuffy Earth's. His lungs sucked it in like a happy bellows. At that moment he felt as if he could have snapped his fingers under the nose of the Sandalphon himself.

"Look out!" screamed Pornsen.

Hal glimpsed out of the corners of his eyes the large antelope-like beast that leaped from the forest onto the road. A half-second later, he twisted the wheel away from it. The jalopy skidded on the dirt. Its rear end swung around. Hal was not well enough grounded in the physics of driving to know that he should have turned the wheels in the direction of the skid to straighten the car out.

His lack of knowledge was not fatal, except to the beast, for its bulk struck the vehicle's side. Checked, the car quit trying to circle. Instead, it angled off the road and ran up a sloping ridge of earth. From there it leaped high into the air and landed with an all-at-once bang of four tires blowing.

Even that did not halt it. A big bush loomed. Hal jerked on the wheel. Too late.

His chest pushed hard against the wheel as if it were trying to telescope the steering shaft against the dashboard. Fobo slammed into Yarrow's back. Both cried out, and the wog fell off.

Then, except for a sharp hissing, there was silence. A pillar of steam from the broken radiator shot through the branches that held Hal's face in a rough barky embrace.

Yarrow stared through steamshapes into big brown eyes. He shook his head. Was he stunned? Eyes. And arms like branches.

Or branches like arms. He thought he was in the grip of a brown-eyed nymph. Or were they called dryads? He couldn't ask anybody. He wasn't supposed to know about such creatures. *Nymph* and *dryad* had even been cut out of such books as Hack's edition of the Revised and Moral Milton. Only an unexpurgated *Paradise Lost* booklegged from Israel, had enabled Hal to learn of Greek mythology.

Thoughts flashed off and on like lights on a spaceship's pilot-board. Nymphs sometimes turned into trees to escape their pursuers. Was this one the fabled forest women staring at him with large and beautiful eyes through the longest lashes he had ever seen?

He shut his lids and wondered if a head injury were responsible for the vision and if it were permanent. If it were, so what? Hallucinations like that were worth keeping.

He opened his eyes. The illusion was gone.

He thought, *It was that antelope looking at me. It got away after all. It ran around the bush and looked back. Antelope eyes.*

✑ Two ✑

He forgot about the eyes. He was choking. A heavy nauseating odor hung around the car. The crash must have frightened the wogs very much, else they would not have released the sphincter muscles which controlled the neck of their "madbags." This organ, a bladder located near the small of their backs, had once been used by the prehumanoid ancestors of the Ozagenians as a powerful weapon of defense in much the same way as a bombardier beetle thwarts attackers. Now an almost vestigial structure, the madbag served as a means of relieving extreme nervous tension. Its function was effective, but it presented problems such as that of the wog psychiatrists, who either had to keep their windows open or else wear gasmasks during therapy.

Hal pushed aside the branches and struggled over the side. Why didn't wogs build doors in their vehicles?

Wong Af Pornsen, assisted by Zugu, crawled out from under

the foliage. His big paunch, the color of his uniform, and the white nylon angel's wings sewed on the back of his jacket made him resemble a fat blue bug. When he stood up and took off his windmask, he showed a bloodless face. His shaking fingers fumbled over the crossed hourglass and sword, symbol of the Haijac Union, before they found the button he was searching for. He pulled out a pack of Merciful Cherubim. Once the cigarette was in his lips, he had a hard time holding the lighter to it.

Hal took out his own and held the glowing coil to the tobacco. It didn't waver.

Only thirty years of discipline could have shoved back the grin he felt deep inside his face muscles.

Pornsen accepted the light. A second later, a tremor of skin around his lips and eyes revealed that he knew he had lost much of his advantage over Yarrow. Trained in psychology, he realized you don't let a man do you a service—even one as slight as his ward's and then crack the whip on him.

He began formally, "Hal Shamshiel Yarrow . . ."

"Shib, abba, I hear."

"You're—uh—much too reckless."

Considering the offense, his voice was milder than it should have been. Now and then he stopped to draw in or puff out smoke.

"The hierarchy has had its eye (puff) upon you for a long time. Though you have not been suspected of any moral turpitude—as regards sex or liquor, that is—you have shown signs of a certain pride and independence. That is not shib, Yarrow. That is not real. It smacks of behavior that does not conform to the structure of the universe as we know it, as it has been revealed to mankind by the Forerunner, real be his name.

"I have (puff)—may the Forerunner forgive them!—sent two dozen men to H. I didn't like it, for I am a tenderhearted man, but it is the duty of the Guardian Angels Pro Tempore to watch out for the diseases of the self that may spread and infect the followers of Isaac Sigmen. Unreality must not be tolerated; the self is too weak and precious to be subjected to temptation.

"I have been your gapt since you were (puff) born. You always were a disobedient child, but you could be whipped into submissiveness, into seeing reality. Not until you were eighteen did you become hard to handle. That was when you decided to become a joat. I thought you'd make a very good specialist, and I warned you that as a joat you'd only get so high in our society. But you persisted. And since we have need of joats, and since I was overridden by my superior, I allowed you to become one.

"That wasn't too (puff) unshib, but when I picked out the woman most suitable to be your wife, I saw just how proud and rebellious you were. She was a woman whom the Urielites, selfdocs, and Sandalphons agreed was the ideal mate as set forth in the Western Talmud. And yet you argued and held out for a year before you consented to marry her. In that year of unreal behavior, you cost the Sturch one self . . ."

Hal's face had paled, and in so doing had revealed seven thin red marks that rayed out fanwise from the left corner of his lips and across his cheek to his ear. They were scars left by Pornsen's lash years before.

"I cost it nothing," blazed Hal. "Mary and I were married ten years, and she proved barren. And it was her fault, not mine, as the tests proved. When that came out, why didn't you insist on our divorce, as your duty required, instead of pigeonholing my petition?"

Pornsen blew out smoke slowly enough, but his voice tensed. He dropped one shoulder lower than the other, a characteristic when he forgot himself, and said, "That's another thing. I was sure when you applied for this expedition that it was not out of desire to serve the Sturch in its quest for new lands for our overcrowded planets. (Puff) I was sure you signed up for one reason. To get away from your wife. Since barrenness, adultery, and space travel are the only legal grounds for divorce, and adultery means going to H, you took the only way out. You became legally dead. You—"

"You can't prove it!" Hal was shaking, and loathed himself because he could not hide his rage.

"Oh, I could have, if I had recommended you for the Elohi-meter. But we needed scientists very much, and my superiors thought it best to overlook your possible motives. Besides, you had an excuse in that sterility report, which was lost through the inefficiency of my secretaries.

"However, the hierarchy has been slowly and regretfully, but surely, coming to the conclusion that you do not have a high enough regard for your self. Or that of others.

"The self, as defined by Isaac Sigmen, is sacred, sacred to God, to the angels both high and low, to the pre-Torah prophets . . ."

Hal listened with only a half-ear. Pornsen was repeating Moral Lecture PT19, which his ward knew by heart. Hal was looking at the beast's body crumpled on the road. Now he remembered the thump the jalopy had made when it struck it. But if it were dead, whose eyes had he seen through the bush?

Fobo, the empathist, was bending over it. He straightened up; large tears filled his blue eyes and ran down the long tubular nose. The antennae rising from his bald forehead waved. He made a circular sign with his index finger over the carcass.

Hal said to Pornsen, "Shut up!"

The gapt stiffened. The lower left shoulder drew level with the other. The cigarette fell from his slack thin lips. Red swarmed up his bull-neck and sagging jowls. His right hand shot to his belt and grabbed the crux ansata on the handle of his whip. He jerked it out and cracked it in the air.

The marks on Yarrow's cheek tingled in remembrance of that other time when the lashes, one for each of the Seven Deadly Unrealities, had cut the flesh.

The gapt said, "How dare you?"

Hal said in a low voice, swiftly, "A moment ago you said some-thing in English. You know French is the only tongue we're allowed to speak under any circumstances."

The whip dropped.

"When—when was that?"

"When you screamed at me just before we struck that animal. Remember? And when you were yelling for help under the bush."

Pornsen stuck the whip back in his belt and lit up another Merciful Seraphim. His fifth that day. Another, and he'd be over his quota.

"You say nothing to the chief," he muttered. "And I'll keep quiet about your sibboleth recklessness."

"Shib," agreed Hal.

He tried to keep the contempt and elation out of his voice. Once a gapt cracked . . .

Pornsen rolled his small green eyes at the approaching Fobo. "Think he heard me?"

"I wouldn't know."

Fobo stopped and looked at them. His antennae became rigid. He said, "Un argument, messieurs?"

Fobo had wept as the dying beast's nervous discharges of grief and pain struck his overtrained, too receptive antennae. Now he smiled the ghastly V-in-V smile of a wogglebug. Though super-sensitive, his nervous system was a hit and run one. Charge and discharge came easily.

"Non!" replied Hal. "No disagreement. We were just wondering how far we'd have to walk to get to the humanoid ruins. Your jalopy's wrecked. Tell Zugu I'm sorry."

"Ca ne fait rien. The walk will be pleasant and stimulating. It is only a mile. Or thereabouts."

"Bien. Allons."

The ward turned away and threw his mask and goggles in the rear seat of the car, where the Ozagenians had laid theirs.

He picked up his suitcase, but left the gapt's on the floor. Let him carry his own.

He said, "Fobo, aren't you afraid the driving-clothes will be stolen?"

"Pardon? What does that mean?"

"Voler. Voler. To take an article of property from someone without their permission, and keep it for yourself. It is a crime, punishable by law."

"Un crime?"

Hal gave up. He shrugged and moved his long legs fast.

Behind him the gapt, afraid of losing dignity if he trailed behind Hal, and angry because his ward was breaking etiquette by forcing him to carry his own case, shouted, "You'll pay for this, you—you joat!"

With which outburst he lost face.

Hal didn't turn. He plunged on ahead. The angry retort he was phrasing beneath his breath fizzed away. Out of the corner of his eye he had caught a flash of white skin in the green summer foliage.

But when he turned to look for it, it was gone. Nor did he see it or its owner the rest of the day.

☙ THREE ❧

Soo Yarrow. Soo Yarrow. B'swa. L'fvayfvoo, Soo Yarrow."

Hal woke up. For a moment, he didn't remember where he was. Then he recalled that he was sleeping in one of the marble rooms of the mammal-humanoid ruins. The moonlight, brighter than Earth's, poured in through the doorway. It shone on a small shape on the floor near the entrance, and on a flying insect that passed above the shape. Something long and thin flickered up and wrapped itself around the flier and pulled it into a suddenly gaping mouth.

The lizard loaned by the ruins custodian was doing a fine job of keeping out pests.

Hal turned his head to look at the open window a foot above him. The bugcatcher there was busily sweeping the area clean of mosquitoes. From beyond that moonwashed square the voice had seemed to come. He listened. Silence. Then a snuffling and rattling jerked him upright. A thing the size of a raccoon stood by the doorway. It was one of the quasi-insects, the so called lungbugs, that prowled the forest at night. It represented a development of arthropod not found on Earth. Unlike its Terran cousins, it no longer depended solely on tracheae, or breathing tubes, for oxygen. A pair of distensible sacs; like a frog's, swelled out and fell in behind its mouth, and enabled it to make the heavy breathing sound.

Though it was shaped like a preying mantis, Hal wasn't worried. Fobo had told him it would not attack without provocation.

A shrilling like that of an alarm clock suddenly filled the room. Pornsen, on the cot across the room, sat up. He saw the insect and yelled. It scurried off. The shrilling, which had come from the mechanism on Pornsen's wrist, stopped.

Pornsen lay down and groaned. "That makes the sixth time those bugs have woke me up."

"Turn off the wristbox," said Hal.

Pornsen did not answer. For about ten minutes he was restless and then he began snoring. Hal's lids felt heavy. He must have dreamed the soft low voice speaking in a tongue neither Terran nor Ozagenian. He must have, because it had been human; and he and the gapt were the only specimens of *Homo sapiens* for at least two hundred miles.

It had been a woman's voice. God! To hear one again. Almost two years now!

And he knew it would probably be five years before he would hear another. That is, if he returned.

"Soo Yarrow. L'fvayfvoo. Say mwa, zh'not w'stinvak."

Hal stood up. His neck was cased in ice. The whisper *was* coming from the window. He turned his head. The outline of a woman's head leaned into the solid box of moonlight that was the window. Moonwash fell off white shoulders. A pale finger crossed the black of mouth.

"Poo lamoo d'b'tyu, soo. Seelahs. F'nay. Feet, seel-fvooplay."

Numbed, but obeying as if shot full of hypno-lipno, he threw aside the sheet over his legs. Slowly, he turned on his buttocks and moved his feet until they touched the stone floor. With a look to make sure Pornsen was still asleep, he rose.

For a second his training almost overcame him and forced him to wake the gapt up. But it was evident the woman was addressing him alone. Her urgency and suppressed fear decided him to take a chance. It also made him wonder if she might not be a member of one of the unreal sects that had fled the Haijac Union two hundred or more years ago—

No. That couldn't be. She spoke in no tongue he knew. For that same reason, it was improbable that she was a party to an expedition from one of the other Earth nations.

Her words had seemed to click something familiar, however— as if he ought to know the language. But he didn't. It wasn't the English or Icelandic or Caucasian of the Haijac Union, or the Hebrew of the Israeli Republics, or the Bazaar or Swahili of the Bantu-Malay Federation. Yet it had sounded like something he'd heard before. And recently.

He picked up his suitcase and shoved it under the sheet. He rolled up a blanket and packed it next to the case. His jacket he folded and laid on the pillow. If Pornsen woke up and took a quick look at the cot, he might be fooled into thinking the bulk under the sheet was Hal's.

Softly, on bare feet, he walked to the doorway. A cylinder the size of a tin can squatted on guard. If any object larger than a mouse came within two feet of the field radiating from the cylinder, it would set up a disturbance which would cause a signal to be transmitted to the small box mounted on a silver bracelet around the gapt's wrist. The box would shrill—as it had at the appearance of the lungbug and up would come Pornsen from the bottom of his ever-watchful sleep.

The watchcan was not only there to insure against trespassers. Its primary purpose was to make certain that Hal would not leave the room without Pornsen's knowledge. As the ruins had no working plumbing, the only permissible excuse to step outside would be to relieve bowel or bladder. The gapt would go along to see that that was what he intended.

Two things Pornsen was watching for. One was unsupervised contact with the wogs. The other was that unreal conduct, punishable by exile to H and cataloged in the Sefer shel ha Chetim, or the Book of Sins, as Onanism. The long space voyage had resulted in the arrest of five men for that very unreality.

Hal picked up one of the flyswatters given them by the ruins custodian. It had a three-foot-long handle made of some flexible wood. Its mass would not be enough to touch off the field.

Though his hand trembled, he grasped the swatter-end and very gently pushed the cylinder to one side with the handle. He had to be careful not to upset it, for that, too, would trigger the alarm. Fortunately, the stone floor was smooth.

When he had stepped outside, he reached back in and slid the cylinder back to its former spot. Then, with his heart pounding under the double burden of tampering with the guard and of meeting a strange woman, he walked around the corner.

She had moved from the window into the shadow of a kneeling goddess' statue about sixty yards away. When Hal began striding toward her, he saw the reason for her hiding. Fobo was strolling towards him. Hal walked faster. He wanted to intercept the wog before he noticed the girl and also before he came so close that their voices might wake up Pornsen.

"Bon soir," greeted Fobo. His antennae described little circles. "You seem nervous. Is it that incident of the forenoon?"

"Non. I am just restless."

Hal looked at the empathist. Ozagen! What was the story? That the discoverer of this planet, upon first seeing the natives, had exclaimed, "Oz again!" because the aborigines had so much resembled Frank Baum's Professor Wogglebug? Their bodies were rather round, and their limbs were skinny in proportion. Their mouths were shaped like two broad and shallow V's, one set inside the other. The lips were thick and lobular. Actually, a wogglebug had four lips, each leg of the two V's separated by a deep seam at the connection. Once, far back on the evolutionary path, those lips had been modified arms. Now they were rudimentary limbs, so disguised as true labial parts that no one who did not know their history would have guessed their origin. When the wide V-in-V mouths opened in a laugh, they startled the Terrans. The teeth were quite human, true, but a fold of skin hung from the roof of the mouth. Once the epipharynx, it was now a vestigial upper tongue, of no use at all except to tell of the wogs' arthropodal ancestry.

Their skins were as unpigmented as Hal's redhead complexion, but where the Earthman's epidermis was pink, theirs was a very faint green. Copper, not iron, carried oxygen in their blood cells.

They had antennae, their forepates were bald, but a stiff cork-screw fuzz rose from their backpates to form a corona. To complete the Oz parallel, their noses were bridgeless and shot straight out from their faces in projectile fashion.

The Terran who first saw them might have been justified by his remark. However, the story wasn't true. Ozagen was the native name for "Mother Earth."

⁍ FOUR ⁍

Wogglebug they were called, yet they were no more insects than the Earthmen. It was true that millions of years ago their ancestors had been a primitive unspecialized wormlike arthropod. But evolution follows parallel paths when aiming at intelligent beings. Realizing the limitations of the anatomy, she had split Fobo's Nth-great-grandfather from the arthropod phylum. When the crustacea, arachnida, and insecta had formed exoskeletons and ventral nervous systems, Grandpa the Nth had declined to go along with his cousins. He had refused to harden his delicate cuticle-skin into chitin and had begun shifting the central nerves from chest and belly to the back and had also erected a skeleton inside the flesh. Both of the latter feats were equal to lifting oneself by the bootstraps.

As the price for that action, by the time the true arthropods were very developed, highly specialized creatures creeping, hopping, and flying by the billions over the hot new globe, Fobo's ancestors were still ugly, flatwormish things hiding from their beautiful, fully rounded-out relatives.

Becoming chordate arthropods—a contradiction in terms, by the way—was a deed that took many millions of years and much humility and self-denial.

Yet it had been worth it. The wogs' fathers had finally made the ventral to dorsal shift and sheathed their bones in muscle. Their cold blood became warm; they developed airsacs and then lungs. Their nerves ramified and grew intricate. The strata-shot eye of the epoch winked, and a monkeylike creature appeared.

Another wink, and it was an ape. After a very long while, as years go, it came down from the trees. Once brachiate, it began walking on two feet. It passed through australopithecoid, pithecanthropoid, and neanderthaloid stages. It became Fobo.

One of the few arthropodal heritages left was the pair of antennae. Eras ago they might have been used, as some insects are supposed to use theirs, for communication. Now their function was rudimentary, but effective. They were so sensitive they could pick up nervous discharges from the skin of other beings. That gift, thought Hal, probably helped make the Ozagen society what it was. No wogglebug could fool another about his emotions. If he pretended friendliness, he would be betrayed. Hate, fear, rage, affection and love were easily read. A wog had to express what he felt, because he could not hide it. And once he had expressed, he had discharged his emotions, rebalanced his organism, and opened himself to rational talk and conduct.

At least, that was the theory. In actual practice, as Fobo said, it was not so easy.

Hal became aware that Fobo was talking to him:

"—this joat that monsieur Pornsen called you when he was so angry and furious. What does that mean?"

The Terran could not tell Fobo that the word was an initial combination, formed from the first letters of jack-of-all-trades. The wog would wonder how they deduced that combination from French.

"It means," he said carefully, "that I am not a specialist in any of the sciences, but one who knows, or is supposed to know, a great deal about all of them. Actually, I am a liaison officer between various scientists and the government. It is my business to summarize and integrate what is going on in science and then report to the hierarchy."

He glanced at the statue. The woman was not in sight.

"Science has become so specialized that intelligible communication even between scientists in the same field is very difficult. Each has a deep vertical knowledge of his own little field, but not much horizontal. The more he knows about his own subject, the less aware he is of what others are doing. It is so bad that a physicist, for instance, who deals in mercury anti-ions will find it hard to talk the same language as one whose study is radioactive isotopes. Or two doctors who specialize in nose dysfunctions. One treats the left nostril; the other, the right. Believe me, that's not exaggerated."

Fobo shrugged his shoulders and threw up his hands. He might have been French.

"But . . . science would come to a standstill!"

"Exactly."

Hal saw a head stick out from the base of the statue. It withdrew. Hal began sweating.

Fobo questioned the joat about the religion of the Forerunner. Hal was as taciturn as possible and replied to some questions not at all. The wog was nothing if not logical, and logic was the light that Hal had never turned upon what he had been taught by the Urielites.

Finally the empathist said, "I feel that this conversation is making you nervous. Perhaps we can pursue it some other time. Tell me, what do you think of these ruins?"

"Very interesting. What I cannot imagine is how these people, who you say once covered this huge continent, could entirely die out."

"Oh, there may be a few in the backwoods or jungles. But most died in the wars with us about five hundred years ago. Since then there's been peace on this planet. It's true we wiped them out, but they were very decadent, quarrelsome and greedy, and forced my ancestors to fight them."

Human, all right, thought Hal.

"I'll tell you later about their decline and fall," Fobo said. "In some ways it is a fantastic story. Right now, I think I'll go to bed."

"I'm restless. If you don't mind, I'll poke around. These ruins are fascinating in the moonlight."

"Reminds me of a poem by our great bard, Shamero. If I could remember it, I'd quote it." Fobo's V-in-V lips yawned. "Bonne nuit."

Hal watched him until he'd disappeared, then turned and walked toward the statue of the Great Mother. When he got to the shadows in its base, he saw the girl slipping into the darkness cast by a mountainous heap of rubble. He followed, only to see her thirty yards ahead, leaning against a monolith. Beyond was the lake, silvery and black in the moonpaint.

"B'swa, soo Yarrow." Her voice was low and throaty.

"Bon soir, mademoiselle," he said mechanically . . . and then paused, struck.

OF COURSE! Now he knew why it had had a familiar ring. B'swa was bon soir! Even though her words were a degraded form, they could not disguise their essential Latinity. B'swa! And l'fvay-fvoo was levez-vous, which was French for "get up." How could he have missed it? It must have been because his mind wasn't expecting the familiar, and therefore had not recognized it. Say mwa. C'est moi. It's I. And soo Yarrow. Could that be monsieur Yarrow? The initial m dropped. Final r also. Abandonment of nasalization plus vowel and consonant shifts in other words. Different, but still subtly Gallic.

"Bon soir, mademoiselle."

How inadequate those words were. Here were two human beings meeting a thousand light-years from Earth, one a man who had not seen a woman for two years, the other a woman obviously hiding; perhaps the only woman left on the planet. And all he could say was "Good evening, miss."

He stepped closer. Suddenly he was flushed with heat. Her white skin was relieved only by two black, narrow strips of cloth, one across her breasts, the other diapered around the hips. In all his life he had seen only one woman who was not clad from neck to floor in thick cloth, and that had been in a semidarkness. She had been his wife.

The heat of his embarrassment was followed by a gasp of astonishment. She was lipsticked! Her lips were scarlet in the moonlight with the forbidden rouge.

His mind gave that problem a quick flip in the air and considered its other side. Cosmetics had gone out with the coming of the Forerunner. They were unreal, immoral. No woman dared . . .

well, that wasn't true . . . it was just in the Haijac Union that they were not used. Israeli and Bantu women wore rouge; but then everybody knew what kind of women they were.

Another step, and Hal breathed hard again. He was close enough to see that the scarlet was natural. That meant that she was not Earthborn but was an Ozagen human being. The murals in the ruins showed red-lipped women, and Fobo had told him they were born with the flaming labile pigment.

But how could that be? She spoke a Terran dialect.

The next moment he forgot about his doubts and paradoxes. She was clinging to him and he had his arms around her, clumsily trying to comfort her. She was pouring out words, one so fast after the other that even though he knew they came from the French he could only make out a word here and a phrase there.

Hal asked her to slow down and go over what she had said. She paused, her head cocked slightly to the left, while he enunciated clearly his request. When he was through, she brushed back the hair over one ear, a gesture he was to find characteristic of her when she was thinking.

Then she repeated.

She began slowly enough. But as she progressed she speeded up, her full lips working like two bright-red things independent of her, packed with their own life and purpose.

Fascinated, Hal watched them. As they worked, they seemed to send stabs of desire into him, almost as if they were heliographing erotic messages.

With an effort he lifted his gaze from them and listened, trying to grasp her whole story.

She told it disconnectedly and with repetition and backtracking. But he could understand that her name was Jeanette, that she came from a plateau in the tropics of Ozagen, that she was one of the few human beings left on the planet, that she had been captured by an exploring party of wogs and taken to Siddo, that she had only recently escaped, that she had been hiding in the ruins and the nearby forest, that she was frightened because of the things that prowled the forest at night, that she lived on wild fruit and berries or on food stolen from wog farmhouses, that she had seen Hal when he crashed the jalopy, that she had followed him and listened to his conversations with the two wogs and with the gapt, that she could tell by her instincts—here she used a word that he did not understand but which he translated as "instincts"—that he was a man she could trust, that he had to do something for her.

That he had to save her.

Tears filled her big dark eyes, and her voice broke. She leaned against him; her shoulders were soft and smooth; her full breasts pressed against his ribs. What her words did not say, her body did.

Yarrow thought swiftly. He had to get back to the room in the ruins before Pornsen woke up. And he couldn't see her tomorrow, because a gig from the ship was picking the two Haijacs up in the morning. Whatever he was going to do would have to be told to her in the next few minutes.

Suddenly he had a plan; it unfolded in an instant from another idea, one he had long carried around buried in the fertile soil of his brain. Its seeds had been in him even before the ship had left Earth. But he hadn't had the courage to carry it out. Now, with the sudden appearance of this girl as a catalyst, he was thrown into action. She was what he needed to spark his guts and make him step onto a path that, once taken, could not be retraced.

"Jeannette," he said rapidly and fiercely, "listen to me! You'll have to wait here every night. No matter what things haunt the dark, you'll have to be here. I can't tell you just when I'll be able to get a gig and fly here. Sometime in the next three weeks, I think. If I'm not here by then, keep waiting. Keep waiting! I'll be here! And when I am, we'll be safe. Safe for a while, at least. Can you do that? Can you hide here? And wait?"

She nodded her head and said, "Vi."

✧ Five ✧

Two weeks later, Yarrow flew from the spaceship *Gabriel* to the ruins. His needle-shaped gig gleamed in the big moon as it floated over the white marble buildings and settled to a stop. The city lay silent and bleached, great stone cubes and hexagons and cylinders and pyramids and statues like toys left scattered while the giant child went to bed and slept forever.

The Terran stepped out, glanced to left and right, and then strode to an enormous arch. His flashlight probed its darkness; his voice echoed from the faraway roof and walls.

"Jeannette. C'est moi. Votre ami, Hal Yarrow. Jeannette. Où êtes vous?"

He walked down the fifty-yard-broad staircase that led to the crypts of the kings. The beam bounced up and down the steps and suddenly splashed against the black and white figure of the girl.

"Hal!" she cried, looking up at him. "Thank the Great Stone Mother! I've waited every night! But I knew you'd come!"

Tears trembled on the long lashes; her scarlet mouth was screwed up as if she were doing her best to keep from sobbing. He wanted to take her in his arms and comfort her, but a lifetime of "you-must-nots" stiffened his arms. It was a terrible thing even to look at a woman as unclothed as she was. To embrace her would be unthinkable. Nevertheless, that was exactly what he was thinking of.

The next minute, as if divining his paralysis, she moved to him and put her head on his chest. Her own shoulders hunched forward as she tried to burrow into him. He found his arms going around her. His muscles tightened, and heat stabbed from his stomach down into his loins.

He released her and looked away. "We'll talk later. We've no time to lose. Come."

She followed him, silently, until they came to the gig. Then she hesitated by the door. He gestured impatiently for her to climb in and sit down beside him.

"You will think I'm a coward," she said. "But I have never been in a flying machine. To leave this solid earth . . ."

Surprised, he could only stare at her. It was hard for him to understand the mental attitude of a person totally unaccustomed to airtravel. Such reactions did not fit into his culture.

"Get in!" he barked.

Obediently enough, she got in and sat down in the co-pilot's seat. She could not keep from trembling, however, or looking with huge brown eyes at the instruments before and around her.

Deciding the best thing to do was to ignore her fear, Hal glanced at his watchphone.

"Ten minutes to get to my apartment in the city. One minute to drop you off there. A half-minute to return to the ship. Fifteen minutes to report on my espionage among the wogs. Thirty seconds to return to the apartment. Not quite half an hour in all. Not bad."

He laughed. "I would have been here two days ago, but I had to wait until all the gigs that were on automatic were in use. Then I pretended that I was in a hurry, that I had forgotten some notes, and that I had to go back to my apartment to pick them up. So I borrowed one of the manually controlled gigs used for exploration outside the city. I never could have gotten permission from the O.D. for that, but he was overwhelmed by this."

Hal touched a large golden badge on his left chest. It bore a Hebrew L.

"That means I'm one of the Chosen. I've passed the 'Meter."

Jeannette had seemingly forgotten her terror and had been looking at Hal's face in the glow from the panel-light. She gave a little cry. "Hal Yarrow! What have they done to you?" Her fingers touched his face.

He looked at her. A deep purple ringed his eyes; his cheeks were sunken, and in one a muscle twitched; a rash spread ever his forehead; and the seven whipmarks stood out against a pale skin.

"Anybody would say I was crazy to do it," he said. "I stuck my head in the lion's mouth. And he didn't bite my head off. Instead, I bit his tongue."

"What do you mean?"

"Listen. Didn't you think it was strange that Pornsen wasn't with me tonight, breathing his sanctimonious breath down my neck? No? Well, you don't know our setup. There was only one way I could get permission to move out of my quarters in the ship and get an apartment in Siddo. That is, without having a gapt living with me to watch my every move. And without having to leave you out here in the forest. And I couldn't do that."

He shook his head. She ran her finger down the line from his nose to the corner of his lip. Ordinarily he would have shrunk from the touch, because he hated close contact with anybody. Now, he didn't shrink.

"Hal," she said softly. "M' sheh."

"Mon cher," he corrected

"Mon cher," she repeated.

He felt a glow. My dear. Well, why not?

To stave off the headiness her touch gave, he said, "There was only one thing to do. Volunteer for the 'Meter."

"Le Mètre? Keskasekasah?"

"It's the only thing that can free you from the constant shadow of a gapt. Once you've passed it, you're pure, above suspicion—theoretically, at least.

"My petition caught the hierarchy off guard. They never expected any of the scientists—let alone me—to volunteer. Urielites and Uzzites have to take it if they hope to advance in the hierarchy—"

"Urielites? Uzzites?"

"To put it in ancient terminology, priests and cops. The Forerunner adopted those terms—the names of angels—for religious-governmental use—from the Talmud. See?"

"Non."

"You'll be clearer about that later. Anyway, only the most zealous ask to face the 'Meter. It's true that many people do but the majority do it because they are compelled to. The Urielites were gloomy about my chances before it, but they were forced by law to let me try my chances. Besides, they were bored, and they wanted to be entertained—in their grim fashion.

He scowled a little at the memory. "So it was that a day later I was told to report to the psych lab at 2300 S.T.—Ship's Time, that is. I went into my cabin—Pornsen was out—opened my labcase, and took out a bottle labeled 'Prophetsfood.' It was supposed to contain a powder whose base was peyote. That's a drug that was once used by American Indian medicine-men."

"Quoi?"

"Just listen. You'll get the main points. Prophetsfood is taken by everybody during Purification Period. That's two days of locking yourself in a cell, fasting, praying, being flagellated by electric whips, and seeing visions induced by hunger and Prophetsfood. Also subjective time-traveling."

"Quoi?"

"Don't keep saying 'What?' I haven't got time to explain dunnology . . . It took me ten years of hard study to understand it and its mathematics. Even then, there were a lot of questions I had. But it's not wise to ask them. You might be thought to be doubting.

"Anyway, my bottle did not hold Prophetsfood. Instead it contained a substitute I'd secretly prepared just before the ship left Earth. That powder was the reason why I dared face the 'Meter. And why I was not as terrified as I should have been . . . though I was scared enough. Believe me."

"I do believe you. You were brave. You overcame your fear."

Hot blood crept beneath his face-skin. It was the first time in his life he had ever been complimented.

"A month before the expedition took off for Ozagen, I had noticed in one of the many scientific journals that passed under my nose an announcement that a certain drug had been synthesized. Its efficacy was in destroying the virus of the so-called Sirian 'rash.' What interested me was a footnote. It was in small print and in Hebrew, which showed that the biochemist must have realized its importance."

"Poow kwa?"

"Why? Well, I imagine it was in Hebrew in order to keep any layman from understanding it. If a secret like that became generally known . . .

"The note commented briefly that it had been found that a man suffering from the 'rash' was temporarily immune to the effects of hypno-lipno. And that the Urielites should take care during any sessions with the 'Meter that their subject was healthy."

"I have trouble understanding you," she said.

"I'll go slower. Hypno-lipno is the most widely used truth-drug. I saw at once the implications in the note. The beginning of the article had described how the Sirian 'rash' was narcotically induced for experimental purposes. The drug used was not named, but it did not take me long to look it and its processing up in other journals. I thought: if the true 'rash' would make a man immune to hypno-lipno, why wouldn't the artificial?

"No sooner said than done. I prepared a batch, inserted a tape of questions about my personal life in a psychotester, injected the 'rash' drug, injected the truth drug, and swore that I would lie to the tester about my life. And I *could* lie, even though shot full of hypno-lipno!"

"You're so intelligent," she murmured.

She squeezed his biceps. He hardened them. It was a vain thing to do, but he wanted her to think he was strong.

"Nonsense!" he clipped. "A blind man would have seen what to do. In fact, I wouldn't be surprised if the Uzzites had arrested the chemist and put out orders for some other truth drug to be used. If they did, they were too late. Our ship left before any such news reached us.

"Anyway, the first day with the 'Meter was nothing to worry about. I took a twelve-hour written and oral test in serialism. That's Dunne's theories of time and Sigmen's amplifications on it. I've been taking that same test for years. Easy but tiring.

"The next day I rose early, bathed, injected what was supposed to be Prophetsfood, and, breakfastless, went into the Purification Cell. Alone, I lay two days on a cot. From time to time I took a drink of water or a shot of the false drug. Now and then I pressed the button that sent the mechanical scourge lashing against me. The more flagellations, you know, the higher your credit.

"I didn't see any visions. I did break out with the 'rash.' That didn't worry me. If anybody got suspicious, I could explain that I had an allergy to Prophetsfood. Some people do."

He looked below. Moonfrosted forest and an occasional square or hexagonal light from a farmhouse. Ahead was the high range of hills that shielded Siddo.

"So," he continued, unconsciously talking faster as the hills loomed closer, "at the end of my purification I rose, dressed, and ate the ceremonial dinner of locusts and honey."

"Ugh!"

"Locusts aren't so bad if you've been eating them since childhood."

"Locusts are delicious," she said. "I've eaten them many times. It's the combination with honey that sickens me."

He shrugged and said, "I'm turning out the cabin lights. Get down on the floor. And put on that cloak and night-mask. You can pass for a wog."

Obediently she slid off the seat. Before he flicked the lights off, he glanced down. She was leaning over while picking up the cloak, and he could not help getting a full glimpse of her superb breasts. Though he jerked his head away, he kept the image in his head. He felt both deeply aroused and ashamed.

He continued uncomfortably: "Then the hierarch came in. Macneff the Sandalphon, that is, the Archurielite, the theologians, and the dunnological specialists: the psychoneural parallelists, the interventionists, the substratumists, the chronentropists, the pseudo-temporalists, the cosmobservists.

"I was seated on a chair. Wires were taped to my body. Needles were stuck in my arms and back. Hypno-lipno was injected. The lights were turned out. Prayers were said; readings from the Western Talmud and the Revised Scriptures were intoned. Then a spotlight shone down from the ceiling upon the Elohimeter . . ."

"Keskasekasah?"

"Elohim is Hebrew for God. Meter is Greek for—well, for those." He pointed at the instrument panel. "The Elohimeter is round and enormous, and its needle, as long as my arm, is straight up and down. The circumference of the dial's face is marked with Hebraic letters that are supposed to mean something to those giving the test.

"Most people are ignorant of what the dipping and rising needle shows. But I'm a joat. I've access to the books that describe the test."

"Then you knew the answers, nespa?"

"Oui. Though that means nothing, because hypno-lipno brings out the truth, the reality . . . unless, of course, you are suffering from Sirian 'rash,' natural or artificial."

His sudden laugh was a mirthless bark.

"Under the drug, Jeannette, all the dirty and foul things you've done and thought, all the hates you've had for your superiors, all the doubts about the realness of the Forerunner's doctrines—these rise up from your lower-level minds like soap released at the bottom of a dirty bathtub. Up it comes, slick and irresistibly buoyant and covered with all the layers of scum.

"But I sat there, and I watched the needle—it's just like watching the face of God, Jeannette—you can't understand that, can you?—and I lied. Oh, I didn't overplay it. I didn't pretend to be incredibly pure and faithful. I confessed to minor unrealities. Then the needle would flicker and go back around the circumference a few square letters. But on the big issues, I answered as if my life depended on them. Which it did.

"And I told them my dreams—my subjective time-traveling."

"Subjectif?"

"Oui. Everybody travels in time subjectively. But the Forerunner is the only man, except his first disciples and a few of the scriptural prophets, who has traveled objectively.

"Anyway, my dreams were beauties—architecturally speaking. Just what they liked to hear. My last, and crowning; creation—or lie—was one in which the Forerunner himself appeared on Ozagen and spoke to the Sandalphon, Macneff. That event is supposed to take place a year from now.

"Oh, Hal!" she breathed. "Why did you tell them that?"

"Because now, ma chère, the expedition will not leave Ozagen until that year is up.. They couldn't go without giving up the chance of seeing Sigmen in the flesh as he voyages up and down the stream of time. Nor without making a liar of him. And of me. So, you see, that colossal lie will make sure that we have at least a year together . . .

"And then?"

"We'll think of something else then." Her throaty voice murmured in the darkness by the seat: "And you would do all that for me . . ."

Hal did not reply. He was too busy keeping the gig close to the rooftop level. Clumps of buildings, widely separated by woods, flashed by. So fast was he going that he almost overshot Fobo's castlelike house. Three stories high, medieval-seeming with its crenellated towers and gargoyle heads of stone beasts and insects leering out from many niches, it was not nearer than a hundred yards to any other building. Wogs built their cities with plenty of elbow-room in mind.

Jeanette put on the long-snouted nightmask; the gig's door swung open; they ran across the sidewalk and into the building. After they dashed through the lobby and up on the steps to the second floor, they had to stop while Hal fumbled for the key. He had had a wog smith make the lock and a wog carpenter install it. He hadn't trusted the carpenter's mate from the ship, because there was too much chance of duplicate keys being made.

He finally found the key, had trouble inserting it. When the door opened, he was breathing hard. He almost pushed Jeannette through. She had taken her mask off.

"Wait, Hal," she said, leaning her weight against his. "Haven't you forgotten something?"

"Oh, *Forerunner!* What could it be? Something serious?"

"No. I only thought," and she smiled and then lowered her lids, "that it was the Terran custom for men to carry their brides across the threshold."

His jaw dropped. Bride! She was certainly taking a lot for granted!

He couldn't take time to argue. Without a word, he swept her up in his arms and carried her into the apartment. There he put her down and said, "Back as soon as possible. If anybody knocks or tries to get in, hide in that special closet I told you about. Don't make a sound or come out until you're sure it's me."

She suddenly put her arms around him and kissed him.

"M'sheh, m'gwa foh."

Things were going too fast. He didn't say a word or even return her kiss. Vaguely he felt that her words, applied to him, were somewhat ridiculous. If he translated her degenerate French right, she had called him her dear, her strong man.

Turning, he closed the door; but not so quickly that he did not see the hall light shine on a white face haloed blackly by a hood. A red red mouth stained the whiteness.

He shook. He had a feeling that Jeannette was not going to be the frigid mate so much admired, officially, by the Sturch.

✑ SIX ✑

Hal was an hour late returning home from the *Gabriel,* because the Sandalphon asked for more details about the prophecy he'd made concerning Sigmen. Then Hal had to dictate his report on the day's espionage to a stenoservo. Afterwards, he ordered a sailor to pilot his gig back to the apartment. While he was walking toward the launching-rack, he met Pornsen.

"Shalom, abba," greeted Hal.

He smiled and rubbed his knuckles against the raised lamech on the shield.

The gapt's left shoulder, always low, sagged even more, as if it were a flag dipping in surrender. His ward was now out of his reach. More, if there were any whipcuts to be given, they would be struck by Yarrow.

The joat puffed out his chest and started to walk on, but Pornsen said, "Just a minute, son. Are you going back to the city?"

"Shib."

"Shib. I'll ride back with you. I have an apartment in the same building. On the third floor, right next door to Fobo's."

Hal opened his mouth to protest, then closed it. It was Pornsen's turn to smile. He knew he had nettled the joat. He turned and led the way. Hal followed with tight lips. Had the gapt perhaps trailed him and seen his meeting with Jeannette? No. If he had, he would have had Hal arrested at once.

The thing was that the gapt was small-minded. He knew his presence would annoy Hal.

Under his breath Hal quoted an old proverb, "A gapt's teeth never let loose."

The sailor was waiting by the gig. They all got in and dropped silently into the night.

At the apartment-building Hal strode into the doorway ahead of Pornsen. He felt a slight glow of satisfaction at thus breaking etiquette and expressing his contempt for the man.

Before opening his door, he paused. The guardian angel passed silently behind him. Hal, struck with a devilish thought, called out in French, "Père!"

Pornsen turned.

"What?"

"Would you care to inspect my rooms and see if I'm hiding a woman in there?"

The little man purpled. He closed his eyes and swayed, dizzy with sheer fury. When he opened them he shouted, "Yarrow! If ever I saw an unreal personality, you're it! I don't care how you stand with the hierarchy! I think you're—you're—just not simply shib!"

Hal looked blank. "I'm sure I don't know what you mean, Pornsen. I'm pure. I've proven there isn't an evil thought in my head."

His voice became strident, harsh. "Pornsen, you've just been talking in English! I'm sorry, but I have to report that in the morning. You know what that means!"

Pornsen's red face was suddenly drained of its blood. He opened his mouth, closed it, looked at Yarrow's merciless face, spun on his bootheels and walked away.

Hal leaned against the doorway. He felt both weak and

triumphant. When he had recovered from the reaction of baiting his guardian, he turned the key in his lock. Around and around in his head flew the thought that it had taken this girl only a few hours to fill him with enough courage to overcome thirty years of fear and submissiveness.

He clicked on the front room lights. Looking beyond into the dining room, he could see the closed kitchen door. The rattling of pots came through it. He sniffed deeply.

Steak!

The pleasure was replaced by a frown. He'd told her to hide until he returned. What if he had been a wog or an Uzzite?

When he swung the door open, the hinges squeaked. Jeannette's back was to him. At the first protest of unoiled iron, she whirled. The spatula in her hand dropped; the other hand flew to her open mouth.

The angry words on his lips died. If he were to scold her now, she would probably break out in embarrassing tears.

"M'tyuh! You startled me!"

He grunted and went by her to lift the lids on the pots.

"You see," she said, her voice trembling as if she divined his anger and were defending herself, "I have lived such a life, being afraid of getting caught, that anything sudden scares me. I am always ready to run."

"How those wogs fooled me!" Hal said sourly. "I thought they were so kind and gentle, and now I find they've kept you prisoner for two years."

She glanced at him out of the side of her large eyes. Her color had come back; her red lips smiled.

"Oh, they weren't so bad. They really were kind. They gave me everything I wanted, except my freedom. They were afraid I'd make my way back to my aunts and sisters."

"What did they care?"

"Oh, they thought there might be some males of my race left in the jungle and that I might give them children. They are terribly frightened of my race becoming numerous and strong again and making war on them. They do not like war."

"Hm! Well, let's eat."

When they had finished, he sighed, patted his stomach, and said, "Ah, Jeannette, the soup was the best I ever tasted. The bread was fresh and hot. The salad was superb. The steak perfect."

"My aunts gave me very good training. Among my people the female is taught at an early age all that will please a man. All. By the time we've grown up, we do it almost instinctively."

Hal leaned back and lit a cigarette. She tried one, coughed, then drew in and blew out smoke like a veteran. She seemed to have an amazing facility for imitation. Show or tell her something once, and she never forgot it.

They smoked awhile, looking at each other. During the meal she had chattered lightly and amusingly about her life with her father and her relatives. She had the trick of raising her eyebrows as she laughed; he was fascinated by them. They were almost bracket-shaped. A thin line rose from the bridge of the nose, turned at right angles, curved slightly while going above the eyesockets, and then made a little hook downwards. He asked her if the shape was a trait of her mother's people. She laughed and said No, she got them from her father. Her laughter was low and musical. It did not get on his nerves, as his ex-wife's had. Lulled by it, he felt pleasant. She seemed to have a sixth sense that guessed his moods and thoughts and exactly what he needed to blunt any gloominess or sharpen any gaiety.

Finally he said, "We'll have to wash the dishes. It would never do for a visitor to see a table set for two. And another thing: we'll have to hide the cigarettes, and air out the rooms frequently. Now that I've been 'Metered, I'm supposed to have renounced such vices as smoking."

Jeannette would not let him help her do the dishes. He smoked and speculated about the chances of getting tobacco. She so enjoyed the cigarettes that he could not stand the idea of her missing out on them. One of the crewmen he knew did not smoke, but instead sold his ration to his mates. Maybe a wog could act as middleman; buy the stuff from the sailor, and pass it on to Hal. He'd have to be careful . . . maybe it wasn't worth it . . .

Hal sighed. Having Jeannette was wonderful, but she was beginning to complicate his life. Here he was, contemplating a criminal action as if it were the most natural thing in the world.

She was standing before him, hands on her hips, eyes shining.

"Now, Hal, mon cher, if we only had something to drink . . . it would make a perfect evening."

He got to his feet. "Sorry. I forgot you wouldn't know how to make coffee."

"Non. Non. It is the liquor I am thinking of. L'alcool. Pas le café."

"Alcohol? Good God, girl, we don't *drink!* That'd be the most disgust—"

He stopped. She was hurt. He mastered himself. After all, she couldn't help it. She came from a different culture. She wasn't even, strictly speaking, all human.

"I'm sorry," he said. "It's a religious matter. Forbidden."

Tears filled her eyes. Her shoulders began to shake. She put her face into her hands and began to sob. "You don't understand. I have to have it. I have to."

"But why?"

She spoke from behind her fingers. "Because during my imprisonment I had little to do but entertain myself. My captors gave me liquor; it helped to pass the time and make me forget how utterly homesick I was. Before I knew it, I was an—an alcoholic."

Hal clenched his fists and growled, "Those sons of bugs!"

"So you see, I have to have a drink. It would make me feel better, just for the time being. And later, maybe later, I can try to overcome it. I know I can, if you'll help me."

He gestured emptily. "But—but where can I get you any?" His stomach revolted at the idea of trafficking in alcohol, but if she needed it, he'd try his best to get it.

Swiftly she said, "Fobo lives on the third floor. Perhaps he could give you some."

"But Fobo was one of your captors! Won't he suspect something if I come asking for alcohol?"

"He'll think it's for you."

"All right," he said, somewhat sullenly, and at the same time guiltily because he was sullen. "But I hate for anybody to think I drink. Even if he is just a wog."

She came up to him and seemed to flow against him. Her lips pressed softly and hotly. Her body tried to pass through his. He held her for a minute and then took his mouth away.

"Do I have to leave you?" he whispered. "Couldn't you pass up the liquor? Just for tonight? Tomorrow I'll get you some."

Her voice broke. "Oh, m'namoow, I wish I could. How I wish I could. But I can't. I just can't. Believe me . . ."

"I believe you."

He released her and walked into the front room, where he took a hood, cloak, and nightmask out of the closet. His head was bent; his shoulders sagged. Everything would be spoiled. He would not be able to get near her, not with her breath stinking with alcohol. And she'd probably wonder why he was cold, and he wouldn't have the nerve to tell how revolting she was, because that would hurt her feelings. To make it worse, she'd be hurt anyway, if he offered no explanation.

Before he left, she kissed him again on his now frozen lips.

"Hurry! I'll be waiting."

"Yeah."

ᕰ Seven ᕰ

Yarrow knocked lightly. Fobo's apartment was next door to Pornsen's. Tonight was not a good time for the gapt to see him visiting the empathist.

When the door opened, he stepped in and shut it quickly. Noise bounced off the walls of the room, large as a basketball court. Screaming, twelve wog children raced around. Abasa, Fobo's wife, was sitting in one corner and chattering with three female visitors. The empathist himself was at a table by the door, reading.

Hal shouted, "How can you concentrate?"

Fobo looked up. "Why, can't you cut out all unwanted noises with an effort of will? That is, turn off certain nerve paths? No?

Well, we wogs can, though how, we don't know. That is one of the subjects for research at the nearby College of Empathology. And now, won't you sit down? I'd offer you a drink, but I'm fresh out."

Hal was sure that his dismay didn't show on his face, but Fobo's antennae must have picked it up.

"Anything wrong?"

Hal decided not to waste time. "Yes. Where can I get a quart of liquor?"

The wog took his night garments down from a hook, put them on, and then buckled on a broad leather belt with sheath and short rapier.

"I was just thinking of going out and getting some. You see, this empathology is very trying on the nerves. I run into so many people who need help; and since I must put myself into their shoes, feel their emotions as they feel them, and then must wrench myself out of their shoes and take an objective look at their problems, I am exhausted and shaken at the end of the day. I find that a drink or two relaxes me. You understand?"

The Terran didn't, but he shook his head yes. He wondered how he was going to explain that he was breaking the law by drinking. He'd have to stress the necessity of saying nothing to Pornsen.

Outside, Hal said, "Why the sword?"

"Oh, there isn't much danger, but it's best to be careful. You see, this is a world of insects whose development and specialization go even beyond your planet. You know the parasites and mimics that infest ant colonies, don't you? The beetles that look like ants and make an easy living from that resemblance? The pygmy ants and other tiny creatures that live in the walls and prey on the eggs and the young? Well, we have things analogous to them. Things that hide in sewers or basements or hollow trees and creep around the city at night. Our streets are well-lighted and patrolled, but they are often separated by wooded stretches . . ."

By the time Fobo had finished talking, they had passed through a park, zigzagged down a dozen blocks of a shopping district, now closed, and stopped before a building in front of which a big electric sign blazed.

"Duroku's Tavern," translated Fobo.

It was in the basement. Hal, after stopping to shudder at the blast of liquor that came up the steps, followed the wog. In the entrance he paused to blink.

Loud odors of alcohol mingled with loud bars of a strange music and even louder talk. Wogs crowded the hexagonal-topped tables and leaned across big pewter steins to shout in each other's face. Antennae wiggled with drunken emotion. Somebody waved his hands uncoordinatedly and sent a stein crashing. A waitress, looking much like her Terran counterpart with her white apron and peaked cap, hurried up with a towel to mop up the mess. When she bent over, she was slapped resoundingly on the rump by a jovial, greenfaced, and very fat wogglebug. His tablemates howled with laughter, their broad V-in-V lips wide open. The waitress laughed, too, and said something to the fat one that must have been witty, for the tables roundabout guffawed.

On a platform at one end of the room a five-piece band slammed out fast and weird notes. Hal saw three instruments that looked Terranlike: a harp, a trumpet, and a drum. A fourth musician, however, was not himself producing any music, but was now and then prodding with a long stick a rabbit-sized locustoid insect in a cage. When so urged, the creature rubbed its hind wings over its back legs and gave four loud chirps followed by a long, nerve-scratching screech.

The fifth player was pumping away at a bellows connected to a bag and three short and narrow pipes. A thin squealing came out.

Fobo shouted, "You mustn't judge Ozagen by this place. It's a lowerclass hangout. Especially, don't think that noise is typical of our music. It's cheap popular stuff. I'll take you to a symphony concert one of these days and you'll hear what great music is like."

The wog led the man to one of the curtained-off booths scattered along the walls. They sat down. A waitress came to them. Sweat ran off her forehead and down her tubular nose.

"Keep your mask on until we've gotten our drinks," said Fobo. "Then we can close the curtains."

The waitress said something in Wog. Fobo repeated in French, "Beer, wine, or alcohol à la beetle. Myself, I wouldn't touch the first two. They're for women and children."

The Terran didn't want to lose face He said with a bravado he didn't feel, "The latter, of course."

"Double shot?"

Hal didn't know what that meant, but he nodded.

Fobo held up two fingers. The waitress returned quickly with two big steins. The wog leaned his nose into the fumes and breathed deeply. He closed his eyes in ecstasy, lifted the stein, and drank a long time. When he put the container down, he belched loudly and then smacked his lips.

"Tastes as good coming up as going down!" he bellowed.

The man felt queasy. Eructation was very frowned upon in the Haijac Union.

"Mais, monsieur! You are not drinking."

Yarrow said weakly, "Damifaino," the Ozagen equivalent of mud-in-your-eye, and drank.

Fire ran down his throat like lava down a volcano's slope. And, like a volcano, Hal erupted. He coughed and wheezed; liquor spurted out of his mouth; his eyes shut and squeezed out big tears.

"Tres bonne, n'est-ce pas?" said Fobo calmly.

"Yes, very good," croaked Yarrow from a throat that seemed to be permanently scarred. Though he had spat most of the stuff out, some of it must have dropped straight through his intestines and into his legs, for he felt a hot tide down there swinging back and forth as if pulled by some invisible moon circling around and around in his head, a big moon that bulged and brushed against the inside of his skull.

"Have another."

The second drink he managed better outwardly, at least, for he did not cough or sputter But inwardly he was not so unconcerned. His belly writhed, and he was sure he would disgrace himself.

After a few deep breaths, he thought he would keep the liquor down. Then he belched. The lava got as far as his throat before he managed to stop it.

"Pardon me," he said, blushing.

"Why?" said Fobo.

Hal thought that was one of the funniest retorts he had ever heard. He laughed loudly and sipped at the stein. If he could empty it swiftly and then buy a quart for Jeannette, he could get back before the night was completely wasted.

When the liquor had receded halfway down the stein, Hal heard Fobo, dimly and faroff as if he were at the end of a long tunnel, ask him if he cared to see where the alcohol was made.

"Shib," Hal agreed.

He rose, but had to put a hand on the table to steady himself. The wog told him to put his mask back on. "Earthmen are still objects of curiosity. We don't want to waste all evening answering questions. Or drinking drinks that'll be forced on us."

They threaded through the noisy crowd to a backroom. There Fobo gestured and said, "Voilà. L'escarbot."

Hal looked. If he had not had some of his inhibitions washed away in the liquorish flood, he might have been overwhelmingly repulsed. As it was, he was curious.

The thing sitting on a chair by the table might at first glance have been taken for a wogglebug. It had the antennae, the blond fuzz, the bald pate, the nose, and the V-shaped mouth. It also had the round body and enormous paunch of some of the Ozagens.

But a second look in the bright light from the unshaded bulb overhead showed a creature whose body was sheathed in a hard and lightly green-tinted chitin. And though it wore a long cloak, the legs and arms were naked. They were not smooth-skinned but were ringed, segmented with the edges of armor-sections, like stovepipes.

Fobo spoke to it in Wog. Yarrow understood some of the words; the others he was able to fill in.

"Ducko, this is Mr. Yarrow. Say hello to Mr. Yarrow, Ducko."

The big blue eyes looked at Hal. There was nothing about them to distinguish them from a wog's, yet they seemed inhuman, thoroughly arthropodal.

"Hello, Mr. Yarrow," Ducko said in a parrot's voice.

"Tell Mr. Yarrow what a fine night it is."

"It's a fine night, Mr. Yarrow."

"Tell him Ducko is happy to see him."

"Ducko is happy to see you."

"And serve him."

"And serve you."

"Show Mr. Yarrow how you make beetlejuice."

A wog standing by the table glanced at his wristwatch. He spoke in rapid Ozagen. Fobo translated.

"He says Ducko ate a half hour ago. He should be ready to serve. These creatures eat a big meal every half hour and then they—watch!"

Duroku hurried up with a huge earthenware bowl and set it on the table. Ducko leaned over it until a half-inch long tube, probably a modified tracheal opening, was poised above the edge. From the tube he shot a clear liquid into the bowl until it was filled to the brim. Duroku grabbed the bowl and carried it off. An Ozagen came from the kitchen with a plate of highly-sugared spaghetti. He set it down, and Ducko began eating from it with a big spoon.

Hal's brain was by then not working very fast, but he began to see what was going on. Frantically, he looked around for a place to throw up. Fobo shoved a drink under his nose. For lack of anything better to do, he swallowed some. Whole hog or none. Surprisingly, the fiery stuff settled his stomach. Or else burned away the rising tide.

"Exactly," replied Fobo to Hal's strangled question. "These creatures are a superb example of parasitical mimicry. Though quasi-insectal, they look much like us. They live among us and earn their board and room by furnishing us with a cheap and smooth alcoholic drink. You noticed its enormous belly, no?

Eh bien, it is there that they so rapidly manufacture the alcohol and so easily upchuck it. Simple and natural, oui? Duroku has two others working for him, but it is their night off, and doubtless they are in some neighborhood tavern, getting drunk. A sailor's holiday . . ."

Hal burst out, "Can't we buy a quart and get out? I feel sick. It must be the closeness of the air. Or something."

"Something, probably," murmured Fobo.

He sent a waitress after two quarts. While they were waiting for her, they saw a short wog in a mask and blue cloak enter. The newcomer stood in the doorway, black boots widespread and the long tubular projection of the mask pointing this way and that like a sub's periscope peering for prey.

Hal gasped and said, "Pornsen!"

"Oui," replied Fobo. "That drooping shoulder and the black boots and the lack of antennae give him away. Who does he think he's fooling?"

The joat looked wildly around. "I've got to get out of here!"

The waitress returned with the bottles. Fobo paid her and gave one to Hal, who automatically put it in the inside pocket of his cloak.

The gapt saw them through the doorway, but he must not have recognized them. Yarrow still wore his mask, while the empathist probably still looked to Pornsen like any other wog. Methodical as always, Pornsen evidently determined to make a thorough search. He brought up his sloping shoulder in a sudden gesture and began parting the curtains of the booths along the walls. Whenever he saw a wog with his or her mask on, he lifted the grotesque covering and looked behind.

Fobo chuckled. "He won't keep that up long. What does he think we Ozagens are? A bunch of rabbits?"

What he had been waiting for happened. A burly wog suddenly stood up as Pornsen reached for his mask and instead lifted the gapt's. Surprised at seeing a non-Ozagenian's features, the wog dropped his jaw and stared for a second. Then he gave a screech, yelled something, and punched the Earthman in the nose.

At once there was bedlam. Pornsen staggered back into a table, knocking it and its steins over, and fell to the floor. Two wogs jumped him. Another hit a fourth. The fourth struck back. Duroku, carrying a short club, hurried up and began thumping his fighting customers on the back and legs. Somebody threw beetlejuice in his face.

And at that moment Fobo threw the switch that plunged the tavern into darkness.

❧ EIGHT ❧

Hal stood bewildered. A hand seized his. "Follow me!" The hand tugged. Hal turned and allowed himself to be led, stumbling, toward what he thought was the backdoor.

Any number of others must have had the same idea. Hal was knocked down and trampled upon. Fobo's hand was torn from his. Yarrow cried out for the wog, but any possible answer was drowned out in a chorus of *Beat it! Get off my back, you dumb son-of-a-bug! Great Larva, we're piled up in the door-way!*

Sharp reports added to the noise. A foul stench choked Hal as the wogs, under nervous stress, released the gas in their madbags. Gasping, he fought his way through the door. A few seconds later his mad scrambling over twisting bodies got him his freedom. He lurched down an alleyway. Once on the street, he ran as fast as he could. He didn't know where he was going. His one thought was to put as much distance as possible between himself and Pornsen.

Arc-lights on top of tall slender iron poles flashed by. He ran with his shoulder almost scraping the buildings. He wanted to stay in the shadows thrown by the many balconies jutting out from the second stories. Presently, he slowed down at a narrow passageway. A glance showed him it wasn't a blind alley. He darted down it until he came to a large square can, one that by its odor must have been used for garbage. Squatting behind it, he tried to lessen his gaspings. After a minute his lungs regained their balance; he no longer had to sob for air. Then he could listen without having his heart thudding in his ears.

He heard no pursuer. After a while he decided it was safe to rise. He felt the bottle in his cloakpocket. Miraculously, it had not been broken. Jeannette would get her liquor. What a story he would have to tell her! After all he had gone through for her, he would surely get a just reward . . .

He shivered with goose-pimples at the thought and began to walk briskly down the alley. Where he was he had no idea, but he carried a map of the city in his pocket. It had been printed in the ship and bore street names in Ozagen with French translations beneath. All he had to do was read the street-signs under one of the many lamps, orient himself with the map, and return home. As for Pornsen, the fellow had no real evidence against him, and would not be able to accuse him until he got some. Hal's possession of the golden lamech made him above suspicion. Pornsen . . .

Pornsen! No sooner had he muttered the name than the flesh appeared. There was a click of hard boot-heels behind him. He turned. A short, cloaked figure was coming down the alley. A lamp's glow outlined the droop of a shoulder and shone on black leather boots. His mask was off.

"Yarrow!" shrilled the gapt. "No use running! Wait!" Triumph was in the voice. "I saw you go in that tavern!"

He clickclacked up to his ward's tall rigid form. "Drinking! I know you were drinking!"

"Yeah?" Hal croaked. "What else?"

"Isn't that enough?" screamed the gapt. "Or are you hiding something in your apartment? Maybe you are! Maybe you've got the place filled with bottles. Come on. Come on. Let's get back to your apartment. We'll go over it and see what we see. I wouldn't be surprised to find all sorts of evidence of your unreal thinking."

Hal hunched his shoulders and clenched his fists, but he said nothing. When the gapt told him to precede him back to Fobo's building, he walked without a sign of resistance. Like conqueror and conquered, they marched from the alley into the street. Yarrow, however, spoiled the picture by reeling a little and having to put his hand to the wall to steady himself.

Pornsen sneered, "You drunken joat! You make me sick to my stomach!"

Hal pointed ahead. "I'm not the only one who's sick. Look at that fellow."

He was not really interested, but he had a wild hope that anything he said or did, however trivial, might put off the final and fatal moment when they would return to his apartment. What he indicated was a large and evidently intoxicated wogglebug hanging onto a lamp post to keep from falling on his tube-shaped nose. The picture might have been one of a nineteenth or twentieth century drunk, complete to top hat, cloak and lamp post. Now and then the creature groaned as if he were deeply disturbed.

"Perhaps we'd better stop and see if he's hurt?" said Hal.

He had to say anything, anything, to delay Pornsen. Before his captor could protest, he went up to the wog. He put his hand on the free arm—the other was wrapped around the post—and spoke in Ozagen.

"Can we help you?"

The big wog looked as if he, too, had been in a brawl. His cloak, besides being ripped down the back, was spotted with dried green blood. He kept his face away from Hal, so that the Earthman had a hard time understanding his muttering.

Pornsen jerked at his arm. "Come on, Yarrow. He'll get by all right. What's one sick bug more or less?"

"Shib," agreed Hal, tonelessly. He let his hand drop and started to walk on. Pornsen, behind, took one step . . . and then bumped into Hal as Hal stopped.

"What are you stopping for, Yarrow?" The gapt's voice was suddenly apprehensive.

And then the voice was screaming in agony.

Hal whirled . . . to see in grim actuality what had flashed across his mind and caused him to stop in his tracks. When he had put his hand on the wog's arm, he had felt, not warm skin, but hard and cool chitin. For a few seconds the meaning of that had not cleared the brain's switchboard. Then it had come through, and he had remembered the talk he and Fobo had had on the way to the tavern, and why Fobo wore a sword. Too late, he had wheeled to warn Pornsen.

Now the gapt was holding both hands to his eyes and shrieking. The big thing that had been leaning against the lamp post was advancing towards Hal. Its body seemed to grow huger with every step. A sac across its chest was swelled until it looked like a palpitating grey balloon; the hideous insectal face, with two vestigial arms waving on each side of its mouth and the funnel-shaped proboscis below the mouth, was pointed at him. It was that proboscis which Hal had mistakenly thought was a wog's nose. In reality, the thing must breath through tracheae and two slits below the enormous eyes.

Hal yelled with fury and as a means of discharging his fear. At the same time he grabbed his cloak and threw it up before his face. His mask might have saved him, but he did not care to take the chance.

Something burned the back of his hand. He yelped with pain, but leaped forward. Before the thing could breath in air to bloat the sac again and expel the acid through the funnel, Hal rammed his head against its paunch.

The thing said, "Oof!" and fell backward where it lay on its back and thrashed its legs and arms like a giant poisonous bug—which it was. Then, as it recovered from the shock and rolled over and tried to get back on its feet, Hal kicked hard. His leather toe drove with a crunching sound through the thin chitin.

The toe withdrew; a greenish blood oozed out; Hal kicked again in the open place. The thing screamed and tried to crawl away on all fours. The Terran leaped upon it with both feet and bore it sprawling to the cement. He pressed his heel against its thin neck and shoved with all the strength of his leg. The neck cracked. The thing lay still. Its lower jaw dropped open and exposed two rows of tiny needle-teeth. The mouth's rudimentary arms wigwagged feebly for a while and then drooped.

Hal's chest heaved in agony. He couldn't get enough air. His guts quivered and threatened to force their way through his throat. Then they did, and Hal bent over, retching.

All at once, he was sober. By that time Pornsen had quit screaming. He was lying huddled on his side in the gutter. Hal turned him over and shuddered at what he saw. The eyes were partly burned out, and the lips were grey with large blisters. The tongue, too, sticking from the mouth, was swollen and lumpy. Evidently Pornsen had swallowed some of the venom. According to Fobo, even a small part was fatal.

Hal straightened up and walked away. A wog patrol would find the gapt's body and turn it over to the Earthmen. Let the hierarchy figure out what had happened. Pornsen was dead, and now that he was, Yarrow admitted to himself what he had never allowed himself to admit before this time. He had hated Pornsen. And he was glad that he was dead. If Pornsen had suffered horribly, so what? His pains were brief, but the pain and grief he had caused Hal had lasted for almost thirty years.

In all that time Hal had kept unconscious his desire to kill the man. Now his feelings, anti-climactically, exploded. Tears ran down his cheeks; his shoulders shook with sobs; he staggered like a drunk. Something was reaching down into his intestines and tearing them apart. It wasn't grief. It was hate, working out like a poison, a swift poison leaving his body but boiling him alive. Still, it was coming out, and though he felt that he was dying while it lasted, by the time he arrived at home he felt much better. Fatigue held his arms and legs down, and he could hardly make it up the steps. But inside, where the heart was, he was stronger than he had ever been in his life.

❧ NINE ❧

A tall ghost in a light blue shroud was waiting for the Terran in the false dawn. It was the empathist, standing in the hexagonal-shaped arch that led into his building. When Hal came close, Fobo threw back the hood and exposed a face that was scratched on one cheek and blacked around the right eye.

He chuckled and said, "Some son of a bug pulled my mask off and plowed me good. But it was fun. It helps if you blow off steam that way now and then. How did you come out? I was afraid you might have been picked up by the police. Normally that wouldn't worry me, but I know your colleagues at the ship would frown upon such activities."

Hal smiled wanly. "Frown misses it by a mile."

He wondered how Fobo knew what the hierarch's reaction would be. How much did these wogs know about the Terrestrials? Were they onto the Haijac game, and waiting to pounce? If so, with what? Their technology, as far as could be determined, was way behind Earth's. True, they seemed to know more of psychic functions than the Terrans did, but that was understandable. The Sturch had long ago decreed that the proper psychology had been perfected and that further research was unnecessary. The result had been a standstill in the psychical sciences.

He shrugged mentally. He was too tired to think of such things. All he wanted was to go to bed.

"I'll tell you later what happened," he said.

Fobo replied, "I can guess. Your hand. You'd better let me fix that burn. Nightlifer venom is nasty."

Like a little child, Hal followed to the wog's apartment and let him put a cooling salve on it.

"Voilà," said Fobo. "Go to bed. Tomorrow you can tell me all about it."

Hal thanked him and walked down to his floor. His hand fumbled with the key. Finally, after using Sigmen's name in vain, he inserted the key. When he had shut and locked the door, he called Jeannette. She must have been hiding in the closet-within-a-closet in the bedroom, for he heard two doors bang. In a moment she was running to him. She threw her arms around him.

"Oh, mon homme, mon homme! Hal, mon amour, what has happened? I was so worried. I thought I would scream when the night went by, and you didn't return."

Though he was sorry he had caused her pain, he could not help a prickling of pleasure because someone cared enough about him to worry. Nobody ever had before.

"There was a brawl," he said. He had decided not to say

anything about the gapt or the nightlifer. Later, when the strain had passed, he'd talk.

She untied his cloak and hood and took off his mask. While she hung them up in the frontroom closet, he sank into a chair and closed his eyes. A moment later they were pulled open by the sound of liquid pouring into a glass. She was standing in front of him and filling a large glass from the quart. The odor of beetle-juice began to turn his stomach, and the picture of a beautiful girl about to drink the nauseating stuff spun it all the way around.

She looked at him. The delicate brackets of her brows rose. "Qu'y a-t-il?"

"Nothing's the matter!" he groaned. "I'm all right."

She put down the glass, picked up his hand, and led him into the bedroom. There she gently sat him down, pressed on his shoulder until he laid down, and then took off his shoes. He didn't resist. After she unbuttoned his shirt, she stroked his hair.

"You're sure you're all right?"

"Shib. I could lick the world with one hand tied behind my back."

"Good."

The bed creaked as she got up and walked out of the room. Before he could fall asleep, she returned. Again, he opened his eyes. Again, she was standing with a glass in her hand.

She said, "Would you like a sip now, Hal?"

"Great Mind, girl, don't you understand?" he barked. Fury poured adrenalin into his tired blood. He sat up. "Why do you think I got sick? I can't stand the stuff! I can't stand to see you drink it. It makes me sick. You make me sick. What's the matter with you? Are you stupid?"

Jeannette's eyes widened. Blood drained from her face and left the pigment of her lips a crimson moon in a white lake. Her hand shook so that the liquor spilled.

"Why—why—" she gasped—"I thought you said you felt fine. I thought you were all right. I thought you wanted to go to bed with me."

Yarrow groaned. He shut his eyes and laid back down. Sarcasm was lost on her. She insisted on taking everything literally. She would have to be re-educated, not only in irony, but in other things. If he weren't so exhausted, he would have been shocked by her open proposal—so much like that of the Scarlet Woman in the Western Talmud when she had tried to seduce the Forerunner.

But he was past being shocked. Moreover, a voice on the edge of his conscience said that she had merely put into hard and unrecallable words what he had planned in his heart all this time. But when you spoke them!

A crash of glass shattered his thoughts. He jerked upright. She was standing there, face twisted, lovely red mouth quivering and tears flowing. Her hand was empty. A large wet patch against the wall, still dripping, showed what had become of the glass.

"I thought you loved me!" she yelled.

Unable to think of anything to say, he stared. She spun and walked away. He heard her go into the front room. Loud sobs forced him to jump out of bed and walk swiftly after her. These rooms were supposed to be soundproof, but one never knew. What if she were overheard?

Anyway, she was twisting something inside him, and he had to straighten it out.

When he entered the front room, she didn't look up. For a while he stood silent, wanting to say something but utterly unable to because he had never been forced to solve such a problem before. Haijac women didn't cry often, or if they did, they wept alone in privacy.

He sat down by her and put his hand on her soft shoulder.

"Jeannette."

She turned quickly and laid her dark hair against his chest and said, between sobs, "I thought maybe you didn't love me. And I couldn't stand it. Not after all I've been through!"

"Well, Jeannette, I didn't . . . I mean I wasn't . . ."

He paused. He had had no intention of saying he loved her. He'd never told any girl he loved her. Nor had any girl ever told him. And here was this girl on a faraway planet, only half-human at that, taking it for granted that he was hers, body and self.

He began speaking in a soft voice. Words came easily, because he was quoting Moral Lecture AT-16:

". . . all beings with their hearts in the right place are brothers . . . Man and woman are brother and sister . . . Love is everywhere . . . but love should be on a higher plane . . . Man and woman should rightly loath the beastly act as something the Great Mind, the Cosmic Observer, has not yet eliminated in man's evolutionary development . . . The time will come when children will be produced otherwise. Meanwhile we must recognize sex as outmoded, and necessary for only one reason: children . . ."

Slap! His head rang, and points of fire whirled off into the blackness before his eyes.

It was a moment before he could realize that Jeannette had leaped to her feet and slammed him hard with the palm of her hand. He saw her standing above him with her eyes slitted and her red mouth open and drawn back in a snarl.

Then she whirled and ran into the bedroom. He got up and followed her. She was lying on the bed, sobbing.

"Jeannette, you don't understand."

"Va t'feh fut!"

When he understood that, he blushed. Then he got mad. He grabbed her by the shoulder and turned her over so that she faced him. Suddenly he was saying, "But I do love you, Jeannette. I do."

He sounded strange, even to himself. The concept of love, as she meant it, was alien to him—rusty, perhaps, if it could be put that way. It would need a lot of polishing. But it would, he knew, be polished. Here in his arms was one whose nature and instinct and education were pointed toward love. He had thought he had drained himself of grief earlier that night, but now, as he forgot his resolve not to tell her what had happened, and as he recounted, step by step, the long and terrible night, tears ran down his face. Thirty years makes a deep well; it takes a long time to pump out all the weeping.

Jeannette, too, cried, and said that she was sorry that she had gotten angry at him. She promised never again to do so. He said it was all right. They kissed again and again until, like two babies who have wept themselves and loved themselves out of frustration and fury, they passed gently into sleep.

✧ Ten ✧

At dawn the Haijac ship, which had been suspended fifty feet high, settled to earth. All day long it would rest there in the middle of a big glade. At nightfall it would rise again. Even though the Terrans had so far seen no evidence of wog aerial flight, except for a few balloons, they took no chances of sudden attack. The sinking sun always saw the *Gabriel* poised above the treetops, radar probing, ready on the instant to accelerate into Ozagen's stratosphere, or, if necessary, into the safety of space.

At 0900 Ship's Time, Yarrow walked into the *Gabriel,* the smell of morning dew on grass in his nostrils. As he had a little time before the conference, he looked up Turnboy, the historian joat. Casually, he asked if Tumboy knew anything of a spaceflight emigration from France during the Forerunner's early days. Turnboy was delighted to show off his knowledge. Yes, the remnants of the Gallic nation had gathered in the Loire country after the Apocalyptic War and had formed the nucleus of what might have become a new France.

But the fastgrowing colonies sent from Iceland to the northern part of France, and from Israel to the southern part, had surrounded the Loire. New France found itself squeezed economically and religiously. Sigmen's disciples invaded the Catholic territory in waves of missionaries. High tariffs had strangled the little state's trade. Finally a group of Frenchmen, seeing the inevitable absorption or conquest of their state, religion, and tongue, had left in six spaceships, three thousand strong, to find another Gaul rotating about some faroff star. Where they had landed, nobody knew.

Hal thanked Turnboy and walked to the conference room. He spoke to many; two years of flight had enabled him to recognize most of the personnel. Half of them, like him, had a Mongolian tinge to their features. They were the English-speaking descendants of Hawaiian and Australian survivor of the same war which had decimated France. Their manytimes great-grandfathers had repopulated Australia, the Americas, and Japan.

Almost half of the crew spoke Icelandic. Their ancestors had sailed from the grim island to spread across northern Europe and Siberia and Manchuria.

About a sixteenth of the crew spoke Georgian when among their fellows from home. Their fathers had moved down from the Caucasus Mountains and resettled the depopulated plains of southern Russia. A minority in the Haijac Union, they were gradually abandoning their native tongue in favor of that of their closest neighbors—the Icelanders.

At 1200 Hal left the conference room. He felt wonderful. First, he had been moved from twentieth place to the Archurielite's left to sixth from his right. The lamech on his chest made the difference. Second, there was little difficulty about Pornsen's death. The gapt was considered as a casualty of war. Everyone was warned about the night-lifers and other things that sometimes prowled Siddo after dusk. It was not, however, suggested that the Haijacs quit their moonlit espionage.

Macneff, the Achurielite, ordered Hal, as the dead gapt's spiritual son, to arrange for the funeral the following day. Then he pulled down a huge map from a long roller on the wall. This was the representation of Earth that would be given to the wogs.

It was a good example of the Haijacs' subtlety and Chinese box-within-a-box thinking. The sheet bore two hemispheres of Earth with colored political boundaries. It was correct as far as the Bantu and Malay states were concerned. But the positions of the Israeli and Haijac nations had been reversed. The legend beneath the map said that green was the color of the Forerunner states and yellow was the Hebrews'. The green portion, however, was a ring around the Mediterranean, covering Palestine, Turkey, the Balkans, Italy, Austria, south Germany, lower France, Spain and northern Africa; it included the Sahara Sea, Arabia, Mesopotamia, and eastern Persia.

In other words, said Macneff, if by any inconceivable chance the Ozagenians were concealing spaceships, or captured the *Gabriel* and built ships with it as a model, and if they managed to find Sol, they would still attack the wrong country. They would think the Israeli Republic was the Union. Unless, that is, they took time to capture and question Terrans and thus found out the truth. But that was unlikely, for the essence of modern war was the surprise attack. The wogs would not want to give their enemies a chance to prepare.

As everyone knew, Macneff added, the deception might have been furthered by having the *Gabriel's* members speak Hebrew. But since that was the holy tongue, not to be used by the lower classes except in religious rituals nor to be used at all in profane matters such as carrying on a war, it was forbidden.

However—due to the excellent suggestion of Yarrow, the linguistic joat—French was being spoken. If the wogs pierced the deception, they would think it was a ruse of the Israeli.

After the conference, still glowing from the Achurielite's compliment, Hal gave orders for the funeral arrangements. Other duties kept him till dark, when he returned home.

♂ Eleven ♂

When Yarrow locked the door behind him, he heard the shower running. He hung his coat up in the closet; the water quit splashing. As he went toward his bedroom door, Jeannette stepped out from the bathroom. She was drying her hair with a big towel, and she was naked.

She said, "Bon jour, Hal," and walked on unselfconsciously into the bedroom.

Hal replied feebly. He turned and went back into the front room. He felt foolish, because of his timorousness, and at the same time vaguely wicked, unreal, because of the pounding of his heart, his heavy breathing, the hot and fluid fingers that wrapped themselves, half-pain, half-delight, around his loins.

She came out dressed in a pale green robe which he had purchased for her and which she had re-cut and re-sewed to fit her figure. Her heavy black hair was piled on her head in a Psyche knot. She kissed him and asked if he wanted to come into the kitchen while she cooked. He said that would be fine.

She began making a sort of spaghetti. He asked her to tell him about her life. Once started, she was not hard to keep going.

". . . and so my father's people found a planet like Earth and settled there. It was a beautiful planet; that is why they called it Luhbawpfey."

"Huh?"

"Le Beau Pays," she enunciated more carefully. "The beautiful land. According to my father, there are about thirty million living there on one continent. My father was not content to live the life his grandfathers had—tilling the soil or running a shop and raising many children. He and some other young men like him took the only spaceship left of the original six that had come there, and they sailed off to the stars. They came to Ozagen. And crashed. No wonder. It was two hundred and fifty years old."

"The obsolete ion-beam drive. Is the wreck still around?"

"Vi. I mean oui. Close to where my sisters and aunts and cousins live."

"Your mother is dead?"

She hesitated, then nodded. "Yes. She died giving birth to me. And my sisters. Father died later. Or rather, we think he did. He went on a hunting-party and never came back."

Hal frowned. "Wait a minute. You told me that your mother and aunts were the last of the native human beings on Ozagen. And you said once before that Rastignac was the only Earthman to get out alive from the wreck. He was your mother's husband, naturally . . . and incredible as it sounds, their union—one of a terrestrial and an extraterrestrial—was fertile! That alone would rock my colleagues on their heels. Amazing! Completely contrary to accepted science, that their body chemistry and chromosomes should match! But—what I'm getting at is that your mother's sister had children, too. If the last Ozagenian human male died years before Rastignac crashed, who was their father?"

"Jean Rastignac. He was the husband of my mother and my four aunts. They all say that he was a superb and very virile lover."

Hal said, "Oh."

Until she had the spaghetti and salad ready, he watched her in silence. By then he had regained some of his perspective. After all, the Frenchman was not too much worse than he himself was. Maybe not as bad. He chuckled. How easy it was to condemn somebody else for giving way to temptation until you yourself faced the same situation. He wondered what Pornsen would have done if Jeannette had contacted him.

". . . and so it was easy to escape from the wogs," she was saying. "They did not watch me closely, and they were through examining me. Mon Dieu, the tests. Questions, questions! That Fobo asked me all sorts of things. Wanted to find out my intelligence, my personality, my etcetera. Put me under all kinds of machines. He and his fellows turned me inside out. Literally, my dear. They took pictures of my insides. Showed me my skeleton and organs and just simply everything. They said it was most interesting. Imagine that! I am exposed as no woman has ever been exposed, and to them I am just most interesting. Indeed!"

"Well," laughed Hal. "You can't expect arthropods to take the viewpoint of a mammal towards a female . . . that is . . ."

She looked archly at him. "And am I a mammal?"

"Obviously, unmistakably, indisputably, and enthusiastically."

"For that you get a kiss."

"Hmmm. I'll bet that was almost as good as the spaghetti is going to be."

"You eat your food, and then I will show you something that is much better than almost as good."

He was learning fast. He didn't even flush.

After the meal he cut a pitcher of beetlejuice with water, poured in a purplish liquid which made the drink smell like grapes, and dropped sprigs of an orange plant on the surface. Poured into a glass of ice cubes, it was cool and even tasted like grapes. It did not gag him at all.

"Why did you pick me, instead of Pornsen?" he asked.

She sat on his lap, one arm around his neck, the other on the table, drink in hand. "Oh, you were so good looking, and he was so ugly. Besides, I eavesdropped, and he sounded mean. You were nice. And I knew I had to be careful. My father had told me about Earthmen. He said they couldn't be trusted."

"How true. But you must have an instinct for doing the right thing, Jeannette. If you had antennae, I'd say you could detect nervous emanations. Here, let's see!" He went to run his fingers through her hair, but she ducked her head and laughed.

He laughed with her and dropped the hand to her shoulder, rubbing the smooth skin. "I was probably the only person on the ship who wouldn't have betrayed you. But I'm in a quandary now. You see, your presence here raises the devil. Here we Haijacs are, speaking French as a sort of camouflage for our real nationality, and all the time the wogs knew our language from the beginning. When we first came here, we were careless of what we said before them, because we figured it would take some time for them to learn French.

"Now our expedition may be in danger. And I can't tell Macneff that, because he would want to know how I knew. That'd give you away. And there's something else. You told me they have x-ray machines. So far we've seen none. Are the wogs hiding them? And if they are, what else are they concealing? And why? It's important that we know; but I can't tell Macneff they've got a hidden technology. So I'm on the horns of a dilemma."

"A dilemma? A beast I never heard of."

He hugged her. "I hope you never do. Listen, Jeannette, this is serious. Sooner or later, and probably sooner, we'll have to make up our minds to leave. Our specialists are working night and day on samples of wogglebug blood. They hope to make an artificial semivirus that will attach itself to the copper in the green blood-cells and change their electrophoretic properties."

"Comment?"

"Don't look so blank. Or giggle. It's deadly serious. It's what killed seven-eighths of Earth's people. Guided missiles by the tens of thousands circling high over the surface. Dropping little knots of protein molecules that locked onto the hemoglobin in the red blood cells and gave them a positive charge so that one end of a globin molecule would bind with the end of another. Which would make the molecules go into a sort of crystallization. Which would twist the doughnut shaped red cells into a scimitar, and cause an artificial sickle cell anemia.

"The lab-created anemia was much swifter and more certain than the natural kind, because every red cell would be affected, not just a small percentage. Every cell would soon break down. The blood would have no carriers of oxygen to various parts of the body. The body would die.

"The body did die, Jeannette—the body of humanity. Almost a planetful of human beings perished from lack of oxygen. Only by accident did any organized governments survive. Most of those were islands that weren't attacked because they were felt to be too small to bother with. Hawaii, and Iceland, and a city in Australia and Bali.

"Palestine got scotfree by sheer coincidence An experiment with short radiowaves interfered with the missiles' guiding beams. None got to the Holy Land. By the time the enemy found out why, they were dead. All over the world—not only in the civilized parts, but in the arctic, the jungles, the mountains—they died. Everywhere the missiles circled; everywhere was the invisible rain of death, the skulls, the bones—"

"Hush!" Jeannette put her finger on his quivering lips. "I don't know what you mean by proteins and molecules and those—those electrofrenetic charges! They're way above my head. But I do know that the longer you've been talking, the more scared you've been getting. Your voice was getting higher, and your eyes were growing wider.

"Somebody has frightened you in the past. No! Don't interrupt! They've scared you, and you've been man enough to hide most of your fear; but they've done such a horribly efficient job that you haven't been able to get over it.

"Well—" and she put her soft lips to his ears and whispered—" I'm going to wipe that fear out, I'm going to lead you out of that valley of fright. No! Don't protest! I know it hurts your ego to think that a woman could know you're afraid. But I don't think any the less of you. I admire you all the more because you've conquered so much of it. I know what courage it took to face the 'Meter. I know you did it because of me. I'm proud that you did. I love you for it. And I know what courage it takes to keep me here, when any time a slip would send you to certain disgrace and death. I know what it all means. It's my nature and instinct and business and love to know.

"Now! Drink with me. We're not outside these walls where we have to worry ourselves about such things and be scared. We're in here. Away from everything except ourselves. Drink. And love me. I'll love you, Hal, and we'll not see the world outside nor need to. For the time being. Forget in my arms."

They drank the purplish liquor. After a while he picked her up and carried her into the bedroom. There he forgot. The only disconcerting item was that she insisted upon keeping her eyes open, even during the climax, as if she were trying to photograph his features upon her mind.

✑ Twelve ✑

On Earth, the alcoholics were not cured but were sent to H. Therefore no psychological or narcotic therapies had been worked out for addicts. Hal, deadended by this fact in his desire to wipe out Jeannette's alcoholism, went for medicine to the very people who had given her the disease. Only he pretended that the cure was for himself.

Fobo said, "There is widespread drinking on Ozagen, but it is light. Our few alcoholics are quickly empathized into normality. Why don't you let me empathize you?"

"Sorry. My government forbids that." He had given Fobo the same excuse for not inviting the wog home.

"You have the most forbidding government," said Fobo, and went into one of his long, howling laughs. When he recovered, he said, "You're forbidden to touch liquor, too, but that doesn't hold you back. Well, there's no accounting for inconsistency. Seriously, though, I have just the thing for you. It's called Easyglow. It's a stimulant which has an effect similar to alcohol's, but which is, in reality, however, depressing. We put it into the daily ration of liquor, increasing slowly the Easyglow and diminishing the alcohol. In two or three weeks the patient is drinking from a fluid 96 percent Easyglow. The taste is much the same; the drinker seldom suspects. Continued treatment eases the patient from his dependence on the alcohol. There is only one drawback."

He paused and said. "The drinker is now addicted to Easyglow!"

He whooped and slapped his thigh and wiggled his antennae and laughed until the tears came.

"Really, though, the peculiar effect of Easyglow is that it opens the patient for discharge of the strains that have driven him to drink. He may then be empathized and at the same time weaned from the stimulant. Since I have no opportunity to slip the stuff to you secretly, I'm taking the chance that you are seriously interested in curing yourself. When you're ready for therapy, tell me."

Hal took the bottle to his apartment. Every day its contents went quietly and carefully into the beetlejuice he got for Jeannette. He hoped that he was psychologist enough to cure her once the Easyglow took effect.

Although he didn't know it, he was himself being "cured" by Fobo. His almost daily talks with the empathist instilled doubts about the religion and science of the Haijacs—or, as their enemies termed them, the Highjackers. Fobo read the biographies of Isaac Sigmen and the Works: the Pre-Torah, the Western Talmud, the Revised Scriptures, the Foundations of Serialism, Time and Theology, The Self and the World-Line. Calmly sitting at his table with a glass of juice in his hand, the wog challenged the mathematics of the dunnologists. Hal proved; Fobo disproved. He pointed out that the math was mainly based on false-to-fact assumptions; that Dunne's and Sigmen's reasoning was buttressed by too many analogs, metaphors and strained interpretations. Remove the buttresses, and the structure fell.

And worse, far worse, he said that the Forerunner's biographies and theological writings revealed him, even through the censor's veil, as a sexually frigid and woman-hating man with a messiah complex and paranoid and schizophrenic tendencies which burst through his icy shell from time to time in religious-scientifical frenzies and fantasies.

"Other men," Fobo said, "have stamped their personality and ideas upon their times. But Sigmen had an advantage over those great leaders who came before him. Because of Earth's rejuvenation serums he lived long enough, not only to set up his kind of society, but to consolidate it and weed out its weaknesses. He didn't die until the cement of his social form had hardened."

"But the Forerunner didn't die," protested Yarrow. "He left in time. He is still with us, traveling down the fields of presentation, skipping here and there, now to the past, now to the future. Always, wherever he is needed to turn pseudo-time into real time, he is there."

"Ah, yes," smiled Fobo. "That was the reason you went to the ruins, was it not? To check up on a mural which hinted that the Ozagen humans had once been visited by a man from outer space. You thought it might have been the Forerunner, didn't you?"

"Macneff did," said Hal, annoyed. "But my report showed that, though the man resembled Sigmen somewhat, the evidence was too inconclusive. The Forerunner may or may not have visited this planet a thousand years ago."

"Be that as it may, I maintain your theses are meaningless. You claim that his prophecies came true. I say, first, that they were couched ambiguously. Second, if they have been realized, it is because your powerful state-church—you may call it the Sturch—has made strenuous efforts to fulfill them.

"Furthermore, this pyramidal society of yours—this guardian-angel administration—where every ten families have a gapt to supervise their most intimate and minute details, and every ten family-gapts have a block-gapt at their head, and every fifty block-gapts are directed by a supervisor-gapt, and so on—this society is based on fear and ignorance and suppression."

Hal, shaken, angered, shocked, would get up to leave. Fobo would call him back and ask him to disprove what he'd said.

Hal would let loose a flood of wrath. Sometimes, when he had finished, he would be asked to sit down and continue the discussion. Sometimes, Fobo would lose his temper; they would shout and scream insults; twice, they fought with fists; Hal got a bloody nose once and Fobo a black eye. Then the wog, weeping, would embrace Hal and ask for his forgiveness, and they would sit down and drink some more until their nerves were calmed.

Yarrow told Jeannette of these incidents. She encouraged him to tell them over and over again until he had talked away the stress and strain of grief and hate and doubt. Afterwards, there was always love such as he had never thought possible. For the first time he knew that man and woman could become one flesh. His wife and he had remained outside the circle of each other, but Jeannette knew the geometry that would take him in and the chemistry that would mix his substance with hers.

Always, too, there was the light and the drink. But they did not bother him. Unknown to her, she was now drinking a liquor almost entirely Easyglow. And he had gotten used to the light above their bed. It was one of her quirks. Fear of the dark wasn't behind it, because it was only while making love that she required a bulb be left on. He didn't understand it. Perhaps she wanted to impress his image on her memory, always to have it if she ever lost him. If so, let her keep the light. By its glow he explored her body with an interest that was part sexual and part anthropological. He was delighted and astonished at the many small differences between her and Terran women. There was a small appendage of skin on the roof of her mouth that might have been the rudiment of some organ whose function was long ago cast aside by evolution. There were two bumps of cartilage on the top of her head, hidden by her thick black hair. She had thirty teeth; the wisdom teeth were missing. That might or might not have been a characteristic of her mother's people.

He suspected that she either had an extra set of pectoral muscles or else an extraordinarily well-developed normal set. Her large and cone-shaped breasts did not sag. They were high and firm and pointed slightly upwards: the ideal of feminine beauty so often portrayed through the ages by male sculptors and painters and so seldom existing in nature.

She was not only a pleasure to look at; she was pleasing to be with. At least once a week she would greet him with a new garment. She loved to sew; out of the materials he gave her she fashioned slips, blouses, skirts and even gowns. Along with the change in dress went new hairdos. She was ever-new and ever-beautiful, and she made Hal realize for the first time that a thing of beauty was a joy, if not for forever, then for at least as long as it lasted.

Her imitativeness was another thing that delighted him. She had switched from her brand of French to his almost overnight. Within a week she was speaking it faster and more expressively than he. As she also knew Ozagen thoroughly, he decided the best way for him to learn it was to have her read wog books to him. He'd lie on the divan while she sat on a chair. Her accent and pronunciation were correct, and trained his ear. Where she saved him time was in his not having to look up each new word in a dictionary—she translated for him.

Jeannette loved to read to him, but she wearied of the dry and technical books he gave her. When he saw that she was tired, he softened and let her stop. He never did, for example, finish Weenai's monumental *Rise and Fall of Man on Ozagen.* That evening Jeannette began, as usual, bravely enough. Her low, throaty voice tried to simulate interest in what her eyes saw. She went through the first chapter, which described the formation of the planet and the beginnings of life. In the second she yawned quite openly and looked at Hal, but he closed his eyes and pretended not to notice. So she read of the rise of the wogs from an arthropod that had changed its mind and decided to become a chordate. Weenai made some heavy jests about the contrariness of the wogglebugs since that fateful day, and then took up, in the third chapter, the story of mammalian evolution on the other large continent of Ozagen. It climaxed in man.

She quoted: "But *Homo sapiens*, like us, had its mimical parasites. One was a different species of the so-called tavern beetle. It, instead of resembling a wog, looked like a man. Like its counterpart, it could fool no intelligent person, but its gift of alcohol made it very acceptable to man. It, too, accompanied its host from primitive times, became an integral part of his civilization, and, finally, a large cause of man's downfall.

"Humanity's disappearance from the face of Ozagen is due not only to the tavern beetle. That creature can be controlled, and has been by us. Like most things, it has benefits to confer. Like most things, it can be abused or its purpose distorted so that it becomes a menace.

"That is what man did with it.

"He had, it must be noted an ally to help him in the misuse of the insect. This was another parasite, one of a somewhat different kind; one that was, indeed, our cousin. That is, it is a so-called chordate arthropod.

"One thing, however, distinguishes it from us, and from man, and from any other animal on this planet with the exception of some very low species. That is, that from the very first fossil evidence we have of it, it was wholly—"

Jeannette put the book down. "I don't know the next word. Hal, do I have to read this? It's so boring."

"No. Forget it. Read me one of those comics that you and the crew like so much."

She smiled, a beautiful sight, and began Vol. 1037, Book 56, of the *Adventures of Leif Magnus, Beloved Disciple of the Forerunner, When He Met the Horror From Arcturus.*

He listened to her translation of the French into vernacular Wog until he grew tired of the banalities and pulled her down to him.

Always, there was the light left on above them.

ᴄ⌵ THIRTEEN ᴄ⌵

It was the following day that Yarrow, returning from the market with a large box, said, "You've sure been putting away the groceries lately. You're not eating for two? Or maybe three?"

She paled. "Mon Dieu! Do you know what you're saying?"

He put the box on a table and grabbed her shoulders.

"Shib. I do. Jeannette, I've been thinking about that very thing for a long time, but I haven't said anything. I didn't want to worry you. Tell me, are you?"

She looked him straight in the eye, but her body was shaking. "Oh, no. It is impossible!"

"Why should it be? We've used no preventives."

"Oui. But I know—don't ask me how—call it instinct, if you wish—that it cannot be. But you must never say things like that. Not even joking. I can't stand it."

He pulled her close and said over her shoulder, "Is it because you can't? Because you know you'll never bear my children?"

Her thick, faintly perfumed hair nodded. "I know. Don't ask me how I know."

He held her at arm's length again. "Listen, Jeannette. I'll tell you what's been troubling you. You and I are really of different species. Your mother and father were, too. Yet they had issue. But you're thinking that the ass and the mare have young, too, but the mule is sterile. The lion and the tigress may breed, but the liget or tigon can't. Isn't that right? You're afraid you're a mule!"

She put her head on his chest and sobbed.

He said, "Let's be real about this, honey. Maybe you are. So what? My God, our situation is bad enough without a baby to complicate it. We'll be lucky if you are . . . uh . . . well, we have each other, haven't we? That's all I want. You.

He couldn't keep from being reflective as he dried her tears and kissed her and helped her put the food in the refrigerator.

The quantities of groceries and milk she had been consuming were more than a normal amount, especially the milk. There had been no telltale change in her superb figure, true. But the stuff was going somewhere.

A month passed. He watched her closely. She ate enormously. Nothing happened.

Yarrow put it down to his ignorance of her alien metabolism.

◌ Fourteen ◌

Another month. Hal was just leaving the ship's library when Turnboy stopped him.

"The rumor is that the techs have finally made the globin-locking molecule," the historian said. "I think that this time the grapevine's right. A conference is called for 1500."

"Shib." Hal kept his despair out of his voice.

When the meeting broke up at 1650, it left him with sagging shoulders. The virus was already in production. In a week a large enough supply would be made to fill the disseminators of six prowler-torpedoes. The plan was to release them to wipe out the city of Siddo. A beachhead would be established there. While the *Gabriel* flew back to Earth, the beachhead would keep making the virus and would send prowlers out in spirals whose range would expand until a large territory would be covered. By the time a huge fleet returned, millions of wogs would be slain. The fleet would then deal with the rest of the planet.

When he got home, he found Jeannette lying in bed. She smiled weakly. Her hair was loose in a black corona on the pillow.

He forgot his mood in a thrill of concern.

"What's the matter, baby?"

He laid his hand on her forehead. The skin was dry and hot and rough.

"I don't know. I haven't been feeling really well for two weeks, but I didn't complain. I thought I'd get over it. Today I felt so bad I just had to go back to bed after breakfast."

"We'll get you well."

He sounded confident. Inside himself, he was lost. If she had contracted a serious disease, she could get no doctor, no medicine—

For the next few days she continued to lie in bed. Her temperature fluctuated from 99.5 in the morning to 100.2 at night. Hal attended her as well as he could. He put wet towels and icebags on her head and gave her aspirin. She had quit eating so much food; all she wanted was liquid. She seemed to be always asking for milk. Even the beetle-juice and the cigarettes were turned down.

Her illness was bad enough, but her silences stung Yarrow into a frenzy. As long as he had known her, she had chattered lightly, merrily, amusingly. She could be quiet, but it was with an interested wordlessness. Now she let him talk, and when he quit, she did not fill his silence with questions or comments.

In an effort to arouse her, he told her of his plan to steal a gig and take her back to her jungle home. A light came into her dulled eyes; the brown looked shiny for the first time. She even sat up while he put a map of the continent on her lap. She indicated the general area where she had lived, and then described the mountain range that rose from the green tropics, and the table-land on its top where her aunts and sisters lived in the ruins of a metropolis.

Hal sat down at the little octagonal-shaped table by the bed and worked out the coordinates from the maps. Now and then he glanced up. She was lying on her side, her white and delicate shoulder rising from her nightgown, her eyes large in the shadows that were beginning to stain rings around them.

"All I have to do is steal a little key," he said. "You see, the milometer on a gig is set at 0 before every flight from the field. The boat will run fifty miles on manual. That gives us leeway to go any place in Siddo and return. But once the tape passes fifty, the gig automatically stops and sends out a location signal. That's to keep anybody from running away. However, the autos can be unlocked and the signal turned off. A little key will do it. I can get it. Don't worry."

"You must love me very much."

"You bet I do!"

He rose and kissed her. Her mouth, once so soft and dewy, felt dry and hard. It was almost as if the skin were turning to horn.

He returned to his calculations. An hour later, a sigh from her made him look up. Her eyes were closed, and her lips were slightly open. Sweat ran down her face.

He hoped her fever had broken. No. The mercury stopped at 100.3.

She said something.

He bent down. "What?"

She was muttering in an unknown language. Delirious. Hal swore. He had to act. No matter what the consequences. He ran into the bathroom, shook from a bottle a ten grain rockabye tablet, went back and propped Jeannette up and got her to wash the pill down with a glass of water.

After he locked her bedroom door, he put on a hood and cloak and walked fast to the nearest pharmacy. There he purchased three 20-gauge needles, three syringes, and some anti-coagulant. Back in his apartment, he tried to insert the needle in an arm vein. The point refused to go in until the fourth attempt when, in a fit of exasperation, he pressed hard.

During none of the jabbings did she open her eyes or jerk her arm.

When the first fluid crept into the glass tube, he gasped with relief. Though he hadn't known it, he had been biting his lower lip and holding his breath. Suddenly he knew that he had for the last month been pushing a horrible suspicion back to the outlands of his mind. Now, he realized the thought had been ridiculous.

The blood was red.

He tried to arouse her in order to get a specimen of urine. She twisted her mouth over strange syllables, then lapsed back into sleep or a coma—he didn't know which. In an anguish of despair he slapped her face, again and again, hoping he could bring her to. He swore once more, for he realized all at once that he should have gotten the specimen before giving her the rockabye pill. How stupid could he get! He wasn't thinking straight; he was too excited over her condition and what he had to do at the ship.

He perked some very strong coffee and managed to get part of it down her. The rest dribbled down her chin and soaked her gown.

Either the caffeine or his desperate tone awoke her, for she opened her eyes long enough to look at him while he explained what he wanted her to do and where he was going afterwards.

Once he'd gotten the urine into a previously boiled jar, he wrapped the syringes and jar in a handkerchief and dropped them into the cloak-pocket.

He had already wristphoned the *Gabriel* for a gig. A horn beeped outside. He took another look at Jeannette, locked the bedroom door, locked the apartment door, and ran down the stairs. The gig hovered above the curb. He entered, sat down, and punched the *Go* button. The boat rose to a thousand feet and then flashed at an 11-degree angle toward the park where the ship squatted.

ᴄᴏ FIFTEEN ᴄᴏ

The medical section was empty, except for one orderly. The fellow dropped his comic and jumped to his feet.

"Take it easy," said Hal. "I just want to use the Labtech. And I don't want to be bothered with making out triplicate forms. This is a little personal matter, see?"

Hal had taken off his cloak. The orderly looked at the bright golden lamech.

"Shib," he grunted.

Hal gave him two cigarettes.

"Geez, thanks." The orderly lit up, sat down, and picked up his *The Forerunner and Delilah in the Wicked City of Gaza*.

Yarrow went around the corner of the Labtech, where the orderly couldn't see him, and set the proper dials. After he inserted his specimens, he sat down. Almost at once he jumped up and began pacing back and forth. Meanwhile, the huge cube of the Labtech purred like a contented cat as it digested its strange food. A half-hour later, it rumbled once and then flashed a green light: ANALYSIS COMPLETE.

Hal pressed a button. Like a tongue out of a metal mouth, a long tape slid out. He read the code. Urine was normal. No infection there. Also normal was the pH and the blood count.

He hadn't been sure the "eye" would recognize the cells in her blood. However, the chances had been strong that her red cells would be Terranlike. Why not? Evolution follows parallel paths; the biconcave disk is the most efficient form for carrying the maximum of oxygen.

The machine chattered. More tape. Unknown hormone! Similar in molecular structure to the parathyroid hormone primarily concerned in the control of calcium metabolism.

What did that mean? Could the mysterious substance loosed in her bloodstream be the cause of her trouble?

More clicks. The calcium content of the blood was 40 mg. per cent.

Strange. Such an abnormally high percentage should mean that the renal threshold was passed and that an excess of calcium should be "spilling" into the urine. Where was it going?

The Labtech flashed a red light: FINISHED.

He took a Hematology book down from the shelf and opened it to the Ca section. When he quit reading, he straightened his shoulders. New hope? Perhaps. Her case sounded as if she had a form of hypercalcemia, which was manifested by any number of diseases ranging from rickets and steomalacia to chronic hypertrophic arthritis. Whatever she had, she was suffering from a malfunction of the parathyroid glands.

The next move was to the Pharm machine. He punched three buttons, dialed a number, stood for two minutes, and then lifted a little door at waist-level. A tray slid out. On it was a cellophane sheath containing a hypodermic needle and a tube holding 30 c.c. of a pale blue fluid. It was Jesper's serum, a "one-shot" readjustor of the parathyroid.

Hal put on his cloak, stuck the package in the inside pocket, and strode out. The orderly didn't even look up.

The next step was the weapons room. There he gave the storekeeper an order—made out in triplicate—for one .1 mm. automatic and a clip of one hundred cartridges. The keeper only glanced over the forged signatures—he, too, was awed by the lamech—and unlocked the door. Hal took the gun, which he could easily hide in the palm of his hand, and stuck it in his pants pocket.

At the key room, two corridors away, he repeated the crime. Or rather, he tried to.

Moto, the officer on duty, looked at the papers, hesitated, and said, "I'm sorry. My orders are to check on any requests with the Chief Uzzite. That won't be possible for about an hour, though. He's in conference with the Archurielite."

Hal picked up his papers. "Never mind. My business'll hold. Be back in the morning."

On the way home, he planned what he'd do. After injecting Jesper's serum in Jeannette, he'd move her into the gig. The floor beneath the gig's control-panel would have to be ripped up, two wires would be unhooked, and one connected to another lead. That would remove the fifty-mile limit. Unfortunately, it would also set off an alarm back in the *Gabriel*. His hope was that he could take off straight up, level off, and dive behind the range of hills to the west of Siddo. The hills would deflect the radar. The autopilot could be set long enough for him to demolish the box that would be sending out the signal by which the *Gabriel* might track him down.

After that, with the gig hedgehopping, he could hope to be free until daybreak. Then he'd submerge in the nearest deep-enough lake or river until nightfall. During the darkness he could rise and speed towards the tropics; and if his radar showed any signs of pursuit, he could plunge again into a body of water.

He left the long needle-shape parked by the curb. His feet pounded the stairs. The key missed the hole the first two tries. He slammed the door without bothering to lock it again.

"Jeannette!" he shouted. Suddenly he was afraid that she might have gotten up while delirious and somehow opened the doors and wandered out.

A low moan answered him. He unlocked the bedroom door and shoved it open. She was lying with her eyes wide.

"Jeannette. Do you feel better?"

"No. Worse. Much worse."

"Don't worry, baby. I've got just the medicine that'll put new life in you. In a couple of hours you'll be sitting up and yelling for steaks. And you won't even want to touch that milk. You'll be drinking Easyglow by the gallon. And then—"

He faltered as he saw her face. It was a stony mask of distress, like the grotesque and twisted wooden faces of the Greek tragedians.

"Oh, no . . . *no!* My God," she moaned. "What did you say? Easyglow?" Her voice rose. "Is that what you've been giving me?"

"Shib, Jeannette. Take it easy. You liked it. What's the difference? The point is that we're going—"

"Oh, Hal, Hal! What have you done?"

Her pitiful face tore at him. Tears were falling; if ever stone could weep, it was weeping now.

He turned and ran into the kitchen where he took out the sheath, removed the contents, and inserted the needle in the tube. He went back into the bedroom. She said nothing as he thrust the point into her vein. For a moment he was afraid the needle would break. The skin was almost brittle.

"This stuff cures Earth people in a jiffy," he said, with what he hoped was a cheery bedside manner.

"Oh, Hal, come here. It's—it's too late now."

He withdrew the needle, rubbed alcohol on the break and put a pad on it. Then he dropped to his knees by the bed and kissed her. Her lips were hard.

"Hal, do you love me?"

"Won't you ever believe me? How many times must I tell you?"

"No matter what you'll find out about me?"

"I know all about you."

"No, you don't. You can't. Oh, Great Mother, if only I'd told you, Hal! Maybe you'd have loved me just as much, anyway. Maybe . . ."

"Jeannette! What's the matter?"

Her lids had closed. Her body shook in a spasm. When the violent trembling passed, she whispered with stiff lips. He bent his head to hear her.

"What did you say? Jeannette! Speak!"

He shook her. The fever must have died, for her shoulder was cold. And hard.

The words came low and slurring.

"Take me to my aunts and sisters. They'll know what to do. Not for me . . . but for the . . ."

"What do you mean?"

"Hal, will you always love . . ."

"Yes, yes. You know that! We've got more important things to do now than talk about that."

If she heard him she gave no sign. Her head was tilted far back with her exquisite nose pointed at the ceiling. Her lids and mouth were closed, and her hands were by her side, palms up. The breasts were motionless. Whatever breath she might have was too feeble to stir them.

☙ Sixteen ☙

Hal ran upstairs to the third floor and pounded on Fobo's door until it opened.

The empathist's wife said, "Bugs, alive, Hal, you startled me!"

"Where's Fobo?"

"He's at a college board meeting."

"I've got to see him at once." Abasa yelled after him, "If it's important, go ahead. Those meetings bore him, anyway."

By the time Yarrow had taken the steps three at a time and bee-lined across the nearby campus, his lungs were on fire. He didn't slacken his pace; he hurtled up the steps of the administration building and burst into the board room.

When he tried to speak, he had to stop and suck in deep breaths.

Fobo jumped out of his chair.

"What's up?"

"You—gasp—you've—got to come. Mater—life—death!"

"Excuse me, gentlemen," said Fobo. The ten wogs nodded their antennae and resumed the conference. The empathist put on his cloak and high-crowned, plumed hat and led Hal out.

"Now, what is it?"

"Listen. I've got to trust you. I know you can't promise me anything. But I think you won't turn me in to my people. You're a real person, Fobo. Not like the Haijac men."

"Get to the point, my friend."

"Listen. You wogs are as advanced as we are in endocrinology. And you've got an advantage. You know Jeannette inside out. You've examined her."

"Jeannette? Oh, Rastignac! The lalitha."

"Yes. I've been hiding her in my apartment."

"I know."

"You . . . know! How?"

"Never mind." The wog put his hand on Hal's shoulder. "Something bad has happened, or you'd not have come to me about her."

By the time Hal had told him, they were at their apartments. Fobo stopped him at the door.

"I may as well tell you. Your countrymen know you're up to something. For the last eight days a man has been living in that building down the street and spying on you. His name is Art Hunah Fedtof."

"An Uzzite!"

"Oui. He lives in the front room on the ground floor. His windows are darkened, but he is probably watching you right now."

"Forget about him!" Yarrow snarled. He bounded up the stairs. Fobo followed him into his rooms. The wog felt Jeannette's forehead and tried to lift her lid to look at her eye. It would not bend.

"Hmm! Calcification of the outer skin layer is far advanced."

With one hand he threw the sheet from her figure and with the other he grabbed her gown by the neckline and ripped the thin cloth down the middle. The two parts fell to either side. She lay nude, as silent and pale and beautiful as a sculptor's masterpiece.

Her lover gave a little cry at what seemed like a violation. But he shut up at once, because he knew that Fobo's move was medical. In any case, the wog would not have been sexually interested.

Puzzled, he watched. Fobo had tapped his fingertips against her flat belly and then put his ear against it. When he stood up, he shook his head.

"I won't deceive you, Hal. Though we'll do the best we can, we may not be good enough. She'll have to go to a surgeon. If we can cut her eggs out before they hatch, that, plus the serum you gave her, may reverse the effect and pull her out."

"Eggs?"

"I'll tell you later. Wrap her up. I'll run upstairs and phone Dr. Kuto."

Yarrow folded a blanket around her. When he rolled her over, she was as stiff as a show-window dummy. He covered her face. The stony look was too much for him.

His wristphone shrilled. Automatically he reached to flick the stud and just in time drew his hand back. It shrilled loudly, insistently. Finally he decided that if he didn't answer, he would stir up their suspicion far faster.

"Yarrow!"

"Shib!"

"Report to the Archurielite. You will be given fifteen minutes."

"Shib."

Fobo came back in and said, "What're you going to do?"

Hal squared his mouth and said, "You take her by the shoulders, and I'll carry her feet. Rigid as she is, we won't need a stretcher."

As they carried her down the steps, he said, "Can you hide us after the operation, Fobo? We won't be able to use the gig now."

"Don't worry," the wog said enigmatically over his shoulder. "The Earthmen are going to be too busy to run after you."

It took sixty seconds to get her in the gig, hop to the hospital, and get her out.

Hal said, "Let's put her on the ground for a minute. I've got to set the gig on auto and send her back to the *Gabriel*. That way, at least, they won't know where I'm at."

"No. Leave it here. You may be able to use it afterward."

"After what?"

"Later. Ah, there's Kuto."

In the waiting room the joat paced back and forth and puffed Merciful Seraphim out in smoke. The empathist sat on a chair and rubbed his bald pate and the thick golden corkscrew fuzz on the back of his head.

"All this could have been avoided," he said unhappily. "But I didn't know until a week ago that the lalitha was living with you. I didn't think there was any hurry to tell you that I knew. Anyway, I was busy working on Project Earthman."

"What was that?" barked Yarrow.

"Oh, for some time we've had our electroencephalographs on you. You Terrans are far ahead of us in most of the physical sciences, but in the psychical sciences we've got you beaten. For instance, you haven't yet found out that below the level of the general brain-waves, which might be likened to 'static,' lie very weak but definite impulses.

"These we call the 'semantic' waves. Our instruments, built with our antennae and nervous system as a model, are so sensitive that they can pick them up at quite a distance and amplify them. The various heights of the semantic waves are then correlated with the spoken syllables of the language. In other words, we have a more or less efficient mind-reader.

"We trained them on you Terrans from the beginning. We thought we would have quite an advantage, because we had learned a type of French from the lalitha. To our consternation, however, we found that you talked to us in one language but tended to do your thinkng in, not one, but four different tongues."

"Those were Hebrew for the theological thinking of the Urielites and technical thinking of some of the scientists," snapped Hal. "English, Icelandic and Georgian for the everyday thoughts. Any other time I'd be interested in this thinkpicker. But for Forerunner's sake, I want to hear about Jeannette!"

"Believe me, Hal, I can feel for and with you." He wiggled his antennae to indicate he was receiving grief and anxiety emanations. "It's necessary and justifiable that I take my explanation in order. Otherwise, I'll be confused and backtracking all the time, which I detest. As I was saying, we were stumped for a while because the semantic waves fluctuations did not match those of the spoken word. However, we kept picking up stray thoughts here and there in French. As well grounded as you all seem to have been in that language, it was inevitable that you would do a certain amount of private thinking in it, regardless of your native tongue. About two weeks ago we managed to work out the complete synchronization in the artificial tongue and also bind up a great many impulses with the other languages words by comparing them with the French."

"Then you know we have perfected the globinlocker?"

Fobo smiled. "Yes, but we were suspicious of that from the beginning. When you asked us for samples of blood, your request was accompanied by too heavy a charge of what we call 'furtive' emanations. We gave you the blood, all right, but it was that of a barnyard creature which uses copper in its blood cells. We wogs use magnesium as the oxygen-carrying element in our cells."

"Our virus is useless!"

"Naturally. Now to get to the personal. My colleagues had their e.c.g's turned on you whenever you came into my room. They didn't think it was any use tapping your waves when you were in your room. You'd be likely to be thinking in the vernacular. About a week ago they did, however, just for experiment, and they were amazed to find the lalitha there. They told me. I was too engrossed with this business with the ship to put two and two together. Otherwise, I'd have known why you were pretending to be an alcoholic. I—"

A nurse entered and said, "Phone, Doctor."

Yarrow paced, and smoked another cigarette. Fobo came back.

He said, We're going to have company. One of my colleagues, who is watching the ship, tells me Macneff and two Uzzites left in a gig a minute ago. They should be arriving at the hospital any second now."

Yarrow stopped in midstride. His jaw dropped. "Here?"

"Don't be afraid."

Hal just stood there. The cigarette, unnoticed, burned until it seared his fingers. He dropped it and crushed it beneath his sole.

Bootheels clicked in the corridor.

Three men entered. One was a tall and gaunt ghost—Macneff, the Archurielite. The others were short and broad-shouldered and clad in black. Their meaty hands, though empty, were hooked, ready to dart into their pockets. Their heavy-lidded eyes stabbed at Fobo and then at Hal.

Macneff strode up to the joat. His pale blue eyes glared; his lipless mouth was drawn back in a skull's smile.

"You unspeakable degenerate!" he shouted.

His arm flashed, and the whip, jerked out of his belt, cracked. Thin red marks crawled out of Yarrow's white face and began oozing blood.

"You will be taken back to Earth in chains and there exhibited as an example of the worst pervert, traitor, and—and—!"

He drooled, unable to find words.

"You—who have passed the Elohimeter, who are supposed to be so pure—you have lusted after and lain with an insect!"

"What! What!"

"Yes. With a thing that is even lower than a beast of the field. What even Moses did not think of when he forbade union between man and beast, what even the Forerunner could not have guessed when he reaffirmed the law and set the death penalty for it, you have done. You, Hal Yarrow, the pure, the lamech wearer!"

Fobo rose and said in a deep voice, "Might I suggest and stress that you are not quite right in your zoological classification? It is not the class of insecta but the class of the chordata pseudarthropoda, or words to that effect."

The joat said, "What?" again. He could not think.

The wog growled, "Shut up, Hal. Let me talk."

He swung to face Macneff. "You know about her?"

"You are shib that I know her! Yarrow thought he was getting away with something. But no matter how clever these unrealists are, they're always tripped up. In this case, it was his asking Turnboy about those Frenchmen that fled Earth two and a half centuries ago. Turnboy, who is very zealous in his attitude towards the Sturch, reported the conversation. It lay among my papers for quite a while. When I came across it, I turned it over to the psychologists. They told me that the joat's question was a deviation from the pattern expected of him; a thing totally irrelevant unless it was connected to something we didn't know about him.

"A man was put on his trail. He saw Yarrow buying twice the groceries he should have. And much cloth and sewing equipment and silk stockings and perfume and earrings. Moreover, when you wogs learned the tobacco habit from us and began making cigarettes too, he bought them from you. The conclusion was obvious. He had a female in his apartment.

"We didn't think it'd be a wog female for she wouldn't have to stay hidden. Therefore she must be human. But we couldn't imagine how she got here on Ozagen. It was impossible for him to have stowed her away on the *Gabriel*. She must either have come here in a different ship, or be descended from people who had.

"It was Yarrow's talk with Turnboy that furnished the clue. Obviously, the French had landed here. She was a great-great-granddaughter. How the joat had found her, we didn't know. It wasn't important. We'll find out, any how."

"You're due to find out some other things, too," Fobo said calmly. "How did you discover she wasn't human?"

Yarrow muttered, "I've got to sit down."

∾ SEVENTEEN ∾

He swayed to the wall and sank into a chair. One of the Uzzites started to move toward him. Macneff waved the man back and said, "Turnboy had been reading the history of man on Ozagen. He came across so many references to the lalitha that the suspicion was bound to rise that the girl might be one.

"Last week one of the wog physicians, while talking to Turnboy, mentioned that he had once examined a lalitha. Later, he said, she had run away. It wasn't hard for us to guess where she had ended up!"

"My boy," said Fobo, turning to Hal, "didn't you read Weenai's book?"

Hal shook his head. "We started it, but Jeannette mislaid it."

"And doubtless saw to it that you had other things to think of . . . they are good at diverting a man's mind. Why not? That is their purpose in life.

"Well, Hal, I'll explain. The lalitha are the highest example of mimetic parasitism known. Also, they are unique among sentient beings. Unique in that all are female.

"You see, if you'd read on in Weenai, you'd have found that fossil evidence shows that about the time that Ozagenian man was still an insectivorous marmoset-like creature, he had in his family group not only his own females but the females of another class, perhaps another phylum. These animals looked and probably stank enough like the females of prehomo marmoset to be able to live and mate with them. They seemed mammalian, but dissection would have indicated very strongly their pseudoarthropodal ancestry.

"It's reasonable to suppose that these precursors of the lalitha were man's parasites long before the marmosetoid stage. They may have met him when he first crawled out of the sea, and promptly adapted their shape, through an evolutionary process, to that of the lung-fish. And later to the amphibian's. And the reptile's and primitive mammal's. And so on.

"What we do know is that the lalitha were Nature's most amazing experiment in parasitism and parallel evolution. As man metamorphosed into higher forms, so she kept pace with him. All female, mind you, depending upon the male of another phylum for the continuance of the species.

"It is astonishing the way they became integrated into the prehuman cultures, the pithecanthropoid and neanderthaloid steps. Only when *Homo sapiens* developed did their troubles begin. Some families and tribes accepted them; others killed them. So they resorted to artifice, and disguised themselves as human women. A thing not hard to do—unless they became pregnant.

"In which case they died."

Hal groaned and put his hands over his face.

"Painful but real, as our acquaintance Macneff would say," said Fobo. "Of course—such a condition required a secret sorority. In those societies where the lalitha was forced to camouflage, she would, once pregnant, have to leave. And perish in some hidden place among her kind, who would then take care of the nymphs—"

here Hal shuddered—"until they were able to go into human cultures. Or else be introduced as foundlings or changelings.

"You'll find quite a tribal lore about them—fables and myths make them central or peripheral characters quite frequently. They were regarded as witches, demons, or worse.

"With the introduction of the alcohol beetle in primitive times, a change for the better came to the lalitha. Alcohol made them sterile. At the same time, barring accident, disease, or murder, it made them *immortal.*

Hal took his hands off his face. "You—you mean Jeannette would have lived—forever? That I cost her that?"

"She could have lived a thousand years, at least. We know that some did. What's more, they remained young. Let me explain. In due order. Some of what I'm going to say will distress you, Hal, but it must be said.

"The long life of the pseudo-woman, sometimes so long that they survived tribes and nations they had joined when first founded, led to their being worshipped as goddesses. They became the repositories of wisdom and wealth. Religions were established with lalitha as the focus and priests and beetles on the circumference as permanent marks of human civilizations. The priests and the kings were their lovers.

"Some cultures barred the lalitha. They could not, however, keep them out. The false women infiltrated. Being always very beautiful, they mated with the most powerful men—the leaders, the rich, the poets, the thinkers. They competed with women and beat them at their own game, hands down, because in the lalitha Nature wrought the complete female.

"You see, they had no male hormone, no male element. They were all woman, and they centered their lives on men. They were instinctively and consciously sensitive to their lovers' desires, whims and moods. Yet they were crafty enough not to be clinging vines. When the time demanded a quarrel, they produced it. They knew what few human females did: the time to speak and the time not to speak.

"You noticed that in Jeannette, didn't you, Hal? No wonder.

As part of their arthropodal heritage they owned two rudimentary antennae—mere bumps on their heads, but still sensitive in detecting the grosser nervous emanations.

"And so they gained mastery over their lovers. Influenced unduly the governments. Caused widespread slavery and whole-sale breeding of beetles and the resulting alcoholism which led to humankind's downfall.

"When we wogs came to this continent, half their cities were ruined. War, liquor, depraved religious rites, falling birth rate, graft, corruption—a hundred factors leveled once mighty man. Yet, though weakened, they fought us. The lalitha urged them to battle, for they saw in us their doom. We could not be influenced by them as their men were. War and disease slew half of them; the rest just seemed to lose interest in living . . ."

A wog nurse with a white mask over her long nose came out of the operating room. Hal sprang up and watched her as she said something to the empathist in a low voice.

Macneff had been pacing back and forth with his hands clutched behind him. Hal wondered, in the back of his mind, why he, Hal, had not been dragged away at once; why the priest had waited to hear Fobo. Then a flash of insight told him that Macneff had wanted the joat to hear all about Jeannette and realize the full enormity of his deeds.

The nurse went back into the operating room. The Archurielite said loudly, "Is the beast of the fields dead yet?"

Fobo, ignoring him, spoke to Hal, who had shaken as if at a blow when he heard the word "dead."

"Your larv—that is, your children, have been removed. They are in an incubator. They are—" he hesitated—"eating well. They will live."

Yarrow could tell from his tone that it was no use asking about the mother.

The wog twitched his antennae. Big tears rolled from his round blue eyes. He did not, however, offer any sympathy. He kept on talking:

"You won't understand, Hal, what has happened unless you

comprehend the Lalitha's unique method of reproduction. To begin, their ovaries furnish the matrix for the bodies of the embryo, all beautiful bodies, the apex of art as practiced by Nature. The male spermatozoa is in no way connected with the genes that lay out the pattern for the body.

"Two things the lalitha needs to reproduce. Those two things must occur simultaneously. They are, excitation from orgasm and the stimulation of the photokinetic nerve."

Fobo paused and seemed to cock an ear, as if he were listening for something outside. Hal, who had absorbed some of the empathy of the wog during his acquaintanceship, felt that he was waiting for something big. Really big. And whatever it was, it involved the fate of the Earthmen.

Suddenly he thrilled to hot and cold tinglings . . . and the knowledge that he was on the wog's side!

"What is this nerve?" Fobo went on. "It is a property of the lalitha, and runs from the retina of the eye, along with the optic nerve, to the hack of the brain. From there it descends the spinal column and leaves the base to enter the uterus. Or, as we term it, the camera obscura uteri. The dark room of the womb. Where the photographs of the father's features are developed. And attached to the daughters' faces.

"Yes, that is one of their unique anatomical marks. The photogenes. A lalitha's chromosomes are connected to the photokinetic nerve. During intercourse, at the moment of the climax, an electrochemical change takes place in that nerve. By the light that the lalitha always requires—an arc-reflex makes it impossible for her to close her eyes at that time—the face of the male is photographed.

"Photographed is an inadequate word, but it is the only one we have for the process. Anyway, if his hair is light brown, that information passes down a string of genes, each of which controls a specific hair color from jet-black down through the hair-spectrum to orange-red. The genes work on a cybernetic parallel. A yes-no binary system. If the gene's color does not correspond to the photokinetic nerve's request, it does not respond. It says no. If it approximates most closely the request, it says yes.

"The same thing happens with the shape and thickness of the hair, the size and shape of the nose and lips, the cheekbones, and jaw, and chin, and the color of the eyes. The shape of the nose, for instance, might have to be turned down a hundred and fifty times before the right combination of genes were struck—"

"You hear that?" exulted Manceff. "You have begat larvae! Monsters of an unholy union. Insect children! And they will have your face as witness of this revolting carnality—"

"Of course, I am no connoisseur of human features," interrupted Fobo, "but the young man's strike me as vigorous and handsome. In a human way, you understand."

He turned to Yarrow. "Now you see why Jeannette desired light. And why she pretended alcoholism. As long as she drank a sufficient amount of liquor before copulation, she was sure that the workings of the delicate photokinetic nerve would be interfered with. No pregnancy that way. No death. But when . . . you cut the beetlejuice with Easyglow . . . unknowing, of course . . ."

Macneff burst into a high-pitched laughter. "What irony! Truly it has been said that the wages of unrealism are death!"

Fobo spoke loudly; "Go ahead, son. Cry, if you like. You'll feel better. You can't, eh? I wish you would.

"Eh, bien. Je continue. The lalitha, no matter how human she looks, cannot escape her arthropod heritage. The nymphs that develop from the larvae can easily pass for babies, but it would pain you to see the larvae themselves. Though they are not any uglier than a five months human embryo. Not to me, anyway.

"It is a sad thing that the lalitha mother must die. Hundreds of millions of years ago, when the primitive pseudo-arthropod was ready to hatch the eggs in her womb, a hormone was released in her body. It calcified the skin and turned her into a womb-tomb. She became a shell. Her larvae ate the organs and the bones, which were softened by the draining away of their calcium. When the young had fulfilled the function of the larva, which is to eat and grow, they rested and became nymphs. Then they broke the shell in its weak place in the belly.

"That weak point is the navel. It alone does not calcify with the epidermis, but remains soft. By the time the nymphs are ready to come out, the soft flesh of the navel has decayed. Its dissolution lets loose a chemical which decalcifies an area that takes in most of the abdomen. The nymphs, though weak as human babies and much smaller, are activated by instinct to kick out the thin and brittle covering.

"You must understand, Hal, that the navel itself is both functional and mimetic. Since the larvae are not connected to the mother by an umbilical cord, they would have no navel. But they grow an excrescence which resembles one.

"The breasts of the adult also have two functions. Like the human female's, they are both sexual and reproductive. They never produce milk, of course, but they are glands. At the time the larvae are ready to hatch from the eggs, the breasts act as two powerful pumps of the hormone which carries out the hardening of the skin.

"Nothing wasted, you see—Nature's economy. The things that enable her to survive in human society also carry out the death process.

"It is a sad thing, but it has not changed in all these epochs. The mothers must give their lives for their young. Yet Nature, as a sort of recompense, has given them a gift. On the analogy of reptiles, which do not stop growing larger as long as they aren't killed, the lalitha will not die if they remain unpregnant. And so—"

Hal leaped to his feet and shouted, "Stop it!"

"I'm sorry," Fobo said softly. "I'm just trying to make you see why Jeannette felt that she couldn't tell you what she truly was. She loved you, Hal; she, possessed the three factors that make love: a genuine passion, a deep affection, and the feeling of being one flesh with you, male and female so inseparable it would be hard to tell where one began and the other ended. I know she did, believe me, for we empathists can put ourselves into somebody else's nervous system and think and feel as they do.

"And feel, despite all this, she must have had a bitter leaven in her love. The belief that if you knew she was of an utterly alien branch of the animal kingdom, separated by millions of years of evolution, barred by her ancestry and anatomy from the true completion of marriage—children—you would turn from her with horror. That belief must have shot with darkness even her brightest moments . . ."

"No! I would have loved her, anyway! It might have been a shock. But I'd have gotten over it. Why, she was human; she was more human than most of the women I've known!"

Macneff sounded as if he were going to retch. When he had recovered himself, he howled, "You absymal thing! How can you stand yourself, now you know what utterly filthy monster you have lain with! Why don't you try to tear out your eyes, which have seen that vile filth! Why don't you bite off your lips, which have kissed that insect mouth! Why don't you cut off your hands, which have pawed with loathsome lust that mockery of a body! Why don't you tear out by the roots those organs of carnal—"

Fobo spoke through the storm of wrath. "Macneff! Macneff!"

The gaunt head swiveled towards the empathist. His eyes stared, and his lips had drawn back into what seemed to be an impossibly large smile; a smile of absolute fury.

"What? What?" he muttered, like a man waking from sleep.

"Macneff. Why don't you tell Yarrow what you were thinking about the other night? When you were alone in your cabin, and supposedly at your prayers. Why don't you tell him what you were planning to do if your agents brought in the lalitha alive? What were you thinking?"

The Sandalphon's jaw fell. Red flooded his face and became purple. The violent color faded, and a corpselike white replaced it.

He screeched like an owl.

"Enough! Uzzites, take this—this thing that calls itself a man to the gig!"

The two men in black circled to come at the joat from front and back. Their approach was based on training, not real caution. Years of taking prisoners had taught them to expect no resistance. The arrested always stood cowed and numb before the representatives of the Sturch. Now, despite the unusual circumstances, and the knowledge that Hal carried a gun, they saw nothing different in him.

Normally, they would have been right. They could not guess that they had met a man whose basically rebellious character was on the point of bursting the lifelong cocoon of repression. He stood with bowed head and hunched shoulders and dangling arms, the typical arrestee.

That was one second; the next, he was a tiger striking.

The agent in front of him reeled back, blood flowing from his mouth and spilling on his black jacket. When he bumped into the wall, he paused to spit out three teeth.

By then Yarrow had whirled and rammed a fist into the big soft belly of the man behind him.

"*Whoof!*" went the Uzzite.

He folded. As he did so, Hal brought his knee up against the unguarded chin. There was a crack of bone breaking, and the agent fell to the floor.

"Watch him!" yelled Macneff. "He's got a gun!"

The Uzzite by the wall shoved his hand under his jacket, feeling for the weapon in his armpit holster. Simultaneously a heavy bronze bookend, thrown by Fobo, struck his temple. He crumpled.

Macneff screamed, "You are resisting, Yarrow! You are resisting!"

Hal bellowed, "You're damn shib I am!"

Head down like a mad bull's, he plunged at the Archurielite.

Macneff slashed with his whip at his attacker's skull. Hal rammed into the grayclad form and knocked it to the floor. When Macneff got to his knees, Yarrow seized him by the throat and squeezed. Macneff turned purple and clutched at the terrible hands.

At that moment a tremendous *boom!* rattled the hospital windows. On its heels came another shock wave. Somewhere outside, the night became day for a second.

Hal unclenched his hands and let Macneff fall.

"What was that?" he demanded.

"I imagine it was the *Gabriel* falling from a height of fifty feet," Fobo said. "Not very far, of course, but the ship is tremendous. Something must have exploded. I hope the damage wasn't too serious, for we want to use the ship as a model to build some for ourselves."

Macneff groaned. Hal, standing over him and breathing hard, stared at the wog.

"We don't have mechanical flying missiles, Hal. But we do have hordes of winged and poisonous insects whose flight may be directed, within limits, by painful or pleasing super or subsonic waves. And who also may be conditioned by the sweat-impregnated clothing of Terrans to bite any Earthmen that come within their sense of smell.

"What happened a moment ago was that our fierce little fighters were sent through the open ports and ventilators of the Gabriel. Once inside, it is probable that they stung everybody on the ship, and that those stung collapsed with half-paralyzed nervous systems. Naturally, I don't know why the ship fell and then exploded. However, that makes it unnecessary for us to board the ship from a ballon which Zugu had powered with a motor."

"You wogs think of everything, don't you?"

Fobo shrugged. "We are peaceful but, unlike you Terrans, we are really 'realists.' If we have to take action against vermin, we exterminate them. On this insect-ridden planet we have had a long history of battling vermin."

He looked at Macneff, who was on all fours, eyes glazed, shaking his head like a wounded bear.

Fobo said, "I do not include you in that vermin, Hal. You are free to go where you want."

Hal sat down again and croaked, "What is there left for me?"

"Plenty, man." Tears ran down Fobo's nose and collected at the end. "You have your daughters to care for, to love. In a few days they will be through with their feeding in the incubator— they survived the Caesarean quite well—and will be beautiful babies. They will be yours as much as any human infants could be. After all, they look like you—in a modified feminine way, of course. Your genes are theirs. What's the difference whether genes act by cellular or photonic means? Genes are genes.

"And there will be women for you. You forget that she has aunts and sisters. All young and beautiful."

"Thanks, Fobo, but that's not for me." He buried his face in his hands.

A nurse stuck her head out of the door of the operating room.

"Doctor Fobo, we are bringing the body out. Does the man care to look?"

Without removing his hands, Hal shook his head.

Two nurses wheeled the carrier out. A white sheet was draped over the form. It clung to the superb curves of the shell beneath.

Hal did not look up.

He moaned, "Jeannette! Jeannette!"

SAIL ON! SAIL ON!

F riar Sparks sat wedged between the wall and the realizer. He sat motionless except for his forefinger and his eyes. From time to time his finger tapped rapidly on the key upon the desk, and now and then his irises, gray-blue as his native Irish sky, swiveled to look through the open door of the *toldilla* in which he crouched, the little shanty on the poop deck. Visibility was low.

Outside was dusk and a lantern by the railing. Two Sailors leaned on it. Beyond them bobbed the bright lights and dark shapes of the *Niña* and the *Pinta*. And beyond them was the smooth horizon-brow of the Atlantic, edged in black and blood by the red dome of the rising moon.

The single carbon filament bulb above the monk's tonsure showed a face lost in fat—and in concentration.

The luminiferous ether crackled and hissed tonight, but the phones clamped over his ears carried, along with them, the steady dots and dashes sent by the operator at the Las Palmas station on the Grand Canary.

"*Zzisss!* So you're out of sherry already . . . *Pop!* . . . Too bad . . . *Crackle* . . . you hardened old winebutt . . . *Zzz* . . . May god have mercy on your sins . . .

"Lots of gossip, news, et cetera . . . *Hisses!* . . . Bend your ear instead of your neck, impious one . . . The Turks are said to be gathering . . . *crackle* . . . an army to march on Austria. It is rumored that the flying sausages, said by so many to have been seen over the capitals of the Christian world, are of Turkish origin. The rumor goes they have been invented by a renegade Rogerian who was converted to the Muslim religion . . . I say . . . *zziss* . . . to that. No one of us would do that. It is a falsity spread by our enemies in the Church to discredit us. But many people believe that . . .

"How close does the Admiral calculate he is to Cipangu now?

"Flash! Savonarola today denounced the Pope, the wealthy of Florence, Greek art and literature, and the experiments of the disciples of Saint Roger Bacon . . . *Zzz!* . . . The man is sincere but misguided and dangerous . . . I predict he'll end up at the state he's always prescribing for us . . .

"*Pop* . . . This will kill you . . . Two Irish mercenaries by the name of Pat and Mike are walking down the street of Granada when a beautiful Saracen lady leaned out of a balcony and emptied a pot of . . . *hiss!* . . . and Pat looked up and . . . *Crackle* . . . Good, hah? Brother Juan told that last night . . .

"PV . . . PV . . . Are you coming in? . . . PV . . . PV . . . Yes, I know it's dangerous to bandy such jests about, but nobody is monitoring us tonight . . . *Zzz* . . . I think they're not, anyway . . ."

And so the ether bent and warped with their messages. And presently Friar Sparks tapped out the PV that ended their talk—the "*Pax vobiscum.*" Then he pulled the plug out that connected his earphones to the set and, lifting them from his ears, clamped them down forward over his temples in the regulation manner.

After sidling bent-kneed from the *toldilla*, punishing his belly against the desk's hard edge as he did so, he walked over to the railing. De Salcedo and de Torres were leaning there and talking in low tones. The big bulb above gleamed on the page's red-gold hair and on the interpreter's full black beard. It also bounced pinkishly off the priest's smooth-shaven jowls and the light scarlet robe of the Rogerian order. His cowl, thrown back, served as a bag for scratch paper, pens, an ink bottle, tiny wrenches and screwdrivers, a book on cryptography, a slide rule, and a manual of angelic principles.

"Well, old rind," said young de Salcedo familiarly, "what do you hear from Las Palmas?"

"Nothing now. Too much interference from that." He pointed to the moon riding the horizon ahead of them. "What an orb!" bellowed the priest. "It's as big and red as my revered nose!"

The two sailors laughed, and de Salcedo said, "But it will get smaller and paler as the night grows, Father. And your proboscis will, on the contrary, become larger and more sparkling in the inverse proportion according to the square of the ascent—"

He stopped and grinned, for the monk had suddenly dipped his nose, like a porpoise diving into the sea, raised it again, like the same animal jumping from a wave, and then once more plunged it into the heavy currents of their breath. Nose to nose, he faced them, his twinkling little eyes seeming to emit sparks like the realizer in his *toldilla*.

Again, porpoiselike, he sniffed and snuffed several times, quite loudly. Then satisfied with what he had gleaned from their breaths, he winked at them. He did not, however, mention his findings at once, preferring to sidle toward the subject.

He said, "This Father Sparks on the Grand Canary is so entertaining. He stimulates me with all sorts of philosophical notions, both valid and fantastic. For instance, tonight, just before we were cut off by that"—he gestured at the huge bloodshot eye in the sky—"he was discussing what he called worlds of parallel time tracks, an idea originated by Dysphagius of Gotham. It's his idea there may be other worlds in coincident but not contacting universes, that God, being infinite and of unlimited creative talent and ability, the Master Alchemist, in other words, has possibly—perhaps necessarily—created a plurality of continua in which every possible event has happened."

"Huh?" grunted de Salcedo.

"Exactly. Thus, Columbus was turned down by Queen Isabella, so this attempt to reach the Indies across the Atlanta was never made. So we could not now be standing here plunging ever deeper into Oceanus in our three cockle-shells, there would be no booster buoys strung out between us and the Canaries, and Father Sparks at Las Palmas and I on the *Santa Maria* would not be carrying on our fascinating conversations across the ether.

"Or, say, Roger Bacon was persecuted by the Church, instead of being encouraged and giving rise to the order whose inventions have done so much to insure the monopoly of the Church on alchemy and its divinely inspired guidance of that formerly pagan and hellish practice."

De Torres opened his mouth, but the priest silenced him with a magnificent and imperious gesture and continued.

"Or, even more ridiculous, but thought-provoking, he speculated just this evening on universes with different physical laws. One, in particular, I thought very droll. As you probably know, Angelo Angelei has proved, by dropping objects from the Leaning Tower of Pisa, that different weights fall at different speeds. My delightful colleague on the Grand Canary is writing a satire which takes place in a universe where Aristotle is made out to be a liar, where all things drop with equal velocities, no matter what their size. Silly stuff, but it helps to pass the time. We keep the ether busy with our little angels."

De Salcedo said, "Uh, I don't want to seem too curious about the secrets of your holy and cryptic order, Friar Sparks. But these little angels your machine realizes intrigue me. Is it a sin to presume to ask about them?"

The monk's bull roar slid to a dove cooing, "Whether it's a sin or not depends. Let me illustrate, young fellows. If you were concealing a bottle of, say, very scarce sherry on you, and you did not offer to share it with a very thirsty old gentlemen, that would be a sin. A sin of omission. But if you were to give the desert-dry, that pilgrim-weary, that devout, humble, and decrepit old soul a long soothing, refreshing, and stimulating draught of livegiving fluid, daughter of the vine, I would find it in my heart to pray for you for that deed of loving-kindness, of encompassing charity. And it would please me so much I might tell you a little of our realizer. Not enough to hurt you, just enough so you might gain more respect for the intelligence and glory of my order."

De Salcedo grinned conspiratorially and passed the monk the bottle he'd hidden under his jacket. As the friar tilted it, and the chug-chug-chug of vanishing sherry became louder, the two sailors glanced meaningfully at each other. No wonder the priest, reputed to be so brilliant in his branch of the alchemical mysteries, had yet been sent off on this halfbaked voyage to devil-knew-where. The Church had calculated that if he survived, well and good. If he didn't, then he would sin no more.

The monk wiped his lips on his sleeve, belched loudly as a horse, and said, "Gracias, boys. From my heart, so deeply buried in this fat, I thank you. An old Irishman, dry as a camel's hoof, choking to death with the dust of abstinence, thanks you. You have saved my life."

"Thank rather that magic nose of yours," replied de Salcedo. "Now, old rind, now that you're well greased again, would you mind explaining as much as you are allowed about that machine of yours?"

Friar Sparks took fifteen minutes. At the end of that time, his listeners asked a few permitted questions.

". . . and you say you broadcast on a frequency of eighteen hundred k.c.?" the page asked. "What does 'k.c.' mean?"

"K stands for the French *kilo*, from a Greek word meaning thousand. And c stands for the Hebrew *cherubim*, the 'little angels.' Angel comes from the Greek *angelos*, meaning messenger. It is our concept that the ether is crammed with these cherubim, these little messengers. Thus, when we Friar Sparkses depress the key of our machine, we are able to realize some of the infinity of 'messengers' waiting for just such a demand for service.

"So, eighteen hundred k.c. means that in a given unit of time one million, eight hundred thousand cherubim line up and hurl themselves across the ether, the nose of one being brushed by the feathertips of the cherub's wings ahead. The height of the wing crests of each little creature is even, so that if you were to draw an outline of the whole train, there would be nothing to distinguish one cherub from the next, the whole column forming that grade of little angels known as C.W."

"C.W.?"

"Continuous wingheight. My machine is a C.W. realizer."

Young de Salcedo said, "My mind reels. Such a concept! Such a revelation! It almost passes comprehension. Imagine, the aerial of your realizer is cut just so long, so that the evil cherubim surging back and forth on it demand a predetermined and equal number of good angels to combat them. And this seduction coil on the realizer crowds 'bad' angels into the left-hand, the sinister, side. And when the bad little cherubim are crowded so closely and numerously that they can't bear each other's evil company, they jump the spark gap and speed around the wire to the 'good' plate. And in this racing back and forth they call themselves to the attention of the 'little messengers,' the yea-saying cherubim. And you, Friar Sparks, by manipulating your machine thus and so, and lifting and lowering your key, you bring these invisible and friendly lines of carriers, your etheric and winged postmen, into reality. And you are able, thus, to communicate at great distances with your brothers of the order."

"Great God!" said de Torres.

It was not a vain oath but a pious exclamation of wonder. His eyes bulged; it was evident that he suddenly saw that man was not alone, that on every side, piled on top of each other, flanked on every angle, stood a host. Black and white, they presented a solid chessboard of the seemingly empty cosmos, black for the nay-sayers, white for the yea-sayers, maintained by a Hand in delicate balance and subject as the fowls of the air and the fish of the sea to exploitation by man.

Yet de Torres, having seen such a vision as has made a saint of many a man, could only ask, "Perhaps you could tell me how many angels may stand on the point of a pin?"

Obviously, de Torres would never wear a halo. He was destined, if he lived, to cover his bony head with the mortar-board of a university teacher.

De Salcedo snorted. "I'll tell you. Philosophically speaking, you may put as many angels on a pinpoint as you want to. Actually speaking, you may only put as many as there is room for. Enough of that. I'm interested in facts, not fancies. Tell me, how could the moon's rising interrupt your reception of the cherubim sent by the Sparks at Las Palmas?"

"Great Caesar, how would I know? Am I a repository of universal knowledge? No, not I! A humble and ignorant friar, I! All I can tell you is that last night it rose like a bloody tumor on the horizon, and that when it was up I had to quit marshalling my little messengers in their short and long columns. The Canary station was quite overpowered, so that both of us gave up. And the same thing happened tonight."

"The moon sends messages?" asked de Torres.

"Not in a code I can decipher. But it sends, yes."

"Santa Maria!"

"Perhaps," suggested de Salcedo, "there are people on that moon, and they are sending."

Friar Sparks blew derision through his nose. Enormous as were his nostrils, his derision was not small bore. Artillery of contempt laid down a barrage that would have silenced any but the strongest of souls.

"Maybe"—de Torres spoke in a low tone—"maybe, if the stars are windows in heaven, as I've heard said, the angels of the higher hierarchy, the big ones, are realizing—uh—the smaller? And they only do it when the moon is up so we may know it is a celestial phenomenon?"

He crossed himself and looked around the vessel.

"You need not fear," said the monk gently. "There is no Inquisitor leaning over your shoulder. Remember, I am the only priest on this expedition. Moreover, your conjecture has nothing to do with dogma. However, that's unimportant. Here's what I don't understand: how can a heavenly body broadcast? Why does it have the same frequency as the one I'm restricted to? Why—"

"I could explain," interrupted de Salcedo with all the brashness and impatience of youth. "I could say that the Admiral and the Rogerians are wrong about the earth's shape. I could say the earth is not round but it is flat. I could say the horizon exists, not because we live upon a globe, but because the earth is curved only a little ways, like a greatly flattened out hemisphere. I could also say that the cherubim are coming, not from Luna, but from a ship such as ours, a vessel which is hanging in the void off the edge of the earth."

"What?" gasped the other two.

"Haven't you heard," said de Salcedo, "that the King of Portugal secretly sent out a ship after he turned down Columbus' proposal? How do we know he did not, that the messages are from our predecessor, that he sailed off the world's rim and is now suspended in the air and becomes exposed at night because it follows the moon around Terra—is, in fact, a much smaller and unseen satellite?"

The monk's laughter woke many men on the ship. "I'll have to tell the Las Palmas operator your tale. He can put it in that novel of his. Next you'll be telling me those messages are from one of those fire-shooting sausages so many credulous laymen have been seeing flying around. No, my dear de Salcedo, let's not be ridiculous. Even the ancient Greeks knew the earth was round. Every university in Europe teaches that. And we Rogerians have measured the circumference. We know for sure that the Indies lie just across the Atlantic. Just as we know for sure, through mathematics, that heavier-than-air-machines are impossible. Our Friar Ripskulls, our mind doctors, have assured us these flying creations are mass hallucinations or else the tricks of heretics or Turks who want to panic the populace.

"That moon radio is no delusion, I'll grant you. What it is, I don't know. But it's not a Spanish or Portuguese ship. What about its different code? Even it if came from Lisbon, that ship would still have a Rogerian operator. And he would, according to our policy, be of a different nationality from the crew so he might the easier stay out of political embroilments. He wouldn't break our laws by using a different code in order to communicate with Lisbon. We disciples of Saint Roger do not stoop to petty boundary intrigues. Moreover, that realizer would not be powerful enough to reach Europe, and must, therefore, be directed at us."

"How can you be sure?" said de Salcedo. "Distressing though

the thought may be to you, a priest could be subverted. Or a layman could learn your secrets and invent a code. I think that a Portuguese ship is sending to another, a ship perhaps not too distant from us."

De Torres shivered and crossed himself again. "Perhaps the angels are warning us of approaching death? Perhaps?"

"Perhaps? Then why don't they use our code? Angels would know it as well as I. No, there is no perhaps. The order does not permit perhaps. It experiments and finds out; nor does it pass judgment until it knows."

"I doubt we'll ever know." said de Salcedo gloomily. "Columbus has promised the crew that if we come across no sign of land by evening tomorrow, we shall turn back. Otherwise"—he drew a finger across his throat—"*kkk!* Another day, and we'll be pointed east and getting away from that evil and bloody-looking moon and its incomprehensible messages."

"It would be a great loss to the order and to the Church," sighed the friar. "But I leave such things in the hands of God and inspect only what He hands me to look at."

With which pious statement Friar Sparks lifted the bottle to ascertain the liquid level. Having determined in a scientific manner its existence, he next measured its quantity and tested its quality by putting all of it in the best of all chemistry tubes, his enormous belly.

Afterward, smacking his lips and ignoring the pained and disappointed looks on the faces of the sailors, he went on to speak enthusiastically of the water screw and the engine which turned it, both of which had been built recently at the St. Jonas College at Genoa. If Isabella's three ships had been equipped with those, he declared, they would not have to depend upon the wind. However, so far, the fathers had forbidden its extended use because it was feared the engine's fumes might poison the air and the terrible speeds it made possible might be fatal to the human body. After which he plunged into a tedious description of the life of his patron saint, the inventor of the first cherubim realizer and receiver, Jonas of Carcassonne, who had been martyred when he grabbed a wire he thought was insulated.

The two sailors found excuses to walk off. The monk was a good fellow, but hagiography bored them. Besides, they wanted to talk of women . . .

If Columbus had not succeeded in persuading his crews to sail one more day, events would have been different.

At dawn the sailors were very much cheered up by the sight of several large birds circling their ships. Land could not be far off; perhaps these winged creatures came from the coast of the fabled Cipangu itself, the country whose houses were roofed with gold.

The birds swooped down. Closer, they were enormous and very strange. Their bodies were flattish and almost saucer-shaped and small in proportion to the wings, which had a spread of at least thirty feet. Nor did they have legs. Only a few sailors saw the significance of that fact. These birds dwelt in the air and never rested upon land or sea.

While they were meditating upon that, they heard a slight sound as of a man clearing his throat. So gentle and far off was the noise that nobody paid any attention to it, for each thought his neighbor had made it.

A few minutes later, the sound had become louder and deeper, like a lute string being twanged.

Everybody looked up. Heads turned west.

Even yet they did not understand that the noise like a finger plucking a wire came from the line that held the earth together, and that the line was stretched to its utmost, and that the violent finger of the sea was what had plucked the line.

It was sometime before they understood. They had run out of horizon.

When they saw that, they were too late.

The dawn had not only come up *like* thunder, it *was* thunder. And though the three ships heeled over at once and tried to sail close-hauled on the port tack, the suddenly speeded-up and relentless current made beating hopeless.

Then it was the Rogerian wished for the Genoese screw and the wood-burning engine that would have made them able to resist the terrible muscles of the charging and bull-like sea. Then it was that some men prayed, some raved, some tried to attack the Admiral, some jumped overboard, and some sank into a stupor.

Only the fearless Columbus and the courageous Friar Sparks stuck to their duties. All that day the fat monk crouched wedged in his little shanty, dot-dashing to his fellow on the Grand Canary. He ceased only when the moon rose like a giant red bubble from the throat of a dying giant. Then he listened intently all night and worked desperately, scribbling and swearing impiously and checking cipher books.

When the dawn came up again in a roar and a rush, he ran from the *toldilla,* a piece of paper clutched in his hand. His eyes were wild, and his lips were moving fast, but nobody could understand that he had cracked the code. They could not hear him shouting, "It is the Portuguese! It is the Portuguese!"

Their ears were too overwhelmed to hear a mere human voice. The throat clearing and the twanging of a string had been the noises preliminary to the concert itself. Now came the mighty overture; as compelling as the blast of Gabriel's horn was the topple of Oceanus into space.

Sestina of the Space Rocket

One thing is sure, O comrades, that the love
That fights to keep us rooted in the earth,
But also urges us to dare the stars,
This irresistible, this ancient power
Wedged in the soul, unshakable, is the light
That burns our roots and leaves us free for Space.

The way is open, comrades, free as Space
Alone is free. The only gold is love,
A coin that we have minted from the light
Of others who have cared for us on Earth
And who have deposited in us the power
That nerves our nerves to seize the burning stars.

Courage, comrades! Let the fire of stars
Reflect their flames in your hearts till men lack space
To say enough of the inexpressible power
That gives the strength to sever us from love
Of beautiful women, strength which makes large Earth,
Once so close, now only a spurt of light.

Philip José Farmer

Eyes forward! Sing a paean to the light
That God gives us to net the distant stars
In eyes that once were blinded with black earth.
Man had no time for aught but toil, no space
For aught but war. Yet God, in His great love,
Has cleared our eyes and given a hint of Power.

Now we have lit a candle to the power
Of atoms; now we know we're heirs of light
Itself and know no more that fleck whose love
And hates are far from us, as far as stars
Once were, now let us swear to leave no space
Unconquered till we find a better earth.

Yes, we hope to seed a new, rich earth.
We hope to breed a race of men whose power
Dwells in hearts as open as all Space
Itself, who ask for nothing but the light
That rinses the heart of hate so that the stars
Above will be below when man has Love.

God, Whose hand holds stars, as we lump earth
In our fingers, give us power, give us light
To hold all love within our breast's small space.

MOTHER

✃ ONE ✃

L ook, mother. The clock is running backwards."
Eddie Fetts pointed to the hands on the pilot room dial.

Dr. Paula Fetts said, "The crash must have reversed it."

"How could it do that?"

"I can't tell you. I don't know everything, son."

"Oh!"

"Well, don't look at me so disappointedly. I'm a pathologist, not an electronician."

"Don't be so cross, mother. I can't stand it. Not now."

He walked out of the pilot room. Anxiously, she followed him. The burial of the crew and her fellow scientists had been very trying for him. Spilled blood had always made him dizzy and sick; he could scarcely control his hands enough to help her sack the scattered bones and entrails.

He had wanted to put the corpses in the nuclear furnace, but she had forbidden that. The Geigers amidships were ticking loudly, warning that there was invisible death in the stern.

The meteor that struck the moment the ship came out of Translation into normal space had probably wrecked the engine-room. So she had understood from the incoherent high-pitched

157

phrases of a colleague before he fled to the pilot room. She had hurried to find Eddie. She feared his cabin door would still be locked, as he had been making a tape of the aria "Heavy Hangs the Albatross" from Gianelli's *Ancient Mariner.*

Fortunately, the emergency system had automatically thrown out the locking circuits. Entering, she had called out his name in fear he'd been hurt. He was lying half-unconscious on the floor, but it was not the accident that had thrown him there. The reason lay in the corner, released from his lax hand; a quart free-fall thermos, rubber-nippled. From Eddie's open mouth charged a breath of rye that not even Nodor pills had been able to conceal.

Sharply she had commanded him to get up and on to the bed. Her voice, the first he had ever heard, pierced through the phalanx of Old Red Star. He struggled up, and she, though smaller, had thrown every ounce of her weight into getting him up and on to the bed.

There she had lain down with him and strapped them both in. She understood that the lifeboat had been wrecked also, and it was up to the captain to bring the yacht down safely to the surface of this charted but unexplored planet, Baudelaire. Everybody else had gone to sit behind the captain, strapped in crashchairs, unable to help except with their silent backing.

Moral support had not been enough. The ship had come in on a shallow slant. Too fast. The wounded motors had not been able to hold her up. The prow had taken the brunt of the punishment. So had those seated in the nose.

Dr. Fetts had held her son's head on her bosom and prayed out loud to her God. Eddie had snored and muttered. Then there was a sound like the clashing of the gates of doom—a tremendous bong as if the ship were a clapper in a gargantuan bell tolling the most frightening message human ears may hear—a blinding blast of light—and darkness and silence.

A few moments later Eddie began crying out in a childish voice, "Don't leave me to die, mother! Come back! Come back!"

Mother was unconscious by his side, but he did not know that. He wept for a while, then he lapsed back into his rye-fogged stupor—if he had ever been out of it—and slept. Again, darkness and silence.

It was the second day since the crash, if "day" could describe that twilight state on Baudelaire. Dr. Fetts followed her son wherever he went. She knew he was very sensitive and easily upset. All his life she had known it and had tried to get between him and anything that would cause trouble. She had succeeded, she thought, fairly well until three months ago when Eddie had eloped.

The girl was Polina Fameux, the ash-blonde, long-legged actress whose tridi image, taped, had been shipped to frontier stars where a small acting talent meant little and a large and shapely bosom much. Since Eddie was a well-known Metro tenor, the marriage made a big splash whose ripples ran around the civilized Galaxy.

Dr. Fetts had felt very bad about the elopement, but she had, she hoped, hidden her grief very well beneath a smiling mask. She didn't regret having to give him up; after all, he was a full-grown man, no longer her little boy. But, really, aside from the seasons at the Met and his tours, he had not been parted from her since he was eight.

That was when she went on a honeymoon with her second husband. And then she and Eddie had not been separated long, for Eddie had got very sick, and she'd had to hurry back and take care of him, as he had insisted she was the only one who could make him well.

Moreover, you couldn't count his days at the opera as a total loss, for he vised her every noon and they had a long talk—no matter how high the vise bills ran.

The ripples caused by her son's marriage were scarcely a week old before they were followed by even bigger ones. They bore the news of the separation of Eddie and his wife. A fortnight later, Polina applied for divorce on grounds of incompatibility. Eddie was handed the papers in his mother's apartment. He had come back to her the day he and Polina had agreed they "couldn't make a go of it," or, as he phrased it to his mother, "couldn't get together."

Dr. Fetts was, of course, very curious about the reason for their parting, but, as she explained to her friends, she "respected" his silence. What she didn't say was that she had told herself the time would come when he would tell her all.

Eddie's "nervous breakdown" started shortly afterwards. He had been very irritable, moody, and depressed, but he got worse the day a so-called friend told Eddie that whenever Polina heard his name mentioned, she laughed loud and long. The friend added that Polina had promised to tell someday the true story of their brief merger.

That night his mother had to call in a doctor.

In the days that followed, she thought of giving up her position as research pathologist at De Kruif and taking all her time to help him "get back on his feet." It was a sign of the struggle going on in her mind that she had not been able to decide within a week's time. Ordinarily given to swift consideration and resolution of a problem, she could not agree to surrender her beloved quest into tissue regeneration.

Just as she was on the verge of doing what was for her the incredible and the shameful, tossing a coin, she had been vised by her superior. He told her she had been chosen to go with a group of biologists on a research cruise to ten preselected planetary systems.

Joyfully, she had thrown away the papers that would turn Eddie over to a sanatorium. And, since he was quite famous, she had used her influence to get the government to allow him to go along. Ostensibly, he was to make a survey of the development of opera on planets colonized by Terrans. That the yacht was not visiting any colonized globes seemed to have been missed by the bureaus concerned. But it was not the first time in the history of a government that its left hand knew not what its right was doing.

Actually, he was to be "rebuilt" by his mother, who thought herself much more capable of curing him than any of the prevalent A, F, J, R, S, K, or H therapies. True, some of her friends reported amazing results with some of the symbol-chasing techniques. On the other hand, two of her close companions had tried them all and had got no benefits from any of them. She was his mother;

she could do more for him than any of those "alphabatties;" he was flesh of her flesh, blood of her blood. Besides, he wasn't so sick. He just got awfully blue sometimes and made theatrical but insincere threats of suicide or else just sat and stared into space. But she could handle him.

ᘉ Two ᘉ

So now it was that she followed him from the backward-running clock to his room. And saw him step inside, look for a second, and then turn to her with a twisted face.

"Neddie is ruined, mother. Absolutely ruined."

She glanced at the piano. It had torn loose from the wallracks at the moment of impact and smashed itself against the opposite wall. To Eddie it wasn't just a piano; it was Neddie. He had a pet name for everything he contacted for more than a brief time. It was as if he hopped from one appellation to the next, like an ancient sailor who felt lost unless he was close to the familiar and designated points of the shoreline. Otherwise, Eddie seemed to be drifting helplessly in a chaotic ocean, one that was anonymous and amorphous.

Or, analogy more typical of him, he was like the night-clubber who feels submerged, drowning, unless he hops from table to table, going from one well-known group of faces to the next, avoiding the featureless and unnamed dummies at the strangers' tables.

He did not cry over Neddie. She wished he would. He had been so apathetic during the voyage. Nothing, not even the unparalleled splendor of the naked stars nor the inexpressible alienness of strange planets had seemed to lift him very long. If he would only weep or laugh loudly or display some sign that he was reacting violently to what was happening. She would even have welcomed his striking her in anger or calling her "bad" names.

But no, not even during the gathering of the mangled corpses, when he looked for a while as if he were going to vomit, would he give way to his body's demand for expression. She understood that if he were to throw up, he would be much better for it, would have got rid of much of the psychic disturbance along with the physical.

He would not. He had kept on raking flesh and bones into the large plastic bags and kept a fixed look of resentment and sullenness.

She hoped now that the loss of his piano would bring tears and shaking shoulders. Then she could take him in her arms and give him sympathy. He would be her little boy again, afraid of the dark, afraid of the dog killed by a car, seeking her arms for the sure safety, the sure love.

"Never mind, baby," she said. "When we're rescued, we'll get you a new one."

"When—!"

He lifted his eyebrows and sat down on the bed's edge. "What do we do now?"

She became very brisk and efficient.

"The ultrad automatically started working the moment the meteor struck. If it's survived the crash, it's still sending SOSs. If not, then there's nothing we can do about it. Neither of us knows how to repair it.

"However, it's possible that in the last five years since this planet was located, other expeditions may have landed here. Not from Earth but from some of the colonies. Or from non-human globes. Who knows? It's worth taking a chance. Let's see."

A single glance was enough to wreck their hopes. The ultrad had been twisted and broken until it was no longer recognizable as the machine that sent swifter-than-light waves through the no-ether.

Dr. Fetts said with false cheeriness, "Well, that's that! So what? It makes things too easy. Let's go into the storeroom and see what we can see."

Eddie shrugged and followed her. There she insisted that each take a panrad. If they had to separate for any reason, they could always communicate and also, using the DFs—the built-in direction finders—locate each other. Having used them before, they knew the instruments' capabilities and how essential they were on scouting or camping trips.

The panrads were lightweight cylinders about two feet high and eight inches in diameter. Crampacked, they held the mechanisms of two dozen different utilities. Their batteries lasted a year without recharging, they were practically indestructible and worked under almost any conditions.

Keeping away from the inside of the ship that had the huge hole in it, they took the panrads outside. The long wave bands were searched by Eddie while his mother moved the dial that ranged up and down the shortwaves. Neither really expected to hear anything, but to search was better than doing nothing.

Finding the modulated wave-frequencies empty of any significant noises, he switched to the continuous waves. He was startled by a dot-dashing.

"Hey, mom! Something in the 100 kilocycles! Unmodulated!"

"Naturally, son," she said with some exasperation in the midst of her elation. "What would you expect from a radio-telegraphic signal?"

She found the band on her own cylinder. He looked blankly at her. "I know nothing about radio, but that's not Morse."

"What? You must be mistaken!"

"I—I don't think so."

"Is it or isn't it? Good God, son, can't you be certain of anything!"

She turned the amplifier up. As both of them had learned Galacto-Morse through sleeplearn techniques, she checked him at once.

"You're right. What do you make of it?"

His quick ear sorted out the pulses.

"No simple dot and dash. Four different time-lengths."

He listened some more.

They've got a certain rhythm, all right. I can make out definite groupings. Ah! That's the sixth time I've caught that particular one. And there's another. And another."

Dr. Fetts shook her ash-blonde head. She could make out nothing but a series of zzt-zzt-zzt's.

Eddie glanced at the DF needle.

"Coming from NE by E. Should we try to locate?"

"Naturally," she replied. "But we'd better eat first. We don't know how far away it is, or what we'll find there. While I fix a hot meal, you get our field trip stuff ready."

"O.K.," he said with more enthusiasm than he had shown for a long time.

When he came back he ate everything in the large dish his mother had prepared on the unwrecked galley stove.

"You always did make the best stew," he said.

"Thank you. I'm glad you're eating again, son. I am surprised. I thought you'd be sick about all this."

He waved vaguely but energetically.

"The challenge of the unknown. I have a sort of feeling this is going to turn out much better than we thought. Much better."

She came close and sniffed his breath. It was clean, innocent even of stew. That meant he'd taken Nodor, which probably meant he'd been sampling some hidden rye. Otherwise, how explain his reckless disregard of the possible dangers? It wasn't like him.

She said nothing, for she knew that if he tried to hide a bottle in his clothes or field sack while they were tracking down the radio signals, she would soon find it. And take it away. He wouldn't even protest, merely let her lift it from his limp hand while his lips swelled with resentment.

ය THREE ය

They set out. Both wore knapsacks and carried the panrads. He carried a gun over his shoulder, and she had snapped on to her sack her small black bag of medical and lab supplies.

High noon of late autumn was topped by a weak red sun that barely managed to make itself seen through the eternal double layer of clouds. Its companion, an even smaller blob of lilac, was setting on the northwestern horizon. They walked in a sort of bright twilight, the best that Baudelaire ever achieved. Yet, despite the lack of light, the air was warm. It was a phenomenon common to certain planets behind the Horsehead—one being investigated but as yet unexplained.

The country was hilly, with many deep ravines. Here and there were prominences high enough and steep-sided enough to be called embryo mountains. Considering the roughness of the land, however, there was a surprising amount of vegetation. Pale green, red and yellow bushes, vines, and little trees clung to every bit of ground, horizontal or vertical. All had comparatively broad leaves that turned with the sun to catch the light.

From time to time, as the two Terrans strode noisily through the forest, small multicolored insect-like and mammal-like creatures scuttled from hiding place to hiding place. Eddie decided to carry his gun in the crook of his arm. Then, after they were forced to scramble up and down ravines and hills and fight their way through thickets that became unexpectedly tangled, he put it back over his shoulder, where it hung from a strap.

Despite their exertions, they did not tire quickly. They weighed about twenty pounds less than they would have on Earth, and, though the air was thinner, it was richer in oxygen.

Dr. Fetts kept up with Eddie. Thirty years the senior of the twenty-three-year-old, she passed even at close inspection for his older sister. Longevity pills took care of that. However, he treated her with all the courtesy and chivalry that one gave one's mother and helped her up the steep inclines, even though the climbs did not appreciably cause her deep chest to demand more air.

They paused once by a creek bank to get their bearings.

"The signals have stopped," he said.

"Obviously," she replied.

At that moment the radar-detector built into the panrad began to ping. Both of them automatically looked upwards.

"There's no ship in the air."

"It can't be coming from either of those hills," she pointed out. "There's nothing but a boulder on top of each one. Tremendous rocks."

"Nevertheless, it's coming from there, I think. Oh! Oh! Did you see what I saw? Looked like a tall stalk of some kind being pulled down behind that big rock."

She peered through the dim light. "I think you were imagining things, son. I saw nothing."

Then, even as the pinging kept up, the zzting started again. After a burst of noise, both stopped.

"Let's go up and see what we shall see," she said.

"Something screwy," he commented. She did not answer.

They forded the creek and began the ascent. Half-way up, they stopped to sniff in puzzlement at a gust of some heavy odor coming downwind.

"Smells like a cageful of monkeys," he said.

"In heat," she added. If his were the keener ears, hers was the sharper nose.

They went on up. The RD began sounding its tiny hysterical gonging. Nonplussed, Eddied stopped. The DF indicated the radar pulses were not coming from the top of the hill they were climbing, as formerly, but from the other hill across the valley. Abruptly, the panrad fell silent.

"What do we do now?"

"Finish what we started. This hill. Then we go to the other one."

He shrugged and then hastened after her tall slim body in its long-legged coveralls. She was hot on the scent, literally, and nothing could stop her. Just before she reached the bungalow-sized boulder topping the hill, he caught up with her. She had stopped to gaze intently at the DF needle, which swung wildly before it stopped at neutral. The monkey-cage odor was very strong.

"Do you suppose it could be some sort of radio-generating mineral?" she asked, disappointedly.

"No. Those groupings were semantic. And that smell . . ."

"Then what—"

He didn't know whether to feel pleased or not that she had so obviously and suddenly thrust the burden of responsibility and action on him. Both pride and a curious shrinking affected him. But he did feel exhilarated. Almost, he thought, he felt as if he were on the verge of discovering what he had been looking for for a long time. What the object of his search had been, he could not say. But he was excited and not very much afraid.

He unslung his weapon, a two-barrelled combination shotgun and rifle. The panrad was still quiet.

"Maybe the boulder is camouflage for a spy outfit," he said. He sounded silly, even to himself.

Behind him, his mother gasped and screamed. He whirled and raised his gun, but there was nothing to shoot. She was pointing at the hilltop across the valley, shaking, and saying something incoherent.

He could make out a long slim antenna seemingly projecting from the monstrous boulder crouched there. At the same time, two thoughts struggled for the first place in his mind: one, that it was more than a coincidence that both hills had almost identical stone structures on their brows, and two, that the antenna must have been recently stuck out, for he was sure he had not seen it the last time he looked.

He never got to tell her his conclusions, for something thin and flexible and irresistible seized him from behind. Lifted into the air, he was borne backwards. He dropped the gun and tried to grab the bands or tentacles around him and tear them off with his bare hands. No use.

He caught one last glimpse of his mother running off down the hillside. Then a curtain snapped down, and he was in total darkness.

✂ FOUR ✂

Eddie sensed himself, still suspended, twirled around. He could not know for sure, of course, but he thought he was facing in exactly the opposite direction. Simultaneously, the tentacles binding his legs and arms were released. Only his waist was still gripped. It was pressed so tightly that he cried out with pain.

Then, boot-toes bumping on some resilient substances, he was carried forward. Halted, facing he knew not what horrible monster, he was suddenly assailed—not by a sharp beak or tooth or knife or some other cutting or mangling instrument—but by a dense cloud of that same monkey perfume.

In other circumstances, he might have vomited. Now his stomach was not given the time to consider whether it should clean house or not. The tentacle lifted him higher and thrust him against something soft and yielding—something fleshlike and womanly—almost breastlike in texture and smoothness and warmth and in its hint of gentle curving.

He put his hands and feet out to brace himself, for he thought for a moment he was going to sink in and be covered up—enfolded—ingested. The idea of a gargantuan amoeba-thing hiding within a hollow rock—or a rock-like shell—made him writhe and yell and shove at the protoplasmic substance.

But nothing of the kind happened. He was not plunged into a smothering and slimy jelly that would strip him of his skin and then his flesh and then dissolve his bones. He was merely shoved repeatedly against the soft swelling. Each time, he pushed or kicked or struck at it. After a dozen of these seemingly purposeless acts, he was held away, as if whatever was doing it was puzzled by his behavior.

He had quit screaming. The only sounds were his harsh breathing and the zzzts and pings from the panrad. Even as he became aware of them, the zzzts changed tempo and settled into a recognizable pattern of bursts—three units that crackled out again and again.

"Who are you? Who are you?"

Of course, it could just as easily have been, "What are you?" or "What the hell!" or "Nor smoz ka pop?"

Or nothing—semantically speaking.

But he didn't think the latter. And when he was gently lowered to the floor, and the tentacle went off to only-God-knew-where in the dark, he was sure that the creature was communicating—or trying to—with him.

It was this thought that kept him from screaming and running around in the lightless and fetid chamber, brainlessly seeking an outlet. He mastered his panic and snapped open a little shutter in the panrad's side and thrust in his right-hand index finger. There he poised it above the key and in a moment, when the thing paused in transmitting, he sent back, as best he could, the pulses he had received. It was not necessary for him to turn on the light and spin the dial that would put him on the 1,000 kc. band. The instrument would automatically key that frequency in with the one he had just received.

The oddest part of the whole procedure was that his whole body was trembling almost uncontrollably—one part excepted. That was his index finger, his one unit that seemed to him to have a definite function in this otherwise meaningless situation. It was the section of him that was helping him to survive—the only part that knew how—at that moment. Even his brain seemed to have no connection with his finger. That digit was himself, and the rest just happened to be linked to it.

When he paused, the transmitter began again. This time the units were unrecognizable. There was a certain rhythm to them, but he could not know what they meant. Meanwhile, the RD was pinging. Something somewhere in the dark hole had a beam held tightly on him.

He pressed a button on the panrad's top, and the built-in flashlight illuminated the area just in front of him. He saw a wall of reddish-grey rubbery substance. On the wall was a roughly circular, light grey swelling about four feet in diameter. Around it, giving it a medusa appearance, were coiled twelve very long, very thin tentacles.

Though he was afraid that if he turned his back to them the tentacles would seize him once more, his curiosity forced him to wheel about and examine his surroundings with the bright beam. He was in an egg-shaped chamber about thirty feet long, twelve wide, and eight to ten high in the middle. It was formed of reddish-grey material, smooth except for irregular intervals of blue or red pipes. Veins and arteries?

A door-sized portion of the wall had a vertical slit running down it. Tentacles fringed it. He guessed it was a sort of iris and that it had opened to drag him inside. Starfish-shaped groupings of tentacles were scattered on the walls or hung from the ceiling. On the wall opposite the iris was a long and flexible stalk with a cartilaginous ruff around its free end. When Eddie moved, it moved, its blind point following him as a radar antenna tracks the thing it is locating. That was what it was. And unless he was wrong, the stalk was also a C.W. transmitter-receiver.

He shot the light around. When it reached the end farthest from him, he gasped. Ten creatures were huddled together facing him! About the size of half-grown pigs, they looked like nothing so much as unshelled snails; they were eyeless, and the stalk growing from the forehead of each was a tiny duplicate of that on the wall. They didn't look dangerous. Their open mouths were little and toothless, and their rate of locomotion must be slow, for they moved like snails, on a large pedestal of flesh—a foot-muscle.

Nevertheless, if he were to fall asleep they could overcome him by force of numbers, and those mouths might drip an acid to digest him, or they might carry a concealed poisonous sting.

His speculations were interrupted violently. He was seized, lifted, and passed on to another group of tentacles. He was carried beyond the antenna-stalk and towards the snail-beings. Just before he reached them, he was halted, facing the wall. An iris, hitherto invisible, opened. His light shone into it, but he could see nothing but convolutions of flesh.

His panrad gave off a new pattern of dit-dot-deet-dats. The iris widened until it was large enough to admit his body, if he were shoved in head first. Or feet first. It didn't matter. The convolutions straightened out and became a tunnel. Or a throat. From thousands of little pits emerged thousands of tiny, razor-sharp teeth. They flashed out and sank back in, and before they had disappeared thousands of other wicked little spears darted out and past the receding fangs.

Meat-grinder.

Beyond the murderous array, at the end of the throat, was a huge pouch of water. Steam came from it, and with it an odor like that of his mother's stew. Dark bits, presumably meat, and pieces of vegetables floated on the seething surface.

Then the iris closed, and he was turned around to face the slugs. Gently, but unmistakably, a tentacle spanked his buttocks. And the panrad zzzted a warning.

Eddie was not stupid. He knew now that the ten creatures were not dangerous unless he molested them. In which case he had just seen where he would go if he did not behave.

Again he was lifted and carried along the wall until he was shoved against the light grey spot. The monkey-cage odor, which had died out, became strong again. Eddie identified its source with a very small hole which appeared in the wall.

When he did not respond—he had no idea yet how he was supposed to act—the tentacles dropped him so unexpectedly that he fell on his back. Unhurt by the yielding flesh, he rose.

What was the next step? Exploration of his resources. Itemization: the panrad. A sleeping-bag, which he wouldn't need as long as the present too-warm temperature kept up. A bottle of Old Red Star capsules. A free-fall thermos with attached nipple. A box of A-2-Z rations. A Foldstove. Cartridges for his double-barrel, now lying outside the creature's boulderish shell. A roll of toilet paper. Toothbrush. Paste. Soap. Towel. Pills: Nodor, hormone, vitamin, longevity, reflex, and sleeping. And a thread-thin wire, a hundred feet long when uncoiled, that held prisoner in its molecular structure a hundred symphonies, eighty operas, a thousand different types of musical pieces, and two thousand great books ranging from Sophocles and Dostoyevsky to the latest bestseller. It could be played inside the panrad.

He inserted it, pushed, a button, and spoke "Eddie Fetts's recording of Puccini's *Che gelida manina,* please."

And while he listened approvingly to his own magnificent voice, he zipped open a can he had found in the bottom of the sack. His mother had put into it the stew left over from their last meal in the ship.

Not knowing what was happening, yet for some reason sure he was for the present safe, he munched meat and vegetables with a contented jaw. Transition from abhorrence to appetite sometimes came easily for Eddie.

He cleaned out the can and finished with some crackers and a chocolate bar. Rationing was out. As long as the food lasted, he would eat well. Then, if nothing turned up, he would . . . But then, he reassured himself as he licked his fingers, his mother, who was free, would find some way to get him out of his trouble.

She always had.

✑ Five ✑

The panrad, silent for a while, began signalling. Eddie spotlighted the antenna and saw it was pointing at the snailbeings, which he had, in accordance with his custom, dubbed familiarly. Sluggos he called them.

The Sluggos crept towards the wall and stopped close to it. Their mouths, placed on the tops of their heads, gaped like so many hungry young birds. The iris opened, and two lips formed into a spout. Out of it streamed steaming-hot water and chunks of meat and vegetables. Stew! Stew that fell exactly into each waiting mouth.

That was how Eddie learned the second phrase of Mother Polyphema's language. The first message had been, "What are you?" This was, "Come and get it!"

He experimented. He tapped out a repetition of what he'd last heard. As one, the Sluggos—except the one then being fed—turned to him and crept a few feet before halting, puzzled."

Inasmuch as Eddie was broadcasting, the Sluggos must have had some sort of built-in DF. Otherwise they wouldn't have been able to distinguish between his pulses and their Mother's.

Immediately after, a tentacle smote Eddie across the shoulders and knocked him down. The panrad zzzted its third intelligible message: "Don't ever do that!"

And then a fourth, to which the ten young obeyed by wheeling and resuming their former positions.

"This way, children."

Yes, they were the offspring, living, eating, sleeping, playing, and learning to communicate in the womb of their Mother—the Mother. They were the mobile brood of this vast immobile entity that had scooped up Eddie as a frog scoops up a fly. This Mother. She who had once been just such a Sluggo until she had grown hog-size and had been pushed out of her Mother's womb. And who, rolled into a tight ball, had free-wheeled down her natal hill, straightened out at the bottom, inched her way up the next hill, rolled down, and so on. Until she found the empty shell of an adult who had died. Or, if she wanted to be a first class citizen in her society and not a prestigeless *occupée*, she found the bare top of a tall hill—any eminence that commanded a big sweep of territory—and there squatted.

And there she put out many thread-thin tendrils into the soil and into the cracks in the rocks, tendrils that drew sustenance from the fat of her body and grew and extended downwards and ramified into other tendrils. Deep underground the rootlets worked, the instinctive chemistry; searched for and found the water, the calcium, the iron, the copper, the nitrogen, the carbons, fondled earthworms and grubs and larvae, teasing them for the secrets of their fats and proteins; broke down the wanted substance into shadowy colloidal particles; sucked them up the thready pipes of the tendrils and back to the pale and slimming body crouched on a flat space atop a ridge, a hill, a peak.

There, using the blueprints stored in the molecules of the cerebellum, her body took the building blocks of elements and fashioned them into a very thin shell of the most available materials, a shield large enough so she could expand to fit it while her natural enemies—the keen and hungry predators that prowled twilighted Baudelaire—nosed and clawed it in vain.

Then, her evergrowing bulk cramped, she would resorb the hard covering. And if no sharp tooth found her during that process of a few days, she would cast another and a larger. And so on through a dozen or more.

Until she had become the monstrous and much reformed body of an adult and virgin female. Outside would be the stuff that so much resembled a boulder, that was, actually, rock; either granite, diorite, marble, basalt, or maybe just plain limestone. Or sometimes iron, glass, or cellulose.

Within was the centrally located brain, probably as large as a man's. Surrounding it, the tons of organs: the nervous system, the mighty heart, or hearts, the four stomachs, the microwave and longwave generators, the kidneys, bowels, tracheae, scent and taste organs, the perfume factory which made odors to attract animals and birds close enough to be seized, and the huge womb. And the antennae—the small one inside for teaching and scanning the young, and a long and powerful stalk on the outside, projecting from the shelltop, retractable if danger came.

The next step was from virgin to Mother, lower-case to upper-case as designated in her pulse-language by a longer pause before a word. Not until she was deflowered could she take a high place in her society. Immodest, unblushing, she herself made the advances, the proposals, and the surrender.

After which, she ate her mate.

The clock in the panrad told Eddie he was in his thirtieth day of imprisonment when he found out that little bit of information. He was shocked, not because it offended his ethics, but because he himself had been intended to be the mate. And the dinner.

His finger tapped, "Tell me, Mother, what you mean."

He had not wondered before how a species that lacked males could reproduce. Now he found that, to the Mothers, all creatures except themselves were male. Mothers were immobile and female. Mobiles were male. Eddie had been mobile. He was, therefore, a male.

He had approached this particular Mother during the mating season, that is, midway through raising a litter of young. She had scanned him as he came along the creek-banks at the valley bottom. When he was at the foot of the hill, she had detected his odor. It was new to her. The closest she could come to it in her memory banks was that of a beast similar to him. From her description, he guessed it to be an ape. So she had released from her repertoire its rut stench. When he seemingly fell into the trap, she had caught him.

He was supposed to attack the conception-spot, that light grey swelling on the wall. After he had ripped and torn it enough to begin the mysterious workings of pregnancy, he would have been popped into her stomach-iris.

Fortunately, he had lacked the sharp beak, the fang, the claw. And she had received her own signals back from the panrad.

Eddie did not understand why it was necessary to use a mobile for mating. A Mother was intelligent enough to pick up a sharp stone and mangle the spot herself.

He was given to understand that conception would not start unless it was accompanied by a certain titillation of the nerves—a frenzy and its satisfaction. Why this emotional state was needed, Mother did not know.

Eddie tried to explain about such things as genes and chromosomes and why they had to be present in highly-developed species.

Mother did not understand.

Eddie wondered if the number of slashes and rips in the spot corresponded to the number of young. Or if there were a large number of potentialities in the heredity-ribbons spread out under the conception-skin. And if the haphazard irritation and consequent stimulation of the genes paralleled the chance combining of genes in human male-female mating. Thus resulting in offspring with traits that were combinations of their parents.

Or did the inevitable devouring of the mobile after the act indicate more than an emotional and nutritional reflex? Did it hint that the mobile caught up scattered gene-nodes, like hard seeds, along with the torn skin, in its claws and tusks, that these genes survived the boiling in the stew-stomach, and were later passed out in the faeces? Where animals and birds picked them up in beak, tooth, or foot, and then, seized by other Mothers in this oblique rape, transmitted the heredity-carrying agents to the conception-spots while attacking them, the nodules being scraped off and implanted in the skin and blood of the swelling even as others were harvested? Later, the mobiles were eaten, digested, and ejected in the obscure but ingenious and never-ending cycle? Thus ensuring the continual, if haphazard, recombining of genes, chances of variations in offspring, opportunities for mutations, and so on?

Mother pulsed that she was nonplussed.

Eddie gave up. He'd never know. After all, did it matter?

He decided not, and rose from his prone position to request water. She pursed up her iris and spouted a tepid quartful into his thermos. He dropped in a pill, swished it around till it dissolved, and drank a reasonable facsimile of Old Red Star. He preferred the harsh and powerful rye, though he could have afforded the smoothest. Quick results were what he wanted. Taste didn't matter, as he disliked all liquor tastes. Thus he drank what the Skid Row bums drank and shuddered even as they did, renaming it Old Rotten Tar and cursing the fate that had brought them so low they had to gag such stuff down.

The rye glowed in his belly and spread quickly through his limbs and up to his head, chilled only by the increasing scarcity of the capsules. When he ran out—then what? It was at times like this that he most missed his mother.

Thinking about her brought a few large tears. He snuffled and drank some more and when the biggest of the Sluggos nudged him for a back-scratching, he gave it instead a shot of Old Red Star. A slug for Sluggo. Idly, he wondered what effect a taste for rye would have on the future of the race when these virgins became Mothers.

At that moment he was shaken by what seemed a lifesaving idea. These creatures could suck up the required elements from the earth and with them duplicate quite complex molecular structures. Provided, of course, they had a sample of the desired substance to brood over in some cryptic organ.

Well, what easier to do than give her one of the cherished capsules? One could become any number. Those, plus the abundance of water pumped up through hollow underground tendrils from the nearby creek, would give enough to make a master-distiller green!

He smacked his lips and was about to key her his request when what she was transmitting penetrated his mind.

Mother

Rather cattily, she remarked that her neighbor across the valley was putting on airs because she, too, held prisoner a communicating mobile.

۵ Six ۵

The Mothers had a society as hierarchical as table-protocol in Washington or peck-order in a barnyard. Prestige was what counted, and prestige was determined by the broadcasting power, the height of the eminence on which the Mother sat, which governed the extent of her radar-territory, and the abundance and novelty and wittiness of her gossip. The creature that had snapped Eddie up was a queen. She had precedence over thirty-odd of her kind; they all had to let her broadcast first, and none dared start pulsing until she quit. Then, the next in order began, and so on down the line. Any of them could be interrupted at any time by Number One, and if any of the lower echelon had something interesting to transmit, she could break in on the one then speaking and get permission from the queen to tell her tale.

Eddie knew this, but he could not listen in directly to the hilltop-gabble. The thick pseudo-granite shell barred him from that and made him dependent upon her womb-stalk for relayed information.

Now and then Mother opened the door and allowed her young to crawl out. There they practiced beaming and broadcasting at the Sluggos of the Mother across the valley. Occasionally that Mother deigned herself to pulse the young, and Eddie's keeper reciprocated to her offspring.

Turnabout.

The first time children had inched through the exit-iris, Eddie had tried, Ulysses-like, to pass himself off as one of them and crawl out in the midst of the flock. Eyeless, but no Polyphemus, Mother had picked him out with her tentacles and hauled him back in.

It was following that incident that he had named her Polyphema.

He knew she had increased her own already powerful prestige

177

tremendously by possession of that unique thing—a transmitting mobile. So much had her importance grown that the Mothers on the fringes of her area passed on the news to others. Before he had learned her language, the entire continent was hooked-up. Polyphema had become a veritable gossip columnist; tens of thousands of hillcrouchers listened in eagerly to her accounts of her dealings with the walking paradox: a semantic male.

That had been fine. Then, very recently, the Mother across the valley had captured a similar creature. And in one bound she had become Number Two in the area and would, at the slightest weakness on Polyphema's part, wrest the top position away.

Eddie became wildly excited at the news. He had often day-dreamed about his mother and wondered what she was doing. Curiously enough, he ended many of his fantasies with lip-mutterings, reproaching her almost audibly for having left him and for making no try to rescue him. When he became aware of his attitude, he was ashamed. Nevertheless, the sense of desertion colored his thoughts.

Now that he knew she was alive and had been caught, probably while trying to get him out, he rose from the lethargy that had lately been making him doze the clock around. He asked Polyphema if she would open the entrance so he could talk directly with the other captive. She said yes. Eager to listen in on a conversation between two mobiles, she was very co-operative. There would be a mountain of gossip in what they would have to say. The only thing that dented her joy was that the other Mother would also have access.

Then, remembering she was still Number One and would broadcast the details first, she trembled so with pride and ecstasy that Eddie felt the floor shaking.

Iris open, he walked through it and looked across the valley. The hillsides were still green, red, and yellow, as the plants on Baudelaire did not lose their leaves during winter. But a few white patches showed that winter had begun. Eddie shivered from the bite of cold air on his naked skin. Long ago he. had taken off his clothes. The womb-warmth had made garments too uncomfortable;

moreover, Eddie, being human, had had to get rid of waste products. And Polyphema, being a Mother, had had periodically to flush out the dirt with warm water from one of her stomachs. Every time the tracheae-vents exploded streams that swept the undesirable elements out through her door-iris, Eddie had become soaked. When he abandoned dress, his clothes had gone floating out. Only by sitting on his pack did he keep it from a like fate.

Afterward, he and the Sluggos had been dried off by warm air pumped through the same vents and originating from the mighty battery of lungs. Eddie was comfortable enough—he'd always liked showers—but the loss of his garments had been one more thing that kept him from escaping. He would soon freeze to death outside unless he found the yacht quickly. And he wasn't sure he remembered the path back.

So now, when he stepped outside, he retreated a pace or two and let the warm air from Polyphema flow like a cloak from his shoulders. Then he peered across the half-mile that separated him from his mother, but he could not see her. The twilight state and the dark of the unlit interior of her captor hid her.

He tapped in Morse, "Switch to the talkie, same frequency." Paula Fetts did so. She began asking him frantically if he were all right.

He replied he was fine.

"Have you missed me terribly, son?"

"Oh, very much."

Even as he said this he wondered vaguely why his voice sounded so hollow. Despair at never again being able to see her, probably.

"I've almost gone crazy, Eddie. When you were caught I ran away as fast as I could. I had no idea what horrible monster it was that was attacking us. And then, halfway down the hill, I fell and broke my leg . . ."

"Oh, no, mother!"

"Yes. But I managed to crawl back to the ship. And there, after I'd set it myself, I gave myself B.K. shots. Only, my system didn't react like it's supposed to. There are people that way, you know, and the healing took twice as long.

"But when I was able to walk, I got a gun and a box of dynamite. I was going to blow up what I thought was a kind of rock-fortress, an outpost for some kind of extee. I'd no idea of the true nature of these beasts. First, though, I decided to reconnoiter. I was going to spy on the boulder from across the valley. But I was trapped by this thing.

"Listen, son. Before I'm cut off, let me tell you not to give up hope. I'll be out of here before long and over to rescue you."

"How?"

"If you remember, my lab kit holds a number of carcino-gens for field work. Well, you know that sometimes a Mother's conception-spot when it is torn up during mating, instead of beget-ting young, goes into cancer—the opposite of pregnancy. I've in-jected a carcinogen into the spot and a beautiful carcinoma has developed. She'll be dead in a few days."

"Mom! You'll be buried in that rotting mass!"

"No. This creature has told me that when one of her species dies, a reflex opens the labia. That's to permit their young—if any—to escape. Listen, I'll—"

A tentacle coiled about him and pulled him back through the iris, which shut.

When he switched back to C.W., he heard, "Why didn't you communicate? What were you doing? Tell me! Tell me!"

Eddie told her. There was a silence that could only be inter-preted as astonishment. After Mother had recovered her wits, she said, "From now on, you will talk to the other male through me."

"Please," he persisted, not knowing how dangerous were the waters he was wading in, "please let me talk to my mother di—"

For the first time, he heard her stutter.

"Wha-wha-what? Your Mo-Mo-Mother?"

"Yes. Of course."

The floor heaved violently beneath his feet. He cried out and braced himself to keep from falling and then flashed on the light. The walls were pulsating like shaken jelly, and the vascular columns had turned from red and blue to gray. The entrance-iris sagged open, like a lax mouth, and the air cooled. He could feel the drop in temperature in her flesh with the soles of his feet.

It was some time before he caught on.

Polyphema was in a state of shock.

What might have happened had she stayed in it, he never knew. She might have died and thus forced him out into the winter before his mother could escape. If so, and he couldn't find the ship, he would die. Huddled in the warmest corner of the egg-shaped chamber, Eddie contemplated that idea and shivered to a degree for which the outside air couldn't account.

✸ SEVEN ✸

However, Polyphema had her own method of recovery. It consisted of spewing out the contents of her stew-stomach, which had doubtless become filled with the poisons draining out of her system from the blow. Her ejection of the stuff was the physical manifestation of the psychical catharsis. So furious was the flood that her foster son was almost swept out in the hot tide, but she, reacting instinctively, had coiled tentacles about him and the Sluggos. Then she followed the first upchucking by emptying her other three water-pouches, the second hot and the third lukewarm and the fourth, just filled, cold.

Eddie yelped as the icy water doused him.

Polyphema's irises closed again. The floor and walls gradually quit quaking; the temperature rose; and her veins and arteries regained their red and blue. She was well again. Or so she seemed.

But when, after waiting twenty-four hours, he cautiously ap-proached the subject, he found she not only would not talk about it, she refused to acknowledge the existence of the other mobile.

Eddie, giving up hope of conversation, thought for quite a while. The only conclusion he could come to, and he was sure he'd grasped enough of her psychology to make it valid, was that the concept of a mobile female was utterly unacceptable.

Her world was split into two: mobile and her kind, the

immobile. Mobile meant food and mating. Mobile meant—male. The Mothers were—female.

How the mobiles reproduced had probably never entered the hillcrouchers' minds. Their science and philosophy were on the instinctive body-level. Whether they had some notion of spontaneous generation or amoeba-like fission being responsible for the continued population of mobiles, or they'd just taken for granted they 'growed,' like Topsy, Eddie never found out. To them, they were female and the rest of the protoplasmic cosmos was male.

That was that. Any other idea was more than foul and obscene and blasphemous. It was—unthinkable.

Polyphema had received a deep trauma from his words. And though she seemed to have recovered, somewhere in those tons of unimaginably complicated flesh a bruise was buried. Like a hidden flower, dark purple, it bloomed, and the shadow it cast was one that cut off a certain memory, a certain tract, from the light of consciousness. That bruise-stained shadow covered that time and event which the Mothers, for reasons unfathomable to the human being, found necessary to mark KEEP OFF.

Thus, though Eddie did not word it, he understood in the cells of his body, he felt and knew, as if his bones were prophesying and his brain did not hear, what came to pass.

Sixty-six hours later by the panrad clock, Polyphemas entrance-lips opened. Her tentacles darted out. They came back in, carrying his helpless and struggling mother.

Eddie, roused out of a doze, horrified, paralyzed, saw her toss her lab kit at him and heard an inarticulate cry from her. And saw her plunged, headforemost, into the stomach-iris.

Polyphema had taken the one sure way of burying the evidence.

Eddie lay face down, nose mashed against the warm and faintly throbbing flesh of the floor. Now and then his hands clutched spasmodically as if he were reaching for something that someone kept putting just within his reach and then moving away.

How long he was there he didn't know, for he never again looked at the clock.

Finally, in the darkness, he sat up and giggled inanely, "Mother always did make good stew."

That set him off. He leaned back on his hands and threw his head back and howled like a wolf under a full moon.

Polyphema, of course, was dead-deaf, but she could radar his posture, and her keen nostrils deduced from his body-scent that he was in terrible fear and anguish.

A tentacle glided out and gently enfolded him.

"What is the matter?" zzted the panrad.

He stuck his finger in the keyhole.

"I have lost my mother!"

"?"

"She's gone away, and she'll never come back."

"I don't understand. *Here I am.*"

Eddie quit weeping and cocked his head, as if he were listening to some inner voice. He snuffled a few times and wiped away the tears, slowly disengaged the tentacle, patted it, walked over to his pack in a corner, and took out the bottle of Old Red Star capsules. One he popped into the thermos; the other he gave to her with the request she duplicate it, if possible. Then he stretched out on his side, propped on one elbow like a Roman in his sensualities, sucked the rye through the nipple, and listened to a medley of Beethoven, Moussorgsky, Verdi, Strauss, Porter, Feinstein, and Waxworth.

So the time—if there were such a thing here—flowed around Eddie. When he was tired of music or plays or books, he listened in on the area hookup. Hungry, he rose and walked—or often just crawled—to the stew-iris. Cans of rations lay in his pack; he had planned to eat those until he was sure that—what was it he was forbidden to eat? Poison? Something had to be devoured by polyphema and the Sluggos. But sometime during the music-rye orgy, he had forgotten. He now ate quite hungrily and with thought for nothing but the satisfaction of his wants.

Sometimes the door-iris opened, and Billy Greengrocer hopped in. Billy looked like a cross between a cricket and a kangaroo. He was the size of a collie, and he bore in a marsupialian pouch vegetables and fruit and nuts. These he extracted with shiny green, chitinous claws and gave to Mother in return for meals of stew. Happy symbiote, he chirruped merrily while his many-faceted eyes, revolving independently of each other, looked one at the Sluggos and the other at Eddie.

Eddie, on impulse, abandoned the 1000 kc. band and roved the frequencies until he found that both Polyphema and Billy were emitting a 108 wave. That, apparently, was their natural signal.

When Billy had his groceries to deliver, he broadcast. Polyphema, in turn, when she needed them, sent back to him. There was nothing intelligent on Billy's part; it was just his instinct to transmit. And the Mother was, aside from the "semantic" frequency, limited to that one band. But it worked out fine.

☙ Eight ☙

Everything was fine. What more could a man want? Free food, unlimited liquor, soft bed, air-conditioning, shower-baths, music, intellectual works (on the tape), interesting conversation (much of it was about him), privacy, and security.

If he had not already named her, he would have called her Mother Gratis.

Nor were creature comforts all. She had given him the answers to all his questions, all . . .

Except one.

That was never expressed vocally by him. Indeed, he would have been incapable of doing so. He was probably unaware that he had such a question.

But Polyphema voiced it one day when she asked him to do her a favor.

Eddie reacted as if outraged.

"One does not—! One does not—!"

He choked, and then he thought, how ridiculous! She is not—

And looked puzzled, and said, "But she is."

He rose and opened the lab kit. While he was looking for a scalpel, he came across the carcinogens. He threw them through the half-opened labia far out and down the hillside.

Then he turned and, scalpel in hand, leaped at the light gray swelling on the wall. And stopped, staring at it, while the instrument fell from his hand. And picked it up and stabbed feebly and did not even scratch the skin. And again let it drop.

"What is it? What is it?" crackled the panrad hanging from his wrist.

Suddenly, a heavy cloud of human odor—mansweat—was puffed in his face from a nearby vent.

"? ? ? ?"

And he stood, bent in a half-crouch, seemingly paralyzed. Until tentacles seized him in fury and dragged him toward the stomach-iris, yawning man-sized.

Eddie screamed and writhed and plunged his finger in the panrad and tapped, "All right! All right!"

And once back before the spot, he lunged with a sudden and wild joy; he slashed savagely; he yelled. "Take that! And that, P. . ." and the rest was lost in a mindless shout.

He did not stop cutting, and he might have gone on and on until he had quite excised the spot had not Polyphema interfered by dragging him toward her stomach-iris again. For ten seconds he hung there, helpless and sobbing with a mixture of fear and glory.

Polyphema's reflexes had almost overcome her brain. Fortunately, a cold spark of reason lit up a corner of the vast, dark, and hot chapel of her frenzy.

The convolutions leading to the steaming, meat-laden pouch closed and the foldings of flesh rearranged themselves. Eddie was suddenly hosed with warm water from what he called the "sanitation" stomach. The iris closed. He was put down. The scalpel was put back in the bag.

For a long time Mother seemed to be shaken by the thought of what she might had done to Eddie. She did not trust herself to transmit until her nerves were settled. When they were, she did not refer to his narrow escape. Nor did he.

He was happy. He felt as if a spring, tight-coiled against his bowels since he and his wife had parted, was now, for some reason, released. The dull vague pain of loss and discontent, the slight fever and cramp in his entrails, and the apathy that sometimes afflicted him, were gone. He felt fine.

Meanwhile, something akin to deep affection had been lighted, like a tiny candle under the drafty and overtowering roof of a cathedral. Mother's shell housed more than Eddie; it now curved over an emotion new to her kind. This was evident by the next event that filled him with terror.

For the wounds in the spot healed and the swelling increased into a large bag. Then the bag burst and ten mouse-sized Sluggos struck the floor. The impact had the same effect as a doctor spanking a newborn baby's bottom; they drew in their first breath with shock and pain; their uncontrolled and feeble pulses filled the ether with shapeless SOS's.

When Eddie was not talking with Polyphema or listening in or drinking or sleeping or eating or bathing or running off the tape, he played with the Sluggos. He was, in a sense, their father. Indeed, as they grew to hog-size, it was hard for their female parent to distinguish him from her young. As he seldom walked anymore, and was often to be found on hands and knees in their midst, she could not scan him too well. Moreover, something in the heavywet air or in the diet had caused every hair on his body to drop off. He grew very fat. Generally speaking, he was one with the pale, soft, round, and bald offspring. A family likeness.

There was one difference. When the time came for the virgins to be expelled, Eddie crept to one end, whimpering, and stayed there until he was sure Mother was not going to thrust him out into the cold, hard, and hungry world. That final crisis over, he came back to the center of the floor. The panic in his breast had died out, but his nerves were still quivering. He filled his thermos and then listened for a while to his own tenor singing the "Sea Things" aria from his favorite opera, Gianelli's *Ancient Mariner*. Suddenly, he burst out and accompanied himself, finding himself thrilled as never before by the concluding words.

And from my neck so free
The Albatross fell off, and sank
Like lead into the sea.

Afterwards, voice silent but heart singing, he switched off the wire and cut in on Polyphema's broadcast

Mother was having trouble. She could not precisely describe to the continent-wide hook-up this new and almost inexpressible emotion she felt about the mobile. It was a concept her language was not prepared for. Nor was she helped any by the gallons of Old Red Star in her bloodstream.

Eddie sucked at the plastic nipple and nodded sympathetically and drowsily at her search for words. Presently, the thermos rolled out of his hand.

He slept on his side, curled in a ball, knees on his chest and arms crossed, neck bent forward. Like the pilot room chronometer whose hands reversed after the crash, the clock of his body was ticking backwards, ticking backwards . . .

In the darkness, in the moistness, safe and warm, well fed, much loved.

LOVERS AND OTHERWISE

The history of "The Lovers" is, I think, worth reading. It is divided into two segments: (1) the actual conception and writing, and (2) what happened to it after it was written. The latter is especially intriguing because it illustrates so well the relationship between authors and editors. And the reverberations that may take a long time a-bouncing before there is complete understanding and agreement between the two species.

I was reminded of that when Mrs. H. L. Gold, known professionally as Evelyn Paige, was introduced to me during the World Science Fiction Convention in Chicago. Mrs. Gold is a striking brunette. She has very dark hair and very white teeth, a quite noticeable and very pleasing contrast. She smiles often, is energetic, intense, articulate, and devoted to her husband, whom she mentions frequently during her conversation. She has, both as wife and as assistant editor for *Galaxy*, been very much wrapped up in its spectacular leap to a place on the top roost of science fiction. (That's a mixed metaphor, but so is the story of "The Lovers'" fate.)

Mrs. Gold was emphatic in asking if I would please broadcast the truth about "The Lovers" and its reception at *Galaxy*. Many people had asked Mr. Gold why he had rejected "The Lovers"; she wished that I would inform those interested that he had not.

I said I'd be glad to. In fact, I was thinking of telling the story in an article for *Fantastic Worlds*. So, before the genesis and development of the story itself is told, I'd like to go sidewise in time. Science fiction fans or anybody interested in the-behind-the-story dealings of editors and writers should be intrigued.

When I finished the MS. of "The Lovers," I was sure I had a pretty good story. Of course, during the writing and even after I'd completed it, I had qualms, moments of doubt, and impulses to rise and throw the pages in the furnace. But these, I'm told, are universal emotions during composition, especially to those who've sold little or nothing. Despite these little plunges into gloom, my general inpression was that the story was, in some respects, fresh and original. This in spite of the fact that the story was framed in a setting as old as science fiction itself.

On finishing, I did what every author does. Look around for the highest-paying magazine. Money mattered. Respect for the editors and prestige of their magazines didn't enter the picture. All three of the editors that I thought of submitting to had my highest respect. And as far as prestige goes—there is no such thing.

Rather, I should say that prestige is a very subjective thing. What you consider the highest ranking, the next fellow thinks is rank. Read the fan columns in the various publications; check my statement. I'm continually amazed that so many people can't see what I do. And vice versa.

Anyway, not having an agent, and getting my information about rates for words, reprint rights, etc., from *Writer's Digest*, I decided that *Galaxy* would be a wonderful place to send it. Mr. Gold had announced, I believe, that a great deal of freedom would be allowed to writers in his magazine. A close and eager reading of *Galaxy* from its inception had convinced me of that.

Moreover, Mr. Gold was one of that triumvirate of science fiction editors who had been kind enough to criticize previous efforts. Believe me, that is one of the best things an editor can do to encourage up-and-coming talent. It's heartening to receive a note, even a small one, in which the defects and virtues of the rejected MS. are pointed out.

After having written and having had turned down about twelve science fiction stories, mostly short-shorts, I began forming a liking for these three men. Perhaps the note was a brief statement to the affect that the story was trite, or that it had an original idea but was treated too heavily. But I preferred that by far to the cold and stony printed slip.

And I noticed as time passed that my stories were receiving lengthier and more favorable comments. I was getting some place and I *knew* it. That was the thing. I could have been closer to my goal, and if I'd not been informed so in so many words—if nothing but formal forms kept popping out of the manila envelopes—how would I know? I might have given up when I was just on the verge of acceptance.

Believe me, I was—and am—grateful for the efforts taken by these very busy men. The result was that I soon began grading editors—from a writer's, not a fan's, viewpoint—into two echelons, upper and lower. Not so strangely, those ranked in the upper echelon also edited, in my opinion, the best and most mature and most entertaining magazines.

So, taking into consideration various factors, I mailed it to Mr. Gold. And became convinced from what it cost me for stamps that "The Lovers" had better sell the first or second time, or I'd go broke kicking it around the weary reject circuit. Actually, though, with the undying optimism of the congenital idiot—I mean, author—I didn't think it would come back.

My only doubt, aside from its sexual-biological content, was its length. The peculiarity of the story was that it had to be wrapped in one package to get its full impact. It wouldn't do for it to be serialized. And that, to my naive mind, offered a problem. *Galaxy* and *Astounding*, I knew, had a limit of 25,000 words for their one-shot novels. *Thrilling Wonder* printed novels of about 30,000; *Startling*, 40-45,000.

Here was the difficulty. I wanted the story to be about 45,000, just dandy for *Startling*. Full development of all I wanted to put in demanded it. Moreover, at that time there were only two editors whom I thought were taboo-free enough to consider "The Lovers." Or three, rather, but Mr. Boucher's magazine did not publish stories that long.

The pot of gold at the end of the rainbow twinkled. Three cents a word versus one point seven. So I compromised. I made it a little too long for *Galaxy* and a little too short for *Startling*. I cut hell out of it, threw out scenes, characters, and action that would have explained the fascinating—to me—social and political set up of the Ozagens. Also, there was much about the Haijac development of Dunne's theories of time that I sliced. The result was that, unless you'd read Dunne or read of him, you wouldn't understand fully the peculiar synthesis of religion and chronoscience.

However, I tried to show through action just how it worked. The reader who knew little or nothing of Dunne but who was intelligent should be able to deduce the needed facts.

After much heartburning blue-pencilling, though I was, in a way, relieved because it meant less typing of the final MS. (typing drives me to frantic, frantic drives me to beer, beer gives me an eye-ache so I can't type), I ended up with a 30,000-word story. This was too long for *Galaxy*, but I thought that if it were good enough it might be published in that length. I didn't think it could be reduced any more without its being weakened.

So I waited the normal period and formed nerves on my nerves, got a bad case of mailboxitis. And so, in normal process, the suitcase-sized package returned.

Gods! Blasphemy! Tearing of garments, gnashing of teeth, pouring of ashes on my heads! *Quelle horreur! Ia! Ia! Cthulhu fhtagn! Ph'nglui mglw'nafh!*

Home again baby?

My tear-filled eyes read the letter enclosed. And found that "The Lovers" was not rejected—in toto. Mr. Gold admitted that my story had a good idea, but that he couldn't accept it in its present form and live with himself. Whatever my attitude toward minorities might be, the story was dangerous. It, in effect, justified discrimination because minorities *might*, if they ever achieved domination, become dictatorial. As far as he, Mr. Gold, was concerned, it didn't matter *now* if they would or they wouldn't. The present fact was that the minorities were under direct or latent attack. And he wouldn't care to add fuel to that blaze.

However, my notion of imitation females could be excellent *sans* racial overtones, if I developed it in a Fortean manner to explain various mysterious phenomena. It would be kept on this planet, and it wouldn't have the elaborate stage I gave it. Should I be interested, and if I thought I could do something with the perceptions and integration of research that E. F. Russell did in his *Sinister Barrier*, he would want to see it. He was even kind enough and interested enough to offer to help in the plotting, though it wouldn't be easy by mail.

In any case, I was to let him know.

That gave me to pause.

As to the first objection, about the dangerous implications, I hadn't even thought about them. At first, I didn't understand what he meant. It was something I wouldn't have dreamed of. It shook me.

The second idea—having the story take place on Earth—had already occurred to me. Indeed, I was halfway through "The Lovers" when such a thought collided head on with me. I stopped and turned it over to examine every facet. And then continued with my original plan. To carry that out would have meant wiping out Ozagen, Fobo, the tavern beetles, etc. I wasn't a world-wrecker; I couldn't do it.

I would have if I'd thought the story and the characters weren't jelling. But they were.

Besides, I was too lazy.

So I sent a long letter to Mr. Gold in which I very carefully—and probably too passionately—defended my position in regard to minorities, persecutions, and prejudices.

Mr. Gold took the trouble and time—and for a very busy science fiction editor this involves a sacrifice—to write a two-page single-spaced reply. In his very forceful and articulate style, he made it clear that, concerning "The Lovers," he didn't consider me bigoted. If he had, he'd have merely returned the story and kept me tagged for future rough handling.

This impressed me as a very mild and conservative attitude. If I were editor, and I received a story from a bigot, I would have voiced in no uncertain terms my opinions and told said author I wanted no more of his stories, even if they were world masterpieces and had nothing to do with racial derogation.

However, I'm not an editor.

Mr. Gold went on to the fact that two friends of mine had read the story before I'd sent it in. Both were involved with discrimination, ethically and personally. One was a preacher; the other, a freethinker of Jewish parentage. Neither had objected to anything in the story or even noticed anything that might be misconstrued. But Mr. Gold said that that should not convince me that my view was correct. The real test would be to give it to someone who *was* bigoted.

I couldn't do that. None of the bigoted people I know read science fiction, nor would they be persuaded to read what they call "that crap." Which speaks volumes for the kind of people they are and illustrates the high type of person, generally speaking, that inhabits the world of science fiction.

Mr. Gold maintained that a bigot would, on reading the story, have the same reaction as any other bigot. The only difference you might get would depend on his literate level. The uneducated would comment that the behavior of the Israeli Republics in the colonization of depopulated France would be just what you'd expect from a Jew or a Negro. Give them a chance and they'd be worse than the worst white men. The educated would have stated the same thing in well-turned phrases and a semblance of logic.

This was not based on guesswork. Part of his opinion was founded on his own dealings with bigots. But most of it came from the reaction stirred up both among biased and militantly unbiased people whenever he'd published a tale with a racial theme. He was, I suppose, referring especially to that wonderful story "Dark Interlude" by Mack Reynolds and Fredric Brown.

The latter people have always been against discrimination. Several of the stories Mr. Gold then had in inventory would, he believed, evoke the same angry reaction. One division of readers, the biased, acutely conscious of the message, would furiously deny its validity. And the unbiased would raise cain because he'd had a character use the word "nigger"—even when his and its significance should be obvious to them.

If you took "The Lovers" apart, you'd find the neo-Judaic society a vicious one. The reader, who must identify himself with a character, is pleased by the revolt against society. A bigot, he'll have his own prejudices fortified by this idea of a culture that hasn't developed and probably never will. A tolerant person will find his emotions fighting each other. Aware there is no Haijac Union, he can be depended upon to recall the Bible and how it tells with remarkable candor the treatment by Hebrews of some of their neighbors. Thus, he might wonder if the same events might not occur again, only on a larger scale.

As Mr. Gold explains it, the tale had mental fish-hooks of which I wasn't aware. His response on reading the story and my explanation was the same as the prayer of Voltaire: "Save me from my friends; I can handle my enemies."

Though he knew that I had the best of intentions, he considered my story potentially more dangerous than the most outrageous rantings of a minority-hater. Why? Because it was well-intentioned and obviously sympathetic and very logical.

By the time I'd received Mr. Gold's second letter, I'd sold the story to Sam Mines.

For some time I'd watched the standards of *Thrilling Wonder* and *Startling Stories* rise under Sam Merwin, Jr. When he quit for free-lancing and Sam Mines took over, I noticed that he had used Merwin's work as a sort of base and took off at right angles, like a rocket with the devil on its tail. Changes were frequent and evident and all for the better. Those who've followed the two magazines know what I'm talking about. Very pleasing to the science fiction heart.

Sam Mines, aided and abetted by Jerry Bixby, announced a policy whose only restrictions would be those of good taste. This, I thought, is my meat, for "The Lovers" will certainly test that policy. I'd made up my mind that I didn't want to rewrite the tale. To do so would have been composing a brand new story. And I didn't, I want to make clear here, think that there would be much, if any, reaction to the use of the Israeli or Haijac societies. The fact that the Haijac was vicious meant nothing. There have been and are sub-societies founded on similar principles. But this is not because the principles are vicious. Far from it. It is because these groups have taken the great and true teachings originated and promulgated by the Hebrew prophets and have hypocritically perverted them.

They have taken what was pure and magnificent and dirtied and twisted it. Sometimes this has been done honestly; sometimes not. In either case, there has been malformation.

So the Haijac Union.

Anyway, I read Sam's letter of acceptance with even more interest than you would expect. Sam stated that he liked "The Lovers" very much, with certain minor reservations. It was off-trail for *Startling* being basically a sex story. But he was serious in his policy of no taboos and anxious to impose no throttling hands upon authors who showed originality and freshness. Some small revisions seemed necessary; he and Jerry could work them out, but he thought I might prefer to do them myself.

Three points needed clarifying:

(1) The ship's purpose and mission ought to be made clear at once instead of late in the story. The reader wonders too long what the humans are after and what their relationahip with the wogs is.

(2) Sam thought the love story would he benefited by an elevation from a simple and slightly sordid sex affair to something a little more noble. The hero could have *some* unselfish motive in offering shelter to the girl besides a desire to get in bed with her. His training in celibacy was strong. His breakdown should be gradual and logically motivated.

(3) And tying the theology of the future to the ancient Hebrews seemed strained, unlikely, and capable of offending the more tolerant who would resent being linked with suppressive

totalitarianism. The story wouldn't suffer in the slightest if the theology were a mythical one, with a mythical god instead of Jahveh. My effect would be the same—might even be better—since it would sound more like the future and less like the past. I could even base it upon the new gods—Einstein, Freud, Edison, Jung, etc.

These changes were slight and would I let him know if I wanted to do them?

Point 1. O.K. I wrote the prolog.

Point 2. I replied that the hero did have some unselfish motive in offering shelter to the girl. She was human (so he thought), she was hiding from the wogs (so he thought), and she would be impounded and treated like a lab animal if he turned her over to his fellows (he knew).

The above was stated or at least implicit in the story. Besides, it was in the nature of the *lalitha* to go to bed with a desirable man and no bones about it. Their whole evolution pointed towards that.

His training in celibacy was very strong, true. On the other hand, a year or two in a space-ship, plus that old devil Sex Urge, plus a congenital rebel, would lead to a quick breakdown. Moreover, Hal Yarrow had a corner on the market. She was the only available human female on the whole wide planet. Such a number of factors would go to a man's head.

Besides, had he ever met Jeannette? Did he know what she could do to a man?

I knew how she was. Take my word for it. St. Anthony himself would have fallen.

As to point three, as you've read, I'd encountered that before. Seeing it again, from another much-admired editor, gave me to pause. Maybe I was wrong.

So I wrote another long letter defending my viewpoint. The gist of it: The Hebrews have, among other things, been noted for the invention of the world's first *really* great religion. It is one so virile, so fecund, so strong in concept and truth, as far as basics go, that it has survived no matter what its enemies do and has given birth to two worldwide religions: the Mohammedan and the Christian.

The latter has split into many sects and subsects, and where it'll go nobody knows. Such a religion as the Hebrews', having already borne two great ones, might yet deliver another. Especially if it were coupled with a historical figure, Isaac Sigmen, the Forerunner, who lived long enough, due to longevity serums, not only to found but to cement the structure of his ideas. One who used scientific gobbledegook to justify his religion and a totalitarian setup—all for the good of his people, of course!—to keep his society static.

Moreover, the reader will see that whereas the neo-Judaic Haijacs were vicious, their enemies, the Israelis, were not. This last point will be made more clearly in the sequel to "The Lovers"— the story called *"Moth and Rust."*

I couldn't buy Sam's idea about a new religion based on the new gods—Einstein, Freud, Jung, etc.

Why?

Because they're scientists, not religious prophets. People don't follow scientists in matters of faith, not religious faith, anyway. And there's nothing in the scientists' works to whip up enthusiasm among disciples. You might take some of their ideas and tie them in with certain aspects or potentialities (for good or bad) of an already established religion. But that's what Sigmen did. I didn't think that the above-named scientists taught anything that could by the longest stretch of imagination be called religious.

Old lightning-wielding Jahweh still lives—in many forms— and it is from Him that you will get your true tablets of stone. Not from pen-wielders.

However, in order to avoid any such thing as Mssrs. Gold and Mines had objected to, I thought it'd be all right if a certain passage were struck out. That is the one referring to the division of France between the Israeli Republic (of Midi) and the Haijacs. A checking upon the story when it appeared in the magazine showed that Sam had come to the same conclusion as mine. Be realistic and logical and trust to the good sense of science fiction fandom, in general, to see what is meant.

After all, a bigot will seize upon anything you say and twist it. As to the militantly unbiased, I'm one, and I wrote the story. I would await the reaction. And while, at the time of writing this article, I haven't seen the letter response in the "The Ether Vibrates" section of *Startling*, I've been told by Sam and Jerry that it's been terrific, unbelievably enthusiastic. The gripes are extremely few.

Another reason I wanted to keep the Israeli Republics. The Hebrews have suffered so much because of their religion, been so persecuted, so much, in short, a minority, that it tickled me to portray a future in which they've become a majority. After millenia of hanging on, they win out. Sheer guts and genius enable them to survive and become, finally, top-dog. And, as I'll show in "Moth and Rust" they are the best among the four great unions left in my highly hypothetical but by no means impossible future. But I don't portray them as superhuman or subhuman. Just human, with the strength and weaknesses of men. Individuals, not types.

I took a chance on being misunderstood, but I think I was, in the main, justified.

As to whether "The Lovers" would have been a better story if set in a modern Terran background, no one will ever know. I'll concede that Mr. Gold might have been right. But I was just too fond of Fobo and my tavern beetles and Jeannette (whose death I regret but could not logically avoid) and the triumphant Israelis to kill them off. Besides being too lazy to do all that rewriting.

But I'm very well satisfied with the way things turned out. So are a number of other people.

Mr. Gold and I did not agree on certain points, but we parted amiably enough. I left still convinced that he was a great science fiction editor, and he probably left convinced that I was a peculiarly hard-headed author, but one who was, apart from that, not so bad.

During my conversation with Evelyn Paige, she told me that her husband was a man who could do the hardest thing in the world, that is, admit he might be wrong. Such honesty and flexibility are things to admire; they are the criteria of a real man. Mr. Gold has done just that; he has evidently changed his mind about one of the objections he had to "The Lovers." For he has published a story in the August issue of *Galaxy* "Education of a Martian," by Joseph Shallit, whose point is that a despised and persecuted person may himself hold towards another group the same attitude from which he suffers.

A bigot could deduce from this that if you don't keep a minority down, they might some day rise and keep you down.

But Mr. Gold has decided that bigots are the rara avis in science fiction fandom and that you may show that minorities possess weaknesses without having someone cry "Shame!" Or that if they do, enough people will understand what you're driving at.

I hope I've summed up fairly this tempest in a teapot.

I'd like to point out that up to three years ago or even later, such a story as "The Lovers" would have been unprintable as it was. Even today, with the policy adopted by Sam Mines in his search for new things in science fiction, such a sexual-biological story has to be offered with a certain amount of trepidation as to its reception. It took courage to print it.

That it has been given such an enthusiastic welcome is a true indication of the so-called "maturity" of science fiction. Basically biological, unavoidably sexual, the story is not sexy or sensational. It is, simply, a realistic treatment of an imaginative theme, one I tried to do honestly.

I'd like to thank Sam Mines and Jerry Bixby for their faith in allowing the story to remain virtually unchanged and the editors of *Fantastic Worlds* for having asked me to do an article on how I wrote "The Lovers." It's true I never got around to doing that, that I talked mainly of its course after being written.

Sometimes, the sideshow is more entertaining than the main attraction.

Attitudes

Roger Tandem crouched behind his pinochle hand as if he were hiding behind a battery of shields. His eyes ran like weasels over the faces of the other players, seated around a table in the lounge of the interstellar liner, *Lady Luck.*

"Father John," he said, "I've got you all figured out. You'll be nice to me, you'll crack jokes, and you'll play pinochle with me, though not for money, of course. You'll even have a beer with me. And, after I begin thinking you're a pretty good guy, you'll lead me gradually to this and that topic. You'll approach them at an angle, slide away when I get annoyed or alarmed, but always circle back. And then, all of a sudden, when I'm not watching, you jerk the lid off hell's flames and invite me to take a look. And you think I'll be so scared I'll jump right back under the wing of Mother Church."

Father John raised his light blue eyes long enough from his cards to say, mildly, "You're right about the last half of your last sentence. As to the rest, who knows?"

"You're smart, Father, with this religious angle. But you'll get no place with me. Know why? It's because you haven't the right attitude."

The eyebrows of the other five players rose as high as they could get. The captain of the *Lady Luck,* Rowds, coughed until he was red in the face and then, sputtering and blowing into a handkerchief, said, "Hang it all, Tandem, what—ah—do you mean by saying that—ah—*he* hasn't got the right attitude?"

Tandem smiled as one who is very sure of himself and replied, "I know you're thinking I've a lot of guts to say that. Here's Roger Tandem, a professional gambler and a collector—and seller—of interstellar *objets d'art,* reproaching a padre. But I've got more to add to that. I not only do not think Father John has the right attitude, I don't think any of you gentlemen have."

Nobody replied. Tandem's lips curved to approximate a sneer, but his fellow-players could not see them because he held his cards in front of his mouth.

"You're all more or less pious," he said. "And why? Because you're afraid to take a chance, that's why. You say to yourself that you're not sure there's life beyond this one, but there just might be. So you decide it's playing safe if you hitch a ride aboard one or another religion. None of you gentlemen belong to the same one, but you all have this in common. You think you have nothing to lose if you profess to believe in this or that god. On the other hand, if you deny one, you might lose out altogether. So, why not profess? It's safer."

He laid his cards down and lit up a cigarette and quickly blew smoke out so it formed a veil before his face.

"I'm not afraid to take a chance. I'm betting big stakes. My so-called eternal soul against the belief that there is nothing beyond this life. Why should I always *not* do what I want to and thus make myself miserable and hypocritical, when I can enjoy myself thoroughly?"

"That," said Father John Carmody, "is where you may be making a mistake. My opinion is that *you* have the wrong attitude. All of us are betting in a game where there is only one way in which we *can* win. That is by faith. But your method of placing your stakes is not, from my viewpoint, the sensible one. Even if you should be proved correct, you would not know it. How would you collect your wager?"

"I collect it while I live, Father," said Tandem.

"That's enough for me. When I'm dead, I don't worry about anyone welshing on me. And I might point out, Father, that you had better have more luck with your faith than you do with your cards. You're not a very good player, you know."

The priest smiled. His round pudgy face was not at all handsome, but, when he was amused, he looked pleasant and likeable. You got the impression he had a tuning fork inside-him, and it was shaking him with a mirth he invited you to share.

Tandem liked it except when the laughter seemed to be at his expense. Then his mouth curved into the expression it so often took when his cards hid it.

At that moment a loud voice came over the intercom, and a yellow light began flashing above the entrance to the lounge room. Captain Rowds rose and said, "Ah, pardon me, gentlemen. The—ah—pilot-room wants me. We're about to come out of Translation. Don't forget that we'll be—ah—in free fall as soon as the red light comes on."

The hand was not finished. The cards were put away in a box whose magnetized side would cling to an iron panel set in the table. The players leaned back to wait until the *Lady Luck* came out of Translation and went into free fall for a period of ten minutes while the automatic computer took its bearings.

If they had emerged from no-space at the desired point, they would then continue to their destination by normal space-drive.

Tandem looked around the lounge and sighed. Pickings had been slim during this trip. Most of his time had been spent playing for fun with Father John, Captain Rowds, the Universal Light missionary, and the two sociology professors. It was too bad his companions had no money and thought of themselves as gentlemen. Had they played for keeps, they would have been offended if anyone had insisted on suspending a PK or ESP indicator above the cardtable. And Tandem would, then, have had no second thoughts about using either of those talents. He reasoned that they had been given to him for a purpose. The question of from whom they had come did not shadow his mind.

He'd made some money during the hop from B Velorum to

Y Scorpii when he had struck up an acquaintance with a rich young dice-enthusiast, the type who was insulted if you set an alarm on the floor. He was a *real* gambler. That is, he understood that one PKer could detect when another was using energies supposedly forbidden during a game. But he also understood that, nowadays, one of the most exciting risks was that of running up against somebody who might be as good as you. Or better.

Whatever happened, when two of the "talented" were in a game with a group of non-PKers, neither would divulge that the other was a cheater. Then it became a duel between the two who thought of themselves as the "aristocrats" of gambling. The plebs were left outside in the cold, and possessed neither wisdom nor money at the game's end. Tandem had had the edge with the rich young man. But, just when he had jockeyed him to the verge of making some big bets, the *Lady Luck* [a misnamed vessel if ever there was one!] had Translated outside their destination, the game had ended, and the sucker had left shortly after.

Now, he was not only getting close to broke, he was, far worse, bored. Even the long argument with Father John—if you could call anything so mild such—no longer titillated him. And now, perhaps, it was that failure to be excited and the vague feeling that the padre had gotten the better of him that made him do what he did. For, as the red light began flashing and the intercom warned the passengers to watch themselves, Tandem unbuckled the belt that held him to the chair. He pushed himself upwards with a slight tap of his foot. As he floated towards the ceiling, he put his hands to his lips in an attitude of prayer and adopted an expression that was a marvelous blend of silliness and saintliness.

"Hey, Father John!" he called. "Look! Joseph of Cupertino!"

There were embarrassed looks and a few nervous laughs from the loungers. Even the apostle of the Universal Light, though the padre's competitor, frowned at what he thought was very bad taste and, in a way, a slight upon his own beliefs.

"Wrong attitude," he muttered, "definitely the wrong attitude."

Father John blinked once before he saw that Tandem was parodying the difficulties that a famous medieval saint had had with involuntary levitations. Far from being offended, however, he calmly took a notebook from his pocket and began writing in it. No matter what the event, he tried to profit from it. Even the devil must be thanked for giving examples. Tandem's antics had inspired him with an idea for an article. If he finished it in time and got it off on a mail-ship, he might have it published in the next issue of his order's periodical.

It would be titled *The Free Fall of Man: Down or Up?*

Tandem had been briefly tempted to get off at the next stop, Wildenwooly. It was a virgin planet that offered much work to its settlers and very few avenues of amusement. Gambling was one. But the trouble with Wildenwooly was that it also did not have many men who had any really big money, and that all were pathologically quick to take offense. Tandem's luck might make them suspicious and, if an indicator were available, it might be used. Nor would it help him much to damp out his powers. The result would be just as extraordinary a streak of bad luck.

Everybody had some PK. The indicators were set too high to register the average energy. Tandem and men like him could not consistently key their output to the normal man's unless they kept a rigid control. And almost always they would get excited during a game, or succumb to temptation, and use an abnormal amount. The result would be their exposure. So, to avoid that, they had to suppress their talent completely. This ended in just as much suspicion. And, while the Woolies could not *prove* that he had been cheating, they might follow their habit of taking the law into their own hands.

As Tandem didn't relish beatings or being ridden out of town on a rail—an unlovely revival of an old American custom—he decided he would stick to the *Lady Luck* until she arrived at Po Chu-I. That was a planet full of Celestials whose pockets bulged with Federation credits and whose eyes were bright with the gleam of their ancient passion for Dame Fortune.

Before the liner got to Po Chu-I, it stopped off at Weizmann and picked up another rich young man. Tandem rubbed his hands and took the sucker for all he could. This was the beauty of the technological age. No matter what the scientific advances, you could find the same old type of human being begging to be fleeced. The rich young man and he located several others who would play with them until the stakes got too high. Tandem's former partners, the captain, the professors, and the two reverends were ignored while he piled up the chips. Unfortunately, just after they took off from Po Chu-I, the rich young man became sullen, argued with him about something unconnected with the gambling, and gave him a black eye.

Tandem did not strike back. He told the rich young man that he would file suit against him in an Earth court for having violated his free will. He had not given anybody permission to strike him. Moreover, he would submit willingly to an injection of Telol. Questioning under the influence of that drug would reveal that he had not been cheating.

For some reason he did not understand, nobody except Father John would speak to Tandem the rest of the trip. And Tandem did not care to talk to the padre. He swore he'd get off at the next stop regardless of what type of world it was.

The *Lady Luck* balked him by setting down upon a planet that was terra incognita as far as Earthmen were concerned. No human settlements had been made there at all. The only reason the liner landed was the need of water to refill its fuel tanks.

Captain Rowds announced to the crew and passengers that they might step out upon the soil of Kubeia and stretch their legs. But they were not to venture beyond the other side of the lake.

"Ah—ladies and gentlemen—ah—it so happens that the Federation Sociological Agent has—ah—made an agreement with the aborigines whereby we may use this area. But we are not to enter into any traffic with the—ah—Kubeians themselves. These people have many peculiar institutions which we—ah—Terrans might offend through—if you will pardon that expression—ignorance. And some of their customs are—ah—if I may so express it, rather—ah—beastly. A word to the wise is—ah—sufficient."

Tandem found out that the ship would take at least four hours for refilling. Therefore, he reasoned, if he cared to do a little exploring, he would have more than enough time. He was determined to get at least a slight view of Kubeia. Their situation inside a little forest-covered valley forbade that. If he were to climb a hill and then a tree, he could see the city of the natives, whose white buildings he had glimpsed from the porthole as the ship sank towards this alien soil. He had no particular interest, really, except that the captain had forbidden it. That, to Tandem, was equal to a command. Even as a child, he had always taken a delicious delight in disobeying his father. And, as an adult, he would not bow to authority.

Head bent slightly downwards, his hand stroking his chin and mouth, he sauntered around the other side of the gigantic liner. There was no one there to order him back. He stepped up his pace. And, at the same time, he heard a voice.

"Wait for me! I'll go with you a way!"

He turned. It was Father John.

Tandem tensed. The priest was smiling, his light blue eyes beaming. And that was the trouble. Tandem did not trust this man because he was altogether too inconsistent. You couldn't predict his behavior. One minute he was smooth as a banana peel; the next, rough as a three-day beard. The gambler dropped his hand to reveal his half smile, half-sneer.

"If I ask you to go with me a mile, Father, you must, according to your belief, go with me at least two miles."

"Gladly, son, except that the captain has forbidden it. And, I presume, with good cause."

"Look, Father, what possible harm could come from just sneaking a glance outside? The natives think this area is tabu. They won't bother us. So, why not take a little walk?"

"There is no good reason to disregard the captain. He has complete temporal jurisdiction over the ship, which is his little world. He knows his business; I respect his orders."

"O.K., Father, wrap yourself up in your little robe of submission. You may be safe in it, but you'll never see or enjoy anything outside it. As for me, I'm going to take a chance. Not that it'll be much of one."

"I hope you're right."

"Look, Father, get that woeful expression off your face. I'm just going up the hill a little ways and climb a tree. Then I'm coming right back down. Anything wrong with that?"

"You know whether or not there is."

"Sure, I do," said Tandem, speaking through his fingers, now held over his mouth. "It all depends on your attitude, Father. Walk boldly, be unafraid, don't hide from anything or anybody, and you'll get out of life just what you put in it."

"I'll agree with you that you get out of life just what you put in it. But as to the former part of your statement, I disagree. You're not walking boldly. You're afraid. You're hiding."

Tandem had turned to stride away, but he halted and spun back.

"What do you mean?"

"I mean that you feel you must hide from someone or something all the time. Otherwise, why do you always cover your lips with your hand, or, if not with that, with a shield of playing cards? And when you are forced to expose your face, then you twist into a rictus of contempt for the world. Why?"

"Now it's psychiatry!" snarled Tandem. "You stay here, Father, stuck in your little valley. I'm going to see what the rest of Kubeia has to offer."

"Don't forget. We leave in four hours."

"I have a watch," said Tandem, and he laughed and added, "I'll let it be my conscience."

"Watches run down."

"So do consciences, Father."

Still laughing, Tandem walked off. Halfway up the hill, he paused to peer back between the trees. Father John was standing there, watching, a lone and little black figure. But he must have turned a trifle at just the right angle, for the sun flashed on the crescent of white collar and struck Tandem in the eyes. He blinked and cursed and lit a cigarette and felt much better as the blue curtain drifted up past his face. There was nothing like a good smoke to relax a man.

It might have been said of Tandem that he had been looking all his life for black sheep to fleece. Nor did he have any trouble finding them now.

From his spy-post near the top of a great tree, he could look down into the next valley. And there he could see the black sheep. Even on Kubeia.

There was no mistaking the purpose of the crowd gathered into two concentric rings at the bottom of the hill. There was the smaller circle of men inside, all on their knees and regarding intently some object in their center. And behind them stood a greater number of people, also watching intently the thing that resembled, as near as he could tell, a weathercock. Obviously, it wasn't that. He could tell from the attitudes of those around it what its purpose was. And his heart leaped. There was no mistake. He was able to smell a crap game a mile away. This might be a slightly different form than the Terran type, but its essence was the same.

Hastily, he climbed down the tree and began threading through the trunks that covered this hill. A glance at his wrist watch showed him he had three and a half hours left. Moreover, it was inconceivable that Captain Rowds would set off without his passenger. Tandem had to watch this Kubeian game of chance. He wouldn't enter it, of course, because he didn't know the rules and had no local currency with which to buy his way in. He'd just observe a while and then leave.

His heart beat fast; his palms grew moist. This was what he lived for, this tension and uncertainty and excitement. Take a chance. Win or lose. Come on, cubes, roll Daddy a natural!

He grinned to himself. What was he thinking of? He couldn't possibly get into the fun. And there was the possibility that the Kubeians would be so upset by the appearance of an Earthman that the game would break up. He doubted that, though. Gamblers were notoriously blase. Nothing but cataclysm or the police could tear them away as long as there was money yet to win.

Before he revealed himself, he examined the players. Humanoid, they had brown skins, round heads covered with short coarse auburn hairs, triangular faces innocent of whiskers except for six semi-cartilaginous bristles on their long upper lips, black noses like boxing gloves, black leathery lips, sharp meat-eater's teeth, and well developed chins. A ruff of auburn hairs grew like a boa around their necks.

All were dressed in long black coats and white knee-length breeches. Only one wore a hat. This native seemed to be a ring-master of some sort, or, as Tandem came to think of him, the Croupier. He was taller and thinner than the others and wore a miter with a big green eyeshade. He stood on one spot, arbitrated disputes about bets, and gave the signal for each play to start. It was the Croupier, Tandem realized, who would govern the temper of the crowd towards the newcomer.

He breathed deeply, adopted the familiar rictus, and stepped out from behind the bush.

He had been right about the attitudes of the Kubeians toward strangers. Those on the outer fringe looked up, widened their somewhat slanting eyes, and pricked up their foxlike ears. But, after glances that assured them he was harmless, they returned to the game. Either they were following a cultural pattern of feigning indifference, or they actually were as adaptable as they seemed to be. Whatever their reasons, he decided to profit by them.

He gently tried to work his way through the throng of specta-tors and found them quite willing to step aside. Before long he was in the front row. He looked squarely at the Croupier, who gave him an enigmatic but searching glance, and then raised both hands above his head. Two of his four fingers on each hand were crossed. The crowd gave a single barking cry and imitated his gesture. Then the Croupier dropped his hands; the game went on as if the Terran had always been there. Tandem, after a moment's shrewd study, was convinced that he had found his element and that this was nothing other than a glorified version of Spin-the-Milk-Bottle.

The center of attention was a six-foot-long statue of a Kubeian. Its two arms were extended at right angles on either side, and its legs were held straight out on a line with its body. It was face downward and whirled freely upon its navel, which was stuck on a rod whose other end was cemented firmly into a large block of marble.

The figure's head was painted white. Its legs were black. One arm was red; the other, green. The body was a steel gray.

Tandem's heart accelerated. The statue, he was sure, was platinum.

He watched. A player took hold of one of the arms and crooned a liturgy to it in his exotic tongue, a chant whose tones matched exactly those used by a pleading Terran before he casts his dice. Then, after a signal from the Croupier, he gave the arm a vigorous shove. The figure spun around and around, the sun glancing off it in red and green and black and white and silver flashes. When it began to slow down, the players crouched in breathless anticipation or else held out their arms to it and pleaded invocations that were Galaxy-wide, no matter what the language.

Meanwhile, both the players and the spectators were making side bets. Each had one or more smaller duplicates of the central statue. As it whirled around, they gesticulated at each other, chattered, then tossed their figures up in the air so they revolved around and around. Tandem was sure these statuettes were of platinum, also.

The spinning figure stopped. Its green arm pointed at one of the players. A cry went up from the crowd. Many stepped forward and piled their figurines before the man. He gave the Whirligig—as Tandem now called it—another shove. Again, it spun around and around.

The Earthman had now analyzed the game. You took one of your little whirligigs and tossed it in the air. If one of its limbs or its head sunk into the soft earth, and it happened to be the same color as the big Whirligig's extension when it pointed to you, you collected the statuettes that had landed upon extensions of a different color. If the Whirligig singled you out, but your statuette had sunk an indicator of another color into the earth, you neither lost nor won but got another try. Otherwise, the person next in line tried his luck.

Tandem rubbed his mental hands. He showed his watch to a neighbor and indicated he'd like to trade it for a whirligig. The naive native, after getting the high sign from the Croupier, readily accepted and seemed quite pleased that he was several thousand credits the loser.

Tandem made several side bets and won. Armed with the whirligigs, he boldly pushed into the inner ring. Once there he coolly exerted his PK to slow the big Whirligig down and stop it at just the right person and on just the right color. He was clever enough not to have it indicate him over a few times; most of his rapidly building fortune was made on side bets. Sometimes, he lost on purpose; sometimes, by chance. He was sure that many of the Kubeians had an unconscious PK that was bound to work for them if enough happened to concentrate on the same color. He could detect little slops of emanations here and there but could not localize them. They were lost in the general shuffle.

It did not matter. The natives would not have his trained talents.

He forgot about that and watched the temper of the crowd. He'd been alone among aliens and had seen them turn ugly when he began to win too steadily. He was ready to start losing so they would cool off, or, if that didn't work, to run. How he expected to make any speed with the weight of his winnings dragging him down, he didn't stop to think. But he was sure that, somehow, he'd come out ahead.

Nothing that he waited for came to pass. The natives lost none of their vaguely vulpine grins, and their rusty-red eyes seemed sincerely friendly. When he won, he was slapped on the back. Some even helped him pile up his whirligigs. He kept an eye on them to make sure they didn't conceal any under their long fuzzy black coats, so much like a Terran preacher's. But, nobody tried to steal.

The afternoon whirled by dizzily in flashing greens and reds and whites and silvers and dull blacks. Not too obviously, the whirligigs at his feet began to build to a small mountain.

Outwardly cool, he was inwardly intoxicated. He was not so far gone that he did not glance occasionally at the watch strapped around the hairy wrist of the Kubeian he had traded it to. Always, he saw that he had plenty of time left to make another killing.

Busy as he was, he noticed also that the crowd of spectators was increasing. This game was like any game of chance anywhere. Let somebody get hot and, through some psychological grapevine that could not be explained, everybody in the neighborhood heard of it. Natives by the dozens were loping through narrow passes into the little valley, pushing the watchers closer to the players, chattering loudly, whistling, applauding with strange barking cries, and building up a mighty stench under the hot sun with the accumulation of sweaty, hairy bodies. Slanting rusty-red eyes gleamed; sharp pointed ears waggled; the auburn airs of the neckruffs stood up; long red tongues with green bulb-tips licked the thin black-leather lips; everywhere, hands lifted to the skies in a peculiar gesture, each with two of its four fingers crossed.

Tandem did not mind. He had heard—and smelled—crowds like this before. When he was winning, he reveled in it.

Let the Whirligig spin! Let the statuettes soar! And let the wealth pile up at his feet! This was living. This was what even drink and women could not do for him!

There came a time when only four natives were left with any whirligigs before them. It was Tandem's turn to spin. He threw his figurine high up, saw it land with its black legs stuck into the soft earth, and stepped forward to give the big figure a whirl. He shot a side-glance at the Croupier and saw tears brightening the rusty eyes.

Tandem was surprised, but he did not try to guess what caused this strange emotion. All he wanted to do was to play, and he had the go-ahead from the native.

But as he laid his hands upon the hard green arm, he heard a cry that shot above the roar of the mob, stilled it, and seized him so he could make no move.

It was Father John's voice, and he was shouting "Stop, Tandem! For the love of God, *stop!*"

"What the hell are you doing here?" snarled Tandem. "Are you trying to queer the deal?"

"I've come the second mile, son," said Father John. "And a good thing for you, too. One more second, and you would have been lost."

Streams of sweat ran down his heavy jowls into his collar, now turning gray with dirt and perspiration. A branch must have raked a three-fingered red furrow across his cheek.

His blue eyes vibrated to the tuning fork deep-buried within his rotund body, but the note was not that of mirth.

"Step back, Carmody," said Tandem. "This is the last spin. Then I'm coming back. Rich!"

"No, you won't. Listen, Tandem, we haven't much time . . . !"

"Get out of the way! These people might want to take advantage of this and stop the game!"

Father John threw a despairing look towards the sky. At the same time the Croupier left the spot on which he had stood during the game, and advanced with his hand held out towards the padre. Hope replaced despair on Father John's face. Eagerly, he began making a series of gestures directed at the Croupier.

Tandem, though exasperated, could do little else than watch and hope that the meddling officious priest would be sent packing. It irritated him almost to weeping to have complete victory so close and now see it destroyed by this long-nosed puritan.

Father John paid no attention to Tandem. Having snared the Croupier's wet and rusty-red eyes, he then pointed to himself and to Tandem and indicated a circle around them. The Croupier did not change expression. Undaunted at this, Father John then pointed his finger at the natives and described a circle around them. He repeated the maneuvers twice. Abruptly, the slanting eyes widened; the rusty-red gleamed. He rotated his head swiftly, an action which seemed to be his equivalent of nodding yes. Apparently he understood that the padre was indicating that the two humans were in a different class from the Kubeians.

Father John then stabbed his index finger at the Whirligig and followed that by pointing at the Croupier. Again the circle was drawn, this time clearly circumscribing the native and the face-downward statue. Then another circle around the two Earthmen. After which, Father John held up the crucifix hung from his neck so that all could clearly see it.

A single-throated cry rose from the mob.

Somehow it held tones of disappointment, not surprise. They

pressed forward, but at a bark from the Croupier, they fell back. He himself came forward and eagerly inspected the symbol. When he was done, he looked at Father John for further signs. Tears streamed from his eyes.

"What're you doing, Carmody?" said Tandem harshly. "Is it going to hurt you if I win something valuable?"

"Quiet, man, I've almost got it through their heads. We may be able to call off the game yet. I don't know, though, you're so deep in it now."

"When I get back to Earth or the nearest big port, I'll sue you for interfering with my free will!"

He knew that was an idle threat, for the law would not apply to this case. But it made him feel better to express it.

Father John had not heard him, anyway. He was now struck into the attitude of a crucifixion, arms straight out, legs together, and an agonized expression on his face. As soon as he saw the Croupier rotate his head in comprehension, the padre pointed again at Tandem. The Croupier looked startled; his black boxing-glove nose twitched with some unknown emotion. He shrugged his shoulders in a gesture that could only be interpreted in a Gallic fashion, and he lifted his hands up, palms turned upwards.

Father John smiled; his whole body seemed to hum with the invisible tuning fork inside him. This time, it was a note of relaxation.

"You were lucky, my boy," he said to Tandem, "that, shortly after you left, I remembered an article I had read in the *Interstellar Journal of Comparative Religions*. This one was written by an anthropologist who had spent some time here on Kubeia, and . . ."

The Croupier interrupted with some vigorous signs. Evidently Father John had mistaken his meaning. The priest's lips and jowls sagged, and he groaned. "This fellow has heard of free will, too, Tandem. He insists that you make up your own mind as to whether you care to . . ."

Tandem did not wait to hear the rest but gave a glad shout.

"Gentlemen, on with the game!"

He scarcely heard the padre's cry of protest as he seized the Whirligig's green arm and gave it a shove that sent it around and around upon its navel. Nor could he have heard any more from Father John, so rapt was he in waiting for the moment when it would slow down to the point where he could begin to exert the tiny shoves or pushes that would bring the black legs pointing straight at him.

Around and around it went, and while it spun, the statuettes of the side-betters flashed in the sun. Fortunes were made or lost among the natives. Tandem stood motionless in a half-crouch, smug in the knowledge that he was not going to lose. The four who faced him did not, individually or collectively, have what he had on the ball. See! Here the Whirligig came, slow, slow, coming around for one more turn. The green arm swept by, then the legs passed him. A little push, a little push would bring them back in their circle, then a small pull, a small pull to keep their speed, and finally, a fraction of a shove to halt them entirely.

This is the way they go. Here they come, long and black with the stylized feet stuck out in the same plane as the legs. Here they come, whoa, whoa, gently, gently . . . aah!

Hah!

The crowd, which had been holding its breath, released it in a mighty burst, a howl of surprise and disappointment.

And Tandem was still frozen in his crouch, his mind not believing what his eyes saw, and the hairs on the back of his neck prickling as he detected the sudden and irresistible power that had leapt out and swung the legs enough to miss him and make the green arm point at one of his opponents.

It was Father John who shook him and said, "Man, come on. You're wiped out."

Numbly, Tandem watched the weeping Croupier signal to natives who swarmed over his pile of figurines and crated them across the circle to the winner. Now, though he had not realized it, the rules had changed. It was winner take all.

Before they could go, the Croupier stepped up to the padre and handed him one of the statuettes. Father John hesitated, then lifted the chain from around his neck and handed the crucifix to him.

"What's that for?"

"Professional courtesy," said the padre as he steered Tandem by the elbow through the mob of wildly howling and leaping Kubeians. "He's a good man. Not the least jealous."

Tandem did not try to decipher that. His rage, sizzling beneath the crust of numbness, broke loose.

"Damn it, those natives were hiding the power of their PK! But, even so, they'd not have been able to catch me off balance if you hadn't stopped the game when you did and allowed them to gang up on me! It was only pure chance that they happened to be working together! If you hadn't been such a puritanical dog-in-the-manger, I'd have won for sure! I'd be rich! Rich!"

"I take full responsibility. Meanwhile, allow me to ex—Oops, watch it!"

Tandem stumbled and would have fallen flat on his face if Father John had not caught him. Tandem recovered and was angrier than before. He wanted to owe the padre absolutely nothing.

Silent, they made their slow way through the heavy vegetation until they came to a break. Here, at Father John's gentle insistence of hand upon his elbow, Tandem turned. He was looking through an avenue in the trees at a full view of the valley.

"You see, Roger Tandem, I had read this article in the *Journal*. It was titled 'Attitudes,' and a good thing for you, for our previous talk about wrong attitudes brought it back to my mind. I decided then and there, to—if you will pardon the seeming egotism of the statement—to go the second mile. Or a third, if need be.

"You see, Roger, when you saw these people, you interpreted the scene in terms of the signs and symbols you are used to. You saw these natives around a device that seemed clearly to be for gambling. You saw further evidences: people on their knees, feverish betting, intent concentration upon the device, and you heard chanting, supplication to Lady Luck, grunts, exclamations, screams of triumph, moans of defeat. You saw a master in charge of ceremonies, the head gambler, the house master.

"What you did not perceive were certain similarities between the postures and sounds adopted during a gambling contest and those that mark the gatherings of certain types of frenetic religious sects in whatever area of the universe you happen to be. They are much the same. Watch the players in a hot crap game and then observe the antics of the less inhibited devout at certain primitive revival meetings. Is there so much difference?"

"What do you mean?"

Father John pointed through the break. "You almost became a convert."

The winner was standing proudly by the great pile of statuettes at his feet. He seemed to be exulting inwardly in his victory, for he stood straight and silent, his hands by his sides. But not for long. A number of the burly players seized him from behind. His arms were straightened out and tied to a beam of wood. Another beam, at right angles to the first, was applied to his back. His legs, waist, and head were strapped to it. Crucifix-wise, he was picked up and carried forward.

At the same time, the Whirligig was taken off the post.

Even then, Tandem did not see what his fate might have been until the native was poised face down over the post and its sharp point inserted into the navel. Then a worshiper seized the extended arm and pushed.

If the living Whirligig gave any cry of pain, he could not have been heard above the howl of the assembled faithful. Until the tip of the post thrust into the wood beam on his back, he spun, and the mob chanted.

Father John prayed half-aloud.

"If I have interfered, I have done so through love for this man and because I must choose according to the dictates of my heart. I knew that one of them must die, Father, and I did not think that the man was ready. Perhaps the man of this world was not ready, either, but I had no way of knowing that. He was playing with full knowledge of what he must do if he won, and this man Tandem was not. And Tandem is a man like unto myself, Father, and I must presume that, unless I have knowledge of signs to the contrary, I must do my best to save him so that, some day, he may do his best to save himself.

"But if I have erred, I have done so through ignorance and through love."

When Father John was finished, he led Tandem, who was pale and trembling, up the hill. "The house always wins," said Father John, who was himself a little pale. "That man that you thought was the Croupier was the head priest. The tears you first saw in his eyes were those of joy at making a convert and those you saw later were those of disappointment at losing one. He wanted you to win in this millennia-old ritual-game. If you had, you could have been the first Earthman to be the living representative of their deity, who was sacrificed in that peculiarly painful fashion. And your winnings would have been buried with you, an offering to the god whose living image you became.

"But, as I said, the house never loses. Later, the head priest would have dug them up and added them to his church's treasury."

"Do you mean that all those signals you were making at the Crou—the priest—were to convince him that I . . . ?"

"Belonged to the God of the Upright Cross, yes. Not the God of the Horizontal Cross. And I almost had him convinced until he must have thought of free will, too, and gave you the chance of joining his sect. I, as you have commented, am not so backward about interfering."

Tandem stopped to light a cigarette. His hand shook, but after a few puffs, with the smoke drifting by in blue veils, he felt better.

Squaring his shoulders and lifting his chin, he said, "Look, Father John, if you think that this is going to scare me so I'll jump in under the shadow of Mother Church's wings, you're wrong. So I made a mistake? It was only a half-error, you'll have to admit, for they *were* gambling. And anybody could have been fooled. I didn't need your help, anyway."

"Really?"

"Well, I suppose it was a good thing that you came along . . . No, it wasn't. I lost; I couldn't have won with those four ganging up on me. So what did I have to lose? I had a good time, and I'm out nothing."

"You lost your watch."

Father John did not seem to have recovered yet from the shadow that had fallen over him since he had led Tandem away from the valley. The tuning fork inside him hummed deep and black.

"Look, Father," said Tandem, "let's drop all those morals and symbols, huh? No comparisons between my watch and my conscience, huh? You can stretch these things all out of proportion, you know."

He walked fast around the great curve of the ship so he could leave the priest behind. But as he did so, he stopped. A thought that had been roosting in the shadows suddenly hopped into light. He turned and walked back.

"Say, Father, what about those four who were left? I'd have sworn they didn't have enough . . ."

He stopped. Father John was about 25 yards away, his back turned to him. His shoulders were thrown back a little more than they had been, and there was something in the set of his whole body that showed that the humming fork was beginning to vibrate to a lighter note.

Tandem perceived that only half-consciously. It was what Father John was doing that seized him and demanded all of his attention.

The priest was whirling the statuette up into the air and watching it land upon its black legs. Four times, he repeated. Always, the legs dug into the dirt.

Even from that distance, Tandem could feel the power.

Totem and Taboo

Kathy Phelan told her fiancé, "Jay, you can take your choice. Give up drinking or give up me."

Jay Martin was convinced she meant it. Her triangular face was set in tense lines, and her slanting green eyes burned.

He made one more protest. "But, kitten, I'm not an alcoholic. Just a light-heavy drinker, almost a middleweight, you might say."

She bared little sharp teeth with extraordinarily long canines.

"Flyweight, shmyweight, what's the difference? You're no champ. You never go more than six rounds before you're flat on your back."

Pretty as a prize Siamese—and her bite was as sharp. Sadly, Jay Martin said he would, of course, not hesitate a moment about his choice. She smiled and purred and ran her little red-pink tongue out to moisten her lips for his good-bye kiss.

Like a wounded crow dragging his broken wing behind him, Jay Martin limped into the Green Lizard Lounge. It was the best place he could think of in which to brood over his decision not to drink anymore. A dry martini was just the thing in which to mingle sorrow and anger.

Ivan Tursiops entered a moment later, almost literally dived into a huge schooner of beer, rolled and reveled in it, then, after blowing and snorting relief and rhapsody, condescended to listen to Jay's story. He was properly sympathetic.

"You can't help your urge toward the bottle, you know," he said. "What you need is a good psychiatrist."

"The only one I know is an alcoholic."

"Oh, now, he's not the only one in the world. The trouble with you, my boy, is you don't hobnob with enough neurotics. Now I've dozens for friends, and every one swears by a different witch doctor. But I've heard recently of one fellow who's so good I'm afraid to see him. I might lose my neurosis, you know, and I couldn't afford that."

"You mean your total inability to hear your mother-in-law?"

"Exactly. Look, here's his address. The new Medical Arts Building."

Dr. Capra pulled on his chin-whiskers and said, "Yes, I'm of a new school of thought. We take the anthropological approach. Have you read the recent authoritative article on our theories in the August *Commuter's Digest*?"

Jay nodded. Dr. Capra looked pleased and glanced at his watch. His waiting room was full.

"Then you know the essentials. Why waste time repeating them? You must be an intelligent man; you graduated from college. Business administration, I believe?"

"Yes, Doctor. Look, Kathy loves me, but she dominates me. She wants to run every minute of my life. And . . ."

"Never mind that, Mr. Martin. Or may I call you Jay? Pay no attention to what your fiancée is doing. I assure you the Freudians and their mother-complexes were way off. It's not at all necessary that I know your personal difficulties. We—"

"But she's made me give up almost everything I like. Now, I don't mind . . ."

"All that's of no consequence at all, Jay. Ha! *Hmm!*"

The doctor was holding up four photographs of Jay, each made from a different angle. He stroked his chin-whiskers. "Excellent. No border case here. You're definitely the avian type."

Ignoring Jay's torrential story of his conflicts with Kathy, he said, "Look at the tall, thin, and gangling body. Stork. Look at the shock of hair. Kingfisher. Big round eyes. Owl. Hooked nose. Falcon. Big and friendly but slightly mocking grin. Laughing jackass."

"Say!" said Jay. "I resent—"

"No doubt of it, young man. You're a classical type. There'll be no trouble at all, at all."

Dr. Capra rubbed his hands in professional glee and then handed Jay Martin a pillbox. "One every two hours, my boy, until your tutelary totem appears."

"What?"

"You read the article, didn't you? You know that primitive societies were quite correct in dividing their people into clans, each of which had a guiding and protecting spirit of totem modeled after a particular animal, don't you? We psychiatrists of the anthropological school have found that the primitives unconsciously stumbled over a great truth. Every man is, in his subconscious, a bear or fox or weasel or magpie or pig, or what have you. Watch your friends. Observe their types of bodies, their faces, their actions, their characters. All modeled upon some zoological prototype.

"This pill is the result of our collaborations with the neurologists and biochemists. It organizes your subconscious so that your subjective totem seems to be projected objectively. In fact, it may be, for all we know, for we've never succeeded in catching one. However . . ."

"But, Doctor, don't you want to hear what my trouble is? Kathy says . . ."

Capra glanced at his wristwatch, stood up, smiling, and gently butted Jay out of the office with his hands.

"Come back at this time next week. I can give you five minutes."

"But, Doc, Kathy says I drink too much!"

Capra stopped, frowned, and pulled on his yellow-brown goatee.

"I knew there was something. Ah, yes, don't drink any liquor while you're taking these pills, my boy. Might disorganize the subconscious, you know."

"But, but . . . !"

"Not now, Mr. Martin."

Ivan Tursiops looked up from the depths of his beer.

"How'd it go?"

"I just told Kathy. Her fur really bristled; I was lucky to get away with only a verbal mauling. She says I should ignore Capra's corn. All I need is a strong will power. If I loved her enough, I'd . . ."

Ivan beckoned to the waitress.

"Dry martini."

"No, thanks," said Jay. "Doctor's orders. And Kathy threatened to scratch my eyes out if I ever came around with liquor on my breath again. Everybody's against me . . ."

The waitress set down the martini. Absently, broodingly, Jay sipped. Ivan said, "Pay no attention to either, my boy. I was just talking to Bob White, and he said he knows a hell of a good psychiatrist who uses the overdo-it approach. Just what you need. If your neurosis is alcohol, you don't try to quit hitting the bottle. You try to drink *too* much."

Jay downed his martini. His eyes were bright. "Yeah? Tell me more."

"Waitress!"

Jay Martin awoke at noon the following day. Because it was Saturday and he didn't have to work, he didn't care that it was so late. But he did mind that he had to wake up at all. Seven martinis before he lost count. That meant a head the size of the *Hindenburg* and one just as ready to burst into flames. He'd be riding a seismograph of nausea and . . .

But he wasn't. His head was clear as a freshly wiped cocktail glass, and his nerves firm as a bartender's hand scooping up a tip.

It was then that he saw, perched on the foot of his bed, the bird.

The jagbird.

It was big as a bald eagle. It *was* bald, and the bags under its squinting bloodshot eyes were packed with dissipation. Its long bulbous red beak hung open to expose a swollen tongue with purple hair. Its frizzled black plumage reeked of stale beer; its breath was the morning-after's.

If Jay had not felt so healthy, he would have sworn that this was the first hallucination of an attack of D.T.'s.

"Go away!" he said.

"Nevermore!" croaked the jagbird.

It was some time before Jay understood that the phrase was not a reply to his request that it leave. It was, literally, Jay's usual vow on awakening after a hard night.

Jay got up and made some coffee. While he was drinking it, the bird flew in and perched on the chair across the table.

"Nevermore!"

If it hadn't been for the creature, Jay would have been able to eat a hearty breakfast, something he hadn't done for several years.

He got up and walked out. The bird flew through the door just as he opened it. And it insisted on perching upon his shoulder and croaking every sixty seconds, regular and monotonous as a metronome, "Nevermore!"

When he brushed it away, it flapped heavily above him so its shadow always fell on Jay's head.

Jay was afraid to visit Kathy, so he went to a movie. The bird flew in with him, nor was it asked for a ticket. When Jay sat down, it perched upon his shoulder. The woman behind Jay did not seem to be bothered by it, so he decided that it must be a hallucination. It was a visual, auditory, tactile, and olfactory triumph for Dr. Capra's little pills. Jay wanted to read the riot act to the psychiatrist, but he was afraid that he would be asked if he'd been drinking liquor while taking the pills. Not only had he done so, he had swallowed all of them at once during a fit of bravado when Ivan Tursiops had said that they were probably nothing but sugar.

At exactly five o'clock, the jagbird disappeared. Puzzled but elated, Jay left the movie a few minutes later. It was not until he was just about to step into the Green Lizard that he remembered his hangovers always left him at that time.

He raised his eyebrows and went on in. His eyebrows soared even higher when he saw the bird sitting on the bar, waiting for him. Jay ignored it and ordered a martini. He lifted it to his lips.

"*Hic!*" belched the bird.

At the same time it breathed in his face.

"Aagh!"

"What's the matter?" said the bartender. "You chokin or somepin?"

"Can't you smell it?" wheezed Jay.

"Smell what?"

"Nothing."

The jagbird had put one heavy foot on the edge of the glass. Its talon, like a waiter's dirty thumb, dipped into the drink. Its red eyes, purple in the lounge's dim light, squinted reproachfully.

"*Hic!*" it said.

"*Haec!*" sneered Jay.

"*Hoc!*" trumped the bird.

"Heck!" groaned Jay.

He left the martini untouched. He couldn't argue with a bird who could decline Latin.

Kathy was so pleased to see Jay sober and with not even the hint of liquor on his breath that she almost purred. Her suspicion-slanted eyes widened into a soft golden-green.

"Oh, Jay, you've really sworn off. You love me!"

Her kiss was more than warm. He didn't enjoy it as much as he should, and she felt it. She stiffened, narrowed her eyes, and put her sharp nails on his arm.

"What's the matter? Aren't you happy? Do you regret doing this for me?"

"Bring me a drink."

"What? I will not!"

"Oh, I won't touch it . . . I think."

Kathy sensed urgency. She went to the liquor cabinet and poured a scotch. He watched her and wondered again why he had to give up drinking when she wouldn't. She had explained that she did not *have* to drink, but he did. Would he be a dog-in-the-manger and ask her to give up her harmless enjoyment because it was for him a vicious habit? Feeling like a selfish brute, he had said no. But he couldn't help a little bitterness.

She handed him the scotch. Instantly, the jagbird stuck its big bulbous beak between cup and lip.

"*Hic!*"

Jay handed the glass back to Kathy.

"See?"

She didn't. He explained. Instead of relaxing, her eyes slitted even more, and her nails scratched his arm.

"Do you mean this bird will *always* be with us? Even after we're married? We'll *never* be alone?"

There was no soft plaintive note in her voice. Only a hiss of anger and determination.

He patted her arm. "It's not a real bird, kitten. You can't see it."

"No, but I'll know it's there! I won't be able to forget it. It'll make me nervous as a cat! Not only that, but I don't like your giving up liquor because of some crazy bird. I want you to do it on your own will power, to stand on your own two feet."

"If it weren't for my totem," he said, "I'd not be standing on my feet now. I'd be under the table at the Green Lizard."

"That's what I thought!" she spat. "Where is the jagbird now?"

He jerked his thumb at the end table, where it perched, sleepy-eyed, upon the ceramic bust of a Silenus. She stared vainly, burst into tears, and said, "Oh, if only I could see it! If only . . ."

She stopped and dried her eyes. She became soft and furry-voiced. "What is the address of this Dr. Capra, honey?"

It was a moment before he could see what she intended doing. She looked unconcernedly at him and even yawned, as if the whole matter had all at once become of no importance.

He blinked rapidly, like a startled owl. The outlines of her body had wavered and then congealed. They had remained fixed for only the space of a wink, but long enough. There was no mistaking the long bristling whiskers, the fangs revealed by the yawn, and the narrow-pupiled eyes. Nor the I'm-about-to-swallow-the-canary expression.

He strode past her, scooped up the jagbird, and lunged through the door.

Kathy screamed, "Jay, come back!"

"Nevermore!" croaked the bird, its head sticking out from under its owner's arm.

Jay Martin is now married to a little woman with a spaniel's big brown eyes. Her devotion to him has been described by their friends as dog-like. They act like two lovebirds. He no longer drinks like a fish, and he has become a whale of a success in the business world. He seems to be gifted with some uncanny instinct which enables him to judge a person's character at a glance. Last year he joined the bulls, cornered the bears, and made a big killing among the wolves of Wall Street.

The Tin Woodman Slams the Door

The Tin Woodman it was who first opened the door for me. He took me around and introduced me so that, in time, I knew them all, Tik-Tok and the Ragged Man and Ozma and the Cowardly Lion and I could go on and use up the rest of this space with just a list of the marvelous citizens.

After many adventures, some of which I untiringly lived through a dozen times through a curious type of time-traveling called rereading, I began to see things in a slightly polarized light. The Woodman's movements began to be a little jerky, the Cowardly Lion had no real reason to be afraid, the Gingerbread Man was just a little too sugary, and the final blow came when I wondered if Dorothy would object if I gave her a kiss. She did object, and so the Tin Woodman, metal jaw cranked to a grim angle, shook his shining axe at me and slammed the door in my face.

I said, "But, but, I didn't really mean any harm!"

No, of course I didn't, but I wasn't aware that if you want a thing to grow up with you it may—quite rightly—refuse, preferring to remain timeless within the walls of the archaic and innocent garden.

During the years after that, I tried many times to sneak back through the door. Always, I was confronted by that shining axe.

Not too long after this deportalization, I was blinded by the garish gateway of Gernsbackis, a wondrous land indeed. I quit sighing over that other lost door. Came the day when that portal was closed, too, when Treemainia, Campbellis, and others beckoned me to evermore fascinating odysseys. Yet, travelling there did not give me the sense of wonder that the yellowbricked highway had. True, I waited with eagerness for what next month's saga would offer in some strange place and puzzling time, but gone was the pristine breathlessness I'd known when knocking on the door to the Emerald City.

And then, one day, when I wasn't even looking for it, a gate swung open, and there he was.

"You?" I said.

"Not exactly. I am his grandson."

It took me a minute. Then I said, "Ike Positronic!"

He grinned tinnily and introduced me to the citizens of this not-quite-verdant metropolis, and I saw the Cowardly Lion's grandsons, which, if you've read *Gratitude Guaranteed*, you have, too, and I saw ten raggedy men with firewater bottles, and quite a few wizards, some mad and some mules, and some writing articles on scientology, and I saw Dorothy, but she was tall and had filled out here and there and didn't seem at all averse to a kiss, and there were also the evil gnomes, though they were bald and psychopathetic, and I could go on.

But I think you get the idea, and you'll be no more surprised than I when the Tin Woodman, in answer to my complaint that this was all very nice but didn't give me the good old-time sense of wonder, replied, "Well, do you think that cybernetic brains and antigravity machines and psionic powers belong more to the world of reality than sawdust brains and flying powders and magic mirrors? It's all just a matter of sounding more adult, you know. Besides, you grew up and gained some things and lost others, and you wouldn't give up all this for that little door you used to knock at, now, would you?"

I answered, "I suppose not," and I really don't think I would, do I?

The 1960s

Philip José Farmer's output had slowed a bit as the 1950s concluded, but it took again off with the advent of the 1960s. Horace Gold, the editor of *Galaxy* magazine, approached Phil about writing science fiction novels with sexual content for a new line of books to be published by Galaxy-Beacon. Phil wrote and sold two of these: *Flesh*, about a space ship crew that returns to earth after eight hundred years in space and finds the U.S. has devolved into an agrarian matriarchal society, and *A Woman a Day*, which was an expansion and revision of an earlier novella, "Moth and Rust."

His groundbreaking story, "The Lovers," was expanded into a novel and published in paperback by Ballantine. He also published his first mainstream novel, *Fire and the Night*; his first Ace Double, *The Cache from Outer Space/The Celestial Blueprint*; and two short story collections, *Strange Relations* and *The Alley God*. He continued to sell stories to *F&SF*, "Open to Me, My Sister," "A Few Miles," and "Prometheus," and cracked a few new markets, selling "Heel" to *Worlds of If*, "Tongues of the Moon," and "How Deep the Grooves" to *Amazing Stories*; "Uproar in Acheron" to *The Saint Mystery Magazine*; and "Some Fabulous Yonder" to *Fantastic Stories of Imagination*. He only published one fanzine article in the early 1960s, "On a Mountain Upside Down," in *JD Argassy*. Phil and Bette also attended WorldCon 20 in Chicago in 1962, and WorldCon 22 in Oakland in 1964.

The second half of the decade was even busier. In 1965, the Farmers moved to Beverly Hills, while Phil worked as a freelance technical writer as well as a science fiction writer.

Phil sent one of his rewrites of *Owe for the Flesh* to Fred Pohl, then the editor of *Worlds of Tomorrow*, *If*, and *Galaxy*. Pohl thought Phil's "Riverworld" idea was too big for one novel, and suggested Phil write several novelettes that Pohl could publish in his magazines. Thus, "The Day of the Great Shout," "The Suicide Express," and "Riverworld" appeared in *Worlds of Tomorrow* (the first two were later published as the novel *To Your Scattered Bodies Go*). "The Felled Star," parts 1 and 2, and "The Fabulous Riverboat," parts 1 and 2, appeared in *Worlds of If* (all four parts were later published as the novel *The Fabulous Riverboat*). He sold several other stories to Fred's magazines as well: "The Blasphemers" and "The King of the Beasts" went to *Galaxy*, while "A Bowl Bigger than Earth," "The Shadow of Space," and "Down in the Black Gang" went to *Worlds of If*.

Phil only sold two stories from 1964–1969 to non-Pohl publications. "The Blind Rowers" went to *Knight*, and "The Jungle Rot Kid on the Nod" went to *Broadside*, both adult magazines.

Gene Roddenberry hired Phil to write a scientific guide for his forthcoming television series, *Star Trek*. The guide was intended to provide prospective script writers a framework of what science might and might not be possible in the future. As far as Phil knew, it was never used. Phil also tried to sell several stories to *Star Trek*, but none were accepted. Phil reworked two of them into the stories "The Shadow of Space," and "Sketches Among the Ruins of My Mind."

Phil also started selling stories to anthologies, a market that opened up due to the success of Harlan Ellison's *Dangerous Visions*, which included Phil's "Riders of the Purple Wage," the 1968 Hugo winner for Best Novella. He also sold "Don't Wash the Carrots" to Damon Knight for *Orbit 3*.

In addition to short fiction, Phil's novel-length output in the latter half of the decade was prolific. He sold two more books to

Phil and Bette Farmer at WorldCon 26 in San Francisco, 1968.

Ballantine, *Inside Outside* and *Dare*. He expanded the novella "Tongues of the Moon" and sold it to Pyramid. Ace published the first three novels in his World of Tiers series: *The Maker of Universes*, *The Gates of Creation*, and *A Private Cosmos*. Belmont published *The Gate of Time* and Berkeley published an expanded version of the novella *Night of Light*.

Going several steps beyond what Galaxy-Beacon did in the early 1960s, porn publisher Brandon House started a new imprint under the name Essex House and reached out to well-established authors for books that would contain explicit sexual content. Sex was to be included because it was important to the story, not merely for titillation. Phil published three controversial books with Essex: *Image of the Beast* and its sequel *Blown*, and *A Feast Unknown*. The latter featured stand-ins for Phil's favorite pulp heroes, Tarzan and Doc Savage, in odd and violent sexual situations. While many pulp fans appreciated that *A Feast Unknown* turned many conventions inside-out, others never forgave him for writing the book.

During this time, Phil also became interested in the Triple Revolution Document, which postulated that due to increased cybernation, governments would be able to switch to systems based on economies of abundance instead of economies of scarcity. His story "Riders of the Purple Wage" describes one such future and his article "Blueprint for Free Beer" delves into the problems and benefits of this shift. As the guest of honor at the 26th WorldCon in San Francisco in 1968, Phil gave a speech on the topic entitled "Reap." Unfortunately, the programming was already running behind schedule, the air conditioning was not working, and Phil's long call to arms to the science fiction community did not go over. He did refer to economies of abundance again a few times in his stories in the 1970s, but lost most of his fervor for the idea. He did later joke that instead of worrying about changing the world, if he had started a religion back in the 1960s he would have been very wealthy.

In March 1969, Phil, along with many other American science fiction writers, attended the Second International Film Festival in Rio de Janeiro. He wrote an interesting report of his trip for the fanzine *Luna*. This year he also wrote the article "Oft I have Travelled (on Solar Pons)" about the character August Derleth created as analogue to Sherlock Holmes.

Shortly before NASA put a man on the moon in 1969, McDonnell-Douglas laid off a large part of their work force, Phil included. He decided that this was the time to once again make a go at writing science fiction full time.

On a Mountain Upside Down

To stand on your head on top of a narrow mountain is not always easy.

I did it once several months ago. Two paths led me there: yoga and the lure of the West.

Although not a conventional Beatnik, I became interested in the physical aspects of yoga to slough off the fat and tighten the slack muscles that working in an office have given me these last three years. One of the first exercises suggested is standing on the head for five minutes. Nehru, I found out, stands on his head half an hour every day, but look at the mess India is in. However, I tried it for three minutes at first, then over a lengthy period of three days built up my endurance to five and a half minutes. To time myself, I placed a clock in front of my face and had no trouble reading the time upside down. At first, the blood drained into my head, and I felt as if my eyes would pop out from pressure. My legs felt empty of all fluid, and my neck muscles quivered.

I also had trouble with my male Siamese sealpoint cat. He is a creature who does not like his routine disturbed, and his slave standing on his head was something he did not care for at all. After pacing back and forth crying (Siamese cats never meow), his tail stiff with extended hairs, he attacked me. He did this by leaping upon my crotch and hanging there—so over he and I went to the floor. I tried again, but this time he bit my face, not enough to bring blood but enough to warn me to quit this crazy posture.

Into the bathroom he went. The door locked on him, his piteous wails ringing through the house, his slave went back to his head-standing. The next day he paced back and forth while I was propped up against the wall, but he did not attack. And now he ignores me, having accepted is as part of routine that I stand on my head for five minutes every night before going to bed.

If you want to get a fresh slant on your living room, stand on your head. The world looks upside down; you get the strange sensation that you are wearing an anti-gravity belt and doing spin-turns through the house. Sometimes, if you stay in this position long enough, you begin to think that it is quite normal for the tables and chairs and sofa and lamps and rugs to be suspended from the ceiling. You get fond of this position; you are sure that people who are content to keep their feet on the ground are a bunch of damn bourgeois. And you are right.

This exercise is supposed to result in improved circulation of blood and will cure anything from colds to cancer. However, though I did begin to feel more stimulated, less tired, I think it was due to changing my routine and a fresher outlook on life. For, about three weeks after I began standing on my head, I came down with one of the worst colds of my life. Had to take almost a week off from work.

And this was in dry sunny Arizona.

Which leads me, unnaturally, to speak of other perils besides sinus and sore throats, in which Arizona is rich. The morning I was to return to work I awoke an hour early. I felt a tingling in my lower lip, which made me think that the damned cat was at his usual practice of getting me up at dawn so I could let him out. But no, he was sleeping on the foot of the bed. Then I felt the tingling increase, and I arose and went into the bathroom to look into the mirror. Suspicion verified. My lower lip was swelling at an alarming rate, ballooning up before my eyes.

By the time the rest of the family was up, the lip was stretched out so huge and taut I looked like a male white Ubangi, or half-

On a Mountain Upside Down

Ubangi. I did not go to work but went instead to see a doctor. He did not think I had been bitten by a spider or nonpoisonous scorpion. He was insistent that the swelling was caused by psychosomatic reasons. Even though I showed him the slight break in labial skin which could have been caused by an insect bite, he wanted to know if I was under unusual pressure, was worried about anything in particular, etc. I told him I wasn't any more nervous or strained that usual. He was dissatisfied with my secure neurological state but gave me a shot of anti-histamine in the hip, which hurt worse than the insect bite(?) and some pills whose chemical composition I don't remember. Probably a placebo, anyway. The swelling went down in two days and I returned to work with my story, which was greeted with guffaws and stares of incredulity.

No matter. The following week-end I went with the Old Prospector on a safari into the desert near the Kofa Mts. The desert in Arizona is guaranteed to cure you of anything unless you get bitten by a rattlesnake or run out of water. And even these have their end.

The Old Prospector is a technical writer who slaves away at the desk beside mine. He is an ex-electrical power engineer who has at least thirty claims staked out all over Arizona and parts of California and Utah. On this trip we were headed for Bronco Ledge, which he is testing for gold or whatever he finds through the equipotential method. This consists of driving a number of iron rods into the grounds and sending a current into the earth to measure the resistance. He says it is a sure-fire method of locating ore deposits; other engineers I've talked to say it is highly unreliable in the type of ground he deals with. I do not care, though I would like to see George strike it rich. While he and his partners slave away, I roam the desert, looking for animals, Indian artifacts, and breath-taking views. On this trip four of us went, two electrical engineers and two technical writers. I rode with George in his pick-up truck; the engineers followed behind in their jeep. After reaching Hassayampa, we cut off the state highway onto a country dirt road, then left that to make our own trail. Our destinations for that evening was Clanton Well.

Out here you have to cross washes by the scores. And often, if your vehicle can't make it down or up a steep bank, you have to build your own road, pile rocks to make a causeway, then fill the gaps in between with sand. And push the truck when it gets stuck in the sand of the wash-beds. Hard work, but a lot of fun. While you're jolting over the rough rocks, going this way and that around the saguaro, mesquite, cholla, and palo verde vegetation and the malapi rocks, jumping out now and then to push or make a road, the moon comes up over the mountains, the biggest orange you ever saw, and the desert is painted with a thin spray of shining tequila-juice. At least, that's how it feels, because you get drunk with its harsh beauty.

Sometimes, you have to go down a wash to see if there's a good crossing for the truck, and you wonder if any big pussycats are around. You know there's a good chance, for your flashlight has picked up many tracks of deer, bobcats, coyotes and mountain lions. How the hell they live out here where the nearest water is forty miles away, you don't know. Maybe they drink each other's blood.

Our first big stopping-place was the abandoned mine which the Clanton boys, and their poppa dug. Very few people have seen this; I felt thrilled. We roamed around a while but didn't go down into the mine because we didn't have a rope ladder. We said that the next time we came out this way we'd bring one. One of the men staked a claim to the mine, just for the hell of it, and we pushed on.

We drove down a wash with very narrow sides and very sandy bottom. The cat-claws reached out and scraped the truck-side; you had to keep your elbows in. George said that this wash was once a road the military had built. After they abandoned it, nature took it back and turned it into a coarse for the spring floods which come down from the snow melting in the mountains.

Our next stop was the Stardust mine. This was once worked by the parents of George's partner (who wasn't with us that night). After the gold vein seemed to peter out, the mine was deserted. But George thinks it might turn up again later on; he's been doing some work on it from time to time. We went down several levels, climbing down a rickety wooden ladder with only our flashlights for illumination. When we reached the bottom, we were a hundred and fifty under. But this wasn't the lowest level. After walking down a high corridor about fifty feet long, we took a tunnel that descended at a fortyfive degree angle into the rock. Went down another wooden ladder, and reached the bottom. Here we found a strange thing; two dried-up corpses of animals intertwined. One looked like a large rat; the other, like a jackrabbit. Apparently these two rodents had locked in mortal combat on the ground above and had fallen down the shaft and been killed when they struck the rock floor. Some of their bones were broken.

Before we left the mine, George gave us sticks of dynamite to carry out for him; these had been stored for some time. But George looked them over to make sure the dynamite wasn't crystallized; when the nitro starts to form crystals, the dynamite is likely to go off with a slight jar.

Our next stop, the final for that night, was Clanton Well. This is where the Clanton clan had a ranch before they went off to Tombstone and became famous. The military had dug a well here, used it as a watering place. Then they abandoned it, and the Clantons moved in with their cows. The Clantons didn't pay much attention to the cattle. They spent most of their time prospecting, knowing that the cows wouldn't stray far because this was the only place they could get water for forty miles roundabout. Now there's nothing left of the old Clanton ranch but a few timbers piled under a tree; somebody had built a cattle-chute and fences here, and a rusty iron windmill stands above the well. There's still water in it, but we had no way of operating the pump.

The next day we pushed on, and by noon got to Bronco Ledge. This heap of malapi rock is only a few miles east of the Kofa Game Refuge; the only sign of civilization is a narrow trail made by the state and the inevitable beer and bean cans. Even these are so few they don't distract.

Part of the afternoon we shot with our pistols and rifles at a beer can in which was a stick of dynamite. Once George, as a joke, threw a stick of dynamite at me, hollering, "Catch!" I didn't jump, because I knew—or hoped—he wouldn't throw crystallized dynamite. Even if it was inclined to explode, there wasn't anything I could do.

One of the engineers, who shall be nameless, had already shown his fear of the explosive in the Stardust. When George asked us to help him carry the stuff out, he had taken up the ladder without a word. I won't say he was pale, but he did look shaken. However we all have our idiosyncrasies; one man's foolishness is another man's fear.

George is quite the practical joker. That first morning at Clanton Well, he rose early and fired his .38 close to the ear of one of the men sleeping under the truck. Naturally, he raised his head, and also, a bump. George laughed and said he'd seen a fox and shot at it.

After target practice was over, and George had gotten a big laugh out of me jumping into the air when a stick went off when I was cooking lunch, having completely forgot about their practice, I hooked my canteen onto my G.I. belt, filled my knapsack with goodies, and stuck my .32 Husquevarna six-shooter into my holster. Then I took off for Puka Peak, a mountain about five miles away, though it looked only two. On its topmost peak was a lone saguaro cactus; I decided to climb the peak and keep it company.

I hadn't gotten more than fifty yards away when I heard a rattle, and there, sure enough, was a diamond-back. He was no danger to me, being too far away, but I didn't want to take a chance of running into him later, so I broke his back and smashed in his head with a malapi. I was genuinely sorry to have to do that, for I think a rattler is a beautiful creature, but I don't like to think about getting bitten. I walked another mile up, and down the hills and across a very steep wash—where there were mountain lion tracks—and then came across the biggest tarantula I've ever seen outside of a zoo. He wanted nothing to do with me, and I wasn't scared because they're not poisonous, contrary to what folklore says. But I was leery; they look as if they belong on the surface of Mars, that is, in Arizona, which from where I was looks as strange and desolate as the surface of the red planet. He scuttled off into a hole.

I entered a valley which was absolutely soundless. No sign that man had ever been there. But I did flush up a jackrabbit, who bounded off toward the west. And the sun shone through the transparent upper parts of his ears, making them look like pale blood. This was, to me, a weird and unforgettable sight, the sun shining pinkly through his ears.

When I reached the bottom of Puka Peak and looked up, the saguaro on top presented the appearance of a sorrowful saint or some hooded figure. It bulged at the top to form a chin and the outline of a face. I named it Saint Puka.

The climb was steep and breath-taking. Being out of condition, I had to stop often and get my wind back and wait until my heart quit pounding. And there were places which were precipitous enough to impress me, though a real mountain-climber wouldn't have given them a second thought. However, being alone, I had to be extra careful.

Close to the top, I passed caves. These looked as if they could harbor big pussycats, but I doubt it, for the climb up and back wouldn't be worth the effort for them.

Finally, I reached the top by the lone saguaro and here sat down to look over the scene. Too bad you couldn't have been there; you could see for over fifty miles away, and all around were the heads of mountains mightier than the one I was on, mountains with strange shapes indeed. One looked like a Chinese pagoda; Another, like an eagle's tail. I strained my eyes, but I couldn't see the Shithouse Mountains, which are designated on the topographical maps as the SH mountain range. These got their name from a series of peaks which look from a distance like a row of outhouses.

From the ridiculous to the sublime. I stood on my head on top of this peak. There was just enough room so that if I lost my balance I wouldn't fall off; my feet would hang over the edge. And I had folded my shirt under my head to keep its top from being hurt by the rock floor.

It was a strange thing, seeing all those mountains hanging down from the upside down earth. Strange, but nothing beyond the imagination to conceive. I rotated slowly, pivoting from east to west, until I was facing the sinking sun. The sun, as anybody knows, looks the same downside up as the other way. Being round has its disadvantages.

Finally, having exhausted the possibilities of this position, and sure that nobody else had stood on their head on this particular peak, or probably on any in Arizona, sure also that nobody but myself gave a damn, I sat down. All was quiet; even the hawk that had been circling this peak and crying as I climbed up was gone; no sound but my breathing. Far away I could see the sun glitter from the white top of the truck at the base of Bronco Ledge; at least, it should have been the truck, for I was too distant from it to make out its outline.

Here, I thought, if a man wanted to practice some aspects of Zen, or just be simpatico with Nature, here is the place. For a while, at least. Eventually, a man would miss his kind; he'd have to climb down and find someone to talk to; after all, Man is part of Nature, too.

I did decide to climb down. By the time I reached the bottom of the mountain, twilight had fallen. And in a short time, darkness. The sky had become clouded over, a rare thing in this part of the country, and the moon and stars were hidden. Fortunately, though the camp was five miles away, I had lined up the intersection of two hills to aim for, knowing the camp would not be too far away. Even in the darkness, the twins loomed up.

Nevertheless, I was nervous. There were mountain lions, bobcats, and the stickly cholla cactus to run into me. And I had not taken along my flashlight. I could have lit up my path for fifty yards ahead by touching off the inflammable needles of cholla; these blaze up like tar torches and give an excellent light. But I did not want to do this. Somehow, it seemed more romantic to be sneaking through the desert night without a light. Though you could hardly call my noisy progress sneaking. Once, I heard a loud snort, then a crash as some large animal bounded away. Undoubtedly a deer. If it had been a cougar I'd have heard nothing.

I put my .32 in my hand and walked along, whirling every now and then to see if some glowing-eyed big cat was trailing me. Naturally, there were none; if they'd wanted me they'd have made sure I didn't see them until it was too late.

Eventually, I passed through the little valley between the two hills and suddenly saw the camp-fires. It took me half an hour to reach them, for I had to take a roundabout way to avoid climbing other hills. When I did get there, I asked them if they had seen me through their binoculars. They said they had. They didn't say a thing about my having stood on my head, so I didn't. I did tell them about filing a claim on top, which I left in an empty Prince Albert tobacco can. Why claim that useless knob of rock? they asked. Just so anybody else who climbed up there would know he wasn't the first, I replied. But somebody else may have been there before you and didn't leave any record of it, they said. Without evidence to the contrary, I am the first, I said, and we left it at that.

Uproar in Acheron

Everybody in the town of Acheron had been wondering for two weeks whom Linda Beeman favored. Now there was no doubt. The smoke of the revolvers had just thinned away when Linda ran into the Lucky Lode saloon and threw herself, sobbing, on the body of Johnny Addeson.

Skeeter Patton, the Colt still in his hand, stood blinking at her like a cat that'd been suddenly awakened. He was pale and shaking, and no wonder. He'd put two bullets into the chest of his best friend and lost forever his chance of marrying Linda. Yet he could have done nothing to stop what had happened.

The two young men had dropped in at the Lucky Lode after work to have a few. Johnny had been moody for about a week, but tonight he was laughing and joking. That is, he was until Skeeter said that he had to leave soon. He had a date to take Linda for a buggy ride.

Johnny's eyes had widened, and he had said, "Quit your fooling! She has a date with me!"

The men along the bar laughed and watched to see who would win the argument. They didn't expect the argument to be anything except the friendly pretend-mad joshing the two gave each other all the time. Johnny and Skeeter had come into Acheron only three weeks ago on the same stagecoach. They had not known each other before that day. Johnny had come from

Tucson, where he'd been studying under a horse doctor. He'd opened his own business next door to the livery stable. Skeeter was fresh into the territory of Arizona from New Orleans, where he'd been a printer's devil. The two had struck it off together like flint and steel. Sparks flew sometimes, but their disputes always ended up with them laughing and backslapping each other. They'd even been agreeable about both courting Linda Beeman, the daughter of the owner of the Beeman Stables.

But Skeeter must have suddenly become serious about Linda. He swore at Johnny and said, "No call for that! And I'm not a liar!"

"This says you are!" shouted Johnny, and he drew his Smith and Wesson .45.

Skeeter struck Johnny's gun upwards with one hand and started to draw his own with the other hand. But Johnny brought his pistol down and fired. He was so close he couldn't have missed. But his bullet struck the far wall.

Skeeter fired his Colt .44 twice at point-blank range. And Johnny jerked backward from the force of the slugs and fell, face up, on the floor. Blood from the two wounds spread outwards on his chest.

There was uproar and confusion. Everybody was paralyzed with shock. A nice young man like Johnny going berserk was the last thing anybody would've thought of.

Old Doc Evans, Acheron's medico, coroner, and undertaker, finished his drink at the bar. Then he felt Johnny's pulse and pulled back one of Johnny's eyelids. When he rose from the body, Doc Evans shook his head.

"Right through the heart," he said. "Deader 'n last week's newspaper."

Pedro, the Lucky Lode's janitor, ran to get Linda. He didn't take long. The stables, over which she lived with her father, were only the throw of a horseshoe away. In two minutes she was sobbing over Johnny's body.

Skeeter hadn't said a word. He was too dazed. Even when Sheriff Douglas said, "Don't worry, son. It was a clear case of self-defense," Skeeter didn't talk. Once, he put his hand out towards

Linda and then, as if knowing it would do no good, withdrew his hand.

Old Doc Evans gave a few orders. Two men picked up Johnny's body and carried it out of the Lucky Lode. They were headed for the doc's house, which was also the undertaking parlor. But they had not gotten halfway across the street before they stopped.

Everybody else stopped, too, for down the main street was a blaze of lanterns, a squeak of wheels, and the high-walled bulk of a van. It was the kind of van a snake-oil man drives around in and lives in and carries his snake oil and fever pills and tonics in. But this van had no big signs on the side or anything to tell what the owner was selling.

The van pulled up just by the two men carrying the body, and the driver looked down from his high seat.

"Had a shooting, friends?" the man said. "Did this young fellow just die? Perhaps I can do something for him."

It was a strange thing to say, and the man who said it was even stranger. He was dressed in a rusty black suit and wore a black bowler from which hair black as stove polish hung. His face was as pale as if he'd just seen Death. He had a handsome face, though it was bony with high cheekbones and a Roman nose and deep hollow eyes and dark rims under the eyes. His neck, sticking out of his white collar, was thin as a colt's leg, and his shoulders were narrow as a cat's.

"I am Doctor Grandtoul," he said in a voice that surprised everybody because it was so deep.

"Always nice to meet another M.D. in this unpopulated territory," said old Doc Evans. He took off his Stetson and placed it over his heart. "But there ain't much you can do for Johnny Addeson. He breathed his last five minutes ago, and his soul has winged on to its reward."

Doctor Grandtoul raised a slim pale hand and pointed a slim pale finger. "Ah, my friend," he said, "that is where you are wrong."

He looked around at the crowd, which was rubbernecking as if they knew something out of the ordinary was coming and they weren't sure they were going to like it.

"Yes," said Doctor Grandtoul, "no discredit to you, my worthy Hippocratian comrade. But perhaps you have not heard of the latest scientific advancement.

"Advancement!" he repeated explosively. "No! Miracle, rather! The miracle of electricity, which is both the stuff of lightning and of life itself!"

He swung down off the seat of the van and landed on his feet as lightly as a catamount.

"Bring the late departed to the back of my van," he said, "and help me place the body on my bed. Then I'll do what I can."

He walked around to the back of the van, opened the doors, and leaped into the van like a long lean black cat. Then he took Johnny from the two men who handed him up, and, with a strength amazing in a man with such pipe-cleaner arms, carried Johnny to the bed on one side of the van. Once he'd placed Johnny there, he ripped off Johnny's shirt. Then he cleaned the wounds and from a jar on a shelf he poured out some powder into his hand.

He turned to the buzzing gaping crowd, bowed, flashed white teeth, and said, "Friends, we can't leave an ugly hole in the departed's chest, can we? I think not, for he'd have trouble breathing, what with the air whistling in and out, a ghastly rune. So we'll just place this *soodoplazum*, a secret of the ancient Tibetan lamas, in the wounds. And, once the lightning of the revitalizing machine surges through the body, the *soodoplazum* will become real flesh."

There weren't many who really heard him, and those who heard didn't understand him. They were too busy staring at the big batteries that lined one side of the van. The batteries looked just like the monsters the telegraph companies used to provide electricity for their copper lines. There were many copper wires, very thin wires, that sprouted out of the main cables from the battery terminals. Doc Grandtoul took the wires, one by one, and attached them to Johnny's wrists and ankles and waist and head with thin copper bands.

Then he paused and said, "Would you gentlemen allow your doctor—Evans, is it?—to come up here? I want him to examine the late departed once more and make absolutely certain the ghost is gone."

"Ain't no need," grumbled Doc Evans, tugging at his white walrus moustache and swaying back and forth because, like always, he had a snootful. But at Doc Grandtoul's insistence Doc Evans climbed into the van and felt Johnny's pulse again and looked into his eyes. Then he said, "I'll stake my professional reputation that Johnny's dead as Julius Caesar's mule."

"Wanta buy a drink if he ain't?" somebody called, and the crowd hooted with laughter because they knew how tight old Doc Evans was when it came to buying a drink for anybody except himself.

Nevertheless, not a man or woman there—and everybody in Acheron except the kids and sick in bed was there—didn't believe Johnny was dead. Old Doc Evans might be closefisted, ornery, and too much a tippler, but he'd seen enough corpses to know a dead ringer from a live one.

Doc Grandtoul took a hypodermic syringe from a box, wiped the needle with alcohol, and plunged it into Johnny's chest. After taking the needle out, he said, "The late departed has just been injected with a serum which, coupled with the electricity coursing through his body should bring the life back."

The crowd gasped. The doctor grinned at them and pulled a huge goldplated watch from his vest pocket. His black eyebrows rose knowingly, and he said, "Three minutes should do it, my friends. The combination of serum and electrical juice in a strong young body as recently deceased as this takes only a short time to accomplish its mission."

Afterwards, there were some that said those were the longest and most terrifying three minutes of their lives. Something about the scene, Johnny's body lying so still in the bed, dimly lit by the kerosene lamp inside the van, the copper wires sprouting from him and running to the huge black batteries, and the calm certain bearing of the mysterious stranger convinced them they were going to see something they'd never seen before, maybe something they shouldn't be seeing.

There wasn't a sound except the hard breathing of the men and women pressing together so they could get closer to the van for a good look.

Then—there was one big gasp, one loud scream, and the sound of running feet. Doc Grandtoul was calling after them, "Come back! There's nothing to be afraid of!"

But he was alone. Even old Doc Evans had bolted.

Not quite alone. Johnny was sitting up in the bed and saying, "What in blue blazes is going on?"

Later, much later, Johnny Addeson, Skeeter Patton, and Doc Grandtoul left the Lucky Lode. Johnny had invited the doctor to stay at the room he shared with Skeeter in Mrs. Lundgren's hotel. The men of Acheron followed the three out of the saloon, for they still hadn't gotten over the wonder of seeing Johnny raised from the dead. They kept touching him and saying, "How was it while you was dead, Johnny?"

And Johnny kept saying, "Just like I was sleeping. I didn't know nothing until I woke up with a strange face looking down at me."

He would laugh and say, "At first I thought it was the devil," and he would whoop with laughter to show how glad he was to be alive.

Skeeter Patton, after making sure that Johnny wasn't still mad at him, was buddies with Johnny again. He swore he didn't have any real interest in Linda Beeman. As far as he was concerned, Johnny could have her all to himself.

That was the strangest thing of all. Linda should have been overjoyed, should have been hanging on to Johnny for all she was worth, shouldn't have wanted him out of her sight. But she hadn't seen Johnny since he sat up and she ran away with the others. Old Doc Evans was with her in her father's house taking care of her. He didn't leave her until Johnny and Skeeter and Doc Grandtoul left the Lucky Lode. He met them just as they crossed the street towards the hotel.

"Doc," said Johnny, "how is Linda? Does she want to see me now?"

Doc Evans shook his head. "Sorry, son. She seems scared to death of you; keeps saying it ain't right you should be living. A dead man ought to stay dead."

"I don't understand that at all," said Johnny, scratching his curly head. "You'd think she'd be thanking God I'm up and jumping."

"She's in a state of shock, son," said Doc Evans. Why don't you try to see her tomorrow, when she'll probably be recovering? After all, it ain't every day a tender young girl sees her boyfriend rise from his death bed."

Doc Evans spoke to Doc Grandtoul. "You've created quite a sensation, to put it mildly. How do you plan to cap what you did tonight?"

Grandtoul lifted his hands, and the crowd fell silent. He looked impressive as Lucifer himself with the light streaming out from a window of the Lucky Lode on his pale handsome face and glistening off his hair and eyes, which were black as malapai rock. His rich baritone boomed out, "Friends, I came to you out of the desert with this miraculous means of revitalizing the dead. I intend eventually to go East. I expect to find fame and fortune there. But I'm in no hurry for it. I don't want to sound like a preacher, but I really am more interested in benefiting mankind than in gaining all the wealth of the world. It makes me happier to think about reuniting you with your beloved dead than in making personal gains. Your happiness is mine.

"So, tomorrow, after I've rested, I'll explain more of what I intend to do. I can't promise you all the dead in your cemetery will be brought back to life. That depends on how they died and how long they've been dead. But I can assure you that if any of those who were taken away from you can be brought back by my revitalizing machine, they will walk once more among you.

"And, to show you my heart is in the right place, I assure you that I will not take one red cent for doing this. I will do everything for free. So you can see that I am not some charlatan who intends to take you for all you have. Good night!"

He walked away with Johnny and Skeeter, leaving behind

him not wild shouts of joy but a silence. Even then, some of the people in Acheron were beginning to see what emptying the graveyard might mean to them.

Late next morning Linda Beeman walked into the lobby of Mrs. Lundgren's hotel. She wanted to speak to Johnny Addeson, but she was told by Mrs. Lundgren she'd have to wait her turn. Johnny was busy working as Doc Grandtoul's secretary. He and Skeeter were ushering in people who wanted to see the doctor. The doctor had rented a room next to Johnny's and was giving interviews to those who wanted to speak to him in private.

Linda spoke to everybody in the crowded lobby. Half of Acheron seemed to be waiting to talk to the doctor. All seemed to be very nervous. As Linda was the last to come, she wasn't called upstairs until noon.

When she entered Johnny's room, she found Johnny and Skeeter and Doc Grandtoul seated around a table. A large carpet-bag was by the doctor's feet.

"Johnny," said Linda, "I'd like to speak to you alone."

"You're not desperate to talk to me?" said Doc Grandtoul. "You're the first."

He rose. "Come along, Skeeter. We'll wet our whistles at the Lucky Lode. Watch that bag, Johnny. It contains all our worldly wealth."

Linda spoke before the doctor could close the door behind him. "Is it true that tomorrow you're going to raise the dead?"

"I'm no miracle-maker," he answered. "Those who are well-preserved will benefit by the scientific means I use. Those who are not, well"—he bowed his head for a second and then continued—"tomorrow I will bring life to the departed and joy into the hearts of the bereaved."

He smiled, bowed, and left. Johnny said, "How're you feeling now, Linda?"

"I'm all over the shock now," she said. She paused, breathed deeply as if to gain strength for what she was going to say, and then spoke. "Johnny, do you think Doctor Grandtoul is doing right by raising the dead?"

"Right?" he said. "Of course! Why, if it wasn't for him I'd be six feet under! You wouldn't like that, would you?"

"No," she said. "Only . . ."

"Only what? What's eating you? I thought you loved me!"

Linda sat down and frowned as if she were thinking deeply. Finally, she said, "Of course I love you. Didn't I tell you so a week ago? And weren't we going to announce our engagement this Sunday after church? But . . . well, Johnny, you didn't know this, but I was engaged to Roy Canton only six months ago. We were going to be married, and . . ."

"What about it?" he said. "You didn't marry him. And you're going to marry me, right?"

"Roy Canton is dead," she said quietly, her wide blue eyes fixed on his face. "He died of fever less than a week after we announced our engagement. He's buried in the cemetery here."

Johnny paled. He swallowed several times and then managed to find his voice. "You don't mean you want him back?"

Suddenly, Linda began weeping. "I don't know what I want!" she sobbed. "When Roy died, I thought I'd die, too. Then I met you. And I fell in love. I wasn't being unfaithful to Roy. You can't be unfaithful to the dead. They're gone; they're never coming back. You're living and can't go on acting as if the dead were just away on a short visit and will be home next week. But now, now, I don't know! I love you, but I never quit loving Roy. And if he comes back, then I won't know what to do! I'll have two living men that I love. And . . . and I don't know what to do!"

Johnny, choking, said, "Maybe I could talk Doc into not raising Roy."

"No, you don't!" said Linda fiercely. "That wouldn't be fair!"

"What am I supposed to do?" said Johnny. "Wait around while you make up your mind? Who *do* you love, Roy or me?"

"If somebody had asked me that yesterday I'd have told him I love you as I love the living. And Roy as I love the dead. But now . . ."

"In other words," said Johnny bitterly, "you'll wait until Roy can ask you again, and then you'll make up your mind which of us you want."

Linda began crying again. Johnny's face twisted as if somebody had stuck a knife in him.

And then he shouted, "There's no use crying, Linda! Roy isn't going to come back from the dead!"

Linda rose from the chair and took a step towards Johnny.

"What do you mean?"

Johnny bit his lip and started to turn away. But Linda caught him by the shoulder and, with a strength surprising for such a small woman, spun him around to face her.

"What do you mean by saying he isn't going to come back from the dead?"

"I'll give it to you straight, Linda." said Johnny. "Doc Grandtoul can't any more put life into a corpse than you or I can!"

Linda gave a little shriek and swayed back and forth for a minute. Johnny caught her in his arms and pulled her to him.

"Oh, Linda, darling, don't be mad at me! I'm a cheat, a liar, a crook! And Skeeter and Doc Grandtoul are cheats, liars, and crooks, too! This whole business is a fraud!"

He dropped his arms from around her and began pacing around the room while he talked loudly and furiously. He would not look directly at her. He seemed to be ashamed and to be afraid he might see scorn on her face.

"I met Doc and Skeeter about six months ago," he said. "In Jumpoff, Nevada. I'd been prospecting and hadn't had any luck. I was broke and hungry. Doc took me in, fed me, clothed me, taught me to be a good poker player. He and Skeeter were dealing for the house for the poker games at the High Stepper Saloon. But Doc wasn't satisfied. He wanted to make more money and faster. He's a great reader, is Doc, well educated. In fact, he's a real doctor, got his M.D. from an Eastern university, though he comes from an old New Orleans family.

"Doc had read something in one of his history books that gave him an idea. It seems that in the Middle Ages there was a band of sharpers that traveled from village to village, announcing they intended to raise the dead from the local cemetery. And things happened there and then just like they did here and now.

Nobody was anxious for the dead to come back. In fact, they were determined they wouldn't come back. Why? Because they'd cause too much consternation and turmoil, make too many problems.

"Doc said people hadn't changed a bit since the 13th century. We have gunpowder and steam trains and telegraph and gas lights. But people are just as superstitious and gullible as in the old days. They don't want their lives disrupted any more than can be helped.

"So Doc, who's a smart man even if he is as crooked as a snake's path, made some hollow wax bullets with red dye in the hollows. When they're fired, the wax doesn't hurt the man it hits, just stings. And the wax just spreads out and splatters the red dye so it looks like a bullet wound."

Linda had seated herself on a chair. She had been staring at him as if she could not understand what he was telling her. But when he paused for breath, she said, "What about Doc Evans? He pronounced you dead. How'd you fool him?"

Johnny, still not looking at her, grinned crookedly: He said, "Skeeter and I always travel ahead of Doc Grandtoul. We stop in a town and look it over. If the local doctor can be bribed or if there ain't no doctors, we stay. Acheron was a setup for us. Old Doc Evans hasn't much money, and he likes his whiskey too well. He agreed to go along with us if we gave him a good cut of the loot. He said he could send his grandson through medical school with the money and have enough to retire on, too."

"Then the whole quarrel over me was arranged by you and Skeeter?"

For the first time since he had started talking, Johnny looked directly at her. Desperately, he said, "Yes! But I wasn't fooling when I said I loved you! I do love you!"

"And just what did you expect me to do when you had to leave town before everybody found out you were a fraud?" she said scornfully. "Go with you? A cheat and a liar!"

"Now, honey," said Johnny, "if you'll think about it, you'll remember that Doc said he'd raise only those that the revitalizing machine can raise. And since it can't raise anybody, well . . . And he also said he wouldn't take a red cent for raising anybody. He won't, either. He's just taken money not to raise certain dead people. Nothing really dishonest in that. Like Doc says, you can't cheat an honest man."

"I don't know what you mean," she said.

"Here's what I mean," said Johnny angrily as he picked up the carpetbag and dumped its contents on the top of the table. "See all this money? Piles and piles of money? This all comes from the people that saw Doc this morning.

"Here's five hundred from rich Mr. Baggs, the banker. Who'd think he was so anxious to make sure his dead partner didn't climb out of the grave and demand his half of the bank back, hah?

"And here's a hundred from Mrs. Tanner. Her first husband, I understand, died under rather mysterious circumstances. And it wasn't much later that she married her foreman. She must have good reason not to want the old boy to appear and clear up just how he did die.

"And here's two hundred from old Mr. Krank. He's about ready to be buried himself, but he wants his last few days to be peaceful and quiet. Which they wouldn't be if Mrs. Krank's tongue was freed from the silence of the tomb. She was quite a shrew.

"And here's five hundred, a contribution of a hundred each from the sons and daughters of Silas Johnson. He was a tyrant and a hypochondriac. Besides, he might want the inheritance back.

"And here's . . . well, why go on? It's the same story in every town we've come to."

"It's not a very nice story," Linda said. "But you've not answered me. What did you expect me to do when you had to leave town?"

"I was going to tell you as soon as I could get the nerve. But I was afraid you wouldn't want anything to do with me when I told you the truth."

"What about Doc Grandtoul and Skeeter?" she said. "Did they know you were going to tell me?"

"No, I supposed they'd be mad at me. However, they couldn't do much about it. Anyway, they've got about as much money as they'll get out of Acheron. They could go on and get another partner somewhere else."

"And how," she said sarcastically, "did you expect to keep from being lynched when people found out they'd been cheated?"

"Well," he said slowly, "I was hoping you'd go with me to some other town. We could get a fresh start there. I can't stay here. We'll have to leave tomorrow. Maybe tonight."

"You must be crazy!" she said. "I can't just run off and leave my father like that! I might go away with you, but not before I explain to my father. But I don't think he'd like me to marry a man like you. You might want to go back to cheating people."

"Don't say that, Linda. I'll admit I made a mistake. But Doc was so nice to me, and I really didn't know we'd be hurting people so much."

Linda walked up to Johnny and stood in front of him and looked him in the eye.

"Johnny, if you'll tell everybody in Acheron what you've done, and say you're sorry, and give them their money back, I'll marry you."

"Use your horse sense," said Johnny. "If I did that, I couldn't ever settle down here. Who'd trust his horses to a man like me? And you couldn't hold your head high in this town, because you'd be the wife of that sharper Johnny Addeson. Give me a chance to straighten this out. I'll go talk with Doc and Skeeter. We'll fix this up somehow. I swear it! And you and I'll be able to live here the rest of our lives. And I'll be good to you, Linda. Good to you and good for this town. You'll be proud of me."

"All right," said Linda. "I'll give you a chance. I do want to live here. And I don't want anybody scorning you or me. Or our children."

Johnny smiled like a kid who's been given a sackful of candy for free. He picked up the bag and scooped the money into it and said, "I think Doc'll be able to help me out of this jam. He's a sharper, and he likes to take a dishonest sucker. But he isn't mean. He really does have a good heart. If anybody's smart enough to figure this out, he is."

He kissed Linda lightly on the lips and then ran out of the room.

Linda sat down again and waited. After a while she rose and went to the window to look out. She was just in time to see Johnny and Skeeter and Doc Grandtoul come out of the saloon across the street. Johnny was still holding the bag of money, and all three looked grim. Linda couldn't hear what they were saying, but they seemed to be arguing. They were talking and waving their hands when they walked into the livery stable.

Linda didn't leave the window. In about half an hour Johnny and Skeeter came out of the stable. Johnny was grinning. Neither of the two had the bag of money. They walked down the street and stopped in front of the Lucky Lode to talk to Doc Evans. The three talked earnestly for about ten minutes, but when some men joined them they quit talking to each other and joined in the general conversation.

The sound of a shot reached Linda through the half-opened window. The men on the street looked startled, milled around for a moment and then ran towards the stable. Linda raced down the hall and down the steps to the street. When she was halfway to the stable, she heard what the whole town of Acheron knew by then.

Doc Grandtoul was dead. He had accidentally shot himself.

Some stories have happy endings. Any story of young love should have a happy ending. It means two young citizens settling down in a town and raising more happy young citizens. And this was what happened in Acheron after the uproar over Doc Grandtoul's sudden and sad demise had quieted down. Doc Grandtoul was pronounced dead by Doc Evans, and the burial took place next day.

Only Linda thought it was peculiar that, when the coffin lid was closed over Doc Grandtoul, Doc Evans was the sole person present. And she noticed that Skeeter left town the same day. She didn't think it was so peculiar that not a word was said about the money paid to Doc Grandtoul. Those who had paid were not going to raise a fuss. Everybody pulled a long face and said what a pity it was that only Doc Grandtoul knew how to operate his machine. But very few moped around because of what had happened.

For a long time Linda never opened her mouth to Johnny about the incident of the revitalizing machine. She was satisfied that the result had been to make her happy. However, one thing bothered her. And one night, years later, when she and Johnny were sitting before the fireplace, after putting the kids to bed, Linda said, unexpectedly, "Johnny, what happened to those people who pronounced you dead in all those towns you three scoundrels fleeced? Weren't they left to face everybody and be branded as sharpers just as Doc Evans would have been if Doc Grandtoul hadn't been killed?"

Johnny was startled, but after coughing a few times he managed to say, "I'm sorry to say that we didn't worry about them."

"If Doc Grandtoul had had an 'accident' in every town," she said, "nobody would have been left holding the bag."

Linda looked into the fireplace a moment, and then she said, "I wonder where Doc Grandtoul is now?"

Johnny pretended to misunderstand her.

"I don't know, darling. I'll bet he went to the Good Place. He brought us together, didn't he?"

The King of the Beasts

The biologist was showing the distinguished visitor through the zoo and laboratory.

"Our budget," he said, "is too limited to re-create all known extinct species. So we bring to life only the higher animals, the beautiful ones that were wantonly exterminated. I'm trying, as it were, to make up for brutality and stupidity. You might say that man struck God in the face every time he wiped out a branch of the animal kingdom."

He paused and they looked across the moats and the force fields. The quagga wheeled and galloped, delight and sun flashing off his flanks. The sea otter poked his humorous whiskers from the water. The gorilla peered from behind bamboo. Passenger pigeons strutted. A rhinoceros trotted like a dainty battleship. With gentle eyes a giraffe looked at them, then resumed eating leaves.

"There's the dodo. Not beautiful but very droll. And very helpless. Come, I'll show you the re-creation itself."

In the great building, they passed between rows of tall and wide tanks. They could see clearly through the windows and the jelly within.

"Those are African Elephant embryos," said the biologist. "We plan to grow a large herd and then release them on the new government preserve."

"You positively radiate," said the distinguished visitor. "You really love the animals, don't you?"

"I love all life."

"Tell me," said the visitor, where do you get the data for recreation?"

"Mostly skeletons and skins from the ancient museums. Excavated books and films that we succeeded in restoring and then translating. Ah, see those huge eggs? The chicks of the giant moa are growing within them. There, almost ready to be taken from the tank, are tiger cubs. They'll be dangerous when grown but will be confined to the preserve."

The visitor stopped before the last of the tanks.

"Just one?" he said. "What is it?"

"Poor little thing," said the biologist, now sad. "It will be so alone. But I shall give it all the love I have."

"Is it so dangerous?" said the visitor. "Worse than elephants, tigers, and bears?"

"I had to get special permission to grow this one," said the biologist. His voice quavered.

The visitor stepped sharply back from the tank. He said, "Then it must be . . . But you wouldn't dare!"

The biologist nodded.

"Yes. It's a man."

Riverworld

Tom Mix had fled on Earth from furious wives, maddened bulls, and desperate creditors. He'd fled on foot, on horse, and in cars. But this was the first time, on his native planet or on the Riverworld, that he had fled in a boat.

It sailed down-River and downwind swiftly, rounding a bend with the pursuer about fifty yards behind. Both craft, the large chaser and the small chased, were bamboo catamarans. They were well-built vessels, though there wasn't a metal nail in them: double-hulled, fore-and-aft rigged and flourishing spinnakers. The sails were made of bamboo fibre.

The sun had two hours to go before setting. People were grouped by the great mushroom-shaped stones lining the banks. It would be some time before the grailstones would roar and spout blue electricity, energy which would be converted in the cylinders on top of the stones into matter. That is, into the evening meal and also, liquor, tobacco, marijuana, and dreamgum. But they had nothing else to do at this time except to lounge around, talk, and hope something exciting might happen.

They would soon be gratified.

The bend which Mix's boat had rounded revealed that the

mile-wide River behind him had suddenly become a three-mile wide lake ahead. There were hundreds of boats there, all filled with fishers who'd set their cylinders on the stones and then put out to augment their regular diet with fish. So many were the craft that Mix suddenly found that there was even less room to maneuver than in the narrower stretch of water behind him.

Tom Mix was at the tiller. Ahead of him on the deck were two other refugees, Bithniah and Yeshua. Both were Hebrew, tied together by blood and religion though separated by twelve hundred years and sixty generations. That made much difference. In some ways Bithniah was less a stranger to Mix than she was to Yeshua; in some ways, Yeshua was closer to Mix than to the woman.

All three, at the moment, shared bruises and contusions given by the same man, Kramer. He wasn't in the boat following their wake, but his men were. If they captured the three, they'd return them to "The Hammer," as Kramer had been called on Earth and was here. If they couldn't take the refugees alive, they'd kill them.

Mix glanced behind him. Every bit of sail on the two-masted catamaran was up. It was slowly gaining on the smaller craft. Mix's boat should have been able to keep its lead, its crew was far lighter, but, during the escape, three spears had gone through the sail. The holes were small, but their effect had accumulated during the chase. In about fifteen minutes the prow of the chaser could be touching the stern of his craft. However, Kramer's men wouldn't try to board from the bow of their boat. They'd come up along-side, throw bone grappling hooks, draw the vessels together, and then swarm over the side.

Ten warriors against three, one a woman, one a man who would run away but who refused on principle to fight, and one a man who'd been in many duels and mass combats but wouldn't last long against such numbers.

People in a fishing boat shouted angrily at him as he took the catamaran too near them. Mix grinned and swept from his head his ten-gallon white hat, made of woven straw fibres painted with a rare pigment. He saluted them with the hat and then donned it. He wore a long white cloak made of towels fastened together with magnetic tabs, a white towel fastened around his waist, and high-heeled cowboy boots of white River-serpent leather. The latter were, in this situation, both an affectation and a handicap. But now that fighting was close, he needed bare feet to get a better grip on the slippery deck.

He called to Yeshua to take over the tiller. His face rigid, unresponsive to Mix's grin, Yeshua hastened to him. He was five feet ten inches tall, exactly Mix's height, but considered tall among the people of his time and place on Earth. His hair was black but with an undercoating which shone reddish in the sun. It was cut just below the nape of the neck. His body was thin but wiry, covered only by a black loincloth; his chest was matted with curly black hair. The face was long and thin, ascetic, that of a beardless scholarly-looking Jewish youth. His eyes were large and dark brown with flecks of green, inherited, he'd said, from Gentile ancestors. The people of his native land, Galilee, were much mixed since it had been both a trade route and a road for invaders for several thousand years.

Yeshua could have been Mix's twin, a double who'd not been eating or sleeping as well as his counterpart. There were slight differences between them. Yeshua's nose was a trifle longer, his lips a little thinner, and Mix had no greenish flecks in his eyes nor red underpigment in his hair. The resemblance was still so great that it took people some time to distinguish between them—as long as they didn't speak.

It was this that had caused Mix to nickname Yeshua as "Handsome."

Now Mix grinned again. He said, "Okay, Handsome. You handle her while I get rid of these."

He sat down and took off his boots, then rose and crossed the deck to drop them and his cloak into a bag hanging from a shroud. When he took over the tiller, he grinned a third time.

"Don't look so grim. We're going to have some fun."

Yeshua spoke in a deep baritone in a heavily accented English.

"Why don't we go ashore? We're far past Kramer's territory now. We can claim sanctuary."

"Claiming's one thing," Mix drawled in a baritone almost as deep. "Getting's another."

"You mean that these people'll be too scared of Kramer to let us take refuge with them?"

"Maybe. Maybe not. I'd just as soon not have to find out. Anyway, if we beach, so will they, and they'll skewer us before the locals can interfere."

"We could run for the hills."

"No. We'll give them a hard time before we take a chance on that. Get back there, help Bithniah with the ropes."

Yeshua and the woman handled the sail while Mix began zig-zagging the boat. Glances over his shoulder showed that the pursuer was following his wake. It could have continued on a straight line in the middle of the River, and so gotten ahead of Mix's craft. But its captain was afraid that one of the zigs or zags would turn out to be a straight line the end of which would terminate at the bank.

Mix gave an order to slacken the sail a little. Bithniah protested. "They'll catch us sooner!"

Mix said, "They think they will. Do as I say. The crew never argues with the master, and I'm the captain."

He smiled and told her what he hoped to do. She shrugged, indicating that if they were going to be boarded, it might as well be sooner as later. It also hinted that she'd known all along that he was a little mad and this was now doubly confirmed.

Yeshua, however, said, "I won't spill blood."

"I know I can't count on you in a fight," Mix said. "But if you help handle the boat, you're indirectly contributing to blood-shed. Put that in your philosophical pipe and smoke it."

Surprisingly, Yeshua grinned. Or perhaps his reaction wasn't so unexpected. He delighted in Mix's Americanisms, and he also liked to discuss subtleties in ethics. But he was going to be too busy to engage in an argument just now.

Mix looked back again. The fox—the chaser was the fox and he was the rabbit—was now almost on his tail. There was a gap of twenty feet between them, and two men at the bows of the double hull were poised, ready to hurl their spears. However, the rapid rise and fall of the decks beneath them would make an accurate cast very difficult.

Mix shouted to his crew—*some* crew!—and swung the tiller hard over. The prow had been pointed at an angle to the righthand bank of the River. Now it turned away suddenly, the boat leaning, the boom of the sail swinging swiftly. Mix ducked as it sang past his head. Bithniah and Yeshua clung to ropes to keep from being shot off the deck. The righthand hull lifted up, clearing the water for a few seconds.

For a moment, Mix thought the boat was going to capsize. Then it righted, and Bithniah and Yeshua were paying out the ropes. Behind him he heard shouting, but he didn't look back. Ahead was more shouting as the crews of two small one-masted fishing boats voiced their anger and fear.

Mix's vessel ran between the two boats in a lane only thirty feet wide. That closed quickly as the two converged. Their steersmen were trying to turn them away, but they had been headed inward on a collision path. Normally, they would have straightened this out, but now the stranger was between them, and its prow was angling toward the boat on the port.

Mix could see the twisted faces of the men and women on this vessel. They were anguished lest his prow crash into their starboard side near their bow. Slowly, it seemed too slowly, the prow of that boat turned. Then its boom began swinging as it was caught in the dead zone.

A woman's voice rose above the others, shrilling an almost unintelligible English at him. A man threw a spear at him, a useless and foolish action but one which would vent some of his anger. The weapon soared within a foot of Mix's head and splashed into the water on the starboard. Mix glanced back. The pursuer had fallen into the trap. Now, if only he could keep from being caught in his own.

His vessel slid by the boat to port, and the end of its boom almost struck the shrouds of the mast tied to the starboard edge of the deck. And then his boat was by.

Behind him, the shouting and screaming increased. The crash of wood striking wood made him smile. He looked swiftly back. The big catamaran had smashed bows first into the side of the fishing boat on his right. It had turned the much smaller single-hulled bamboo vessel around at right angles to its former course. The crew of both boats had been knocked to the deck, including the steersmen. Three of Kramer's men had gone over the side and were struggling in the water. Count them out. That left seven to deal with.

ᘓ Two ᘓ

The rabbit became a fox; the attacked, the attacker. His craft turned as swiftly as Mix dared take it and began beating against the wind toward the two that had collided. This took some time, but Kramer's vessel was in no shape to counter-maneuver. Both it and the fishing boat had stove-in hulls and were settling down slowly. Water was pouring in through the hulls. The captain of the catamaran was gesturing, his mouth open, his voice drowned by all those on his boat and the others, plus the yelling from the many other crafts. His men must have heard him, though, or interpreted his furious signs. They picked themselves up, got their weapons, and started toward the vessel they'd run into. Mix didn't understand why they were going to board it. That would be deserting a sinking ship for another, jumping from the boiling kettle into the fire. Perhaps it was just a reflex, a mindless reaction. They were angry, and they meant to take it out on the nearest available persons.

If so, they were frustrated. The two men and two women on the fisher leaped overboard and began swimming. Another boat sailed toward them to pick them up. Its sail slid down as it neared the swimmers, and men leaned over its side to extend helping hands. Two of Kramer's men, having gotten on the smaller vessel, ran to the other side and heaved spears at the people in the water.

"They must be out of their mind," Mix muttered. "They'll have this whole area at their throats."

That was agreeable to him. He could leave the pursuers to the mercy of the locals. But he didn't intend to. He had a debt to pay. Unlike most debts, this would be a pleasure to discharge.

He told Yeshua to take over the tiller, and he got a war boomerang from the weapons box on the deck. It was two feet long, fashioned by sharp flint from a piece of heavy white oak. One of its ends turned at an angle of 30 degrees. A formidable weapon in the hand of a skilled thrower, it could break a man's arm even if hurled from five hundred feet away.

The weapons box contained three chert-headed axes, four more boomerangs, several oak spear shafts with flint tips, and two leather slings and two bags of sling-stones. Mix braced himself by the box, waited until his boat had drawn up alongside the enemy's on the portside, and he threw the boomerang. The up-and-down movement of the deck made calculation difficult. But the boomerang flew toward its target, the sun flashing off its whirling pale surface, and it struck a man in the neck. Despite the noise of voices, Mix faintly heard the crack as the neck broke. The man fell sidewise on the deck; the boomerang slid against the railing.

The dead man's comrades yelled and turned toward Mix.

The captain recalled the four men aboard the sinking fisher. They threw clubs and spears, and Mix and his crew dropped flat onto the deck. Some of the missiles bounced off the wood or stuck quivering in it. The nearest, a spear with a fire-hardened wooden point, landed a few inches from Yeshua's ear and slid off into the water.

Mix jumped up, braced himself, and when the starboard side of the craft rolled downward, hurled a spear. It fell short of its mark, the chest of a man, but it pierced his foot. He screamed and yanked the point loose from the deck, but he didn't have courage enough to withdraw it from his foot. He hobbled around the deck, shrilling his pain, until two men got him down and yanked the shaft out. The head was dislodged from the shaft and remained half-sticking out from the top of his foot.

Meanwhile, the second fisher, the one which Mix's boat had almost struck, had come alongside the sinking fisher. Three men leaped onto it and began securing ropes to lash the two boats together. Several rowboats and three canoes came up to the fisher, and their occupants climbed aboard it. Evidently, the locals were angry about the attack and intended to take immediate measures. Mix thought they would have been smarter to have waited until the big catamaran sank and then speared the crew members as they swam. On the other hand, by attacking Kramer's men, they were getting deeply involved. This could be the start of war. In which case, the refugees would be welcomed here.

However, a catamaran, because of its two hulls, didn't sink easily. It might even be able to get away, if not back to its homeport, at least out of this area. The locals didn't want this to happen.

The enemy captain, seeing what was coming, had ordered his men to attack. Leading them, he boarded the sinking fisher, crossed it, and hurled himself at the nearest man on the fisher. A woman whirled a sling above her head, loosed one end, and the stone smashed into the captain's solar plexus. He fell on his back, unconscious or dead.

Another of Kramer's warriors fell with a spear sticking through his arm. His comrade stumbled over him and received the point of a spear with the full weight of its wielder behind it.

The woman who'd slung the stone staggered backward with a spear sticking out of her chest and toppled into the water.

Then both sides closed, and there was a melee.

Yeshua brought the catamaran up alongside the portside of Kramer's while Bithniah and Mix let the sail down and then threw grappling hooks onto the railing. While Bithniah and Yeshua sweated to tie the two boats together, Tom Mix used his sling. He had practiced on land and water for hundreds of hours with this weapon, and so he worked smoothly with great speed and finesse. He had to wait until an enemy was separated from the crowd to prevent accidentally hitting a local. Three times he struck his target. One stone caught a man in the side of his neck. Another hit the base of a spine. The third smashed a kneecap, and the writhing man was caught and held down by some locals while a flint knife slashed his jugular.

Mix threw a spear which plunged deep into a man's thigh. Then, gripping a heavy axe, he leaped onto the catamaran and his axe rose and fell twice on the backs of heads.

The two enemy survivors tried to dive overboard. Only one made it. Mix picked up the boomerang from the deck, lifted it to throw at the bobbing head, then lowered it. Boomerangs were too hard to come by to waste on someone who was no longer dangerous.

Suddenly, except for the groaning of the wounded and the weeping of a woman, there was silence. Even the onlookers, now coming swiftly toward the scene of the battle, were voiceless. The battlers looked pale and spent. The fire was gone from them.

Mix liked to be dressed for the occasion, and this was one of victory. He returned to his boat, winked at Yeshua and Bithniah, and put on his boots and cloak. His ten-gallon hat had remained on his head throughout. He returned to the fisher, removed his hat with a flourish, grinned, and spoke.

"Tom Mix, Esquire, at your service, ladies and gentlemen. My heartfelt thanks for your help, and my apologies for any inconvenience our presence caused you."

The captain of the rescue boat said, "Bare bones o' God, I scarce comprehend your speech. Yet it seems to be somewhat English."

Mix put his hat back on and rolled his eyes as if asking for help from above.

"Still in the seventeenth century! Well, at least I can understand your lingo a little bit."

He spoke more slowly and carefully. "What's your handle, amigo?"

"Handle? Amigo?"

"Your name, friend. And who's your boss? I'd like to offer myself as a mercenary. I need him, and I think he's going to need me."

"John Wickel Stafford is the lord-mayor of New Albion," a woman said. She and others were looking strangely at him and Yeshua.

He grinned and said, "No, he's not my twin brother, or any

sort of brother to me, aside from the kinship that comes from being human. And you know how thin that is. He was born about one thousand eight hundred and eighty years before me. In Palestine. Which is a hell of a long way off from my native Pennsylvania. It's only a trick of fate he resembles me so. A lucky one for him, otherwise he might not've slipped the noose Kramer'd tied around his neck."

Apparently, some of his audience understood some of what he'd said. The trouble was not so much vocabulary, though there were some significant differences, as with the intonation and the pronunciation. Theirs somewhat resembled the speech of some Australians he'd met. God knew what they thought his was like.

"Any of you know Esperanto?" he said.

The captain said, "We've heard of that tongue, sir. It is being taught by some of that new sect, the Church of the Second Chance, or so I understand. So far, though, none has come into this area."

"Too bad. So we'll make do with what we have. My friends and I have had a tough time the last couple of days. We're tired and hungry. I'd like permission to stay in your spread for a few days before we go on down the River. Or maybe join up with you. Do you think your boss, uh, lord-mayor, would object?"

"Far from it, sir," the woman said. "He welcomes good fighting men and women in the hope they'll stay. And he rewards them well. But tell us, those men, Kramer's they must be, why were they so hot for your blood? They chased you here, yet they knew they were forbidden to come here under pain of death."

"That's a long story, ma'am," Mix said.

He smiled. His smile was very attractive, and he knew it. The woman was pretty, a short blonde with a buxom figure, and possibly she was unattached at the moment or thinking of being so. Certainly, there was nothing shy about her.

"You evidently are acquainted with Kramer the Hammer, Kramer the Burner. These two, Bithniah and Yeshua, were prisoners of his, ripe for the stake because they were heretics, according to his lights, and that's what counts in his land. Also they were

Jewish, which made it worse. I got them loose, along with a bunch of others. We three were the only ones made it to a boat. The rest you know."

The captain decided he might as well introduce himself.

"I am Robert Nickard. This woman is Angela Doverton. Be not deceived by her immodest manner, Master Mix. She talks boldly and without regard to her sex, unmindful of her place. She is my wife, though there is neither giving nor taking of marriage in heaven or hell."

Angela smiled and winked at Mix. Fortunately, the eye was turned away from Nickard.

"As for this business of heretics, New Albion does not care—officially, anyway—what the religion of a man or woman be. Or indeed if he be an atheist, though how any could be after having been resurrected from the dead, I cannot understand. We welcome all as citizens, so they be hard-working and dutiful, clean and comparatively sober. We even accept Jews."

"That must be quite a change from when you were alive," Mix said.

Quickly, before Nickard could comment on that, he said, "Where do we report, sir?"

Nickard gave him directions. Mix told his crew to return to their craft. They untied the ropes, retrieved the grappling hooks, hoisted sail, and departed down-River. Not, however, before Mix saw Angela Doverton slip him another wink. He had already decided to steer clear of her, desirable though she was. He didn't believe in making love to another man's mate. On the other hand, if she were to leave Nickard, which seemed likely, then . . . no, she seemed like a troublemaker. Still . . .

Behind him the business of getting the two damaged boats in to shore before they sank had begun. The lone survivor of the Kramer force had been pulled out of the water and was being taken, bound, to the shore. Mix wondered what would happen to him, not that he cared.

The woman Bithniah steered the catamaran while Yeshua took care of the ropes. Tom Mix stood in the prow, one hand on a shroud to support himself, his long white cloak flapping. He must seem a strange and dramatic figure to the locals. At least, he hoped so. Wherever he was, if he found drama lacking, he drummed up some.

✑ Three ✑

As almost everywhere in the never-ending valley, both sides of the River were bordered with plains. These were usually from a mile to a mile and half wide. They were as unbumpy as the floor of a house but sloped gently toward the foothills. A shortbladed grass that no amount of trampling could kill covered them. Here and there were some trees.

Beyond the plains, the hills started out as mounds twenty feet high and sixty feet broad. As they neared the mountains, they became broader and higher and finally converged. The hills were thick with forest. Eighty out of every hundred were usually the indestructible "irontrees," deep-rooted monsters the bark of which resisted fire and shrugged off the edge of even steel axes—though very few of these existed in this metal-poor world. Beneath the trees grew long-bladed grass and bamboo—some only two feet high, some over a hundred. Unlike every other area he'd been in, this lacked ash and yew trees and so the bow and arrow were seldom seen. Most of the bows were made from the mouth of a huge fish, but apparently the people here had not caught many of these. Even the bamboo here wasn't suitable for use as bows.

Beyond the hills, the mountains soared. The lower parts were rugged with small canyons and fissures and little plateaus. At the five-thousand-foot height, the mountains became unbroken cliffs, smooth as glass. Then they climbed straight up for another five thousand feet or leaned outward near the top. They were unclimbable. If a man wished to get to the valley on the other side of them, he'd have to follow The River, and that might take him years. The Rivervalley was a world-snake, winding down from the headwaters at the North Pole and around the South Pole and back up the other hemisphere to the mouth at the North Pole.

Or so it was said. Nobody had yet proved it.

In this area, unlike some he'd been in, huge vines encircled the trees and even some of the bamboo stands. From the vines grew perennial flowers of many sizes, shapes, and exhibiting every shade of the spectrum.

For ten thousand miles the Rivervalley would be a silent, frozen explosion of color. Then, just as abruptly as it had started, the trees would resume their unadorned ascetic green.

But this stretch of The River trumpeted a flourish of hue.

A mile from the scene of the battle, Mix ordered that Bithniah steer toward the lefthand bank. Presently, Yeshua lowered the sail, and the catamaran slid its nose up onto a slope of the bank. The three got off, and many hands among the crowd grabbed the hulls and pulled it entirely on land. Men and women surrounded the newcomers and asked many questions. Mix started to answer one from a good-looking woman when he was interrupted by soldiers. These wore fish-leather bone-reinforced helmets and cuirasses, modelled after those used in the time of Charles I and Oliver Cromwell. They carried small round shields of leather-covered oak and long stone-tipped or wooden-ended spears or heavy war-axes or big clubs. Thick fish-leather boots protected their legs to just above the knees.

Their ensign, Alfred Regius Swinford, heard Mix's report half-way through. Mix interrupted himself then, saying, "We're hungry. Couldn't we wait until we charge our buckets?"

He gestured at the nearest mushroom-shaped stone, six feet high and several feet broad. The bottoms of the grey cylinders of the bystanders were inserted in the depressions on its top.

"Buckets?" the ensign said. "We name them copias, stranger. Short for cornucopia. Give me your copias. We'll charge them for you, and you can fill your bellies after Lord Stafford's talked to you. I'll see that they're properly identified."

Mix shrugged. He was in no position to argue, though, like everybody else, he was uneasy if his "holy bucket" was out of his sight. The three walked among the soldiers across the plain toward a hill. They went past many one-room bamboo huts. On top of the hill was a larger circular wall of logs. They went through the gateway into a huge yard. The Council House, their destination, was a long triangular log building in the center of the stockade. There were many observation towers and a broad walkway behind the outer walls. The sharp-pointed logs towered above this, but windows and slits for defenders to throw spears or pour out burning fish oil on attackers were plentiful. There were also wooden cranes which could be swung over the walls to dump nets full of large rocks.

Mix saw ten large wooden tanks filled with water and sheds which he supposed held stores of dried fish and acorn bread and weapons.

Out of one of the sheds, though, came men carrying baskets of earth. These would be digging a secret underground tunnel to the outside for escape or for a rear attack on the enemy. It wasn't much of a secret if they allowed strangers to see evidence of it. He felt chilled momentarily. Perhaps no stranger who knew of the tunnel would be allowed to leave.

Mix said nothing. He might as well play dumb, though he doubted that the ensign would think he was that unobservant. No. He should try something, however weak.

"Digging a well," he said. "That's a good idea. If you're besieged, you needn't worry about water."

"Exactly," Swinford said. "We should have dug it a long time ago. But then we were shorthanded for a while."

Mix didn't think that he'd fooled the ensign, but at least he'd tried. By then the sun had reached the peaks of the western mountain range. A moment later it sank, and the valley thundered with the eruption of the copiastones along the banks. Dinner was ready.

Stafford and his council were sitting at a round table of pine on a platform at the far end of the hall. Between this and the entrance was a long rectangular table with many bamboo chairs around it. Trap doors in the ceiling were open to let in the light, but this was fading fast. Pine torches impregnated with fish oil had already been lit and set in brackets on the walls or in stands on the dirt floor. The smoke rose toward the high blackened beams and rafters, and the stench of fish heavied the air. Underlying it was another stink—unwashed human bodies. Mix thought that there might have been an excuse for this uncleanliness in seventeenth-century England, but there was none here. The River was within comfortable walking distance. However, he knew that old habits clung hard, despite which they were changing slowly. With the constant passage of people who came from cultures which did bathe frequently, a sense of cleanliness and the shame associated with uncleanliness were spreading. In ten or fifteen years these Englishmen would be soaping regularly in The River. Well, most of them would be, anyway. There were always persons in every culture who would think that water was for drinking only.

Actually, aside from the offensiveness of body odor and the aesthetics of a clean body, there was no reason why they should wash frequently. There were no diseases of the body on the Riverworld. Plenty of diseases of the mind, though.

The ensign halted below the platform and reported to Stafford. The others at the table, twenty in all, stared at the newcomers. Many smoked copia-supplied cigarettes or cigars, unknown to them in their time on Earth when pipes only were used.

Stafford rose from the table to greet his guests courteously. He was a tall man, six feet two inches, broad-shouldered, long-armed, slimly built. His face was long and narrow, his eyebrows very thick and tangled, his eyes grey, his nose long and pointed, his lips thin, his chin out-thrusting and deeply cleft. His brownish hair hung to just below his shoulders and was curled at the ends.

In a pleasant voice thick with a Northern burr—he was a native of Carlisle, near the Scottish border—he asked them to sit at the table. He offered them their choice of wine, whiskey, or liqueur. Mix, knowing that the supply was limited, took the offer as a good sign. Stafford would not be so generous with expensive commodities to those he thought were hostiles. Mix sniffed, smiled at the scent of excellent bourbon, and sipped. He would have liked to pour it down, but this would have meant that his hosts would have to offer him another immediately.

Stafford asked Tom Mix to make his own report. This involved a long tale, during which fires were lit in the two great hearths on each side of the central part of the hall. Mix noticed that some of those bringing in the wood were short, very swarthy Mongolianish men and women. These, he supposed, were from the other side of The River, which was occupied by Huns. From what he'd heard, these had been born about the time Attila had invaded Europe, the fifth century A.D. Whether they were slaves or refugees from across The River, he could not know.

Stafford and the others listened to Mix with only a few comments while they drank. Presently, their copias were brought in, and all ate. Tom was pleasantly surprised by this evening's offering of his bucket. It was Mexican: tacos, enchiladas, burritos, a bean salad, and the liquor was tequila with a slice of lemon and some salt. It made him feel more at home, especially when the tobacco turned out to be some slim-twisted dark cigars.

Stafford didn't seem to like the liquor he got. He smelled it, then looked around. Mix interpreted his expression correctly. He said, "Would you like to trade?"

The lord-mayor said, "What is it you have?"

This made for an extended explanation. Stafford had lived when North America was first being colonized by the English, but he knew very little of it. Also, in his time, Mexico was an area conquered by the Spanish, and he had almost no data on it. But after listening to Mix's lengthy exposition, he handed his cup to Mix.

Tom sniffed at it and said, "Well, I don't know what it is, but I ain't afraid of it. Here, try the tequila."

Stafford followed the recommended procedure: the drink at once succeeded by the salt and the lemon.

"Zounds! It feels as if fire were leaping from my ears!"

He sighed and said, "Most strange. But most pleasant and exhilarating. What about yours?"

Mix sipped. "Ah! I don't know what the hell brand it is! But it tastes great, though it's a little gross. Whatever its origin, it's wine—of a sort. Maybe it's what the ancient Babylonians used to push. Maybe it's Egyptian, maybe it's Malayan or early Japanese saki, rice wine. Did the Aztecs have wine? I don't know, but it's powerful stuff, and it's rank yet appealing.

"Tequila is a distilled spirit gotten from the heart-sap of the century or agave plant. Well, here's to international brotherhood, no discrimination against foreign alcohol, and your good health."

"Hear, hear!"

Having finished his supply from the copia, Stafford ordered a keg of lichen liquor in. This was composed of alcohol distilled from the green-blue lichen that grew on the mountain cliffs and then cut with water, the flavor provided by powdered dried leaves from the tree-vines. After quaffing half a cupful, Stafford said, "I don't know why Kramer's men were so eager to kill you that they dared trespass on my waters."

Speaking carefully and slowly, so that they could understand him easier, Mix began his story. Now and then Stafford nodded to an officer to give Mix another drink. Mix was aware that this generosity was not just based on hospitality. If Stafford got his guest drunk enough, he might, if he were a spy, say something he shouldn't. Mix, however, was a long way from having enough to make him loose-tongued. Moreover, he had nothing to hide. Well, not much.

"How far do you want me to go back in my story?"

Stafford laughed, and his slowly reddening eyes looked merry.

"For the present, omit your Earthy life. And condense it previously to your first meeting with Kramer."

"Well, ever since All Souls' Day"—one of the names for the day on which Earthpeople had first been raised from the dead— "I've been wandering down The River. Though I was born in 1880 A.D. in America and died in 1940, I wasn't resurrected among people of my own time and place. I found myself in an area occupied by fifteenth-century Poles. Across The River were some sort of American Indian pygmies. Until then I hadn't known that such existed, though the Cherokee Indians have legends of them. I know that because I'm part Cherokee myself."

That was a lie, one which a movie studio had originated to

glamorize him. But he'd said it so often that he half believed it. It couldn't hurt to spread it on a little.

Stafford belched, and said, "I thought when I first saw you that you had some redskin blood in you."

"My grandfather was a chief of the Cherokees," Mix said. He hoped that his English, Pennsylvania Dutch, and Irish ancestors would forgive him.

"Anyway, I didn't hang around the Poles very long. I wanted to get to some place where I could understand the language. I shook the dust off my feet and took off like a stripe-assed ape."

Stafford laughed and said, "What droll imagery!"

"It didn't take me long to find out there weren't any horses on this world, or any animals except man, earthworms, and fish. So I built me a boat. And I started looking for folks of my own time, hoping I'd run into people I'd known. Or people who'd heard of me. I had some fame during my lifetime; millions knew about me. But I won't go into that now.

"I figured out that if people were strung along The River according to when they'd been born, though there were many exceptions, me being one, the twentieth-century people ought to be near the River's mouth. That, as I found out, wasn't necessarily so. Anyway, I had about ten men and women with me, and we sailed with the wind and the current for, let's see, close to five years. Now and then we'd stop to rest or to work on land."

"Work?"

"As mercenaries. We picked up extra cigarettes, booze, good food. In return, we helped out people that needed helping real bad and had a good cause. Most of the men were veterans of wars on Earth and so were some of the women. I'm a graduate of Virginia Military Institute . . ."

Another movie prevarication.

"Virginia I've heard about," Stafford said. "But . . ."

Tom Mix had to pause in his narrative to ask just how much Stafford knew of history since his death. The Englishman replied that he'd gotten some information from a wandering Albanian who'd died in 1901 and a Persian who'd died in 1897. At least, he supposed they had those dates right. Both had been Moslems, which made it difficult to correlate their calendar with the Christian. Also, neither had known much about world history. One had mentioned that the American colonies had gained their independence after a war. He hadn't known whether or not to believe the man. It was so absurd.

"Canada remained loyal," Mix said. "I see I have a lot to tell you. Anyway, I fought in the Spanish-American War, the Boxer Rebellion, the Philippine Insurrection, and the Boer War. I'll explain what these were later."

Mix had fought in none of these, but what the hell. Anyway, he would have if he'd had a chance to do so. He'd deserted the US cavalry in his second hitch because he wanted to get to the front lines and the damned brass had kept him home.

"A couple of times we were captured by slavers when we landed at some seemingly friendly place. We escaped, but the time came when I was the only one left of the original group.

The rest were either killed or quit because they were tired of travelling. My lovely little Egyptian, a daughter of a Pharaoh . . . well, she was killed, too."

Actually, Miriam was the child of a Cairo shopkeeper and was born sometime in the eighteenth century. But he was a cowboy, and cowboys always embellished the truth a little. Maybe more than a little. Anyway, figuratively, she was a daughter of the Pharaohs. And what counted in this world, as in the last one, was not facts but what people believed were the facts.

He said, "Maybe I'll run into her again someday. The others, too. They could've just as well been re-resurrected down-River as up-River."

He paused, then said, "It's funny. Among the millions, maybe billions of faces I've seen while sailing along, I've not seen one I knew on Earth."

Stafford said, "I met a philosopher who calculated that there could be at least thirty-five billion people along The River."

Mix nodded.

"Yeah, I wouldn't be surprised. But you'd think that in five years just one . . . well, it's bound to happen someday. So, I built this last boat about five thousand miles back, a year ago. My new crew and I did pretty well until we put in at a small rocky island for a meal. We hadn't used our buckets for some time because we'd heard the people were mighty ornery in that area. But we were tired of eating fish and bamboo shoots and acorn bread from our stores. And we were out of cigarettes and the last booze we'd had had been long gone. We were aching for the good things of life. So, we took a chance on going ashore, and we lost. We were brought before the local high muckymuck, Kramer himself, a fat ugly guy from fifteenth-century Germany.

"Like a lot of nuts, and begging your pardon if there's any like him among you, he hadn't accepted the fact that this world isn't near what he thought the afterlife was going to be. He was a bigshot on Earth, a priest, an inquisitor. He'd burned a hell of a lot of men, women, and children after torturing them for the greater glory of God."

Yeshua, sitting near Mix, muttered something. Mix fell silent for a moment. He was not sure that he had not gone too far.

Although he had seen no signs of such, it was possible that Stafford and his people might just be as lunatic in their way as Kramer was in his. During their Terrestrial existence, most of the seventeenth-centurians had had a rock-fast conviction in their religious beliefs. Finding themselves here in the strange place neither heaven nor hell, they had suffered a great shock. Some of them had not yet recovered.

There were those adaptable enough to cast aside their former religion and seek the truth. But too many, like Kramer, had rationalized their environment. Kramer, for instance, maintained that this world was a purgatory. He had been shaken to find that not only Christians but all heathens were here. He had insisted that the teaching of the Church had been misunderstood on Earth. They had been deliberately perverted in their presentation by Satan-inspired priests. But he clearly saw The Truth now.

However, those who did not see the truth as he did must be shown it. Kramer's method of revelation, as on Earth, was the wheel and the fire.

When Mix had been told this, he had not argued with Kramer's theory. On the contrary, he was enthusiastic—outwardly—in offering his services. He did not fear death, because he knew that he would be resurrected twenty-four hours later elsewhere along The River. But he did not want to be stretched on the wheel and then burned.

He waited for his chance to escape.

One evening a group had been seized by Kramer as they stepped off a boat. Mix pitied the captives, for he had witnessed Kramer's means of changing a man's mind. Yet there was nothing he could do for them. If they were stupid enough to refuse to pretend that they agreed with Kramer, they must suffer.

"But this man Yeshua bothered me," Mix said. "In the first place, he looked too much like me. Having to see him burn would be like seeing myself in the flames. Moreover, he didn't get a chance to say yes or no. Kramer asked him if he was Jewish. Yeshua said he had been on Earth, but he now had no religion.

"Kramer said he would have given Yeshua a chance to become a convert, that is, believe as Kramer did. This was a lie, but Kramer is a mealy-mouthed slob who has to find justification for every rotten thing he does. He said that he gave Christians and all heathens a chance to escape the fire—except Jews. They were the ones who'd crucified Jesus, and they should all pay. Besides, a Jew couldn't be trusted. He'd lie to save his own skin.

"The whole boatload was condemned because they were all Jews. Kramer asked where they'd been headed, and Yeshua said they were looking for a place where nobody had ever heard of a Jew. Kramer said there wasn't any such place; God would find them out no matter where they went. Yeshua lost his temper and called Kramer a hypocrite and an anti-Christ. Kramer got madder than hell and told Yeshua he wasn't going to die as quickly as the others.

"About then, I almost got thrown into prison with them. Kramer had noticed how much we looked alike. He asked me if I'd lied to him when I told him I wasn't a Jew. How come I looked like a Jew if I wasn't? Of course, this was the first time he thought of me looking like a Jew, which I don't. If I was darker, I could pass for one of my Cherokee ancestors.

"So I grinned at him, although the sweat was pouring out of me so fast it was trickling down my legs, and I said that he had it backwards. Yeshua looked like a Gentile, that's why he resembled me. I used one of his own remarks to help me; I reminded him he'd said Jewish women were notoriously adulterous. So maybe Yeshua was half-Gentile and didn't know it.

"Kramer gave one of those sickening belly laughs of his; he drools until the spit runs down his chin when he's laughing. And he said I was right. But I knew my days were numbered. He'd get to thinking about my looks later, and he'd decide that I was lying. To hell with that, I thought, I'm getting out tonight.

"But I couldn't get Yeshua out of my mind. I decided that I wasn't just going to run like a cur with its tail between its legs. I was going to make Kramer so sick with my memory his pig's belly would ache like a boil every time he thought of me. That night, just as it began to rain, I killed the two guards with my axe and opened the stockade gates. But somebody was awake and gave the alarm. We ran for my boat, had to fight our way to it, and only Yeshua, Bithniah and I got away. Kramer must have given orders that the men who went after us had better not return without our heads. They weren't about to give up."

Stafford said, "God was good enough to give us eternal youth in this beautiful world. We are free from want, hunger, hard labor, and disease. Or should be. Yet men like Kramer want to turn this Garden of Eden into hell. Why? I do not know. One of these days, he'll be marching on us, as he has on the people to the north of his original area. If you would like to help us fight him, welcome!"

"I hate the murdering devil!" Mix said. "I could tell you things . . . never mind, you must know them."

"To my everlasting shame," Stafford replied. "I must confess that I witnessed many cruelties and injustices on Earth, and I not only did not protest, I encouraged them. I thought that law and order and religion, to be maintained, needed torture and persecution.

Yet I was often sickened. So when I found myself in a new world, I determined to start anew. What had been right and necessary on Earth did not have to be so here."

"You're an extraordinary man," Mix said. "Most people have continued to think exactly what they thought on Earth. But I think the Riverworld is slowly changing a lot of them."

ꝏ FOUR ꝏ

The food from the copias had been put on wooden plates. Mix, glancing at Yeshua, saw that he had not eaten his meat. Bithniah, catching Mix's look, laughed.

"Even though his mind has renounced the faith of his fathers, his stomach clings to the laws of Moses."

Stafford, not understanding her heavily accented English, asked Mix to translate. Mix told him what she'd said.

Stafford said, "But isn't she Hebrew, too?"

Mix said that she was. Bithniah understood their exchange. She spoke more slowly.

"Yes, I am a Hebrew. But I have abandoned my religion, though, to tell the truth, I was never what you would call devout. Of course, I didn't voice any doubts on Earth. I would've been killed or at least sent into exile. But when we were roaming the desert, I ate anything, clean or unclean, that would fill my belly. I made sure, though, that no one saw me. I suspect others were doing the same. Many, however, would rather starve than put an unclean thing in their mouths, and some did starve. The fools!"

She picked up a piece of ham on her plate and, grinning, offered it to Yeshua. He turned his head away with an expression of disgust.

Mix said, "For Christ's sake, Yeshua. I've told you time and again that I'll trade my steak for your ham. I don't like to see you go hungry."

"I can't be sure that the cow was slaughtered or prepared correctly," Yeshua said.

"There's no kosher involved. The buckets must somehow

convert energy into matter. The power that the bucketstones give off is transformed by a mechanism in the false bottom of the bucket. The transformer is programmed, since there's a different meal every day.

"The scientist that explained all that to me said, though he admitted he was guessing, that there are matrices in the buckets that contain models for certain kinds of matter. They put together the atoms and molecules formed from the energy to make steaks, cigars, what have you. So, there's no slaughter, kosher or unkosher."

"But there must have been an original cow that was killed," Yeshua said. "The beef which was the model for the matrix came from a beast which, presumably, lived and died on Earth. But was it slaughtered in the correct manner?"

"Maybe it was," Mix said. "But the meat I just ate isn't from the cow. It's a reproduction, just energy converted into matter. Properly speaking, it was made by a machine. It has no direct connection with the meat of the beast. If what that scientist said was true, some kind of recording was made of the atomic structure of the piece of beef. I've explained what recordings and atoms are to you. Anyway, the meat in our buckets is untouched by human hands. Or nonhuman, for that matter.

"So, how can it be unclean?"

"That is a question which would occupy rabbis for many centuries," Yeshua said. "And I suppose that even after that long a time they would still disagree. No. The safest way is not to eat it."

"Then be a vegetarian!" Mix said, throwing his hands up. "And go hungry!"

"Still," Yeshua said, "there was a man in my time, one who was considered very wise and who, it was said, talked to God, who did not mind if his disciples sat down with dirty hands at the table if there was no water to wash them or there were mitigating circumstances. He was rebuked by the Pharisees for this, but he knew that the laws of God were made for man and not man for the laws.

"That made good sense then and it makes good sense now. Perhaps I am being overstrict, Pharasaical, more devoted to the letter than to the spirit of the law. Actually, I should pay no attention to the law regarding what is ritually clean and what unclean. I no longer believe in the law.

"But even if I should decide to eat meat, I could not put the flesh of swine in my mouth if I knew what it was. I would vomit it. My stomach has no mind, but it knows what is fit for it. It is a Hebrew stomach, and it is descended from hundreds of generations of such stomachs. The tablets of Moses lie as heavy as a mountain in it."

"Which doesn't keep Bithniah from eating pork and bacon," Mix said.

"Ah! That woman! She is the reincarnation of some abominable pagan!"

"You don't even believe in reincarnation," Bithniah said, and she laughed.

Stafford had understood part of the conversation. He said, eagerly, "Then you, Master Yeshua, lived in the time of Our Lord! Did you know him?"

"As much as I know of any man," Yeshua said.

Everybody at the table began plying him with many questions. Stafford ordered more lichen-liquor brought in.

How long had he known Jesus?

Since his birth.

Was it true that Herod massacred the innocents?

No. Herod wouldn't have had the authority if he had wished to do so. He would have been removed by the Romans and perhaps executed. Moreover, such a deed would have caused a violent revolution. No. That tale, which he had never heard until he came to The Riverworld, was not true. It must be a folk story which had originated after Jesus was dead. Probably, though, it was based on an earlier tale about Isaac. Then that meant that Jesus, Joseph, and Mary did not flee to Egypt?

They didn't. Why should they?

What about the angel who appeared to Mary and announced that she would give birth though she was a virgin?

How could that be when Jesus had older brothers and sisters, all fathered by Joseph and borne by Mary? Anyway, Mary, whom he knew well, had never said anything about an angel.

Mix, observing that the redness of some faces was not wholly caused by the liquor, leaned close to Yeshua.

"Careful," he whispered. "These guys may have decided that their religion was false, but they still don't like to hear denied what they were taught all their life was true. And a lot of them are like Kramer. They believe, even if they won't say it, that they're in a kind of purgatory. They're still going to Heaven. This is just a way station."

Yeshua shrugged and said, "Let them kill me. I will rise again elsewhere in a place neither worse nor better than this."

One of the councillors, Nicholas Hyde, began banging his stone mug on the table.

"I don't believe you, Jew!" he bellowed. "If you *are* a Jew! You are lying! What are you doing, trying to create dissension among us with these diabolical lies? Or perhaps you are the *devil?*"

Stafford put his hand on Hyde's arm. "Restrain yourself, dear sir. Your accusations make no sense. Just the other day I heard you say that God was nowhere on The River. If He isn't here, then Satan is also absent. Or is it easier to believe in Old Nick than in the Creator? This man is here as our guest, and as long as he is such, we will treat him courteously."

He turned to Yeshua. "Pray continue."

The questions were many and swift. Finally, Stafford said, "It's getting late. Our guests have gone through much today, and we have much work tomorrow. I'll allow one more."

He looked at a tall distinguished-looking youth who'd been introduced as William Grey.

"Milord, care you to put it?"

Grey stood up somewhat unsteadily.

"Thank you, my lord-mayor. Now, Master Yeshua, were you present when Christ was crucified? And did you see him when he had risen? Or talk to someone reliable who had seen him, perhaps on the road to Emmaus?"

"That is more than one question," Stafford said. "But I'll allow it."

Yeshua was silent for a moment. When he spoke, he did so even more slowly.

"Yes, I was present when he was crucified and when he died. As for events after that, I will testify only to one thing. That is, he did not rise from the dead on Earth. I have no doubt that he rose here, though."

A clamor burst out, Hyde's voice rising above the others and demanding that the lying Jew be thrown out.

Stafford stood up, banging a gavel on the table, and cried, "Please, silence, gentlemen! There will be no more questions."

He gave orders to a Sergeant Channing to conduct the three to their quarters. Then he said, "Master Mix, I will speak with you three in the morning. God gives you a pleasant sleep."

Mix, Yeshua, and Bithniah followed the sergeant, who held a torch, though it was not needed. The night sky, blazing with giant star clusters and luminous gasclouds, cast a brighter light than Earth's full moon. The River sparkled. Mix asked the soldier if they could bathe before retiring. Channing said that they could do so if they hurried. The three walked into the water with their kilt-towels on. When with people who bathed nude, Mix did so also. When with the more modest, he observed their proprieties.

Using soap provided by the copias, they washed the grime and sweat off. Mix watched Bithniah. She was short and dark, full-bosomed, narrow-waisted, and shapely-legged. Her hips, however, were too broad for his tastes, though he was willing to overlook this imperfection. Especially now, when he was full of liquor. She had long, thick, glossy blue-black hair and a pretty face, if you liked long noses, which he did. His fourth wife, Vicky Forde, had had one, and he'd loved her more than any other woman. Bithniah's eyes were huge and dark, and even during the flight they had given Mix some curious glances. He told himself that Yeshua had better watch her closely. She radiated the heat of a female alleycat in mating season.

Yeshua now, he was something different. The only resemblance he had to Mix was physical. He was quiet and withdrawn, except for that one outburst against Kramer, and he seemed to be always thinking of something far away. Despite his silence, he gave the impression of great authority—rather, of a man who had once had it but was now deliberately suppressing it.

Channing said, "You're clean enough. Come on out."

"You know," Mix said to Yeshua, "shortly before I came to Kramer's territory, something puzzling happened to me. A little dark man rushed at me crying out in a foreign tongue. He tried to embrace me; he was weeping and moaning, and he kept repeating a name over and over. I had a hell of a time convincing him he'd made a mistake. Maybe I didn't. He tried to get me to take him along, but I didn't want anything to do with him. He made me nervous, the way he kept on staring at me.

"I forgot about him until just now. I'll bet he thought I was you. Come to think of it, he did say your name quite a few times."

Yeshua came out of his absorption. "Did he say what his name was?"

"I don't know. He tried four or five different languages on me, including English, and I couldn't understand him in any of them. But he did repeat a word more than once. Mattithayah. Mean anything to you?"

Yeshua did not reply. He shivered and draped a long towel over his shoulders. Mix knew that something inside Yeshua was chilling him. The heat of the daytime, which reached an estimated 80 °F. at high noon (there were no thermometers), faded away slowly. The high humidity of the valley (in this area, anyway) retained the heat until the invariable rains fell a few hours after midnight. Then the temperature dropped swiftly to an estimated 65 F. and stayed there until dawn.

Channing led them to their residences. These were two small square one-room bamboo huts, the roofs thatched with the huge leaves of the irontree. Inside each was a table, several chairs, and a low bed, all of bamboo. There were also wooden towel racks and a rack for spears and other weapons. A baked-clay nightjar stood in one corner. The floor was a slightly raised bamboo platform. Real class. Most huts had bare earth floors.

Yeshua and Bithniah went into one hut; Mix, into the other. Channing started to say good night, but Mix asked him if he minded talking a little while. To bribe the sergeant, he gave him a cigar from his grail. At one time on Earth Mix had smoked, but he had given up the habit to preserve his image as a "cleancut" hero for his vast audiences of young movie-goers. Here, he alternated between long stretches of indulgences or abstinences. For the past year, he had laid off tobacco. But he thought it might make the sergeant chummier if he smoked with him. He lit up a cigarette, coughed, and became dizzy for a moment. The tobacco certainly tasted good, though.

Micah Shepstone Channing was a short, muscular, and heavy-boned redhead. He'd been born in 1621 in the village of Havant, Hampshire, where he became a parchment maker. When the civil war broke out, he'd joined the forces against Charles I. Badly wounded at the battle of Naseby, he returned home, resumed his trade, married, had eight children of whom four survived to adulthood, and died of a fever in 1687.

Mix asked him a number of questions. Though his interest was mainly to establish a friendly feeling, he was curious about the man. He liked people in general.

He then went on to other matters, the personalities of the important men of New Albion, the setup of the government, and the relations with neighboring states, especially Kramer's Deusvolens, which the Albions pronounced as Doocevolenz.

During the English Civil War, Stafford had served under the Earl of Manchester. But, losing a hand from an infected wound, he went to live in Sussex and became a beekeeper. In time he became quite prosperous and branched out from honey to general merchandising. Later, he specialized in naval provisions. In 1679 he died during a storm off Dover. He was, Channing said, a good man, a born leader, quite tolerant, and had from the first been instrumental in establishing this state.

"Twas he who suggested that we do away with titles of nobility or royalty and elect our leaders. He's now serving his second term as lord-mayor."

"Are women allowed to vote?" Mix said.

"They weren't at first, but last year they insisted they get their rights, and after some agitation, they got them. There's no holding them," Channing said, looking somewhat sour. "They can pick up any time they want and leave, since there's little property involved and no children to take care of and blessed little housework or cooking to do. They've become mighty independent."

Anglia, on the south border of New Albion, had a similar system of government, but its elected chief was titled the sheriff. Ormondia, to the north, was inhabited chiefly by those royalists who'd been faithful to Charles I and Charles II during the troubles. They were ruled by James Butler, first Duke of Ormonde, lord-lieutenant of Ireland under Charles I and Charles II, and chancellor of Oxford University.

"It's *milord* and *your grace* in Ormondia," Channing said. "Ye'd think that England had been transplanted from old Earth to The River. Despite which, the titles are mainly honorary, ye might say, since all but the duke are elected, and their council has in it more men born poor but honest and deserving than nobles. What's more, when their women found out ours was getting the vote, they set up a howl and there was nothing His Grace could do but swallow the bitter pill and smile like he was enjoying it."

Though relations between the two tiny states had never been cordial, they were united against Kramer. The main trouble was that their joint military staffs didn't get along too well. The duke didn't like the idea of having to consult the lord-mayor or deferring to him in any way.

"Far as that goes, I don't like it either," Channing said. "There should be one supreme general during a war. This is a case where two heads be not better than one."

The Huns across The River had caused much trouble in the early years, but for some time now they'd been friendly. Actually, only about one-fourth of them were Huns, according to Channing. They'd fought among themselves for so long they'd killed off each other. These had been replaced by people from other places along The River. They spoke a Hunnish pidgin with words from other languages making up a fourth of the vocabulary. The state directly across from New Albion was at the moment ruled by a Sikh, Govind Singh, a very strong military leader.

"As I said," Channing said, "for three hundred miles along here on this side the people resurrected were mainly British of the 1600's. But there's some ten-mile stretches where they aren't. Thirty miles down are some thirteenth-century Cipangese, fierce little slant-eyed yellow bastards. And there's Doocevolenz, which is fourteenth-century and half-German and half-Spanish."

Mix thanked him for the information and then said that he had to turn in. Channing bade him a good night.

☙ FIVE ❧

Mix fell asleep at once. Sometime during the night he dreamed that he was making love to Victoria Forde, his fourth wife, the one woman whom he still loved. Drums and blarings from many fish-bone horns woke him up. He opened his eyes. It was still dark, but its paleness indicated that the sun would soon come up over the mountains. He could see through the open window the greying sky and fast-fading stars and gas clouds.

He closed his eyes and drew the edge of the double blanket-length towels over his head. Oh, for a little more sleep! But a lifetime of discipline as a cowboy, a movie actor, and a circus star on Earth, and as a mercenary on this world, got him out of bed. Shivering in the cold, he put on a towel-kilt and splashed icy water from a shallow fired-clay basin onto his face. Then he removed the kilt to wash his loins. His dream-Vicky had been as good in bed as the real Vicky.

He ran his hand over his jaw and cheeks. It was a habit he'd never overcome despite the fact that he did not have to shave and never would. All men had been resurrected permanently beardless. Tom didn't know why. Maybe whoever had done it didn't like facial hair. If so, they had no distaste for pubic or armpit hairs. But they had also made sure that hair didn't grow in the ears and nose hairs only grew to a certain length.

The unknowns responsible for the Riverworld had also made certain adjustments in the faces and bodies of some. Women who'd had huge breasts on Earth had wakened from death here to find that their mammaries had been reduced in size. Women with very small breasts had been given "normal"-sized breasts. And no woman had sagging breasts.

Not all were delighted. By no means. There were those who'd liked what they had had. And of course there had been societies in which huge dangling breasts were much admired and others in which the size and shape of the female breast meant nothing at all in terms of beauty or sex. They were just there to provide milk for the babies.

Men with very small penises on Earth here had penises which would not cause ridicule or shame. Mix had never heard any complaints about this. But a man who'd secretly yearned on Earth to be a woman had once, while drunk, poured his grievances into Mix's ear. Why couldn't the mysterious beings who'd corrected so many physical faults have given him a female body?

"Why didn't you tell them what you wanted?" Mix had said and he'd laughed. Of course, the man couldn't have informed the Whoevers. He'd died, and then awakened on the banks of The River, and in between he'd been dead.

The man had hit Tom in the eye then and given him a black whopper. Tom had had to knock him out to prevent further injury to himself.

Other deficiencies or deviations from the "normal" had also been corrected. Tom had once met a very handsome, perhaps too handsome Englishman—eighteenth century—who'd been a nobleman. From the groin upward, he'd been perfect, but his legs had been only a foot and a half long. Now he stood six feet two inches high. No complaints from him. But his grotesqueness on Earth had seemingly twisted his character. Though now a beautiful man in body, he was still embittered, savagely cynical, insulting, and, though he was a great "lover," hated women.

Tom had had a run-in with him, too, and broken the limey's nose. After they'd recovered from their injuries, they became friends. Strangely, now that the Englishman's handsomeness was ruined by the flat and askew nose, he'd become a better person. Much of his hatefulness had disappeared.

It was often hard to figure out human beings.

While Tom had been drying himself, he'd been thinking about what the Whoevers had done in the physical area to people. Now he wrapped himself in a cloak made of long towels held together with magnetic tabs inside the cloth, and he picked up a roll of toilet paper. This, too, had been provided by the copias, though there were societies who didn't use it for the intended purpose. He left the hut and walked toward the nearest latrine. This was a ditch over which was a long bamboo hut. It had two entrances. On the horizontal plank above each, a crude figure of a man, full-face, had been incised. The women's crapper was about twenty yards distant from it, and over its entrances crude profiles of women had been cut into the wood.

If the custom of daily bathing was not yet widespread in this area, other sanitation was enforced. Sergeant Channing had informed Mix that no one was allowed to crap just anywhere he or she pleased. (He did not use the word "crap," however, since this had been unknown in the seventeenth century.) Unless there were mitigating circumstances, a person caught defecating outside the public toilets was exiled—after his or her face had been rubbed in the excrement.

Urinating in public was lawful under certain situations, but the urinator must take care to be unobserved if the opposite sex was present.

"But it's a custom more honored in the breach than in the observance," Channing had said, quoting Shakespeare without knowing it. (He'd never heard of the Bard of Avon.) "In the wild lawless time just after the resurrection, people became rather shameless. There was little modesty then, and people, if you'll pardon the phrase, just didn't give a shit. Haw, haw!"

At regular intervals, the latrine deposits were hauled up to the mountains and dropped into a deep and appropriately named canyon.

"But some day it's going to be so high that the wind'll bring the stink down to us. I don't know what we'll do then. Throw it into The River and let the fish eat it, I suppose. That's what those disgusting Huns across The River do."

"Well," Mix had drawled, "that seems to me the sensible way to do it. The turds don't last long. The fish clean them up right away, almost before the stuff hits the water."

"Yes, but then we catch the fish and eat them!"

"It don't affect their taste any," Mix had said. "Listen, you said you lived on a farm for a couple of years, didn't you? Well, then you know that chickens and hogs eat cow and horse flop if they get a chance, and they often do. That didn't affect their taste when they were on the table, did it?"

Channing had grimaced. "It don't seem the same. Anyway, hogs and chickens eat cow manure, and there's a big difference between that and human ordure."

Mix had said, "I wouldn't really know. I never ate either."

He paused. "Say, I got an idea. You know the big earthworms eat human stuff. Why don't you people drag them out of the ground and throw them into the shit pit? They'd get rid of the crap, and the worms'd be as happy as an Irishman with a free bottle of whiskey."

Channing had been amazed. "That's a splendid idea! I wonder why none of us thought of it?"

He'd then complimented Mix on his intelligence. Mix hadn't told him that he'd been through many areas in which his "new" idea was a long-standing practice.

These places, like this one, had been lacking in sulphur. Otherwise, they would have processed nitrate crystals from the excrement and mixed it with charcoal and sulphur to make gunpowder. The explosive was then put into bamboo cases to be used as bombs or warheads for rockets.

Mix went into the latrine shed and sat down on one of the twelve holes. During the short time he was there, he picked up some gossip, mostly about the affair one of the councilmen was having with a major's woman. He also heard a dirty joke he'd never heard before, and he'd thought he'd heard them all on Earth. After washing his hands in a trough connected to a nearby stream, he hastened back to his hut. He picked up his grail and walked forty yards to Yeshua's hut. He'd intended to knock on the door and invite the couple to go with him to the nearest charging stone. But he halted a few paces from the door.

Yeshua and Bithniah were arguing loudly in heavily accented English of the seventeenth century. Mix wondered why they weren't using Hebrew. Later, he would find out that English was the only language they had in common, though they could carry on a very limited conversation in sixteenth-century Andalusian Spanish and fourteenth-century High German. Though Bithniah's native tongue was Hebrew, it was at least twelve hundred years older than Yeshua's. Its grammar was, from Yeshua's viewpoint, archaic, and its vocabulary was loaded with Egyptian loanwords and Hebrew items which had dropped out of the speech long before he was born.

Moreover, though born in Palestine of devout Jewish parents, Yeshua's native tongue was Aramaic. He knew Hebrew mainly as a liturgical tool, though he could read the Torah, the first five books of the Old Testament, with some difficulty.

As it was, Mix had some difficulty in understanding half of what they said. Not only did their Hebrew and Aramaic pronunciations distort their words, they had learned their English in an area occupied by seventeenth-century Yorkshire people, and that accent further bent their speech. But Mix could fill in what he didn't grasp. Usually.

"I'll not go with you to live in the mountains!" Bithniah was shouting. "I don't want to be alone! I hate being alone! I have to have many people around me! I don't want to sit on top of a rock with no one but a walking tomb to talk to! I won't go! I won't go!"

"You're exaggerating, as usual," Yeshua said loudly but much more quietly than Bithniah. "In the first place, you will have to go down to the nearest foothill copiastone three times a day. And you may go down to the bank and talk whenever you feel like it.

Also, I don't plan to live up there all the time. Now and then I'll go down to work, probably as a carpenter, but I don't . . ."

Mix couldn't understand the rest of what the man said even though he spoke almost as loudly as before. He had no trouble comprehending most of Bithniah's words, however.

"I don't know why I stay with you! Certainly it's not because no one else wants me! I've had plenty of offers, let me tell you! And I've been tempted, very tempted, to accept some!

"I do know why you want me around! It's certainly not because you're in love with my intelligence or my body! If it were, you'd delight in them, you'd be talking to me more and have me on my back far more than you do!

"The only reason you stick with me is that you know that I knew Aharon and Mosheh, and I was with the tribes when we left Egypt and when we invaded Canaan! Your only interest in me is to drain me of all I know about your great and holy hero, Mosheh!"

Mix's ears figuratively stood up. Well, well! Here was a man who'd known Christ, or at least claimed to, living with a woman who'd known Aaron and Moses, or at least claimed to. One or both of them, however, could be liars. There were so many along The River. He ought to know. It took one to recognize one, though his lies were mainly just harmless prevarications.

Bithniah screamed, "Let me tell you, Yeshua, Mosheh was a louse! He was always preaching against adultery and against lying with heathen women, but I happen to know what he practiced! Why, he even married one, a Kushi from Midian! And he tried to keep his son from being circumcised!"

"I've heard all that many times before," Yeshua said.

"But you don't really believe I'm telling the truth, do you? You can't accept that what you believed so devoutly all your life is a bunch of lies! Why should I lie? What would I gain by that?"

"You like to torture me, woman."

"Oh, I don't have to lie to do that. There are plenty of other ways! Anyway, it's true that Mosheh not only had many wives, he would take other men's women if he got a chance! I should know;

I was one of them. But he was a real man, a bull! Not like you! You can only become a real man when you've taken dreamgum and are out of your mind! What kind of a man is that, I ask you?"

"Peace, woman," Yeshua said softly.

"Then don't call me a liar!"

"I have never done that."

"You don't have to! I can see in your eyes, hear in your voice, that you don't believe me!"

"No. Though there are times—most of the time, in fact—when I wish I'd never heard your tales. But great is the truth, no matter how much it hurts."

He continued in Hebrew or Aramaic. The tone of his voice indicated that he was quoting something.

"Stick to English!" Bithniah screamed. "I got so disgusted with the so-called holy men always quoting moral proverbs, and all the time their own sins stank like a sick camel! You sound like them! And you even claim to have been a holy man! Perchance you were! But I think that your devoutness ruined you! I wouldn't know, though! You've never actually told me much about your life! I found out more about you when you were talking to the councilmen than you've ever told me!"

Yeshua's voice, which had been getting lower, suddenly became so soft that Mix couldn't make out a word of it. He glanced at the eastern mountains. A few minutes more, and the sun would clear the peaks. Then the stones would give up their thundering, blazing energy. If they didn't hurry, they'd have to go breakfastless. That is, unless they ate dried fish and acorn bread, the thought of which made him slightly nauseated.

He knocked loudly on the door. The two within fell silent. Bithniah swung the door open violently, but she managed to smile at him as if nothing had occurred.

"Yes, I know. We'll be with you at once."

"Not I," Yeshua said. "I don't feel hungry now."

"That's right!" Bithniah said loudly. "Try to make me feel guilty, blame your upset stomach on me. Well, I'm hungry, and I'm going to eat, and you can sit here and sulk for all I care!"

"No matter what you say, I am going to live in the mountains."

"Go ahead! You must have something to hide! Who's after you? Who are you that you're so afraid of meeting people? Well, *I* have nothing to hide!"

Bithniah picked up her copia by the handle and stormed out. Mix walked along with her and tried to make pleasant conversation. But she was too angry to co-operate. As it was, they had just come into sight of the nearest mushroom-shaped rock, located between two hills, when blue flames soared up from the top and a roar like a colossal lion's came to them. Bithniah stopped and burst into her native language. Obviously she was cursing. Mix contented himself with one short word.

After she'd quieted down, she said, "Got a smoke?"

"In my hut. But you'll have to pay me back later. I usually trade my cigarettes for liquor."

"Cigarettes? That's your word for pipekins?"

He nodded, and they returned to his hut. Yeshua was not in sight. Mix purposely left his door open. He trusted neither Bithniah nor himself.

Bithniah glanced at the door.

"You must think me a fool. Right next door to Yeshua!"

Mix grinned.

"You never lived in Hollywood!"

He gave her a cigarette. She used the lighter that the copia had furnished; a thin metallic box which extended a whitely glowing wire when pressed on the side.

"You must have overheard us," she said. "Both of us were shouting our fool heads off. He's a very difficult man. Sometimes he frightens me, and I don't scare easily. There's something very deep—and very different, almost alien, maybe unhuman, about him. Not that he isn't very kind or doesn't understand people. He does, too much so.

"But he seems so aloof most of the time. Sometimes, he laughs very much, and he makes me laugh, for he has a wonderful sense of humor. Other times, though, he delivers harsh judgements, so harsh they hurt me because I know that I'm included in the indictment. Now, I don't have any illusions about men or women. I know what they are and what to expect. But I accept this. People are people, although they often pretend to be better than they are. But expect the worst, I say, and you now and then get a pleasant surprise because you don't get the worst."

"That's pretty much my attitude," Mix said. "Even horses aren't predictable, and men are much more complicated. So you can't always tell what a horse or a man's going to do or what's driving him. One thing you can bet on. You're Number One to yourself, but to the other guy, Number One is himself or herself. If somebody acts like you're Number One, and she's sacrificing herself for you, she's just fooling herself."

"You sound as if you'd had some trouble with your wife."

"Wives. That, by the way, is one of the things I like about this world. You don't have to go through any courts or pay any alimony when you split up. You just pick up your bucket, towels, and weapons, and take off. No property settlements, no in-laws, no kids to worry about."

"I bore twelve children," she said. "All but six died before they were two years old. Thank God, I don't have to go through that here."

"Whoever sterilized us knew what he was doing," Mix said. "If we could have kids, this valley'd be jammed tight as a pig-trough at feeding time."

He moved close to her and grinned.

"Anyway, we men still have our guns, even if they're loaded with blanks."

"You can stop where you are," she said, although she was still smiling. "Even if I leave Yeshua, I may not want you. You look too much like him."

"I might show you the difference," he said.

But he moved away from her and picked up a piece of dried fish from his leather bag. Between bites, he asked her about Mosheh.

"Would you get angry or beat me if I told you the truth?" she said.

"No, why should I?"

"Because I've learned to keep my mouth shut about my Earthly life. The first time I told about it, that was less than a year after the Day of the Great Shout, I was badly beaten and thrown into The River. The people who did it were outraged, though I don't know why they should have been. They knew that their religion was false. They had to know that the moment they rose from the dead on this world. But I was lucky not to have been tortured and then burned alive."

"I'd like to hear the real story of the exodus," he said. "It won't bother me that it's not what I learned in Sunday school."

"You promise not to tell anybody else?"

"Cross my heart and hope to fall off Tony."

♋ Six ♋

She looked blank.

"Is that an oath?"

"As good as any."

She was, she said, born in the land of Goshen, which was in the land of Mizraim, that is, Egypt. Her tribe was that of Levi, and it had come with other tribes of Eber into Mizraim some four hundred years before.

Famine in their own land had driven them there. Besides, Yoseph—in English, Joseph—had invited them to come. He was the vizier of the Pharaoh of Egypt and so was able to get the tribes into the land of plenty just east of the great delta of the Nile.

Mix said, "You mean, the story of Joseph is true? He *was* sold into slavery by his brothers, and he *did* become the Pharaoh's righthand man?"

Bithniah smiled and said, "You must remember that all that happened four hundred years before I was born. It may or may not have been true, but that was the story I was told."

"It's hard for me to believe that a Pharaoh would make a nomadic Hebrew his chief minister. Why wouldn't he choose an Egyptian, a civilized man who'd know all the complicated problems of administering a great nation?"

"I don't know. But the Pharaoh of lower Egypt then, when my ancestors came into Egypt, was not an Egyptian. He was a foreigner, one of those invaders from the deserts whom the English call the shepherd-kings. They spoke a language much like Hebrew, or so I was told. He would have regarded Joseph as more or less a cousin. One of a kindred people, anyway, and more to be trusted than a native Egyptian. Still, I don't know if the story is true, since I did not see Joseph with my own eyes, of course. But while my people were in Goshen, the people of upper Egypt conquered the shepherd-kings and set up one of their own as Pharaoh of all Egypt."

That, said, Bithniah, was when the lot of the sons of Eber and of Jacob began to worsen. They had entered Mizraim as free men, working under contract, but then they became slaves, in effect if not officially.

"Still, it was not so bad until the great Raamses became Pharaoh. He was a mighty warrior and a builder of forts and cities, and the Hebrews were among the many people set to build these."

"Was this Raamses the first or the second?" Mix said.

"I don't know. The Pharaoh before him was named Seti."

"He would have been Raamses II," Mix said. "So *he* was the Pharaoh of the Oppression! And was the man who succeeded him named Merneptah?"

"You pronounce his name strangely, but, yes, it was."

"The Pharaoh of the exodus."

"Yes, the going-forth. We were able to escape our bondage because Mizraim was in turmoil then. The people of the seas, as the English call them, and as they were called in my time, invaded. They were, I hear, beaten back, but during the time of troubles we took the opportunity to flee Mizraim."

"Moses, I mean Mosheh, didn't go to the Pharaoh and demand that his people be allowed to go free?"

"He wouldn't have dared. He would have been tortured and then executed. And many of us would have been slain as an example."

"You've heard of the plagues visited upon the Egyptians by

God because of Moses' requests? The Nile turning to blood, the plague of frogs, the slaying of the firstborn male children of all the Egyptians and the marking with blood of the doorposts of the Hebrews so that their sons might be spared?"

She laughed and said, "Not until I came to this world. There was a plague raging throughout the land, but it killed Hebrew as well as Egyptian. My two brothers and a sister died of it, and I was sick with it, but I survived."

Mix questioned her about the religion of the tribes. She said that there was a mixture of religions in the tribes. Her mother had worshipped, among others, El, the chief god that the Hebrews had brought with them when they had entered the land of Goshen. Her father had favored the gods of Egypt, especially Ra. But he had participated in offering sacrifices to El, though these were few. He couldn't afford to pay for many.

She had known Mosheh since she was very young. He was a wild kid (her own words), half-Hebrew, half-Mizraimite. The mixture was nothing unusual. The women slaves were often raped by their masters or gave themselves willingly to get more food and creature comforts. Or sometimes just because they liked to have sexual intercourse. There was even some doubt about whether or not one of her sisters had a Hebrew or an Egyptian father.

There was also some doubt about the identity of Mosheh's father.

"When Mosheh was ten years old he was adopted by an Egyptian priest who'd lost his two sons to a plague. Why would the priest have adopted Mosheh instead of an Egyptian boy unless the priest was Mosheh's father? Mosheh's mother had worked for the priest for a while."

When Mosheh was fifteen, he had returned to the Hebrews and was once again a slave. The story was that his fosterfather had been executed because he was secretly practising the forbidden religion of Aton, founded by the accursed Pharaoh Akhenaton. But Bithniah suspected that it was because Mosheh was suspected by his father of lying with one of his concubines.

"Didn't he have to flee to Midian later on when he killed an

Egyptian overseer of slaves? He is supposed to have murdered the man when he caught him maltreating a Hebrew slave."

Bithniah laughed.

"The truth is probably that the Egyptian caught him with his wife, and Mosheh was forced to kill him to keep from being killed. But he did escape to Midian. Or so he said when he returned some years later under a false name."

"Moses must have been horny as hell," Mix said.

"The kid grows up to be a goat."

On returning with his Midianite wife, Mosheh announced that the sons of Eber had been adopted by a god. This god was Yahweh. The announcement came as a surprise to the Hebrews, most of whom had never heard of Yahweh until then. But Yahweh had spoken from a burning bush to Mosheh, and Mosheh had been charged to lead his people from bondage. He was inspiring and spoke with great authority, he seemed truly to burn as brightly with the light of Yahweh as the burning bush he described.

"What about the parting of the Red Sea and the drowning of Pharaoh and his soldiers when they pursued you Hebrews?"

"Those Hebrews who lived long after we did and wrote those books I've been told about were liars. Or perchance they weren't liars but just believed tales that had been told for many centuries."

"What about the golden calf?"

"You mean the statue of the god that Mosheh's brother Aharon made while Mosheh was on the mountain talking to Yahweh? It was a calf, the Mizraimite god Hapi as a calf. But it wasn't made of gold. It was made of clay. Where would we get gold in that desert?"

"I thought you slaves carried off a lot of loot when you left?"

"We were lucky to have our clothes and our weapons. We left in a hurry, and we didn't want to be burdened down any more than we could help, if the soldiers came after us. Fortunately, the garrisons were undermanned at that time. Many soldiers had been called to the coast to fight against the people of the sea."

"Moses did make the tablets of stone?"

"Yes. But there weren't ten commandments on them. And they were in Egyptian sign-writing. I couldn't read them; three-fourths of us couldn't. Anyway, there wasn't room on the tablets to write out ten commandments in Egyptian signs. And the writing didn't last long. The paint was poor, and the hot winds and the sand soon flaked the paint off."

✂ SEVEN ✂

Mix wanted to keep on questioning her, but a soldier knocked on the doorpost. He said that Stafford wanted to see the three at once. Mix called Yeshua out of his hut, and they followed the soldier to the council hall. Nobody said a word all the way.

Stafford said good morning and asked them if they intended to stay in New Albion.

The three said that they would like to be citizens.

Stafford said, "Very well. But you have to realize that a citizen owes the state certain duties in return for its protection. I'll enumerate these later. Now, what position in the army or navy are you particularly fitted for? If any?"

Mix had already told him what his skills were, but he repeated them. The lord-mayor told him that he would have to start as a private, though his experience qualified him to be a commissioned officer.

"I apologize for this, but it is our policy to start all newcomers at the bottom of the ranks. This prevents unhappiness and jealousy among those who've been here for a long time. However, since you have stone weapons of your own, and these are scarce in this area, I can assign you to the axeman squad. Axemen are treated as elite, as something special. After a few months, you may be promoted to sergeant if you do well, and I'm sure you will."

"That suits me fine," Tom said. "But I can also make boomerangs and instruct your people in throwing them."

Stafford said "Hmm!" and drummed his fingers on the desk for a moment.

"Since that'll make you a specialist, you deserve to be sergeant immediately. But when you're with the axe squad, you'll still have to take orders from the corporals and sergeants. Let's see. It's an awkward situation. But . . . I can make you a nonactive sergeant when you're in the squad and an active sergeant when you're in the capacity of boomerang instructor."

"That's a new one on me," Mix said grinning. "Okay."

"What?" Stafford said.

"Okay means 'all right.' It's agreeable with me."

"Oh! Very well. Now, Yeshua, what would you like to do?"

Yeshua said that he had been a carpenter on Earth and had also done considerable work in this field here. In addition, he had learned how to flake stone. Moreover, he had a small supply of flint and chert. The boat they'd fled in happened to have a leather bag full of unworked stone brought down from a distant area.

"Good!" Stafford said. "You can start by working with Mr Mix. You can help him make boomerangs."

"I'm sorry," Yeshua said. "I can't do that."

Stafford's eyes widened. "Why not?"

"I am under a vow not to shed the blood of any human being nor to take part in any activity which results in the shedding of blood."

"But what about when you were running away? Didn't you fight then?"

"No, I did not."

"You mean that if you'd been captured you would not have defended yourself? You'd have just stood there and allowed yourself to be slain?"

"I would."

Stafford drummed his fingers again while his skin became slowly red. Then he said, "I know little of this Church of the Second Chance, but I have heard some reports that its members refuse to fight. Are you one of them?"

Yeshua shook his head.

"No. My vow is a private one."

"There isn't any such thing," Stafford said. "Once you've told others of your vow, it becomes a public thing. What you mean is that you made this vow to your god."

"I don't believe in gods or a God," Yeshua said in a low but firm voice. "Once I did believe, and I believed very strongly. In fact, it was more than a belief. It was knowledge. I *knew*. But I was wrong.

"Now I believe only in myself. Not because I know myself. No man really knows anything, including himself, or perhaps I should say that no man knows much. But I do know this. That I can make a vow to myself which I will keep."

Stafford gripped the edge of his desk as if he were testing its reality.

"If you don't believe in God, then why make such a vow? What do you care if you shed blood while defending yourself? It would only be natural. And where there is no God, there is no sin. A man may do what he wants to do, no matter how he harms others, and it is right because all things are right or all things are wrong if there is no Upper Law. Human laws do not matter."

"The vow is the only true thing in the world."

Bithniah laughed and said, "He's crazy! You won't get any sense out of him! I think that he refuses to kill to keep from being killed because he wants to be killed! He would like to die, but he doesn't have guts enough to commit suicide! Besides, what good would it do! He'd only be resurrected some other place!"

"Which," Stafford said, "makes your vow meaningless. You can't really kill anybody here. You can put out a person's breath, and he will become a corpse. But twenty-four hours later, he will be a new body, a whole body, though he had been cut into a thousand pieces."

Yeshua shrugged. "That doesn't matter. Not to me, anyway. I have made my vow, and I will not break it."

"Crazy!" Bithniah said.

"You're not intending to start a new religion, are you?" Mix said.

Yeshua looked at Mix as if he were stupid.

"I just said that I don't believe in God."

Stafford sighed. "I don't have time to dispute theology or philosophy with you. This issue is easily disposed of, however. You can leave our state at once, and I mean this very minute. Or you can stay here but as an undercitizen. There are ten such living in New Albion now. They, like you, won't fight, though for different reasons from yours. But they have their duties, their work, just like all citizens. They do not, however, get any of the bonuses given to citizens every three months by the state, the extra cigarettes, liquor, and food. They are required to contribute a certain amount from their copias to the state treasury. And they must work extra shifts as latrine-cleaners. Also, in case of war, they will be kept in a stockade until the war is over. This is so they will not get in the way of the military. Another reason for this is that we can't be sure of their loyalty."

"I agree to this," Yeshua said. "I will build you fishing boats and houses and anything else that is required as long as they are not directly connected with the making of war."

"That isn't always easy to discern," Stafford said. "But, never mind, we can use you."

After they were dismissed and had gone outside, Bithniah stopped Yeshua.

Glaring, she said, "Goodbye, Yeshua. I'm leaving you. I can't endure your insanity any longer."

Yeshua looked even sadder. "I won't argue with you. It will be best if we do separate. I was making you unhappy, and it is not good to thrust one's unhappiness upon another."

"No, you're wrong about that," she said. Tears trickled down her cheeks. "I don't mind sharing unhappiness if I can help relieve it, if I can do something about it. But I can't help you. I tried, and I failed, though I don't blame myself for failing."

Yeshua walked away.

Bithniah said, "Tom, there goes the unhappiest man in the world. I wish I knew why he is so sad and lonely."

Mix glanced at his near-double, walking swiftly away as if he had some place to go, and said, "There but for the grace of God go I."

And he wondered again what strange meeting of genes had resulted in two men, born about one thousand eight hundred and eighty years apart in lands five thousand miles apart, of totally different ancestry, looking like twins. How many such coincidences had happened during man's existence on Earth?

Bithniah left to report to a woman's labor force. Mix looked up a Captain Hawkins and transmitted Stafford's orders to him. He spent an hour in close-order drill with his company and the rest of the morning practising mock-fighting with axe and shield and some spear-throwing. That afternoon, he showed some crafts-men how to make boomerangs. In a few days he would be giving instruction in the art of throwing the boomerang.

Several hours before dusk, he was dismissed. After bathing in The River, he returned to his hut. Bithniah was in hers, but Yeshua had left.

"He went up into the mountains," she said. "He said some-thing about purifying himself and meditating."

Mix said, "He can do what he wants with his free time. Well, Bithniah, what about moving in with me? I like you, and I think you like me."

"I'd be tempted if you didn't look so much like Yeshua," she said, smiling.

"I may be his spitting image, but I'm not a gloomy cuss. We'd have fun, and I don't need dreamgum to make love."

"You'd still remind me of him," she said. Suddenly she began weeping, and she ran into her hut.

Mix shrugged and went to the nearest stone to put his copia upon it.

⋐ Eight ⋑

While eating the goodies provided by his copia, holy bucket, miracle pail, grail, or whatever, he struck up a conversation with a pretty but lonely-looking blonde. She was Delores Rambaut, born in Cincinnati, Ohio, in 1945. She'd been living in the state across The River until this very afternoon. Her hutmate had driven her crazy with his unreasonable jealousy, and so, after putting up with him for a long time, she'd fled out of the hut, but he was likely to try to kill her.

"How was it living with all those Huns?" he said.

She looked surprised.

"Huns? Those people aren't Huns. They're what we call Scythians. At least, I think they are. They're mostly a fairly tall white-skinned people, Caucasians. They were great horsemen on Earth, you know, and they conquered a wide territory in southern Russia. In the seventh century B.C., if I remember right what I read about them."

"The people here call them Huns," he said. "Maybe it's just an insulting term and has no relation to their race or nationality. Or whatever. Anyway, I'm glad you're here. I don't have a mate, and I'm lonely."

She laughed and said, "You're kind of rushing it, aren't you? Tom Mix, heh? You couldn't be . . . ?"

"The one and only," he said. "And just as horseless as the ancient Scythians are now."

"I should have known. I saw enough pictures of you when I was a child. My father was a great admirer of yours. He had a lot of newspaper clippings about you, an autographed photo, and even a movie poster. *Tom Mix in Arabia*. He said it was the greatest movie you ever made. In fact, he said it was one of the best movies he ever saw."

"I kind of liked it myself," he said smiling.

"Yes. It was rather sad, though. Oh, I don't mean the movie. I mean about all your movies. You made . . . how many?"

"Two hundred and sixty—I think."

"Wow! That many? Anyway, my father said, oh, it was years later, when he was a very old man, that all of them had disappeared. The studios didn't have any, and the few still existing were privately owned and fading fast."

Tom winced, and he said, "Sic transit gloria mundi. However, I made a hell of a lot of money and enjoyed blowing it. So, what the hell!"

Delores had been born five years after he'd rammed his car into a barricade near Florence on the highway between Tucson and Phoenix. He'd been travelling as advance agent for a circus and was carrying a metal suitcase full of money with which to pay bills. As usual, he was driving fast, ninety miles an hour at the time. He'd seen the warning on a barrier that the highway was being repaired. But, also as usual, he'd paid no attention to the sign. One moment, the road was clear. The next . . . there was no way he could avoid the crashing into the barricade.

"My father said you died instantly. The suitcase was behind you, and it snapped your neck."

Tom winced again.

"I always was lucky."

"He said the suitcase flew open, and there were thousand-dollar bills flying all over the place. It was a money shower. The workmen didn't pay any attention to you at first. They were running around like chickens with a fox loose in the henhouse, catching the money, stuffing it in their pockets and under their shirts. But they didn't know who you were until later. You got a big funeral, and you were buried in Forest Lawn Cemetery."

"I had class," he said. "Even if I did die almost broke. Was Victoria Forde, my fourth wife, at the funeral?"

"I don't know. Well, what do you know? I'm eating and talking with a famous movie star!"

Tom had felt hurt that the workers had been more interested in scooping up the money that was whirling like green snowflakes than in finding out whether he was dead or not. But he quickly smiled to himself. If he'd been in their skins, he might have done the same thing. The sight of a thousand-dollar bill blown by the wind was very tempting—to those who didn't earn in ten years what he'd made in a week. He couldn't really blame the slobs.

"They put up a monument at the site of the accident," she said. "My father stopped off to see it when he took us on a vacation trip through the Southwest. I hope knowing that makes you feel better."

"I wish the locals knew what a big shot I was on Earth," he said. "Maybe they'd give me a rank higher than sergeant. But they hadn't heard of movies until they came here, of course, and they can't even visualize them."

After two hours, Delores decided that they'd known each other long enough so that he was no longer rushing it. She accepted his invitation to move into his hut. They had just reached its door when Channing appeared. He'd been sent to summon Mix at once to the lord-mayor.

Stafford was waiting for him in the Council Hall.

"Master Mix, you know so much about Kramer and have such an excellent military background that I'm attaching you to my staff. Don't waste time thanking me.

"My spies in Kramer's land tell me he's getting ready for a big attack. His military and naval forces are completely mobilized, and only a small force is left for defense. But they don't know where the invasion will be. Kramer hasn't told even his staff, as yet. He knows we have spies there, just as he has his spies here."

"I hope you still don't suspect that I might be one of his men," Mix said.

Stafford smiled slightly.

"No. My spies have reported that your story is true. You're not a spy unless you're part of a diabolically clever plot to sacrifice a good boat and some fighting men to convince me you're what you claim to be. I doubt it, for Kramer is not the man to let go of Jewish prisoners for any reason whatsoever."

Stafford, Mix learned, had been impressed by the showing of Mix in the fight on The River and by the reports of Mix's superiors. Also, Mix's Earthly military experiences had given Stafford some thought. Tom felt a little guilty then, but it quickly passed. Moreover, Mix knew the topography and the defenses of Deusvolens well. And he had said the night before that the only way to defeat Kramer was to beat him to the punch.

"A curious turn of phrase but clear in its meaning," Stafford had said.

"From what I've heard," Mix said, "Kramer's method of expansion is to leapfrog one state and conquer the one beyond it. After he consolidates his conquest, he squeezes the bypassed area between his two armies. That's fine, but it wouldn't work if the other states would unite against Kramer. They know he's going to gobble them all up eventually. Despite which, they're so damned suspicious they don't trust each other. Maybe they got good reason, I don't know. Also, as I understand it, no one state's willing to submit itself to another's general. I guess you know about that.

"I think that if we could deliver one crippling blow, and somehow capture or kill Kramer and his Spanish sidekick, Don Esteban de Falla, we would weaken Deusvolens considerably. Then the other states would come galloping in like Comanches so they could really crush Deusvolens and grab all the loot that's for the grabbing.

"So, my idea is to make a night raid, by boat, of course, a massive one that would catch Kramer with his pants down. We'd burn his fleet and burst in on Kramer and de Falla and cut their throats. Knock off the heads of the state, and the body surrenders. His people would fall apart."

"I've sent assassins after him, and they've failed," Stafford said. "I could try again. If we make enough diversion, they might succeed this time. However, I don't see how we could carry this off. Sailing up-River is slow work, and we couldn't reach Kramer's land while it's still dark if we left at dusk. We'd be observed by his spies long before we got there, most probably when we amassed our boats. Kramer would be ready for us. That would be fatal for us. We have to have surprise."

"Yeah," Mix said. "But you're forgetting the Huns across The River. Oh, by the way, I just found out they're not really Huns, they're ancient Scythians."

"I know that," Stafford said. "They were mistakenly called Huns in the old days because of their savagery and our ignorance. The terminology doesn't matter. Stick to the relevant points."

"Sorry. Well, so far, Kramer has been working on this side of The River only. He's not bothered the Huns. But they aren't dumb, according to what I've just heard."

"Ah, yes, from the woman, Delores Rambaut," Stafford said.

Tom Mix tried to repress his surprise. "You've got spies spying on your own people."

"Not officially. I don't have to appoint people to spy on their own countrymen. There are enough volunteers to come running to me with accounts of everything that goes on here. They're gossips, and they're nuisances. Occasionally, though, they tell me something important."

"Well, what I meant when I said the Huns weren't dumb was that they know that Kramer's going to attack them when he has enough states on this side of The River under his belt. They must know he'll move against them then so he can consolidate this whole area. They know it'll be some years from now, but they know it's coming. So, they might be receptive to some ideas I've been hatching. Here's what we could do."

They talked for another hour. At the end, Stafford said that he'd do what he could to develop Mix's plan. It was a desperate one, in his opinion, chiefly because of the very little time left to carry it out. It meant staying up all night and working hard. Every minute that passed gave Kramer's spies just that much more opportunity to find out what was happening. But it had to be done. He didn't intend to sit passively and wait for Kramer to attack. It was better to take a chance than to *let Kramer call the shots*. Stafford was beginning to pick up some of Mix's twentieth-century Americanisms.

⁓ Nine ⁓

Intelligence reported that Kramer was not using his entire force. Though he theoretically had available enough soldiers and sailors to overwhelm both New Albion and Ormondia, in fact he was afraid to withdraw many from his subject states. His garrisons there were composed of a minority of men from Deusvolens and a majority of collaborators in the occupied states. They kept the people terrorized and had built earth and wooden walls on the borders and stationed troops in forts along these. The copias of most citizens were stored in well-guarded places and only passed out during charging times. Anyone who wished to flee either had to steal his copia or kill himself and rise somewhere else on The River with a new copia. The former was almost impossible to do, and the latter course was taken only by the bravest or most desperate.

Nevertheless, if Kramer weakened the garrisons too much, he would have a dozen revolutions at once.

From what Stafford's spies said, Kramer had quietly taken two out of every ten of his soldiers and sailors in the subject states and brought them to Deusvolens and Felipia, the state adjoining his north border. His fleet was stationed along the banks of The River in a long line. But the soldiers and the boats might be amassed at any time during the night. What night was, of course, unknown.

"Kramer's spies know that you and Yeshua and Bithniah are here," Stafford said to Mix. "You think that he'll attack New Albion just to get you three back. I don't believe it. Why should you three be so important to him?"

"Others have escaped him," Mix said, "but never in such a public manner. The news has gotten around, he knows it, and he feels humiliated. Also, he's afraid that others might get the same idea. However, I think that he's been planning to extend his conquests, and we've just stimulated him to act sooner than he'd intended.

"What he'll do, he'll bypass Freedom and Ormondia and attack us. If he takes New Albion, he'll then start his squeeze play."

Messengers had been sent to Ormondia, and the duke and his council had met Stafford and his council at the border. Half the night had been spent in trying to get the duke to agree to join in a surprise attack. The rest of the night and all morning had been taken up in arguing about who the supreme general should be. Finally, Stafford had agreed that Ormonde should be in command. He didn't like to do so, since he thought the duke wasn't as capable as himself. Also, the New Albionians would not be happy about serving under him. But Stafford needed the Ormondians.

Not stopping for even a short nap, Stafford then crossed The River to confer with the rulers of the two "Hunnish" states. Their spies had informed them that Kramer was planning another invasion. They hadn't been much concerned about it, since Kramer had never attacked across The River. Stafford finally convinced them that Kramer would get to them eventually. They bargained, however, for the majority of the loot. Stafford and the duke's agent, Robert Abercrombie, reluctantly agreed to this.

The rest of the day was taken up in making plans for the disposition of the Hunnish boats. There was much trouble about this. Hartashershes and Dherwishawyash, the rulers, argued about who would take precedence in the attack. Mix suggested to Stafford that he suggest to them that the boats carrying the rulers should sail side by side. The two could then land at the same time. From then on it would be every man for himself.

"But all of this may go awry," he said to Mix. "Who knows what Kramer's spies have found out? There may even be some in my own staff or among the Huns. If not, the watchers in the hills will have observed us."

Soldiers in New Albion and Ormondia were scouring the hills, searching for spies. These would be hiding, unable to light signal fires or beat on their relay drums. Some would have slipped through the hunters to carry their information on foot or by boat. That, however, would take time.

Meanwhile, envoys from New Albion had gone to three of the states south of its border. They would attempt to get these to furnish personnel and craft in the attack.

Tom had, by the end of the night, been commissioned a captain. He was supposed to don the leather, bone-reinforced casque and cuirass of the Albionian soldier, but he'd insisted that he keep his cowboy hat. Stafford was too weary to oppose him.

Two days and nights passed. During this time, Mix managed to get some sleep. In the afternoon of the third day, he decided that he'd like to get away from all the bustle and noise. There was so much going on that he could find no quiet place to sleep. He'd go up into the hills and find a silent spot to snooze, if that was possible. There were still search parties there.

First, though, he stopped at Bithniah's to see how she was doing. She was, he found, now living with a man whose mate had been killed during the River-fight. She seemed fairly happy with him. No, she hadn't seen "the crazy monk," Yeshua. Mix told her he'd seen him at a distance now and then. Yeshua had been cutting down some pine trees with a flint axe, but Mix didn't know for what purpose.

On the way to the hills, he ran into Delores. She was on a work party which was hauling logs of the giant bamboo down to the banks. These were being set up to reinforce the wooden walls lining the waterside of New Albion's border. She looked tired and dirty and not at all happy. It wasn't just the hard labor that made her glare at Mix, however. Not once had they had time or the energy to make love.

Tom grinned at her and called, "Don't worry, dear! We'll get together after this is all over! And I'll make you the happiest woman alive!"

Delores told him what he could do with his hat.

Tom laughed and said, "You'll get over that."

She didn't reply. She bent her back to the rope attached to the log and strained with the other women to get it up over the crest of the hill.

"It'll be all downhill from now on," he said.

"Not for you it won't," she called back.

He laughed again, but, when he turned away, he frowned. It wasn't his fault that she'd been drafted into a work party. And he regretted as much as she, maybe more, that they hadn't had a honeymoon.

The next hill was busy and loud with the ring of stone axes chopping at the huge bamboo plants, the grunting of the choppers, and the shouted orders of the foremen and forewomen. Presently, he was on a still higher hill, only to discover that it, too, was far from conducive to sleep. He continued, knowing that when he got to the mountain itself, he would run into no human beings there. He was getting tired and impatient, though.

He stopped near the top of the last hill to sit down and catch his breath. Here the great irontrees grew closely together, and among them were the tall grasses. He could see no one, but he could hear the axes and the voices faintly. Maybe he should just lie down here. The grass was not soft, and it was itchy, but he was so fatigued that he wouldn't mind that. He'd spread out his cloak and put his hat over his face and pass out quickly into a much-deserved sleep. There were no insects to crawl over him or sting him, no pestiferous ants, flies, or mosquitoes. Nor would any loud bird cries disturb him.

He rose and removed his white cloak and placed it on the grass. The sun's hot rays came down between two irontrees on him; the long grass made a wall around him. Ah!

Stafford might be looking for him right now. If so, it was just too bad.

He stretched out, then decided he'd take his military boots off. His feet were hot and sweating. He sat up and slid one boot from his right foot and started to remove the woven-grass sock. He stopped. Had he heard a rustle in the grass not made by the wind?

His weapons lay by him, a chert tomahawk and a flint knife and a boomerang, all in straps in his belt. He took all three out, laying the boomerang on the cloak, and he held the tomahawk in his right hand and the knife in his left.

The rustling had stopped, but after a minute it resumed. He rose cautiously and looked over the top of the grass. There, twenty feet away, toward the mountain, the grass was bending down, then springing up. For a while he couldn't see the passerby. Either he was shorter than the tall blades or he was bending over.

Then he saw a head rise above the green. It was a man's, dark-skinned, black-haired, and Spanish-featured. That wasn't significant, since there were plenty like him in the area, good citizens all, some of them refugees from Deusvolens and Felipia. The stealthiness of the man, however, indicated that he wasn't behaving like one who belonged here.

He could be a spy who'd eluded the search parties.

The man had been looking toward the mountain, presenting his profile to the watcher. Mix ducked down before the stranger turned his head toward him. He crouched, listening. The rustling had stopped. After a while, it started again. Was the man aware that somebody else was here and so was trying to locate him?

He got down on his knees and put his ear to the ground. Like

most valleydwellers, the fellow was probably barefooted or wore
sandals. But he might step on a twig, though there weren't too
many of those from the bushes. Or he might stumble.

After a minute of intent listening, Mix got up. Now he couldn't
even hear the noise of the man's passage. Nor was there any movement of the grass caused by anything except the breeze. Yes! There
was! The fellow had resumed walking. The back of his head was
moving away from Mix.

He quickly strapped on his belt, fastened his cloak around
his neck, and put the boot back on. With his white hat held by
the brim in his teeth, the knife in one hand, the tomahawk in
the other, he went after the stranger. He did so slowly, however,
raising his head now and then above the grass. Inevitably, the
followed and the follower looked at each other at the same time.

The man dropped at once. Now that he'd been discovered,
Mix saw no reason to duck down. He watched the grass as it
waved, betraying the crawler beneath as water disturbed by a
swimmer close to the surface. He breasted the grass, striding
swiftly toward the telltale passage but ready to disappear himself if
the green wake ceased.

Suddenly, the dark man's head popped up. Surprisingly, he
placed a finger on his lips. Mix stopped. What in hell was he
doing? Then the man pointed beyond Mix. For a second, Mix
refused to look. It seemed too much like a trick, but what could
the man gain by it? He was too far away to get any advantage by
charging when Mix was looking behind him.

Trick or not, Mix had too much curiosity. He turned to look
over the territory. And there was the grass moving as if an invisible
snake were crawling over it.

He considered the situation quickly. Was that other person an
ally of the dark man and sneaking up on himself? No. If he were,
the dark man wouldn't be pointing him out. What had happened
was that the dark man was an Albionian who had detected a spy.
He'd been trailing him when Mix had mistaken him for a spy.

Mix had no time then to think about how he might have
killed one of his own people. He dropped down and began

approaching the place where the third person was—had been, rather, since by the time he got there the unknown would probably be some place else. Every twelve feet or so he rose to check on the unknown's progress. Now the ripples were moving toward the mountain, away from both himself and the dark man. The latter, as indicated by the moving grass, was crawling directly toward where Mix had been.

Tired of the silent and slow play, sure that a sudden and violent action would flush out the quarry, Mix whooped. And he ran through the grass as swiftly as it would allow him.

The afternoon was certainly full of surprises. Two heads shot up where he had expected one. One was blond, and the other was a redhead. The woman had been in front of the man as they had crawled and crouched and risen briefly like human periscopes, though he hadn't actually seen them coming up to observe.

Mix stopped. If he'd made a mistake about the identity of the first person, could he be doing the same with these two?

He shouted to them, telling them who he was and what he was doing here. The dark man then called out, saying that he was Raimondo de la Reina, a citizen of New Albion. The redhead and the blond then identified themselves: Eric Simons and Guindilla Tashent, also citizens of the same state.

Mix wanted to laugh at this comedy of errors, but he still wasn't sure. Simons and Tashent might be lying so that the others would let down their guard.

Tom stayed where he was. He said, "What were you two doing here?"

"For God's sake," the man said, "we were making love! But please do not bruit this about. My woman is very jealous, and Guindilla's man would not be very pleased if he heard about this, either!"

"Your secret is safe with me," Mix called.

He turned toward de la Reina, who was walking toward him. "What about you, pard? There isn't any reason to say anything about this, is there? Especially since it makes all of us look like fools?"

There was another problem. The two lovers were probably shirking their duties. This could be a serious, a court-martial business, if the authorities learned about it. Mix had no intention of reporting it, but the Spaniard might feel that it must be brought to the attention of the authorities. If he insisted, then Mix couldn't argue with him. Not too strongly, anyway.

He, Simons, and Tashent hadn't moved. De la Reina was ploughing through the grass toward him, probably to talk the situation over with him. Or perhaps he thought that the pair wasn't to be trusted. Which made sense, Mix thought. They could be spies who'd invented this tale when found out. Or, more likely, prepared it in case they were discovered.

But Mix didn't really think this was so.

Presently, the Spaniard was a few feet from him. Now Mix could clearly see his features, long and narrow, aquiline, a very aristocratic Hispanic face. He was as tall as Mix. Through the bending grass Mix glimpsed a green towel-kilt, a leather belt holding two flint knives, and a tomahawk. One hand was behind his back; the other was empty.

Mix wouldn't allow anybody to get near him who hid one hand. He said, "Stop there, amigo!"

De la Reina did so. He smiled but at the same time looked puzzled.

"What's the matter, friend?"

He spoke seventeenth-century English with a heavy foreign accent, and it was possible that he had trouble understanding Mix's twentieth-century American pronunciation. He was given the benefit of the doubt, though not very much.

Tom spoke slowly. "Your hand. The one behind your back. Bring it out. Slowly."

He chanced to look at the others. They were moving toward him, though slowly. They looked scared.

The Spaniard said, "Of course, friend."

And de la Reina was leaping toward him, shouting, the hand now revealed, clutching a flint blade. There were only a few inches showing, but there was enough to slash a jugular vein or a throat. If the Spaniard had been smarter, he could have concealed the entire weapon in his hand and let the hand swing naturally. But he had been afraid to do that.

Tom Mix swung the tomahawk. Its edge cracked against de la Reina's temple. He dropped. The blade fell from his grip.

Tom called to the two. "Stop where you are!"

They looked at each other uneasily, but they halted.

"Hold your hands up," he said. "High above your heads!"

The hands went up as high as they could go. Simons, the red-head, said, "What happened?"

"Get over under that irontree!"

The two started to walk toward the indicated place. An abandoned hut stood under it, but the grass around it had been recently cut. It had grown back to a height of a foot, enabling Mix to see if they carried weapons or not.

He bent down and examined the Spaniard. The fellow was still breathing, though harshly. He might or might not recover, and if he did, he might never have all his wits about him. It would be far better for him if he died, since he was bound to be tortured. That was the fate of all spies in this area who failed to kill themselves when facing inevitable capture. This one would be stretched over a wooden wheel until the ropes on his wrists and ankles pulled his joints apart. If he wouldn't give any worthwhile information or he was thought to be lying, he'd be suspended naked over a low fire and slowly seared.

During his turnings on the spit, he might have one eye or both poked out or an ear sliced off. Should he still refuse to talk, he'd be taken down and cooled off with water. Then his finger-nails and toenails might be pulled out or tiny cuts made in his genitals. A hot flint tip might be thrust up his anus. One finger at a time might be severed and the stump immediately thereafter cauterized with a hot rock.

The list of possible tortures was long and didn't bear thinking about by any sensitive imaginative person.

Mix hadn't seen the Albionians put any spies to the question. But he had witnessed some inquisitions while Kramer's prisoner, and so he knew too well the horrors awaiting the Spaniard.

What could this poor devil tell that was worth hearing? Nothing, Mix was sure.

He straightened up to check on Simons and Tashent. They were under the branches of the tree now, standing near the hut.

He stooped and slashed the man's jugular vein. Having made sure that he was dead and having collected the valuable weapons, he walked toward the tree. The fellow would be resurrected in a whole body somewhere along The River far from here. Maybe someday Mix would run into him again, and he could tell him about his act of mercy.

Halfway toward the tree, he halted. From above, somewhere on the mountain, the wild skirling of a bamboo syrinx floated down.

Who could be up there wasting time when everybody was supposed to be working hard? Another pair of lovers, one of whom was entertaining the other with music between the couplings? Or was the skirling some sort of signal by a spy? Not very likely but he had to consider all possibilities.

The blonde and the redhead still had their hands up. Both were naked. The woman certainly had a beautiful body, and her thick pubic hair was just the red-gold that especially excited him. She reminded him of a starlet he'd run around with just after his divorce from Vicky.

"Turn around," he said.

Simons said, "Why?" But he obeyed.

"Okay," Mix said. "You can put your hands down now."

He didn't tell them that he'd once been stabbed by a naked prisoner who'd gripped a knife between the cheeks of his buttocks until he was close to his captor.

"Now, what happened?"

Events had been much as he'd thought. The two had sneaked off from a work-party to make love in the grass. While lying in the grass between bouts, getting ready to light up cigarettes, they'd heard the spy walking nearby. Picking up their weapons, they'd started to trail him. They were sure that the stranger was up to no good.

Then they'd seen Mix following de la Reina and were just

about to join him when the Spaniard had seen them. He'd been a quick thinker in trying to deceive Mix into believing that they were the spies.

"He might've succeeded if he hadn't tried to kill me at once instead of waiting for a better time," Tom said. "Well, you two get back to your duty."

Guindilla said, "You aren't going to tell anybody about this, are you?"

Tom said, grinning, "Maybe, maybe not. Why?"

"If you keep quiet about this, I could make it worth your while."

Eric Simons snarled, "Guin! You wouldn't, would you?"

She shrugged, causing intriguing ripples.

"What could it hurt? It'd be just this once. You know what'll happen if he turns us in. We'll be put on acorn bread and water for a week, publicly humiliated, and . . . well, you know how Robert is. He'll beat me, and he'll try to kill you."

"We could just run off," Simons said.

He looked very nasty. "Or would you like to tumble this man, you slut!"

Tom laughed again, and said, "If you got caught while deserting, you'd be executed. Don't worry. I'm not a blackmailer, a lecherous hard-hearted Rudolf Rassendale."

They looked blank. "Rassendale?" Simons said.

"Never mind. You wouldn't know. You two get going. I'm not telling anybody the whole truth. I'll just say I was alone when I discovered the Spaniard. But tell me, who's playing the syrinx up there?"

They said they had no idea. As they walked away into the grass to retrieve their weapons and clothes, they quarreled loudly. Mix didn't think their passion for each other would survive this incident.

When their wrangling voices faded out, Tom turned to the mountain. Should he go back to the plain and report that he'd killed a spy? Go up the mountain to check out the syrinx player? Or do what he had come here for, that is, sleep?

Curiosity won out. It always did with him.

Telling himself he should have been a cat, one who'd already used up one of his nine lives, he began climbing. There were fissures along the face of the mountain, ledges, little plateaus, and steep narrow paths. Only a mountain goat or a very determined or crazy person would use these to get up the cliff, however. A sensible man would look up it and perhaps admire it, but he'd stay below and loaf or sleep or roll a pretty woman in the grass. Best of all, he'd do all three, not to mention pouring down some good bourbon or whatever his copia gave him in the way of booze.

Sweating despite the shade, he pulled himself over the edge of one of the small plateaus. A building that was more of an enclosed leanto than a hut was in the middle of the tablerock. Beyond it was a small cascade, one of the many waterfalls that presumably originated from unseen snows on top of the mountains. The cascades were another mystery of this planet, which had no seasons and thus should rotate at an unvarying 90 degrees to the ecliptic. If the snows had no thawing period, where did the water come from?

Yeshua was by the waterfall. He was naked and blowing on the pan's pipe and dancing as wildly as one of the goat-footed worshippers of The Great God. Around and around he spun. He leaped high, he skipped, he bent forward and backward, he kicked, he bent his legs, he pirouetted, he swayed. His eyes were closed, and he came perilously close to the edge of the plateau.

Like David dancing after the return of the ark of God, Mix thought. But Yeshua was doing this for an invisible audience. And he certainly had nothing to celebrate.

Mix was embarrassed. He felt like a window-peeper. He almost decided to retreat and leave Yeshua to whatever was possessing him. But the thought of the difficulty of the climb and the time he had taken made him change his mind.

He called. Yeshua stopped dancing and staggered backward as if an arrow had struck him. Mix walked up to him and saw that he was weeping.

Yeshua turned, kneeled and splashed the icy water from a pool by the side of the cataract, then turned to face Mix. His tears had stopped, but his eyes were wide and wild.

"I was not dancing because I was happy or filled with the glory of God," he said. "On Earth, in the desert by the Dead Sea, I used to dance. No one around but myself and The Father. I was a harp, and His fingers plucked the strings of ecstasy. I was a flute, and He sounded through my body the songs of Heaven.

"But no more. Now I dance because, if I do not, I would scream my anguish until my throat caught fire, and I would leap over the cliff and fall to a longed-for death. What use in that? In this world, a man cannot commit suicide. Not permanently. A few hours later, he must face himself and the world again. Fortunately, he does not have to face his god again. There is none left to face."

Mix felt even more embarrassed and awkward.

"Things can't be that bad," he said. "Maybe this world didn't turn out to be what you thought it was going to be. So what? You can't blame yourself for being wrong. Who could possibly have guessed the truth about the unguessable? Anyway, this world has many good things that Earth didn't have. Enjoy them. It's true it's not always a picnic here, but when was it on Earth? At least, you don't have to worry about growing old, there are plenty of good-looking women, you don't have to sit up nights wondering where your next meal is coming from or how you're going to pay your taxes or alimony. Hell, even if there aren't any horses or cars or movies here, I'll take this world anytime! You lose one thing; you gain another."

"You don't understand, my friend," Yeshua said. "Only a man like myself, a man who has seen through the veil that the matter of this physical universe presents, seen the reality beyond, felt the flooding of The Light within . . ."

He stopped, stared upward, clenched his fists, and uttered a long ululating cry. Mix had heard only one cry like that—in Africa, when a Boer soldier had fallen over a cliff. No, he hadn't really heard any Boer soldier. Once more, he was mixing fantasy with reality. "Mix" was a good name for him.

"Maybe I better go," Mix said. "I know when there's nothing to be done. I'm sorry that—"

"I don't want to be alone!" Yeshua said. "I am a human being; I need to talk and to listen, to see smiles and hear laughter, and know love! But I cannot forgive myself for being . . . what I was!"

Mix wondered what he was talking about. He turned and started to walk to the edge of the plateau. Yeshua came after him.

"If only I had stayed there with the Sons of Zadok, the Sons of Light! But no! I thought that the world of men and women needed me! The rocks of the desert unrolled before me like a scroll, and I read therein that which must come to pass, and soon, because God was showing me what would be. I left my brothers in their caves and their cells and went to the cities because my brothers and sisters and the little children there must know, so that they would have a chance to save themselves."

"I got to get going," Mix said. "I feel sorry for whatever's riding you, but I can't help you unless I know what it is. And I doubt that I'd be much help then."

"You've been sent to help me! It's no coincidence that you look so much like me and that our paths crossed."

"I'm no brain doctor," Mix said. "Forget it. I can't straighten you out."

Abruptly, Yeshua dropped the hand held out to Mix, and he spoke softly.

"What am I saying? Will I never learn? Of course you haven't been sent. There's Nobody to send you. It's just chance."

"I'll see you later."

He began climbing down. Once he looked upward, and he saw Yeshua's face, his own face, staring down at him. He felt angry then, as if he should have stayed and at least given some encouragement to the man. He could have listened until Yeshua talked himself into feeling better.

By the time he had reached the hills and started walking back, he had a different attitude. He doubted that he could really aid the poor devil.

Yeshua must be half cracked. Certainly he was half baked. And that was a peculiar thing about this world and the resurrection.

Everybody else had not only been awakened from the dead with the body of a twenty-five-year-old—except, of course, for those who had died on Earth before that age—but all who had suffered a mental illness on Earth had been restored mentally whole.

However, as time passed, and the problems of the new world pressed in, many began to sicken again in their minds. There wasn't much schizophrenia; but he understood from talking to a twentieth-centurian that at least three-quarters of schizophrenia had been proved to be due to a physical imbalance and was primarily genetic in origin.

Nevertheless, five years of life in the Rivervalley had produced a number of insane people, though not in the relative proportions known on Earth. And the resurrection had not been successful in converting the majority of the so-called sane to a new viewpoint, a different attitude, one that phased in with reality.

Whatever reality was.

As on Earth, most of humanity was often irrational, though rationalising, and was impervious to logic it didn't like. Mix had always known the world was half mad and behaved accordingly, usually to his benefit.

Or so he had thought then. Now, since he had time sometimes to contemplate the Terrestrial past, he saw that he had been as half-mad as most people. He hoped he'd learned his lessons, but there were plenty of times when he doubted it. Anyway, except for a few deeds, he'd been able to forgive himself for his sins.

But Yeshua, miserable fellow, could not forgive himself for whatever he had been or had done on Earth.

ఴ Ten ఴ

After telling Stafford about de la Reina, he went to his hut, and he drank the last of his whiskey, four ounces.

Whoever would have thought that there'd be a dead ringer for Tom Mix, and an ancient Jew at that, for Christ's sake? It was too bad Yeshua hadn't been born at the same time as he had. Yeshua could have made good money as his stand-in.

Despite the noise still swirling around the hut, he managed to sleep well. The rest didn't last long, though. Two hours later, Channing woke him up. Tom told him to shove off. Channing continued to shake his shoulder, then gave up on that method of wakening, and emptied a skin-bucket full of water on his face. Sputtering, swearing, striking out with his fists, Mix came up off the bed. The sergeant ran out of the hut laughing.

The council lasted an hour, and he went back to the hut for some more shut-eye. He was roused momentarily when the copiastones thundered. Fortunately, he'd promised some cigarettes to a man if he'd place Mix's copia for him so he wouldn't go supperless.

Sometime later, Delores came in, set down their copias, and then tried to wake him up for their first, and possibly last, love-making. He told her to go away, but she did something that very few men could ignore. Afterward, they ate and then smoked a couple of cigarettes. Since he might not come out of the invasion alive, one coffin nail wouldn't hurt him. Anyway, Delores didn't like smoking alone after being plumbed.

The cigarette, however, made him cough, and he felt dizzy. He swore off again though the tobacco certainly had tasted delicious. A moment later, having forgotten his resolve, he lit up another.

A corporal came after him then. Tom kissed Delores. She cried and said that she was sure she'd never ever see him again.

"I appreciate your sentiments," Tom said. "But they aren't exactly comforting."

The fleets of Anglia and New Cornwall, a neighboring state which had decided at the last minute to join the invasion, were approaching the New Albion shores. Tom, dressed in his ten-gallon hat, cloak, vest, kilt, and Wellington boots, got onto the flagship. It was the biggest man-of-war in New Albion, three-masted, carrying ten catapults. Behind it came the other largest boats, four men-of-war. After it trailed twenty frigates, as the two-masters were called, though they looked little like the frigates of Earth. After them came forty cruisers, single-masted warcanoes, hollowed out of giant bamboo logs.

The night-sky blazed down on a River in which the traffic of tacking vessels was thick. There were a few unavoidable collisions, but little damage resulted, though they caused a lot of shouting and cursing. The danger increased as the Hunnish, or Scythian, fleets put out. Bull's-eye lanterns burning fish oil signalled every-where. An observer in the hills would have been reminded of the dance of fireflies on Earth. But if there were any spies left, they didn't light signal fires or beat drums. They were lying low, still hiding from the search parties. All the male soldiers left behind were manning the forts and other important posts. Armed women were beating the hills now.

The miles dropped by slowly. Then the Ormondian fleet sailed out to join them, the duke's flagship in the van. More signals were rayed out.

Just north of Ormondia was the determinedly neutral state of Jacobea. Stafford and Ormonde had debated inviting it to be an ally, but had finally decided against it. There was little chance of its joining, and even if it had, its security couldn't be trusted. Now, as the fleet ventured into Jacobean waters, the cries of sentinels came to it. Its crews saw torchlights flare up, and they heard the booming of the hollow-log and fish-skin drums. The Jacobeans, fearing an invasion, poured out of their huts, their weapons in hand, and began falling into formation.

Up in the hills, signal fires began building up. These were tended by Kramer's spies, which Jacobea allowed to operate unmolested.

However, the clouds were forming in the skies. Fifteen minutes later, they emptied their contents, drowning out the fires. If Stafford's planning went as hoped for, there would be no relay of warning signals to Kramer.

The signal-man on the duke's boat flashed a message to the Jacobeans. It identified the fleets and said that they intended no harm. They were sailing against Kramer, and if Jacobea cared to join them, they'd be welcome.

"They won't do it, of course," Stafford said. He laughed. "But it'll throw them into a frenzy. They won't know what to do, and they'll end up doing nothing. If they follow us into battle, and we lose, God forbid, then Kramer will take his vengeance on them. If we win by God's good will, then they will be in our bad graces, and we might invade them. 'Twould only be justice if we did, and it would serve the scurvy curs right. But we have no desire to bring more sorrow and bloodshed upon this land. They won't know that, though."

"In other words," Mix said, "they won't know whether to shit or go blind."

"What? Oh! I see what you mean. It's a powerful phrase but most distasteful. Just like the excrement you referred to."

Grimacing, he turned away.

Whatever changes the Riverworld had made in Stafford, one had not been a tolerance for obscene language. He no longer believed in the god of the Old and New Testament, though he still used His name, but he reacted as strongly here as on Earth to "dirty" words. Half a Nonconformist still lived within him. Which must give him daily pain, Mix thought, since the ex-royalists and the ex-peasants in this area were not averse to earthy speech.

The boats passed the state just below Deusvolens as the fog rose up from The River and rolled down from the hills on schedule. From then on, the men in the crow's nests above the grey clouds directed the sailing by pulling on ropes. The men handling these on the decks told the steersmen which way to turn the tiller and when to expect the great booms to swing over. It was dangerous navigation, and twice Mix heard the crash of boats colliding.

After what seemed an endless time, the signal was given that Deusvolens had been sighted. At least, they hoped that it was their destination. Sailing so blindly, with the plains as well as The River concealed in fog, they could not be sure.

Shortly before the sky was due to turn pale under the greater blaze of the rising sun, the capital "city" of Fides was sighted. One of the watchmen came down to report.

"There be great lights all over the place. Something's stirring, my lord-mayor."

A moment later there was a cry from aloft.

"Boats! Many boats! They're heading straight for us! Beware, milord!"

Stafford revealed that he could curse as well as any when under great pressure.

"God's wounds! It's Kramer's fleet! The goddamned swine! He's setting out on his own invasion! What damnable timing! May he rot in the devil's ass forever!"

Ahead of them came the clamor of war, men shouting, the blowing of flutes, beating of drums, then, faintly, the sound of great vessels in the vanguard ramming into each other, screams as men fell into the water or were speared, knifed, clubbed, or axed.

Stafford ordered that his craft ignore the Kramerian fleet, if possible, and head for Fides. He also commanded that signals be sent by his watchman to the other Albionian boats.

"Let the duke and the Cornishmen and the Huns take care of the enemy on the water!" he said. "We'll storm ashore as planned!"

As the sun cleared the mountains on their left, it disclosed a high earth and rock rampart on top of which was a wall of upright logs extending as far as the eye could see. At its base the fog was a woollen covering, but this would soon be burned away by the sun. There were thousands of helmeted heads behind the wall and above them the heads of thousands of spears. The huge alarm-drums were still booming, the echoes rolling back from the mountain behind it.

Amidst the deafening bruit, the flagship, *Invincible*, pulled up alongside the main gate, just past the end of the piers, and loosed, one by one, great stones from its catapults. These smashed in the main gates. Other boats, in Indian file, came up and loosed their boulders. Some struck too high, some too low. Nevertheless, five other huge holes were breached in the wooden walls and a few defenders smashed.

Instead of turning around to use the catapults on the other sides, a maneuver that would have taken much time, the boats sailed along the banks. They had to tack some to keep from grounding and so being rammed by those behind them. When the flagship had gone far enough to give room for its followers to stop, its sails were dropped, and its bow turned toward shore. Anchors, large stones tied to ropes, dropped into the shallows. At once, the small boats were launched, and since there was no room in them for all those aboard, many soldiers leaped into the water.

They swarmed ashore under a hail of spears, clubs, sling-stones, and axes onto the strip of land between the bases of the ramparts and the edge of the banks. They ran toward the smashed gateway, many carrying tall ladders.

Mix was among those in the lead. He saw men fall in front and on both sides of him, but he escaped being struck. After a minute, he was forced to slow his pace. The gateway was still a half mile away; he'd be too tired to fight at once if he ran full speed. The strategy of Stafford and the Council didn't seem so good now. They were losing too many men trying to amass at the breaches for a massive assault. Still, if the plans had gone as hoped, they might have worked quite well. The other fleets were to sail along the walls and throw the big rocks at intervals above and below where Stafford's vessels were. Thus, fifty different breaches could have been stormed and the Deusvolentians would have had to spread out their forces to deal with these.

If only Kramer's fleet hadn't decided to set out just before the big attack came. If only . . . that was the motto of generals, not to mention the poor devils of soldiers who had to pay for the if-only's.

As he ran he glanced now and then toward The River. The fog was almost gone now. He could see . . .

The deafening thunder of the copiastones erupting almost made his heart stop. He'd completely forgotten about them. They were inside the earth walls, set within log wells. At least the enemy wasn't going to have time to eat breakfast.

He looked to his right again. Out in The River were at least fifty vessels grappled in pairs, the crews of each trying to board the other. Many others were still manoeuvring, trying to run alongside the foe so that they could release missiles: fish-oil firebombs, stones, spears hurled by atlatls, clubs, stones tied to wooden shafts. It was too bad that there hadn't been time to make boomerangs and train men how to use them. They would have been very effective.

He couldn't determine how the battle on the water was going. Two ships were on fire. Whether they were enemy or friend, he didn't know. He saw a big warcanoe sink, a hole in its bottom made by a boulder cast by a catapult. A frigate was riding over the stern of a large catamaran. It was too early to say on whom Victory was smiling. She was a treacherous bitch, anyway. Just as you thought you couldn't lose, she slipped in something that resulted in you running like hell to get away from the defeated-suddenly-become-conquerors.

Now the attackers had joined in front of the gateway or before the other breaches. He had to catch his breath, and so did most of the others. However, men who'd landed from boats that had stopped close to these were already storming up the rampart and going through the holes in the walls. Trying to, anyway. Many dead or wounded lay on the slopes and in the entrances. Above them the Kramerians cast spears or hurled stones or poured burning fish oil from leather buckets into down-tilted stone troughs.

Tom cast his spear and had the satisfaction of seeing it plunge into one of the faces above the pointed ends of the log wall. He pulled his heavy axe from his belt and ran on.

Only so many defenders could get on the walkways behind the walls, and many of these had been struck by spears or large, unworked stones attached to wooden shafts.

On the ground behind the walls would be massed many soldiers, far outnumbering the invaders. At first, they'd crowded across the gateway, but now, as the first wave of Albionians crumbled, the Deusvolentians retreated. They were waiting for the next wave to come through. Then they would spread out, surround them, and close in.

A major shouted for the next charge to begin. Mix was glad that he couldn't be in that. Not unless those ahead of him were so successful that everybody got in.

Stafford, standing near Mix, shouted at the major to hold the attack. Two frigates were coming in. They'd be able to throw their catapults over the anchored ships and over the walls and into the men beyond them. The major couldn't hear him in the din. If he had, he wouldn't have been able to stop. Those behind forced him through the gate. Mix glimpsed him getting a spear in the chest, then he toppled forward out of sight.

Presently, Tom was being forced ahead by those axemen behind him. He fell once over a body, was kicked hard several times, struggled up, and began climbing up the steep slope of earth. Then he was through the gateway, walking over bodies, slipping, catching himself, and he was in a melee.

He fought as well as he could in the press, but he had no sooner engaged a spearman than he was whirled away, and he was fighting somebody else, a short dark man with a leather shield and a spear. Mix battered the man's shield aside with his axe and knocked the spear downward. He brought the axe upward, striking the man on the chin. The fellow reeled back, but something hit Mix's wrist, and he dropped his axe.

Quickly, Tom pulled out his tomahawk with his left hand and leaped on the man, knocking him down. Astride him, he brought the weapon down, splitting the skull between the eyes. He rose, panting. An Albionian staggered back and fell against him, flattening him. He writhed out from under and got to his feet. He wiped the blood from his eyes, not knowing if it was his or the soldier's who'd fallen over him. Certainly, he hadn't been aware of any head wound.

Panting, he glared around. The battle was going against the invaders. At least a fourth were casualties, and another fourth would soon be. Now was the time for a strategic withdrawal. But between him and the gateway were at least one hundred men, facing inward, their spears thrust out, waiting. The invaders were trapped.

Beyond them, at the other breaches, the fight was still going on. There were, however, so many Kramerians between him and the entrances that he couldn't make out the details.

Stafford, bloody, his helmet knocked off, his eyes wide, gripped his arm.

"We'll have to form men for a charge back through the gateway!"

That was a good idea, but how were they to do it?

Suddenly, by that unexplained but undeniable telepathy that exists among soldiers in combat, all the Albionians came to the same decision. They turned and fled toward those blocking the exit. They were speared in the back as they ran, hurled forward by clubs and axes from behind, or knocked over by weapons from the sides. Stafford tried to marshal them for a disciplined attack. He must have known that it was too late, though he tried valiantly nevertheless. He was bowled over by two men, rose, and fell again. He lay on his back, his mouth open, one eye staring up at the sky. The other was pierced by a spearhead.

Slowly, pulled by the weight of the shaft, his head turned, and his one eye was looking straight at Mix.

Something struck Tom in the back of the head and his knees loosened. He was vaguely aware that he was falling, but he had no idea who he was or where he was, and he had no time to try to figure it all out.

ℰ⅋ ELEVEN ℰ⅋

Tom Mix awoke, and he was sorry that he had.

He was lying on his back, a throbbing pain in the back of his head and a twisting in his stomach. The face looking down was blurry and doubled, wavering in and out. It was long and thin and hatchety, dark, black-eyed, a grim smile showing rows of white teeth in which the two front lower were missing.

Tom groaned. The face belonged to de Falla, Kramer's ramrod. The teeth had been knocked out by Tom himself while making his escape from this very place, Fides. He didn't think he'd be doing a repeat performance.

The Spaniard spoke in excellent only slightly accented English.

"Welcome to Deusvolens."

Mix forced a smile.

"I don't suppose I bought a return ticket?"

De Falla said, "What?"

Mix said, "Never mind. So what kind of cards are you planning to deal me?"

"Whatever they are, you'll accept them," de Falla said.

"You're in the driver's seat."

He sat up and leaned on one arm. His vision wasn't any better, and the movement made him want to throw up. Unfortunately, his last meal had long been digested. He suffered from the dry heaves, which made the pain in the back of his head even worse.

De Falla looked amused. No doubt, he was.

"Now, my friend, the shoe, as you English say, is on the other foot. Though you don't have any footwear."

He was right. Mix had been stripped of everything. He looked around and saw his hat on a man nearby and beyond that someone wearing his boots. Four men, actually. He must have had a concussion, no slight one. Well, he'd had worse injuries and survived to be better than ever. The chances for living long, though, didn't seem good.

There were bodies everywhere on the ground, none of which was moving or making a sound. He supposed that all but the lightly wounded had been put out of their pain. Not for the sake of mercy but for economy. There was no use wasting food on them.

Someone had pulled the spear out of Stafford's eye.

De Falla said, "There's still a battle on The River. But there's no doubt who'll win now."

The Spaniard gestured to two soldiers. They lifted Mix between them and started to march him across the plain, detouring around corpses. When his legs gave way, they dragged him, but de Falla came running. He told them to get a stretcher. Mix didn't need to ask why he was being so well treated, relatively speaking. He was a special prisoner to be saved for special reasons. He was so sick and weak that, at the moment, he didn't even care about the reasons.

They carried him to where the huts began and down a street and out past the huts to a compound. This was very large, though it held only a few prisoners. The log gate was swung open, and he was taken to an enclosure of upright logs set into the ground. Within this was a small hut. He was in a compound within a compound.

The two soldiers set him down inside the hut and checked on the amount of water in a baked-clay pot, his drinking supply. The nightjar was looked into, and one of the soldiers bellowed out a name. A short, thin worried-looking man ran up and got chewed out for not emptying it. Mix thought that he must indeed be special if such details were being taken care of.

Apparently, the previous occupant had not been so highly regarded. The stench was appalling even though the lid was on the thunder mug.

Seven days passed. Mix became better, his strength waxed, though it did not reach its fullness. Occasionally, he was troubled with recurrences of double vision. His only exercise was walking around the hut, around and around. He ate three times a day but not well. He had identified his copia which had been taken off the flagship by his captives, but he was allowed only half the food it gave and none of the cigarettes or liquor. His guards took these for themselves. Though he had smoked only two cigarettes in the past two years, he now yearned fiercely for more.

Daytime wasn't so bad, but late at night he suffered from the cold and the dampness. Most of all he suffered from not being able to talk to anybody. Unlike most of the guards he'd encountered during a dozen periods of incarceration, these refused to say a single word to him. They even seemed to be reserved with their grunts.

On the morning of the eighth day, Kramer and his victorious forces returned. From what he could overhear of the guards' conversation, New Albion, Ormondia, and Anglia had been conquered. There would be plenty of loot and women for all, including those who had not participated in the invasion.

Tom thought Kramer was celebrating too soon. He still had New Cornwall and the Huns to deal with. But he supposed that the defeat of their navies had made them pull in their necks for a while.

The other prisoners, about fifty, were hustled from their repair work on the ramparts back into the compound. Sounds of jubilation came from the area around the main gateway, drums beating, flutes shrilling, cheering. Kramer came through first—even at this distance Mix recognized the fat body and the piggish features—on a big chair carried by four men. The crowds shouted their greeting and tried to swarm around him but were pushed back by his bodyguard. After him came his staff and then the first of the returned soldiers, all grinning widely.

The chair was deposited in front of Kramer's "palace," a huge log structure on top of a low hill. De Falla came to greet him then, and both made speeches. Mix was too far away to hear what they said.

Some naked prisoners were marched in at spear point and double-stepped to the compound. Among the dirty, bruised, bloodied bunch was Yeshua. He sat down at once with his back to the wall, and his head sank as if he were completely dejected. Tom yelled at him until a man asked him whom he wanted. The man went across the compound and spoke to Yeshua. At first, Tom thought that Yeshua was going to ignore him. He looked at Tom for a moment and then let his head hang again. But after a while he rose, somewhat unsteadily, and walked slowly to the circular enclosure. He looked through the spaces between the logs, his eyes dull. He had been beaten about the face and body.

"Where's Bithniah?" Tom said.

Yeshua looked down again. He said, hollowly, "She was being raped by many men the last I saw of her. She must have died while they were doing it. She'd stopped screaming by the time I was taken to the boat."

Mix gestured at some female prisoners.

"What about them?"

"Kramer said he wanted some alive . . . to burn."

Mix grunted, and said, "I was afraid that was why they didn't kill me. Kramer's going to get a special revenge out of me."

He didn't add, though he was thinking it, that Yeshua would also be in the "privileged" class. Yeshua must know it, anyway.

He said, "If we start a ruckus, we might force them to kill some of us. If we're lucky, we'll be among the late unlamented."

Yeshua raised his head. His eyes were wild and staring.

"If only a man did not have to live again! If he could be dust forever, his sadness and his agonies dissolved into the soil, eaten by the worms as his flesh is eaten! But no, there's no escape! He is forced to live again! And again! And again! God will permit him no release!"

"God?" Tom said.

"It's just a manner of speech. Old habits die hard."

"It's tough just now," Tom said, "but in between the bad times it's not so bad. Hell, I'm sure that someday all this fighting will stop. Most of it, anyway. It's a time of troubles now. We're still getting straightened out, too many people are behaving like they did on Earth. But the setup's different here. You can't hold a man down. You can't tie him to his job and his house because he carries his own food supply with him and it doesn't take long to build a house. You can enslave him for a while, but he'll either escape or kill himself or make his captors kill him, and he's alive again and free and has another chance for the good life.

"Look here! We can make those buggers kill us now so we don't have to go through all the pain Kramer's figuring to give us. The guards aren't here now. Pull back the bar on the gate and let me out. As you can see, I can't reach through to do it myself. Once I'm out, I'll organise the others, and we'll go out fighting."

Yeshua hesitated, then gripped the big knob at the end of the massive bolt and, straining hard, withdrew it. Mix pushed the heavy gate open and left his prison within a prison.

Though there were no guards within the compound, there were many on the platforms outside the walls and in the towers. These saw Mix leave, but they did not object, which, Tom thought, meant that they knew he had to be released from it soon, anyway. He was just saving them the trouble of opening the gate.

It wouldn't be long before the prisoners would be herded out of the compound.

He called to the others, about sixty, to gather around him.

"Listen, you poor bastards! Kramer's got you marked for torture! He's going to put on a big show, a Roman circus! We're all going to wish soon we were never born, though I guess you know that! So I say we should cheat them! And save ourselves all that pain! Here's what I think we should do!"

His plan seemed wild to them, though mainly because it was

unheard of. But it offered escape of a sort which once would not have been regarded as such. It was better than just sitting there like sick sheep waiting to be slain. Their tired eyes took on some life; their exhausted and abused bodies lost their shrunken appearance, swelling up with hope.

Only Yeshua demurred.

"I cannot take a human life."

Tom said, in an exasperated tone, "You won't be doing that! Not in the sense we knew on Earth! You'll be giving your man his life! And saving him from torture!"

A man said, "He doesn't have to take anybody's life. He can volunteer to be one of those that'll die."

"Yeah, that's right," Tom said. "How about it, Yeshua?"

"No. That would make me a collaborator in murder, hence, a murderer, even if the one murdered was myself. Besides, that would be suicide, and I cannot kill myself. That, too, would be a sin, against . . ."

He bit his lower lip.

"Look!" Tom said. "We don't have time to argue. The guards are getting mighty curious now. First thing you know, they'll be storming in here."

"That is what you want," Yeshua said.

Angrily, Tom cried out, "I don't know what you did or where you were when you were on Earth, but whatever it was or who-ever you were, you really haven't changed! I've heard you say you've lost your religion, yet you act like you haven't lost a shred of it! You don't believe in God anymore, yet you were just about to spout off about not going against God! Are you crazy, man?"

"I think I've been crazy all my life," Yeshua said. "But there are some things I will not do. They are against my principles, even though I no longer believe in The Principle."

By then the captain of the guards was shouting at the prisoners, demanding to know what they were up to.

"Forget the mad Jew," a woman said. "Let's get this over with before they get here."

"Line up then," Mix said.

All except Yeshua got into one of two lines in which each person faced another. That was just as well since they were, without him, even-numbered. Opposite Mix was a woman, a brunette whom he vaguely remembered seeing in New Albion. She was pale and trembling but game enough.

He lifted the chamberpot by its rim and said, "You call it."

He swung the brown pot up, loosed it, and watched it turn over and over. Sixty-two pairs of eyes were fastened upon it.

"Open end!" The woman called out loudly but shakily.

The container, turning, fell. It landed on its bottom and cracked in two.

"Don't hesitate!" Tom shouted. "We don't have much time, and you might lose your nerve!"

The woman closed her eyes as Tom stepped up to her and gripped her throat. For a few seconds she held her arms out at right angles to her body. She was attempting to put up no resistance, to make the job easier for him and quicker for her. The will to live was, however, too strong for her. She grabbed his wrists and tried to break his grip. Her eyes opened wide as if she were pleading with him. He squeezed her throat more tightly. She writhed and kicked, driving her knee up between his legs. He bent away though not swiftly enough to avoid getting the knee in the belly.

"Hell, this ain't going to work!" he said.

He released her. Her face was blue by then, and she was gasping. He hit her in the chin, and she dropped onto the ground. Before she could regain consciousness, he was choking her again. It only took a few seconds to still her breath. Wanting to make sure, he held on a little longer.

"You're the lucky one, sister," he said, and he rose.

The people in his line, which had won the toss or lost it, depending upon the viewpoint, were having the same trouble he'd had. Though the other line had agreed beforehand not to fight against their stranglers, most of them had been unable to keep their promise. Some had torn loose and were slugging it out with their would-be killers. A few were running away, pursued. Some were dead, and some were now trying to choke their chokers.

He looked at the big gate. It was swinging open. Behind it was a horde of guards, all armed with spears.

"Stop it!" he roared. "It's too late now! Attack the guards!"

Without waiting to see how many had heard him, he ran toward the first of the spearmen. He yelled to give himself courage and to startle the guards into self-defense. But what did they have to fear from an unarmed, naked, and enfeebled man?

The guards nearest him did, however, raise their spears.

Good! He'd hurl himself onto the points, arms out, catching some in his belly and some in his chest.

But the captain bellowed out an order, and they reversed their weapons. The shafts would be used as clubs.

Nevertheless, he leaped, and he saw the butt end of the spear that would knock him senseless.

ᴄᴏ Twelve ᴄᴏ

When he awoke, he had two pains in his head, the new one far worse than the old. He also was suffering again from diplopia. He sat up and looked around at the blurred scene. There were bodies of the prisoners here and there. Some had been killed by the others, and some had been beaten to death by the guards. Three of the guards lay on the dirt, one dead, the others bleeding. Apparently, some prisoners had wrested the spears away from the guards and gotten some small revenge before being killed.

Yeshua was standing away from the rest of the prisoners, his eyes closed and his mouth moving. He looked as if he were praying, but Mix doubted that he was.

When he looked back, he saw about twenty spearmen marching through the compound gate. Kramer was leading them. Mix watched the short, fat youth with the dark-brown hair and very pale blue eyes walking toward him. His piggish face looked pleased. Probably, Mix thought, he was happy that Mix and Yeshua had not been slain.

Kramer stopped a few feet away from Mix. He looked ridiculous, though he must think he made a splendid figure. He wore a crown of oak wood each of the seven points of which sported a round button cut from mussel shells. His upper eyelids were painted blue, an affectation of the males of his land, an affectation which Mix thought was fruity. The upper ends of his black towel-cape were secured around his fat neck with a huge brooch made from copper, an exceedingly rare and expensive metal. On one plump finger was an oak ring in which was set an uncut emerald, also a scarce item. A black towel-kilt was around his paunch, and his knee-length boots were of black fish-leather. In his right hand he held a long shepherd's crook, symbol that he was the protector of his sheep—his people. It also signified that he had been appointed by God for that role.

Behind Kramer were two bloodied and bruised and naked prisoners, whom Mix had not seen before. They were short dark men with Levantine features.

Mix squinted. He was wrong. He did know one of the two. He was Mattithayah, the little man who had mistaken Mix for Yeshua when they had first been Kramer's prisoners.

Kramer pointed at Yeshua and spoke in English.

"Iss zat ze man?"

Mattithayah broke into a storm of unintelligible but recognizable English. Kramer whirled and sent him staggering backward with a blow of his left fist against the jaw. Kramer said something to the other prisoner. This one answered in English as heavily accented as Kramer's, but his native tongue was obviously different.

Then he cried, "Yeshua! Rabbi! We have looked for you for many years! And now *you* are *here*, too!"

He began to weep, and he opened his arms and walked toward Yeshua. A guard banged the butt of his spear on his back, over the kidney area, and the little man groaned and fell on his knees, his face twisted with pain.

Yeshua had looked once at the two men and had groaned. Now he stood with downcast eyes.

Kramer, scowling and muttering, strode up to Yeshua and seized his long hair. He jerked it, forcing Yeshua to raise his head.

"Madman! Anti-Christ!" he shouted. "You'll pay for your blasphemies! Yust ass your two crazedt friendss vill pay!"

Yeshua closed his eyes. His lips moved soundlessly. Kramer struck him in the mouth with the back of his hand, rocking Yeshua's head. Blood flowed from the right corner of Yeshua's lips.

Kramer screamed, "Shpeak, you filt! Do you indeedt claim to be Christ?"

Yeshua opened his eyes, and spoke softly.

"I claim only to be a man named Yeshua, just another son of man. If this Christ of yours did exist and if he were here, he would be horrified, driven to madness with despair, at what had happened on Earth to his teachings after he died."

Kramer, yelling, hit Yeshua alongside the head with his staff. Yeshua fell to his knees and then crumpled forward, his head hitting the earth with a soft thud. Kramer drove the toe of his boot against the fallen man's ribs.

"Renounce your blasphemiess! Recant your Satanic ravingks! You vill excape mush pain in zis worlt if you do, ant you may safe your zoul in the next!"

Yeshua raised his head, but he said nothing until he had regained his breath.

"Do what you will to me, you unclean Gentile."

Kramer shouted, "Shut your dirty mous, you inzane monshter!"

Yeshua grunted as Kramer's boot toe drove into his side again, and he moaned for a little while thereafter.

Kramer, his black cloak flapping after him, strode to Mattithayah and his companion.

"Do you shtill maintain zat zis lunatic iss ze Blessedt Zon of Godt?"

The two were pale beneath their dark skins, and their faces looked as if they were made of melting wax. Neither replied to Kramer.

"Answer me, you svine!" he cried.

He began to beat them with the shepherd's staff. They backed away, their hands up to protect themselves, but they were seized by the guards and kept from retreating.

Yeshua struggled to his feet. Loudly, he said, "He is so savage because he fears that they speak the truth!"

Mix said, "What truth?"

His double vision was increasing, and he felt as if he should vomit. He was beginning to lose interest in everything but himself. God, if only he could die before he was tied to the stake and the wood set afire!

"I've heard that question before," Yeshua said.

Mix didn't know for a moment what Yeshua meant. Then illumination flooded in. Yeshua had thought he'd said, "What *is* truth?"

After Kramer had beaten Mattithayah and his friend into unconsciousness, they were dragged out through the gate by their legs, their heads bumping, their arms trailing along behind their heads. Kramer started to walk toward Yeshua, his staff lifted high as if he intended to give him the same treatment. Mix hoped that he would. Perhaps, in his rage, he'd kill Yeshua now and thus save him from the fire.

The joke would certainly be on Kramer then.

But a sweating panting man ran through the gate, and he cried out Kramer's name. It was thirty seconds, though, before he caught his wind. He was the bearer of ill news.

Apparently, there were two fleets approaching, one from up-River, one from down-River. Both were enormous. The states to the north of Kramer's and the states to the south of the newly conquered territories had been galvanized into allied action against Kramer, and the Huns across from them had joined them. They finally realised that they must band together and attack Kramer before he moved against them.

Kramer turned pale, and he struck the messenger over the head with his staff. The man fell without a sound.

Kramer was in a bad way. Half of his own fleet had been destroyed in its victory, and the number of his soldiers had been considerably reduced. He wouldn't be ready for a long time to launch another attack nor was he well fitted to withstand an invasion from such a huge force.

He was doomed, and he knew it.

Despite Mix's pain and the knowledge of the fire waiting for him, he managed a smile. If Kramer were captured, he would undoubtedly be tortured and then burned alive. It was only just that he should be. Perhaps if Kramer himself felt the awful flames, he might not be so eager to subject others to them when he rose again.

But Mix doubted that.

Kramer shouted orders to his generals and admirals to prepare for the invasion. After they had left, he turned, panting, toward Yeshua. Mix called to him.

"Kramer! If Yeshua is who those two men claim he is, and they've no reason to lie, then what about you? You've tortured and killed for nothing! And you've put your own soul in the gravest jeopardy!"

Kramer reacted as Mix had hoped he would. Screaming, he ran at Mix with the staff raised. Mix saw it come down on him.

Kramer must have pulled his punch. Mix awoke some time later, though not fully. He was upright and tied to a great bamboo stake. Below him was a pile of small bamboo logs and pine needles.

Through the blur, he could see Kramer applying the torch. He hoped that the wind would not blow the smoke away from him. If it rose straight up, then he would die of asphyxiation and would never feel the flames on his feet.

The wood crackled. His luck was not with him. The wind was blowing the smoke away from him. Suddenly, he began coughing. He looked to his right and saw, vaguely, that Yeshua was tied to another stake very near him. Upwind. Good, he thought. Poor old Yeshua will burn, but the smoke from his fire will kill me before I burn.

He began coughing violently. The pains in his head struck him like fists. Vision faded entirely. He fell toward oblivion.

But he heard Yeshua's voice, distorted, far away, like thunder over a distant mountain.

"Father, they *do* know what they're doing!"

THE BLIND ROWERS

O ver the railing and into the Aegean Sea hurtled Joan McReady. She fell six feet, struck the water with her left shoulder, and went down. Two strokes upward brought her head above the surface. She looked up to see Platon Neusis standing in the moonlight.

He shook his fist at her and screamed in Romaic, reverting in his fury to his native tongue. He was a handsome man of thirty-five, but for the past six hours he had been getting uglier with each drink of Scotch and each refusal from her. Son of a multi-millionaire's widow, tall, blond, athletic, cosmopolitan, he was used to having his way with the women who accepted an invitation to go yacht-cruising with him. But he had not gotten his way.

Joan McReady, a secretary for a UN health unit, had met Platon at a party in Athens. From the first, she had had misgivings about his intentions. Even after dating him for two weeks, during which he had not gone beyond goodnight kisses, she did not trust him. Her friends had told her that he was a Don Juan. Also, she knew that the men of his country took "nice" girls to meet their mothers. So far, he had talked much of his mother, too much, but had not even hinted that he would like to introduce Joan to her.

When she had been invited to go on a cruise to Sikia, his native city on the northern coast of the Aegean, she had replied that she would love to go. That is, she would if others were going also. He assured her she would not be alone. There was another couple, a charming French couple. But they had gotten off at a small village south of Sikia, where they intended to stay for several weeks. Platon had suggested that he would like to continue to Sikia and see an uncle.

Once more, Joan had asked if she would be the only one aboard. He was smooth, as smooth as a hawk slipping through the air, and had never made a move or said a word that she might consider objectionable. He assured her again, and the ship left for Sikia on a moonlight cruise.

The captain and two crewmen were not on the yacht. Joan asked about them; Platon replied that they were on liberty. She reminded him of his promise. Smiling, he said that she was not alone. He was there.

The ship was then only half a mile from shore, and she could easily have swum the distance. She shrugged and told herself not to act like a fool. She could take care of herself. She was a little edgy for a while. Platon talked of the beauty of the landscape of his hometown and of the accomplishments of his uncle. Joan relaxed.

The ship moved on, and after an hour and a half, Platon, commenting that the sea was so smooth and beautiful, stopped the motors. He began drinking and soon, under the full moon and a full load of Scotch, made the proposals that were at first circuitous and then outright and even obscene. Joan did not try to be diplomatic. She was furious. Soon, they were yelling at each other. He tried to grab her; she clawed him; over the railing she went.

Joan refused to give him the satisfaction of hearing her scream or beg for help. She was so angry that she almost yielded to the impulse to try to swim to shore. Even when he continued to rage at her and showed no signs of throwing a ladder down to her, she did not get frightened. But when he disappeared and the motors coughed, and the yacht drew away, she became panicky. Still, she would not plead with him. Only when the white hull of the yacht was on the point of vanishing did she call out.

There was no answer, no moonlit whiteness getting larger. She was alone with the waves.

She still could not believe that he would not cool off and return after he had taught her a "lesson." But what if, when he came back, he could not find her? She was so small, and the sea was so large. And what if—unthinkable but nevertheless thought—he did not return?

The mainland shore was now at least fifteen miles away. The waters were not rough, and she was an excellent swimmer. She could stay afloat a long time, but she could not swim fifteen miles. Even if she could, she did not know which way to go. The moon was directly overhead. If only she had been more observant of the constellations and could guide herself by them . . .

She thought, *I'll panic if I don't do something. I can't just float here, waiting for that bastard Platon to come back. I'll swim in the direction his yacht went. No. He wasn't headed back to the shore. Or was he?*

First, she had to get rid of even the slight weight of her clothes. Her blouse and skirt slid off. After a slight hesitation, she removed her bra and panties. Modesty was non-survival. No man could see her, and the heaviness of watersoaked underclothing might mean a mile or two less of swimming.

Like a broad heavy hand, the sea closed around her. Its grip was not strong, but it promised a tighter squeeze later. It was not cold now, but it would become cold.

She swam slowly so that she could save her strength. Now and then she turned on her back and floated, though this resulted several times in a choking mouthful or stinging noseful.

But she kept on, and dawn swam out across the waves to meet her. The sun shone on nothing but water.

It seemed an easy thing to do, to quit moving her arms and legs and slide down into the waters and let the sea take her.

Twenty-five years old, and no one has taken me, she thought. *No man. I have resisted too strongly. I have said no too many times. I wanted it all to be right and proper, and no man was quite right. Now, I will be taken anyway. But by no man.*

Something long and hard slipped along her thigh and brushed against her crotch. She shrieked and turned and glimpsed the silver-and-black length of a fish.

Sharks? Were there sharks in the Aegean? She had never seen any. And that was no shark. A little fish not more than six or seven inches long

"I will swim until I have no strength left," she said.

An hour later, if the climb of the sun was a correct indication of time, she had reached the end of her strength. Treading, gasping, arms and legs heavy, as if logged with salt and water, she looked around the horizon. And she saw, to her right, a mass breaking the smooth line.

Clouds or land?

Whichever they were, she had to find out. Somehow, she would get there.

Fortunately, the current was carrying her towards the darkness. She floated and resisted the temptation to swim. Slowly, the infringement on the copyright of horizon became not clouds, but land. A squat hill, shaped like a crooked sausage, bent at an angle in the middle. There were large grey buildings halfway up. Later, a black sand beach at the foot of the hill.

A man was standing on the beach, a tall bearded man in a black robe and black cylindrical hat. He saw her, but he made no effort to help her. He turned and ran away, flapping his arms, the wide sleeves like the wings of a great clumsy bird attempting to take off. He ran up a flight of wooden steps zigzagging up the face of the cliff.

Why doesn't the damn fool come in after me and get me? she thought. *He can see I'm on the point of drowning. I can't stay up much longer. Can't he swim?*

Even though the shore was now only fifty yards away, she had to turn on her back and float. She did not have the energy to make two more strokes. Looking up at the sky, she thought, *Maybe that monk thinks I'm Venus riding out of the waves, having slipped off my scallop shell. And he's gone to spread abroad the news of another miracle, reinstate the old pagan religion. Or something.*

She giggled in near-hysteria. Then, hearing the growl of surf become a roar, she turned over and tried feebly to swim. She went up and down a valley, slid down its white-crested and green slope, and rolled over and over, going under at the bottom of the slope.

Coughing, she came up out of the waters. Now there were four men on the black sand, and others running down the crazy wooden steps. All were in robes and bearded. One of the men on the beach was white-haired and white-bearded. All had their heads turned away from her.

"Look at me!" she screamed. The wind tore her words apart. The waves swept her into the shallows, and she was on her hands and knees, sand grinding and cutting into her palms and knees, the receding sea trying to suck her back into the deep.

"Help me! *Look* at me!"

Two monks sidled towards her like huge black crabs. They held long poles, and their heads were turned away. One, however, was watching her out of the corner of his eyes. He thrust the end of the long wooden staff at her, and she grabbed for it and clung with all the strength—it was not much—that she had.

The monk shouted something and tore the pole from her grasp. Then it drove back at her. She put up her hands to stave it off but felt its hard end grinding into her breastbone. The monk lunged, and she was driven back out into a wave and knocked over by it.

"What are you doing? Are you crazy?" she screamed. Her lungs burned with the effort.

The white-haired man, his eyes shut, walked toward her. Two men, each holding an elbow, directed him, although they could see her no better than he. When the three felt the water of the dying thrust of the surf on their bare feet, they stopped.

She had thought that they had not heard her, but the old monk, instead of speaking Romaic, used broken but fluent English. What was she doing *here?* His words came to her against the wind and the crash of surf, and she could make out only a word here, a phrase there. She heard enough to catch the sense. Sense? It was senseless.

What a question! An idiot could see she was a castaway. Did he really think that she had deliberately swum from the mainland to this insane place to entice these men with her naked body?

Summoning strength from a reservoir she had thought emptied, she shouted, "You fools! I fell off a ship! I mean, I was thrown off! Please let me ashore! I'll die if you don't! Die!"

The old man took two more steps into the water, and he cried, "No female, animal or human, has set foot on this island for a thousand years, my daughter! We cannot allow you even to touch the shore!"

"For the love of God, I'll die! Please!"

The old monk roared, "We cannot have the sanctity of this island violated! It would be unclean forever! Indeed, how do we know what lusts of the devil would be unleashed if you came among us! Naked in your shamelessness! The man who first saw you said you were as naked as our mother Eve. He will pay a heavy penance for seeing you. He might even blind himself to make sure this does not happen again!"

Death, which had seemed to recede into the sea, was as close as ever. These men were fanatics. Reason, compassion, humanity— these meant nothing.

"Give me a robe!" she yelled. "I'll cover my body! And my face, too, if that offends you! Please! I can't last much longer! I don't want to die!"

The old man opened his mouth wide in a grimace, and she saw that he had only a few teeth and these were black. At the same time, the young monk who had shoved her back with the pole turned his head fully towards her. He smiled. His teeth were even and healthy-looking. His eyes were large, moist, dark, and long-lashed. Even with his thick curly beard, he was handsome.

"I'm coming ashore!" she screamed. "You'll have to kill me to stop me! And my blood will be on your hands! You murdering eunuchs!"

For answer, the old man pointed to his left. Fifty yards away, six monks were bending their backs into shoving a rowboat into the surf.

"You must get into that! You will be given a robe to cover your nakedness! My brothers will row you to the mainland! But you will have to steer! They will be blindfolded to remove them from temptation! Go straight, west, keeping the hill as a landmark! When it is out of sight, keep steering westward! Follow the sun! Then you will see the mountains of the mainland!"

He covered his eyes with his hands and said, "Do not speak to my brothers or touch them! They will have to scourge themselves, and even then . . ."

Joan did not wait to hear the rest. She had to get to the boat before she collapsed. Everything, the island, the sky, the sun, the sea, was shifting, flowing into each other. Only the old monk was stable and definite, a black tower in chaos.

Too tired to wade, she floated and paddled weakly toward the boat. The waves kept driving her into shore. They knocked her over on her side and carried her, bumping and scraping against the sand, to the edge of the beach. Twice, she tried to crawl upon the sand and get out of reach of the waves. Each time, the young monk placed the blunt end of the pole against her ribs and shoved. She winced with the pain and glared with anger at him. He stared directly at her, seemingly not caring if the others saw that his eyes were open. But then, they had their eyes shut and could not see him. Or, if they did, they could not accuse him without accusing themselves.

Moreover, he could not be expected to push her away with the pole unless he could see her. Perhaps he had been authorized by the old monk to do so.

When she managed to reach the boat, which was now two waves out and lifting and rising in one spot, kept from drifting back by the rowers, she was reeling. She stretched out a hand to a monk who was standing up and holding out a robe to her. His head was turned away. The others were blindfolded.

She grabbed the edge of the robe and pulled. The monk, losing his balance, toppled over into the sea beside her. The robe, which had slipped out of both their grasps, floated billowing towards the shore. The monk rose out of the water, risked one look, turned his head away from her, and struck out from the beach. He looked frightened.

Joan was trying to get the strength to call to the others in the boat and tell them they had to help her aboard when she felt a strong hand on her elbow. Another hand seized her buttocks in a powerful bowler's grip.

She cried out with pain, surprise, and injured dignity. A man laughed behind her. Up she went, kicking, forgetting her weakness in the shock of feeling those fingers. She went over the side of the boat and onto the deck, scraping the skin off her shins. She turned over on her back to see the face of the young monk appear, followed by his soaking black robes.

He now had on a blindfold, but it was placed high enough for him to peer out from beneath it. He said, "The abbot . . . say . . . you go to mainland. He give you . . . directions? We keeping the . . . what you call them . . . blindfooleds? . . . over eyes. You steer. You know how steer?"

"I know," she said. She took the tiller while he sat down in the position vacated by the monk who had fallen into the water. The young monk chanted, and the six began to row. Presently, Joan turned her head to look behind her. The figures on the beach were tiny.

"Do you have food and water? Especially water? I'm dying!"

The young monk, eyes bright from the reflection of her body, jerked his head at a basket and said, "Bread, wine, water there. But you not die. You too good flesh to die. Strong, healthy flesh."

She left the tiller and crawled to the basket. As she grasped its handle, she felt the monk's bare foot sliding over her breast. She recoiled but did not let the basket go.

He grinned at her and said, "You eat. Get strong. Weak woman is no good . . ."

She returned to the tiller and opened the bottle of water and drank, forcing herself to swallow the water slowly. Then she ate half a piece of bread, holding it with one hand while she steered with the other. Her eyes became heavy; the sun warmed her body; there were a million tiny golden needles, hypodermics all, shooting sleep into her. She shook her head and told herself she had to stay awake.

Suddenly, she was being shaken by the young monk. One hand

was on her shoulder, and it was some time before she became aware of what his other hand was doing.

Her voice was like a crow's. She squawked harshly, "Quit that! Or I'll scream!"

He stepped back from her, but he was smiling. He said, "You sleeping for two, maybe three hours. Plenty time yet. I steering. We not going straight, but not in a hurry. You eat more, get strength quick."

She ate rapidly, biting off huge chunks of the black bread and parts of the cold fish, and washing them down with long swallows of water. Food had never been so exquisite, and she did not care if the water was sanitary or not.

It was no wonder they were going in circles, she thought. The young monk had not been rowing and was not now. He stood near her while he finished off a bottle of wine.

"You strong now?" he said in a low voice.

"A little," she replied. She looked around the boat. "Don't you have anything I can cover myself with? What will I do when I get to the mainland?"

He grinned and slipped off his robe. He was wearing nothing under the robe. "Here. You want my robes?"

"You dirty peasant," she said. "Get back to your bench and start rowing. And tell me which way to steer. If you don't do it— right now!—I'll tell your friends what you're doing."

"They not understand English," he said. "And they not believe you. The abbot tell them not listen to you. Devil try seduce them through you. Maybe you what you say; maybe not. They to stop their . . . airs? . . . if you talk. And if they stop their airs, they not able to row. So you keep mouth shut."

He threw the bottle into the sea and said, "You true blonde, heh? You not dye your hair, right?"

"I'll scream so loudly they'll have to listen. And if you think they won't take their blindfolds off, you don't know men."

He inched towards her. His hands were half-closed, moving inwards towards each other and towards her. They were long slim hands with delicate fingers. They reminded her of the hands of

Platon Neusis. He played a piano beautifully; he often spoke of playing for hours for his mother. And shortly before he had thrown her overboard, he had boasted of how his hands played women, played symphonies with them.

"You scream; I throw you to the fish. Please. Not make me add one more sin. If it is sin to kill a devil sent to make men sin."

"And how will you explain my disappearance?" she said. "You can't get away with it."

"I tell them you crazy. You come out of sea, a crazy naked woman, a devil. You go back into sea. They be happy."

He stopped his hands a few inches from her and leaned toward her. His skin was like dark, fine-grained marble. However, long dark hairs sprouted out of his nostrils. *Like horns,* she thought. *What made me think of horns?*

"You're the devil!" she said. "Stay away from me!"

"Don't be scared. You keep mouth shut. I won't hurt you. What you expect, anyway? You can't go naked like this."

He pointed at her breasts and hips. "You white there. You take sunbath with coverings for evil things of woman. You white like the flesh in my dreams. You white!"

"You have a lot of guts talking about the evil things of women! You're the evil one! You'd rape me! Murder me!"

"I can't help," he said. "It's you sin, you fault. Three years I fight off devil at night when I try sleep. Even so, he sends womans—white like ghosts but solid like flesh—to my dreams. Then I wake up and pray. Night go by. Dawn come. I not sleep. Three years of fighting the devil. Now, just as I defeat the devil, can sleep, forget womans, you come out of the sea. Like the devil send you. And I tired of fighting!"

He launched himself at her, his hands closing around her throat and the force of his body throwing her backwards. Her head struck the wood of the deck with a shock that made her see bright planets with rings around them. His mouth was on hers, and it was no young god's, unless the Olympians were fond of garlic.

Joan fought, convinced that it made little difference in the eventual outcome whether she submitted, cooperated, or resisted.

He would have to kill her to keep her from talking, and he knew it. So she would fight.

Suddenly, his lips left hers, his hands loosened, and his face twisted. Shaking, moaning, he rolled away from her.

"Too much years. All this in me, all the womans in my dreams. I burst, like a goatskin with too much wine in it."

Joan gripped the tiller handle to keep from falling. She felt faint. But she managed to snarl feebly at him.

"Goatskin? You smell like a goat! I hope you're satisfied now."

She could see that he was not.

She rose, wobbling, and grabbed the blindfold of the nearest rower and pulled it upwards and off his head. He cried out and snatched for the cloth, though he still kept his eyes shut. Joan lunged past the young monk and began to pull the blindfold off another monk. Then, seeing the young monk coming towards her, she struck the two rowers in the faces with her fists. The nose of one began to bleed and the mouth of the other was cut with a finger-nail. They beat the air with their hands but refused to open their eyes.

"Are you all crazy?" she yelled. "Help! Help!"

The rowers sat stiffly, their oars motionless, faces rigid. They seemed to be listening to inward voices. They were silent; the young monk was silent; the only noise was the sea muttering and a gull mewing overhead.

"All right, all right, you deaf and dumb statues! Then I'll do it!"

She tore an oar from the hands of a grey-haired monk and raised it over her head. It felt heavy, too heavy, but she kept it up and then brought it down towards the young monk. He lifted his hands to protect himself and jumped backward. The blade of the oar hissed and thunked into the deck. The shaft flew from her hands and struck a monk on the shoulder. He cried out and half-rose, then sat back down.

The young monk charged, hurled into her, and bore her down. She fell heavily, her breath driven from her. There was an inch of water on the deck, and she was rowed backwards over it by the monk. By the time she had regained her wind, it was over. At least, for the time being.

"Now, you be a good girl," he said. "I not kill you, it not is necessary, see? Just keep mouth shut. Who knows? Nobody believe you anyway."

Joan had two older brothers who had told her what to do if she were attacked. It was too late for defense but not for revenge. She knew exactly where to squeeze with all the strength left.

He writhed, his teeth clamped to keep from crying out. She rose and picked up the empty bottle of water and struck him against the side of the head. She was too weak to swing with much force, and his thick hair gave him some protection. Nevertheless, his eyes unfocused for several seconds.

He struggled to his feet while clenching his groin with both hands. She ran at him. He lifted his hands to ward off her raised bottle. It struck his wrist and was torn from her fist, but she grappled with him. She hooked her heel behind his and pushed. They fell, this time with her on top, and toppled over the side of the boat and into the sea.

On striking the water, she loosed her hold on him and began swimming toward the boat. A scream and a cry in Romaic made her turn around. She saw his hands, reaching upwards for something to hold, slide beneath the surface.

There was nothing she could for him—or wanted to do. She lacked the strength even to save herself. The monks were rowing again and the boat was drawing away at speed beyond her ability to match.

No use calling out. Only one thing to do. Hope. Hope that the boat because it had no steersman and lacked one rower, might come back in a circle. It did not turn back to her. It dwindled, became a dot, then nothing.

Once again, she was alone, blue around, blue overhead, blue underneath. Somewhere down there, the young monk, his passion spent, was sinking to the bottom. And if help did not come soon, she would be joining him.

Coldly, wearily, she thought. *This is life for you. I fight for virtue. Why? I would rather lose it than my life. What good am I to anyone but the fish if I drown? Never again. Let them do what they want to. I want to live . . .*

The only lover I ever knew. No lover, really. And he died, just as I will die. For his sins? No, because the fool never learned how to swim.

Well, what if he couldn't? I can swim. And a fat lot of good it does me. This is life for you. Never again. If I'm saved—oh, God, I hope I'm Saved!—I'll become the biggest . . .

Something flashed white on the horizon.

It became larger while she fought to keep from screaming wildly and wasting her energy. It was the yacht, and it was soon alongside her. Platon, his face anxious, threw her a lifebelt and then hauled her aboard.

He wrapped a blanket around her, helped her below-decks and into a bunk. He gave her hot coffee, bread and cold meat. And after she had eaten, she looked at him, wondering if it was all to begin over.

"I am sorry, sorry beyond words!" he said. "I cooled off fifteen minutes after I—ah—pitched you off the ship. I came back, but I couldn't find you. I've been looking for you ever since, praying, cursing myself for a drunken swine, a murderer."

His eyes were bloodshot and puffy; his face, lined; his voice, shaky.

"Have you really been swimming all this time? What a woman! I would not have thought it possible! It is a miracle! And you have suffered so much because I thought you were one of those easy American girls playing hard to get. What an idiot, what a criminal, I am! Please forgive me!"

You don't know how easy it would be for you now, she thought. I have neither strength nor will to fight, I don't think I want to fight, ever again. Not physically, anyway. But what am I saying? In the water, I swore . . .

Platon took her hand in his. He said, "I think you are the most beautiful and the most amazing woman I have ever met. Even more than my mother! Yes, I say it openly. More than my mother! To prefer drowning to seduction by me, me, at whom women throw themselves! And to swim so far, so long, until I find you again! I tell you, it's a miracle!"

He kissed her hand. "Joan. I love you! I will take you to meet my mother! And I will say to her . . ."

She smiled slightly. If it turned out that Platon had saved more than one life when he had picked her up from the sea, if she felt life stirring within her in a few months . . . well, he was as much responsible for what had happened as the young monk. No, much more. Much, much more.

She said, "Yes. I'd like to meet your mother. But don't jump to any conclusions. I'm not so sure I want to even consider a man who's capable of murder."

"Murder! I would not dream of lifting my hand against you! You are a saint! I worship you!"

"And after you've gotten over your spasm of conscience?" she said. "Help me back to the deck, Platon. I feel stifled down here."

Near the railing, she turned to him. He was blond and blue-eyed and handsome, and his eyelashes were long and thick and dark. They reminded her of the lashes of the young monk. They were rotting now or being torn by fish or dissolving in the belly of a fish.

Platon took her hand again and kissed it. He said, "Your hand is so cold, my darling. But I swear that I will warm it and keep it warm forever.

She seized his hand and pulled him towards her, reached down, and squeezed. He shrieked and doubled over and then went over the railing as she shoved him with her foot.

She stood at the railing and looked down as he writhed and splashed and shouted. For a moment, she thought of taking the ship away and leaving him there. Then she thought. *No. He must live*. She threw down the ladder.

Platon crawled aboard. He lay gasping for a while and then said. "I do not blame you. You must have been very angry. You must have suffered terribly. But now you've paid me back. We can start off even again, can't we?"

She looked down at him. She felt cold, but she did not shiver. She thought. *Paid back? You have just started to pay.*

362

Riders of the Purple Wage

If Jules Verne could really have looked into the future, say 1966 A.D., he would have crapped in his pants. And 2166, oh, my!

—from Grandpa Winnegan's unpublished MS. *How I Screwed Uncle Sam & Other Private Ejaculations.*

THE COCK THAT CROWED BACKWARDS

Un and Sub, the giants, are grinding him for bread.

Broken pieces float up through the wine of sleep. Vast treadings crush abysmal grapes for the incubus sacrament.

He as Simple Simon fishes in his soul as pail for the leviathan.

He groans, half-wakes, turns over, sweating dark oceans, and groans again. Un and Sub, putting their backs to their work, turn the stone wheels of the sunken mill, muttering Fie, fye, fo, fum. Eyes glittering orange-red as a cat's in a cubbyhole, teeth dull white digits in the murky arithmetic.

Un and Sub, Simple Simons themselves, busily mix metaphors non-self-consciously.

Dunghill and cock's egg: up rises the cockatrice and gives first crow, two more to come, in the flushrush of blood of dawn of I-am-the erection-and-the-strife.

It grows out and out until weight and length merge to curve it over, a not-yet weeping willow or broken reed. The one-eyed red head peeks over the edge of bed. It rests its chinless jaw, then, as body swells, slides over and down. Looking monocularly this way and those, it sniffs archaically across the floor and heads for the door, left open by the lapsus linguae of malingering sentinels.

A loud braying from the center of the room makes it turn back. The three-legged ass, Baalim's easel, is heehawing. On the easel is the "canvas," an oval shallow pan of irradiated plastic, specially treated. The canvas is seven feet high and eighteen inches deep. Within the painting is a scene that must be finished by tomorrow.

As much sculpture as painting, the figures are in alto-relief, rounded, some nearer the back of the pan than others. They glow with light from outside and also from the self-luminous plastic of the "canvas." The light seems to enter the figures, soak awhile, then break loose. The light is pale red, the red of dawn, of blood watered with tears, of anger, of ink on the debit side of the ledger.

This is one of his Dog Series: *Dogmas from a Dog, The Aerial Dogfight, Dog Days, The Sundog, Dog Reversed, The Dog of Flinders, Dog Berries, Dog Catcher, Lying Doggo, The Dog of the Right Angle,* and *Improvisations on a Dog.*

Socrates, Ben Jonson, Cellini, Swedenborg, Li Po, and Hiawatha are roistering in the Mermaid Tavern. Through a window, Daedalus is seen on top of the battlements of Cnossus, shoving a rocket up the ass of his son, Icarus, to give him a jet-assisted takeoff for his famous flight. In one corner crouches Og, Son of Fire. He gnaws on a sabertooth bone and paints bison and mammoths on the mildewed plaster. The barmaid, Athena, is bending over the table where she is serving nectar and pretzels to her distinguished customers. Aristotle, wearing goat's horns, is behind her. He has lifted her skirt and is tupping her from behind. The ashes from the cigarette dangling from his smirking lips have fallen onto her skirt, which is beginning to smoke. In the doorway of the men's room, a drunken Batman succumbs to a long-repressed desire and attempts to bugger the Boy Wonder. Through another window is a lake on the surface of which a man is walking, a green-tarnished halo hovering over his head. Behind him a periscope sticks out of the water.

Prehensile, the penisnake wraps itself around the brush and begins to paint. The brush is a small cylinder attached at one end to a hose which runs to a dome-shaped machine. From the other end of the cylinder extends a nozzle. The aperture of this can be decreased or increased by rotation of a thumb-dial on the cylinder. The paint which the nozzle deposits in a fine spray or in a thick stream or in whatever color or hue desired is controlled by several dials on the cylinder.

Furiously, proboscisean, it builds up another figure layer by layer. Then, it sniffs a musty odor of must and drops the brush and slides out the door and down the bend of wall of oval hall, describing the scrawl of legless creatures, a writing in the sand which all may read but few understand. Blood pumppumps in rhythm with the mills of Un and Sub to feed and swill the hot-blooded reptile. But the walls, detecting intrusive mass and extrusive desire, glow.

He groans, and the glandular cobra rises and sways to the fluting of his wish for cuntcealment. Let there not be light! The nights must be his cloaka. Speed past mother's room, nearest the exit. Ah! Sighs softly in relief but air whistles through the vertical and tight mouth, announcing the departure of the exsupress for Desideratum.

The door has become archaic; it has a keyhole. Quick! Up the ramp and out of the house through the keyhole and out onto the street. One person abroad a broad, a young woman with phosphorescent silver hair and snatch to match.

Out and down the street and coiling around her ankle. She looks down with surprise and then fear. He likes this; too willing were too many. He's found a diamond in the ruff.

Up around her kitten-ear-soft leg, around and around, and sliding across the dale of groin. Nuzzling the tender corkscrewed hairs and then, self-Tantalus, detouring up the slight convex of belly, saying hello to the belly-button, pressing on it to ring upstairs, around and around the narrow waist and shyly and quickling snatching a kiss from each nipple. Then back down to form an expedition for climbing the mons veneris and planting the flag thereon.

Oh, delectation tabu and sickersacrosanct! There's a baby in there, ectoplasm beginning to form in eager preanticipation of actuality. Drop, egg, and shoot the chutychutes of flesh, hastening to gulp the lucky Micromoby Dick, outwriggling its million million brothers, survival of the fightingest.

A vast croaking fills the hall. The hot breath chills the skin. He sweats. Icicles coat the tumorous fuselage, and it sags under the weight of ice, and fog rolls around, whistling past the struts, and the ailerons and elevators are locked in ice, and he's losing altiattitude fast. Get up, get up! Venusberg somewhere ahead in the mists; Tannhäuser, blow your strumpets, send up your flares, I'm in a nosedive.

Mother's door has opened. A toad squatfills the ovoid doorway. Its dewlap rises and falls bellows-like; its toothless mouth gawps. Ginungagap. Forked tongue shoots out and curls around the boar cuntstrictor. He cries out with both mouths and jerks this way and those. The waves of denial run through. Two webbed paws bend and tie the flopping body into a knot—a runny shapeshank, of course.

The woman strolls on. Wait for me! Out the flood roars, crashes into the knot, roars back, ebb clashing with flood. Too much and only one way to go. He jerkspurts, the firmament of waters falling, no Noah's ark or arc; he novas, a shatter of millions of glowing wriggling meteors, flashes in the pan of existence.

Thigh kingdom come. Groin and belly encased in musty armor, and he cold, wet, and trembling.

GOD'S PATENT ON DAWN EXPIRES

. . . the following spoken by Alfred Melophon Voxpopper, of the Aurora Pushups and Coffee Hour, Channel 69B. Lines taped during the 50th Folk Art Center Annual Demonstration and Competition, Beverly Hills, level 14. Spoken by Omar Bacchylides Runic, extemporaneously if you discount some forethought during the previous evening at the nonpublic tavern The Private Universe, and you may because Runic did not remember a thing about that evening. Despite which he won First Laurel Wreath A, there being no Second, Third, etc., wreaths classified as A through Z, God bless our democracy.

> A gray-pink salmon leaping up the falls of night
> Into the spawning pool of another day.

> Dawn—the red roar of the heliac bull
> Charging over the horizon.

> The photonic blood of bleeding night,
> Stabbed by the assassin sun.

and so on for fifty lines punctuated and fractured by cheers, hand-claps, boos, hisses, and yelps.

Chib is half-awake. He peeps down into the narrowing dark as the dream roars off into the subway tunnel. He peeps through barely opened lids at the other reality: consciousness.

"Let my peeper go!" he groans with Moses and so, thinking of long beards and horns (courtesy of Michelangelo), he thinks of his great-great-grand-father.

The will, a crowbar, forces his eyelids open. He sees the fido which spans the wall opposite him and curves up over half the ceiling. Dawn, the paladin of the sun, is flinging its gray gauntlet down.

Channel 69B, YOUR FAVORITE CHANNEL, LA's own, brings you dawn. (Deception in depth. Nature's false dawn shadowed forth with electrons shaped by devices shaped by man.)

Wake up with the sun in your heart and a song on your lips! Thrill to the stirring lines of Omar Runic! See dawn as the birds in the trees, as God, see it!

Voxpopper chants the lines softly while Grieg's *Anitra* wells softly. The old Norwegian never dreamed of this audience and just as well. A young man, Chibiabos Elgreco Winnegan, has a sticky wick, courtesy of a late gusher in the oilfield of the unconscious.

"Off your ass and onto your steed," Chib says. "Pegasus runs today."

He speaks, thinks, lives in the present tensely.

Chib climbs out of bed and shoves it into the wall. To leave the bed sticking out, rumpled as an old drunkard's tongue, would fracture the aesthetics of his room, destroy that curve that is the reflection of the basic universe, and hinder him in his work.

The room is a huge ovoid and in a corner is a small ovoid, the toilet and shower. He comes out of it looking like one of Homer's god-like Achaeans, massively thighed, great-armed, golden-brown-skinned, blue-eyed, auburn-haired—although beardless. The phone is simulating the tocsin of a South American tree frog he once heard over Channel 122.

"Open O sesame!"

INTER CAECOS REGNAT LUSCUS

The face of Rex Luscus spreads across the fido, the pores of skin like the cratered fields of a World War I battlefield. He wears a black monocle over the left eye, ripped out in a brawl among art critics during the *I Love Rembrandt Lecture Series*, Channel 109. Although he has enough pull to get a priority for eye-replacement, he has refused.

"*Inter caecos regnat luscus*," he says when asked about it and quite often when not. "Translation: among the blind, the one-eyed man is king. That's why I renamed myself Rex Luscus, that is, King One-eyed."

There is a rumor, fostered by Luscus, that he will permit the bioboys to put in an artificial protein eye when he sees the works of an artist great enough to justify focal vision. It is also rumored that he may do so soon, because of his discovery of Chibiabos Elgreco Winnegan.

Luscus looks hungrily (he swears by adverbs) at Chib's tomentum and outlying regions. Chib swells, not with tumescence but with anger.

Luscus says, smoothly, "Honey, I just want to reassure myself that you're up and about the tremendously important business of this day. You must be ready for the showing, must! But now I see you, I'm reminded I've not eaten yet. What about breakfast with me?"

"What're we eating?" Chib says. He does not wait for a reply. "No. I've too much to do today. Close O sesame!"

Rex Luscus' face fades away, goatlike, or, as he prefers to describe it, the face of Pan, a Faunus of the arts. He has even had his ears trimmed to a point. Real cute.

"Baa-aa-aa!" Chib bleats at the phantom. "Ba! Humbuggery! I'll never kiss your ass, Luscus, or let you kiss mine. Even if I lose the grant!"

The phone bells again. The dark face of Rousseau Red Hawk appears. His nose is as the eagle's, and his eyes are broken black glass. His broad forehead is bound with a strip of red cloth, which circles the straight black hair that glides down to his shoulders. His shirt is buckskin; a necklace of beads hangs from his neck. He looks like a Plains Indian, although Sitting Bull, Crazy Horse, or the noblest Roman Nose of them all would have kicked him out of the tribe. Not that they were anti-Semitic, they just could not have respected a brave who broke out into hives when near a horse.

Born Julius Applebaum, he legally became Rousseau Red Hawk on his Naming Day. Just returned from the forest reprimevalized, he is now reveling in the accursed fleshpots of a decadent civilization.

"How're you, Chib? The gang's wondering how soon you'll get here?"

"Join you? I haven't had breakfast yet, and I've a thousand things to do to get ready for the showing. I'll see you at noon!"

"You missed out on the fun last night. Some goddam Egyptians tried to feel the girls up, but we salaamed them against the walls."

Rousseau vanished like the last of the red men.

Chib thinks of breakfast just as the intercom whistles. Open O sesame! He sees the living room. Smoke, too thick and furious for the air-conditioning to whisk away, roils. At the far end of the ovoid, his little half-brother and half-sister sleep on a flato. Playing Mama-and-friend, they fell asleep, their mouths open in blessed innocence, beautiful as only sleeping children can be.

Opposite the closed eyes of each is an unwinking eye like that of a
Mongolian Cyclops.

"Ain't they cute?" Mama says. "The darlings were just too
tired to toddle off."

The table is round. The aged knights and ladies are gathered
around it for the latest quest of the ace, king, queen, and jack.
They are armored only in layer upon layer of fat. Mama's jowls
hang down like banners on a windless day. Her breasts creep and
quiver on the table, bulge, and ripple.

"A gam of gamblers," he says aloud, looking at the fat faces,
the tremendous tits, the rampant rumps. They raise their eyebrows. What the hell's the mad genius talking about now?

"Is your kid really retarded?" says one of Mama's friends, and
they laugh and drink some more beer. Angela Ninon, not wanting
to miss out on this deal and figuring Mama will soon turn on the
sprayers anyway, pisses down her leg. They laugh at this, and
William Conqueror says, "I open."

"I'm always open," Mama says, and they shriek with laughter.

Chib would like to cry. He does not cry, although he has been
encouraged from childhood to cry any time he feels like it.

> —It makes you feel better and look at the Vikings,
> what men they were and they cried like babies
> whenever they felt like it

Courtesy of Channel 202 on the popular program *What's A
Mother Done?*

He does not cry because he feels like a man who thinks about
the mother he loved and who is dead but who died a long time
ago. His mother has been long buried under a landslide of flesh.
When he was sixteen, he had had a lovely mother.

Then she cut him off.

THE FAMILY THAT BLOWS IS THE FAMILY THAT GROWS

—from a poem by Edgar A. Grist, via Channel 88

"Son, I don't get much out of this. I just do it because I love you."

Then, fat, fat, fat! Where did she go? Down into the adipose abyss. Disappearing as she grew larger.

"Sonny, you could at least wrestle with me a little now and then."

"You cut me off, Mama. That was all right. I'm a big boy now. But you haven't any right to expect me to want to take it up again."

"You don't love me any more!"

"What's for breakfast, Mama?" Chib says.

"I'm holding a good hand, Chibby," Mama says. "As you've told me so many times, you're a big boy. Just this once, get your own breakfast."

"What'd you call me for?"

"I forgot when your exhibition starts. I wanted to get some sleep before I went."

"14:30, Mama, but you don't have to go."

Rouged green lips part like a gangrened wound. She scratches one rouged nipple. "Oh, I want to be there. I don't want to miss my own son's artistic triumphs. Do you think you'll get the grant?"

"If I don't, it's Egypt for us," he says.

"Those stinking Arabs!" says William Conqueror.

"It's the Bureau that's doing it, not the Arabs," Chib says. "The Arabs moved for the same reason we may have to move."

From Grandpa's unpublished MS.:
> Whoever would have thought that Beverly Hills
> would become anti-Semitic?

"I don't want to go to Egypt!" Mama wails. "You got to get that grant, Chibby. I don't want to leave the clutch. I was born and raised here, well, on the tenth level, anyway, and when I moved all my friends went along. I won't go!"

"Don't cry, Mama," Chib says, feeling distress despite himself.

"Don't cry. The government can't force you to go, you know. You got your rights."

"If you want to keep on having goodies, you'll go," says Conqueror. "Unless Chib wins the grant, that is. And I wouldn't blame him if he didn't even try to win it. It ain't his fault you can't say no to Uncle Sam. You got your purple and the yap Chib makes from selling his paintings. Yet it ain't enough. You spend faster than you get it."

Mama screams with fury at William, and they're off. Chib cuts off fido. Hell with breakfast; he'll eat later. His final painting for the Festival must be finished by noon. He presses a plate, and the bare egg-shaped room opens here and there, and painting equipment comes out like a gift from the electronic gods. Zeuxis would flip and Van Gogh would get the shakes if they could see the canvas and palette and brush Chib uses.

The process of painting involves the individual bending and twisting of thousands of wires into different shapes at various depths. The wires are so thin they can be seen only with magnifiers and manipulated with exceedingly delicate pliers. Hence, the goggles he wears and the long almost-gossamer instrument in his hand when he is in the first stages of creating a painting. After hundreds of hours of slow and patient labor (of love), the wires are arranged.

Chib removes his goggles to perceive the overall effect. He then uses the paint-sprayer to cover the wires with the colors and hues he desires. The paint dries hard within a few minutes. Chib attaches electrical leads to the pan and presses a button to deliver a tiny voltage through the wires. These glow beneath the paint and, Lilliputian fuses, disappear in blue smoke.

The result is a three-dimensional work composed of hard shells of paint on several levels below the exterior shell. The shells are of varying thicknesses and all are so thin that light slips through the upper to the inner shell when the painting is turned at angles. Parts of the shells are simply reflectors to intensify the light so that the inner images may be more visible.

When being shown, the painting is on a self-moving pedestal

which turns the painting 12 degrees to the left from the center and then 12 degrees to the right from the center.

The fido tocsins. Chib, cursing, thinks of disconnecting it. At least, it's not the intercom with his mother calling hysterically. Not yet, anyway. She'll call soon enough if she loses heavily at poker.

Open O sesame!

SING, O MEWS, OF UNCLE SAM

Grandpa writes in his *Private Ejaculations*:

> Twenty-five years after I fled with twenty billion dollars and then supposedly died of a heart attack, Falco Accipiter is on my trail again. The IRB detective who named himself Falcon Hawk when he entered his profession. What an egotist! Yet, he is as sharp-eyed and relentless as a bird of prey, and I would shiver if I were not too old to be frightened by mere human beings. Who loosed the jesses and hood? How did he pick up the old and cold scent?

Accipiter's face is that of an overly suspicious peregrine that tries to look everywhere while it soars, that peers up its own anus to make sure that no duck has taken refuge there. The pale blue eyes fling glances like knives shot out of a shirtsleeve and hurled with a twist of the wrist. They scan all with sherlockian intake of minute and significant detail. His head turns back and forth, ears twitching, nostrils expanding and collapsing, all radar and sonar and odar.

"Mr. Winnegan, I'm sorry to call so early. Did I get you out of bed?"

"It's obvious you didn't!" Chib says. "Don't bother to introduce yourself. I know you. You've been shadowing me for three days."

Accipiter does not redden. Master of control, he does all his blushing in the depths of his bowels, where no one can see. "If you know me, perhaps you can tell me why I'm calling you?"

"Would I be dumbshit enough to tell you?"

"Mr. Winnegan, I'd like to talk to you about your great-great-grandfather."

"He's been dead for twenty-five years!" Chib cries. "Forget him. And don't bother me. Don't try for a search warrant. No judge would give you one. A man's home is his hassle . . . I mean castle."

He thinks of Mama and what the day is going to be like unless he gets out soon. But he has to finish the painting.

"Fade off, Accipiter," Chib says. "I think I'll report you to the BPHR. I'm sure you got a fido inside that silly-looking hat of yours."

Accipiter's face is as smooth and unmoving as an alabaster carving of the falcon-god Horus. He may have a little gas bulging his intestines. If so, he slips it out unnoticed.

"Very well, Mr. Winnegan. But you're not getting rid of me that easily. After all . . ."

"Fade out!"

The intercom whistles thrice. What I tell you three times is Grandpa. "I was eavesdropping," says the 120-year-old voice, hollow and deep as an echo from a Pharaoh's tomb. "I want to see you before you leave. That is, if you can spare the Ancient of Daze a few minutes."

"Always, Grandpa," Chib says, thinking of how much he loves the old man. "You need any food?"

"Yes, and for the mind, too."

Der Tag. Dies Irae. Götterdammerung. Armageddon. Things are closing in. Make-or-break day. Go-no-go time. All these calls and a feeling of more to come. What will the end of the day bring?

THE TROCHE SUN SLIPS INTO THE SORE THROAT
OF NIGHT

—from Omar Runic

Chib walks towards the convex door, which rolls into the interstices between the walls. The focus of the house is the oval family room. In the first quadrant, going clockwise, is the kitchen, separated from the family room by six-meter-high accordion screens, painted with scenes from Egyptian tombs by Chib, his too subtle comment on modern food. Seven slim pillars around the family room mark the borders of room and corridor. Between the pillars are more tall accordion screens, painted by Chib during his Amerind mythology phase.

The corridor is also oval-shaped; every room in the house opens onto it. There are seven rooms, six bedroom-workroom-study-toilet-shower combinations. The seventh is a storeroom.

Little eggs within bigger eggs within great eggs within a mega-monolith on a planetary pear within an ovoid universe, the latest cosmogony indicating that infinity has the form of a hen's fruit. God broods over the abyss and cackles every trillion years or so.

Chib cuts across the hall, passes between two pillars, carved by him into nymphet caryatids, and enters the family room. His mother looks sidewise at her son, who she thinks is rapidly approaching insanity if he has not already overshot his mark. It's partly her fault; she shouldn't have gotten disgusted and in a moment of wackiness called It off. Now, she's fat and ugly, oh, God, so fat and ugly. She can't reasonably or even unreasonably hope to start up again.

It's only natural, she keeps telling herself, sighing, resentful, teary, that he's abandoned the love of his mother for the strange, firm, shapely delights of young women. But to give them up, too? He's not a fairy. He quit all that when he was thirteen. So what's the reason for his chastity? He isn't in love with the fornixator, either, which she would understand, even if she did not approve.

Oh, God, where did I go wrong? And then, There's nothing wrong with me. He's going crazy like his father—Raleigh Renaissance, I think his name was—and his aunt and his great-great-grandfather. It's all that painting and those radicals, the Young Radishes, he runs around with. He's too artistic, too sensitive. Oh, God, if something happens to my little boy, I'll have to go to Egypt.

Chib knows her thoughts since she's voiced them so many times and is not capable of having new ones. He passes the round table without a word. The knights and ladies of the canned Camelot see him through a beery veil.

In the kitchen, he opens an oval door in the wall. He removes a tray with food in covered dishes and cups, all wrapped in plastic.

"Aren't you going to eat with us?"

"Don't whine, Mama," he says and goes back to his room to pick up some cigars for his Grandpa. The door, detecting, amplifying, and transmitting the shifting but recognizable eidolon of epidermal electrical fields to the activating mechanism, balks. Chib is too upset. Magnetic maelstroms rage over his skin and distort the spectral configuration. The door half-rolls out, rolls in, changes its mind again, rolls out, rolls in.

Chib kicks the door and it becomes completely blocked. He decides he'll have a video or vocal sesame put in. Trouble is, he's short of units and coupons and can't buy the materials. He shrugs and walks along the curving, one-walled hall and stops in front of Grandpa's door, hidden from view of those in the living room by the kitchen screens.

> For he sang of peace and freedom,
> Sang of beauty, love, and longing;
> Sang of death, and life undying
> In the Islands of the Blessed,
> In the kingdom of Ponemah,
> In the land of the Hereafter.
> Very dear to Hiawatha
> Was the gentle Chibiabos.

Chib chants the passwords; the door rolls back.

Light glares out, a yellowish red-tinged light that is Grandpa's own creation. Looking into the convex oval door is like looking into the lens of a madman's eyeball. Grandpa, in the middle of the room, has a white beard falling to midthigh and white hair cataracting to just below the back of his knees. Although beard and headhair conceal his nakedness, and he is not out in public, he wears a pair of shorts. Grandpa is somewhat old-fashioned, forgivable in a man of twelve decadencies.

Like Rex Luscus, he is one-eyed. He smiles with his own teeth, grown from buds transplanted thirty years ago. A big green cigar sticks out of one corner of his full red mouth. His nose is broad and smeared as if time had stepped upon it with a heavy foot. His forehead and cheeks are broad, perhaps due to a shot of Ojibway blood in his veins, though he was born Finnegan and even sweats celtically, giving off an aroma of whiskey. He holds his head high, and the blue-gray eye is like a pool at the bottom of a prediluvian pothole, remnant of a melted glacier.

All in all, Grandpa's face is Odin's as he returns from the Well of Mimir, wondering if he paid too great a price. Or it is the face of the windbeaten, sandblown Sphinx of Gizeh.

"Forty centuries of hysteria look down upon you, to paraphrase Napoleon," Grandpa says. "The rockhead of the ages. *What, then, is Man?* sayeth the New Sphinx, Edipus having resolved the question of the Old Sphinx and settling nothing because She had already delivered another of her kind, a smartass kid with a question nobody's been able to answer yet. And perhaps just as well it can't be."

"You talk funny," Chib says. "But I like it."

He grins at Grandpa, loving him.

"You sneak into here every day, not so much from love for me as to gain knowledge and insight. I have seen all, heard everything, and thought more than a little. I voyaged much before I took refuge in this room a quarter of a century ago. Yet confinement here has been the greatest Odyssey of all.

THE ANCIENT MARINATOR

I call myself. A marinade of wisdom steeped in the brine of over-salted cynicism and too long a life."

"You smile so, you must have just had a woman," Chib teases.

"No, my boy. I lost the tension in my ramrod thirty years

ago. And I thank God for that, since it removes from me the temptation of fornication, not to mention masturbation. However, I have other energies left, hence, scope for other sins, and these are even more serious.

"Aside from the sin of sexual commission, which paradoxically involves the sin of sexual emission, I had other reasons for not asking that Old Black Magician Science for shots to starch me out again. I was too old for young girls to be attracted to me for anything but money. And I was too much a poet, a lover of beauty, to take on the wrinkled blisters of my generation or several just before mine.

"So now you see, my son. My clapper swings limberly in the bell of my sex. Ding, dong, ding, dong. A lot of dong but not much ding."

Grandpa laughs deeply, a lion's roar with a spray of doves.

"I am but the mouthpiece of the ancients, a shyster pleading for long-dead clients. Come not to bury but to praise and forced by my sense of fairness to admit the faults of the past, too. I'm a queer crabbed old man, pent like Merlin in his tree trunk. Samolxis, the Thracian bear god, hibernating in his cave. The Last of the Seven Sleepers."

Grandpa goes to the slender plastic tube depending from the ceiling and pulls down the folding handles of the eyepiece.

"Accipiter is hovering outside our house. He smells something rotten in Beverly Hills, level 14. Could it be that Win-again Winnegan isn't dead? Uncle Sam is like a diplodocus kicked in the ass. It takes twenty-five years for the message to reach its brain."

Tears appear in Chib's eyes. He says, "Oh, God, Grandpa, I don't want anything to happen to you."

"What can happen to a 120-year-old man besides failure of brain or kidneys?"

"With all due respect, Grandpa," Chib says, "you do rattle on."

"Call me Id's mill," Grandpa says. "The flour it yields is baked in the strange oven of my ego—or half-baked, if you please."

Chib grins through his tears and says, "They taught me at school that puns are cheap and vulgar."

"What's good enough for Homer, Aristophanes, Rabelais, and Shakespeare is good enough for me. By the way, speaking of cheap and vulgar, I met your mother in the hall last night, before the poker party started. I was just leaving the kitchen with a bottle of booze. She almost fainted. But she recovered fast and pretended not to see me. Maybe she did think she'd seen a ghost. I doubt it. She'd have been blabbing all over town about it."

"She may have told her doctor," Chib says. "She saw you several weeks ago, remember? She may have mentioned it while she was bitching about her so-called dizzy spells and hallucinations."

"And the old sawbones, knowing the family history, called the IRB. Maybe."

Chib looks through the periscope's eyepiece. He rotates it and turns the knobs on the handle-ends to raise and lower the cyclops on the end of the tube outside. Accipiter is stalking around the aggregate of seven eggs, each on the end of a broad thin curved branchlike walk projecting from the central pedestal. Accipiter goes up the steps of a branch to the door of Mrs. Applebaum's. The door opens.

"He must have caught her away from the fornixator," Chib says. "And she must be lonely; she's not talking to him over fido. My God, she's fatter than Mama!"

"Why not?" Grandpa says. "Mr. and Mrs. Everyman sit on their asses all day, drink, eat, and watch fido, and their brains run to mud and their bodies to sludge. Caesar would have had no trouble surrounding himself with fat friends these days. You ate, too, Brutus?"

Grandpa's comment, however, should not apply to Mrs. Applebaum. She has a hole in her head, and people addicted to fornixation seldom get fat. They sit or lie all day and part of the night, the needle in the fornix area of the brain delivering a series of minute electrical jolts. Indescribable ecstasy floods through their bodies with every impulse, a delight far surpassing any of food, drink, or sex. It's illegal, but the government never bothers a user unless it wants to get him for something else, since a fornic rarely has children. Twenty per cent of LA have had holes drilled in their heads and tiny shafts inserted for access of the needle. Five per cent are addicted; they waste away, seldom eating, their distended bladders spilling poisons into the bloodstream.

Chib says, "My brother and sister must have seen you sometimes when you were sneaking out to mass. Could they . . . ?"

"They think I'm a ghost, too. In this day and age! Still, maybe it's a good sign that they can believe in something, even a spook."

"You better stop sneaking out to church."

"The Church, and you, are the only things that keep me going. It was a sad day, though, when you told me you couldn't believe. You would have made a good priest—with faults, of course—and I could have had private mass and confession in this room."

Chib says nothing. He's gone to instruction and observed services just to please Grandpa. The church was an egg-shaped seashell which, held to the ear, gave only the distant roar of God receding like an ebb tide.

THERE ARE UNIVERSES BEGGING FOR GODS
yet He hangs around this one looking for work.

—from Grandpa's MS.

Grandpa takes over the eyepiece. He laughs. "The Internal Revenue Bureau! I thought it'd been disbanded! Who the hell has an income big enough to report on any more? Do you suppose it's still active just because of me? Could be."

He calls Chib back to the scope, directed towards the center of Beverly Hills. Chib has a lane of vision between the seven-egged clutches on the branched pedestals. He can see part of the central plaza, the giant ovoids of the city hall, the federal bureaus, the Folk Center, part of the massive spiral on which sit the houses of worship, and the dora (from pandora) where those on the purple wage get their goods and those with extra income get their goodies. One end of the big artificial lake is visible; boats and canoes sail on it and people fish.

The irradiated plastic dome that enfolds the clutches of Beverly Hills is sky-blue. The electronic sun climbs towards the zenith. There are a few white genuine-looking images of clouds and even a V of geese migrating south, their honks coming down faintly. Very nice for those who have never been outside the walls of LA. But Chib spent two years in the World Nature Rehabilitation and Conservation Corps—the WNRCC—and he knows the difference. Almost, he decided to desert with Rousseau Red Hawk and join the neo-Amerinds. Then, he was going to become a forest ranger. But this might mean he'd end up shooting or arresting Red Hawk. Besides, he didn't want to become a sammer. And he wanted more than anything to paint.

"There's Rex Luscus," Chib says. "He's being interviewed outside the Folk Center. Quite a crowd."

THE PELLUCIDAR BREAKTHROUGH

Luscus' middle name should have been Upmanship. A man of great erudition, with privileged access to the Library of Greater LA computer, and of Ulyssean sneakiness, he is always scoring over his colleagues.

He it was who founded the Go-Go School of Criticism.

Primalux Ruskinson, his great competitor, did some extensive research when Luscus announced the title of his new philosophy. Ruskinson triumphantly announced that Luscus had taken the phrase from obsolete slang, current in the mid-twentieth century.

Luscus, in the fido interview next day, said that Ruskinson was a rather shallow scholar, which was to be expected.

Go-go was taken from the Hottentot language. In Hottentot, *go-go* meant to examine, that is, to keep looking until something about the object—in this case, the artist and his works—has been observed.

The critics got in line to sign up at the new school. Ruskinson thought of committing suicide, but instead accused Luscus of having blown his way up the ladder of success.

Luscus replied on fido that his personal life was his own, and

Ruskinson was in danger of being sued for violation of privacy. However, he deserved no more effort than a man striking at a mosquito.

"What the hell's a mosquito?" say millions of viewers. "Wish the bighead would talk language we could understand."

Luscus' voice fades off for a minute while the interpreters explain, having just been slipped a note from a monitor who's run off the word through the station's encyclopedia.

Luscus rode on the novelty of the Go-Go School for two years.

Then he re-established his prestige, which had been slipping somewhat, with his philosophy of the Totipotent Man.

This was so popular that the Bureau of Cultural Development and Recreation requisitioned a daily one-hour slot for a year-and-a-half in the initial program of totipotentializing.

Grandpa Winnegan's penned comment in his *Private Ejaculations*:

What about The Totipotent Man, that apotheosis of individuality and complete psychosomatic development, the democratic Übermensch, as recommended by Rex Luscus, the sexually one-sided? Poor old Uncle Sam! Trying to force the proteus of his citizens into a single stabilized shape so he can control them. And at the same time trying to encourage each and every to bring to flower his inherent capabilities—if any! The poor old long-legged, chin-whiskered, milk-hearted, flint-brained schizophrenic! Verily, the left hand knows not what the right hand is doing. As a matter of fact, the right hand doesn't know what the right hand is doing.

"What about the totipotent man?" Luscus replied to the chairman during the fourth session of the *Luscan Lecture Series*. "How does he conflict with the contemporary Zeitgeist? He doesn't. The totipotent man is the imperative of our times. He must come into being before the Golden World can be realized. How can you have a Utopia without Utopians, a Golden World with men of brass?"

It was during this Memorable Day that Luscus gave his talk on The Pellucidar Breakthrough and thereby made Chibiabos Winnegan famous. And more than incidentally gave Luscus his biggest score over his competitors.

"Pellucidar? Pellucidar?" Ruskinson mutters. "Oh, God, what's Tinker Bell doing now?"

"It'll take me some time to explain why I use this phrase to describe Winnegan's stroke of genius," Luscus continues. "First, let me seem to detour.

FROM THE ARCTIC TO ILLINOIS

"Now, Confucius once said that a bear could not fart at the North Pole without causing a big wind in Chicago.

"By this he meant that all events, therefore, all men, are interconnected in an unbreakable web. What one man does, no matter how seemingly insignificant, vibrates through the strands and affects every man."

Ho Chung Ko, before his fido on the 30th level of Lhasa, Tibet, says to his wife, "That white prick has got it all wrong. Confucius didn't say that. Lenin preserve us! I'm going to call him up and give him hell."

His wife says, "Let's change the channel. Pai Ting Place is on now, and . . ."

Ngombe, 10th level, Nairobi: "The critics here are a bunch of black bastards. Now you take Luscus; he could see my genius in a second. I'm going to apply for emigration in the morning."

Wife: "You might at least ask me if I want to go! What about the kids . . . mother . . . friends . . . dog . . . ?" and so on into the lionless night of self-luminous Africa.

". . . ex-president Radinoff," Luscus continues, "once said that this is the 'Age of the Plugged-In Man.' Some rather vulgar remarks have been made about this, to me, insighted phrase. But Radinoff did not mean that human society is a daisy chain. He meant that the current of modern society flows through the circuit of which we are all part. This is the Age of Complete Interconnection. No wires can hang loose; otherwise we all short-circuit. Yet, it is undeniable that life without individuality is not worth living. Every man must be a *hapax legomenon* . . ."

Ruskinson jumps up from his chair and screams, "I know that phrase! I got you this time, Luscus!"

He is so excited he falls over in a faint, symptom of a wide-spread hereditary defect. When he recovers, the lecture is over. He springs to the recorder to run off what he missed. But Luscus has carefully avoided defining The Pellucidar Breakthrough. He will explain it at another lecture.

Grandpa, back at the scope, whistles. "I feel like an astronomer. The planets are in orbit around our house, the sun. There's Accipiter, the closest, Mercury, although he's not the god of thieves but their nemesis. Next, Benedictine, your sad-sack Venus. Hard, hard, hard! The sperm would batter their heads flat against that stony ovum. You sure she's pregnant?

"Your Mama's out there, dressed fit to kill and I wish some-one would. Mother Earth headed for the perigee of the gummint store to waste your substance."

Grandpa braces himself as if on a rolling deck, the blue-black veins on his legs thick as strangling vines on an ancient oak. "Brief departure from the role of Herr Doktor Sternscheissdreckschnuppe, the great astronomer, to that of der Unterseeboot Kapitan von Schooten die Fischen in der Barrel. Ach! I zee yet das tramp Schteamer, Deine Mama, yawing, pitching, rolling in the seas of alcohol. Compass lost; rhumb dumb. Three sheets to the wind. Paddlewheels spinning in the air. The black gang sweating their balls off, stoking the furnaces of frustration. Propellers tangled in the nets of neurosis. And the Great White Whale a glimmer in the black depths but coming up fast, intent on broaching her bottom, too big to miss. Poor damned vessel, I weep for her. I also vomit with disgust.

"Fire one! Fire two! Baroom! Mama rolls over, a jagged hole in her hull but not the one you're thinking of. Down she goes, nose first, as befits a devoted fellationeer, her huge aft rising into the air. Blub, blub! Full fathom five!

"And so back from undersea to outer space. Your sylvan Mars, Red Hawk, has just stepped out of the tavern. And Luscus, Jupiter, the one-eyed All-Father of Art, if you'll pardon my mixing of Nordic and Latin mythologies, is surrounded by his swarm of satellites."

EXCRETION IS THE BITTER PART OF VALOR

Luscus says to the fido interviewers. "By this I mean that Winnegan, like every artist, great or not, produces art that is, first, secretion, unique to himself, then excretion. Excretion in the original sense of 'sifting out.' Creative excretion or discrete excretion. I know that my distinguished colleagues will make fun of this analogy, so I hereby challenge them to a fido debate whenever it can be arranged.

"The valor comes from the courage of the artist in showing his inner products to the public. The bitter part comes from the fact that the artist may be rejected or misunderstood in his time. Also from the terrible war that takes place in the artist with the disconnected or chaotic elements, often contradictory, which he must unite and then mold into a unique entity. Hence my 'discrete excretion' phrase."

Fido interviewer: "Are we to understand that everything is a big pile of shit but that art makes a strange sea-change, forms it into something golden and illuminating?"

"Not exactly. But you're close. I'll elaborate and expound at a later date. At present, I want to talk about Winnegan. Now, the lesser artists give only the surface of things; they are photographers. But the great ones give the interiority of objects and beings.

Winnegan, however, is the first to reveal more than one interiority in a single work of art. His invention of the alto-relief multilevel technique enables him to epiphanize—show forth—subterranean layer upon layer."

Primalux Ruskinson, loudly, "The Great Onion Peeler of Painting!"

Luscus, calmly after the laughter has died: "In one sense, that is well put. Great art, like an onion, brings tears to the eyes. However, the light on Winnegan's paintings is not just a reflection; it is sucked in, digested, and then fractured forth. Each of the broken beams makes visible, not various aspects of the figures beneath, but whole figures. Worlds, I might say.

"I call this The Pellucidar Breakthrough. Pellucidar is the hollow interior of our planet, as depicted in a now forgotten fantasy-romance of the twentieth-century writer, Edgar Rice Burroughs, creator of the immortal Tarzan."

Ruskinson moans and feels faint again. "Pellucid! Pellucidar! Luscus, you punning exhumist bastard!"

"Burroughs' hero penetrated the crust of Earth to discover another world inside. This was, in some ways, the reverse of the exterior, continents where the surface seas are, and vice versa. Just so, Winnegan has discovered an inner world, the obverse of the public image Everyman projects. And, like Burroughs' hero, he has returned with a stunning narrative of psychic dangers and exploration.

"And just as the fictional hero found his Pellucidar to be populated with stone-age men and dinosaurs, so Winnegan's world is, though absolutely modern in one sense, archaic in another. Abysmally pristine. Yet, in the illumination of Winnegan's world, there is an evil and inscrutable patch of blackness, and that is paralleled in Pellucidar by the tiny fixed moon which casts a chilling and unmoving shadow.

"Now, I did intend that the ordinary 'pellucid' should be part of Pellucidar. Yet 'pellucid' means 'reflecting light evenly from all surfaces' or 'admitting maximum passage of light without diffusion or distortion.' Winnegan's paintings do just the opposite.

But—under the broken and twisted light, the acute observer can see a primeval luminosity, even and straight. This is the light that links all the fractures and multilevels, the light I was thinking of in my earlier discussion of the 'Age of the Plugged-In Man' and the polar bear.

"By intent scrutiny, a viewer may detect this, feel, as it were, the photonic fremitus of the heartbeat of Winnegan's world."

Ruskinson almost faints. Luscus' smile and black monocle make him look like a pirate who has just taken a Spanish galleon loaded with gold.

Grandpa, still at the scope, says, "And there's Maryam bint Yusuf, the Egyptian backwoodswoman you were telling me about. Your Saturn, aloof, regal, cold, and wearing one of those suspended whirling manycolored hats that're all the rage. Saturn's rings? Or a halo?"

"She's beautiful, and she'd make a wonderful mother for my children," Chib says.

"The chic of Araby. Your Saturn has two moons, mother and aunt. Chaperones! You say she'd make a good mother! How good a wife! Is she intelligent?"

"She's as smart as Benedictine."

"A dumbshit then. You sure can pick them. How do you know you're in love with her? You've been in love with twenty women in the last six months."

"I love her. This is it."

"Until the next one. Can you really love anything but your painting? Benedictine's going to have an abortion, right?"

"Not if I can talk her out of it," Chib says. "To tell the truth, I don't even like her any more. But she's carrying my child."

"Let me look at your pelvis. No, you're male. For a moment, I wasn't sure, you're so crazy to have a baby."

"A baby is a miracle to stagger sextillions of infidels."

"It beats a mouse. But don't you know that Uncle Sam has been propagandizing his heart out to cut down on propagation? Where've you been all your life?"

"I got to go, Grandpa."

Chib kisses the old man and returns to his room to finish his latest painting. The door still refuses to recognize him, and he calls the gummint repair shop, only to be told that all technicians are at the Folk Festival. He leaves the house in a red rage. The bunting and balloons are waving and bobbing in the artificial wind, increased for this occasion, and an orchestra is playing by the lake.

Through the scope, Grandpa watches him walk away.

"Poor devil! I ache for his ache. He wants a baby, and he is ripped up inside because that poor devil Benedictine is aborting their child. Part of his agony, though he doesn't know it, is identification with the doomed infant. His own mother has had innumerable—well, quite a few—abortions. But for the grace of God, he would have been one of them, another nothingness. He wants this baby to have a chance, too. But there is nothing he can do about it, nothing.

"And there is another feeling, one which he shares with most of humankind. He knows he's screwed up his life, or something has twisted it. Every thinking man and woman knows this. Even the smug and dimwitted realize this unconsciously. But a baby, that beautiful being, that unsmirched blank tablet, unformed angel, represents a new hope. Perhaps it won't screw up. Perhaps it'll grow up to be a healthy confident reasonable good-humored unselfish loving man or woman. 'It won't be like me or my next-door neighbor,' the proud, but apprehensive, parent swears.

"Chib thinks this and swears that his baby will be different. But, like everybody else, he's fooling himself. A child has one father and mother, but it has trillions of aunts and uncles. Not only those that are its contemporaries; the dead, too. Even if Chib fled into the wilderness and raised the infant himself, he'd be giving it his own unconscious assumptions. The baby would grow up with beliefs and attitudes that the father was not even aware of. Moreover, being raised in isolation, the baby would be a very peculiar human being indeed.

"And if Chib raises the child in this society, it's inevitable that it will accept at least part of the attitudes of its playmates, teachers, and so on ad nauseam.

"So, forget about making a new Adam out of your wonderful potential-teeming child, Chib. If it grows up to become at least half-sane, it's because you gave it love and discipline and it was lucky in its social contacts and it was also blessed at birth with the right combination of genes. That is, your son or daughter is now both a fighter and a lover."

ONE MAN'S NIGHTMARE IS ANOTHER MAN'S WET DREAM

Grandpa says.

"I was talking to Dante Alighieri just the other day, and he was telling me what an inferno of stupidity, cruelty, perversity, atheism, and outright peril the sixteenth century was. The nineteenth left him gibbering, hopelessly searching for adequate enough invectives.

"As for this age, it gave him such high-blood pressure, I had to slip him a tranquilizer and ship him out via time machine with an attendant nurse. She looked much like Beatrice and so should have been just the medicine he needed—maybe."

Grandpa chuckles, remembering that Chib, as a child, took him seriously when he described his time-machine visitors, such notables as Nebuchadnezzar, King of the Grass-Eaters; Samson, Bronze Age Riddler and Scourge of the Philistines; Moses, who stole a god from his Kenite father-in-law and who fought against circumcision all his life; Buddha, the Original Beatnik; No-Moss Sisyphus, taking a vacation from his stone-rolling; Androcles and his buddy, the Cowardly Lion of Oz; Baron von Richthofen, the Red Knight of Germany; Beowulf; Al Capone; Hiawatha; Ivan the Terrible; and hundreds of others.

The time came when Grandpa became alarmed and decided that Chib was confusing fantasy with reality. He hated to tell the little boy that he had been making up all those wonderful stories, mostly to teach him history. It was like telling a kid there wasn't any Santa Claus.

And then, while he was reluctantly breaking the news to his grandson, he became aware of Chib's barely suppressed grin and knew that it was his turn to have his leg pulled. Chib had never been fooled or else had caught on without any shock. So, both had a big laugh and Grandpa continued to tell of his visitors.

"There are no time machines," Grandpa says. "Like it or not, Miniver Cheevy, you have to live in this your time.

"The machines work in the utility-factory levels in a silence broken only by the chatter of a few mahouts. The great pipes at the bottom of the seas suck up water and bottom sludge. The stuff is automatically carried through pipes to the ten production levels of LA. There the inorganic chemicals are converted into energy and then into the matter of food, drink, medicines, and artifacts. There is very little agriculture or animal husbandry outside the city walls, but there is superabundance for all. Artificial but exact duplication of organic stuff, so who knows the difference?

"There is no more starvation or want anywhere, except among the self-exiles wandering in the woods. And the food and goods are shipped to the pandoras and dispensed to the receivers of the purple wage. *The purple wage.* A madison-avenue euphemism with connotations of royalty and divine right. Earned by just being born.

"Other ages would regard ours as a delirium, yet ours has benefits others lacked. To combat transiency and rootlessness, the megalopolis is compartmented into small communities. A man can live all his life in one place without having to go elsewhere to get anything he needs. With this has come a provincialism, a small-town patriotism and hostility towards outsiders. Hence, the bloody juvenile gang-fights between towns. The intense and vicious gossip. The insistence on conformity to local mores.

"At the same time, the small-town citizen has fido, which enables him to see events anywhere in the world. Intermingled with the trash and the propaganda, which the government thinks is good for the people, is any amount of superb programs. A man may get the equivalent of a Ph.D. without stirring out of his house.

"Another Renaissance has come, a fruition of the arts compara-ble to that of Pericles' Athens and the city-states of Michelangelo's Italy or Shakespeare's England. Paradox. More illiterates than ever before in the world's history. But also more literates. Speakers of classical Latin outnumber those of Caesar's day. The world of aesthetics bears a fabulous fruit. And, of course, fruits.

"To dilute the provincialism and also to make international war even more unlikely, we have the world policy of *homogenization*. The voluntary exchange of a part of one nation's population with another's. Hostages to peace and brotherly love. Those citizens who can't get along on just the purple wage or who think they'll be happier elsewhere are induced to emigrate with bribes.

"A Golden World in some respects; a nightmare in others. So what's new with the world? It was always thus in every age. Ours has had to deal with overpopulation and automation. How else could the problem be solved? It's Buridan's ass (actually, the ass was a dog) all over again, as in every time. Buridan's ass, dying of hunger because it can't make up its mind which of two equal amounts of food to eat.

"History: a *pons asinorum* with men the asses on the bridge of time.

"No, those two comparisons are not fair or right. It's Hobson's horse, the only choice being the beast in the nearest stall. Zeitgeist rides tonight, and the devil take the hindmost!

"The mid-twentieth-century writers of the Triple Revolution document forecast accurately in some respects. But they de-emphasized what lack of work would do to Mr. Everyman. They believed that all men have equal potentialities in developing artistic tendencies, that all could busy themselves with arts, crafts, and hobbies or education for education's sake. They wouldn't face the 'undemocratic' reality that only about ten per cent of the population—if that—are inherently capable of producing any-thing worth while, or even mildly interesting, in the arts. Crafts, hobbies, and a lifelong academic education pale after a while, so back to the booze, fido, and adultery.

"Lacking self-respect, the fathers become free-floaters, nomads on the steppes of sex. Mother, with a capital M, becomes the dominant figure in the family. She may be playing around, too, but she's taking care of the kids; she's around most of the time. Thus, with father a lower-case figure, absent, weak, or indifferent, the children often become homosexual or ambisexual. The wonderland is also a fairyland.

"Some features of this time could have been predicted. Sexual permissiveness was one, although no one could have seen how far it would go. But then no one could have foreknown of the Panamorite sect, even if America has spawned lunatic-fringe cults as a frog spawns tadpoles. Yesterday's monomaniac is tomorrow's messiah, and so Sheltey and his disciples survived through years of persecution and today their precepts are embedded in our culture."

Grandpa again fixes the cross-reticules of the scope on Chib.

"There he goes, my beautiful grandson, bearing gifts to the Greeks. So far, that Hercules has failed to clean up his psychic Augean stable. Yet, he may succeed, that stumblebum Apollo, that Edipus Wrecked. He's luckier than most of his contemporaries. He's had a permanent father, even if a secret one, a zany old man hiding from so-called justice. He has gotten love, discipline, and a superb education in this starred chamber. He's also fortunate in having a profession.

"But Mama spends far too much and also is addicted to gambling, a vice which deprives her of her full guaranteed income. I'm supposed to be dead, so I don't get the purple wage. Chib has to make up for all this by selling or trading his paintings. Luscus has helped him by publicizing him, but at any moment Luscus may turn against him. The money from the paintings is still not enough. After all, money is not the basis of our economy; it's a scarce auxiliary. Chib needs the grant but won't get it unless he lets Luscus make love to him.

"It's not that Chib rejects homosexual relations. Like most of his contemporaries, he's sexually ambivalent. I think that he and Omar Runic still blow each other occasionally. And why not? They love each other. But Chib rejects Luscus as a matter of principle. He won't be a whore to advance his career. Moreover, Chib makes a distinction which is deeply embedded in this society. He thinks that uncompulsive homosexuality is natural (whatever that means?) but that compulsive homosexuality is, to use an old term, queer. Valid or not, the distinction is made.

"So, Chib may go to Egypt. But what happens to me then?

"Never mind me or your mother, Chib. No matter what. Don't give in to Luscus. Remember the dying words of Singleton, Bureau of Relocation and Rehabilitation Director, who shot himself because he couldn't adjust to the new times.

"'What if a man gain the world and lose his ass?'"

At this moment, Grandpa sees his grandson, who has been walking along with somewhat drooping shoulders, suddenly straighten them. And he sees Chib break into a dance, a little improvised shuffle followed by a series of whirls. It is evident that Chib is whooping. The pedestrians around him are grinning.

Grandpa groans and then laughs. "Oh, God, the goatish energy of youth, the unpredictable shift of spectrum from black sorrow to bright orange joy! Dance, Chib, dance your crazy head off! Be happy, if only for a moment! You're young yet, you've got the bubbling of unconquerable hope deep in your springs! Dance, Chib, dance!"

He laughs and wipes a tear away.

SEXUAL IMPLICATIONS OF THE CHARGE OF THE LIGHT BRIGADE

is so fascinating a book that Doctor Jespersen Joyce Bathymens, psycholinguist for the federal Bureau of Group Reconfiguration and Intercommunicability, hates to stop reading. But duty beckons.

"A radish is not necessarily reddish," he says into the recorder. "The Young Radishes so named their group because a radish is a radicle, hence, radical. Also, there's a play on roots and on red-ass, a slang term for anger, and possibly on ruttish and rattish. And undoubtedly on rude-ickle, Beverly Hills dialectical term for a repulsive, unruly, and socially ungraceful person.

"Yet the Young Radishes are not what I would call Left Wing; they represent the current resentment against Life-In-General and advocate no radical policy of reconstruction. They howl against Things As They Are, like monkeys in a tree, but never give constructive criticism. They want to destroy without any thought of what to do after the destruction.

"In short, they represent the average citizen's grousing and bitching, being different in that they are more articulate. There are thousands of groups like them in LA and possibly millions all over the world. They had normal life as children. In fact, they were born and raised in the same clutch, which is one reason why they were chosen for this study. What phenomenon produced ten such creative persons, all mothered in the seven houses of Area 69-14, all about the same time, all practically raised together, since they were put together in the playpen on top of the pedestal while one mother took her turn baby-sitting and the others did whatever they had to do, which . . . where was I?

"Oh, yes, they had a normal life, went to the same school, palled around, enjoyed the usual sexual play among themselves, joined the juvenile gangs and engaged in some rather bloody warfare with the Westwood and other gangs. All were distinguished, however, by an intense intellectual curiosity and all become active in the creative arts.

"It has been suggested—and might be true—that that mysterious stranger, Raleigh Renaissance, was the father of all ten. This is possible but can't be proved. Raleigh Renaissance was living in the house of Mrs. Winnegan at the time, but he seems to have been unusually active in the clutch and, indeed, all over Beverly Hills. Where this man came from, who he was, and where he went are still unknown despite intensive search by various agencies. He had no ID or other cards of any kind, yet he went unchallenged for a long time. He seems to have had something on the Chief of Police of Beverly Hills and possibly on some of the Federal agents stationed in Beverly Hills.

"He lived for two years with Mrs. Winnegan, then dropped out of sight. It is rumored that he left LA to join a tribe of white neo-Amerinds, sometimes called the Seminal Indians.

"Anyway, back to the Young (pun on Jung?) Radishes. They are revolting against the Father Image of Uncle Sam, whom they both love and hate. Uncle is, of course, linked by their subconsciouses with *unco*, a Scottish word meaning strange, uncanny, weird, this indicating that their own fathers were strangers to them. All come from homes where the father was missing or weak, a phenomenon regrettably common in our culture.

"I never knew my own father . . . Tooney, wipe that out as irrelevant. *Unco* also means news or tidings, indicating that the unfortunate young men are eagerly awaiting news of the return of their fathers and perhaps secretly hoping for reconciliation with Uncle Sam, that is, their fathers.

"Uncle Sam. Sam is short for Samuel, from the Hebrew *Shemu'el*, meaning Name of God. All the Radishes are atheists, although some, notably Omar Runic and Chibiabos Winnegan, were given religious instruction as children (Panamorite and Roman Catholic, respectively).

"Young Winnegan's revolt against God, and against the Catholic Church, was undoubtedly reinforced by the fact that his mother forced strong *cath*artics upon him when he had a chronic constipation. He probably also resented having to learn his *cat*echism when he preferred to play. And there is the deeply significant and traumatic incident in which a *cath*eter was used on him. (This refusal to excrete when young will be analyzed in a later report.)

"Uncle Sam, the Father Figure. *Figure* is so obvious a play that I won't bother to point it out. Also perhaps on *figger*, in the sense of 'a fig on thee!'—look this up in Dante's *Inferno*, some Italian or other in Hell said, 'A fig on thee, God!' biting his thumb in the ancient gesture of defiance and disrespect. Hmm? Biting the thumb—an infantile characteristic?

"Sam is also a multileveled pun on phonetically, orthographically, and semisemantically linked words. It is significant that young Winnegan can't stand to be called *dear*; he claims that his mother called him that so many times it nauseates him. Yet the word has a deeper meaning to him. For instance, *sambar* is an

Asiatic *deer* with *three*-pointed antlers. (Note the *sam*, also.) Obviously, the three points symbolize, to him, the Triple Revolution document, the historic dating point of the beginning of our era, which Chib claims to hate so. The three points are also archetypes of the Holy Trinity, which the Young Radishes frequently blaspheme against.

"I might point out that in this the group differs from others I've studied. The others expressed an infrequent and mild blasphemy in keeping with the mild, indeed pale, religious spirit prevalent nowadays. Strong blasphemers thrive only when strong believers thrive.

"Sam also stands for *same*, indicating the Radishes' subconscious desire to conform.

"Possibly, although this particular analysis may be invalid, Sam corresponds to Samekh, the fifteenth letter of the Hebrew alphabet. (Sam! Ech!?) In the old style of English spelling, which the Radishes learned in their childhood, the fifteenth letter of the Roman alphabet is O. In the Alphabet Table of my dictionary, Webster's 128th New Collegiate, the Roman O is in the same horizontal column as the Arabic Dad. Also with the Hebrew Mem. So we get a double connection with the missing and longed-for Father (or Dad) and with the overdominating Mother (or Mem).

"I can make nothing out of the Greek Omicron, also in the same horizontal column. But give me time; this takes study.

"Omicron. The little O! The lower-case omicron has an egg shape. The little egg is their father's sperm fertilized? The womb? The basic shape of modern architecture?

"Sam Hill, an archaic euphemism for Hell. Uncle Sam is a Sam Hill of a father? Better strike that out, Tooney. It's possible that these highly educated youths have read about this obsolete phrase, but it's not confirmable. I don't want to suggest any connections that might make me look ridiculous.

"Let's see. Samisen. A Japanese musical instrument with *three* strings. The Triple Revolution document and the Trinity again. Trinity? Father, Son, and Holy Ghost. Mother the thoroughly despised figure, hence, the Wholly Goose? Well, maybe not. Wipe that out, Tooney.

"Samisen. Son of Sam? Which leads naturally to Samson, who pulled down the temple of the Philistines on them and on himself. These boys talk of doing the same thing. Chuckle. Reminds me of myself when I was their age, before I matured. Strike out that last remark, Tooney.

"Samovar. The Russian word means, literally, self-boiler. There's no doubt the Radishes are boiling with revolutionary fervor. Yet their disturbed psyches know, deep down, that Uncle Sam is their ever-loving Father-Mother, that he has only their best interests at heart. But they force themselves to hate him, hence, they self-boil.

"A samlet is a young salmon. Cooked salmon is a yellowish pink or pale red, near to a radish in color, in their unconsciouses, anyway. Samlet equals Young Radish; they feel they're being cooked in the great pressure cooker of modern society.

"How's that for a trinely furned phase—I mean, finely turned phrase, Tooney? Run this off, edit as indicated, smooth it out, you know how, and send it off to the boss. I got to go. I'm late for lunch with Mother; she gets very upset if I'm not there on the dot.

"Oh, postscript! I recommend that the agents watch Winnegan more closely. His friends are blowing off psychic steam through talk and drink, but he has suddenly altered his behavior pattern. He has long periods of silence, he's given up smoking, drinking, and sex."

A PROFIT IS NOT WITHOUT HONOR

even in this day. The gummint has no overt objection to privately owned taverns, run by citizens who have paid all license fees, passed all examinations, posted all bonds, and bribed the local politicians and police chief. Since there is no provision made for them, no large buildings available for rent, the taverns are in the homes of the owners themselves.

The Private Universe is Chib's favorite, partly because the proprietor is operating illegally. Dionysus Gobrinus, unable to hew his way through the roadblocks, prise-de-chevaux, barbed wire, and booby-traps of official procedure, has quit his efforts to get a license.

Openly, he paints the name of his establishment over the mathematical equations that once distinguished the exterior of the house. (Math prof at Beverly Hills U. 14, named Al-Khwarizmi Descartes Lobachevsky, he has resigned and changed his name again.) The atrium and several bedrooms have been converted for drinking and carousing. There are no Egyptian customers, probably because of their supersensitivity about the flowery sentiments painted by patrons on the inside walls.

A BAS, ABU
MOHAMMED WAS THE SON OF A VIRGIN DOG
THE SPHINX STINKS
REMEMBER THE RED SEA!
THE PROPHET HAS A CAMEL FETISH

Some of those who wrote the taunts have fathers, grand-fathers, and great-grandfathers who were themselves the objects of similar insults. But their descendants are thoroughly assimilated, Beverly Hillsians to the core. Of such is the kingdom of men.

Gobrinus, a squat cube of a man, stands behind the bar, which is square as a protest against the ovoid. Above him is a big sign:

ONE MAN'S MEAD IS ANOTHER MAN'S POISSON

Gobrinus has explained this pun many times, not always to his listener's satisfaction. Suffice it that Poisson was a mathematician and that Poisson's frequency distribution is a good approximation to the binomial distribution as the number of trials increases and probability of success in a single trial is small.

When a customer gets too drunk to be permitted one more

drink, he is hurled headlong from the tavern with furious combustion and utter ruin by Gobrinus, who cries, "Poisson! Poisson!"

Chib's friends, the Young Radishes, sitting at a hexagonal table, greet him, and their words unconsciously echo those of the Federal psycholinguist's estimate of his recent behavior.

"Chib, monk! Chibber as ever! Looking for a chibbie, no doubt! Take your pick!"

Madame Trismegista, sitting at a little table with a Seal-of-Solomon-shape top, greets him. She has been Gobrinus' wife for two years, a record, because she will knife him if he leaves her. Also, he believes that she can somehow juggle his destiny with the cards she deals. In this age of enlightenment, the soothsayer and astrologer flourish. As science pushes forward, ignorance and superstition gallop around the flanks and bite science in the rear with big dark teeth.

Gobrinus himself, a Ph.D., holder of the torch of knowledge (until lately, anyway), does not believe in God. But he is sure the stars are marching towards a baleful conjunction for him. With a strange logic, he thinks that his wife's cards control the stars; he is unaware that card-divination and astrology are entirely separate fields.

What can you expect of a man who claims that the universe is asymmetric?

Chib waves his hand at Madame Trismegista and walks to another table. Here sits

A TYPICAL TEEMAGER

Benedictine Serinus Melba. She is tall and slim and has narrow lemurlike hips and slender legs but big breasts. Her hair, black as the pupils of her eyes, is parted in the middle, plastered with perfumed spray to the skull, and braided into two long pigtails. These are brought over her bare shoulders and held together with a golden brooch just below her throat. From the brooch, which is in the form of a musical note, the braids part again, one looping under each breast. Another brooch secures them, and they separate to circle around behind her back, are brooched again, and come back to meet on her belly. Another brooch holds them, and the twin waterfalls flow blackly over the front of her bell-shaped skirt.

Her face is thickly farded with green, aquamarine, a shamrock beauty mark, and topaz. She wears a yellow bra with artificial pink nipples; frilly lace ribbons hang from the bra. A demicorselet of bright green with black rosettes circles her waist. Over the corselet, half-concealing it, is a wire structure covered with a shimmering pink quilty material. It extends out in back to form a semifuselage or a bird's long tail, to which are attached long yellow and crimson artificial feathers.

An ankle-length diaphanous skirt billows out. It does not hide the yellow and dark-green striped lace-fringed garter-panties, white thighs, and black net stockings with green clocks in the shape of musical notes. Her shoes are bright blue with topaz high heels.

Benedictine is costumed to sing at the Folk Festival; the only thing missing is her singer's hat. Yet, she came to complain, among other things, that Chib has forced her to cancel her appearance and so lose her chance at a great career.

She is with five girls, all between sixteen and twenty-one, all drinking P (for popskull).

"Can't we talk in private, Benny?" Chib says.

"What for?" Her voice is a lovely contralto ugly with inflection.

"You got me down here to make a public scene," Chib says.

"For God's sake, what other kind of scene is there?" she shrills. "Look at him! He wants to talk to me alone!"

It is then that he realizes she is afraid to be alone with him. More than that, she is incapable of being alone. Now he knows why she insisted on leaving the bedroom door open with her girl-friend, Bela, within calling distance. And listening distance.

"You said you was just going to use your finger!" she shouts. She points at the slightly rounded belly. "I'm going to have a baby! You rotten smooth-talking sick bastard!"

"That isn't true at all," Chib says. "You told me it was all right, you loved me."

"'Love! Love!' he says! What the hell do I know what I said, you got me so excited! Anyway, I didn't say you could stick it in! I'd never say that, never! And then what you *did! What* you did! My God, I could hardly walk for a week, you bastard, you!"

Chib sweats. Except for Beethoven's Pastoral welling from the fido, the room is silent. His friends grin. Gobrinus, his back turned, is drinking scotch. Madame Trismegista shuffles her cards, and she farts with a fiery conjunction of beer and onions. Benedictine's friends look at their Mandarin-long fluorescent fingernails or glare at him. Her hurt and indignity is theirs and vice versa.

"I can't take those pills. They make me break out and give me eye trouble and screw up my monthlies! You know that! And I can't stand those mechanical uteruses! And you lied to me, anyway! You said you took a pill!"

Chib realizes she's contradicting herself, but there's no use trying to be logical. She's furious because she's pregnant; she doesn't want to be inconvenienced with an abortion at this time, and she's out for revenge.

Now how, Chib wonders, how could she get pregnant that night? No woman, no matter how fertile, could have managed that. She must have been knocked up before or after. Yet she swears that it was that night, the night he was

THE KNIGHT OF THE BURNING PESTLE
or
FOAM, FOAM ON THE RANGE

"No, no!" Benedictine cries.

"Why not? I love you," Chib says. "I want to marry you."

Benedictine screams, and her friend Bela, out in the hall, yells, "What's the matter? What happened?"

Benedictine does not reply. Raging, shaking as if in the grip of a fever, she scrambles out of bed, pushing Chib to one side. She runs to the small egg of the bathroom in the corner, and he follows her.

"I hope you're not going to do what I think . . . ?" he says.

Benedictine moans, "You sneaky no-good son of a bitch!"

In the bathroom, she pulls down a section of wall, which becomes a shelf. On its top, attached by magnetic bottoms to the shelf, are many containers. She seizes a long thin can of spermatocide, squats, and inserts it. She presses the button on its bottom, and it foams with a hissing sound even its cover of flesh cannot silence.

Chib is paralyzed for a moment. Then he roars.

Benedictine shouts, "Stay away from me, you rude-ickle!"

From the door to the bedroom comes Bela's timid, "Are you all right, Benny?"

"I'll all-right her!" Chib bellows.

He jumps forward and takes a can of tempoxy glue from the shelf. The glue is used by Benedictine to attach her wigs to her head and will hold anything forever unless softened by a specific defixative.

Benedictine and Bela both cry out as Chib lifts Benedictine up and then lowers her to the floor. She fights, but he manages to spray the glue over the can and the skin and hairs around it.

"What're you doing?" she screams.

He pushes the button on the bottom of the can to full-on position and then sprays the bottom with glue. While she struggles, he holds her arms tight against her body and keeps her from rolling over and so moving the can in or out. Silently, Chib counts to thirty, then to thirty more to make sure the glue is thoroughly dried. He releases her.

The foam is billowing out around her groin and down her legs and spreading out across the floor. The fluid in the can is under enormous pressure in the indestructible unpunchable can, and the foam expands vastly if exposed to open air.

Chib takes the can of defixative from the shelf and clutches it in his hand, determined that she will not have it. Benedictine jumps up and swings at him. Laughing like a hyena in a tentful of nitrous oxide, Chib blocks her fist and shoves her away. Slipping on the foam, which is ankle-deep by now, Benedictine falls and then slides backward out of the bedroom on her buttocks, the can clunking.

She gets to her feet and only then realizes fully what Chib has done. Her scream goes up, and she follows it. She dances around, yanking at the can, her screams intensifying with every tug and resultant pain. Then she turns and runs out of the room or tries to. She skids; Bela is in her way; they cling together and both ski out of the room, doing a half-turn while going through the door. The foam swirls out so that the two look like Venus and friend rising from the bubble-capped waves of the Cyprian Sea.

Benedictine shoves Bela away but not without losing some flesh to Bela's long sharp fingernails. Bela shoots backwards through the door toward Chib. She is like a novice ice skater trying to maintain her balance. She does not succeed and shoots by Chib, wailing, on her back, her feet up in the air.

Chib slides his bare feet across the floor gingerly, stops at the bed to pick up his clothes, but decides he'd be wiser to wait until he's outside before he puts them on. He gets to the circular hall just in time to see Benedictine crawling past one of the columns that divides the corridor from the atrium. Her parents, two middle-aged behemoths, are still sitting on a flato, beer cans in hand, eyes wide, mouths open, quivering.

Chib does not even say goodnight to them as he passes along the hall. But then he sees the fido and realizes that her parents had switched it from EXT. to INT. and then to Benedictine's room. Father and mother have been watching Chib and daughter, and it is evident from father's not-quite dwindled condition that father was very excited by this show, superior to anything seen on exterior fido.

"You peeping bastards!" Chib roars.

Benedictine has gotten to them and on her feet and she is stammering, weeping, indicating the can and then stabbing her finger at Chib. At Chib's roar, the parents heave up from the flato as two leviathans from the deep. Benedictine turns and starts to run towards him, her arms outstretched, her long-nailed fingers curved, her face a medusa's. Behind her streams the wake of the livid witch and father and mother on the foam.

Chib shoves up against a pillar and rebounds and skitters

off, helpless to keep himself from turning sidewise during the maneuver. But he keeps his balance. Mama and Papa have gone down together with a crash that shakes even the solid house. They are up, eyes rolling and bellowing like hippos surfacing. They charge him but separate, Mama shrieking now, her face, despite the fat, Benedictine's. Papa goes around one side of the pillar; Mama, the other. Benedictine has rounded another pillar, holding to it with one hand to keep her from slipping. She is between Chib and the door to the outside.

Chib slams against the wall of the corridor, in an area free of foam. Benedictine runs towards him. He dives across the floor, hits it, and rolls between two pillars and out into the atrium.

Mama and Papa converge in a collision course. The Titanic meets the iceberg, and both plunge swiftly. They skid on their faces and bellies towards Benedictine. She leaps into the air, trailing foam on them as they pass beneath her.

By now it is evident that the government's claim that the can is good for 40,000 shots of death-to-sperm, or for 40,000 copulations, is justified. Foam is all over the place, ankle-deep—knee-high in some places—and still pouring out.

Bela is on her back now and on the atrium floor, her head driven into the soft folds of the flato.

Chib gets up slowly and stands for a moment, glaring around him, his knees bent, ready to jump from danger but hoping he won't have to since his feet will undoubtedly fly away from under him.

"Hold it, you rotten son of a bitch!" Papa roars. "I'm going to kill you! You can't do this to my daughter!"

Chib watches him turn over like a whale in a heavy sea and try to get to his feet. Down he goes again, grunting as if hit by a harpoon. Mama is no more successful than he.

Seeing that his way is unbarred—Benedictine having disappeared somewhere—Chib skis across the atrium until he reaches an unfoamed area near the exit. Clothes over his arm, still holding the defixative, he struts towards the door.

At this moment Benedictine calls his name. He turns to see her sliding from the kitchen at him. In her hand is a tall glass.

He wonders what she intends to do with it. Certainly, she is not offering him the hospitality of a drink.

Then she scoots into the dry region of the floor and topples forward with a scream. Nevertheless, she throws the contents of the glass accurately.

Chib screams when he feels the boiling hot water, painful as if he had been circumcised unanesthetized.

Benedictine, on the floor, laughs. Chib, after jumping around and shrieking, the can and clothes dropped, his hands holding the scalded parts, manages to control himself. He stops his antics, seizes Benedictine's right hand, and drags her out into the streets of Beverly Hills. There are quite a few people out this night, and they follow the two. Not until Chib reaches the lake does he stop and there he goes into the water to cool off the burn, Benedictine with him.

The crowd has much to talk about later, after Benedictine and Chib have crawled out of the lake and then run home. The crowd talks and laughs quite a while as they watch the sanitation department people clean the foam off the lake surface and the streets.

"I was so sore I couldn't walk for a month!" Benedictine screams.

"You had it coming," Chib says. "You've got no complaints. You said you wanted my baby, and you talked as if you meant it."

"I must've been out of my mind!" Benedictine says. "No, I wasn't! I never said no such thing! You lied to me! You forced me!"

"I would never force anybody," Chib said. "You know that. Quit your bitching. You're a free agent, and you consented freely. You have free will."

Omar Runic, the poet, stands up from his chair. He is a tall thin red-bronze youth with an aquiline nose and very thick red lips. His curly hair grows long and is cut into the shape of the *Pequod*, that fabled vessel which bore mad Captain Ahab and his mad crew and the sole survivor Ishmael after the white whale. The coiffure is formed with a bowsprit and hull and three masts and yardarms and even a boat hanging on davits.

Omar Runic claps his hands and shouts, "Bravo! A philosopher! Free will it is; free will to seek the Eternal Verities—if any—or Death and Damnation! I'll drink to free will! A toast, gentlemen! Stand up, Young Radishes, a toast to our leader!"

And so begins

THE MAD P PARTY

Madame Trismegista calls, "Tell your fortune, Chib! See what the stars tell through the cards!"

He sits down at her table while his friends crowd around.

"O.K., Madame. How do I get out of this mess?"

She shuffles and turns over the top card.

"Jesus! The ace of spades!"

"You're going on a long journey!"

"Egypt!" Rousseau Red Hawk cries. "Oh, no, you don't want to go there, Chib! Come with me to where the buffalo roam and . . ."

Up comes another card.

"You will soon meet a beautiful dark lady."

"A goddam Arab! Oh, no, Chib, tell me it's not true!"

"You will win great honors soon."

"Chib's going to get the grant!"

"If I get the grant, I don't have to go to Egypt," Chib says. "Madame Trismegista, with all due respect, you're full of crap."

"Don't mock, young man. I'm not a computer. I'm tuned to the spectrum of psychic vibrations."

Flip. "You will be in great danger, physically and morally."

Chib says, "That happens at least once a day."

Flip. "A man very close to you will die twice."

Chib pales, rallies, and says, "A coward dies a thousand deaths."

"You will travel in time, return to the past."

"Zow!" Red Hawk says. "You're outdoing yourself, Madame. Careful! You'll get a psychic hernia, have to wear an ectoplasmic truss!"

"Scoff if you want to, you dumbshits," Madame says. "There are more worlds than one. The cards don't lie, not when I deal them."

"Gobrinus!" Chib calls. "Another pitcher of beer for the Madame."

The Young Radishes return to their table, a legless disc held up in the air by a graviton field. Benedictine glares at them and goes into a huddle with the other teemagers. At a table nearby sits Pinkerton Legrand, a gummint agent, facing them so that the fido under his one-way window of a jacket beams in on them. They know he's doing this. He knows they know and has reported so to his superior. He frowns when he sees Falco Accipiter enter. Legrand does not like an agent from another department messing around on his case. Accipiter does not even look at Legrand. He orders a pot of tea and then pretends to drop into the teapot a pill that combines with tannic acid to become P.

Rousseau Red Hawk winks at Chib and says, "Do you really think it's possible to paralyze all of LA with a single bomb?"

"Three bombs!" Chib says loudly so that Legrand's fido will pick up the words. "One for the control console of the desalinization plant, a second for the backup console, the third for the nexus of the big pipe that carries the water to the reservoir on the 20th level."

Pinkerton Legrand turns pale. He downs all the whiskey in his glass and orders another, although he has already had too many. He presses the plate on his fido to transmit a triple top-priority. Lights blink redly in HQ; a gong clangs repeatedly; the chief wakes up so suddenly he falls off his chair.

Accipiter also hears, but he sits stiff, dark, and brooding as the diorite image of a Pharaoh's falcon. Monomaniac, he is not to be diverted by talk of inundating all LA, even if it will lead to action. On Grandpa's trail, he is now here because he hopes to use Chib as the key to the house. One "mouse"—as he thinks of his criminals—one "mouse" will run to the hole of another.

"When do you think we can go into action?" Huga Wells-Erb Heinsturbury, the science-fiction authoress, says.

"In about three weeks," Chib says.

At HQ, the chief curses Legrand for disturbing him.

There are thousands of young men and women blowing off steam with these plots of destruction, assassination, and revolt. He does not understand why the young punks talk like this, since they have everything handed them free. If he had his way, he'd throw them into jail and kick them around a little or more than.

"After we do it, we'll have to take off for the big outdoors," Red Hawk says. His eyes glisten. "I'm telling you, boys, being a free man in the forest is the greatest. You're a genuine individual, not just one of the faceless breed."

Red Hawk believes in this plot to destroy LA. He is happy because, though he hasn't said so, he has grieved while in Mother Nature's lap for intellectual companionship. The other savages can hear a deer at a hundred yards, detect a rattlesnake in the bushes, but they're deaf to the footfalls of philosophy, the neigh of Nietzsche, the rattle of Russell, the honkings of Hegel.

"The illiterate swine!" he says aloud. The others say, "What?"

"Nothing. Listen, you guys must know how wonderful it is. You were in the WNRCC."

"I was 4-F," Omar Runic says. "I got hay fever."

"I was working on my second M.A.," Gibbon Tacitus says.

"I was in the WNRCC band," Sibelius Amadeus Yehudi says. "We only got outside when we played the camps, and that wasn't often."

"Chib, you were in the Corps. You loved it, didn't you?"

Chib nods but says, "Being a neo-Amerind takes all your time just to survive. When could I paint? And who would see the paintings if I did get time? Anyway, that's no life for a woman or a baby."

Red Hawk looks hurt and orders a whiskey mixed with P.

Pinkerton Legrand doesn't want to interrupt his monitoring, yet he can't stand the pressure in his bladder. He walks towards the room used as the customers' catch-all. Red Hawk, in a nasty mood caused by rejection, sticks his leg out. Legrand trips, catches himself, and stumbles forward. Benedictine puts out her leg. Legrand falls on his face. He no longer has any reason to go to the urinal except to wash himself off.

Everybody except Legrand and Accipiter laugh. Legrand jumps

up, his fists doubled. Benedictine ignores him and walks over to Chib, her friends following. Chib stiffens. She says, "You perverted bastard! You told me you were just going to use your finger!"

"You're repeating yourself," Chib says. "The important thing is, what's going to happen to the baby?"

"What do you care?" Benedictine says. "For all you know, it might not even be yours!"

"That'd be a relief," Chib says, "if it weren't. Even so, the baby should have a say in this. He might want to live—even with you as his mother."

"In this miserable life!" she cries. "I'm going to do it a favor. I'm going to the hospital and get rid of it. Because of you, I have to miss out on my big chance at the Folk Festival! There'll be agents from all over there, and I won't get a chance to sing for them!"

"You're a liar," Chib says. "You're all dressed up to sing."

Benedictine's face is red; her eyes, wide; her nostrils, flaring. "You spoiled my fun!"

She shouts, "Hey, everybody, want to hear a howler! This great artist, this big hunk of manhood, Chib the divine, he can't get a hardon unless he's gone down on!"

Chib's friends look at each other. What's the bitch screaming about? So what's new?

From Grandpa's *Private Ejaculations*:

Some of the features of the Panamorite religion, so reviled and loathed in the 21st century, have become everyday facts in modern times. Love, love, love, physical and spiritual! It's not enough to just kiss your children and hug them. But oral stimulation of the genitals of infants by the parents and relatives has resulted in some curious conditioned reflexes. I could write a book about this aspect of mid-22nd century life and probably will.

Legrand comes out of the washroom. Benedictine slaps Chib's face. Chib slaps her back. Gobrinus lifts up a section of the bar and hurtles through the opening, crying, "Poisson! Poisson!"

He collides with Legrand, who lurches into Bela, who screams, whirls, and slaps Legrand, who slaps back. Benedictine empties a glass of P in Chib's face. Howling, he jumps up and swings his fist. Benedictine ducks, and the fist goes over her shoulder into a girlfriend's chest.

Red Hawk leaps up on the table and shouts, "I'm a regular bearcat, half-alligator, half . . ."

The table, held up in a graviton field, can't bear much weight. It tilts and catapults him into the girls, and all go down. They bite and scratch Red Hawk, and Benedictine squeezes his testicles. He screams, writhes, and hurls Benedictine with his feet onto the top of the table. It has regained its normal height and altitude, but now it flips over again, tossing her to the other side. Legrand, tippytoeing through the crowd on his way to the exit, is knocked down. He loses some front teeth against somebody's knee cap. Spitting blood and teeth, he jumps up and slugs a bystander.

Gobrinus fires off a gun that shoots a tiny Very light. It's supposed to blind the brawlers and so bring them to their senses while they're regaining their sight. It hangs in the air and shines like

A STAR OVER BEDLAM

The Police Chief is talking via fido to a man in a public booth. The man has turned off the video and is disguising his voice.

"They're beating the shit out of each other in *The Private Universe*."

The Chief groans. The Festival has just begun, and They are at it already.

"Thanks. The boys'll be on the way. What's your name? I'd like to recommend you for a Citizen's Medal."

"What! And get the shit knocked out of me, too! I ain't no stoolie; just doing my duty. Besides, I don't like Gobrinus or his customers. They're a bunch of snobs."

The Chief issues orders to the riot squad, leans back, and drinks a beer while he watches the operation on fido. What's the matter with these people, anyway? They're always mad about something.

The sirens scream. Although the bolgani ride electrically driven noiseless tricycles, they're still clinging to the centuries-old tradition of warning the criminals that they're coming. Five trikes pull up before the open door of *The Private Universe*. The police dismount and confer. Their two-storied cylindrical helmets are black and have scarlet roaches. They wear goggles for some reason although their vehicles can't go over 15 m.p.h. Their jackets are black and fuzzy, like a teddy bear's fur, and huge golden epaulets decorate their shoulders. The shorts are electric-blue and fuzzy; the jackboots, glossy black. They carry electric shock sticks and guns that fire chokegas pellets.

Gobrinus blocks the entrance. Sergeant O'Hara says, "Come on, let us in. No, I don't have a warrant of entry. But I'll get one."

"If you do, I'll sue," Gobrinus says. He smiles. While it is true that government red tape was so tangled he quit trying to acquire a tavern legally, it is also true that the government will protect him in this issue. Invasion of privacy is a tough rap for the police to break.

O'Hara looks inside the doorway at the two bodies on the floor, at those holding their heads and sides and wiping off blood, and at Accipiter, sitting like a vulture dreaming of carrion. One of the bodies gets up on all fours and crawls through between Gobrinus' legs out into the street.

"Sergeant, arrest that man!" Gobrinus says. "He's wearing an illegal fido. I accuse him of invasion of privacy."

O'Hara's face lights up. At least he'll get one arrest to his credit. Legrand is placed in the paddywagon, which arrives just after the ambulance. Red Hawk is carried out as far as the doorway by his friends. He opens his eyes just as he's being carried on a stretcher to the ambulance and he mutters.

O'Hara leans over him. "What?"

"I fought a bear once with only my knife, and I came out better than with those cunts. I charge them with assault and battery, murder and mayhem."

O'Hara's attempt to get Red Hawk to sign a warrant fails because Red Hawk is now unconscious. He curses. By the time Red Hawk begins feeling better, he'll refuse to sign the warrant. He won't want the girls and their boy friends laying for him, not if he has any sense at all.

Through the barred window of the paddywagon, Legrand screams, "I'm a gummint agent! You can't arrest me!"

The police get a hurry-up call to go to the front of the Folk Center, where a fight between local youths and Westwood invaders is threatening to become a riot. Benedictine leaves the tavern. Despite several blows in the shoulders and stomach, a kick in the buttocks, and a bang on the head, she shows no signs of losing the fetus.

Chib, half-sad, half-glad, watches her go. He feels a dull grief that the baby is to be denied life. By now he realizes that part of his objection to the abortion is identification with the fetus; he knows what Grandpa thinks he does not know. He realizes that his birth was an accident—lucky or unlucky. If things had gone otherwise, he would not have been born. The thought of his non-existence—no painting, no friends, no laughter, no hope, no love—horrifies him. His mother, drunkenly negligent about contraception, has had any number of abortions, and he could have been one of them.

Watching Benedictine swagger away (despite her torn clothes), he wonders what he could ever have seen in her. Life with her, even with a child, would have been gritty.

> In the hope-lined nest of the mouth
> Love flies once more, nestles down,
> Coos, flashes feathered glory, dazzles,
> And then flies away, crapping,
> As is the wont of birds,
> To jet-assist the takeoff.
> —Omar Runic

Chib returns to his home, but he still can't get back into his room. He goes to the storeroom. The painting is seven-eighths finished but was not completed because he was dissatisfied with it. Now he takes it from the house and carries it to Runic's house, which is in the same clutch as his. Runic is at the Center, but he always leaves his doors open when he's gone. He has equipment which Chib uses to finish the painting, working with a sureness and intensity he lacked the first time he was creating it. He then leaves Runic's house with the huge oval canvas held above his head.

He strides past the pedestals and under their curving branches with the ovoids at their ends. He skirts several small grassy parks with trees, walks beneath more houses, and in ten minutes is nearing the heart of Beverly Hills. Here mercurial Chib sees

ALL IN THE GOLDEN AFTERNOON, THREE LEADEN LADIES

drifting in a canoe on Lake Issus. Maryam bint Yusuf, her mother, and aunt listlessly hold fishing poles and look towards the gay colors, music, and the chattering crowd before the Folk Center. By now the police have broken up the juvenile fight and are standing around to make sure nobody else makes trouble.

The three women are dressed in the somber clothes, completely body-concealing, of the Mohammedan Wahhabi fundamentalist sect. They do not wear veils; not even the Wahhabi now insist on this. Their Egyptian brethren ashore are clad in modern garments, shameful and sinful. Despite which, the ladies stare at them.

Their menfolk are at the edge of the crowd. Bearded and costumed like sheiks in a Foreign Legion fido show, they mutter gargling oaths and hiss at the iniquitous display of female flesh. But they stare.

This small group has come from the zoological preserves of Abyssinia, where they were caught poaching. Their gummint gave them three choices. Imprisonment in a rehabilitation center, where they would be treated until they became good citizens if it took the rest of their lives. Emigration to the megalopolis of Haifa, Israel. Or emigration to Beverly Hills, LA.

What, dwell among the accursed Jews of Israel? They spat and chose Beverly Hills. Alas, Allah had mocked them! They were now surrounded by Finkelsteins, Applebaums, Siegels, Weintraubs, and others of the infidel tribes of Isaac. Even worse, Beverly Hills had no mosque. They either traveled forty kilometers every day to the 16th level, where a mosque was available, or used a private home.

Chib hastens to the edge of the plastic-edged lake and puts down his painting and bows low, whipping off his somewhat battered hat. Maryam smiles at him but loses the smile when the two chaperones reprimand her.

"*Ya kelb! Ya ibn kelb!*" the two shout at him.

Chib grins at them, waves his hat, and says, "Charmed, I'm sure, mesdames! Oh, you lovely ladies remind me of the Three Graces."

He then cries out, "I love you, Maryam! I love you! Thou art like the Rose of Sharon to me! Beautiful, doe-eyed, virginal! A fortress of innocence and strength, filled with a fierce motherhood and utter faithfulness to thy one true love! I love thee, thou art the only light in a black sky of dead stars! I cry to you across the void!"

Maryam understands World English, but the wind carries his words away from her. She simpers, and Chib cannot help feeling a momentary repulsion, a flash of anger as if she has somehow betrayed him. Nevertheless, he rallies and shouts, "I invite you to come with me to the showing! You and your mother and aunt will be my guests. You can see my paintings, my soul, and know what kind of man is going to carry you off on his Pegasus, my dove!"

There is nothing as ridiculous as the verbal out-pourings of a young poet in love. Outrageously exaggerated. I laugh. But I am also touched. Old as I am, I remember my first loves, the fire, the torrents of words, lightning-sheathed, ache-winged. Dear lasses, most of you are dead; the rest, withered. I blow you a kiss.

—Grandpa

Maryam's mother stands up in the canoe. For a second, her profile is to Chib, and he sees intimations of the hawk that Maryam will be when she is her mother's age. Maryam now has a gently aquiline face—"the sweep of the sword of love"—Chib has called that nose. Bold but beautiful. However, her mother does look like a dirty old eagle. And her aunt—uneaglish but something of the camel in those features.

Chib suppresses these unfavorable, even treacherous, comparisons. But he cannot suppress the three bearded, robed, and unwashed men who gather around him.

Chib smiles but says, "I don't remember inviting you."

They look blank since rapidly spoken LA English is a huftymagufty to them. Abu—generic name for any Egyptian in Beverly Hills—rasps an oath so ancient even the pre-Mohammed Meccans knew it. He forms a fist. Another Arab steps towards the painting and draws back a foot as if to kick it.

At this moment, Maryam's mother discovers that it is as dangerous to stand in a canoe as on a camel. It is worse, because the three women cannot swim.

Neither can the middle-aged Arab who attacks Chib, only to find his victim sidestepping and then urging him on into the lake with a foot in the rear. One of the young men rushes Chib; the other starts to kick at the painting. Both halt on hearing the three women scream and on seeing them go over into the water.

Then the two run to the edge of the lake, where they also go into the water, propelled by one of Chib's hands in each of their backs. A bolgan hears the six of them screaming and thrashing around and runs over to Chib. Chib is becoming concerned because Maryam is having trouble staying above the water. Her terror is not faked.

What Chib does not understand is why they are all carrying on so. Their feet must be on the bottom; the surface is below their chins. Despite which, Maryam looks as if she is going to drown. So do the others, but he is not interested in them. He should go in after Maryam. However, if he does, he will have to get a change of clothes before going to the showing.

At this thought, he laughs loudly and then even more loudly as the bolgan goes in after the women. He picks up the painting and walks off laughing. Before he reaches the Center, he sobers.

"Now, how come Grandpa was so right? How does he read me so well? Am I fickle, too shallow? No, I have been too deeply in love too many times. Can I help it if I love Beauty, and the beauties I love do not have enough Beauty? My eye is too demanding; it cancels the urgings of my heart."

THE MASSACRE OF THE INNER SENSE

The entrance hall (one of twelve) which Chib enters was designed by Grandpa Winnegan. The visitor comes into a long curving tube lined with mirrors at various angles. He sees a triangular door at the end of the corridor. The door seems to be too tiny for anybody over nine years old to enter. The illusion makes the visitor feel as if he's walking up the wall as he progresses towards the door. At the end of the tube, the visitor is convinced he's standing on the ceiling.

But the door gets larger as he approaches until it becomes huge. Commentators have guessed that this entrance is the architect's symbolic representation of the gateway to the world of art. One should stand on his head before entering the wonderland of aesthetics.

On going in, the visitor thinks at first that the tremendous room is inside out or reversed. He gets even dizzier. The far wall actually seems the near wall until the visitor gets reorientated. Some people can't adjust and have to get out before they faint or vomit.

On the right hand is a hatrack with a sign: HANG YOUR HEAD HERE. A double pun by Grandpa, who always carries a joke too far for most people. If Grandpa goes beyond the bounds of verbal good taste, his great-great-grandson has overshot the moon in his paintings. Thirty of his latest have been revealed, including the last three of his Dog Series: *Dog Star, Dog Would,* and *Dog Tiered.* Ruskinson and his disciples are threatening to throw up.

Luscus and his flock praise, but they're restrained. Luscus has told them to wait until he talks to young Winnegan before they go all-out. The fido men are busy shooting and interviewing both and trying to provoke a quarrel.

The main room of the building is a huge hemisphere with a bright ceiling which runs through the complete spectrum every nine minutes. The floor is a giant chessboard, and in the center of each square is a face, each of a great in the various arts. Michelangelo, Mozart, Balzac, Zeuxis, Beethoven, Li Po, Twain, Dostoyevsky, Farmisto, Mbuzi, Cupel, Krishnagurti, etc. Ten squares are left faceless so that future generations may add their own nominees for immortality.

The lower part of the wall is painted with murals depicting significant events in the lives of the artists. Against the curving wall are nine stages, one for each of the Muses. On a console above each stage is a giant statue of the presiding goddess. They are naked and have overripe figures: huge-breasted, broad-hipped, sturdy-legged, as if the sculptor thought of them as Earth goddesses, not refined intellectual types.

The faces are basically structured like the smooth placid faces of classical Greek statues, but they have an unsettling expression around the mouths and eyes. The lips are smiling but seem ready to break into a snarl. The eyes are deep and menacing. DON'T SELL ME OUT, they say. IF YOU DO . . .

A transparent plastic hemisphere extends over each stage and has acoustic properties which keep people who are not beneath the shell from hearing the sounds emanating from the stage and vice versa.

Chib makes his way through the noisy crowd towards the stage of Polyhymnia, the Muse who includes painting in her province. He passes the stage on which Benedictine is standing and pouring her lead heart out in an alchemy of golden notes. She sees Chib and manages somehow to glare at him and at the same time to keep smiling at her audience. Chib ignores her but observes that she has replaced the dress ripped in the tavern. He sees also the many policemen stationed around the building. The crowd does not seem in an explosive mood. Indeed, it seems happy, if boisterous. But the police know how deceptive this can be. One spark . . .

Chib goes by the stage of Calliope, where Omar Runic is extemporizing. He comes to Polyhymnia's, nods at Rex Luscus, who waves at him, and sets his painting on the stage. It is titled *The Massacre of the Innocents* (subtitle: *Dog in the Manger*).

The painting depicts a stable.

The stable is a grotto with curiously shaped stalactites. The light that breaks—or fractures—through the cave is Chib's red. It penetrates every object, doubles its strength, and then rays out jaggedly. The viewer, moving from side to side to get a complete look, can actually see the many levels of light as he moves, and thus he catches glimpses of the figures under the exterior figures.

The cows, sheep, and horses are in stalls at the end of the cave. Some are looking with horror at Mary and the infant. Others have their mouths open, evidently trying to warn Mary. Chib has used the legend that the animals in the manger were able to talk to each other the night Christ was born.

Joseph, a tired old man, so slumped he seems backboneless, is in a corner. He wears two horns, but each has a halo, so it's all right.

Mary's back is to the bed of straw on which the infant is supposed to be. From a trapdoor in the floor of the cave, a man is reaching to place a huge egg on the straw bed. He is in a cave beneath the cave and is dressed in modern clothes, has a boozy expression, and, like Joseph, slumps as if invertebrate. Behind him a grossly fat woman, looking remarkably like Chib's mother, has the baby, which the man passed on to her before putting the foundling egg on the straw bed.

The baby has an exquisitely beautiful face and is suffused with a white glow from his halo. The woman has removed the halo from his head and is using the sharp edge to butcher the baby.

Chib has a deep knowledge of anatomy, since he has dissected many corpses while getting his Ph.D. in art at Beverly Hills U. The body of the infant is not unnaturally elongated, as so many of

Chib's figures are. It is more than photographic; it seems to be an actual baby. Its viscera is unraveled through a large bloody hole.

The onlookers are struck in their viscera as if this were not a painting but a real infant, slashed and disemboweled, found on their doorsteps as they left home.

The egg has a semitransparent shell. In its murky yolk floats a hideous little devil, horns, hooves, tail. Its blurred features resemble a combination of Henry Ford's and Uncle Sam's. When the viewers shift to one side or the other, the faces of others appear: prominents in the development of modern society.

The window is crowded with wild animals that have come to adore but have stayed to scream soundlessly in horror. The beasts in the foreground are those that have been exterminated by man or survive only in zoos and natural preserves. The dodo, the blue whale, the passenger pigeon, the quagga, the gorilla, orangutan, polar bear, cougar, lion, tiger, grizzly bear, California condor, kangaroo, wombat, rhinoceros, bald eagle.

Behind them are other animals and, on a hill, the dark crouching shapes of the Tasmanian aborigine and Haitian Indian.

"What is your considered opinion of this rather remarkable painting, Doctor Luscus?" a fido interviewer asks.

Luscus smiles and says, "I'll have a considered judgment in a few minutes. Perhaps you'd better talk to Doctor Ruskinson first. He seems to have made up his mind at once. Fools and angels, you know."

Ruskinson's red face and scream of fury are transmitted over the fido.

"The shit heard around the world!" Chib says loudly.

"INSULT! SPITTLE! PLASTIC DUNG! A BLOW IN THE FACE OF ART AND A KICK IN THE BUTT FOR HUMANITY! INSULT! INSULT!"

"Why is it such an insult, Doctor Ruskinson?" the fido man says. "Because it mocks the Christian faith, and also the Panamorite faith? It doesn't seem to me it does that. It seems to me that Winnegan is trying to say that men have perverted Christianity, maybe all religions, all ideals, for their own greedy self-destructive purposes, that man is basically a killer and a perverter. At least, that's what I get out of it, although of course I'm only a simple layman, and . . ."

"Let the critics make the analysis, young man!" Ruskinson snaps. "Do you have a double Ph.D., one in psychiatry and one in art? Have you been certified as a critic by the government?

"Winnegan, who has no talent whatsoever, let alone this genius that various self-deluded blowhards prate about, this abomination from Beverly Hills, presents his junk—actually a mishmash which has attracted attention solely because of a new technique that any electronic technician could invent—I am enraged that a mere gimmick, a trifling novelty, can not only fool certain sectors of the public but highly educated and federally certified critics such as Doctor Luscus here—although there will always be scholarly asses who bray so loudly, pompously, and obscurely that . . ."

"Isn't it true," the fido man says, "that many painters we now call great, Van Gogh for one, were condemned or ignored by their contemporary critics? And . . ."

The fido man, skilled in provoking anger for the benefit of his viewers, pauses. Ruskinson swells, his head a bloodvessel just before aneurysm.

"I'm no ignorant layman!" he screams. "I can't help it that there have been Luscuses in the past! I know what I'm talking about! Winnegan is only a micrometeorite in the heaven of Art, not fit to shine the shoes of the great luminaries of painting. His reputation has been pumped up by a certain clique so it can shine in the reflected glory, the hyenas, biting the hand that feeds them, like mad dogs . . ."

"Aren't you mixing your metaphors a little bit?" the fido man says.

Luscus takes Chib's hand tenderly and draws him to one side where they're out of fido range.

"Darling Chib," he coos, "now is the time to declare yourself. You know how vastly I love you, not only as an artist but for yourself. It must be impossible for you to resist any longer the deeply sympathetic vibrations that leap unhindered between us.

God, if you only knew how I dreamed of you, my glorious god-like Chib, with . . ."

"If you think I'm going to say yes just because you have the power to make or break my reputation, to deny me the grant, you're wrong," Chib says. He jerks his hand away.

Luscus' good eye glares. He says, "Do you find me repulsive? Surely it can't be on moral grounds . . ."

"It's the principle of the thing," Chib says. "Even if I were in love with you, which I'm not, I wouldn't let you make love to me. I want to be judged on my merit alone, that only. Come to think of it, I don't give a damn about anybody's judgment. I don't want to hear praise or blame from you or anybody. Look at my paintings and talk to each other, you jackals. But don't try to make me agree with your little images of me."

THE ONLY GOOD CRITIC IS A DEAD CRITIC

Omar Runic has left his dais and now stands before Chib's paintings. He places one hand on his naked left chest, on which is tattooed the face of Herman Melville, Homer occupying the other place of honor on his right breast. He shouts loudly, his black eyes like furnace doors blown out by explosion. As has happened before, he is seized with inspiration derived from Chib's paintings.

> Call me Ahab, not Ishmael.
> For I have hooked the Leviathan.
> I am the wild ass's colt born to a man.
> Lo, my eye has seen it all!
> My bosom is like wine that has no vent.
> I am a sea with doors, but the doors are stuck.
> Watch out! The skin will burst; the doors will break.
>
> You are Nimrod, I say to my friend, Chib.
> And now is the hour when God says to his angels,
> If this is what he can do as a beginning, then
> Nothing is impossible for him.

He will be blowing his horn before
The ramparts of Heaven and shouting for
The Moon as hostage, the Virgin as wife,
And demanding a cut on the profits
From the Great Whore of Babylon.

"Stop that son of a bitch!" the Festival Director shouts. "He'll cause a riot like he did last year!"

The bolgani begin to move in. Chib watches Luscus, who is talking to the fido man. Chib can't hear Luscus, but he's sure Luscus is not saying complimentary things about him.

Melville wrote of me long before I was born.
I'm the man who wants to comprehend
The Universe but comprehend on my terms.
I am Ahab whose hate must pierce, shatter,
All impediment of Time, Space, or Subject
Mortality and hurl my fierce
Incandescence into the Womb of Creation,
Disturbing in its Lair whatever Force or
Unknown Thing-in-Itself crouches there,
Remote, removed, unrevealed.

The Director gestures at the police to remove Runic. Ruskinson is still shouting, although the cameras are pointing at Runic or Luscus. One of the Young Radishes, Huga Wells-Erb Heinsturbury, the science-fiction authoress, is shaking with hysteria generated by Runic's voice and with a lust for revenge. She is sneaking up on a *Time* fido man. *Time* has long ago ceased to be a magazine, since there are no magazines, but became a government-supported communications bureau. *Time* is an example of Uncle Sam's left-hand, right-hand, hands-off policy of providing communications bureaus with all they need and at the same time permitting the bureau executives to determine the bureau policies. Thus, government provision and free speech are united. This is fine, in theory, anyway.

Time has preserved several of its original policies, that is, truth and objectivity must be sacrificed for the sake of a witticism and science-fiction must be put down. *Time* has sneered at every one of Heinsturbury's works, and so she is out to get some personal satisfaction for the hurt caused by the unfair reviews.

Quid nunc? Cui bono?
Time? Space? Substance? Accident?
When you die—Hell? Nirvana?
Nothing is nothing to think about.
The canons of philosophy boom.
Their projectiles are duds.
The ammo heaps of theology blow up,
Set off by the saboteur Reason.

Call me Ephraim, for I was halted
At the Ford of God and could not tongue
The sibilance to let me pass.
Well, I can't pronounce shibboleth,
But I can say shit!

Huga Wells-Erb Heinsturbury kicks the *Time* fido man in the balls. He throws up his hands, and the football-shaped, football-sized camera sails from his hands and strikes a youth on the head. The youth is a Young Radish, Ludwig Euterpe Mahlzart. He is smoldering with rage because of the damnation of his tone poem, *Jetting The Stuff Of Future Hells*, and the camera is the extra fuel needed to make him blaze up uncontrollably. He punches the chief musical critic in his fat belly.

Huga, not the *Time* man, is screaming with pain. Her bare toes have struck the hard plastic armor with which the *Time* man, recipient of many such a kick, protects his genitals. Huga hops around on one foot while holding the injured foot in her hands. She twirls into a girl, and there is a chain effect. A man falls against the *Time* man, who is stooping over to pick up his camera.

"Ahaaa!" Huga screams and tears off the *Time* man's helmet and straddles him and beats him over the head with the optical end of the camera. Since the solid-state camera is still working, it is sending to billions of viewers some very intriguing, if dizzying, pictures. Blood obscures one side of the picture, but not so much that the viewers are wholly cheated. And then they get another novel shot as the camera flies into the air again, turning over and over.

A bolgan has shoved his shock-stick against her back, causing her to stiffen and propel the camera in a high arc behind her. Huga's current lover grapples with the bolgan; they roll on the floor; a Westwood juvenile picks up the shock-stick and has a fine time goosing the adults around him until a local youth jumps him.

"Riots are the opium of the people," the police chief groans. He calls in all units and puts in a call to the chief of police of Westwood, who is, however, having his own troubles.

Runic beats his breast and howls

> Sir, I exist! And don't tell me,
> As you did Crane, that that creates
> No obligation in you towards me.
> I am a man; I am unique.
> I've thrown the Bread out the window,
> Pissed in the Wine, pulled the plug
> From the bottom of the Ark, cut the Tree
> For firewood, and if there were a Holy
> Ghost, I'd goose him.
> But I know that it all does not mean
> A God damned thing,
> That nothing means nothing,
> That is is is and not-is not is is-not
> That a rose is a rose is a
> That we are here and will not be
> And that is all we can know!

Ruskinson sees Chib coming towards him, squawks, and tries to escape. Chib seizes the canvas of *Dogmas from a Dog* and batters Ruskinson over the head with it. Luscus protests in horror, not because of the damage done to Ruskinson but because the painting might be damaged. Chib turns around and batters Luscus in the stomach with the oval's edge.

> The earth lurches like a ship going down,
> Its back almost broken by the flood of
> Excrement from the heavens and the deeps,
> What God in His terrible munificence
> Has granted on hearing Ahab cry,
> Bullshit! Bullshit!
>
> I weep to think that this is Man
> And this his end. But wait!
> On the crest of the flood, a three-master
> Of antique shape. The Flying Dutchman!
> And Ahab is astride a ship's deck once more.
> Laugh, you Fates, and mock, you Norns!
> For I am Ahab and I am Man,
> And though I cannot break a hole
> Through the wall of What Seems
> To grab a handful of What Is,
> Yet, I will keep on punching.
> And I and my crew will not give up,
> Though the timbers split beneath our feet
> And we sink to become indistinguishable
> From the general excrement.
>
> For a moment that will burn on the
> Eye of God forever, Ahab stands
> Outlined against the blaze of Orion,
> Fist clenched, a bloody phallus,
> Like Zeus exhibiting the trophy of
> The unmanning of his father Cronus.

And then he and his crew and ship
Dip and hurtle headlong over
The edge of the world.
And from what I hear, they are still

F
a
l
l
I
n
g

Chib is shocked into a quivering mass by a jolt from a bolgan's electrical riot stick. While he is recovering, he hears his Grandpa's voice issuing from the transceiver in his hat.

"Chib, come quick! Accipiter has broken in and is trying to get through the door of my room!"

Chib gets up and fights and shoves his way to the exit. When he arrives, panting, at his home he finds that the door to Grandpa's room has been opened. The IRB men and electronic technicians are standing in the hallway. Chib bursts into Grandpa's room. Accipiter is standing in its middle and is quivering and pale. Nervous stone. He sees Chib and shrinks back, saying, "It wasn't my fault. I had to break in. It was the only way I could find out for sure. It wasn't my fault; I didn't touch him."

Chib's throat is closing in on itself. He cannot speak. He kneels down and takes Grandpa's hand. Grandpa has a slight smile on his blue lips. Once and for all, he has eluded Accipiter. In his hand is the latest sheet of his MS.

THROUGH BALAKLAVAS OF HATE, THEY CHARGE TOWARDS GOD

For most of my life, I have seen only a truly devout few and a great majority of truly indifferent. But there is a new spirit abroad. So many young men and women have revived, not a love for God, but a violent antipathy towards Him. This excites and restores me. Youths like my grandson and Runic shout blasphemies and so worship Him. If they did not believe, they would never think about Him. I now have some confidence in the future.

TO THE STICKS VIA THE STYX

Dressed in black, Chib and his mother go down the tube entrance to level 13B. It's luminous-walled, spacious, and the fare is free. Chib tells the ticket-fido his destination. Behind the wall, the protein computer, no larger than a human brain, calculates. A coded ticket slides out of a slot. Chib takes the ticket, and they go to the bay, a great incurve, where he sticks the ticket into a slot. Another ticket protrudes, and a mechanical voice repeats the information on the ticket in World and LA English, in case they can't read.

Gondolas shoot into the bay and decelerate to a stop. Wheelless, they float in a continually rebalancing graviton field. Sections of the bay slide back to make ports for the gondolas. Passengers step into the cages designated for them. The cages move forward; their doors open automatically. The passengers step into the gondolas. They sit down and wait while the safety meshmold closes over them. From the recesses of the chassis, transparent plastic curves rise and meet to form a dome.

Automatically timed, monitored by redundant protein computers for safety, the gondolas wait until the coast is clear. On receiving the go-ahead, they move slowly out of the bay to the tube. They pause while getting another affirmation, trebly checked in micro-seconds. Then they move swiftly into the tube.

Whoosh! Whoosh! Other gondolas pass them. The tube glows yellowly as if filled with electrified gas. The gondola accelerates rapidly. A few are still passing it, but Chib's speeds up and soon none can catch up with it. The round posterior of a gondola ahead is a glimmering quarry that will not be caught until it slows before mooring at its destined bay. There are not many gondolas in the tube. Despite a 100-million population, there is little traffic on the north-south route. Most LAers stay in the self-sufficient walls of their clutches. There is more traffic on the east-west tubes, since a small percentage prefer the public ocean beaches to the municipality swimming pools.

The vehicle screams southward. After a few minutes, the tube begins to slope down, and suddenly it is at a 45-degree angle to the horizontal. They flash by level after level.

Through the transparent walls, Chib glimpses the people and architecture of other cities. Level 8, Long Beach, is interesting. Its homes look like two cut-quartz pie plates, one on top of another, open end on open end, and the unit mounted on a column of carved figures, the exit-entrance ramp a flying buttress.

At level 3A, the tube straightens out. Now the gondola races past establishments the sight of which causes Mama to shut her eyes. Chib squeezes his mother's hand and thinks of the half-brother and cousin who are behind the yellowish plastic. This level contains fifteen percent of the population, the retarded, the incurable insane, the too-ugly, the monstrous, the senile aged. They swarm here, the vacant or twisted faces pressed against the tube wall to watch the pretty cars float by.

"Humanitarian" medical science keeps alive the babies that *should*—by Nature's imperative—have died. Ever since the 20th century, humans with defective genes have been saved from death. Hence, the continual spread of these genes. The tragic thing is that science can now detect and correct defective genes in the ovum and sperm. Theoretically, all human beings could be blessed with totally healthy bodies and physically perfect brains. But the rub is that we don't have near enough doctors and facilities to keep up with the births. This despite the ever decreasing drop in the birth rate.

Medical science keeps people living so long that senility strikes. So, more and more slobbering mindless decrepits. And also an accelerating addition of the mentally addled. There are therapies and drugs to restore most of them to "normalcy," but not enough doctors and facilities. Some day there may be, but that doesn't help the contemporary unfortunate.

What to do now? The ancient Greeks placed defective babies in the fields to die. The Eskimos shipped out their old people on ice floes. Should we gas our abnormal infants and seniles? Sometimes, I think it's the merciful thing to do. But I can't ask somebody else to pull the switch when I won't.

I would shoot the first man to reach for it.
                    —from Grandpa's *Private Ejaculations*

The gondola approaches one of the rare intersections. Its passengers see down the broad-mouthed tube to their right. An express flies towards them; it looms. Collision course. They know better, but they can't keep from gripping the mesh, gritting their teeth, and bracing their legs. Mama gives a small shriek. The flier hurtles over them and disappears, the flapping scream of air a soul on its way to underworld judgment.

The tube dips again until it levels out on 1. They see the ground below and the massive self-adjusting pillars supporting the megapolis. They whiz by over a little town, quaint, early 21st century LA preserved as a museum, one of many beneath the cube.

Fifteen minutes after embarking, the Winnegans reach the end of the line. An elevator takes them to the ground, where they enter a big black limousine. This is furnished by a private-enterprise mortuary, since Uncle Sam or the LA government will pay for cremation but not for burial. The Church no longer insists on interment, leaving it to the religionists to choose between being wind-blown ashes or underground corpses.

The sun is halfway towards the zenith. Mama begins to have trouble breathing and her arms and neck redden and swell. The three times she's been outside the walls, she's been attacked with this allergy despite the air conditioning of the limousine. Chib pats her hand while they're riding over a roughly patched road. The archaic eighty-year-old, fuel-cell-powered, electric-motor-driven vehicle is, however, rough-riding only by comparison with the gondola. It covers the ten kilometers to the cemetery speedily, stopping once to let deer cross the road.

Father Fellini greets them. He is distressed because he is forced to tell them that the Church feels that Grandpa has committed sacrilege. To substitute another man's body for his corpse, to have mass said over it, to have it buried in sacred ground is to blaspheme. Moreover, Grandpa died an unrepentant criminal. At least, to the knowledge of the Church, he made no contrition just before he died.

Chib expects this refusal. St. Mary's of BH-14 has declined to perform services for Grandpa within its walls. But Grandpa has often told Chib that he wants to be buried beside his ancestors, and Chib is determined that Grandpa will get his wish.

Chib says, "I'll bury him myself! Right on the edge of the graveyard!"

"You can't do that!" the priest, mortuary officials, and a federal agent say simultaneously.

"The hell I can't! Where's the shovel?"

It is then that he sees the thin dark face and falciform nose of Accipiter. The agent is supervising the digging up of Grandpa's (first) coffin. Nearby are at least fifty fido men shooting with their minicameras, the transceivers floating a few decameters near them. Grandpa is getting full coverage, as befits the Last Of The Billionaires and The Greatest Criminal Of The Century.

Fido interviewer: "Mr. Accipiter, could we have a few words from you? I'm not exaggerating when I say that there are probably at least ten billion people watching this historic event. After all, even the grade-school kids know of Win-again Winnegan.

"How do you feel about this? You've been on the case for 26 years. The successful conclusion must give you great satisfaction."

Accipiter, unsmiling as the essence of diorite: "Well, actually, I've not devoted full time to this case. Only about three years of accumulative time. But since I've spent at least several days each month on it, you might say I've been on Winnegan's trail for 26 years."

Interviewer: "It's been said that the ending of this case also means the end of the IRB. If we've not been misinformed, the IRB was only kept functioning because of Winnegan. You had other business, of course, during this time, but the tracking down of counterfeiters and gamblers who don't report their income has been turned over to other bureaus. Is this true? If so, what do you plan to do?"

Accipiter, voice flashing a crystal of emotion: "Yes, the IRB is being disbanded. But not until after the case against Winnegan's grand-daughter and her son is finished. They harbored him and are, therefore, accessories after the fact.

"In fact, almost the entire population of Beverly Hills, level 14, should be on trial. I know, but can't prove it as yet, that everybody, including the municipal chief of police, was well aware that Winnegan was hiding in that house. Even Winnegan's priest knew it, since Winnegan frequently went to mass and to confession. His priest claims that he urged Winnegan to turn himself in and also refused to give him absolution unless he did so.

"But Winnegan, a hardened 'mouse'—I mean, criminal, if ever I saw one, refused to follow the priest's urgings. He claimed that he had not committed a crime, that, believe it or not, Uncle Sam was the criminal. Imagine the effrontery, the depravity, of the man!"

Interviewer: "Surely you don't plan to arrest the entire population of Beverly Hills 14?"

Accipiter: "I have been advised not to."

Interviewer: "Do you plan on retiring after this case is wound up?"

Accipiter: "No. I intend to transfer to the Greater LA Homicide Bureau. Murder for profit hardly exists any more, but there are still crimes of passion, thank God!"

Interviewer: "Of course, if young Winnegan should win his case against you—he has charged you with invasion of domestic privacy, illegal housebreaking, and directly causing his great-great-grandfather's death—then you won't be able to work for the Homicide Bureau or any police department."

Accipiter, flashing several crystals of emotion: "It's no wonder we law enforcers have such a hard time operating effectively! Sometimes, not only the majority of citizens seem to be on the law-breaker's side but my own employers . . ."

Interviewer: "Would you care to complete that statement? I'm sure your employers are watching this channel. No? I understand that Winnegan's trial and yours are, for some reason, scheduled to take place *at the same time.* How do you plan to be present at both trials? Heh, heh! Some fido-casters are calling you The Simultaneous Man!"

Accipiter, face darkening: "Some idiot clerk did that! He incorrectly fed the data into the legal computer. And he, or somebody, turned off the error-override circuit, and the computer burned up. The clerk is suspected of deliberately making the error—by me anyway, and let the idiot sue me if he wishes—anyway, there have been too many cases like this, and . . ."

Interviewer: "Would you mind summing up the course of this case for our viewers' benefit? Just the highlights, please."

Accipiter: "Well, ah, as you know, fifty years ago all large private-enterprise businesses had become government bureaus. All except the building construction firm, the Finnegan Fifty-three States Company, of which the president was Finn Finnegan. He was the father of the man who is to be buried—somewhere—today.

"Also, all unions except the largest, the construction union, were dissolved or were government unions. Actually, the company and its union were one, because all employees got ninety-five per cent of the money, distributed more or less equally among them. Old Finnegan was both the company president and union business agent-secretary.

"By hook or crook, mainly by crook, I believe, the firm-union had resisted the inevitable absorption. There were investigations into Finnegan's methods: coercion and blackmail of U.S. Senators and even U.S. Supreme Court Justices. Nothing was, however, proved."

Interviewer: "For the benefit of our viewers who may be a little hazy on their history, even fifty years ago money was used only for the purchase of nonguaranteed items. Its other use, as today, was as an index of prestige and social esteem. At one time, the government was thinking of getting rid of currency entirely, but a study revealed that it had great psychological value. The income tax was also kept, although the government had no use for money, because the size of a man's tax determined prestige and also because it enabled the government to remove a large amount of currency from circulation."

Accipiter: "Anyway, when old Finnegan died, the federal government renewed its pressure to incorporate the construction workers and the company officials as civil servants. But young Finnegan proved to be as foxy and vicious as his old man. I don't suggest, of course, that the fact that his uncle was President of the U.S. at that time had anything to do with young Finnegan's success."

Interviewer: "Young Finnegan was seventy years old when his father died."

Accipiter: "During this struggle, which went on for many years, Finnegan decided to rename himself Winnegan. It's a pun on Win Again. He seems to have had a childish, even imbecilic, delight in puns, which, frankly, I don't understand. Puns, I mean."

Interviewer: "For the benefit of our non-American viewers, who may not know of our national custom of Naming Day . . . this was originated by the Panamorites. When a citizen comes of age, he may at any time thereafter take a new name, one which he believes to be appropriate to his temperament or goal in life. I might point out that Uncle Sam, who's been unfairly accused of trying to impose conformity upon his citizens, encourages this individualistic approach to life. This despite the increased record-keeping required on the government's part.

"I might also point out something else of interest. The government claimed that Grandpa Winnegan was mentally incompetent. My listeners will pardon me, I hope, if I take up a moment of your time to explain the basis of Uncle Sam's assertion. Now, for the benefit of those among you who are unacquainted with an early 20th-century classic, *Finnegan's Wake*, despite your government's wish for you to have a free lifelong education, the author, James Joyce, derived the title from an old vaudeville song."

(Half-fadeout while a monitor briefly explains "vaudeville.")

"The song was about Tim Finnegan, an Irish hod carrier who fell off a ladder while drunk and was supposedly killed. During the Irish wake held for Finnegan, the corpse is accidentally splashed with whiskey. Finnegan, feeling the touch of the whiskey, the 'water of life,' sits up in his coffin and then climbs out to drink and dance with the mourners.

"Grandpa Winnegan always claimed that the vaudeville song was based on reality, you can't keep a good man down, and that the original Tim Finnegan was his ancestor. This preposterous statement was used by the government in its suit against Winnegan.

"However, Winnegan produced documents to substantiate his assertion. Later—too late—the documents were proved to be forgeries."

Accipiter: "The government's case against Winnegan was strengthened by the rank and file's sympathy with the government. Citizens were complaining that the business-union was undemocratic and discriminatory. The officials and workers were getting relatively high wages, but many citizens had to be contented with their guaranteed income. So, Winnegan was brought to trial and accused, justly, of course, of various crimes, among which were subversion of democracy.

"Seeing the inevitable, Winnegan capped his criminal career. He somehow managed to steal 20 billion dollars from the federal deposit vault. This sum, by the way, was equal to half the currency then existing in Greater LA. Winnegan disappeared with the money, which he had not only stolen but had not paid income tax on. Unforgivable. I don't know why so many people have glamorized this villain's feat. Why, I've even seen fido shows with him as the hero, thinly disguised under another name, of course."

Interviewer: "Yes, folks, Winnegan committed the Crime Of The Age. And, although he has finally been located, and is to be buried today—somewhere—the case is not completely closed. The Federal government says it is. But where is the money, the 20 billion dollars?"

Accipiter: "Actually, the money has no value now except as collector's items. Shortly after the theft, the government called in all currency and then issued new bills that could not be mistaken for the old. The government had been wanting to do something like this for a long time, anyway, because it believed that there was too much currency, and it only reissued half the amount taken in.

"I'd like very much to know where the money is. I won't rest until I do. I'll hunt it down if I have to do it on my own time."

Interviewer: "You may have plenty of time to do that if young Winnegan wins his case. Well, folks, as most of you may know, Winnegan was found dead in a lower level of San Francisco about a year after he disappeared. His grand-daughter identified the body, and the fingerprints, earprints, retina-prints, teethprints, blood-type, hair-type, and a dozen other identity prints matched out."

Chib, who has been listening, thinks that Grandpa must have spent several millions of the stolen money arranging this. He does not know, but he suspects that a research lab somewhere in the world grew the duplicate in a biotank.

This happened two years after Chib was born. When Chib was five, his grandpa showed up. Without letting Mama know he was back, he moved in. Only Chib was his confidant. It was, of course, impossible for Grandpa to go completely unnoticed by Mama, yet she now insisted that she had never seen him. Chib thought that this was to avoid prosecution for being an accessory after the crime. He was not sure. Perhaps she had blocked off his "visitations" from the rest of her mind. For her it would be easy, since she never knew whether today was Tuesday or Thursday and could not tell you what year it was.

Chib ignores the mortuarians, who want to know what to do with the body. He walks over to the grave. The top of the ovoid coffin is visible now, with the long elephantlike snout of the digging machine sonically crumbling the dirt and then sucking it up. Accipiter, breaking through his lifelong control, is smiling at the fidomen and rubbing his hands.

"Dance a little, you son of a bitch," Chib says, his anger the only block to the tears and the wail building up in him.

The area around the coffin is cleared to make room for the grappling arms of the machine. These descend, hook under, and lift the black, irradiated-plastic, mocksilver-arabesqued coffin up and out and onto the grass. Chib, seeing the IRB men begin to open the coffin, starts to say something but closes his mouth. He watches intently, his knees bent as if getting ready to jump. The fidomen close in, their eyeball-shaped cameras pointing at the group around the coffin.

Groaning, the lid rises. There is a big bang. Dense dark smoke billows. Accipiter and his men, blackened, eyes wide and white, coughing, stagger out of the cloud. The fidomen are running every -which way or stooping to pick up their cameras. Those who were standing far enough back can see that the explosion took place at the bottom of the grave. Only Chib knows that the raising of the coffin lid has activated the detonating device in the grave.

He is also the first to look up into the sky at the projectile soaring from the grave because only he expected it. The rocket climbs up to five hundred feet while the fidomen train their cameras on it. It bursts apart and from it a ribbon unfolds between two round objects. The objects expand to become balloons while the ribbon becomes a huge banner.

On it, in big black letters, are the words

WINNEGAN'S FAKE!

Twenty billions of dollars buried beneath the supposed bottom of the grave burn furiously. Some bills, blown up in the geyser of fireworks, are carried by the wind while IRB men, fidomen, mortuary officials, and municipality officials chase them.

Mama is stunned.

Accipiter looks as if he is having a stroke.

Chib cries and then laughs and rolls on the ground.

Grandpa has again screwed Uncle Sam and has also pulled his greatest pun where all the world can see it.

"Oh, you old man!" Chib sobs between laughing fits. "Oh, you old man! How I love you!"

While he is rolling on the ground again, roaring so hard his ribs hurt, he feels a paper in his hand. He stops laughing and gets on his knees and calls after the man who gave it to him. The man says, "I was paid by your grand-father to hand it to you when he was buried."

Chib reads:

I hope nobody was hurt, not even the IRB men.

Final advice from the Wise Old Man In The Cave. Tear loose. Leave LA. Leave the country. Go to Egypt. Let your mother ride the purple wage on her own. She can do it if she practices thrift and self-denial. If she can't, that's not your fault.

You are fortunate indeed to have been born with talent, if not genius, and to be strong enough to want to rip out the umbilical cord. So do it. Go to Egypt. Steep yourself in the ancient culture. Stand before the Sphinx. Ask her (actually, it's a he) the Question.

Then visit one of the zoological preserves south of the Nile. Live for a while in a reasonable facsimile of Nature as she was before mankind dishonored and disfigured her. There, where *Homo sapiens*(?) evolved from the killer ape, absorb the spirit of that ancient place and time.

You've been painting with your penis, which I'm afraid was more stiffened with bile than with passion for life. Learn to paint with your heart. Only thus will you become great and true.

Paint.

Then, go wherever you want to go. I'll be with you as long as you're alive to remember me. To quote Runic, "I'll be the Northern Lights of your soul."

Hold fast to the belief that there will be others to love you just as much as I did or even more. What is more important, you must love them as much as they love you.

Can you do this?

Tht Junglt Rot Kid on tht Nod

I f William Burroughs instead of Edgar Rice Burroughs had
written the Tarzan novels . . .

Foreword
Tapes cut and respliced at random by Brachiate Bruce,
the old mainliner chimp, the Kid's asshole buddy, cool
blue in the orgone box

from the speech in Parliament of Lord Greystoke alias The
Jungle Rot Kid, a full house, SRO, the Kid really packing them in.
—Capitalistic pricks! Don't send me no more foreign aid!
You corrupting my simple black folks, they driving around the
old plantation way down on the Zambezi River in air-conditioned
Cadillacs, shooting horse, flapping ubangi at me . . . Bwana him
not in the cole cole ground but him sure as shit gonna be soon.
Them M-16s, tanks, mortars, flamethrowers coming up the jungle
trail, Ole Mao Charley promised us!
Lords, Ladies, Third Sex! I tole you about apeomorphine but
you dont lissen! You got too much invested in the Mafia and
General Motors, I say you gotta kick the money habit too. Get
them green things offen your back . . . nothing to lose but your
chains that is stocks, bonds, castles, Rollses, whores, soft toilet

paper, connection with The Man . . . it a long long way to the jungle but it worth it, build up your muscle and character cut/

. . . you call me here at my own expense to degrade humiliate me strip me of loincloth and ancient honored title! You hate me cause you hung up on civilization and I never been hooked. You over a barrel with smog freeways TV oily beaches taxes inflation frozen dinners timeclocks carcinogens neckties all that shit. Call me noble savage . . . me tell you how it is where its at with my personal tarzanic purusharta . . . involves kissing off dharma and artha and getting a fix on moksha through karma . . .

Old Lord Bromley-Rimmer who wear a merkin on his bald head and got pecker and balls look like dried up grapes on top a huge hairy cut-in fold-out thing it disgust you to see it, he grip young Lord Materfutter's crotch and say—Dearie what kinda gibberish that, Swahili, what?

Young Lord Materfutter say—Bajove, kinda African cricket doncha know what?

. . . them fuckin Ayrabs run off with my Jane again . . . intersolar communist venusian bankers plot . . . so it back to the jungle again, hit the arboreal trail, through the middle tearass, dig Numa the lion, the lost civilizations kick, tell my troubles to Sam Tantor alias The Long Dong Kid. Old Sam always writing amendments to the protocols of the elders of mars, dipping his trunk in the blood of innocent bystanders, writing amendments in the sand with blood and no one could read what he had written there selah

Me, I'm only fuckin free man in the world . . . live in state of anarchy, up trees . . . every kid and lotsa grown-ups (so-called) dream of the Big Tree Fix, of swinging on vines, freedom, live by the knife and unwritten code of the jungle . . .

Ole Morphodite Lord Bromley-Rimmer say—Dearie, that Anarchy, that one a them new African nations what?

The Jungle Rot Kid bellowing in the House of Lords like he calling ole Sam Tantor to come running help him outta his mess, he really laying it on them blueblood pricks.

. . . I got satyagraha in the ole original Sanskrit sense of course up the ass, you fat fruits. I quit, So long. Back to the

Dark Continent . . . them sheiks of the desert run off with Jane again . . . blood will flow . . .

Fadeout. Lord Materfutter's face phantom of erection wheezing paregoric breath. —Dig that leopardskin jockstrap what price glory what? cut/

This here extracted from John Clayton's diary which he write in French God only know why . . . Sacre bleu! Nom d'un con! Alice she dead, who gonna blow me now? The kid screaming his head off, he sure don't look like black-haired gray-eyed fine-chiseled featured scion of noble British family which come over with Willie the Bastard and his squarehead-frog goons on the Anglo-Saxon Lark. No more milk for him no more ass for me, carry me back to old Norfolk / / double cut

The Gorilla Thing fumbling at the lock on the door of old log cabin which John Clayton built hisself. Eyes stabbing through the window. Red as two diamonds in a catamite's ass. John Clayton, he rush out with a big axe, gonna chop me some anthropoid wood.

Big hairy paws strong as hold of pusher on old junkie whirl Clayton around. Stinking breath. Must smoke banana peels. *Whoo! Whoo!* Gorilla Express dingdonging up black tunnel of my rectum. Piles burst like rotten tomatoes, sighing softly. Death come. And come. And come. Blazing bloody orgasms. Not a bad way to go . . . but you cant touch my inviolate white soul . . . too late to make a deal with the Gorilla Thing? Give him my title, Jaguar, moated castle, ole faithful family retainer he go down on you, opera box . . . ma tante de pisse . . . who take care of the baby, carry on family name? Vive la bourgerie! cut/

"Twenty years later give take a couple, the Jungle Rot Kid trail the killer of Big Ape Mama what snatch him from cradle and raise him as her own with discipline security warm memory of hairy teats hot unpasteurized milk . . . the Kid swinging big on vines from tree to tree, fastern hot baboonshit through a tin horn. Ant hordes blitzkrieg him like agenbite of intwat, red insect-things which is exteriorized thoughts of the Monster Ant-Mother of the Crab Nebula in secret war to take over this small planet, this Peoria Earth.

Monkey on his back, Nkima, eat the red insect-things, wipe

out trillions with flanking bowel movement, Ant-Mother close up galactic shop for the day . . .

The Kid drop his noose around the black-assed motherkiller and haul him up by the neck into the tree in front of God and local citizens which is called gomangani in ape vernacular.

—You gone too far this time the Kid say as he core out the motherkillers asshole with fathers old hunting knife and bugger him old Turkish custom while the motherkiller rockin and rollin in death agony.

Heavy metal Congo jissom ejaculate catherinewheeling all over local gomangani, they say—Looka that!

Old junkie witch doctor coughing his lungs out in sick gray African morning, shuffling through silver dust of old kraal.

—You say my son's dead, kilt by the Kid?

Jungle drums beat like aged wino's temples morning after.

Get Whitey!

The Kid sometime known as Genocide John really liquidate them dumbshit gomangani. Sure is a shame to waste all that black gash the Kid say but it the code of the jungle. Noblesse obleege.

The locals say—We dont haffa put up with this shit and they split. The Kid dont have no fun nomore and this chimp ass mighty hairy not to mention chimp habit of crapping when having orgasm. Then along come Jane alias Baltimore Blondie, she on the lam from Rudolph Rassendale type snarling—You marry me Jane or else I foreclose on your father's ass.

The Kid rescue Jane and they make the domestic scene big, go to Europe on The Civilized Caper but the kid find out fast that the code of jungle conflict with local ordinances. The fuzz say you cant go around putting a full-nelson on them criminals and breaken their necks even if they did assault you they got civil rights too. The Kid's picture hang on post office and police station walls everywhere, he known as Archetype Archie and by the Paris fuzz as La Magnifique Merde—50,000 francs dead or alive. With the heat moving in, the Kid and Baltimore Blondie cut out for the tree house.

Along come La sometimes known as Sacrifice Sal elsewhere as

Disembowelment Daisy. She queen of Opar, ruler of hairy little man-things of the hidden colony of ancient Atlantis, the Kid always dig the lost cities kick. So the Kid split with Jane for awhile to ball La.

—Along come them fuckin Ayrabs again and abduct Jane, gangbang her . . . she aint been worth a shit since . . . cost me all the jewels and golden ingots I heisted offa Opar to get rid of her clap, syph, yaws, crabs, pyorrhea, double-barreled dysentery, busted rectum, split urethra, torn nostrils, pierced eardrums, bruised kidneys, nymphomania, old hashish habit, and things too disgusting to mention . . .

Along come The Rumble To End All Rumbles 1914 style, and them fuckin Huns abduct Jane . . . they got preying-mantis eyes with insect lust. Black anti-orgone Horbigerian Weltanschauung, they take orders from green venusians who telepath through von Hindenburg.

—Ja Wohl! bark Leutnant Herrlipp von Dreckfinger at his Kolonel, Bombastus von Arschangst. —Ve use die Baltimore snatch to trap der gottverdammerungt Jungle Rot Kid, dot pseudu-Aryan Oberaffenmensch, unt ve kill him unt den all Afrika iss ours! Drei cheers for Der Kaiser unt die Krupp Familie!

The Kid balling La again but he drop her like old junkie drop pants for a shot of horse, he track down the Hun, it the code of the jungle.

Cool blue orgone bubbles sift down from evening sky, the sinking sun a bloody kotex which spread stinking scarlet gash-worms over the big dungball of Earth. Night move in like fuzz with Black Maria. Mysterious sounds of tropical wilds . . . Numa roar, wild boars grunt like they constipated, parrots with sick pukegreen feathers and yellow eyes like old goofball bum Panama 1910 cry Rache!

Hun blood flow, kraut necks crack like cinnamon sticks, the Kid put his foot on dead ass of slain Teuton and give the victory cry of the bull ape, it even scare the shit outta Numa King of the Beasts fadeout.

The Kid and his mate live in the old tree house now . . . surohc lakcaj fo mhtyhr ot ffo kcaj[1] chimps, Numa roar, Sheeta the panther cough like an old junkie. Jane alias The Baltimore Bitch nag, squawk, whine about them mosquitoes tsetse flies ant-things hyenas and them uppity gomangani moved into the neighborhood, they'll turn a decent jungle into slums in three days, I aint prejudiced ya unnerstand some of my best friends are Waziris, whynt ya ever take me out to dinner, Nairobi only a thousand miles away, they really swingin there for chrissakes and cut/

. . . trees chopped down for the saw mills, animals kilt off, rivers stiff stinking with dugout-sized tapeworm turds, broken gin bottles, contraceptive jelly and all them disgusting things snatches use, detergents, cigarette filters . . . and the great apes shipped off to USA zoos, they send telegram: SOUTHERN CALIFORNIA CLIMATE AND WELFARE PROGRAM SIMPLY FABULOUS STOP NO TROUBLE GETTING A FIX STOP CLOSE TO TIAJUANA STOP WHAT PRICE FREEDOM INDIVIDUALITY EXISTENTIAL PHILOSOPHY CRAP STOP

. . . Opar a tourist trap, La running the native-art made-in-Japan concession and you cant turn around without rubbing sparks off black asses.

The African drag really got the Kid down now . . . Jane's voice and the jungle noises glimmering off like a comet leaving Earth forever for the cold interstellar abysms . . .

The Kid never move a muscle staring at his big toe, thinking of nothing—wouldn't you?—not even La's diamond-studded snatch, he off the woman kick, off the everything kick, fulla horse, on the nod, lower spine ten degrees below absolute zero like he got a direct connection with The Liquid Hydrogen Man at Cape Kennedy . . .

The Kid ride with a one-way ticket on the Hegelian Express thesis antithesis synthesis, sucking in them cool blue orgone bubbles and sucking off the Eternal Absolute . . .

[1] Old Brachiate Bruce splice in tape backward here.

My Father the Ripper

AN EXCERPT FROM *A Feast Unknown*

I was conceived and born in 1888.

Jack the Ripper was my father.

I am certain of this, although I have no evidence that would stand up in court. I have only the diary of my legal father. He was, in fact, my uncle, although he was married to my mother.

My legal father kept a diary almost up to the moment of his death. Shortly after he had locked it inside a desk, he was killed. His last written words recorded his despair because his wife had just died and I, only a year old, was wailing for milk. And there were no human beings within hundreds of miles, as far as he knew.

I alone have read the entire diary. I have never permitted anyone else to read any of the diary preceding the moment when my uncle and my mother sailed from England for Africa.

My "Biographer" would have been too horrified by the truth to have written it if I had been unkind enough to reveal it to him. He was a romanticist and, in many ways, a Victorian. He would have made up a story of his own, ignoring the real story, as he did with so many of my adventures. He was interested mainly in adventure for its own sake although he did describe my psychology, my *Weltanschauung*. However, he never really transmitted the half-infrahuman cast of my mind.

Perhaps he could not understand that part of me, although I tried to communicate it as well as I could. He tried to understand, but he was human, all-too-human, as my favorite poet says. He could never grasp, with the human hands of his psyche, the non-human shape of mine.

That part of the diary which I had forbidden others to read describes how my mother happened to be with her husband in Whitechapel on that fog-smothered night. She had insisted on going with him to look for his brother, who had escaped from the cell in the castle in the Cumberland County. Private detectives had quietly tracked John Cloamby to the Whitechapel district of London. His brother, James Cloamby, Viscount Grandrith, had joined the hunt. My mother, Alexandra Applethwaite, related to the noble family of Bedford, had insisted on accompanying him.

My uncle objected to bringing his wife along for several reasons. The strongest was that his brother had attempted to rape her when he had broken out of his cell after bending several iron bars and uprooting them from their stone sockets. Only her screams and the prompt appearance of two manservants armed with pistols had saved her. Alexandra, however, persisted in her insane belief that she alone could make him surrender voluntarily when he was found. Also, she said that she alone could locate him exactly. There was, she claimed, a psychic bond between them, "vibrations" which enabled her to point toward and track him as if she were a human lodestone.

I use the word "insane" in describing this belief because later developments (described by my "biographer" and by me in Vol. I) revealed her mental instability.

She also said that if she were not allowed to go with her husband in the search, she would inform the police and the news-papers of what had happened.

My uncle gave in to her. He had a horror of publicity of any kind and especially of this kind. Also, he might have been arrested for concealing evidence of murder. He was, in fact, an accessory after the fact of murder, if, indeed, there was a fact.

My uncle believed that his brother was responsible for the

disappearance of two whores from villages only a few miles from the estates. A severed breast was found on the shore of a tarn; this was all. The locals presumed that somebody had done away with the two women and buried them somewhere. My uncle connected his brother to the murders because of his ravings while in the cell about killing all whores, including his mother. Especially his mother.

His mother, of course, was safe from him. She had killed herself when James, John, and Patrick, her three sons, were quite young. Her husband had killed himself because he suspected that a Swedish gentleman was the father of the boys and that she may have killed herself because her conscience made life unbearable. Their aunt raised the three boys and was much loved by them. But John Cloamby never forgave his mother, although he had never spoken of her until his madness took him.

Later, my uncle believed that John was Jack the Ripper. Before his breakdown, John had been a medical doctor. His real motive in becoming a physician was not in curing the sick. He wanted to know everything about the human body because he intended to find out the secret of immortality. To this end, he had meant to learn much more of chemistry and botany than any medical doctor had ever known.

This obsession was supposed to be the cause of his sickness, Instead, it was the symptom.

It was ironic that he did not find that secret but that I, his son, did. I supposed this, only to have to change my mind.

If my mother and uncle had not gone to Africa primarily to put my father behind them, I would not have become immortal (have a very long prolonged youth, to be exact). Or so I thought.

I am immortal in the sense that I will be thirty-two years of age in body for a very very long time. However, accident, murder, and suicide can reduce me to the rotting corpse which others usually become before their hundredth birthday.

I omitted disease from the fatal list. The same elixir that gives me a potentiality of thirty thousand years or more also preserves me from disease. This does not, however, explain my seeming immunity from all the diseases so common in tropical Africa before I became thirty-two.

My uncle's diary recounts in an elegant style, reading like a prose Racine, a ride through the dark fog of the night on March 21. He glimpsed his brother after hours of driving through the mists, and he leaped out of his carriage and ran shouting after him. My mother sat shivering with cold and fear in the carriage while she tried to peer through the wet grayness. A gas lamp nearby shot a ghastly half-light through the swirls. She was alone. Her husband had not wanted a coachman because he might report the peculiar occurrences of the evening to the police.

For a while, there was silence. Then she heard the clicking of hard heels on the stones. A man appeared like a ship sailing through the fog. He stopped and turned, and by the dim light she saw her husband's mad brother.

When James Cloamby returned, he found his wife unconscious on the seat of the carriage. Her skirt and petticoats were up over her face, and her undergarments had been cut off, probably with the scalpel that later took apart the bodies of the Whitechapel whores in such grisly fashion.

My uncle was to reason that his brother had not killed her because she was not a whore. But John did hate his older brother, and he may have raped Alexandra for revenge, or possibly because she was not a whore and so was better than his mother, whom, in one part of him, he must still have loved. Also, since John loved Alexandra, or had said he loved her, it was possible that this was his act of love. Who knew what the madman was thinking?

My uncle lit a match when she did not reply to his cry of alarm. He saw the white legs, stripped of the black stockings, and the black, exceptionally hairy vagina out of which oozed my father's spermatic fluid and some of her blood.

The strange thing, to me, anyway, was that this was the first time my uncle had seen any of his wife's body below the shoulders.

Although they had been married for a month, the two had not had any sexual intercourse beyond some kissing and slipping his hand down her bodice and over her breasts. The day of the wedding, she had begun menstruating and would not stop. He, being a Victorian, could not bed her while she was "unclean." (Although there were plenty of Victorians who would have done so.)

The day before John broke loose from the cell, Alexandra had ceased to flow. My uncle (as recorded in his diary) was ecstatic. He could quit masturbating now and could stop eyeing his wife's maid.

Then my father-to-be got out of his cell in the north tower of the half-ruined Castle of Grandrith. He and his wife were too upset for some time to consider sexual intercourse. At least, she was.

Now, in the London fog, James Cloamby pulled his wife's skirts down and revived her. She became hysterical, and not until the next day did he discover that his brother had attacked his wife.

His wife seemed to recover. A few months afterward, they sailed for West Africa, where James was to conduct a secret investigation for the Colonial Office. (This was not the investigation which my "biographer" described, however. He knew the true reason, but he chose to give a spurious one.)

Alexandra now refused to have intercourse with James. She said that she was too "ashamed," felt "too unclean," and, besides, wanted to make certain that she was or was not pregnant. If she was to have a child, she wanted to be certain of its paternity.

Before they sailed, the first known murder by Jack the Ripper occurred on Easter Tuesday, April 3, 1888, on Osborn Street. My uncle heard about this (it was not reported in the *Times*) and wondered in his diary if it could be the work of his brother. Later, he was certain that it was. Yet, so great was his dread of the shame and disgrace if John should be caught, he did not inform the police.

He did continue the search on his own through private detectives. When he sailed for Africa, he sent an anonymous note to the police, describing his brother but not naming him. This note is not in the official records. Research has convinced me that it was suppressed by politically powerful influences.

My father disappeared when Jack the Ripper disappeared. It was not until 1968, the year of this narrative, that I found out what had happened to him.

Alexandra Grandrith was finally able to accept her husband in bed. But by then she was too big with child. My uncle continued to suffer and then backslid, as he put it, to masturbation and, once, a few days before sailing, to the maid. These necessary discharges caused much breast beating in private and many mea culpas.

The events that led to the Grandriths being stranded on the West African coast are familiar to the readers of my "biographer." The reality was somewhat different, but the result was much as depicted in the romances based on my life. James Cloamby built a strong house on the shore near the jungle, and they survived the first twenty months.

I was born November 21, 1888, at 11:45 P.M.

My mother's mind was never thereafter quite in Africa. She spent most of her time in a dream England, a country much better than the one she knew in reality, I'm sure. Despite this, she was very competent in taking care of me, if I am to believe my uncle's diary. James could not make love to her then because it would have been too much like taking advantage of an idiot. So my poor uncle suffered, and I think he may have been glad when death came at the hands of the chief of a tribe of The Folk. Any horror he felt would have been for his nephew, a twelve-month-old baby crying for food and for his mother's milk.

I was to get no more of that because she had died in her sleep a few hours before my uncle was killed. I did get a mother's milk, though it was not quite human milk.

Kickaha's Escape

AN EXCERPT FROM *A Private Cosmos*

Kickaha and Anana rode in the center of the party. Their hands were tied with ropes but loosely, so they could handle the reins. They stopped at noon. They were just finishing their cooked rabbit and greens boiled in little pots, when a lookout on a hill nearby called out. He came galloping toward them, and, when he was closer, he could be heard.

"Half-Horses!"

The pots were emptied on top of the fire, dirt was kicked over the wet ashes, and the soldiers packed away most of their utensils. The two captives were made to remount, and the party started off southward, toward the trade trail, many miles away.

It was then that the soldiers saw the wave of buffalo moving across the plains. It was a tremendous herd several miles across and of a seemingly interminable length. The right flank was three miles from them, but the earth quivered under the impact of perhaps a quarter of a million hooves.

For some reason known only to the buffalo, they were in flight. They were stampeding westward, and they were going so swiftly that the Tishquetmoac party might not be able to get across the trade path in time. They had a chance, but they would not know how good it was until they got much closer to the herd.

The Half-Horses had seen the humans, and they were into full gallop. There were about thirty of them: a chief with a full-feathered and long-tailed bonnet, a number of blooded warriors with feathered headbands, and three or four unblooded juveniles.

Kickaha groaned; it seemed to him that they were of the Shoyshatel tribe. They were so far away that the markings were not quite distinct. But he thought that the bearing of the chief was that of the Half-Horse who had shouted threats at him when Kickaha had taken refuge at the Tishquetmoac fort.

Then he laughed. It did not matter which tribe it was. All Half-Horse tribes hated Kickaha and all would treat him as cruelly as possible if they caught him.

He yelled at Takwoc, the leader of the soldiers, "Cut the ropes from our wrists! They're handicapping us! We can't get away from you, don't worry!"

Takwoc looked for a moment as if he might actually cut the ropes. The danger involved in riding so close to Kickaha, the danger of the horses knocking each other down or Kickaha knocking him off the saddle, probably made him change his mind. He shook his head.

Kickaha cursed and then crouched over the neck of the stallion and tried to evoke from him every muscle-stretching-contracting quota of energy in his magnificent body. The stallion did not respond because he was already running as swiftly as he could.

Kickaha's horse, though fleet, was half a body-length behind the stallion which Anana rode. Perhaps they were about equal in running ability, but Anana's lighter weight made the difference. The others were not too far behind and were spread out in a rough crescent, with horns curving away from him, three on each side. The Half-Horses were just coming over the rise; they slowed down a moment, probably in amazement at the sight of the tremendous herd. Then they waved their weapons and charged on down the hill.

The herd was rumbling westward. The Tishquetmoac and prisoners were coming on the buffalos' right at an angle of forty-five degrees. The Half-Horses had swung a little to the west before coming over the hill and their greater speed had enabled them to squeeze the distance down between them and their intended victims.

Kickaha, watching the corner formed by the flank of the great column of beasts and the front part—almost square—saw that the party could get across in front of the herd. From then on, speed and luck meant safety to the other side or being overwhelmed by the racing buffalo. The party could not directly cut across the advance; it would have to run ahead of the beasts and at an angle at the same time.

Whether or not the horses could keep up their present speed, whether or not a horse or all horses might slip, that would be known in a very short time.

He shouted encouragement at Anana as she looked briefly behind, but the rumble of the hooves, shaking the earth and sounding like a volcano ready to blow its crust, tore his voice to shreds.

The roar, the odor of the beasts, the dust, frightened Kickaha. At the same time, he was exhilarated. This wasn't the first time that he had been raised by his fright out of fright and into near-ecstasy. Events seemed to be on such a grand scale all of a sudden, and the race was such a fine one, with the prize sudden safety or sudden death, that he felt as if he were kin to the gods, if not a god. That moment when mortality was so near, and so probable, was the moment he felt immortal.

It was quickly gone, but while it lasted he knew that he was experiencing a mystical state.

Then he was seemingly heading for a collision with the angle formed by the flank and front of the herd.

Now he could see the towering shaggy brown sides of the giant buffalo, the humps heaving up and down like the bodies of porpoises soaring from wave to wave, the dark-brown foreheads, massive and lowering, the dripping black snouts, the red eyes, the black eyes, the red-shot white eyes, the legs working so swiftly they were almost a blur, foam curving from the open foam-toothed mouths onto thick shaggy chests and the upper parts of the legs.

He could hear nothing at first but that rumbling as of the earth splitting open, so powerful that he expected, for a second, to see the plain open beneath the hooves and fire and smoke spurt out.

He could smell a million buffalo, beasts extinct for ten thousand years on Earth, monsters with horns ten feet across, sweating with panic and the heart-shredding labor of their flight, excrement of fear befouling them and their companions, and something that smelled to him like a mixture of foam from mouth and blood from lungs, but that, of course, was his imagination.

There was also the stink of his horse, sweat of panic and labor of flight and of foam from its mouth.

"Haiyeeee!" Kickaha shouted, turning to scream at the Half-Horses, wishing his hands were not tied and he had a weapon to shake at them. He could not hear his own defiance, but he hoped that the Half-Horses would see his open mouth and his grin and know that he was mocking them.

By now, the centaurs were within a hundred and fifty yards of their quarry. They were frenzied in their efforts to catch up; their great dark broad-cheekboned faces were twisted in agony.

They could not close swiftly enough, and they knew it. By the time their quarry had shot across the right shoulder of the herd at an angle, they would still be fifty or so yards behind. And by the time they reached the front of the herd, their quarry would be too far ahead. And after that, they would slowly lose ground before the buffalo, and before they could get to the other side, they would go down under the shelving brows and curving horns and cutting hooves.

Despite this, the Half-Horses galloped on. An unblooded, a juvenile whose headband was innocent of scalp or feather, had managed to get ahead of the others. He left the others behind at such a rate that Kickaha's eyes widened. He had never seen so swift a Half-Horse before, and he had seen many. The unblooded came on and on, his face twisted with an effort so intense that Kickaha would not have been surprised to see the muscles of the face tear loose.

The Half-Horse's arm came back and then forward, and the lance flew ahead of him, arcing down, and suddenly Kickaha saw that what he had thought would be impossible was happening.

The lance was going to strike the hind quarters or the legs of his stallion. It was coming down in a curve that would fly over the Tishquetmoac riders behind him and would plunge into some part of his horse.

He pulled the reins to direct the stallion to the left, but the stallion pulled its head to one side and slowed down just a trifle. Then he felt a slight shock, and he knew that the lance had sunk into its flesh.

The horse was going over, its front legs crumpling, the back still driving and sending the rump into the air. The neck shot away from before him, and he was soaring through the air.

Kickaha did not know how he did it. Something took over in him as it had done before, and he did not fall or slide into the ground. He landed running on his feet with the black and brown wall of the herd to his left. Behind him, so close that he could hear it even above the rumble-roar of the herd, was the thunk of horses' hooves. Then the sound was all around him, and he could no longer stay upright because of his momentum, and he went into the grass on his face and slid.

A shadow swooped over him; it was that of a horse and rider as the horse jumped him. Then all seven were past him; he saw Anana looking back over her shoulder just before the advancing herd cut her—cut all the Tishquetmoac, too—from his sight.

There was nothing they could do for him. To delay even a second meant death for them under the hooves of the buffalo or the spears of the Half-Horses. He would have done the same if he had been on his horse and she had fallen off hers.

Surely the Half-Horses must have been yelling in triumph now. The stallion of Kickaha was dead, a lance projecting from its rump and its neck broken. Their greatest enemy, the trickster who had so often given them the slip when they knew they had him, even he could not now escape. Not unless he were to throw himself under the hooves of the titans thundering not ten feet away!

This thought may have struck them, because they swept toward him with the unblooded who had thrown the lance trying to cut him off. The others had thrown their lances and tomahawks and clubs and knives away and were charging with bare hands. They wanted to take him alive. Kickaha did not hesitate. He had gotten up as soon as he was able and now he ran toward the herd. The flanks of the beasts swelled before him; they were six feet high at the shoulder and running as if time itself were behind them and threatening to make them extinct like their brothers on Earth.

Kickaha ran toward them, seeing out of the corner of his eyes the young unblooded galloping in. Kickaha gave a savage yell and leaped upward, his hands held before him. His foot struck a massive shoulder and he grabbed a shag of fur. He kicked upward and slipped and fell forward and was on his stomach on the back of a bull!

He was looking down the steep valley formed by the right and left sides of two buffalo. He was going up and down swiftly, was getting sick, and also was slowly sliding backward.

After loosing his hold on the tuft of hair, he grabbed another one to his right and managed to work himself around so that his legs straddled the back of the beast. The hump was in front of him; he was hanging onto the hair of it.

If Kickaha believed only a little in what had happened, the Half-Horse youth who had thought he had Kickaha in his hands believed it not at all.

He raced alongside the bull on which Kickaha was seated, and his eyes were wide and his mouth worked. His arms were extended in front of him as if he still thought he would scoop Kickaha up in them.

Kickaha did not want to let loose of his hold, insecure though it was, but he knew that the Half-Horse would recover in a moment. Then he would pull a knife or tomahawk from the belt around the lower part of his human torso, and he would throw it at Kickaha. If he missed, he had weapons in reserve.

Kickaha brought his legs up so that he was squatting on top of the spine of the great bull, his feet together, one hand clenching buffalo hair. He turned slowly, managing to balance himself despite the up-and-down jarring movement. Then he launched himself outward and onto the back of the next buffalo, which was running shoulder to shoulder with the animal he had just left.

Something dark rotated over his right shoulder. It struck the hump of a buffalo nearby and bounced up and fell between two animals. It was a tomahawk.

Kickaha pulled himself up again, this time more swiftly, and he got his feet under him and jumped. One foot slipped as he left the back, but he was so close to the other that he grabbed fur with both hands. He hung there while his toes just touched the ground whenever the beast came down in its galloping motion. Then he let himself slide down a little, pushed against the ground, and swung himself upward. He got one leg over the back and came up and was astride it.

The young Half-Horse was still keeping pace with him. The others had dropped back a little; perhaps they thought he had fallen down between the buffalo and so was ground into shreds. If so, they must have been shocked to see him rise from the supposed dead, the Trickster, slippery, cunning, many-turning, the enemy who mocked them from within death's mouth.

The unblooded must have been driven a little crazy when he saw Kickaha. Suddenly, his great body, four hooves flying, soared up and he was momentarily standing on the back of a buffalo at the edge of the herd. He sprang forward to the next one, onto its hump, like a mountain goat skipping on moving mountains.

Now it was Kickaha's turn to be amazed and dismayed. The Half-Horse held a knife in his hand, and he grinned at Kickaha as if to say, "At last, you are going to die, Kickaha! And I, I will be sung of throughout the halls and tepees of the Nations of the prairies and the mountains, by men and Half-Horses everywhere!"

Some such thoughts must have been in that huge head. And he would have become the most famous of all dwellers on and about the Plains, if he had succeeded. Trickster killer he would have been named.

He Who Skipped Over Mad Buffalo To Cut Kickaha's Throat.

But on the third hump, a hoof slipped and he plunged on over the hump and fell down between two buffalo, his back legs flying and tail straight up. And that was the end of him, though Kickaha could not see what the buffalo hooves were doing.

Still, the attempt had been magnificent and had almost succeeded, and Kickaha honored him even if he was a Half-Horse. Then he began to think again about surviving.

The Josés from Rio

The Rio airport is hot, sticky, and noisy. We're standing in line, waiting to board the plane for New York, wondering if this evening, a nightmare (though comic at times), will ever end. Brazilians crowd around Jonathan Harris, the Mr. Smith of *Lost in Space* to worship and to get his autograph. Behind the worshippers are Bester, Clarke, Ellison, Farmer, Harrison, Moskowitz, and Van Vogt, none of whom are recognized.

So people do knot themselves around the lead character in a silly-ass space opera. This is natural, I tell myself. One picture worth ten thousand words.

Harris is a friendly likeable person, we find out later, and I wish him continuing good fortune. Moreover, I wonder what would happen if SF were as big as TV and we were the ones being surrounded? I find it inconceivable that the majority of the population would ever dig "good" SF. If they did, then you'd have a different kind of human being. In fact, mankind's history would have been slightly different. I don't say it would have been for the better. It would have been different.

What does this have to do with my impressions of the trip to Rio as a guest of the International Film Festival?

Everything. If I must write a travelogue, I'll write one of the mind.

Finally, we board the Argentinean Airlines plane. It takes a hell of a long time getting off the ground, as if it were overloaded. I have a fantasy that the plane never does manage to get into the air. It keeps on going. The lights of Rio have wheeled away. We're in darkness tunneled out by the plane's lights. We keep going and at last the pilot comes out of his numbness (which, it turns out, is not internally generated). The plane stops, after a while, we get out. The ground is wet and grassy. The time for sunrise comes. No sun. Sentients riding animals glowing with biological light appear, and we know we're in another world.

But the plane does take off. Harry passes me his quart of Scotch. The stewardess brings drinks. I think of what Ziva Sheckley said when we were on a trip to the Corcovado, on top of which is the Stoned Christ of Rio, and we had stopped at a restaurant hanging out over a cliff. Ziva is from New York City and everything Midwest is funny anyway. But she rings the changes on my middle name, speaking of Bob José Bloch and Bob José Sheckley and Brian José Aldiss and J. José Ballard, who were with us. There was more of that later on, but now I see that Ziva spoke true even in her joking. I've always had the feeling that SF people are a community with a peculiar simpatico, that, in one sense I am as merged with the others and they with me. Their middle names are José, even when they don't come up to my ideals and even when they have a deep antipathy towards me. Thus, John W. José Juggernaut and Jim José Kaltfisch and Robert José Zounds and Ted José Blanko, although they've disliked me from the first, still are, in an underground sense, me.

And, at this moment, after our seat belts are unstrapped, I feel more than ever that the writers aboard are more than brothers (since my own brothers would only read SF at the point of a gun and wouldn't understand it if their lives depended on it). The aisle explodes with voices, most of them happy. Maybe they're happy because they're going home, but I like to think it's also because we're together, having a little convention. Behind me, two mortal enemies (in print) Harry José Harrison and Sam José Minostentor are talking, bellowing rather. They seem so polite, yet what invectives and nasty put-downs they've been hurling at each other in fanzines!

Sam, standing in the aisle, is leaning far over the tray of the person in the aisle seat so he can talk to Harry. He feels he has to get close to Harry, though God knows why. That roar can be heard the length of the plane and possibly even in the pilots' compartment. (I see them frantically testing controls, lights flashing, buzzers zinging, CRTs jumping with sine and square waves and dots as the crew probe for the sudden and fearful noise the jets have developed.)

Beside Harry is a small brown-skinned, brown-eyed, dark-haired, bespectacled little girl, fifteen years old, from Austria. Her sandwich is on a plate on the snap-down table before her. She eyes the sandwich and the toothpick skewering it. Sam Minostentor's massive codpiece hangs an inch above it; no wonder she looks as if she's lost her appetite. I'm worried, Sam is like a big zeppelin lowering to land, the pouch containing his genitals is the gondola, and if he doesn't maneuver better, the anchor tower of the tooth-pick is going to drive up through the gondola.

I think about calling his wife, Jacqueline José the Ripper, to carry him off to safety under her arm, but she is Indian wrestling with Jonathan Harris and winning. Sam is bellowing something about the New Wave pricks at Harry. The conversation is taking a nasty turn, or do my ears deceive me? Sam lifts his zeppelin body and the gondola and floats back to his seat. The young Austrian looks at her untouched sandwich and when the stewardess comes by tells her to take it away.

We settle down. A Spanish movie is shown, despite the efforts of Sam and wife to get up a petition to cancel it. Harry passes the bottle to me a few more times. Good Scotch. In Rio, imported hard liquor is very expensive, which is why I usually drank the beer. The beer is better than most U.S. beers and comes in a 24-oz. bottle and costs about a quarter or 20,000 cruzeiros. I think of the article I promised to write. What were the highlights? Getting away from Rio into the heights above the city was one. Being in the poison-green jungle, close to the clouds, in the quiet, was delightful. But part of the delight came from being with people I liked. Bob Bloch, the Sheckleys, Ballard, Aldiss, Souto, Gasca, our girl guide, Monica Leib, Mrs. Bester.

The cable car ride to Sugar Loaf was even more exciting and memorable. From there you get a view of the bays and the jungle or the steep mountains in the middle of Rio. A haze hangs over the waters and the islands. You can understand how awed the first white men felt when they sailed their dirty, rickety vessels into these magnificent waters. It is hard to believe that the beautiful white-towered city below is a hell of streets filled with fender-raking, bumper touching, gas-belching, noise-farting, out-to-kill cars, mostly Volkswagens.

Up here it's serene and cool and beautiful, I hate to go back down. But I do.

Although I don't love the city, I don't hate it. It has a hustling driving air with an overlay of good humor or congeniality which American cities lack. The young generation, the under 25s, are taller than their elders. Apparently they've been well fed and are following the trend for tallness which prevails in the youth of the world. The girls are pretty and sometimes even beautiful, ranging from German type blondes to Sicilian brunettes. They dress quite mod, wear microskirts, and an air of sex hangs over the city, like an invisible cobweb.

At New York, we split. Van Vogt, Leigh Chapman, and myself go on to LA. Howlin José Hellzapoppinson says goodbye sadly. It has not been a pleasant or rewarding trip for him, for several reasons, and I'm sad because I love Howlin and wish him happiness. Success he has, but there's always a storm raging around him because there's always one raging inside him. He's like a rocket that would like to go into a parking orbit but can't turn off the fuel and so must keep going, on into extra-solar space.

I say goodbye to Harry José Harrison, whom I also love. Harry is speaking at the University of Chicago. Subject: science-fiction. You've come a long way baby. Guest lecturer at great universities and guest of the International Film Festival in Rio. We've all come a long long way, baby. I sigh. I'm happy for him and the others, but the pleasure of being in a ghetto is slowly fading away.

The customs held us up so long, we missed our plane. We stand by and get one with no trouble. The beautiful Leigh sits by herself and Van Vogt and I are side by side again and continue our conversation.

Again, I find myself revising my opinion of him. I am always doing this with Van. It seems that I came to wrong conclusions, although they're based on what he says or what he's written. He is one of SF's greats, whatever you think of his work, and he's also one of the great off-beats, the originals, a unique, and, to some, a weirdo. Personally, I've always found him very charming, amusing, educational, and rational. I remember what Daimon José Gnight, whom I met at Rio for the first time, said about Van Vogt.

Daimon once wrote a long article which should have destroyed Van utterly but seems to have affected his career or the esteem of the general public not one whit. Daimon gets a wry joy out of this, because, despite his big-bertha blasting, he likes Van's stories. There is, Daimon says, something vast and slimy and intriguing going on down below, way below, in the substructure of the universes of Van's stories. This analysis catches my attention and delight. Something slimy. Now I've always thought Van's stories were based on the philosophy that this universe is founded on nothing, absolutely nothing. Except Maya perhaps.

However, at one of the negative feedback lectures held during the festival in the mornings in an almost empty theater, Van made some statements which rotated me like Charlie Brown catching a ball. Van said he was one of the few men left who believe in a world-wide Communist plot to take over Earth. Also, he stated that we're all golden fruits on a cosmic tree. In addition, he upheld Lysenko's genetics.

At that point in the speech, I said to Howlin, "Van's out of his fucking mind."

So here I am, homeward bound, finding out that I am wrong again. Van says nothing of the Communist plot, though he speaks of the other matters in his lecture. No matter. The Communists have never been backward about admitting they are out for world conquest. But there is also a capitalist plot, although the master blueprint lies scattered in a hundred thousand fragmentary phrases in a thousand books. And the Communists are fighting among themselves, as any student of human nature knew would happen.

Van explains that his statements about the golden fruits of the tree of the cosmos and about Lysenko are only statements that his (Van's) behavior and thinking are based on an as-if philosophy. In other words, he follows Vaihinger; he acts "as if" Lysenkoism were true but he would not deny that it could be false. I don't say anything about Vaihinger to Van. I remember him vaguely from my college days, when I loved philosophers, before I found out that most of them were suffering from syphilis of the psyche.

Once again, I am charmed into believing that Van is right, though I wonder if he isn't playing the flute to my cobra.

The movie begins. *Bullitt.* I decide to watch It. I'm crazy about private eyes or rugged policemen who fight the mafia and their own corrupted or stupid colleagues. The movie is exciting, fast, and bloody, but illogical. More illogical than the typical comic book or cartoon, but I don't fully realize this until I see it again on the broad screen, a few weeks later.

Just after the tremendously exciting—and dumb—chase through San Francisco, lightning streaks through my head. It's as if a switch had been thrown. And this, in a way, is just what happened.

I've long held that the creators, composers, painters, inventors, poets, philosophers, psychoanalysts, writers, etc., are born with their vivid imaginations. That is, in the casting of the lots, which is what, essentially, genetics is, the creative brain cells come up. Rather, the combination of cells which result in the configuration of heightened imagination. The brain cells have a peculiar hookup which enables them to perceive connections between things thought unrelated.

This happy configuration of cells may die or be repressed and, in our society, often does and is. But if the configuration is nourished, it grows, and new nerve networks grow and grow. And every once in a while, one configuration grows into another, and inspiration, revelation, comes like current when a circuit is completed. The nerves creep out like tentacles and when they touch: Light.

This sudden light in my head was the result of going to Brazil. The experience in a far country, in a strange land, opened doors of perception.

What shall I call it, the result of this light? We seem to have a need to categorize, to label, to tag. I don't want to label, but if I don't, somebody else will.

Subjectivity? Interiority?

These terms are not accurate and have too many carryovers from long usage.

In-with-ness?

That's good enough for the time being.

I won't know what it realy means until after digging down, layer after layer, until I get to the core, break through into my personal Pellucidar. Down there may be nothing or something vast and slimy or a fire bed of crushed protons.

In-with-ness.

What it means is writing that has little reliance on latitude or longitude, on chronometers or barometers, photographs and tape recordings, histories and newspapers, or word of mouth. In short, it's a writing which won't be concerned with accuracy about the so-called objective world. It won't rely on indications from instruments or instrument-interpreters. In-with-ness will interpret the world as it sees and remembers it. In-with-ness is a system of logic, an internal logic, just as a language does not conform to the rules of classical or symbolic logic but has its own peculiar logic. Thus English has its system and Iroquois its own and Macri its own. Each works within its own enclosed rules and yet each can be translated with more or less exactness into the other.

There is some foreshadowing, a tentativeness, a nuclear cell in the yolk, in this report on the Rio trip. For instance, my statement that the Rio beer bottles are 24 oz. bottles. I don't know that this is objectively valid, instrument-true. It seemed to me that it was. Thus I report it.

I don't know if the Sugar Loaf was east, west, or south of Rio. It seemed to me that it was east, but the next time I think of it, it may be south. It will be south, according to my internal compass.

I don't know that I'm reporting Van's speech correctly. Or as he would report it. A copy of it lies in a nearby desk; I can refer to it. But I prefer to report the impression of the speech, its conversion into the system of my logic.

But in-with-ness is not subjectivism. Subjectivism is too occupied with personal imagery. The reader does not understand the references because he is not the writer. In-with-ness is concerned with the inner latitude and longitude but is also concerned with communication. Its goal is communication. It interprets. There may be something lost in the interpretation but better a loss than impenetrability.

In-with-ness will not experiment with style in that sense that Joyce and Burroughs did. The English will be straight enough (most of the time), but the difference is in the translation. Joyce and Burroughs and Ballard, for instance, are also translators, but the first two are experimenters in style, as if they were trying to create new languages. Ballard uses the conventional language in conventional syntax, but he seems to be trying to speak Iroquois with an English vocabulary.

Joyce is like bits of wreckage floating up from the bottom of the mind-dark sea. Burroughs is fluid and shifting and non-sequential, like bits of a horror film spliced at random. Ballard is a somnambulist carving images out of a quartz landscape.

In-with-ness won't show up immediately in my work. I will brood on it and with it and let it brood on me. For the present, I'll finish up the novels and short stories I've already started in the same style I began them. To rework them would spoil the stories and also the concept of in-with-ness. And I will use the old styles and approaches in series I've been publishing for some time: the Riverworld and Wolff-Kickaha series.

This is what going to Brazil means to me, this is the travelog of the mind.

NOTE: A friend to whom I showed this said, "You're one of the nuts on the cosmic tree Van talked about!"

So be it.

THE 1970S

"Like most things from the Seventies, this is Philip José Farmer's fault... If you don't like it, don't write me. Write to Philip José Farmer."   —Howard Waldrop in an introduction to the story
"The Adventure of the Grinder's Whistle"

After Phil committed to writing fiction full time again, the Farmers moved from Beverley Hills back to Peoria, Illinois. Phil and Bette became the darlings of the Midwest science fiction convention circuit, more often than not with Phil as a featured guest, or the Guest of Honor. They attended the Dum-Dum Banquet in Detroit in 1970 (where he was awarded the prestigious Golden Lion Award by the Burroughs Bibliophiles); Marcon in Columbus in 1971; Pecon 2 and 3 in Peoria, in 1971 and 72; the Mid-America Con in Kansas City in 1972; the 30th WorldCon in L.A. in 1972; CreationCon II in New York City in 1972; and the 31st WorldCon in Toronto in 1973.

Despite all that travel, the 1970s began with an explosion of creativity. In the first couple of years, he published the fourth World of Tiers novel, *Behind the Walls of Terra*, and the first two Riverworld novels, *To Your Scattered Bodies Go* (which won the Hugo for Best Novel) and *The Fabulous Riverboat*. He sold his fourth and final X-rated novel, *Love Song*, but Essex House had folded so it was brought out by their parent company, Brandon House. Ace

Books published three new novels. These were *The Stone God Awakens* and two concurrent sequels to *A Feast Unknown*: *Lord of the Tress* and *The Mad Goblin*, which were published as a (PG-rated) Ace Double. Continuing with the Tarzan theme, Doubleday published *Lord Tyger* in hardcover. The book was about a millionaire's attempts to create his own jungle lord. Ballantine brought out *Time's Last Gift*, which had its own Tarzan connection, and *Traitor to the Living*.

Having now written three novels with a Tarzan-like character, Phil was getting back to one of his first loves, and started to do a lot of research, creating a Tarzan coat of arms and publishing a number of articles about the ape-man: "The Arms of Tarzan," "Tarzan's Coat of Arms," "The Two Lord Ruftons," The Great Korak-Time Discrepancy," "The Lord Mountford Mystery," "From Erb to Ygg," and "A Language for Opar."

Phil also continued to sell stories to science fiction magazines, which where a science fiction writer's bread and butter in those days. "The Oögenesis of Bird City" (a prequel to "Riders of the Purple Wage") went to *Amazing Stories*; "Only Who Can Make a Tree?" and "Skinburn" went to *F&SF*; and "Seventy Years of Decpop" went to *Galaxy*.

And he sold even more stories to a wide variety of anthologies as the market continued to change: "The Voice of the Sonar in My Vermiform Appendix" and "Brass and Gold" to *Quark 2* and *4*, respectively; "The Sliced-Crosswise Only-on-Tuesday World" to *New Dimensions 1*; "The Sumerian Oath" and "Sketches Among the Ruins of My Mind" to *Nova 2* and *3*, respectively; "Father's in the Basement" to *Orbit 11*; "Toward the Beloved City" to *Signs and Wonders*; "Mother Earth Wants You" to *And Now Walk Gently Through the Fire*; "Monolog" to *Demon Kind*; "After King Kong Fell" to *Omega*; "Opening the Door" to *Children of Infinity*; and a series of four connected stories, "The Two-Edged Gift," "The Startouched," "The Evolution of Paul Eyre," and "Passing On" to *Continuum 1–4*.

Phil also began writing biographies during this period. First was "The Obscure Life and Hard Times of Kilgore Trout," followed by two book-length works: *Tarzan Alive* and *Doc Savage: His*

Apocalyptic Life. In all three cases he claimed that their subjects were based on actual living people.

As part of the publicity for *Tarzan Alive*, Phil published "Tarzan Lives," an interview with Lord Greystoke in *Esquire* magazine. A reporter from a national television news program contacted the publisher of *Tarzan Alive* to arrange an interview with Phil about meeting the real Lord Greystoke. Unfortunately the none-too-smart person at the publishing company who answered the phone said the whole thing was a hoax.

During his research for *Tarzan Alive,* Phil made an astounding discovery: the Wold Cottage meteorite, which fell near Wold Newton, Yorkshire, England, on December 13, 1795, had caused genetic mutations in the occupants of two passing coaches due to ionization. Many of their descendants were thus endowed with extremely high intelligence and strength, as well as an exceptional capacity and drive to perform good or evil deeds. Notable descendants of the coach passengers included: Tarzan; Doc Savage; Sherlock Holmes; Solomon Kane; Captain Blood; The Scarlet Pimpernel; Professor Moriarty; Phileas Fogg; Allan Quatermain; A. J. Raffles; Professor Challenger; Fu Manchu and his adversary, Sir Denis Nayland Smith; The Shadow; Sam Spade; Nero Wolfe; Philip Marlowe; James Bond; Travis McGee; and many others. This Wold Newton Family, discovered by Phil, connecting so many diverse characters from literature, has become a fan favorite and led to others expanding the "Wold Newton Universe" by several methods, including conducting research and writing scholarly articles, just as Phil did, and by discovering "crossovers" where various literary characters interact.

While Phil did continue to publish at a furious pace throughout the 1970s, he was in fact experiencing a writer's block. While his fans were clamoring for the next World of Tiers adventure, and his publishers were begging for the next Riverworld novel, he just couldn't produce them. Instead, his creativity was fired by reimagining the works of others: *The Wind Whales of Ishmael,* a science fiction sequel to *Moby Dick*; *The Other Log of Phileas Fogg,* the "truth" behind Jules Verne's *Around the World in Eighty Days*; *The Adventure of the Peerless Peer,* a short novel in which Sherlock

Unused back cover photo for *Venus on the Half-Shell.*

Holmes meets Lord Greystoke; *Hadon of Ancient Opar* and *Flight to Opar*, set in the distant past hinted at by Edgar Rice Burroughs and H. Rider Haggard; a translation and "retelling" of a French novel by J. H. Rosny, *Ironcastle*; and *Venus on the Half-Shell* "by Kilgore Trout."

For *Venus*, Phil received permission from Kurt Vonnegut, Jr., to take on the persona of his sad-sack science fiction author, and write a novel he believed Trout would have written. It was a ninety-day sensation as *Locus Magazine*, *Science Fiction Review*, and others weighed in on who they believed Trout to actually be. The publisher, Dell, was even going to sponsor a "Who is Kilgore

Trout?" contest. Phil appeared at UCLA as guest speaker around the same time the school's paper ran a review of *Venus* "proving" Vonnegut had written the book. They had to print a retraction the following week after the *New York Times* reported that Trout was a "well-known science fiction author from Peoria," and the cat was out of the bag.

However, Phil was so inspired by writing as a fictional author that he gave the main character of *Venus* his own favorite author, Jonathon Somers Swift, III. Phil did this deliberately so he could later write stories under that byline. He also contacted other authors, such as Rex Stout, P.G. Wodehouse, and Robert Bloch, and asked for permission to write stories "by" fictional authors they had created. In all, he wrote two stories by Somers, "The Scarletin Study" and "The Doge Whose Barque Was Worse Than His Bight," as well as "The Problem of the Sore Bridge—Among Others" by Harry "Bunny" Manders; "The Volcano," by Paul Chapin; and "It's the Queen of Darkness, Pal" by Rod Keen. All of these appeared in *F&SF* (which also printed a two-part abridged serial of *Venus on the Half-Shell*). He also wrote "Osiris on Crutches," with Leo Queequeg Tincrowdor; "The Impotency of Bad Karma" by Cordwainer Bird; and "Savage Shadow" by Maxwell Grant.

He also invited several other authors to the party. He contacted Arthur Jean Cox, Philip K. Dick, Leslie Fiedler, Ron Goulart, and Gene Wolfe, and asked them to write fictional author stories and publish them in *F&SF*; eventually Phil would reprint them in an anthology. Sadly this never happened. Howard Waldrop got wind of this however, and wrote a fictional author story himself. Hence, the Waldrop quote at the beginning of this section.

In addition to all the Tarzan-related articles and three biographies, he also published "Writing the Biography of Doc Savage"; "Jonathan Swift Somers III: Cosmic Traveller in a Wheelchair," a biography of the fictional author he created in *Venus on the Half-Shell*; and an article about Forrest J Ackerman for a convention program. He also edited *Mother Was a Lovely Beast*, an anthology of stories about humans being raised by animals, which included his "Extracts from the Memoirs of 'Lord Greystoke.'"

During this middle part of the decade, Phil and Bette attended even more conventions. In fact, in 1975 alone they attended Minicon 10 in Minneapolis; Solarcon I in El Paso; RiverCon in Louisville; Star Trek Chicago; and the NASFIC in Los Angeles. In 1976, they went to the Fantasy and Science Fiction Festival in Metz, France; the 34th WorldCon in Kansas City; and Classicon II in Lansing, Michigan. In 1977 they visited Balticon 11 in Baltimore; the Science Fiction, Horror and Fantasy World Exposition in Tucson; Summercon 77 in Toronto; Fabula 77 in Copenhagen; and, closer to home, the first meeting of The Hansoms of John Clayton, a Sherlock Holmes Scion Society that Phil helped found in Peoria.

Phil was at the height of his career during this period. DAW published a short story collection, *The Book of Philip José Farmer*, and not one, but two, different fanzines dedicated to him began in the late 1970s. *The Wold Atlas*, published by the The Wold Newton Meteorics Society, ran for five issues from January 1977 to the Fall of 1978. The first issue contained a letter from Phil, and there were some reviews of his books, but the fanzine mostly contained "Wold Newton" fan fiction. *Farmerage*, published by the Philip José Farmer Society, only ran for three issues, June 1978 to February 1979, but each issue was completely by or about Phil, containing reprints of early stories, articles about his work, book reviews, speeches, etc.

In the latter part of the decade, Phil got over his writer's block and returned to more original works. He wrote three Greatheart Silver stories for *Weird Heroes*; two stories for *Playboy*, "The Henry Miller Dawn Patrol," and "The Leaser of Two Evils"; "Fundamental Issue" for *Amazing*; "The Freshman," a rare horror story, for *F&SF*; and "J. C. on the Dude Ranch," which was published for the first time in the collection *Riverworld and Other Stories*. He also wrote an article, "Creating Artificial Worlds," in which he described the process of world-building used in the 1966 novel *The Gate of Time*, which he expanded and retitled *Two Hawks from Earth* in 1979.

He also finally wrote the third Riverworld novel, *The Dark Design*, with the fourth coming soon, as well as the fifth Tiers novel, *The Lavalite World*, and two standalone novels: *Dark is the Sun* and *Jesus on Mars*.

Only Who Can Make a Tree?

"You'll have to admit that Serendipitous Laboratories cleared away the smog," Dr. Kerls said.

Bobbing, he danced, the toe of his left shoe striking the floor and seeming to catch and pull him backward. He was a very short, middle-aged, and fat chemist. The top of his head looked like the back of a hog, and his voice was high and thin.

"Smog, shmog!" Dr. van Skant said. He snorted as if he had a noseful of nitrogen oxide. "What kind of pollution problem you think a few trillion moths produce, eh? Godalmighty, they're still bulldozing them off the freeways. And I had to stop twice to clean them out of my exhaust pipe! Twice! Godalmighty!"

Kerls grinned and bobbed his head and rubbed his hands together.

"Except for a failure, the experiment was a success, you'll have to admit that."

The Federal inspector-scientist did not reply. He looked around the huge laboratory. Tubes and retorts were bubbling, booping, and beeping. Colored liquids were racing up and down and around transparent plastic and glass pipes. A control panel was pulsing with lights and squeaking and pinging. Tapes were running this way and that. Generators were hurling wormy sparks back and forth, like robot baseball players warming up before a game.

Two white-coated men were pouring chemicals into tubes, and the tubes were throwing off frosty, evil-smelling, evil-looking clouds.

"Where in hell is the table?" van Skant snarled. He was a very tall and huge-paunched man with glasses and a thick blond moustache, and he spoke from behind, or through, a big green cigar at all times.

"What table?" Dr. Kerls said squeakily. He cringed.

"The table with the sheet under which is the monster waiting for the lightning stroke to bring it to life, you nitwit!"

Kerls laughed nervously. "Oh, you're joking! It is impressive, ain't it?"

"Should be," van Skant growled. "You jerks set it up just to impress me."

Kerls looked around helplessly.

Dr. Lorenzo smiled and waved at van Skant. He was very short and thin and had a bald forehead with a great Einsteinian foliage of hair behind the baldness to compensate.

Dr. Mough, very short, stern-faced, his hair cut in stylish bangs across his forehead, grimaced at Kerls.

"You jest, of course?" Kerls said. He danced backward while he cracked his knuckles to the tune of *The Pirates of Penzance* overture.

"Does this place hire nothing but psychotics?" van Skant said.

"Serendipitous Laboratories hires nothing but the best," Kerls said.

Van Skant stopped and stared. Dr. Lorenzo had poured the contents of a tall beaker into a rubber boot, and Dr. Mough, holding the top of the boot shut, was shaking it.

"I think they're testing out a new type of vulcanizer," Kerls said.

Mough set the boot upright on the floor, and he and Lorenzo stepped back.

The boot, stiff as a sailor at the end of a three-day leave, rumbled. Then it leaped like a kangaroo down the aisle between tables, hit the wall, bounced, and did not fall but erupted.

The brownish fluid sprayed over half of the huge room.

Drs. Kerls and van Skant were caught with their mouths open.

"Coffee!" van Skant howled. "You guys are making coffee! On government time!"

"Gee, is that it?" Kerls said, licking his lips. "Not bad. Better than what they usually make. But they were actually trying to make instant cement. Hyungh! Hyungh!"

Van Skant wiped the brown stuff from his face with a handkerchief.

"I'll shut this place down! Cut off the Federal funds! You're working on a government contract to combat pollution!"

Dr. Mough, the little man with the bangs, said, "Quite true, my dear Dr. van Skant. But we're on our coffee break, and we don't have to account for what we do then."

He turned to Dr. Kerls.

"Clean this mess up."

Kerls looked indignant. "Me? You and Lorenzo made the mess."

Mough made the peace sign with his two fingers, poked Kerls in the eyes with them, rapped him on the head with the butt of his palm, punched him in the belly and hammered his forehead again when Kerls doubled up.

"Don't talk back to the assistant project director!"

Kerls staggered off while van Skant, goggle-eyed, watched him.

"Not too much trouble with discipline here," Dr. Mough said. "We run a tight ship."

Van Skant followed Mough. Kerls seemed to be alleviating his pain with liquid from a flask he had taken from his hip pocket.

"Inspiration is found in many places," Mough said, noting van Skant's questioning expression. "Dr. Kerls often comes up with an idea after drinking from his fount of wisdom, as he calls it, hah, hah!"

"I wish to see Dr. Legzenbreins immediately," van Skant said.

"Yeah, there she is, just going into her office," Dr. Mough said. "Ain't she too much? I'm in love with her, and so are my two colleagues, the imbeciles! But she's too dedicated to get married as yet. She's a beautiful young scientist."

"And who's that?" van Skant said, pointing at a huge, pimply-faced girl in a laboratory coat who had just waddled out of the office.

"That's her mad daughter."

"Mad? You mean, angry?"

"Nuts," Mough said. "Oh, don't mean to you, Doctor! She's nuts, out of her skull, real woo-woo, you know. But a brilliant idea man! She's the one thought of the moths."

"That figures," van Skant said.

As he put the handkerchief back in his pocket, he felt something flutter. The insect that he removed and threw away was a large white moth with a scoop-shaped mouth. It flapped around and around the big room until it passed through the steam from an open tube in which bubbled a dark red liquid. The moth dropped as if it had had a heart attack and fell into the tube, where it disintegrated.

The red liquid turned a bright yellow.

Dr. Lorenzo yelped, apparently with delight, and he motioned for his colleagues and the fat girl to hasten to the tube. Kerls had just picked up a ten-foot-long glass pipe to fit onto a partially assembled setup. He turned when Lorenzo yelled, and the end of the pipe swung around and struck Mough in the back of his head. The cracking noise carried across the huge room.

Kerls dropped the pipe on Mough's head as he struggled to get up from the floor. Kerls ran, ducked behind a table, and reappeared by Lorenzo.

Mough staggered up off the floor, feeling the back of his head.

Van Skant strode up to the group, pushing his big belly as if it contained mail from the President, and he said, "What's so interesting?"

Mough's eyes had lost their glaze by then. He was looking suspiciously at Kerls, who was bending over the tube, rubbing his hands, and humming. Mough said, "Ah, Dr. van Skant, I presume? Yes, the moth undoubtedly contains the missing element, or elements, or combination thereof. We've been looking for a long time . . ."

"On government time?"

"On our lunch hour," Dr. Lorenzo said.

"It'll be easier just to use moths than to try to analyze a moth and determine the particular stuff responsible for the reaction," Dr. Kerls said. "Hyungh! Hyungh!"

"No trouble there," Dr. Lorenzo said. "We just send the janitor outside with a shovel and a bucket."

"What is that stuff?" Dr. van Skant bellowed, his face red.

"A universal solvent," Dr. Mough said, smiling proudly.

Van Skant struggled for breath and then pointed his finger at the tube. "A universal solvent? But that tube . . ."

"Oh, the reaction takes time," Kerls said, cracking his knuckles and then looking at his wristwatch, the large white-gloved hands of which were at 12:32. "In fact . . ."

The tube disappeared, and the yellow fluid splashed over the mica-topped table.

One corner of the table and a leg were gone.

A hole appeared in the floor, and a scream from the room below came up through it. And then, far below, there was a hiss of severed steam pipes. Presently, intermingled with the hiss, was a gurgle. A moment later, a splash.

"Possibly sheared plumbing," Dr. Mough said, smiling.

Van Skant's face had turned from red to gray.

"My God!" he yelled when he had finally gotten his breath again. "It'll go all the way to the center of the Earth!"

Dr. Mough passed his hand over his bangs and his face and then cried, "You jerks! You shoulda used less solvent like I told you!"

Kerls was on his right; Lorenzo, his left. His fists caught each in the mouth simultaneously, and they staggered back clutching their faces.

"How deep will that stuff really go?" van Skant screamed.

Mough blinked, rubbed the back of his head, and said, "What? Oh, that! The solvent evaporates within half an hour, so there's no problem there."

A low rumbling noise shook the building, and then the hole in the floor gushed black liquid.

Later on, after much litigation, it was established that the oil well was the property of the Federal government. A few days after the suit was settled, very little mattered. But that was some time in the future.

Van Skant, in his report, admitted that he didn't remember much of anything from the moment he heard the rumble. He thought that Dr. Kerls had picked up a big plastic pipe to insert into the hole in the floor as a plug. He thought, but could not swear to it, that the end of the pipe had struck him across the forehead when Dr. Kerls turned around with it on his shoulder. He made a very poor witness for the government, and so the suit against Serendipitous Laboratories and its head, the beautiful young scientist, Dr. Legzenbreins, was dropped.

By the time that Serendipitous had moved into a new building, the oil well had been capped and Southern California was cleansed of its moths. Dr. Mough, during a news interview, said, "How were my colleagues and I to know that one of the atmospheric toxics which the moths were mutated to eat would be a sex stimulant and that the mutants would breed entirely out of hand? Uh, please don't quote that last remark."

Dr. Mough revealed that Serendipitous was mutating bats which could, as it were, vacuum-clean the air. The company was also mutating goats to eat land pollutants and refuse, and sharks which would digest oceanic pollutants.

At that very moment, Dr. Legzenbreins was in her office with her daughter.

"I need a man," Desdemona whined.

"Who doesn't?" her mother said.

Desdemona blew out her bubble gum and looked cross-eyed at the iridescent bubble. Her mother became tense. Was Desdemona getting another fabulous idea?

The big bubble collapsed into the big mouth.

"You need a man?" Desdemona said. "You? The most beautiful woman in the world?"

"That's what scares them off," Dr. Legzenbreins said. "And the few that don't scare, the studs with low IQ's, I can't stand. So I'm in as bad a way as you are. Ironic, ain't it?"

"Drs. Kerls, Lorenzo. and Mough would marry you within a minute, and they're PhDs," the daughter said, drooling.

"They're five feet tall, and I'm six feet two," the mother said. "Besides, I'm not sure they're not punch-drunk."

"They're brilliant!"

"The two states are not necessarily incompatible."

"I don't want big words. I want a man. I'm twenty-five!"

"I have a man for you," the mother said. "A psychoanalyst." She added. "In a very high-class private sanitorium."

But she did not mean it. Her daughter provided the creative genius of Serendipitous. She herself, though a genius, was basically an analytic scientist, and her three assistants were basically synthesizers. Without madness, science would get no place, and Dr. Legzenbrains knew it.

She put on a very tight peekaboo dress and called in the three for a conference.

"I won't marry until my daughter marries and quits bugging me about her sex life or lack thereof. I'd suggest a lover. But she is, as you know, quite insane, and insists on remaining a virgin until she has a husband. Now, each of you goofballs has asked me many times to marry him."

Dr. Kerls stood up, danced backward, cracked his knuckles, and said, "I repeat my offer."

Dr. Mough kicked him in the knee and slapped him twice in the face before he hit the floor. As Dr. Kerls tried to get up, he was hit on the head with the coffee tray, which bent to form a semihelmet.

"Don't interrupt!" Dr. Mough said.

Dr. Legzenbreins told them what they must do.

There was a long silence when she had finished. It was finally broken by Desdemona's "Eureka!" from the laboratory. At any other time, all would have stampeded through the door to find out what new idea she had just stubbed her mental toe on.

Dr. Legzenbreins leaned back and stretched her arms and arched her back.

"The two survivors, uh, the two that don't marry her, will be permitted to put their names on my marriage lottery list."

Dr. Mough grabbed Dr. Lorenzo's bushy hair and yanked out a fistful. Lorenzo screamed and grabbed the top of his head and moaned.

"Don't ever let me catch you looking at her again like that." Mough said. "It ain't decent."

"Thank you, Dr. Mough," she said. "I can't stand naked lust. Especially in a scientist. It's so unprofessional."

"My pleasure," Dr, Mough said, beaming.

"What I don't like about this," Dr. Kerls said, shrinking from Mough, "is that the loser has to settle for Desdemona."

"Is any sacrifice too great for Science?" Dr. Mough said, shuddering.

"What's Science got to do with this?" Kerls said. "Unless everything reminds you of Science?"

Dr. Legzenbreins said, "I leave it up to you gentlemen to decide who's going to be put on the, uh, go to the altar with her."

She rose and stretched again, and the three moaned.

"Shall we see what Desdemona has thought of this time?"

"I was thinking," Desdemona said, "that this food tastes more like sawdust every day. So I was going to have to find another delicatessen. And then I thought, sawdust. Termites eat wood and get fat on it. Their guts contain protozoa, you know, them teeny little parasitical animals. Protozoa use enzymes to digest the cellulose in the wood and convert it into stuff fit to digest. OK, so thousands of tons of sawdust and chips of wood are just thrown away every year. Why couldn't these be saved and fed to people? If . . ."

"If we could mutate protozoa to live in the human gut, right?" Dr. Lorenzo said.

Dr. Mough banged him on the forehead with his fist.

"Imbecile! How do you get people to eat wood?"

"You make it palatable, indeed, delicious," Desdemona said.

"Just what I was about to say in reply to my rhetorical question," Dr. Mough said.

"I wish you'd just give me rhetorical blows," Dr. Lorenzo said. "Them real blows hurt, you know."

"If I quit hitting you, you'd say I didn't love you no more," Dr. Mough said. "Quit bellyaching; get to work."

Desdemona, being mad, could not be trusted to work with the dangerous chemicals and expensive apparatus.

But she was permitted to use cheap chemicals and equipment while searching for something to make sawdust tasty. Dr. Kerls supervised her every move. As Dr. Mough later said, this was a fortunate decision on his part, even though he was criticized for making Dr. Kerls her watchdog.

Dr. Kerls, carrying a long glass pipe to attach to Desdemona's setup, turned around when Dr. Mough called to him. The pipe knocked over a tube of hydrocyanic acid onto Desdemona's experiment for the day. The result was a minor explosion which caused Dr. Kerls to whirl around and bang Dr. Lorenzo across the eyes with the pipe and a salt which, sprinkled over sawdust, would bring tears of joy to a gourmet. Sawdust hamburgers became Desdemona's favorite food.

She forgot that she needed protozoa to convert cellulose into food and that the protozoa had not been successfully mutated yet so it could live in the human gut. She lost weight. But the sad thing was that she was as ugly as ever, if not more so. The fat had hidden a very unaesthetic bone structure.

"Takes after her father," Dr. Legzenbreins said.

One day, Dr. Kerls sneezed into a test tube of protozoa, and the next day the animalcules were turning sawdust into protein. Desdemona drank a cupful of the little beasts and soon began to gain weight on a diet that only a termite should have loved.

A week later, Dr. Lorenzo got mad at Dr. Mough and threw a beaker of protozoa at him. Mough ducked, and the beaker flew through the door of the men's room as Dr. Kerls stepped out. Dr. Mough said there was nothing to worry about, even if the protozoa were circulating in the city's sewage system. The protozoa couldn't get back into the drinking water, and what if they did?

The next day, Dr. van Skant called them all in and asked for a progress report on the antipollution projects.

"Eureka!" Desdemona cried, interrupting the conference.

"How about a virus which you can put into gasoline or any fuels burned in cars and factories? It's quiescent until blown out the exhaust with the gases. Then it combines with the gases to render them physically inert, or it attacks the pollutants and decomposes them rapidly. You kill the toxics at the source. The viruses multiply as they float through the air, and they continue to eat up the combustion products. And we can make aquatic viruses for the rivers, lakes, and oceans."

The three scientists shook hands with each other while the mother beamed at the daughter.

Van Skant said, "That's fine. But I want a report on what's been done, not on what you're going to do in some cloud-cuckoo-land future."

"Certainly; step this way," Dr. Mough said.

He led the Federal man to a large table on which was a complicated array of very busy apparatus.

"My colleagues and I have put in many hours toiling to build this thingamajig. It's designed to make a substance to coat lungs. This coating will filter out the air pollutants and admit only pure air. How's that grab you, Doctor?"

"I don't know," van Skant said slowly. "There's something wrong in your approach to the pollution problem. But I can't quite put my finger on it."

Mough and van Skant put on protective suits and went into the biological room. There Mough showed him the mutated bats, sharks, and winged goats.

"You'll notice the goats don't have any feet," Dr. Mough said. "That means that they have to fly to get from one place to another on land. And while they're flying, being big animals, they're really breathing hard to keep themselves aloft. So they take in vast quantities of polluted air, and their specialized stomachs and lungs burn up the bad stuff. That leaves a swath of clean air behind them. What the winged goats don't get, the bats will. Or maybe it's the other way around."

"Wouldn't flying elephants burn up even more bad air?" van Skant said, sneering.

"Please don't be absurd," Dr. Mough said.

"There's something I can't quite put my finger on," van Skant said, shaking his head.

Dr. Mough didn't tell him, but the thingamajig was also being used as a matrimonial roulette wheel. There were three special chemicals in the setup, each of which was presently colorless but would eventually change into a primary color. One would be red; one, purple; one, green. Mough's color was red; Lorenzo's, purple; Kerls', green. A random selector had dumped the chemicals into the setup, and so the three colleagues did not know which chemical would change color first. It was all up to chance.

The man whose color appeared first would win Desdemona's hand.

"And, God help him, the rest of her!" moaned Dr. Mough.

One day, the winged goats were gone, having eaten through the steel bars and the glass walls imprisoning them.

Several days later, the three scientists and Desdemona were having lunch in the laboratory when Dr. Legzenbreins walked out of her office. She was completely covered with a helmet and suit, being on her way to the virus section to run a late phase of an experiment. She waved at the group as she went by; the men stopped eating to groan and moan.

A moment later, Dr. van Skant, purple-faced, charged into the room.

"You're closed down!" he bellowed. "Your goddamn flying goats ate half my car in the parking lot! This is the last straw! I'm canceling all your government contracts!"

Drs. Kerls, Lorenzo, and Mough sprang to their feet and their heads met. The result was a loud thunk and cries of pain as they reeled back clutching their heads.

The alarm attached to the thingamajig whooped, and a bright orange light flashed.

"Oh, my God!" Kerls screamed. "It's happened!"

"What? What?" van Skant and Desdemona cried. Desdemona had been behaving rather woodenly lately, but she was aroused now.

Dr. Kerls, half-fainting, grabbed Mough.

A green thread was streaking through the mud-brown liquid in the pipes of the thingamajig.

Dr. Mough felt so sorry for his colleague, he did not hit him for having put his hands on him.

Dr. Legzenbreins raced out of the virus section, leaving the door open.

"What is it? What is"?

Dr. Mough said, "It's the biggest . . ."

Boom!

Clouds of brown vapor and sprays of green liquid filled the laboratory.

By the time the scientists and Desdemona got back onto their feet, they could see clearly. The clouds were gone, revealing a wrecked laboratory and ruptured walls behind which had been the virus section and the zoological room.

"The green doesn't count," Kerls mumbled. "I had my fingers crossed when we swore to abide by the decision of the thingamajig."

"You'll marry Desdemona or else," Dr. Mough said.

"Or else what?' Kerls squeaked.

"Or else this!" Mough said, and he broke a beaker of yellow liquid over Kerl's head and then rammed the flaming end of a Bunsen burner against Kerls' rear when Kerls turned away from him.

Desdemona spat out green liquid.

"Gee, I feel funny," she muttered. She walked out of the laboratory as if she were made of wood,

"Think she's all right?" van Skant said. "That virus got blown all over the place, and God knows what the chemicals in the thingamajig will do."

"Won't hurt nothing," Mough said. "I stake my reputation on that."

"We're lost!" van Skant said, and he staggered out of the room.

Desdemona wandered around, singing, until she found a vacant lot, one in which the good earth was uncovered. And there she stood motionless, arms extended to the sides, while roots, still half-fresh, sprouted and drove into the ground through her shoes.

The fourth day, she put out buds.

The sixth day, a pigeon spotted her and landed to build a nest.

By then, hundreds of thousands of Southern Californians were undergoing similar metamorphoses.

The polluters were changing into something which could not pollute and which converted carbon dioxide into the much-needed oxygen. Serendipitous had found the ideal solution.

Only one was left unmetamorphosed. She had been wearing a protective suit at the time of the explosion and had not taken it off until she was certain that the danger was over.

She was the only human being left in the world.

The doorbell rang.

She got up out of bed, walked through the house, and opened the front door.

Three man-sized trees stood on the porch.

"Kerls, Lorenzo, and Mough!" Dr. Legzenbreins cried.

Somehow, they had dragged up their roots and tracked her down. Love conquers all.

They tried to get through the door at the same time. Even if they had still been human beings, they would have gotten stuck. But with their extended arms—branches—they could never make it through alone.

Dr. Legzenbreins finally led them around to the backyard, where they took root with a shudder of relief. She went back to bed without closing the window, which was a mistake. She awoke with two branches caressing what she considered to be intimate places.

The other trees were hitting their branches against the one that had hold of her.

She reached up and plucked some of Mough's fruits—she thought it was Mough—and the tree quivered. Then the branches drooped and relaxed their hold.

The others continued to beat him with their branches.

But the next day all three were as rigid and motionless as trees should be, and their skin had become completely bark.

Spring came. Something popped deep within Dr. Legzen-breins.

She wished that she had not eaten Mough's fruit.

The Sliced-Crosswise Only-on-Tuesday World

Getting into Wednesday was almost impossible.

Tom Pym had thought about living on other days of the week. Almost everybody with any imagination did. There were even TV shows speculating on this. Tom Pym had even acted in two of these. But he had no genuine desire to move out of his own world. Then his house burned down.

This was on the last day of the eight days of spring. He awoke to look out the door at the ashes and the firemen. A man in a white asbestos suit motioned for him to stay inside. After fifteen minutes, another man in a suit gestured that it was safe. He pressed the button by the door, and it swung open. He sank down in the ashes to his ankles; they were a trifle warm under the inch-thick coat of water-soaked crust.

There was no need to ask what had happened, but he did, anyway.

The firemen said, "A short-circuit, I suppose. Actually, we don't know. It started shortly after midnight, between the time that Monday quit and we took over."

Tom Pym thought that it must be strange to be a fireman or a policeman. Their hours were so different, even though they were still limited by the walls of midnight.

By then the others were stepping out of their stoners or "coffins" as they were often called. That left sixty still occupied.

They were due for work at 08:00. The problem of getting new clothes and a place to live would have to be put off until off-hours, because the TV studio where they worked was behind in the big special it was due to put on in 144 days.

They ate breakfast at an emergency center. Tom Pym asked a grip if he knew of any place he could stay. Though the government would find one for him, it might not look very hard for a convenient place.

The grip told him about a house only six blocks from his former house. A makeup man had died, and as far as he knew the vacancy had not been filled. Tom got onto the phone at once, since he wasn't needed at that moment, but the office wouldn't be open until ten, as the recording informed him. The recording was a very pretty girl with red hair, tourmaline eyes, and a very sexy voice. Tom would have been more impressed if he had not known her. She had played in some small parts in two of his shows, and the maddening voice was not hers. Neither was the color of her eyes.

At noon he called again, got through after a ten-minute wait, and asked Mrs. Bellefield if she would put through a request for him. Mrs. Bellefield reprimanded him for not having phoned sooner; she was not sure that anything could be done today. He tried to tell her his circumstances and then gave up. Bureaucrats! That evening he went to a public emergency place, slept for the required four hours while the inductive field speeded up his dreaming, woke up, and got into the upright cylinder of eternium. He stood for ten seconds, gazing out through the transparent door at other cylinders with their still figures, and then he pressed the button. Approximately fifteen seconds later he became unconscious.

He had to spend three more nights in the public stoner. Three days of fall were gone; only five left. Not that that mattered in California so much. When he had lived in Chicago, winter was like a white blanket being shaken by a madwoman. Spring was a green explosion. Summer was a bright roar and a hot breath. Fall was the topple of a drunken jester in garish motley.

The fourth day, he received notice that he could move into the very house he had picked. This surprised and pleased him. He knew of a dozen who had spent a whole year—forty-eight days or so—in a public station while waiting. He moved in the fifth day with three days of spring to enjoy. But he would have to use up his two days off to shop for clothes, bring in groceries and other goods, and get acquainted with his housemates. Sometimes, he wished he had not been born with the compulsion to act. TV'ers worked five days at a stretch, sometimes six, while a plumber, for instance, only put in three days out of seven.

The house was as large as the other, and the six extra blocks to walk would be good for him. It held eight people per day, counting himself. He moved in that evening, introduced himself, and got Mabel Curta, who worked as a secretary for a producer, to fill him in on the household routine. After he made sure that his stoner had been moved into the stoner room, he could relax somewhat.

Mabel Curta had accompanied him into the stoner room, since she had appointed herself his guide. She was a short, overly curved woman of about thirty-five (Tuesday time). She had been divorced three times, and marriage was no more for her unless, of course, Mr. Right came along. Tom was between marriages himself, but he did not tell her so.

"We'll take a look at your bedroom," Mabel said. "It's small but it's soundproofed, thank God."

He started after her, then stopped. She looked back through the doorway and said, "What is it?"

"This girl . . ."

There were sixty-three of the tall gray eternium cylinders. He was looking through the door of the nearest at the girl within.

"Wow! Really beautiful!"

If Mabel felt any jealousy, she suppressed it.

"Yes, isn't she!"

The girl had long, black, slightly curly hair, a face that could have launched him a thousand times times a thousand times, a figure that had enough but not too much, and long legs. Her eyes were open; in the dim light they looked a purplish-blue. She wore a thin silvery dress.

The plate by the top of the door gave her vital data. Jennie Marlowe. Born 2031 A.D., San Marino, California. She would be twenty-four years old. Actress. Unmarried. Wednesday's child.

"What's the matter?" Mabel said.

"Nothing."

How could he tell her that he felt sick in his stomach from a desire that could never be satisfied? Sick from beauty?

For will in us is over-ruled by fate.
Who ever loved, that loved not at first sight?

"What?" Mabel said, and then, after laughing, "You must be kidding?"

She wasn't angry. She realized that Jennie Marlowe was no more competition than if she were dead. She was right. Better for him to busy himself with the living of this world. Mabel wasn't too bad, cuddly, really, and, after a few drinks, rather stimulating.

They went downstairs after 18:00 to the TV room. Most of the others were there, too. Some had their ear plugs in; some were looking at the screen but talking. The newscast was on, of course. Everybody was filling up on what had happened last Tuesday and today. The Speaker of the House was retiring after his term was up. His days of usefulness were over and his recent ill health showed no signs of disappearing. There was a shot of the family graveyard in Mississippi with the pedestal reserved for him. When science someday learned how to rejuvenate, he would come out of stonerment.

"That'll be the day!" Mabel said. She squirmed on his lap.

"Oh, I think they'll crack it," he said. "They're already on the track; they've succeeded in stopping the aging of rabbits."

"I don't mean that," she said. "Sure, they'll find out how to rejuvenate people. But then what? You think they're going to bring them all back? With all the people they got now and then they'll double, maybe triple, maybe quadruple, the population? You think they won't just leave them standing there?" She giggled, and said, "What would the pigeons do without them?"

He squeezed her waist. At the same time, he had a vision of himself squeezing *that* girl's waist. Hers would be soft enough but with no hint of fat.

Forget about her. Think of now. Watch the news.

A Mrs. Wilder had stabbed her husband and then herself with a kitchen knife. Both had been stonered immediately after the police arrived, and they had been taken to the hospital. An investigation of a work slowdown in the county government offices was taking place. The complaints were that Monday's people were not setting up the computers for Tuesday's. The case was being referred to the proper authorities of both days. The Ganymede base reported that the Great Red Spot of Jupiter was emitting weak but definite pulses that did not seem to be random.

The last five minutes of the program was a precis devoted to outstanding events of the other days. Mrs. Cuthmar, the house-mother, turned the channel to a situation comedy with no protests from anybody.

Tom left the room, after telling Mabel that he was going to bed early—alone, and to sleep. He had a hard day tomorrow.

He tiptoed down the hall and the stairs and into the stoner room. The lights were soft, there were many shadows, and it was quiet. The sixty-three cylinders were like ancient granite columns of an underground chamber of a buried city. Fifty-five faces were white blurs behind the clear metal. Some had their eyes open; most had closed them while waiting for the field radiated from the machine in the base. He looked through Jennie Marlowe's door. He felt sick again. Out of his reach; never for him. Wednesday was only a day away. No, it was only a little less than four and a half hours away.

He touched the door. It was slick and only a little cold. She stared at him. Her right forearm was bent to hold the strap of a large purse. When the door opened, she would step out, ready to go. Some people took their showers and fixed their faces as soon as they got up from their sleep and then went directly into the stoner. When the field was automatically radiated at 05:00, they stepped out a minute later, ready for the day.

He would like to step out of his "coffin," too, at the same time.

But he was barred by Wednesday.

He turned away. He was acting like a sixteen-year-old kid. He had been sixteen about one hundred and six years ago, not that that made any difference. Physiologically, he was thirty.

As he started up to the second floor, he almost turned around and went back for another look. But he took himself by his neck-collar and pulled himself up to his room. There he decided he would get to sleep at once. Perhaps he would dream about her. If dreams were wish-fulfillments, they would bring her to him. It still had not been "proved" that dreams always expressed wishes, but it had been proved that man deprived of dreaming did go mad. And so the somniums radiated a field that put man into a state in which he got all the sleep, and all the dreams, that he needed within a four-hour period. Then he was awakened and a little later went into the stoner where the field suspended all atomic and subatomic activity. He would remain in that state forever unless the activating field came on.

He slept, and Jennie Marlowe did not come to him. Or, if she did, he did not remember. He awoke, washed his face, went down eagerly to the stoner, where he found the entire household standing around, getting in one last smoke, talking, laughing. Then they would step into their cylinders, and a silence like that at the heart of a mountain would fall.

He had often wondered what would happen if he did not go into the stoner. How would he feel? Would he be panicked? All his life, he had known only Tuesdays. Would Wednesday rush at him, roaring, like a tidal wave? Pick him up and hurl him against the reefs of a strange time?

What if he made some excuse and went back upstairs and did not go back down until the field had come on? By then, he could not enter. The door to his cylinder would not open again until the proper time. He could still run down to the public emergency stoners only three blocks away. But if he stayed in his room, waiting for Wednesday?

Such things happened. If the breaker of the law did not have a reasonable excuse, he was put on trial. It was a felony second only to murder to "break time," and the unexcused were stoned. All felons, sane or insane, were stoned. Or *mañanaed*, as some said. The *mañanaed* criminal waited in immobility and unconsciousness, preserved unharmed until science had techniques to cure the insane, the neurotic, the criminal, the sick. *Mañana*.

"What was it like in Wednesday?" Tom had asked a man who had been unavoidably left behind because of an accident.

"How would I know? I was knocked out except for about fifteen minutes. I was in the same city, and I had never seen the faces of the ambulance men, of course, but then I've never seen them here. They stoned me and left me in the hospital for Tuesday to take care of."

He must have it bad, he thought. Bad. Even to think of such a thing was crazy. Getting into Wednesday was almost impossible. Almost. But it could be done. It would take time and patience, but it could be done.

He stood in front of his stoner for a moment. The others said, "See you! So long! Next Tuesday!" Mabel called, "Good night, lover!"

"Good night," he muttered.

"What?" she shouted.

"Good night!"

He glanced at the beautiful face behind the door. Then he smiled. He had been afraid that she might hear him say good night to a woman who called him lover.

He had ten minutes yet. The intercom alarms were whooping. Get going, everybody! Time to take the six-day trip! Run! Remember the penalties!

He remembered, but he wanted to leave a message. The recorder was on a table. He activated it, and said, "Dear Miss Jennie Marlowe. My name is Tom Pym, and my stoner is next to yours. I am an actor, too; in fact, I work at the same studio as you. I know this is presumptuous of me, but I have never seen anybody so beautiful. Do you have a talent to match your beauty? I would like to see some run-offs of your shows. Would you please leave some in room five? I'm sure the occupant won't mind. Yours, Tom Pym."

He ran it back. It was certainly bold enough, and that might be just what was needed. Too flowery or too pressing would have made her leery. He had commented on her beauty twice but not overstressed it. And the appeal to her pride in her acting would be difficult to resist. Nobody knew better than he about that.

He whistled a little on his way to the cylinder. Inside, he pressed the button and looked at his watch. Five minutes to midnight. The light on the huge screen above the computer in the police station would not be flashing for him. Ten minutes from now, Wednesday's police would step out of their stoners in the precinct station, and they would take over their duties.

There was a ten-minute hiatus between the two days in the police station. All hell could break loose in these few minutes and it sometimes did. But a price had to be paid to maintain the walls of time.

He opened his eyes. His knees sagged a little and his head bent. The activation was a million microseconds fast—from eternium to flesh and blood almost instantaneously and the heart never knew that it had been stopped for such a long time. Even so, there was a little delay in the muscles' response to a standing position.

He pressed the button, opened the door, and it was as if his button had launched the day. Mabel had made herself up last night so that she looked dawn-fresh. He complimented her and she smiled happily. But he told her he would meet her for breakfast. Halfway up the staircase, he stopped, and waited until the hall was empty. Then he sneaked back down and into the stoner room. He turned on the recorder.

A voice, husky but also melodious, said, "Dear Mister Pym. I've had a few messages from other days. It was fun to talk back and forth across the abyss between the worlds, if you don't mind my exaggerating a little. But there is really no sense in it, once the novelty has worn off. If you become interested in the other person, you're frustrating yourself. That person can only be a voice in a recorder and a cold waxy face in a metal coffin. I wax poetic. Pardon me. If the person doesn't interest you, why continue to communicate?

There is no sense in either case. And I *may* be beautiful. Anyway, I thank you for the compliment, but I am also sensible.

"I should have just not bothered to reply. But I want to be nice; I didn't want to hurt your feelings. So please don't leave any more messages."

He waited while silence was played. Maybe she was pausing for effect. Now would come a chuckle or a low honey-throated laugh, and she would say, "However, I don't like to disappoint my public. The run-offs are in your room."

The silence stretched out. He turned off the machine and went to the dining room for breakfast.

Siesta time at work was from 14:40 to 14:45. He lay down on the bunk and pressed the button. Within a minute he was asleep. He did dream of Jennie this time; she was a white shimmering figure solidifying out of the darkness and floating toward him. She was even more beautiful than she had been in her stoner.

The shooting ran overtime that afternoon so that he got home just in time for supper. Even the studio would not dare keep a man past his supper hour, especially since the studio was authorized to serve food only at noon.

He had time to look at Jennie for a minute before Mrs. Cuthmar's voice screeched over the intercom. As he walked down the hall, he thought, "I'm getting barnacled on her. It's ridiculous. I'm a grown man. Maybe . . . maybe I should see a psycher."

Sure, make your petition, and wait until a psycher has time for you. Say about three hundred days from now, if you are lucky. And if the psycher doesn't work out for you, then petition for another, and wait six hundred days.

Petition. He slowed down. Petition. What about a request, not to see a psycher, but to move? Why not? What did he have to lose? It would probably be turned down, but he could at least try.

Even obtaining a form for the request was not easy. He spent two nonwork days standing in line at the Center City Bureau before he got the proper forms. The first time, he was handed the wrong form and had to start all over again. There was no line set aside for those who wanted to change their days. There were not enough who wished to do this to justify such a line. So he had to queue up before the Miscellaneous Office counter of the Mobility Section of the Vital Exchange Department of the Interchange and Cross Transfer Bureau. None of these titles had anything to do with emigration to another day.

When he got his form the second time, he refused to move from the office window until he had checked the number of the form and asked the clerk to double-check. He ignored the cries and the mutterings behind him. Then he went to one side of the vast room and stood in line before the punch machines. After two hours, he got to sit down at a small rolltop desk-shaped machine, above which was a large screen. He inserted the form into the slot, looked at the projection of the form, and punched buttons to mark the proper spaces opposite the proper questions. After that, all he had to do was to drop the form into a slot and hope it did not get lost. Or hope he would not have to go through the same procedure because he had improperly punched the form.

That evening, he put his head against the hard metal and murmured to the rigid face behind the door, "I must really love you to go through all this. And you don't even know it. And, worse, if you did, you might not care one bit."

To prove to himself that he had kept his gray stuff, he went out with Mabel that evening to a party given by Sol Voremwolf, a producer. Voremwolf had just passed a civil service examination giving him an A-13 rating. This meant that, in time, with some luck and the proper pull, he would become an executive vice-president of the studio.

The party was a qualified success. Tom and Mabel returned about half an hour before stoner time. Tom had managed to refrain from too many blowminds and liquor, so he was not tempted by Mabel. Even so, he knew that when he became unstonered, he would be half-loaded and he'd have to take some dreadful counter-actives. He would look and feel like hell at work, since he had missed his sleep.

He put Mabel off with an excuse, and went down to the stoner room ahead of the others. Not that that would do him any good if he wanted to get stonered early. The stoners only activated within narrow time limits.

He leaned against the cylinder and patted the door. "I tried not to think about you all evening. I wanted to be fair to Mabel, it's not fair to go out with her and think about you all the time."

All's fair in love . . .

He left another message for her, then wiped it out. What was the use? Besides, he knew that his speech was a little thick. He wanted to appear at his best for her.

Why should he? What did she care for him?

The answer was, he did care, and there was no reason or logic connected with it. He loved this forbidden, untouchable, far-away-in-time, yet-so-near woman.

Mabel had come in silently. She said, "You're sick!"

Tom jumped away. Now why had he done that? He had nothing to be ashamed of. Then why was he so angry with her? His embarrassment was understandable but his anger was not.

Mabel laughed at him, and he was glad. Now he could snarl at her. He did so, and she turned away and walked out. But she was back in a few minutes with the others. It would soon be midnight.

By then he was standing inside the cylinder. A few seconds later, he left it, pushed Jennie's backward on its wheels, and pushed his around so that it faced hers. He went back in, pressed the button, and stood there. The double doors only slightly distorted his view. But she seemed even more removed in distance, in time, and in unattainability.

Three days later, well into winter, he received a letter. The box inside the entrance hall buzzed just as he entered the front door. He went back and waited until the letter was printed and had dropped out from the slot. It was the reply to his request to move to Wednesday.

Denied. Reason: he had no reasonable reason to move.

That was true. But he could not give his real motive. It would have been even less impressive than the one he had given. He had punched the box opposite No. 12. REASON: TO GET INTO AN ENVIRONMENT WHERE MY TALENTS WILL BE MORE LIKELY TO BE ENCOURAGED.

He cursed and he raged. It was his human, his civil right to move into any day he pleased. That is, it should be his right. What if a move did cause much effort? What if it required a transfer of his I.D. and all the records connected with him from the moment of his birth? What if . . . ?

He could rage all he wanted to, but it would not change a thing. He was stuck in the world of Tuesday.

Not yet, he muttered. Not yet. Fortunately, there is no limit to the number of requests I can make in my own day. I'll send out another. They think they can wear me out, huh? Well, I'll wear them out. Man against the machine. Man against the system. Man against the bureaucracy and the hard cold rules.

Winter's twenty days had sped by. Spring's eight days rocketed by. It was summer again. On the second day of the twelve days of summer, he received a reply to his second request.

It was neither a denial nor an acceptance. It stated that if he thought he would be better off psychologically in Wednesday because his astrologer said so, then he would have to get a psycher's critique of the astrologer's analysis. Tom Pym jumped into the air and clicked his sandaled heels together. Thank God that he lived in an age that did not classify astrologers as charlatans! The people— the masses—had protested that astrology was a necessity and that it should be legalized and honored. So laws were passed, and because of that, Tom Pym had a chance.

He went down to the stoner room and kissed the door of the cylinder and told Jennie Marlowe the good news. She did not respond, though he thought he saw her eyes brighten just a little. That was, of course, only his imagination, but he liked his imagination.

Getting a psycher for a consultation and getting through the three sessions took another year, another forty-eight days. Doctor Sigmund Traurig was a friend of Doctor Stelhela, the astrologer, and so that made things easier for Tom.

"I've studied Doctor Stelhela's chart carefully and analyzed carefully your obsession for this woman," he said. "I agree with Doctor Stelhela that you will always be unhappy in Tuesday, but I don't quite agree with him that you will be happier in Wednesday.

However, you have this thing going for this Miss Marlowe, so I think you should go to Wednesday. But only if you sign papers agreeing to see a psycher there for extended therapy."

Only later did Tom Pym realize that Doctor Traurig might have wanted to get rid of him because he had too many patients. But that was an uncharitable thought. He had to wait while the proper papers were transmitted to Wednesday's authorities. His battle was only half-won. The other officials could turn him down. And if he did get to his goal, then what? She could reject him without giving him a second chance.

It was unthinkable, but she could.

He caressed the door and then pressed his lips against it.

"Pygmalion could at least touch Galatea," he said. "Surely, the gods—the big dumb bureaucrats—will take pity on me, who can't even touch you. Surely."

The psycher had said that he was incapable of a true and lasting bond with a woman, as so many men were in this world of easy-come-easy-go liaisons. He had fallen in love with Jennie Marlowe for several reasons. She may have resembled somebody he had loved when he was very young. His mother, perhaps? No? Well, never mind. He would find out in Wednesday—perhaps. The deep, the important, truth was that he loved Miss Marlowe because she could never reject him, kick him out, or become tiresome, complain, weep, yell, insult, and so forth. He loved her because she was unattainable and silent.

"I love her as Achilles must have loved Helen when he saw her on top of the walls of Troy," Tom said.

"I wasn't aware that Achilles was ever in love with Helen of Troy," Doctor Traurig said drily.

"Homer never said so, but I *know* that he must have been! Who could see her and *not* love her?"

"How the hell would I know? I never saw her! If I had suspected these delusions would intensify . . ."

"I am a poet!" Tom said.

"Over imaginative, you mean! Hmmm. She must be a douser! I don't have anything particular to do this evening. I'll tell you what . . . my curiosity is aroused . . . I'll come down to your place tonight and take a look at this fabulous beauty, your Helen of Troy."

Doctor Traurig appeared immediately after supper, and Tom Pym ushered him down the hall and into the stoner room at the rear of the big house as if he were a guide conducting a famous critic to a just-discovered Rembrandt.

The doctor stood for a long time in front of the cylinder. He hmmmed several times and checked her vital-data plate several times. Then he turned and said, "I see what you mean, Mr. Pym. Very well. I'll give the go-ahead."

"Ain't she something?" Tom said on the porch. "She's out of this world, literally and figuratively, of course."

"Very beautiful. But I believe that you are facing a great disappointment, perhaps heartbreak, perhaps, who knows, even madness, much as I hate to use that unscientific term."

"I'll take the chance," Tom said. "I know I sound nuts, but where would we be if it weren't for nuts? Look at the man who invented the wheel, at Columbus, at James Watt, at the Wright brothers, at Pasteur, you name them."

"You can scarcely compare these pioneers of science with their passion for truth with you and your desire to marry a woman. But, as I have observed, she is strikingly beautiful. Still, that makes me exceedingly cautious. Why isn't she married? What's wrong with her?"

"For all I know, she may have been married a dozen times!" Tom said. "The point is, she isn't now! Maybe she's disappointed and she's sworn to wait until the right man comes along. Maybe. . ."

"There's no maybe about it, you're neurotic," Traurig said. "But I actually believe that it would be more dangerous for you not to go to Wednesday than it would be to go."

"Then you'll say yes!" Tom said, grabbing the doctor's hand and shaking it.

"Perhaps. I have some doubts."

The doctor had a faraway look. Tom laughed and released the hand and slapped the doctor on the shoulder. "Admit it! You were really struck by her! You'd have to be dead not to!"

"She's all right," the doctor said. "But you must think this over. If you do go there and she turns you down, you might go off the deep end, much as I hate to use such a poetical term."

"No, I won't. I wouldn't be a bit the worse off. Better off, in fact. I'll at least get to see her in the flesh."

Spring and summer zipped by. Then, a morning he would never forget, the letter of acceptance. With it, instructions on how to get to Wednesday. These were simple enough. He was to make sure that the technicians came to his stoner sometime during the day and readjusted the timer within the base. He could not figure out why he could not just stay out of the stoner and let Wednesday catch up to him, but by now he was past trying to fathom the bureaucratic mind.

He did not intend to tell anyone at the house, mainly because of Mabel. But Mabel found out from someone at the studio. She wept when she saw him at supper time, and she ran upstairs to her room. He felt badly, but he did not follow to console her.

That evening, his heart beating hard, he opened the door to his stoner. The others had found out by then; he had been unable to keep the business to himself. Actually, he was glad that he had told them. They seemed happy for him, and they brought in drinks and had many rounds of toasts. Finally, Mabel came downstairs, wiping her eyes, and she said she wished him luck, too. She had known that he was not really in love with her. But she did wish someone would fall in love with her just by looking inside her stoner.

When she found out that he had gone to see Doctor Traurig, she said, "He's a very influential man. Sol Voremwolf had him for his analyst. He says he's even got influence on other days. He edits the *Psyche Crosscurrents*, you know, one of the few periodicals read by other people."

Other, of course, meant those who lived in Wednesdays through Mondays.

Tom said he was glad he had gotten Traurig. Perhaps he had used his influence to get the Wednesday authorities to push through his request so swiftly. The walls between the worlds were seldom broken, but it was suspected that the very influential did it when they pleased.

Now, quivering, he stood before Jennie's cylinder again. The last time, he thought, that I'll see her stonered. Next time, she'll be warm, colorful, touchable flesh.

"*Ave atque vale!*" he said aloud. The others cheered. Mabel said, "How corny!" They thought he was addressing them, and perhaps he had included them.

He stepped inside the cylinder, closed the door, and pressed the button. He would keep his eyes open, so that . . .

And today was Wednesday. Though the view was exactly the same, it was like being on Mars.

He pushed open the door and stepped out. The seven people had faces he knew and names he had read on their plates. But he did not know them.

He started to say hello, and then he stopped.

Jennie Marlowe's cylinder was gone.

He seized the nearest man by the arm.

"Where's Jennie Marlowe?"

"Let go. You're hurting me. She's gone. To Tuesday."

"*Tuesday! Tuesday?*"

"Sure. She'd been trying to get out of here for a long time. She had something about this day being unlucky for her. She was unhappy, that's for sure. Just two days ago, she said her application had finally been accepted. Apparently, some Tuesday psycher had used his influence. He came down and saw her in her stoner and that was it, brother."

The walls and the people and the stoners seemed to be distorted. Time was bending itself this way and that. He wasn't in Wednesday; he wasn't in Tuesday. He wasn't in any day. He was stuck inside himself at some crazy date that should never have existed.

"She can't do that!"

"Oh, no! She just did that!"

"But . . . you can't transfer more than once!"

"That's her problem."

It was his, too.

"I should never have brought him down to look at her!" Tom said. "The swine! The unethical swine!"

Tom Pym stood there for a long time, and then he went into the kitchen. It was the same environment, if you discounted the people. Later, he went to the studio and got a part in a situation play which was, really, just like all those in Tuesday. He watched the newscaster that night. The President of the U.S.A. had a different name and face, but the words of his speech could have been those of Tuesday's President. He was introduced to a secretary of a producer; her name wasn't Mabel, but it might as well have been.

The difference here was that Jennie was gone, and oh, what a world of difference it made to him.

An Exclusive Interview with Lord Greystoke

A subgenre of biographical literature is that which claims that certain people thought to be fictional are, or were, very much living. Splendid examples of this are Blakeney's *Sir Percy Blakeney: Fact or Fiction?* (a biography of the Scarlet Pimpernel), Baring-Gould's *Sherlock Holmes of Baker Street* and *Nero Wolfe of West Thirty-Fifth Street*, Parkinson's *The Life and Times of Horatio Hornblower*, and the Flashman Papers (three volumes so far) by Fraser. In fact, some public libraries stock these in the "B" or biography section. (The Blakeney book is in the "B" section of the Peoria, Illinois, public library.)

I've written two such "lives": *Tarzan Alive* and *Doc Savage: His Apocalyptic Life* (tentative title). (The former is in the biography section of the Yuma City, California, library.) I plan to write biographies of The Shadow, Allan Quatermain, Fu Manchu, d'Artagnan, Travis McGee, and a number of others. Fu Manchu, by the way, may have been based on a real-life model, a Vietnamese named Hanoi Shan whose operations in early twentieth-century France were every bit as sinister and fantastic as Rohmer's creation. I was informed of this after I'd made the statement in *Tarzan Alive* that Fu Manchu had no living counterpart.

This form of apologia is a lot of fun and much hard work. It requires as much imagination as the writing of science fiction but more discipline. Historical facts must not be ignored. Baring-Gould, in writing his Holmes biography, had an enormous amount of scholarship, articles published in The Baker Street Journal and other periodicals, to draw upon. But he had not only to read all these but to study them and make decisions. He found many conflicting theories, and he had to pick the one that seemed most valid. In addition, where theories or speculations were lacking, he had to generate his own. He had to explain discrepancies, which are numerous in Watson's account of Holmes's life. And, I might add, Burroughs, in his semifictional narratives of Greystoke's career, left many discrepancies for the scholar to reconcile, if he could. There are also gaps in the life of the hero which the biographer must fill in. And if the original writer has neglected the hero's genealogy, the biographer must research this.

Sometimes, a biographer makes a statement which be cannot substantiate. Thus, Baring-Gould said that Holmes was a cousin of Professor Challenger. He has been much criticized by the Sherlockian scholars for this because he presented no evidence from the Canon. Fortunately, in my *Tarzan Alive*, I was able to validate the relationship. The fact that Tarzan's mother was a Rutherford gave me the clue needed to track down the cousinhood.

The following article is part of my interview with "Lord Greystoke" and appeared in the April, 1972, issue of *Esquire* under the title of "Tarzan Lives." It was accompanied by the first authentic portrait of Greystoke, a photograph of a painting by Jean-Paul Goude. The staff of Esquire went to great lengths and much trouble to acquire this, for which they should be thanked. The report that Goude got the commission to do the painting because he is a relative of Admiral Paul d'Arnot of the French navy, Greystoke's closest friend, is being checked. It is said that Goude, like Holmes, is a descendant of Antoine Vernet, father of four famous French painters.

Editor's Note: For a number of years Mr. Farmer, who recorded the following interview, has been engaged in writing a definitive biography of the man Edgar Rice Burroughs called Tarzan of the Apes. Mr. Farmer's book, Tarzan Alive, *to be published by Doubleday in April of this year, is similar in method to Baring-Gould's* Sherlock Holmes of Baker Street *and Parkinson's* The Life and Times of Horatio Hornblower, *with the very important difference that Mr. Farmer firmly avers that "Lord Greystoke" or "Tarzan" is really alive. In fact, Mr. Farmer was able to track his subject to earth in a hotel in Libreville, Gabon, on the coast of Western Africa just above the equator, where he was granted this interview. "I met him," Mr. Farmer tells us, "in his hotel room— fittingly enough, on September 1, Edgar Rice Burroughs' birthday. He is six feet three and, I suppose, about two hundred forty pounds. I did not have the opportunity to see him in action, of course, but just from the way he moved about the room I could guess at his immense physical strength. As Burroughs said, he is much more like Apollo than Hercules; his power lies in the quality not the quantity of his muscles. I don't hesitate to admit that I was awed. I was concerned, of course, that after all my research I might still have been the victim of a hoax; but from the moment I knocked on the door and heard that deep, rich voice say 'Enter,' I knew I had the right man. And of course I was even more convinced when I saw him move—like a leopard, like water falling." The text of Mr. Farmer's interview follows.*

TARZAN: How do you do, Mr. Farmer.

FARMER: How do you do, Your Grace.

T: If you don't mind, Mr. Farmer, I should prefer simply to be called John Clayton. I own a good many titles, both real and fictional, but John Clayton is, as it were, my real name. Though not my true *identity*, so to speak. As you apparently know.

F: Excuse me, sir—Mr. Clayton. Mr. Clayton, you told me over the phone that you would see me for fifteen minutes only, so I'd better work fast. I'll start asking questions right now, if you don't mind?

T: By all means. You don't have a tape recorder on you, do you? No? Good.

F: May I ask first, sir, why you were kind enough to grant this interview?

T: Mr. Farmer, my reasons are my own. But I will say that I appreciate the very great efforts you have gone to in researching the details of my life. It is very flattering to me, and I am not entirely immune to that. Besides, you seem to have information about my family that even I myself don't know. Your genealogical researches provoke my own curiosity, which has always been ample. I may ask you a few questions myself.

F: Of course. First, though, may I ask how it happens that you seem to speak English as you do, with more or less of an American accent? You speak as though you came from Illinois, which is my own home state. I seem to recall that on the phone you spoke— well, as I imagine dukes speak, the educated British accent.

T: I speak more or less as I am spoken *to*. You will recall that English is not my first spoken language—though it was my first *written* language—very unusual business, that—or even my first spoken *European* language. But the first English-speaking country I visited was the United States, Wisconsin in particular, back in 1909. I was not quite twenty-one years old at the time. So when English was fairly new to me, I had rather a large dose of American. Nevertheless, in Britain I do speak British. I have a gift for mimicry, I suppose you might call it, and I conform pretty much to the dialect of my interlocutors. When I gave my first and only speech in the House of Lords I did speak as dukes speak, or at least as dukes think they speak. You seem nervous, by the way. Would you care for a drink? I believe I will join you in a small Scotch.

F: Thank you. But I'm surprised to find you a drinking man. I thought—

T: That I was an abstainer? For many years I was. In my early days among civilized people I not only saw the results of excess but, I'm afraid, committed it myself. For many years I abstained completely. However, I believe the rash impulses of youth are safely behind me now. I can be abstemious without being teetotal. After all, I am—

F: You are eighty-two years old. When this interview is published, you will be eighty-three. But I suppose as far as physical appearance is concerned, you look about thirty-five. It must be true, then, that story about the grateful witch doctor who gave you the immortality treatment—

T: That was in 1912. I was twenty-four then, so as you see I have apparently aged about ten years since. The treatment merely slows down the aging process. Burroughs exaggerated its effects slightly, as he often did. I'll be an old man by the time I'm a hundred and fifty or so.

F: I'd like to return to your physical condition. But since you bring up Burroughs, and since Burroughs is the principal source of information about your life and family—

T: You would like to discuss the accuracy of Burroughs? Go ahead.

F: In *Tarzan of the Apes*, the first Tarzan book, Burroughs says that in 1888 your mother, then pregnant, accompanied your father on a secret mission to Africa for the British government. They hired a small ship, but the crew mutinied and stranded your parents on the coast of Africa. They were left on the shores of Portuguese Angola at approximately ten degrees south latitude, or about fifteen hundred miles north of Cape Town. But it seems to me that many of the scenes in the book could not have taken place in Angola.

T: That is correct. Actually, my parents were marooned on the shore of this very country, Gabon, which was then part of French Equatorial Africa. I was born about 190 miles south of here, in what is now the Parc National du Petit Loango. Any researcher, I believe, could have deduced that from the facts. There were gorillas in my natal territory, but there are no gorillas south of the Congo, and Angola extends far to the south of the Congo. Also, it was a French cruiser that landed near the same spot years later and rescued the party of Professor Porter, including my wife-to-be Jane, but left behind Lieutenant d'Arnot, my first civilized friend. Why would a French warship be patrolling the shores of Angola, a Portuguese possession?

F: Nor are there any lions, zebras, or rhinoceroses in the Gabonese rain forests. What about the lioness whose neck Burroughs said you broke with a full nelson when she was trying to get into your parents' cabin after Jane?

T: The lioness was actually a leopard. It was about the size of a small lioness, one of the big leopards that the natives call *injogu*. I did break its neck. As you know, I had independently invented the full nelson a few months before when I fought the big mangani ape that Burroughs calls Terkoz.

F: Well, then, how do you explain the discrepancies between Burroughs and the facts?

T: Mr. Farmer, the relationship between my life and Burroughs' narration of my life is exceedingly complex. I don't choose, for various reasons, to tell you all that I know about Burroughs' methods or my own; but I can tell you a number of his motives, some of which you may have figured out for yourself. First of all, Burroughs was essentially a romancer. He was not obligated to stick to the facts, and even if I had chosen to try to compel him, litigation would have been involved, and I would have had to appear in court and submit to questioning, which I would rather not have done. I entirely appreciate the feelings of your own Mr. Howard Hughes in this regard. In fact, after Burroughs wrote *Tarzan of the Apes*, I communicated with him, and I told him he should continue to make the narratives highly romantic, even fantastic. Jane advised that, because she said that if people found out I was not a fictional character, I would never again have a moment of privacy.

In the second place, Burroughs himself was not always fully informed. He first heard of me in the winter of 1911. I had then been known to the civilized world for only perhaps two years, and the records of my existence—including my father's diary, which he kept until his death in Africa—were then in England. By the way, here are some photostats of that diary. You may examine them, but you may not take them with you. In any case, Burroughs had not been to England, much less to Africa, and had his information by word of mouth at several removes. In many cases he had to fill in gaps by sheer guesswork, some of which is accurate, some not. For the sake of verisimilitude, Burroughs pretended to be much closer to his sources than was in fact the case.

Finally, certain facts are disguised in the books because they are best left disguised. Burroughs gives directions for getting to the lost city of Opar, with its spires and domes and vaults of gold and jewels. But those directions will lead the curious nowhere. Not that it matters so much in that case, because I have long since disguised the ruins of Opar completely. You could go there today and never know you were there. But I hope you won't try.

A few of Burroughs' stories are pure fiction. In *Jungle Tales of Tarzan*, I am supposed to have shot arrows into the sky in an effort to stop an eclipse of the moon. But the story happens in 1908, and in fact there was no such eclipse visible from my part of Africa that year. Sheer fabrication.

F: I see from your father's diary that he delivered you himself, though he had nothing but some medical books to go by. You were born a few minutes after midnight of November 22, 1888. On the cusp of Sagittarius and Scorpio. Scorpio the passionate and Sagittarius the hunter.

T: I know that. I have read much about astrology, though I believe in it about as much as I do in the speeches of politicians. Still, Sagittarius, the centaur with the bow, could not be a better symbol of the half-animal, half-man that I have been. And I am a very good archer indeed. And Scorpios are supposed to be ingenious, creative, true friends, and dangerous enemies, all of which I am. We're also supposed to exude sexual power. Hmm.

F: Burroughs gives many instances of women attempting to seduce you. You are certainly not the inarticulate ape-man of the movies. What you say about being a good archer, however, reminds me of some critics who maintain you could not have accomplished this. They refer to Marshall McLuhan's thesis that only literate peoples can produce excellent marksmen.

T: I've read *The Mechanical Bride* and *Understanding Media*. McLuhan forgets the medieval English bowman, who was certainly illiterate but undoubtedly a great marksman. And the critics forget that I taught myself to read and write English. I was not illiterate, though I couldn't *speak* the language.

F: What do you think of the Tarzan movies?

T: I saw the first one in 1920, the one with Elmo Lincoln. I came very near to leaping up onto the stage and tearing the picture apart. That fake jungle, those doped-up, scraggly circus cats! Lincoln was built more like a gorilla than like me, and he wore a head-band, which I have never done. All that swinging on a vine is movie invention as well, as is Cheetah the chimpanzee. Nowhere even in Burroughs will you find me swinging on vines, though it's true that he did greatly exaggerate my tree-traveling abilities. I'm too heavy to go skipping along the, ah, arboreal avenues like a monkey. And the chimpanzees would never trust me because they identified me with the great apes who brought me up. We—that is, they—used to eat chimps when they could catch them. But later on I began to find the Tarzan movies more amusing than disgusting. Jane helped me to learn to tolerate them.

F: Arthur Koestler wrote an article claiming that you couldn't have escaped being mentally retarded. He said there had been a few authentic cases of children raised by baboons or wolves and then found by humans. These were unable to master any language. Apparently, if the child doesn't experience language before a certain age, it is forever incapable of learning speech.

T: Koestler must not have bothered to read the Tarzan books. Otherwise he would have learned that the great apes *did* have a language. He should have deduced, as many have, that the great apes, or mangani, were really near-humans. Hominids, in fact. Remember what I said about the sketchy information upon which Burroughs' early books were based? He supplied missing data with imagination or even misinformation. He made up names. He put animals in the Gabonese jungles that did not belong there. He described the mangani as great apes. My father had thought they were apes, and so called them in his diary. But my father was not a zoologist or a paleontologist.

The mangani were a very rare, nearly extinct—even eighty years ago—genus of hominids, halfway between ape and man.

They might have been a giant variety of Australopithecus robustus. The fossil remains of this hominid have been found by Leakey in East Africa, you know. The mangani—and I use Burroughs' word for them, since their own term is an unpronounceable jaw-breaker—had crested skulls and massive jaws. They had long arms and often used their knuckles to assist them in walking, but they had manlike hips and leg bones. They could walk upright when they chose.

Burroughs later had better information about his *great apes*. However, for the sake of consistency he described them in the later novels as he had done earlier on. He slipped in the sixth book, *Jungle Tales of Tarzan*, when he said they walked upright and were manlike.

I can speak mangani fluently, of course. But can't pronounce it quite perfectly. The mangani oral structure is different from man's, and many of their speech sounds have no exact equivalent in human speech. So though I can speak English with any of several accents, I always speak mangani with a *human* accent.

F: Did the big mangani, Terkoz, really abduct Jane and try to rape her? And you killed him with your father's hunting knife?

T: Yes. And there you see, by the way, another reason why the mangani should not be classified as apes. They are capable of raping a human being, whereas a gorilla is not. I once read in the memoirs of Trader Horn about a white trader who put a male gorilla in a cage with a native girl. The gorilla did nothing but sulk in one corner while the poor girl wept in the other. Horn said he shot the white man when he found out about it. In any case, gorillas have forty-eight chromosomes, humans only forty-six, so a gorilla-human hybrid is not possible. But Burroughs knew of instances of offspring being born to a human and a mangani.

F: Albert Schweitzer maintained that Trader Horn, aside from some trifling discrepancies, was generally accurate. Did you know that Schweitzer built his house on the site of Horn's trading post?

T: Yes, at Adolinanongo, a little distance above Lambaréné on the Ogowe River. I know it well. There's a Catholic mission there, founded in 1886. That's where Lieutenant d'Arnot and I came out of the jungle on our trek to civilization.

F: Would you care to comment on how you taught yourself to read and write English? As far as I know this is a unique intellectual feat, especially since you had never heard a word of it spoken.

T: I was about ten years old when I discovered how to unlock the door to my parents' cabin, and there I found, as you have read in Burroughs, a number of books, all of them perfectly meaningless to me, of course. But one of them was a big illustrated children's alphabet book with pictures of bowmen and the like, you know, and legends like "A is for Archer, who shoots with the bow," that sort of thing. Finally it dawned on me that the writing had something to do with the picture, and I spent I don't know how long puzzling it out. When I was seventeen I could read a child's primer. I called the letters "little bugs," or the mangani equivalent rather, and I knew how they worked. One detail you may find rather amusing is this: I had to invent, and did invent, my own manner of pronouncing the English words, which had nothing to do of course with real English but was governed by the usages of mangani grammar. Mangani has two genders, indicated by the prefixes *bu* for the masculine and *mu* for the feminine. Now I supposed that the capital letters were masculine, since they were bigger, and the rest feminine. And as children will do when they know the alphabet but don't yet know how to read, I pronounced each letter separately, using arbitrary syllables taken from mangani. Does this all seem terribly complicated? For example, I pronounced *g* as *la*; *o* as *tu*; and *d* as *mo*. Now take the English word God; adding the prefixes, I pronounced it *Bulamutumumo*. The equivalent in English would be *he-g-she-o-she-d*. Now that's very cumbersome, of course, but it worked. I could read my father's books and know what I was reading.

I had no idea how to write my mangani name, but I had seen a picture of a little white boy, which in Anglo-Mangani, I suppose you might call it, is *Bumudomutumuro*, or *He-she-b-she-o-she-y*. That's what I called myself.

F: Burroughs says that when you discovered intruders had messed up the cabin, you printed a threatening note to them. You signed it with your mangani name. How could you do that if you didn't know how to write it in English?

T: I didn't. I printed a translation of my mangani name: White Skin. When Burroughs wrote *Tarzan of the Apes*, he had no record of the exact text of the note. He made up the text, and he did not care to take time out from the action to explain that I couldn't use my mangani name. Remember he was first and last a storyteller.

F: Your reading must have given you some strange ideas about the outside world. You had no proper references to give you a full comprehension of the books.

T: My ideas were no stranger than the reality. My initial encounters with human beings were extremely unpleasant. The first human being I ever saw had just murdered my foster mother. To him she was an ape, but to me she was the most beautiful and loving and lovable person in the world. The first time I saw white men, one was murdering another. I am fortunate that that didn't make me shun mankind forever. Otherwise I'd never have known human love.

F: When you matured and discovered that you were not an ape but a man, didn't you think of turning to the native tribes for companionship?

T: No. I hated them all for a long time, because I blamed them for my foster mother's death. Also, they were cannibals, and anybody not of their tribe was meat to them. And they had had unfortunate experiences with white men. In addition to that, the women coated their bodies and hair with rancid palm-nut oil. I have an unusually keen sense of smell, and consequently they repelled me. Still, if Jane hadn't come along—

F: Burroughs portrays you as free of racial prejudice.

T: Like Mark Twain, I have only one prejudice. That is against the human race.

F: Let me not pursue *that* further. Many readers have found your behavior with Jane when you were alone in the jungle incredibly chivalrous. Burroughs attributes this to heredity, but no one today would accept this explanation.

T: Remember, I read all the novels—Victorian novels, mind you—in my father's library. And I read Malory's book about King Arthur and the knights and the fair ladies. I believed in chivalry quite literally. And I was in love with Jane and did not want to offend her. Besides, the mangani have a code of ethics, you know. They are not apes. They do not copulate in public; they demand, though they do not always get, marital fidelity; they punish rape with death, if the injured party wishes it. Consider all the factors and you'll find my behavior credible enough.

F: You became chief of a black tribe which Burroughs called the Waziri. Are you aware that Robert Lewis Taylor, in his biography of W. C, Fields, says that Fields once went with Tex Rickard on a world tour? And that Fields entertained a tribe of naked Waziri? That would have been in 1906 or 1907, several years before you encountered the Waziri. Did your Waziri ever say anything about Fields?

T: I have no comment on that, I'm afraid.

F: How much of Burroughs' *Tarzan and the Lion Man* is true? It seems to me that Burroughs wrote it mainly to satirize Hollywood.

T: Yes, nearly everything in that book is fiction. But I did visit Hollywood once, though I told no one except Burroughs who I was, of course.

F: Did you actually try out for the role of Tarzan in a movie? And were you rejected because the producer said you weren't the type?

T: No, though I wouldn't be surprised if such a thing were to happen. In any case, I went there too late to try out for the Weissmuller movie *Tarzan the Ape Man*, and too early for the Buster Crabbe movie *Tarzan the Fearless*. I did meet Burroughs, secretly of course. I liked him very much. He was gentle and broad-minded and he didn't take himself or his works too seriously. He saw many things wrong in civilization, many sickening things, and he satirized them in his books, you know, but his mockery was Voltaire's, not Swift's. He was never soured or snarly. But since we are now discussing authors, let me indulge my curiosity a moment. I gather that you have been led to me by a fairly elaborate trail. Would you mind explaining to me how you first caught my scent, as it were?

F: I had long suspected that Burroughs, Arthur Conan Doyle, and George Bernard Shaw had all written stories about your family. Each, however, used more or less sophisticated systems of code names for your various relatives. If these codes could be cracked, and used as guides to the right places—Burke's Peerage, for instance—they would lead me right to you. And as you see, they have. The reasoning I have employed is long and complex, and I hope you'll be willing to delay a full understanding until I can send you a copy of my book, since our time today is short. Suffice it to say that I have shown you are closely related to the men who were the living prototypes of Doc Savage, Nero Wolfe, Bulldog Drummond, Sherlock Holmes, Lord Peter Wimsey, Leopold Bloom, and Richard Wentworth (also known as G-8, the Spider, and the Shadow), and a number of other notable characters in nineteenth- and twentieth-century fiction.

T: Indeed.

F: I have also found the explanation for the remarkable, almost superhuman powers exhibited by yourself and many members of your family. As you know, a monument marks the spot today where a meteorite hit Wold Newton, Yorkshire, in 1795. It just so happened that three coaches were passing by when the meteorite struck, and in them were the third Duke of Greystoke and his wife, the rich gentleman Fitzwilliam Darcy of Pemberley House and his wife Elizabeth Bennet—the heroine of *Pride and Prejudice*—Sherlock Holmes's great-grandparents, and a number of others. All the ladies were pregnant. Everybody was exposed to the radiation from the meteorite. Ionization accompanies the fall of these, you know. And the radiation must have caused favorable mutations in the party. Otherwise how do you explain the nova of genetic splendor in the descendants of these people, including yourself?

T: I will not say that I am entirely convinced. Nevertheless yours is a very probable theory. My own skeletal bones are half again as thick as normal, which might well indicate that I am a mutant. Moreover, even before I received the immortality treatment from the witch doctor, I was developing oddly, though I had no one of my own race to compare myself with at the time. I was six feet tall at eighteen years of age, and grew three more inches in the next two years. I did not have to shave until I was twenty. I have never been ill or had a toothache. So your mutation theory seems likely enough. And now, I'm afraid, our interview is over. May I have the photostats back, please?

F: My time's up? But—

T: I don't need a watch to know how many minutes have passed. Good-bye. I won't be seeing you again. May I ask you to remain in this room a few minutes and allow me to leave first? I have already checked out and shall soon be gone.

F: May I ask where you're going?

T: To arrange a seemingly fatal accident. Too many people are wondering why I look so young. One reason I gave you this interview is that I'm disappearing. Your book won't help anyone find me. But I hold you to your promise not to reveal my true identity for ten years. I'll be living incognito with Jane in various countries under various names. Occasionally I'll return to the jungle. There are still vast tracts in the rain forests of Gabon and the Ituri where the only men are a few pygmies. The rain forests may disappear someday. But I think that the worldwide pollution is going to result in a collapse of civilization and a drastic reduction of population. Perhaps the forests will be spared after all, and many of the species now threatened with extinction will come back. In any case, I intend to survive. If I don't, well, death gets us sooner or later, and I won't be able to worry about its being sooner if I'm dead. As I told you, I'll be old anyhow when I'm a hundred and fifty. Send your book to my bankers in Zurich.

Then, Mr. Farmer tells us, he left the room and was gone.

SKETCHES AMONG THE RUINS OF MY MIND

✑ ONE ✑

June 1, 1980

It is now 11:00 P.M., and I am afraid to go to bed. I am not alone. The whole world is afraid of sleep.

This morning I got up at 6:30 A.M., as I do every Wednesday. While I shaved and showered, I considered the case of the state of Illinois against Joseph Lankers, accused of murder. It was beginning to stink as if it were a three-day-old fish. My star witness would undoubtedly be charged with perjury.

I dressed, went downstairs, and kissed Carole good morning. She poured me a cup of coffee and said, "The paper's late."

That put me in a bad temper. I need both coffee and the morning newspaper to get me started.

Twice during breakfast, I left the table to look outside. Neither paper nor newsboy had appeared.

At seven, Carole went upstairs to wake up Mike and Tom, aged ten and eight respectively. Saturdays and Sundays they rise early even though I'd like them to stay in bed so their horsing around won't wake me. School days they have to be dragged out.

The third time I looked out of the door, Joe Gale, the paper-boy, was next door. My paper lay on the stoop.

I felt disorientated, as if I'd walked into the wrong courtroom or the judge had given my client, a shoplifter, a life sentence. I was out of phase with the world. This couldn't be Sunday. So what was the Sunday issue, bright in its covering of the colored comic section, doing here? Today was Wednesday.

I stepped out to pick it up and saw old Mrs. Douglas, my neighbor to the left. She was looking at the front page of her paper as if she could not believe it.

The world rearranged itself into the correct lines of polarization. My thin panic dwindled into nothing. I thought, the *Star* has really goofed this time. That's what comes from depending so much on a computer to put it together. One little short circuit, and Wednesday's paper comes out in Sunday's format.

The *Star*'s night shift must have decided to let it go through; it was too late for them to rectify the error,

I said, "Good morning, Mrs. Douglas! Tell me, what day is it?"

"The twenty-eighth of May," she said. "I think . . ."

I walked out into the yard and shouted after Joe. Reluctantly, he wheeled his bike around.

"What is this?" I said, shaking the paper at him. "Did the *Star* screw up?"

"I don't know, Mr. Franham," he said. "None of us knows, honest to God."

By "us" he must have meant the other boys he met in the morning at the paper drop.

"We all thought it was Wednesday. That's why I'm late. We couldn't understand what was happening, so we talked a long time and then Bill Ambers called the office. Gates, he's the circulation manager, was just as bongo as we was."

"Were," I said.

"What?" he said.

"We *were*, not *was*, just as bongo, whatever that means," I said.

"For God's sake, Mr. Franham who cares!" he said.

"Some of us still do," I said. "All right, what did Gates say?"

"He was upset as hell," Joe said. "He said heads were gonna roll. The night staff had fallen asleep for a couple of hours, and some joker had diddled up the computers, or . . ."

"That's all it is?" I said. I felt relieved.

When I went inside, I got out the papers for the last four days from the cycler. I sat down on the sofa and scanned them.

I didn't remember reading them. I didn't remember the past four days at all!

Wednesday's headline was: MYSTERIOUS OBJECT ORBITS EARTH.

I did remember Tuesday's articles, which stated that the big round object was heading for a point between the Earth and the moon. It had been detected three weeks ago when it was passing through the so-called asteroid belt. It was at that time traveling approximately 57,000 kilometers per hour, relative to the sun. Then it had slowed down, had changed course several times, and it became obvious that, unless it changed course again, it was going to come near Earth.

By the time it was eleven million miles away, the radars had defined its size and shape, though not its composition. It was perfectly spherical and exactly half a kilometer in diameter. It did not reflect much light. Since it had altered its path so often, it had to be artificial. Strange hands, or strange somethings, had built it.

I remembered the panic and the many wild articles in the papers and magazines and the TV specials made overnight to discuss its implications.

It had failed to make any response whatever to the radio and laser signals sent from Earth. Many scientists said that it probably contained no living passengers. It had to be of interstellar origin. The sentient beings of some planet circling some star had sent it out equipped with automatic equipment of some sort. No being could live long enough to travel between the stars. It would take over four years to get from the nearest star to Earth even if the object could travel at the speed of light, and that was impossible. Even one-sixteenth the speed of light seemed incredible because of the vast energy requirements. No, this thing had been launched with only electromechanical devices as passengers, had attained its top speed, turned off its power, and coasted until it came within the outer reaches of our solar system.

According to the experts, it must be unable to land on Earth because of its size and weight. It was probably just a surveying vessel, and after it had taken some photographs and made some radar/laser sweeps, it would proceed to wherever it was supposed to go, probably back to an orbit around its home planet.

ᘓᗝ Two ᘓᗝ

Last Wednesday night, the president had told us that we had nothing to fear. And he'd tried to end on an optimistic note. At least, that's what Wednesday's paper said. The beings who had sent The Ball must be more advanced than we, and they must have many good things to give us. And we might be able to make beneficial contributions to them. Like what? I thought.

Some photographs of The Ball, taken from one of the manned orbiting laboratories, were on the second page. It looked just like a giant black billiard ball. One TV comic had suggested that the other side might bear a big white 8. I may have thought that this was funny last Wednesday, but I didn't think so now. It seemed highly probable to me that The Ball was connected with the four-days' loss of memory. How, I had no idea.

I turned on the 7:30 news channels, but they weren't much help except in telling us that the same thing had happened to everybody all over the world. Even those in the deepest diamond mines or submarines had been affected. The president was in conference, but he'd be making a statement over the networks sometime today. Meantime, it was known that no radiation of any sort had been detected emanating from The Ball. There was no evidence whatsoever that the object had caused the loss of memory. Or, as the jargon-crazy casters were already calling it, "memloss."

I'm a lawyer, and I like to think logically, not only about what has happened but what might happen. So I extrapolated on the basis of what little evidence, or data, there was.

On the first of June, a Sunday, we woke up with all memory of May 31 back through May 28 completely gone. We had thought that yesterday was the twenty-seventh and that this morning was that of the twenty-eighth.

If The Ball had caused this, why had it only taken four days of our memory? I didn't know. Nobody knew. But perhaps The Ball, its devices, that is, were limited in scope. Perhaps they couldn't strip off more than four days of memory at a time from everybody on Earth.

Postulate that this is the case. Then, what if the same thing happens tomorrow? We'll wake up tomorrow, June 2, with all memory of yesterday, June 1, and three more days of May, the twenty-seventh through the twenty-fifth, gone. Eight days in one solid stretch.

And if this ghastly thing should occur the following day, June 3, we'll lose another four days. All memory of June 2 will have disappeared. With it will go the memory of three more days, from May twenty-fourth through the twenty-second. Twelve days in all from June 2 backward!

And the next day? June 3 lost, too, along with May 21 through May 19. Sixteen days of a total blank. And the next day? And the next?

No, it's too hideous, and too fantastic, to think about.

While we were watching TV, Carole and the boys besieged me with questions. She was frantic. The boys seemed to be enjoying the mystery. They'd awakened expecting to go to school, and now they were having a holiday.

To all their questions, I said, "I don't know. Nobody knows."

I wasn't going to frighten them with my extrapolations. Besides, I didn't believe them myself.

"You'd better call up your office and tell them you can't come in today," Carole said. "Surely Judge Payne'll call off the session today."

"Carole, it's Sunday, not Wednesday, remember?" I said.

She cried for a minute. After she'd wiped away the tears, she said, "That's just it! I *don't* remember! My God, what's happening?"

The newscasters also reported that the White House was flooded with telegrams and phone calls demanding that rockets with H-bomb warheads be launched against The Ball. The specials, which came on after the news, were devoted to The Ball. These had various authorities, scientists, military men, ministers, and a few science-fiction authors. None of them radiated confidence, but they were all temperate in their approach to the problem. I suppose they had been picked for their level-headedness. The networks had screened out the hotheads and the crackpots. They didn't want to be generating any more hysteria.

But Anel Robertson, a fundamentalist faith healer with a powerful radio/TV station of his own, had already declared that The Ball was a judgment of God on a sinful planet. It was The Destroying Angel. I knew that because Mrs. Douglas, no fanatic but certainly a zealot, had phoned me and told me to dial him in. Robertson had been speaking for an hour, she said, and he was going to talk all day.

She sounded frightened, and yet, beneath the fear was a note of joy. Obviously, she didn't think that she was going to be among the goats when the last days arrived. She'd be right in there with the whitest of the sheep. My curiosity finally overcame my repugnance for Robertson. I dialed the correct number but got nothing except a pattern. Later today, I found out his station had been shut down for some infraction of FCC regulations. At least, that was the explanation given on the news, but I suspected that the government regarded him as a hysteria monger.

At eleven, Carole reminded me that it was Sunday and that if we didn't hurry, we'd miss church.

The Forrest Hill Presbyterian has a good attendance, but its huge parking lot has always been adequate. This morning, we had to park two blocks up the street and walk to church. Every seat was filled. We had to stand in the anteroom near the front door. The crowd stank of fear. Their faces were pale and set; their eyes, big. The air conditioning labored unsuccessfully to carry away the heat and humidity of the packed and sweating bodies. The choir was loud but quavering; their "Rock of Ages" was crumbling.

Dr. Boynton would have prepared his sermon on Saturday afternoon, as he always did. But today he spoke impromptu. Perhaps, he said, this loss of memory *had* been caused by The Ball. Perhaps there were living beings in it who had taken four days away from us, not as a hostile move but merely to demonstrate their immense powers. There was no reason to anticipate that we would suffer another loss of memory. These beings merely wanted to show us that we were hopelessly inferior in science and that we could not launch a successful attack against them.

"What the hell's he doing?" I thought. "Is he trying to scare us to death?"

Boynton hastened then to say that beings with such powers, of such obvious advancement, would not, could not, be hostile. They would be on too high an ethical plane for such evil things as war, unless they were attacked, of course. They would regard us as beings who had not yet progressed to their level but had the potentiality, the God-given potentiality, to be brought up to a high level. He was sure that, when they made contact with us, they would tell us that all was for the best.

They would tell us that we must, like it or not, become true Christians. At least, we must all, Buddhists, Moslems and so forth, become Christian in spirit, whatever our religion or lack thereof. They would teach us how to live as brothers and sisters, how to be happy, how to truly love. Assuredly, God had sent The Ball, since nothing happened without His knowledge and consent. He had sent these beings, whoever they were, not as Destroying Angels but as Sharers of Peace, Love and Prosperity.

That last, with the big P, seemed to settle down most of the congregation. Boynton had not forgotten that most of his flock were of the big-business and professional classes. Nor had he forgotten that, inscribed on the arch above the church entrance was, THEY SHALL PROSPER WHO LOVE THEE.

☙ Three ☙

We poured out into a bright warm June afternoon. I looked up into the sky but could see no Ball, of course. The news media had said that, despite its great distance from Earth, it was circling Earth every sixty-five minutes. It wasn't in a free fall orbit. It was applying continuous power to keep it on its path, although there were no detectable emanations of energy from it.

The memory loss had occurred all over the world between 1:00 A.M. and 2:00 A.M. Central Standard Time. Those who were not already asleep fell asleep for a minimum of an hour. This had, of course, caused hundreds of thousands of accidents. Planes not on automatic pilot had crashed, trains had collided or been derailed, ships had sunk, and more than two hundred thousand had been killed or seriously injured. At least a million vehicle drivers and passengers had been injured. The ambulance and hospital services had found it impossible to handle the situation. The fact that their personnel had been asleep for at least an hour and that it had taken them some time to recover from their confusion on awakening had aggravated the situation considerably. Many had died who might have lived if immediate service had been available.

There were many fires, too, the largest of which were still raging in Tokyo, Athens, Naples, Harlem, and Baltimore.

I thought, Would beings on a high ethical plane have put us to sleep knowing that so many people would be killed and badly hurt?

One curious item was about two rangers who had been thinning a herd of elephants in Kenya. While sleeping, they had been trampled to death. Whatever it is that's causing this, it's very specific. Only human beings are affected.

The optimism, which Boynton had given us in the church, melted in the sun. Many must have been thinking, as I was, that if Boynton's words were prophetic, we were helpless. Whatever the things in The Ball, whether living or mechanical, decided to do for us, or to us, we were no longer masters of our own fate. Some of them must have been thinking about what the technologically superior whites had done to various aboriginal cultures. All in the name of progress and God.

But this would be, must be, different, I thought. Boynton must be right. Surely such an advanced people would not be as we were. Even we are not what we were in the bad old days. We have learned.

But then an advanced technology does not necessarily accompany an advanced ethics.

"Or whatever," I murmured.

"What did you say, dear?" Carole said.

I said, "Nothing," and shook her hand off my arm. She had clung to it tightly all through the services, as if *I* were the rock of the ages. I walked over to Judge Payne, who's sixty years old but looked this morning as if he were eighty. The many broken veins on his face were red, but underneath them was a grayishness.

I said hello and then asked him if things would be normal tomorrow. He didn't seem to know what I was getting at, so I said, "The trial will start on time tomorrow?"

"Oh, yes, the trial," he said. "Of course, Mark."

He laughed whinnyingly and said, "Provided that we all haven't forgotten today when we wake up tomorrow."

That seemed incredible, and I told him so.

"It's not law school that makes good lawyers," he said. "It's experience. And experience tells us that the same damned thing, with some trifling variations, occurs over and over, day after day. So what makes you think this evil thing won't happen again? And if it does, how're you going to learn from it when you can't remember it?"

I had no logical argument, and he didn't want to talk any more. He grabbed his wife by the arm, and they waded through the crowd as if they thought they were going to step in a sinkhole and drown in a sea of bodies.

This evening, I decided to record on tape what's happened today. Now I lay me down to sleep, I pray the Lord my memory to keep, if I forget while I sleep . . .

Most of the rest of today, I've spent before the TV. Carole wasted hours trying to get through the lines to her friends for phone conversations. Three-fourths of the time, she got a busy signal. There were bulletins on the TV asking people not to use the phone except for emergencies, but she paid no attention to it until eight o'clock. A TV bulletin, for the sixth time in an hour, asked that the lines be kept open. About twenty fires had broken out over the town, and the firemen couldn't be informed of them because of the tie-up. Calls to hospitals had been similarly blocked.

I told Carole to knock it off, and we quarreled. Our suppressed hysteria broke loose, and the boys retreated upstairs to their room behind a closed door. Eventually, Carole started crying and threw herself into my arms, and then I cried. We kissed and made up. The boys came down looking as if we had failed them, which we had. For them, it was no longer a fun-adventure from some science-fiction story.

Mike said, "Dad, could you help me go over my arithmetic lessons?"

I didn't feel like it, but I wanted to make it up to him for that savage scene. I said sure and then, when I saw what he had to do, I said, "But all this? What's the matter with your teacher? I never saw so much . . ."

I stopped. Of course, he had forgotten all he'd learned in the last three days of school. He had to do his lessons all over again.

This took us until eleven, though we might have gone faster if I hadn't insisted on watching the news every half-hour for at least ten minutes. A full thirty minutes were used listening to the president who came on at 9:30. He had nothing to add to what the newsmen had said except that, within thirty days, The Ball would be completely dealt with—one way or another. If it didn't make some response to our signals within two days, then we would send up a four-man expedition, which would explore The Ball.

If it can get inside, I thought.

If, however, The Ball should commit any more hostile acts, then the United States would immediately launch, in conjunction with other nations, rockets armed with H-bombs.

Meanwhile, would we all join the president in an inter-denominational prayer?

We certainly would.

At eleven, we put the kids to bed. Tom went to sleep before we were out of the room. But about half an hour later, as I passed their door, I heard a low voice from the TV. I didn't say anything to Mike, even if he did have to go to school next day.

At twelve, I made the first part of this tape.

But here it is, one minute to one o'clock in the morning. If the same thing happens tonight as happened yesterday, then the nightside hemisphere will be affected first. People in the time zone which bisects the South and North Atlantic oceans and covers the eastern half of Greenland, will fall asleep. Just in case it does happen again, all airplanes have been grounded. Right now, the TV is showing the bridge and the salon of the trans-Atlantic liner *Pax*. It's five o'clock there, but the salon is crowded. The passengers are wearing party hats and confetti, and balloons are floating everywhere. I don't know what they could be celebrating. The captain said a little while ago that the ship's on automatic, but he doesn't expect a repetition of last night. The interviewer said that the governments of the dayside nations have not been successful keeping people home. We've been getting shots from everywhere, the sirens are wailing all over the world, but, except for the totalitarian nations, the streets of the daytime world are filled with cars. The damned fools just didn't believe it would happen again.

Back to the bridge and the salon of the ship. My God! They *are* falling asleep!

The announcers are repeating warnings. Everybody lie down so they won't get hurt by falling. Make sure all home appliances, which might cause fires, are turned off. And so on and so on.

I'm sitting in a chair with a tilted back. Carole is on the sofa.

Now I'm on the sofa. Carole just said she wanted to be holding on to me when this horrible thing comes.

The announcers are getting hysterical. In a few minutes, New York will be hit. The eastern half of South America is under. The central section is going under.

✌ Four ✌

True date: June 2, 1980. Subjective date: May 25, 1980

My God! How many times have I said, "My God!" in the last two days?

I awoke on the sofa beside Carole and Mike. The clock indicated three in the morning. Chris Turner was on the TV. I didn't know what he was talking about. All I could understand was that he was trying to reassure his viewers that everything was all right and that everything would be explained shortly.

What was I doing on the sofa? I'd gone to bed about eleven the night of May 24, a Saturday. Carole and I had had a little quarrel because I'd spent all day working on the Lankers case, and she said that I'd promised to take her to see *Nova Express*. And so I had—if I finished work before eight, which I obviously had not done. So what were we doing on the sofa, where had Mike come from, and what did Turner mean by saying that today was June 2?

The tape recorder was on the table near me, but it didn't occur to me to turn it on.

I shook Carole awake, and we confusedly asked each other what had happened. Finally, Turner's insistent voice got our attention, and he explained the situation for about the fifth time so far. Later, he said that an alarm clock placed by his ear had awakened him at two-thirty.

Carole made some coffee, and we drank four cups apiece. We talked wildly, with occasional breaks to listen to Turner, before we became half-convinced that we had indeed lost all memory of the last eight days. Mike slept on through it, and finally I carried him up to his bed. His TV was still on. Nate Frobisher, Mike's favorite spieler, was talking hysterically. I turned him off and went back downstairs. I figured out later that Mike had gotten scared and come downstairs to sit with us.

Dawn found us rereading the papers from May 24 through June 1. It was like getting news from Mars. Carole took a tranquilizer to quiet herself down, but I preferred Wild Turkey. After she'd seen me down six ounces, Carole said I should lay off the bourbon. I wouldn't be fit to go to work. I told her that if she thought anybody'd be working today, she was out of her mind.

At seven, I went out to pick up the paper. It wasn't there. At a quarter to eight, Joe delivered it. I tried to talk to him, but he wouldn't stop. All he said, as he pedaled away, was, "It ain't Saturday!"

I went back in. The entire front page was devoted to The Ball and this morning's events up to four o'clock. Part of the paper had been set up before one o'clock. According to a notice at the bottom of the page, the staff had awakened about three. It took them an hour to straighten themselves out, and then they'd gotten together the latest news and made up the front page and some of section C. They'd have never made it when they did if it wasn't for the computer, which printed justified lines from voice input.

Despite what I'd said earlier, I decided to go to work, First, I had to straighten the boys out. At ten, they went off to school. It seemed to me that it was useless for them to do so. But they were eager to talk with their classmates about this situation. To tell the truth, I wanted to get down to the office and the courthouse for the same reason. I wanted to talk this over with my colleagues. Staying home all day with Carole seemed a waste of time. We just kept saying the same thing over and over again.

Carole didn't want me to leave. She was too frightened to stay home by herself. Both our parents are dead, but she does have a sister who lives in Hannah, a small town nearby. I told her it'd do her good to get out of the house. And I just had to get to the courthouse. I couldn't find out what was happening there because the phone lines were tied up.

When I went outside to get into my car, Carole ran down after me. Her long blonde hair was straggling; she had big bags under her eyes; she looked like a witch.

"Mark! Mark!" she said.

I took my finger off the starter button and said, "What is it?"

"I know you'll think I'm crazy, Mark," she said. "But I'm about to fall apart!"

"Who isn't?" I said.

"Mark," she said, "what if I go out to my sister's and then forget how to get back? What if I forgot *you?*"

"This thing only happens at night," I said.

"So far!" she screamed. "So far!"

"Honey," I said, "I'll be home early, I promise. If you don't want to go, stay here. Go over and talk to Mrs. Knight. I see her looking out her window. She'll talk your leg off all day."

I didn't tell her to visit any of her close friends, because she didn't have any. Her best friend had died of cancer last year, and two others with whom she was familiar had moved away.

"If you do go to your sister's," I said, "make a note on a map reminding you where you live and stick it on top of the dashboard where you can see it."

"You son of a bitch," she said. "It isn't funny!"

"I'm not being funny," I said. "I got a feeling . . ."

"What about?" she said.

"Well, we'll be making notes to ourselves soon. If this keeps up," I said.

I thought I was kidding then. Thinking about it later today I see that that is the only way to get orientated in the morning. Well, not the only way, but it'll have to be the way to get started when you wake up.

Put a note where you can't overlook it, and it'll tell you to turn on a recording, which will, in turn, summarize the situation. Then you turn on the TV and get some more information.

I might as well have stayed home. Only half of the courthouse personnel showed up, and they were hopelessly inefficient. Judge Payne wasn't there and never will be. He'd had a fatal stroke at six that morning while listening to the TV. Walter Barbindale, my partner, said that the judge probably would have had a stroke sometime in the near future, anyway. But this situation must certainly have hastened it.

"The stock market's about hit bottom," he said. "One more day of this, and we'll have another world-wide depression. Nineteen twenty-nine won't hold a candle to it. And I can't even get through to my broker to tell him to sell everything."

"If everybody sells, then the market *will* crash," I said.

"Are you hanging onto your stocks?" he said.

"I've been too busy to even think about it," I said. "You might say I forgot."

"That isn't funny," he said.

"That's what my wife said," I answered. "But I'm not trying to be funny, though God knows I could use a good laugh. Well, what're we going to do about Lankers?"

"I went over some of the records," he said. "We haven't got a chance. I tell you, it was a shock finding out, for the second time, mind you, though I don't remember the first, that our star witness is in jail on a perjury charge."

Since all was chaos in the courthouse, it wasn't much use trying to find out who the judge would be for the new trial for Lankers. To tell the truth, I didn't much care. There were far more important things to worry about than the fate of an undoubtedly guilty murderer.

I went to Grover's Rover Bar, which is a block from the courthouse. As an aside, for my reference or for whoever might be listening to this someday, why am I telling myself things I know perfectly well, like the location of Grover's? Maybe it's because I think I might forget them some day.

Grover's, at least, I remembered well, as I should, since I'd been going there ever since it was built, five years ago. The air was thick with tobacco and pot smoke and the odors of pot, beer and booze. And noisy. Everybody was talking fast and loud, which is to be expected in a place filled with members of the legal profession. I bellied up to the bar and bought the DA a shot of Wild Turkey. We talked about what we'd done that morning, and then he told me he had to release two burglars that day. They'd been caught and jailed two days before. The arresting officers had, of course, filed their reports. But that wasn't going to be enough when the trial came up. Neither the burglars nor the victims and the officers remembered a thing about the case.

"Also," the D.A. said, "at two-ten this morning, the police got a call from the Black Shadow Tavern on Washington Street. They didn't get there until three-thirty because they were too disorientated to do anything for an hour or more. When they did get to the tavern, they found a dead man. He'd been beaten badly and then stabbed in the stomach. Nobody remembered anything, of course. But from what we could piece together, the dead man must've gotten into a drunken brawl with a person or persons unknown shortly before 1:00 A.M. Thirty people must've witnessed the murder. So we have a murderer or murderers walking the streets today who don't even remember the killing or anything leading up to it."

"They might know they're guilty if they'd been planning it for a long time," I said.

He grinned and said, "But he, or they, won't be telling anybody. No one except the corpse had blood on him nor did anybody have bruised knuckles. Two were arrested for carrying saps, but so what? They'll be out soon, and nobody, but nobody, can prove they used the saps. The knife was still half-sticking in the deceased's belly, and his efforts to pull it out destroyed any fingerprints."

∾ Five ∾

We talked and drank a lot, and suddenly it was 6:00 p.m. I was in no condition to drive and had sense enough to know it. I tried calling Carole to come down and get me, but I couldn't get through. At 6:30 and 7:00, I tried again without success. I decided to take a taxi. But after another drink, I tried again and this time got through.

"Where've you been?" she said. "I called your office, but nobody answered. I was thinking about calling the police."

"As if they haven't got enough to do," I said. "When did you get home?"

"You're slurring," she said coldly.

I repeated the question.

"Two hours ago," she said.

"The lines were tied up," I said. "I tried."

"You knew how scared I was, and you didn't even care," she said.

"Can I help it if the D.A. insisted on conducting business at the Rover?" I said. "Besides, I was trying to forget."

"Forget what?" she said.

"Whatever it was I forgot," I said.

"You ass!" she screamed. "Take a taxi!"

The phone clicked off.

She didn't make a scene when I got home. She'd decided to play it cool because of the kids, I suppose. She was drinking gin and tonic when I entered, and she said, in a level voice, "You'll have some coffee. And after a while you can listen to the tape you made yesterday. It's interesting, but spooky."

"What tape?" I said.

"Mike was fooling around with it," she said. "And he found out you'd recorded what happened yesterday."

"That kid!" I said. "He's always snooping around. I told him to leave my stuff alone. Can't a man have any privacy around here?"

"Well, don't say anything to him," she said. "He's upset as it is. Anyway, it's a good thing he did turn it on. Otherwise, you'd have forgotten all about it. I think you should make a daily record."

"So you think it'll happen again?" I said.

She burst into tears. After a moment, I put my arms around her. I felt like crying, too. But she pushed me away, saying, "You stink of rotten whiskey!"

"That's because it's mostly bar whiskey," I said. "I can't afford Wild Turkey at three dollars a shot."

I drank four cups of black coffee and munched on some shrimp dip. As an aside, I can't really afford that, either, since I only make forty-five thousand dollars a year.

When we went to bed, we went to bed. Afterward, Carole said, "I'm sorry, darling, but my heart wasn't really in it."

"That wasn't all," I said.

"You've got a dirty mind," she said. "What I meant was I couldn't stop thinking, even while we were doing it, that it wasn't any good doing it. We won't remember it tomorrow, I thought."

"How many do we really remember?" I said. "Sufficient unto the day is the, uh, good thereof."

"It's a good thing you didn't try to fulfill your childhood dream of becoming a preacher," she said. "You're a born shyster. You'd have made a lousy minister."

"Look," I said, "I remember the especially good ones. And I'll never forget our honeymoon. But we need sleep. We haven't had any to speak of for twenty-four hours. Let's hit the hay and forget everything until tomorrow. In which case . . ."

She stared at me and then said, "Poor dear, no wonder you're so belligerently flippant! It's a defense against fear!

I slammed my fist into my palm and shouted, "I know! I know! For God's sake, how long is this going on?"

I went into the bathroom. The face in the mirror looked as if it were trying to flirt with me. The left eye wouldn't stop winking.

When I returned to the bedroom, Carole reminded me that I'd not made today's recording. I didn't want to do it because I was so tired. But the possibility of losing another day's memory spurred me. No, not another day, I thought. If this occurs tomorrow, I'll lose another four days. Tomorrow and the three preceding May 25. I'll wake up June 3 and think it's the morning of the twenty-second.

I'm making this downstairs in my study. I wouldn't want Carole to hear some of my comments. Until tomorrow then. It's not tomorrow but yesterday that won't come. I'll make a note to myself and stick it in a corner of the case which holds my glasses.

↷ Six ↶

True date: June 3, 1980

I woke up thinking that today was my birthday, May 22. I rolled over, saw the piece of paper half-stuck from my glasses case, put on my glasses and read the note.

It didn't enlighten me: I didn't remember writing the note. And why should I go downstairs and turn on the recorder? But I did so.

As I listened to the machine, my heart thudded as if it were a judge's gavel. My voice kept fading in and out. Was I going to faint?

And so half of today was wasted trying to regain twelve days in my mind. I didn't go to the office, and the kids went to school late. And what about the kids in school on the dayside of Earth? If they sleep during their geometry class, say, then they have to go through that class again on the same day. And that shoves the schedule forward, or is it backward, for that day. And then there's the time workers will lose on their jobs. They have to make it up, which means they get out an hour later. Only it takes more than an hour to recover from the confusion and get orientated. What a mess it has been! What a mess it'll be if this keeps on!

At eleven, Carole and I were straightened out enough to go to the supermarket. It was Tuesday, but Carole wanted me to be with her, so I tried to phone in and tell my secretary I'd be absent. The lines were tied up, and I doubt that she was at work. So I said to hell with it.

Our supermarket usually opens at eight. Not today. We had to stand in a long line, which kept getting longer. The doors opened at twelve. The manager, clerks and boys had had just as much trouble as we did unconfusing themselves, of course. Some didn't show at all. And some of the trucks which were to bring fresh stores never appeared.

By the time Carole and I got inside, those ahead of us had cleaned out half the supplies. They had the same idea we had. Load up now so there wouldn't be any standing in line so many times. The fresh milk was all gone, and the powdered milk shelf had one box left. I started for it but some teenager beat me to it. I felt like hitting him, but I didn't, of course.

The prices for everything were being upped by a fourth even as we shopped. Some of the stuff was being marked upward once more while we stood in line at the checkout counter. From the time we entered the line until we pushed out three overflowing carts, four hours had passed.

While Carole put away the groceries, I drove to another super-market. The line there was a block long; it would be emptied and closed up before I ever got to its doors.

The next two supermarkets and a corner grocery store were just as hopeless. And the three liquor stores I went to were no better. The fourth only had about thirty men in line, so I tried that. When I got inside, all the beer was gone, which didn't bother me any, but the only hard stuff left was a fifth of rotgut. I drank it when I went to college because I couldn't afford anything better. I put the terrible stuff and a half-gallon of cheap muscatel on the counter. Anything was better than nothing, even though the prices had been doubled.

I started to take out the check, but the clerk said, "Sorry, sir. Cash only."

"What?" I said.

"Haven't you heard, sir?" he said.

"The banks were closed at 2:00 P.M. today."

"The banks are closed?" I said. I sounded stupid even to myself.

"Yes, sir," he said. "By the federal government. It's only temporary, sir, at least that's what the TV said. They'll be reopened after the stock market mess is cleared up."

"But . . ." I said.

"It's destructed," he said.

"Destroyed," I said autonomically. "You mean, it's another Black Friday?"

"It's Tuesday today," he said.

"You're too young to know the reference," I said. And too uneducated, too, I thought.

"The president is going to set up a rationing system," he said. "For the interim. And price controls, too. Turner said so on TV an hour ago. The president is going to lay it all out at six tonight."

When I came home, I found Carole in front of the TV. She was pale and wide-eyed.

"There's going to be another depression!" she said. "Oh, Mark, what are we going to do?"

"I don't know," I said. "I'm not the president, you know." And I slumped down onto the sofa. I had lost my flippancy. Neither of us, having been born in 1945, knew what a Depression, with a big capital D, was; that is, we hadn't experienced it personally. But we'd heard our parents, who were kids when it happened, talk about it. Carole's parents had gotten along, though they didn't live well, but my father used to tell me about days when he had nothing but stale bread and turnips to eat and was happy to get them.

The president's TV speech was mostly about the depression, which he claimed would be temporary. At the end of half an hour of optimistic talk, he revealed why he thought the situation wouldn't last. The federal government wasn't going to wait for the sentients in The Ball—if there were any there—to communicate with us. Obviously, The Ball was hostile. So the survey expedition had been canceled. Tomorrow, the USA, the USSR, France, West Germany, Israel, India, Japan and China would send up an armada of rockets tipped with H-bombs. The orbits and the order of battle were determined this morning by computers; one after the other, the missiles would zero in until The Ball was completely destroyed. It would be overkill with a vengeance.

"That ought to bring up the stock market!" I said.

And so, after I've finished recording, to bed. Tomorrow, we'll follow our instructions on the notes, relisten to the tapes, reread certain sections of the newspapers and await the news on the TV. To hell with going to the courthouse; nobody's going to be there anyway.

Oh, yes. With all this confusion and excitement, everybody, myself included, forgot that today was my birthday. Wait a minute! It's *not* my birthday!

True date: June 5, 1980. Subjective date: May 16, 1980

I woke up mad at Carole because of our argument the previous day. Not that of June 4, of course, but our brawl of May 15. We'd been at a party given by the Burlingtons, where I met a beautiful young artist, Roberta Gardner. Carole thought I was paying too much attention to her because she looked like Myrna. Maybe I was. On the other hand, I really was interested in her paintings. It seemed to me that she had a genuine talent. When we got home, Carole tore into me, accused me of still being in love with Myrna. My protests did no good whatsoever. Finally, I told her we might as well get a divorce if she couldn't forgive and forget. She ran crying out of the room and slept on the sofa downstairs.

I don't remember what reconciled us, of course, but we must have worked it out, otherwise we wouldn't still be married.

Anyway, I woke up determined to see a divorce lawyer today. I was sick about what Mike and Tom would have to go through. But it would be better for them to be spared our terrible quarrels. I can remember my reactions when I was an adolescent and overheard my parents fighting. It was a relief, though a sad one, when they separated.

Thinking this, I reached for my glasses. And I found the note. And so another voyage into confusion, disbelief and horror.

Now that the panic has eased off somewhat, May 16 is back in the saddle—somewhat. Carole and I are, in a sense, still in that day, and things are a bit cool.

It's 1:00 P.M. now. We just watched the first rockets take off. Ten of them, one after the other.

It's 1:35 P.M. Via satellite, we watched the Japanese missiles.

We just heard that the Chinese and Russian rockets are being launched. When the other nations send theirs up, there will be thirty-seven in all.

No news at 12:30 A.M., June 5. In this case, no news must be bad news. But what could have happened? The newscasters won't say; they just talk around the subject.

ᏸ SEVEN ᏸ

True date: June 6, 1980. Subjective date: May 13, 1980

My records say that this morning was just like the other four. Hell.

One o'clock. The president, looking like a sad old man, though he's only forty-four, reported the catastrophe. All thirty-seven rockets were blown up by their own H-bombs about three thousand miles from The Ball. We saw some photographs of them taken from the orbiting labs. They weren't very impressive. No mushroom clouds, of course, and not even much light.

The Ball has weapons we can't hope to match. And if it can

activate our H-bombs out in space, it should be able to do the same to those on Earth's surface. My God! It could wipe out all life if it wished to do so!

Near the end of the speech, the president did throw out a line of hope. With a weak smile—he was trying desperately to give us his big vote-winning one—he said that all was not lost by any means. A new plan, called Project Toro, was being drawn up even as he spoke.

Toro was Spanish for bull, I thought, but I didn't say so. Carole and the kids wouldn't have thought it funny, and I didn't think it was so funny myself. Anyway, I thought, maybe it's a Japanese word meaning *victory* or *destruction* or something like that.

Toro, as it turned out, was the name of a small irregularly shaped asteroid about 2.413 kilometers long and 1.609 kilometers wide. Its peculiar orbit had been calculated in 1972 by an L. Danielsson of the Swedish Royal Institute of Technology and a W. H. Ip of the University of California at San Diego. Toro, the president said, was bound into a resonant orbit with the Earth. Each time Toro came near the Earth—"near" was sometimes 12.6 million miles—it got exactly enough energy or "kick" from the Earth to push it on around so that it would come back for another near passage.

But the orbit was unstable, which meant that both Earth and Venus take turns controlling the asteroid. For a few centuries, Earth governs Toro; then Venus takes over. Earth has controlled Toro since A.D. 1580, Venus will take over in 2200. Earth grabs it again in 2350; Venus gets it back in 2800.

I was wondering what all this stuff about this celestial Ping-Pong game was about. Then the president said that it was possible to land rockets on Toro. In fact, the plan called for many shuttles to land there carrying parts of huge rocket motors, which would be assembled on Toro.

When the motors were erected on massive and deep stands, power would be applied to nudge Toro out of its orbit. This would require many trips by many rockets with cargoes of fuel and spare parts for the motors. The motors would burn out a number of times. Eventually, though, the asteroid would be placed in an orbit that would end in a direct collision with The Ball. Toro's millions of tons of hard rock and nickel-steel would destroy The Ball utterly, would turn it into pure energy.

"Yes," I said aloud, "but what's to keep The Ball from just changing its orbit? Its sensors will detect the asteroid; it'll change course; Toro will go on by it, like a train on a track."

This was the next point of the president's speech. The failure of the attack had revealed at least one item of information, or, rather, verified it. The radiation of the H-bombs had blocked off, disrupted, all control and observation of the rockets by radar and laser. In their final approach, the rockets had gone in blind, as it were, unable to be regulated from Earth. But if the bombs did this to our sensors, they must be doing the same to The Ball's.

So, just before Toro's course is altered to send it into its final path, H-bombs will be set off all around The Ball. In effect, it will be enclosed in a sphere of radiation. It will have no sensor capabilities. Nor will The Ball believe that it will have to alter its orbit to dodge Toro. It will have calculated that Toro's orbit won't endanger it. After the radiation fills the space around it, it won't be able to see that Toro is being given a final series of nudges to push it into a collision course.

The project is going to require immense amounts of materials and manpower. The USA can't handle it alone; Toro is going to be a completely international job. What one nation can't provide, the other will.

The president ended with a few words about how Project Toro, plus the situation of memory loss, is going to bring about a radical revision of the economic setup. He's going to announce the outlines of the new structure—not just policy but structure—two days from now.

It'll be designed, so he says, to restore prosperity and, not incidentally, rid society of many problems plaguing it since the industrial revolution.

"Yes, but how long will Project Toro take?" I said. "Oh, Lord, how long?"

Six years, the president said, as if he'd heard me. Perhaps longer. Six years!

I didn't tell Carole what I could see coming. But she's no dummy.

She could figure out some of the things that were to happen in six years, and none of them were good.

I never felt so hopeless in my life, and neither did she. But we do have each other, and so we clung tightly for a while. May 16 isn't forgotten, but it seems so unimportant. Mike and Tom cried, I suppose because they knew that this exhibition of love meant something terrible for all of us. Poor kids! They get upset by our hatreds and then become even more upset by our love.

When we realized what we were doing to them we tried to be jolly. But we couldn't get them to smile.

True date: middle of 1981. Subjective date: middle of 1977

I'm writing this, since I couldn't get any new tapes today. The shortage is only temporary, I'm told. I could erase part of the old ones and use them, but it'd be like losing a vital part of myself. And God knows I've lost enough.

Old Mrs. Douglas next door is dead. Killed herself, according to my note on the calendar, April 2 of this year. I never would have thought she'd do it. She was such a strong fundamentalist, and these believe as strongly as the Roman Catholics that suicide is well-nigh unforgivable. I suspect that the double shock of her husband's death caused her to take her own life. April 2 of 1976 was the day he died. She had to be hospitalized because of the shock and grief for two weeks after his death. Carole and I had her over to dinner a few times after she came home, and all she could talk about was her dead husband. So I presume that, as she traveled backward to the day of his death, the grief became daily more unbearable. She couldn't face the arrival of the day he died.

Hers is not the only empty house on the block. Jack Bridger killed his wife and his three kids and his mother-in-law and himself last month—according to my records. Nobody knows why, but

I suspect that he couldn't stand seeing his three-year-old girl become no more than an idiot. She'd retrogressed to the day of her birth and beyond. She'd lost her language abilities and could no longer feed herself. Strangely, she could still walk, and her intelligence potential was high. She had the brain of a three-year-old, fully developed but lacking all postbirth experience. It would have been better if she hadn't been able to walk. Confined to a cradle, she would at least not have had to be watched every minute.

Little Ann's fate is going to be Tom's. He talks like a five-year-old now. And Mike's fate . . . my fate . . . Carole's . . . God! We'll end up like Ann! I can't stand thinking about it.

Carole. She has the toughest job. I'm away part of the day, she has to take care of what are, in effect, a five-year-old and an eight-year-old, getting younger every day. There is no relief for her, since they're always home. All educational institutions, except for certain research laboratories, are closed.

The president says we're going to convert ninety percent of all industries to cybernation. In fact, anything that can be cybernated will be. They have to be. Almost everything, from the mines to the loading equipment to the railroads and trucks and the unloading equipment and the arrangement and dispersal of the final goods at central distribution points.

Are six years enough to do this?

And who's going to pay for this? Never mind, he says. Money is on its way out. The president is a goddamned radical. He's taking advantage of this situation to put over his own ideas, which he sure as hell never revealed during his campaign for election. Sometimes I wonder who put The Ball up there. But that idea is sheer paranoia. At least, this gigantic WPA project is giving work to those who are able to work. The rest are on, or going to be on, a minimum guaranteed income, and I mean minimum. But the president says that, in time, everybody will have all he needs, and more, in the way of food, housing, schooling, clothing, etc. *He* says! What if Project Toro doesn't work? And what if it does work? Are we then going to return to the old economy? Of course not! It'll be impossible to abandon everything we've worked on; the new establishment will see to that.

I tried to find out where Myrna lived. I'm making this record in my office, so Carole isn't going to get hold of it. I love her— Myrna, I mean—passionately. I hired her two weeks ago and fell headlong, burningly, in love with her. All this was in 1977 of course, but today, inside of *me*, is 1977.

Carole doesn't know about this, of course. According to the letters and notes from Myrna, which I should have destroyed but, thank God; never had the heart to do, Carole didn't find out about Myrna until two years later. At least that's what this letter from Myrna says. She was away visiting her sister then and wrote to me in answer to my letter. A good thing, too, otherwise I wouldn't know what went on then.

My reason tells me to forget about Myrna. And so I will.

I've traveled backward in our affair, from our final bitter parting, to this state, when I was most in love with her. I know this because I've just reread the records of our relationship. It began deteriorating about six months before we split up, but I don't feel those emotions now, of course. And in two weeks I won't feel anything for her. If I don't refer to the records, I won't even know she ever existed.

This thought is intolerable. I have to find her, but I've had no success at all so far. In fourteen days, no, five, since every day ahead takes three more of the past, I'll have no drive to locate her. Because I won't know what I'm missing.

I don't hate Carole. I love her, but with a cool much-married love. Myrna makes me feel like a boy again. I burn exquisitely.

But where is Myrna?

True date: October 30, 1981

I ran into Brackwell Lee, the old mystery story writer today. Like most writers who haven't gone to work for the government propaganda office, he's in a bad way financially. He's surviving on his GMI, but for him there are no more first editions of rare books, new sports cars, Western Reserve or young girls. I stood him three shots of the rotgut which is the only whiskey now served at

Grover's and listened to the funny stories he told to pay me for the drinks. But I also had to listen to his tales of woe.

Nobody buys fiction, or, in fact, any long works of any kind anymore. Even if you're a speed reader and go through a whole novel in one day, you have to start all over again the next time you pick it up. TV writing, except for the propaganda shows, is no alternative. The same old shows are shown every day and enjoyed just as much as yesterday or last year. According to my records, I've seen the hilarious pilot movie of the "Soap Opera Blues" series fifty times.

When old Lee talked about how he had been dropped by the young girls, he got obnoxiously weepy. I told him that that didn't say much for him or the girls either. But if he didn't want to be hurt, why didn't he erase those records that noted his rejections?

He didn't want to do that, though he could give me no logical reason why he shouldn't.

"Listen," I said with a sudden drunken inspiration, "why don't you erase the old records and make some new ones? How you laid this and that beautiful young thing. Describe your conquests in detail. You'll think you're the greatest Casanova that ever lived."

"But that wouldn't be true!" he said.

"You, a writer of lies, say that?" I said. "Anyway, you wouldn't know that they weren't the truth."

"Yeah," he said, "but if I get all charged up and come barreling down here to pick up some tail, I'll be rejected and so'll be right back where I was."

"Leave a stern note to yourself to listen to them only late at night, say, an hour before The Ball puts all to sleep. That way, you won't ever get hurt."

George Palmer wandered in then. I asked him how things were doing.

"I'm up to here handling cases for kids who can't get drivers' licenses," he said. "It's true you can teach anybody how to drive in a day, but the lessons are forgotten the next day. Anyway, it's experience that makes a good driver, and . . . need I explain more?

The kids have to have cars, so they drive them regardless. Hence, as you no doubt have forgotten, the traffic accidents and violations are going up and up."

"Is that right?" I said.

"Yeah. There aren't too many in the mornings, since most people don't go to work until noon. However, the new transit system should take care of that when we get it, sometime in 1984 or 5."

"What new transit system?" I said.

"It's been in the papers," he said. "I reread some of last week's this morning. The city of Los Angeles is equipped with a model system now, and it's working so well it's going to be extended throughout Los Angeles County. Eventually, every city of any size in the country'll have it. Nobody'll have to walk more than four blocks to get to a line. It'll cut air pollution by half and the traffic load by three-thirds. Of course, it'll be compulsory; you'll have to show cause to drive a car. And I hate to think about the mess that's going to be, the paperwork, the pile-up in the courts and so forth. But after the way the government handled the L.A. riot, the rest of the country should get in line."

"How will the rest of the country know how the government handled it unless they're told?" I said.

"They'll be told. Every day," he said.

"Eventually, there won't be enough time in the day for the news channels to tell us all we'll need to know," I said. "And even if there were enough time, we'd have to spend all day watching TV. So who's going to get the work done?"

"Each person will have to develop his own viewing specialty," he said. "They'll just have to watch the news that concerns them and ignore the rest."

"And how can they do that if they won't know what concerns them until they've run through everything?" I said. "Day after day."

"I'll buy a drink," he said. "Liquor's good for one thing. It makes you forget what you're afraid not to forget."

❦ Eight ❦

True date: late 1982. Subjective date: late 1974

She came into my office, and I knew at once that she was going to be more than just another client. I'd been suffering all day from the "mirror syndrome," but the sight of her stabilized me. I forgot the thirty-seven-year-old face my twenty-nine-year-old mind had seen in the bathroom that morning. She is a beautiful woman, only twenty-seven. I had trouble at first listening to her story; all I wanted to do was to look at her. I finally understood that she wanted me to get her husband out of jail on a murder rap. It seemed he'd been in since 1976 (real time). She wanted me to get the case reopened, to use the new plea of rehabilitation by retrogression.

I was supposed to know that, but I had to take a quick look through my resumé before I could tell her what chance she had. Under RBR was the definition of the term and a notation that a number of people had been released because of it. The main idea behind it is that criminals are not the same people they were before they became criminals, if they have lost all memory of the crime. They've traveled backward to goodness, you might say. Of course, RBR doesn't apply to hardened criminals or to someone who'd planned a crime a long time before it was actually committed.

I asked her why she would want to help a man who had killed his mistress in a fit of rage when he'd found her cheating on him?

"I love him," she said.

And I love you, I thought.

She gave me some documents from the big rec bag she carried. I looked through them and said, "But you divorced him in 1977?"

"Yes, he's really my ex-husband," she said. "But I think of him now as my husband."

No need to ask her why.

"I'll study the case," I said. "You make a note to see me tomorrow. Meantime, how about a drink at the Rover bar so we can discuss our strategy?"

That's how it all started—again.

It wasn't until a week later, when I was going over some old recs, that I discovered it was *again*. It made no difference. I love her. I also love Carole, rather, *a* Carole. The one who married me six years ago, that is, six years ago in my memory.

But there is the other Carole, the one existing today, the poor miserable wretch who can't get out of the house until I come home. And I can't come home until late evening because I can't get started to work until about twelve noon. It's true that I could come home earlier than I do if it weren't for Myrna. I try. No use. I have to see Myrna.

I tell myself I'm a bastard, which I am, because Carole and the children need me very much. Tom is ten and acts as if he's two. Mike is a four-year-old in a twelve-year-old body. I come home from Myrna to bedlam every clay, according to my records, and every day must be like today.

That I feel both guilt and shame doesn't help. I become enraged; I try to suppress my anger, which is born out of my desperation and helplessness and guilt and shame. But it comes boiling out, and then bedlam becomes hell.

I tell myself that Carole and the kids need a tower of strength now. One who can be calm and reassuring and, above all, loving. One who can handle the thousand tedious and aggravating problems that infest every household in this world of diminishing memory. In short, a hero. Because the real heroes, and heroines, are those who deal heroically with the everyday cares of life, though God knows they've been multiplied enormously. It's not the guy who kills a dragon once in his lifetime and then retires that's a hero. It's the guy who kills cockroaches and rats every day, day after day, and doesn't rest on his laurels until he's an old man, if then.

What am I talking about? Maybe I could handle the problems if it weren't for this memory loss. I can't adjust because I can't ever get used to it. My whole being, body and mind, must get the same high-voltage jolt every morning.

The insurance companies have canceled all policies for anybody under twelve. The government's contemplated taking over these policies but has decided against it. It will, however, pay for the burials, since this service is necessary. I don't really think that many children are being "accidentally" killed because of the insurance money. Most fatalities are obviously just results of neglect or parents going berserk.

I'm getting away from Myrna, trying to, anyway, because I wish to forget my guilt. I love her, but if I didn't see her tomorrow, I'd forget her. But I *will* see her tomorrow. My notes will make sure of that. And each day is, for me, love at first sight. It's a wonderful feeling, and I wish it could go on forever.

If I just had the guts to destroy all reference to her tonight. But I won't. The thought of losing her makes me panic.

✑ Nine ✑

True date: middle of 1984. Subjective date: middle of 1968

I was surprised that I woke up so early.

Yesterday, Carole and I had been married at noon. We'd driven up to this classy motel near Lake Geneva. We'd spent most of our time in bed after we got there, naturally, though we did get up for dinner and champagne. We finally fell asleep about four in the morning. That was why I hadn't expected to wake up at dawn. I reached over to touch Carole, wondering if she would be too sleepy. But she wasn't there.

She's gone to the bathroom, I thought. I'll catch her on the way back.

Then I sat up, my heart beating as if it had suddenly discovered it was alive. The edges of the room got fuzzy, and then the fuzziness raced in toward me.

The dawn light was filtered by the blinds, but I had seen that the furniture was not familiar. I'd never been in this place before.

I sprang out of bed and did not, of course, notice the note sticking out of my glass case. Why should I? I didn't wear glasses then.

Bellowing, "Carole!" I ran down a long and utterly strange hall and past the bedroom door, which was open, and into the room at the end of the hall. Inside it, I stopped. This was a kids' bedroom: bunks, pennants, slogans, photographs of two young boys, posters and blowups of faces I'd never seen, except one of Laurel and Hardy, some science fiction and Tolkien and Tarzan books, some school texts, and a large flat piece of equipment hanging on the wall. I would not have known that it was a TV set if its controls had not made its purpose obvious.

The bunks had not been slept in. The first rays of the sun fell on thick dust on a table.

I ran back down the hall, looked into the bathroom again, though I knew no one was there, saw dirty towels, underwear and socks heaped in a corner, and ran back to my bedroom. The blinds did not let enough light in, so I looked for a light switch on the wall. There wasn't any, though there was a small round plate of brass where the switch should have been. I touched it, and the ceiling lights came on.

Carole's side of the bed had not been slept in.

The mirror over the bureau caught me, drew me and held me. Who was this haggard old man staring out from my twenty-three-year-old self? I had gray hair, big bags under my eyes, thickening and sagging features, and a long scar on my right cheek.

After a while, still dazed and trembling, I picked up a book from the bureau and looked at it. At this close distance, I could just barely make out the title, and, when I opened it, the print was a blur.

I put the book down, *Be Your Own Handyman around Your House*, and proceeded to go through the house from attic to basement. Several times, I whimpered, "Carole! Carole!" Finding no one, I left the house and walked to the house next door and beat on its door. No one answered; no lights came on inside.

I ran to the next house and tried to wake up the people in it. But there weren't any.

A woman in a house across the street shouted at me. I ran to her, babbling. She was about fifty years old and also hysterical.

A moment later, a man her age appeared behind her. Neither listened to me; they kept asking me questions, the same questions I was asking them. Then I saw a black and white police car of a model unknown to me come around the corner half a block away. I ran toward it, then stopped. The car was so silent that I knew even in my panic that it was electrically powered. The two cops wore strange uniforms, charcoal gray with white helmets topped by red panaches. Their aluminum badges were in the shape of a spread eagle.

I found out later that the police throughout the country had been federalized. These two were on the night shift and so had had enough time to get reorientated. Even so, one had such a case of the shakes that the other told him to get back into the car and take it easy for a while.

After he got us calmed down, he asked us why we hadn't listened to our tapes.

"What tapes?" we said.

'Where's your bedroom?" he said to the couple.

They led him to it, and he turned on a machine on the bedside table "Good morning," a voice said. I recognized it as the husband's.

"Don't panic. Stay in bed and listen to me. Listen to everything I say."

The rest was a resumé, by no means short, of the main events since the first day of memory loss. It ended by directing the two to a notebook that would tell them personal things they needed to know, such as where their jobs were, how they could get to them, where the area central distributing stores were, how to use their I.D. cards and so on.

The policeman said, "You have the rec set to turn on at 6:30, but you woke up before then. Happens a lot."

I went back, reluctantly, to the house I'd fled. It was mine, but I felt as if I were a stranger. I ran off my own recs twice. Then I put my glasses on and started to put together my life. The daily rerun of "Narrative of an Old-Young Man Shipwrecked on the Shoals of Time."

I didn't go any place today. Why should I? I had no job. Who needs a lawyer who isn't through law school yet? I did have, I found out, an application in for a position on the police force. The police force was getting bigger and bigger but at the same time was having a large turnover. My recs said that I was to appear at the City Hall for an interview tomorrow.

If I feel tomorrow as I do today, and I will, I probably won't be able to make myself go to the interview. I'm too grief-stricken to do anything but sit and stare or, now and then, get up and pace back and forth, like a sick leopard in a cage made by Time. Even the tranquilizers haven't helped me much.

I have lost my bride the day after we were married. And I love Carole deeply. We were going to live a long happy life and have two children. We would raise them in a house filled with love.

But the recs say that the oldest boy escaped from the house and was killed by a car and Carole, in a fit of anguish and despair, killed the youngest boy and then herself.

They're buried in Springdale Cemetery. I can't feel a retroactive grief for those strangers called Mike and Tom.

But Carole, lovely laughing Carole, lives in my mind.

Oh, God, why don't I just erase all my recs? Then I'd not have to suffer remorse for all I've done or failed to do. I wouldn't know what a bastard I'd been.

Why don't I do it? Take the past and shed its heartbreaks and its guilts as a snake sheds its skin. Or as the legislature cancels old laws. Press a button, fill the wastebasket, and you're clean and easy again, innocent again. That's the logical thing to do, and I'm a lawyer, dedicated to logic.

Why not? Why not?

But I can't. Maybe I like to suffer. I've liked to inflict suffering and, according to what I understand, those who like to inflict, unconsciously hope to be inflicted upon.

No, that can't be it. At least, not all of it. My main reason for hanging on to the recs is that I don't want to lose my identity. A major part of me, a unique person, is not in the neurons of my mind, where it belongs, but in an electro-mechanical device or in tracings of lead or ink on paper. The protein, the flesh for which I owe, can't hang on to me.

I'm becoming less and less, dwindling away, like the wicked witch on whom Dorothy poured water. I'll become a puddle, a wailing voice of hopeless despair, and then . . . nothing.

God, haven't I suffered enough! I said I owe for the flesh and I'm down in Your books. Why do I have to struggle each day against becoming a dumb brute, a thing without memory? Why not rid myself of the struggle? Press the button, fill the waste-basket, discharge my grief in a chaos of magnetic lines and pulped paper?

Sufficient unto the day is the evil thereof.

I didn't realize, Lord, what that really meant.

∾ TEN ∾

I will marry Carole in three days. No, I would have. No, I did.

I remember reading a collection of Krazy Kat comic strips when I was twenty-one. One was captioned: COMA REIGNS. Coconing County was in the doldrums, comatose. Nobody, Krazy Kat, Ignatz Mouse, Officer Pupp, nobody had the energy to do anything. Mouse was too lazy even to think about hurling his brickbat. Strange how that sticks in my mind. Strange to think that it won't be long before it becomes forever unstuck.

Coma reigns today over the world.

Except for Project Toro, the TV says. And that is behind schedule. But the Earth, Ignatz Mouse, will not allow itself to forget that it must hurl the brickbat, the asteroid. But where Ignatz expressed his love, in a queer perverted fashion, by banging Kat in the back of the head with his brick, the world is expressing its hatred, and its desperation, by throwing Toro at The Ball.

I did manage today to go downtown to my appointment. I did it only to keep from going mad with grief. I was late, but Chief Moberly seemed to expect that I would be. Almost everybody is, he said. One reason for my tardiness was that I got lost. This residential area was nothing in 1968 but a forest out past the edge of town. I don't have a car and the house is in the middle of the area, which has many winding streets. I do have a map of the area, which I forgot about. I kept going eastward and finally carne to a main thoroughfare. This was Route 98, over which I've traveled many times since I was a child. But the road itself, and the houses along it, were strange. The private airport which should have been across the road was gone, replaced by a number of large industrial buildings.

A big sign near a roofed bench told me to wait there for the RTS bus. One would be along every ten minutes, the sign stated.

I waited an hour. The bus, when it came, was not the fully automated vehicle promised by the sign. It held a sleepy-looking driver and ten nervous passengers. The driver didn't ask me for money, so I didn't offer any. I sat down and watched him with an occasional look out of the window. He didn't have a steering wheel. When he wanted the bus to slow down or stop he pushed a lever forward. To speed it up, he pulled back on the lever. The bus was apparently following a single aluminum rail in the middle of the right-hand lane. My recs told me later that the automatic pilot and door-opening equipment had never been delivered and probably wouldn't be for some years—if ever. The grand plan of cybernating everything possible had failed. There aren't enough people who can provide the know-how or the man-hours. In fact, everything is going to hell.

The police chief, Adam Moberly, is fifty years old and looks as if he's sixty-five. He talked to me for about fifteen minutes and then had me put through a short physical and intelligence test. Three hours after I had walked into the station, I was sworn in. He suggested that I room with two other officers, one of whom was a sixty-year-old veteran, in the hotel across the street from the station. If I had company, I'd get over the morning disorientation more quickly. Besides, the policemen who lived in the central area of the city got preferential treatment in many things, including the rationed supplies.

I refused to move. I couldn't claim that my house was a home to me, but I feel that it's a link to the past, I mean the future, no, I mean the past. Leaving it would be cutting out one more part of me.

Philip José Farmer

True date: late 1984. Subjective date: early 1967

My mother died today. That is, as far as I'm concerned, she did. The days ahead of me are going to be full of anxiety and grief. She took a long time to die. She found out she had cancer two weeks after my father died. So I'll be voyaging backward in sorrow through my mother and then through my father, who was also sick for a long time.

Thank God I won't have to go through every day of that, though. Only a third of them. And these are the last words I'm going to record about their illnesses.

But how can I not record them unless I make a recording reminding me not to do so?

I found out from my recs how I'd gotten this big scar on my face. Myrna's ex-husband slashed me before I laid him out with a big ashtray. He was shipped off this time to a hospital for the criminally insane where he died a few months later in the fire that burned every prisoner in his building. I haven't the faintest idea what happened to Myrna after that. Apparently I decided not to record it.

I feel dead tired tonight, and, according to my recs, every night. It's no wonder, if every day is like today. Fires, murders, suicides, accidents and insane people. Babies up to fourteen years old abandoned. And a police department which is ninety percent composed, in effect, of raw rookies. The victims are taken to hospitals where the nurses are only half-trained, if that, and the doctors are mostly old geezers hauled out of retirement.

I'm going to bed soon even if it's only nine o'clock. I'm so exhausted that even Jayne Mansfield couldn't keep me awake. And I dread tomorrow. Besides the usual reasons for loathing it, I have one which I can hardly stand thinking about.

Tomorrow my memory will have slid past the day I met Carole I won't remember her at all.

Why do I cry because I'll be relieved of a great sorrow?

ℭℌ Eleven ℭℌ

True date: 1986. Subjective date: 1962

I'm nuts about Jean, and I'm way down because I can't find her. According to my recs, she went to Canada in 1965. Why? We surely didn't fall in and then out of love? Our love would never die. Her parents must've moved to Canada. And so here we both are in 1962, in effect. Halfway in 1962, anyway. Amphibians of time. Is she thinking about me now? Is she unable to think about me, about anything, because she's dead or crazy? Tomorrow I'll start the official wheels grinding. The Canadian government should be able to find her through the International Information Computer Network, according to the recs. Meanwhile, I burn, though with a low flame. I'm so goddamn tired.

Even Marilyn Monroe couldn't get a rise out of me tonight. But Jean. Yeah, Jean. I see her as seventeen years old, tall, slim but full-busted, with creamy white skin and a high forehead and huge blue eyes and glossy black hair and the most kissable lips ever. And broadcasting sex waves so thick you can see them, like heat waves. Wow!

And so tired old Wow goes to bed.

February 6, 1987

While I was watching TV to get orientated this morning, a news flash interrupted the program. The president of the United States had died of a heart attack a few minutes before.

"My God!" I said. "Old Eisenhower is dead!"

But the picture of the president certainly wasn't that of Eisenhower. And the name was one I never heard, of course.

I can't feel bad for a guy I never knew.

I got to thinking about him, though. Was he as confused every morning as I was? Imagine a guy waking up, thinking he's a senator in Washington and then he finds he's the president? At least, he knows something about running the country. But it's no wonder the old pump conked out. The TV says we've had five prexies, mostly real old guys, in the last seven years. One was shot; one dived out of the White House window onto his head; two had heart attacks; one went crazy and almost caused a war, as if we didn't have grief enough, for crying out loud.

Even after the orientation, I really didn't get it. I guess I'm too dumb for anything to percolate through my dome.

A policeman called and told me I'd better get my ass down to work. I said I didn't feel up to it, besides, why would I want to be a cop? He said that if I didn't show, I might go to jail. So I showed.

True date: late 1988. Subjective date: 1956

Here I am, eleven years old, going on ten.

In one way, that is. The other way, here I am forty-three and going on about sixty. At least, that's what my face looks like to me. Sixty.

This place is just like a prison except some of us get treated like trusties. According to the work chart, I leave through the big iron gates every day at twelve noon with a demolition crew. We tore down five partly burned houses today. The gang chief, old Rogers, says it's just WPA work, whatever that is. Anyway, one of the guys I work with kept looking more and more familiar. Suddenly, I felt like I was going to pass out. I put down my sledge hammer and walked over to him, and I said, "Aren't you Stinky Davis?"

He looked funny and then he said, "Jesus! You're Gabby! Gabby Franham!"

I didn't like his using the Lord's name in vain, but I guess he can be excused.

Nothing would've tasted good the way I felt, but the sandwiches we got for breakfast, lunch and supper tasted like they had a dash of oil in them. Engine oil, I mean. The head honcho, he's eighty if he's a day, says his recs tell him they're derived from petroleum. The oil is converted into a kind of protein and then flavoring and stuff is added. Oil-burgers, they call them.

Tonight, before lights-out, we watched the prez give a speech. He said that, within a month, Project Toro will be finished. One way or the other. And all this memory loss should stop. I can't quite get it even if I was briefed this morning. Men on the moon, unmanned ships on Venus and Mars, all since I was eleven years old. And The Black Ball, the thing from outer space. And now we're pushing asteroids around. Talk about your science fiction!

☙ Twelve ☙

September 4, 1988

Today's the day.

Actually, the big collision'll be tomorrow, ten minutes before 1:00 A.M. . . . but I think of it as today. Toro, going 15,000 miles an hour, will run head-on into The Ball. Maybe.

Here I am again, Mark Franham, recording just in case The Ball does dodge out of the way and I have to depend on my recs. It's 7:00 P.M. and after that raunchy supper of oil-burgers, potato soup and canned carrots, fifty of us gathered around set No. 8. There's a couple of scientists talking now, discussing theories about just what The Ball is and why it's been taking our memories away from us. Old Doctor Charles Presley—any relation to Elvis?—thinks The Ball is some sort of unmanned survey ship. When it finds a planet inhabited by sentient life, sentient means intelligent, it takes specimens. Specimens of the mind that is. It unpeels people's minds four days' worth at a time, because that's all it's capable of. But it can do it to billions of specimens. It's like it was reading our minds but destroying the mind at the same time. Presley said it was like some sort of Heisenberg principle of the mind. The Ball can't observe our memories closely without disturbing them.

This Ball, Presley says, takes our memories and stores them. And when it's through with us, sucked us dry, it'll take off for another planet circling some far-off star. Someday, it'll return to its home planet, and the scientists there will study the recordings of our minds.

The other scientist, Dr. Marbles—he's still got his, ha! ha!—asked why any species advanced enough to be able to do this could be so callous? Surely, the extees must know what great damage they're doing to us. Wouldn't they be too ethical for this?

559

Doc Presley says maybe they think of us as animals, they are so far above us. Doc Marbles says that could be. But it could also be that whoever built The Ball have different brains than we do. Their mind-reading ray, or whatever it is, when used on themselves doesn't disturb the memory patterns. But we're different. The extees don't know this, of course. Not now, anyway. When The Ball goes home, and the extees read our minds, they'll be shocked at what they've done to us. But it'll be too late then.

Presley and Marbles got into an argument about how the extees would be able to interpret their recordings. How could they translate our languages when they have no references—I mean referents? How're they going to translate *chair* and *recs* and *rock and roll* and *yucky* and so on when they don't have anybody to tell them their meanings. Marbles said they wouldn't have just words; they'd have mental images to associate with the words. And so on. Some of the stuff they spouted I didn't understand at all.

I do know one thing, though, and I'm sure those bigdomes do, too. But they wouldn't be allowed to say it over TV because we'd be even more gloomy and hopeless-feeling. That is, what if right now the computers in The Ball are translating our languages, reading our minds, as they're recorded? Then they know all about Project Toro. They'll be ready for the asteroid, destroy it if they have the weapons to do it, or, if they haven't, they'll just move The Ball into a different orbit.

I'm not going to say anything to the other guys about this. Why make them feel worse?

It's ten o'clock now. According to regulations posted up all over the place, it's time to go to bed. But nobody is. Not tonight. You don't sleep when the End of the World may be coming up.

I wish my Mom and Dad were here. I cried this morning when I found they weren't in this dump, and I asked the chief where they were. He said they were working in a city nearby, but they'd be visiting me soon. I think he lied.

Stinky saw me crying, but he didn't say anything. Why should he? I'll bet he's shed a few when he thought nobody was looking, too.

Twelve o'clock. Midnight. Less than an hour to go. Then, the big smash! Or, I hate to think about it, the big flop. We won't be able to see it directly because the skies are cloudy over most of North America.

But we've got a system worked out so we can see it on TV. If there's a gigantic flash when the Toro and The Ball collide, that is.

What if there isn't? Then we'll soon be just like those grown-up kids, some of them twenty years old, that they keep locked up in the big building in the northwest corner of this place. Saying nothing but Da Da or Ma Ma, drooling, filling their diapers. If they got diapers, because old Rogers says he heard, today, of course, they don't wear nothing. The nurses come in once a day and hose them and the place down. The nurses don't have time to change and wash diapers and give personal baths. They got enough to do just spoon-feeding them.

Three and a half more hours to go, and I'll be just like them. Unless, before then, I flip, and they put me in that building old Rogers calls the puzzle factory. They're all completely out of their skulls, he says, and even if memloss stops tonight, they won't change any.

Old Rogers says there's fifty million less people in the United States than there were in 1980, according to the recs. And a good thing, too, he says, because it's all we can do to feed what we got.

Come on, Toro! You're our last chance!

If Toro doesn't make it, I'll kill myself! I will! I'm not going to let myself become an idiot. Anyway, by the time I do become one, there won't be enough food to go around for those that do have their minds.

I'll be starving to death. I'd rather get it over with now than go through that.

God'll forgive me.

God, You know I want to be a minister of the gospel when I grow up and that I want to help people. I'll marry a good woman, and we'll have children that'll be brought up right. And we'll thank You every day for the good things of life and battle the bad things.

Love, that's what I got, Lord. Love for You and love for Your people. So don't make me hate You. Guide Toro right into The Ball, and get us started on the right path again.

I wish Mom and Dad were here.

Twelve-thirty. In twenty minutes, we'll know.

The TV says the H-bombs are still going off all around The Ball.

The TV says the people on the East Coast are falling asleep. The rays, or whatever The Ball uses, aren't being affected by the H-bomb radiation. But that doesn't mean that its sensors aren't. I pray to God that they are cut off.

Ten minutes to go. Toro's got twenty-five thousand miles to go.

Our sensors can't tell whether or not The Ball's still on its original orbit. I hope it is; I hope it is! If it's changed its path, then we're through! Done! Finished! Wiped out!

Five minutes to go; twelve thousand five hundred miles to go.

I can see in my mind's eye The Ball, almost half a mile in diameter, hurtling on its orbit, blind as a bat, I hope and pray, the bombs, the last of the five thousand bombs, flashing, and Toro, a mile and a half long, a mile wide, millions of tons of rock and nickel-steel, charging toward its destined spot.

If it *is* destined.

But space *is* big, and even the Ball and Toro are small compared to all that emptiness out there. What if the mathematics of the scientists is just a little off, or the rocket motors on Toro aren't working just like they're supposed to, and Toro just tears on by The Ball? It's got to meet The Ball at the exact time and place, it's just got to!

I wish the radars and lasers could see what's going on.

Maybe it's better they can't. If we knew that The Ball had changed course . . . but this way we still got hope.

If Toro misses, I'll kill myself, I swear it.

Two minutes to go. One hundred and twenty seconds. The big room is silent except for kids like me praying or talking quietly into our recs or praying and talking and sobbing.

The TV says the bombs have quit exploding. No more flashes until Toro hits The Ball—if it does. Oh, God, let it hit, let it hit!

The unmanned satellites are going to open their camera lenses at the exact second of impact and take a quick shot. The cameras are encased in lead, the shutters are lead, and the equipment is special, mostly mechanical, not electrical, almost like a human eyeball. If the cameras see the big flash, they'll send an electrical impulse through circuits, also encased in lead, to a mechanism that'll shoot a big thin-shelled ball out. This is crammed with flashpowder, the same stuff photographers use, and mixed with oxygen pellets so the powder will ignite.

There's to be three of the biggest flashes you ever saw. Three. Three for Victory.

If Toro misses, then only one flashball'll be set off.

Oh, Lord, don't let it happen!

Planes with automatic pilots'll be cruising above the clouds, and their equipment will see the flashes and transmit them to the ground TV equipment.

One minute to go.

Come on, God!

Don't let it happen, please don't let it happen, that some place way out there, some thousands of years from now, some weird-looking character reads this and finds out to his horror what his people have done to us. Will he feel bad about it? Lot of good that'll do. You, out there, I hate you! God, how I hate you!

Our Father which art in Heaven, fifteen seconds, Hallowed be Thy name, ten seconds, Thy will be done, five seconds, Thy will be done, but if it's thumbs, down, God, why? Why? What did I ever do to You?

The screen's blank! Oh, my God, the screen's blank! What happened? Transmission trouble? Or they're afraid to tell us the truth?

It's on! It's on!

YAAAAAAY!

⟋ THIRTEEN ⟋

July 4, A.D. 2002

I may erase this. If I have any sense, I will. If I had any sense, I wouldn't make it in the first place.

Independence Day, and we're still under an iron rule. But old Dick the Dictator insists that when there's no longer a need for strict control, the Constitution will be restored, and we'll be a democracy again.

He's ninety-five years old and can't last much longer. The vice-president is only eighty, but he's as tough an octogenarian as ever lived. And he's even more of a totalitarian than Dick. And when have men ever voluntarily relinquished power?

I'm one of the elite, so I don't have it so bad. Just being fifty-seven years old makes me a candidate for that class. In addition, I have my Ph.D. in education and I'm a part-time minister. I don't know why I say part-time, since there aren't any full-time ministers outside of the executives of the North American Council of Churches. The People can't afford full-time divines. Everybody has to work at least a ten hours a day. But I'm better off than many. I've been eating fresh beef and pork for three years now. I have a nice house I don't have to share with another family. The house isn't the one my recs say I once owned.

The People took it over to pay for back taxes. It did me no good to protest that property taxes had been canceled during The Interim. That, say the People, ended when The Ball was destroyed.

But how could I pay taxes on it when I was only eleven years old, in effect?

I went out this afternoon, it being a holiday, with Leona to Springdale. We put flowers on her parents' and sisters' graves, none of whom she remembers, and on my parents' and Carole's and the children's graves, whom I know only through the recs. I prayed for the forgiveness of Carole and the boys.

Near Carole's grave was Stinky Davis's. Poor fellow, he went berserk the night The Ball was destroyed and had to be put in a padded cell. Still mad, he died five years later.

I sometimes wonder why I didn't go mad, too. The daily shocks and jars of memloss should have made everyone fall apart. But a certain number of us were very tough, tougher than we deserved. Even so, the day-to-day attack by alarm syndromes did its damage. I'm sure that years of life were cut off the hardiest of us. We're the shattered generation. And this is bad for the younger ones, who'll have no older people to lead them in the next ten years or so.

Or is it such a bad thing?

At least, those who were in their early twenties or younger when The Ball was smashed are coming along fine. Leona herself was twenty then. She became one of my students in high school. She's thirty-five physically but only fifteen in what the kids call "intage" or internal age. But since education goes faster for adults, and all those humanities courses have been eliminated, she graduated from high school last June. She still wants to be a doctor of medicine, and God knows we need M.D.'s. She'll be forty before she gets her degree. We're planning on having two children, the maximum allowed, and it's going to be tough raising them while she's in school. But God will see us through.

As we were leaving the cemetery, Margie Oleander, a very pretty girl of twenty-five, approached us. She asked me if she could speak privately to me. Leona didn't like that, but I told her that Margie probably wanted to talk to me about her grades in my geometry class.

Margie did talk somewhat about her troubles with her lessons. But then she began to ask some questions about the political system. Yes, I'd better erase this, and if it weren't for old habits, I'd not be doing this now.

After a few minutes, I became uneasy. She sounded as if she were trying to get me to show some resentment about the current situation.

Is she an agent provocateur or was she testing me for potential membership in the underground?

Whatever she was doing, she was in dangerous waters. So was I. I told her to ask her political philosophy teacher for answers. She said she'd read the textbook, which is provided by the government. I muttered something about, "Render unto Caesar's what is Caesar's," and walked away.

But she came after me, and asked if I could talk to her in my office tomorrow. I hesitated and then said I would.

I wonder if I would have agreed if she weren't so beautiful?

When we got home, Leona made a scene. She accused me of chasing after the younger girls because she was too old to stimulate me. I told her that I was no senile King David, which she should be well aware of, and she said she's listened to my recs and she knew what kind of man I was. I told her I'd learned from my mistakes. I've gone over the recs of the missing years many times.

"Yes," she said, "you know about them intellectually. But you don't *feel* them!"

Which is true.

I'm outside now and looking up into the night. Up there, out there, loose atoms and molecules float around, cold and alone, debris of the memory records of The Ball, atoms and molecules of what were once incredibly complex patterns, the memories of thirty-two years of the lives of four and a half billion human beings. Forever lost, except in the mind of One.

Oh, Lord, I started all over again as an eleven-year-old. Don't let me make the same mistakes again.

You've given us tomorrow again, but we've very little past to guide us.

Tomorrow I'll be very cool and very professional with Margie. Not too much, of course, since there should be a certain warmth between teacher and pupil.

If only she did not remind me of . . . whom?

But that's impossible. I can remember nothing from The Interim. Absolutely nothing.

But what if there are different kinds of memory?

After King Kong Fell

The first half of the movie was grim and gray and somewhat tedious. Mr. Howller did not mind. That was, after all, realism. Those times had been grim and gray. Moreover, behind the tediousness was the promise of something vast and horrifying. The creeping pace and the measured ritualistic movements of the actors gave intimations of the workings of the gods. Unhurriedly, but with utmost confidence, the gods were directing events toward the climax.

Howller had felt that at the age of fifteen, and he felt it now while watching the show on TV at the age of fifty-five. Of course, when he first saw it in 1933, he had known what was coming. Hadn't he lived through some of the events only two years before that?

The old freighter, the *Wanderer*, was nosing blindly through the fog toward the surflike roar of the natives' drums. And then: the commercial. Mr. Howller rose and stepped into the hall and called down the steps loudly enough for Jill to hear him on the front porch. He thought, commercials could be a blessing. They give us time to get into the bathroom or the kitchen, or time to light up a cigarette and decide about continuing to watch this show or go on to that show.

And why couldn't real life have its commercials?

Wouldn't it be something to be grateful for if reality stopped in mid-course while the Big Salesman made His pitch? The car about to smash into you, the bullet on its way to your brain, the first cancer cell about to break loose, the boss reaching for the phone to call you in so he can fire you, the spermatozoon about to be launched toward the ovum, the final insult about to be hurled at the once, and perhaps still, beloved, the final drink of alcohol which would rupture the abused blood vessel, the decision which would lead to the light that would surely fail?

If only you could step out while the commercial interrupted these, think about it, talk about it, and then, returning to the set, switch it to another channel.

But that one is having technical difficulties, and the one after that is a talk show whose guest is the archangel Gabriel himself and after some urging by the host he agrees to blow his trumpet, and . . .

Jill entered, sat down, and began to munch the cookies and drink the lemonade he had prepared for her. Jill was six and a half years old and beautiful, but then what granddaughter wasn't beautiful? Jill was also unhappy because she had just quarreled with her best friend, Amy, who had stalked off with threats never to see Jill again. Mr. Howller reminded her that this had happened before and that Amy always came back the next day, if not sooner. To take her mind off of Amy, Mr. Howller gave her a brief outline of what had happened in the movie. Jill listened without enthusiasm, but she became excited enough once the movie had resumed. And when Kong was feeling over the edge of the abyss for John Driscoll, played by Bruce Cabot, she got into her grandfather's lap. She gave a little scream and put her hands over her eyes when Kong carried Ann Redman into the jungle (Ann played by Fay Wray).

But by the time Kong lay dead on Fifth Avenue, she was rooting for him, as millions had before her. Mr. Howller squeezed her and kissed her and said, "When your mother was about your age, I took her to see this. And when it was over, she was crying, too."

Jill sniffled and let him dry the tears with his handkerchief. When the Roadrunner cartoon came on, she got off his lap and went back to her cookie-munching. After a while she said, "Grandpa, the coyote falls off the cliff so far you can't even see him. When he hits, the whole earth shakes. But he always comes back, good as new. Why can he fall so far and not get hurt? Why couldn't King Kong fall and be just like new?"

Her grandparents and her mother had explained many times the distinction between a "live" and a "taped" show. It did not seem to make any difference how many times they explained. Somehow, in the years of watching TV, she had gotten the fixed idea that people in "live" shows actually suffered pain, sorrow, and death. The only shows she could endure seeing were those that her elders labeled as "taped." This worried Mr. Howller more than he admitted to his wife and daughter. Jill was a very bright child, but what if too many TV shows at too early an age had done her some irreparable harm? What if, a few years from now, she could easily see, and even define, the distinction between reality and unreality on the screen but deep down in her there was a child that still could not distinguish?

"You know that the Roadrunner is a series of pictures that move. People draw pictures, and people can do anything with pictures. So the Roadrunner is drawn again and again, and he's back in the next show with his wounds all healed and he's ready to make a jackass of himself again."

"A jackass? But he's a coyote."

"Now . . ."

Mr. Howller stopped. Jill was grinning.

"O.K., now you're pulling my leg."

"But is King Kong alive or is he taped?"

"Taped. Like the Disney I took you to see last week. *Bedknobs and Broomsticks.*"

"Then *King Kong* didn't happen?"

"Oh, yes, it really happened. But this is a movie they made about King Kong after what really happened was all over. So it's not exactly like it really was, and actors took the parts of Ann Redman and Carl Denham and all the others. Except King Kong himself. He was a toy model."

Jill was silent for a minute and then she said, "You mean, there really was a King Kong? How do you know, Grandpa?"

"Because I was there in New York when Kong went on his rampage. I was in the theater when he broke loose, and I was in the crowd that gathered around Kong's body after he fell off the Empire State Building. I was thirteen then, just seven years older than you are now. I was with my parents, and they were visiting my Aunt Thea. She was beautiful, and she had golden hair just like Fay Wray's—I mean, Ann Redman's. She'd married a very rich man, and they had a big apartment high up in the clouds. In the Empire State Building itself."

"High up in the clouds! That must've been fun, Grandpa!"

It would have been, he thought, if there had not been so much tension in that apartment. Uncle Nate and Aunt Thea should have been happy because they were so rich and lived in such a swell place. But they weren't. No one said anything to young Tim Howller, but he felt the suppressed anger, heard the bite of tone, and saw the tightening lips. His aunt and uncle were having trouble of some sort, and his parents were upset by it. But they all tried to pretend everything was as sweet as honey when he was around.

Young Howller had been eager to accept the pretense. He didn't like to think that anybody could be mad at his tall, blonde, and beautiful aunt. He was passionately in love with her; he ached for her in the daytime; at nights he had fantasies about her of which he was ashamed when he awoke. But not for long. She was a thousand times more desirable than Fay Wray or Claudette Colbert or Elissa Landi.

But that night, when they were all going to see the premiere of *The Eighth Wonder of the World*, King Kong himself, young Howller had managed to ignore whatever it was that was bugging his elders. And even they seemed to be having a good time. Uncle Nate, over his parents' weak protests, had purchased orchestra seats for them. These were twenty dollars apiece, big money in Depression days, enough to feed a family for a month. Everybody got all dressed up, and Aunt Thea looked too beautiful to be real.

Young Howller was so excited that he thought his heart was going to climb up and out through his throat. For days the newspapers had been full of stories about King Kong—speculations, rather, since Carl Denham wasn't telling them much. And he, Tim Howller, would be one of the lucky few to see the monster first.

Boy, wait until he got back to the kids in seventh grade in Busiris, Illinois! Would their eyes pop when he told them all about it!

But his happiness was too good to last. Aunt Thea suddenly said she had a headache and couldn't possibly go. Then she and Uncle Nate went into their bedroom, and even in the front room, three rooms and a hallway distant, young Tim could hear their voices. After a while Uncle Nate, slamming doors behind him, came out. He was red-faced and scowling, but he wasn't going to call the party off. All four of them, very uncomfortable and silent, rode in a taxi to the theater on Times Square. But when they got inside, even Uncle Nate forgot the quarrel or at least he seemed to. There was the big stage with its towering silvery curtains and through the curtains came a vibration of excitement and of delicious danger. And even through the curtains the hot hairy apestink filled the theater.

"Did King Kong get loose just like in the movie?" Jill said.

Mr. Howller started. "What? Oh, yes, he sure did. Just like in the movie."

"Were you scared, Grandpa? Did you run away like everybody else?"

He hesitated. Jill's image of her grandfather had been cast in a heroic mold. To her he was a giant of Herculean strength and perfect courage, her defender and champion. So far he had managed to live up to the image, mainly because the demands she made were not too much for him. In time she would see the cracks and the sawdust oozing out. But she was too young to disillusion now.

"No, I didn't run," he said. "I waited until the theater was cleared of the crowd."

This was true. The big man who'd been sitting in the seat before him had leaped up yelling as Kong began tearing the bars out of his cage, had whirled and jumped over the back of his seat, and his knee had hit young Howller on the jaw. And so young Howller had been stretched out senseless on the floor under the seats while the mob screamed and tore at each other and trampled the fallen.

Later he was glad that he had been knocked out. It gave him a good excuse for not keeping cool, for not acting heroically in the situation. He knew that if he had not been unconscious, he would have been as frenzied as the others, and he would have abandoned his parents, thinking only in his terror of his own salvation. Of course, his parents had deserted him, though they claimed that they had been swept away from him by the mob. This *could* be true; maybe his folks had actually tried to get to him. But he had not really thought they had, and for years he had looked down on them because of their flight. When he got older, he realized that he would have done the same thing, and he knew that his contempt for them was really a disguised contempt for himself.

He had awakened with a sore jaw and a headache. The police and the ambulance men were there and starting to take care of the hurt and to haul away the dead. He staggered past them out into the lobby and, not seeing his parents there, went outside. The sidewalks and the streets were plugged with thousands of men, women, and children, on foot and in cars, fleeing northward.

He had not known where Kong was. He should have been able to figure it out, since the frantic mob was leaving the midtown part of Manhattan. But he could think of only two things. Where were his parents? And was Aunt Thea safe? And then he had a third thing to consider. He discovered that he had wet his pants. When he had seen the great ape burst loose, he had wet his pants.

Under the circumstances, he should have paid no attention to this. Certainly no one else did. But he was a very sensitive and shy boy of thirteen, and, for some reason, the need for getting dry underwear and trousers seemed even more important than finding his parents. In retrospect he would tell himself that he would have gone south anyway. But he knew deep down that if his pants had not been wet he might not have dared return to the Empire State Building.

It was impossible to buck the flow of the thousands moving like lava up Broadway. He went east on 43rd Street until he came to Fifth Avenue, where he started southward. There was a crowd to fight against here, too, but it was much smaller than that on Broadway. He was able to thread his way through it, though he often had to go out into the street and dodge the cars. These, fortunately, were not able to move faster than about three miles an hour.

"Many people got impatient because the cars wouldn't go faster," he told Jill, "and they just abandoned them and struck out on foot."

"Wasn't it noisy, Grandpa?"

"Noisy? I've never heard such noise. I think that everyone in Manhattan, except those hiding under their beds, was yelling or talking. And every driver in Manhattan was blowing his car's horn. And then there were the sirens of the fire trucks and police cars and ambulances. Yes, it was noisy."

Several times he tried to stop a fugitive so he could find out what was going on. But even when he did succeed in halting someone for a few seconds, he couldn't make himself heard. By then, as he found out later, the radio had broadcast the news. Kong had chased John Driscoll and Ann Redman out of the theater and across the street to their hotel. They had gone up to Driscoll's room, where they thought they were safe. But Kong had climbed up, using windows as ladder steps, reached into the room, knocked Driscoll out, and grabbed Ann, and had then leaped away with her. He had headed, as Carl Denham figured he would, toward the tallest structure on the island. On King Kong's own island, he lived on the highest point, Skull Mountain, where he was truly monarch of all he surveyed. Here he would climb to the top of the Empire State Building, Manhattan's Skull Mountain.

Tim Howller had not known this, but he was able to infer that Kong had traveled down Fifth Avenue from 38th Street on.

He passed a dozen cars with their tops flattened down by the ape's fist or turned over on their sides or tops. He saw three sheet-covered bodies on the sidewalks, and he overheard a policeman telling a reporter that Kong had climbed up several buildings on his way south and reached into windows and pulled people out and thrown them down onto the pavement.

"But you said King Kong was carrying Ann Redman in the crook of his arm, Grandpa," Jill said. "He only had one arm to climb with, Grandpa, so . . . so wouldn't he fall off the building when he reached in to grab those poor people?"

"A very shrewd observation, my little chickadee," Mr. Howller said, using the W. C. Fields voice that usually sent her into giggles. "But his arms were long enough for him to drape Ann Redman over the arm he used to hang on with while he reached in with the other. And to forestall your next question, even if you had not thought of it, he could turn over an automobile with only one hand."

"But . . . but why'd he take time out to do that if he wanted to get to the top of the Empire State Building?"

"I don't know why *people* often do the things they do," Mr. Howller said. "So how would I know why an *ape* does the things he does?"

When he was a block away from the Empire State Building, a plane crashed onto the middle of the avenue two blocks behind him and burned furiously. Tim Howller watched it for a few minutes, then he looked upward and saw the red and green lights of the five planes and the silvery bodies slipping in and out of the searchlights.

"Five airplanes, Grandpa? But the movie . . ."

"Yes, I know. The movie showed about fourteen or fifteen. But the book says that there were six to begin with, and the book is much more accurate. The movie also shows King Kong's last stand taking place in the daylight. But it didn't; it was still nighttime."

The Army Air Force plane must have been going at least 250 mph as it dived down toward the giant ape standing on the top of the observation tower. Kong had put Ann Redman by his feet so he could hang on to the tower with one hand and grab out with the other at the planes. One had come too close, and he had seized the left biplane structure and ripped it off. Given the energy of the plane, his hand should have been torn off, too, or at least he should have been pulled loose from his hold on the tower and gone down with the plane. But he hadn't let loose, and that told something of the enormous strength of that towering body. It also told something of the relative fragility of the biplane.

Young Howller had watched the efforts of the firemen to extinuish the fire and then he had turned back toward the Empire State Building. By then it was all over. All over for King Kong, anyway. It was, in after years, one of Mr. Howller's greatest regrets that he had not seen the monstrous dark body falling through the beams of the searchlights—blackness, then the flash of blackness through the whiteness of the highest beam, blackness, the flash through the next beam, blackness, the flash through the third beam, blackness, the flash through the lowest beam. Dot, dash, dot, dash, Mr. Howller was to think afterward. A code transmitted unconsciously by the great ape and received unconsciously by those who witnessed the fall. Or by those who would hear of it and think about it. Or was he going too far in conceiving this? Wasn't he always looking for codes? And, when he found them, unable to decipher them?

Since he had been thirteen, he had been trying to equate the great falls in man's myths and legends and to find some sort of intelligence in them. The fall of the tower of Babel, of Lucifer, of Vulcan, of Icarus, and, finally, of King Kong. But he wasn't equal to the task; he didn't have the genius to perceive what the falls meant, he couldn't screen out the—to use an electronic term—the "noise." All he could come up with were folk adages. What goes up must come down. The bigger they are, the harder they fall.

"What'd you say, Grandpa?"

"I was thinking out loud, if you can call that thinking," Mr. Howller said.

Young Howller had been one of the first on the scene, and so he got a place in the front of the crowd. He had not completely forgotten his parents or Aunt Thea, but the danger was over, and he could not make himself leave to search for them. And he had even forgotten about his soaked pants. The body was only about thirty feet from him. It lay on its back on the sidewalk, just as in the movie. But the dead Kong did not look as big or as dignified as in the movie. He was spread out more like an apeskin rug than a body, and blood and bowels and their contents had splashed out around him.

After a while Carl Denham, the man responsible for capturing Kong and bringing him to New York, appeared. As in the movie, Denham spoke his classical lines by the body: "It was Beauty. As always, Beauty killed the Beast."

This was the most appropriately dramatic place for the lines to be spoken, of course, and the proper place to end the movie.

But the book had Denham speaking these lines as he leaned over the parapet of the observation tower to look down at Kong on the sidewalk. His only audience was a police sergeant.

Both the book and the movie were true. Or half true. Denham did speak those lines way up on the 102nd floor of the tower. But, showman that he was, he also spoke them when he got down to the sidewalk, where the newsmen could hear them.

Young Howller didn't hear Denham's remarks. He was too far away. Besides, at that moment he felt a tap on his shoulder and heard a man say, "Hey, kid, there's somebody trying to get your attention!"

Young Howller went into his mother's arms and wept for at least a minute. His father reached past his mother and touched him briefly on the forehead, as if blessing him, and then gave his shoulder a squeeze.

When he was able to talk, Tim Howller asked his mother what had happened to them. They, as near as they could remember, had been pushed out by the crowd, though they had fought to get to him, and had run up Broadway after they found themselves in the street because King Kong had appeared. They had managed to get back to the theater, had not been able to locate Tim, and had walked back to the Empire State Building.

"What happened to Uncle Nate?" Tim said.

Uncle Nate, his mother said, had caught up with them on Fifth Avenue and just now was trying to get past the police cordon into the building so he could check on Aunt Thea. "She must be all right!" young Howller said. "The ape climbed up her side of the building, but she could easily get away from him, her apartment's so big!"

"Well, yes," his father had said. "But if she went to bed with her headache, she would've been right next to the window. But don't worry. If she'd been hurt, we'd know it. And maybe she wasn't even home."

Young Tim had asked him what he meant by that, but his father had only shrugged. The three of them stood in the front line of the crowd, waiting for Uncle Nate to bring news of Aunt Thea, even though they weren't really worried about her, and waiting to see what happened to Kong. Mayor Jimmy Walker showed up and conferred with the officials. Then the governor himself, Franklin Delano Roosevelt, arrived with much noise of siren and motorcycle. A minute later a big black limousine with flashing red lights and a siren pulled up. Standing on the running-board was a giant with bronze hair and strange-looking gold-flecked eyes. He jumped off the runningboard and strode up to the mayor, governor, and police commissioner and talked briefly with them. Tim Howller asked the man next to him what the giant's name was, but the man replied that he didn't know because he was from out of town also. The giant finished talking and strode up to the crowd, which opened for him as if it were the Red Sea and he were Moses, and he had no trouble at all getting through the police cordon. Tim then asked the man on the right of his parents if he knew the yellow-eyed giant's name. This man, tall and thin, was with a beautiful woman dressed up in an evening gown and a mink coat. He turned his head when Tim called to him and presented a hawklike face and eyes that burned so brightly that Tim wondered if he took dope. Those eyes also told him that here was a man who asked questions, not one who gave answers. Tim didn't repeat his question, and a moment later the man said, in a whispering voice that still carried a long distance, "Come on, Margo. I've work to do." And the two melted into the crowd.

Mr. Howller told Jill about the two men, and she said, "What about them, Grandpa?"

"I don't really know," he said. "Often 'I've wondered . . . Well, never mind. Whoever they were, they're irrelevant to what happened to King Kong. But I'll say one thing about New York— you sure see a lot of strange characters there."

Young Howller had expected that the mess would quickly be cleaned up. And it was true that the sanitation department had sent a big truck with a big crane and a number of men with hoses, scoop shovels, and brooms. But a dozen people at least stopped the cleanup almost before it began. Carl Denham wanted no one to touch the body except the taxidermists he had called in. If he couldn't exhibit a live Kong, he would exhibit a dead one. A colonel from Roosevelt Field claimed the body and, when asked why the Air Force wanted it, could not give an explanation. Rather, he refused to give one, and it was not until an hour later that a phone call from the White House forced him to reveal the real reason. A general wanted the skin for a trophy because Kong was the only ape ever shot down in aerial combat.

A lawyer for the owners of the Empire State Building appeared with a claim for possession of the body. His clients wanted reimbursement for the damage done to the building.

A representative of the transit system wanted Kong's body so it could be sold to help pay for the damage the ape had done to the Sixth Avenue Elevated.

The owner of the theater from which Kong had escaped arrived with his lawyer and announced he intended to sue Denham for an amount which would cover the sums he would have to pay to those who were inevitably going to sue him.

The police ordered the body seized as evidence in the trial for involuntary manslaughter and criminal negligence in which

Denham and the theater owner would be defendants in due process.

The manslaughter charges were later dropped, but Denham did serve a year before being paroled. On being released, he was killed by a religious fanatic, a native brought back by the second expedition to Kong's island. He was, in fact, the witch doctor. He had murdered Denham because Denham had abducted and slain his god, Kong.

His Majesty's New York consul showed up with papers which proved that Kong's island was in British waters. Therefore, Denham had no right to anything removed from the island without permission of His Majesty's government.

Denham was in a lot of trouble. But the worst blow of all was to come next day. He would be handed notification that he was being sued by Ann Redman. She wanted compensation to the tune of ten million dollars for various physical indignities and injuries suffered during her two abductions by the ape, plus the mental anguish these had caused her. Unfortunately for her, Denham went to prison without a penny in his pocket, and she dropped the suit. Thus, the public never found out exactly what the "physical indignities and injuries" were, but this did not keep it from making many speculations. Ann Redman also sued John Driscoll, though for a different reason. She claimed breach of promise. Driscoll, interviewed by newsmen, made his famous remark that she should have been suing Kong, not him.

This convinced most of the public that what it had suspected had indeed happened. Just how it could have been done was difficult to explain, but the public had never lacked wiseacres who would not only attempt the difficult but would not draw back even at the impossible.

Actually, Howller thought, the deed was not beyond possibility. Take an adult male gorilla who stood six feet high and weighed 350 pounds. According to Swiss zoo director Ernst Lang, he would have a full erection only two inches long. How did Professor Lang know this? Did he enter the cage during a mating and measure the phallus? Not very likely. Even the timid and amiable gorilla would scarcely submit to this type of handling in that kind of situation. Never mind. Professor Lang said it was so, and so it must be. Perhaps he used a telescope with gradations across the lens like those on a submarine's periscope. In any event, until someone entered the cage and slapped down a ruler during the action, Professor Lang's word would have to be taken as the last word.

By mathematical extrapolation, using the square-cube law, a gorilla twenty feet tall would have an erect penis about twenty-one inches long. What the diameter would be was another guess and perhaps a vital one, for Ann Redman anyway. Whatever anyone else thought about the possibility, Kong must have decided that he would never know unless he tried. Just how well he succeeded, only he and his victim knew, since the attempt would have taken place before Driscoll and Denham got to the observation tower and before the searchlight beams centered on their target.

But Ann Redman must have told her lover, John Driscoll, the truth, and he turned out not to be such a strong man after all.

"What're you thinking about, Grandpa?"

Mr. Howller looked at the screen. The Roadrunner had been succeeded by the Pink Panther, who was enduring as much pain and violence as the poor old coyote.

"Nothing," he said. "I'm just watching the Pink Panther with you."

"But you didn't say what happened to King Kong," she said.

"'Oh," he said, "we stood around until dawn, and then the big shots finally came to some sort of agreement. The body just couldn't be left there much longer, if for no other reason than that it was blocking traffic. Blocking traffic meant that business would be held up. And lots of people would lose lots of money. And so Kong's body was taken away by the Police Department, though it used the Sanitation Department's crane, and it was kept in an icehouse until its ownership could be thrashed out."

"Poor Kong."

"No," he said, "not poor Kong. He was dead and out of it."

"He went to heaven?"

"As much as anybody," Mr. Howller said.

"But he killed a lot of people, and he carried off that nice girl. Wasn't he bad?"

"No, he wasn't bad. He was an animal, and he didn't know the difference between good and evil. Anyway, even if he'd been human, he would've been doing what any human would have done."

"What do you mean, Grandpa?"

"Well, if you were captured by people only a foot tall and carried off to a far place and put in a cage, wouldn't you try to escape? And if these people tried to put you back in, or got so scared that they tried to kill you right now, wouldn't you step on them?"

"Sure, I'd step on them, Grandpa."

"You'd be justified, too. And King Kong was justified. He was only acting according to the dictates of his instincts."

"What?"

"He was an animal, and so he can't be blamed, no matter what he did. He wasn't evil. It was what happened around Kong that was evil."

"What do you mean?" Jill said.

"He brought out the bad and the good in the people."

But mostly bad, he thought, and he encouraged Jill to forget about Kong and concentrate on the Pink Panther. And as he looked at the screen, he saw it through tears. Even after forty-two years, he thought, tears. This was what the fall of Kong had meant to him.

The crane had hooked the corpse and lifted it up. And there were two flattened-out bodies under Kong; he must have dropped them onto the sidewalk on his way up and then fallen on them from the tower. But how explain the nakedness of the corpses of the man and the woman?

The hair of the woman was long and, in a small area not covered by blood, yellow. And part of her face was recognizable.

Young Tim had not known until then that Uncle Nate had returned from looking for Aunt Thea. Uncle Nate gave a long wailing cry that sounded as if he, too, were falling from the top of the Empire State Building.

A second later young Tim Howller was wailing. But where Uncle Nate's was the cry of betrayal, and perhaps of revenge satisfied, Tim's was both of betrayal and of grief for the death of one he had passionately loved with a thirteen-year-old's love, for one whom the thirteen-year-old in him still loved.

"Grandpa, are there any more King Kongs?"

"No," Mr. Howller said. To say yes would force him to try to explain something that she could not understand. When she got older, she would know that every dawn saw the death of the old Kong and the birth of the new.

Writing Doc's Biography

Just as I sat down to start writing this article, the galley sheets of *Doc Savage: His Apocalyptic Life* arrived. That was the morning of April 19. Not until today, April 23, was I able to return to writing the galleys. Hopefully, all my corrections will be in the book. Such was not the case for *Tarzan Alive*, my biography of Lord Greystoke. For some reason, Doubleday did not incorporate my corrections, and I've never been able to get an explanation out of them why this omission occurred.

Things may be different this time, however. My title for the Tarzan biography was not used nor was I consulted about the dust jacket illustration. I didn't like either. But Doubleday is using my title for the Savage book and is following my suggestion that the "real," the "original," Doc be portrayed on the dust jacket. I had been afraid that the illustration would be based on those that Bama has been doing for the Bantam reprints.

As we all know, however striking Bama's covers are, his Doc Savage has little relation to that described by Dent and illustrated by Baumhofer or succeeding artists for the Street and Smith magazine originals. As a friend of mine, Jack Cordes, said, Bama portrays Doc as he would have looked like if Nazi Germany had won the war. (A cross between the Jolly Green Giant, and a Nazi Stormtrooper! . . . RW[1]). In my opinion, Bama's Doc looks like a middle-aged, habitual criminal, or a 55-year old ex-Mr. Universe down on his luck.

When Ace Books published my Doc Savage pastiche, *The Mad Goblin*, I asked Don Wollheim, the editor, why Gray Morrow had not portrayed Doc as described by Dent and myself. That is, as a man about thirty, handsome, and with straight bronze-red hair. Why was the cover illustration based on Bama's crewcut, widow-peaked, golden-haired monster?

Wollheim replied that the Bama was the only one most readers knew. The Bama-type cover would sell the Ace pastiche much better than a faithful picture of Doc. I replied that I was a purist and preferred the Baumhofer version. Besides, my Doc Caliban is not a Doc Savage imitation, but a pastiche, a continuation of the original. But when I write my next Doc Caliban, tentatively titled *Some Unspeakable Dweller*,[2] Doc may be shown as he really was. Wollheim will be buying it, and he is now vice-president and editor of DAW Books, and so he can pick his own covers.

Bantam, by the way, sent a note to Ace after *The Mad Goblin* appeared. Bantam objected, not to the book, but to the cover because it was too Bamaish. Wollheim's comment on this was that Bantam did not have a copyright on a torn shirt.

Thus, I was pleased when Doubleday asked me to send them some copies of the Street and Smith Savage magazines, one of which would be used on the dust jacket. I made my choice from the Baumhofers. Baumhofer is, in my opinion, the best illustrator of Doc, though Emery Clarke is very good. Doubleday did have on hand the cover for *Quest of Qui* (July 1935), which is a head and shoulders portrait of Doc. I like this, but it has no action, and action is the essence of Doc. After consideration, I narrowed my choice to the covers for *Fear Cay* (Sept. 1934) and *The Spook Legion* (April 1935). The former shows Patricia Savage, Doc, and (presumably) Renny caught in a net. Doc is tearing apart the thick ropes of the net, and we see lovely Pat full-face. *The Spook Legion* cover was my top choice because it shows Doc in a classical pose, riding a running-board. Monk is at the wheel of the roadster; New York City buildings form a silhouette in the background.

Diane Cleaver and the Doubleday artists agreed with me that this was the best. This made me happy, though I hated to omit Pat. As I say in the book, I fell in love with her when I was fifteen. (This explains why the chapter on Pat is twice as long as the chapters on the five assistant archenemies of evil. On the other hand, Monk Mayfair was my favorite character, perhaps because being so inhibited myself, I loved my opposite, the noisy, brawling, skirt-chasing, ungrammatical, vulgar, and violent Monk.)

The acceptance of my title and my choice of dust jacket illustration pleased me. I suspect, however, this came about because I was the only one involved in the book who knew anything at all about Doc. The Doubleday staff thought they knew about Tarzan, but Doc was an unknown quantity.

The full title, as it appears on the title page is:

DOC SAVAGE:
His Apocalyptic Life

As the Archangel of Technopolis and Exotica
As the Golden-eyed Hero of 181 Supersagas
As the Bronze Knight of the Running Board
Including His Final Battle Against the Forces
of Hell Itself

The table of contents is as follows:

1. The Fourfold Vision
2. Lester Dent, the Revelator from Missouri
3. Son of Storm and Child of Destiny
4. The Bronze Hero of Technopolis and Exotica
5. The Skyscraper
6. The Eighty-Sixth Floor
7. The Hidalgo Trading Company and Its Craft
8. The Crime College
9. The Fortress of Solitude

10. Monk, the Ape in Wolf's Clothing
11. Ham, the Eagle with a Cane
12. Habeus Corpus and Chemistry
13. Renny, Door-Buster and Holy-cower
14. Neoverbalist Johnny
15. Patricia Savage, Lady Auxiliary and Bronze Knockout
16. Long Tom, Wizard of the Juice and Misogynist
17. Doc the Gadgeteer
18. Some of the Great Villains and Their World-Threatening Gadgets

Addendum

1. The Fabulous Family Tree of Doc Savage
2. Chronology
3. List of Doc Savage Stories

I give the table of contents so the reader may get some idea of the structure of the book. When I did *Tarzan Alive*, I modeled its structure somewhat after William B. Baring Gould's biography. *Sherlock Holmes of Baker Street*. This demanded placing all of the stories in the sequence in which they happened, not in the publishing sequence. They were then summarized and the blanks left by Burroughs were filled in by me. I also tried to reconcile the discrepancies among the various stories and generated various theories or used those of various ERB scholars to explain certain difficult points.

But in writing Doc's life, I wasn't about to summarize all 181 of the supersagas. To do this would not only make the book about three times as long as it is, but it would appall and bore the general reader, who is no Savage specialist. So I structured Doc's biography on Baring Gould's *Nero Wolfe of West Thirty-Fifth Street*. Even this summarized the forty-four Wolfe books published up to 1968. I knew that my summaries would be longer than Baring Gould's and would probably amount to about 181 typewritten pages if I kept restraints on myself.

But there are enough references to various stories throughout the book to give the nonspecialist the feel and color of the supersagas.

The first chapter, "The Fourfold Vision," is a comparison of four writers who have something in common: apocalypticism. These are Dr. E.E. Smith (author of the Skylark and Gray Lensman series), Henry Miller (author of *Tropic of Capricorn*), William Burroughs (author of *Nova Express*, *The Soft Machine*, et al.), and Lester Dent.

The second chapter, "Lester Dent, the Revelator from Missouri," is a biographical sketch of Dent. To get details of his life and to ensure accuracy, I twice visited Mrs. Dent in her home in La Plate, Missouri. She was very charming and helpful, and it was a thrill to see Dent's home, his studio, the Baumhofer originals, and the collection of manuscripts. He was a remarkable man.

Chapter 3, "Son of Storm and Child of Destiny," recounts Doc's immediate ancestry, his birth in a ship off Andros Island, his early training, his World War I experiences, and his deeds just before he moved into the Empire State Building.

(Yes, I know the actual 86th floor of the ESB is the observation floor and never was occupied by an individual, and I know that Dent never named Doc's skyscraper. But I explain this, satisfactorily, I hope, in the book.)

The fourth chapter, "The Bronze Hero of Technopolis and Exotica," sketches Doc and his activities and his character development during his adventures in the big cities and the jungles and deserts.

Since "the skyscraper" and the 86th floor are as much characters as the living beings in the stories, chapters 5 and 6 are devoted to them. Chapter 5, "The Skyscraper," contains a line drawing of the ESB and the Hidalgo Trading Company. Floors prominent in the stories are called out, and the various secret express elevators, the subbasement garage, the giant underground pneumatic tube, the secret tunnel to the Broadway subway, and several other features are shown.

The sixth chapter contains a diagram of the 86th floor. This is to be referred to during the reading of the text of this chapter.

This includes many, though by no means all, of the devices, furniture, lab equipment, secret wall panels, doors and various items (including the portrait of Doc's father and the mounted lion, etc.). It wasn't easy making the floor layout or placing many of the items. I had to reconcile the many discrepancies perpetrated by four writers trying to beat a deadline. But, in writing a biography of a "fictional" character, half the fun is in explaining away the discrepancies. It also generates much that wasn't in the originals, and it enables the biographer to fill in the blanks.

I put fictional in quotes because this book, like *Tarzan Alive*, *Sherlock Holmes of Baker Street*, *Nero Wolfe of West Thirty-Fifth Street*, *The Life and Times of Horatio Hornblower*, *Sir Percy Blakeney: Fact or Fiction*, and *Yankee Lawyer, The Auto-biography of Ephraim Tutt*, is based on the premise that Doc Savage was a living person. Of course, his exploits were considerably exaggerated and distorted, some of them being entirely fictional. Doc himself complained of the exaggerations in the memo he sent to Dent in *No Light to Die By* (May/June 1947).

The contents of the remaining chapters are self-evident by their titles, Addendum 1, subtitled "Another Excursion into Creative Mythography," is an extension of addendum 2 of my *Tarzan Alive*. Doc's ancestry and relatives are described in this and end-paper genealogical charts are provided as aids for the reader of addendum 1. This chart, unlike that in *Tarzan Alive*, spells out the names of the major characters and gives the initials of the minor people. The names initialed on the chart are spelled out in the text.

Perhaps some, reading this article, will be surprised to learn that Doc is a descendant of Solomon Kane, Captain Peter Blood, Raphael Hythloday (of More's *Utopia*), and Manual of Poictesme (of James Branch Caball's *Figures of Earth*, *Jurgen*, et al). And he/she may also be surprised to discover that Doc is related to Sam Spade, Richard Hannay, James Bond, Richard Bensen, Fu Manchu, Carl Peterson, Professor Moriarty, Captain Nemo, and Doctor Caber (of Dunsany's *The Fourth Book of Jorkens*).

On the other hand, if the reader is acquainted with *Tarzan Alive*, he may not be surprised.

Addendum 2 is a chronology of the supersagas, an attempt to put the stories in the sequence in which they must have happened, which was not always by any means, the order in which they were published. I had a hell of a time with this. Some of the problems are described in the foreword to the chronology. Very few of the stories specify the dates or the day and the year of the particular event. A few specify both, and some of these presented additional problems because of this. Its axiomatic that an adventure has to occur before it can be written and published, and in some cases, the dates were too close to the publication date to be regarded as accurate.

Fear Cay enabled me to determine the year in which it took place because of the age of Dan Thunden. *The Squeaking Goblin* refers to a book published exactly one hundred years ago. Both of these adventures can thus be set in 1934, but both had to occur early in the year to have been written up and gone through the publishing process before appearing on the stands. *The Squeaking Goblin* (August 1934) appeared on the stands in July. Though Dent probably only took three or four days to write it, the editing and printing of it even at the speed with which pulp magazines put out issues, must have taken a minimum of a month and a half. I would have preferred to place the story in early spring, but *Goblin* definitely takes place during summer, during vacation time. I settled for the first seven days of June, when the rich could be vacationing early.

Many of the stories contain definite references to the season or seasonal data, and these enabled me to determine if the super-saga occurred in fall, winter, spring or summer.

Doc was often said to have just returned from one of his six month stints at the Fortress of Solitude. This stretched the chronology to impossible lengths, and I determined that only in 1933 could he have spent that much time at the Strange Blue Dome. He could have spent five months there in the first part of 1934.

Another problem was presented by the absence of the five aides on projects which required a very long time. These would also expand the chronology; the times of their absences had to be accounted for. I finally concluded that Doc's assistants couldn't have seen these projects through from beginning to end. Thus, when Renny is building a road or airport in China and Johnny is digging in Inca ruins, or Monk is rebuilding a chemical plant in post-war Germany, they were on these projects only as consultants. They flew in, looked around, straightened out the biggest problems, and flew back in time to join Doc in his latest exploit.

In the early years of the magazine, the stories often ended with a preview of the next adventure. These were supposed to follow immediately the story at hand. But this often just could not be. So I presumed that the editors wrote these previews to intrigue the reader. The facts were ignored. It was evident that Dent and his associates did not write the stories in the sequence in which they had actually happened. Not always, anyway.

It was necessary to classify some of the stories as all fiction. *World's Fair Goblin* was obviously written before the World's Fair at New York opened. And I classified *Land of Long Juju* (January 1937) as fiction, and abominable fiction at that; just as a story, it's ridiculous. But the description of and references to East African customs and peoples are absurd. Danberg knew nothing of this area, made up the whole thing, and committed an abomination. Why Bantam did not save this as the last to be printed in the series, why Bantam picked this one when there were so many better stories to publish, I don't know. But, I suspect that the editor of the Bantam stories does not read them before he chooses which one will be issued. More on this later.

The first three supersagas, *The Man of Bronze*, *The Land of Terror*, and *The Quest of the Spider*, occurred in the published sequence. Doc was at the fortress, but only for two weeks, between *Land and Quest*. The fourth story in my chronology, *The Red Skull* (August 1933), was the sixth published. *The Polar Treasure* (June 1933), the fourth published, must have been the eighteenth in chronological sequence.

The Purple Dragon (Sept. 1940), one of my favorites, is definitely set in August 1939 by the text. The "1940" has to be a typo of Dent's or the printer's, and so I put *Dragon* in the

August 1-3 slot of 1939. This is a reasonable move, since the stories have many typos, and errors, including the names of characters who are not in the particular scene.

I suspect that some Savageologists will take issue with me on some of my chronology, or will want to know how I arrived at a certain decision. Don't write me about these, because I don't have time to answer such questions. Write an article for *Pulp* or some Savagezine and if I happen to have enough time, I might answer the article. Some of the slots into which I put certain stories were the result of many factors which had to he weighed against each other. Where discrepancies which existed were found, I favored that which had the most evidence on its side.

Addendum 3 is a list of the stories in published sequence. Date of publication, author, and Bantam reprint (if any) are given. The list of Bantams stop with the middle February, 1973 issue, *The Seven Agate Devils.*

I wrote the Bantam publishers to get their publication figures and also to find out what method was used to pick those stories published. In fact, I wrote three letters, none of which were answered. I mentioned in each that I wanted the information for the biography, which would be published in August by Double-day. It was to Bantam's advantage to reply, since my book will give the Doc Savage stories some publicity.

It's my opinion that the editor of the Bantam Savage books has a very contemptuous attitude towards them. I doubt that he has ever read any of them, though somebody at Bantam has to have skimmed through them to get the blurbs which are on the back of the books.

This indifference seems to extend to the mail-order department. Some years ago, I ordered a batch of Savages through the mail. The package I received was lacking *Meteor Menace* and *The Monsters.* I wrote three letters asking for the books or a refund. No reply. I gave up.

Interim note relating to "biographies." I just strolled over to the Book Emporium on my lunch hour and looked for copies of the soft-cover *Tarzan Alive,* which appeared on most stands at least three weeks ago. (But, to my horror, Popular Library had omitted the end-paper charts, referred to in addendum 2 and essential to help the reader.) I could not understand why no copies had been received by the Emporium. Then, while strolling around, I passed the Biography section. And a certain cover caught my eyes. Yes, there it was, *Tarzan Alive*, nestled in with books on Hitler, Jennie Churchill, Hornblower, Einstein, Lincoln, Louis XIV, Dorothy Parker, et al.

I wonder what the fate of the Savage biography will be in this particular bookstore.

In conclusion, though the biography was hard work, it was also fun. I could have written three novels in the time I took to do it and could have made three times as much money. But, I'm glad I did it. I loved the Doc Savage stories when I was a kid. I still get a charge out of reading them, even if they're not great literature. And, I was finally able to fulfill a boyhood ambition, the writing of a book about my hero, Doctor Clark Savage, Jr.

---

[1] Robert Weinberg, editor and publisher of *The Man Behind Doc Savage*.

[2] Although this book was never completed, Phil did write a chapter for the book, and this was printed in the *World Fantasy Convention Program*, 1983, under the title *The Monster on Hold*.

Sherlock Holmes and Sufism

A Speech to the Baker Street Irregulars

Members of the Baker Street Irregulars, fellow guests, I am indeed honored to be here. And rather happy about it, too. This is for me a unique occasion—so far. This is the first time I've ever spoken at a BSI occasion and is, in fact, my first attendance at one.

I hope that this is the first step, or prelude, to a closer association. I am not a member of any scion, but I hope that some day I will be invited to join one. Unfortunately, my residence is in Peoria, Ill., located about halfway between Chicago and St. Louis (or St. Lewis, if you prefer). It would tax my time and money to travel to monthly meetings. But the main problem is that, so far, no one has invited me to become a member—a consummation devoutly to be wished for.

Perhaps it's just as well. I didn't pass an on-the-spot examination re Holmesiana. Though I've read and reread the Sacred Writings since 1929—the first two stories in that year were "A Scandal in Bohemia" and "The Red-Headed League." I have a bad memory. I'd have to swot for some time before I'd be able to pass a verbal examination. I do better on written tests anyway.

As some of you know, my lifelong interest in Holmes and Watson has resulted in certain unsacred writings. There is much about the immortal twain and related persons—in my biography of Lord Greystoke—also known as Tarzan. Another biography, my *Doc Savage: His Apocalyptic Life*, also contains certain material about Holmes, and his great enemy, Professor Moriarty.

In addition, my science-fictional novel, *The Other Log of Phileas Fogg*, has as its chief antagonist, or villain, that spinner of dark webs, Moriarty, not to mention lesser villains from the works of Jules Verne and R. L. Stevenson.

All three books, by the way, owe much to Professor William Starr, a distinguished member of the Sons of the Copper Beeches, Philadelphia, Penn.

In addition, I have contributed an article to the *Baker Street Journal*—"The Two Lord Ruftons"—in which I pointed out a connection between Brigadier Gerard and Lady Frances Carfax. Gerard, it scarcely needs mentioning, was one of Napoleon's most famous soldiers. Possibly he was also the dumbest.

And then there is my recent *The Adventure of the Peerless Peer*, in which I achieved my long-desired ambition to bring together Holmes, Watson, and Lord Greystoke. Not to mention G-8, the Shadow, a zeppelin, and certain descendants of certain friends of Allan Quatermain.

I plan a sequel in which Holmes and Watson are deeply involved in a mystery in Ireland—during which they fall in with Leopold Bloom, whose biography was written by the famous J. Joyce. One of the persons the three encounter is, of course, an Irishman named Finnegan.

I have also written into a movie treatment a Holmes-Watson vignette. I returned from Hollywood—or Burbank, to be precise, only two days before setting out for the equally exotic land of El Paso, Texas, with George Pal, a producer at Warner Studios, I worked out—and wrote—a treatment for the second Doc Savage movie. A treatment is a story, in essence, a prose outline on which the script is based. Doc Savage is the hero of 181 pulp magazine novels published during the 1930's and 1940's. He was equal in popularity to the other pulp magazine hero—the Shadow.

Bantam Books began reprinting the Savage supersagas in 1965, and these were so popular that George Pal purchased the options to all 181 novels. Pal, for those of you not familiar with movie producers and directors, made such films as *The Time Machine, War of the Worlds, Destination Moon, The Naked Jungle,* and *The Wonderful World of the Brothers Grimm.*

The first Savage movie, *Doc Savage: The Man of Bronze,* is ready to be shown in the summer. I had nothing to do with that; Mr. Pal and I couldn't come to financial terms.

The second movie, however, *Doc Savage: Archenemy of Evil,* will, I hope, be all a Savagephile could desire. I mention it only because I wrote into it a Holmes-Watson vignette.

While Doc and his fabulous five aides are crossing the Atlantic in their fabulous dirigible, Doc sends a radio message to England. This is to one of the men who taught him the art of criminal detection. The Great Detective, in fact.

Doc wants to find out all about the fabled long-lost city of Tasunan, located somewhere deep in the Sahara. The Great Detective, now retired, has written a not-so-trifling monograph on the language of the now-extinct Tasunanians.

And so the camera zooms across the seaside Sussex Downs. It closes on a small villa, outside of which are rows on rows of bee hives.

The camera then enters the villa, where Watson is visiting Holmes. Holmes is playing his violin when someone knocks at the door. It's a messenger, delivering Doc's wirelessed inquiry.

Holmes, talking to Watson, reveals that he tutored some promising pupils after he retired. Doc Savage was his best student. He tells them how and why Doc Savage was dedicated by his father to the battle against crime. Doc's father is James Wilder, the illegitimate son of the Duke of Holdernesse.

The scene ends with Holmes opening a book he's removed from a shelf, his monograph on the Tasunan tablet.

I must warn you, however, that it is possible that the scene will be cut before the film is issued. Exigencies of money, movie-length, etc. and the external and infernal interferences from the financial backers—not to mention their wives and mothers-in-law—not to mention the major actors, who are very jealous of any time taken from them—might result in deletion of the vignette.

Let us hope not.

And now to the main subject, *Sherlock Holmes and Sufism.* First I must beg your indulgence. Between the time I was told I'd be addressing you, and the time I boarded the plane for El Paso, I had no time to write this discourse. I was too busy. In fact, I wasn't sure what the subject would be until last Tuesday. It was on that day that I wrote this. The next day I left for Texas.

Thus, I had no opportunity to do extensive research. But I plan to rewrite this part of my trifling effort when I return to Peoria. I will then submit it to Dr. Wolff for possible publication in the *Baker Street Journal.*

As you know, there has been—is—much controversy about Holmes's activities during the Great Hiatus—between May 1891 to April 1894—according to William S. Baring-Gould.

There's no need to go into detail re this before this body of Sherlockians.

Holmes wandered far and wide, mostly in Asia and Middle Asia and northeast Africa, while hiding from Col. Sebastian Moran and his gang of black-handed, red-handed villains. According to what he told Watson on his return ("The Adventure of the Empty House"), he travelled for two years in Tibet, amusing himself by visiting Lhasa and spending some days with the Head Llama. (Incidentally, Watson amused his readers by spelling Lama with a double-l. Though Watson did have a sense of humor, this is undoubtedly one of the many examples of Watson's difficulty with spelling. This orthographic disease is not unknown among many present-day medical doctors, present company excepted, of course.)

Presumably he visited Tibet because of well-established interest in Buddhism.

He then passed through Persia, looked in at Mecca, and paid a short but interesting visit to the Khalifa at Khartoum. Various scholars have objected to the whole account. The late great Edgar W. Smith maintains that *no* European came anywhere near the forbidden city of Lhasa until 1903. And then the penetration of the holy city was made by force of British arms. I say—true, if you count "historically recorded" visits. But Sherlock Holmes was a master of disguise. Just what disguise he could have used is a subject for an article itself, so I won't go into that here. And, possibly, the Head Lama or Regent had read Watson's adventures, though not in Tibetan translations.

He knew of Holmes, after all, "I hear of you everywhere—" and would also know of Holmes's interest in Buddhism.

However, my interest here is on Holmes's visits to Persia, Arabia, and the Sudan. That is, among *Moslems*, not Buddhists. Again, objectioners maintain that Holmes would not have travelled through these countries. Persia was in the midst of troubles: all English and Russians were suspect, since both Great Britain and Russia were struggling to gain ascendancy here. A civil war was raging in Mecca. And the Caliph of Khartoum, Abdullah, would have been more likely to execute any Englishman than to have a friendly chat with him.

But Mr. Benson Murray, an authority on Persian history, pooh-poohs Mr. Smith's statements. He presents documented proof as intense or widespread as Mr. Smith claims.

As for Mecca, Mr. Murray maintains again via histories of that period, that there was no civil war in Mecca, merely a struggle between the Ottoman (or Turkish) administration and the Sherif of Mecca.

Nor were visits to Mecca by Europeans unknown. Twenty-eight (and Sherlock Holmes's visit) were made between 1503 and 1931. The most famous was probably Sir Richard Francis Burton's Hadj (or Pilgrimage), in 1853. Burton went half-disguised as a half-Persian, half Afghani hakim (or physician). I suggest that Holmes adopted a similar disguise. Indeed, he may even have prepared himself for this trip by conversing with Burton himself. But this would have been before 1890—the year of Burton's death in Trieste. This speculation, again, will be the subject of a separate article.

We know—or can safely assume—that Holmes' visit to Tibet was inspired by his interest in Buddhism.

But why would he go to Persia and Arabia and Egypt? What was his interest there?

I suggest that it was because Sherlock Homes was as intrigued by Sufism as Buddhism. Perhaps even more so.

First, what is Sufism?

Webster's New Collegiate Dictionary – 1963 – defines *Sufi* thus: n. [Ar. sufiy, lit. man of wool] : a Muslim mystic.

The *Encyclopedia Britannica* – 1964 – contains a page and a quote on *Sufism*. Summarized, it states that Sufism (tasawwuf) is formed from Sufi, applied in the second century of Islam to men or women who adopted an ascetic or quietistic way of life.

It was originally a practical religion, not a speculative system. It is pantheistic. It was heavily influenced by Christianity and Buddhism.

Both *Webster's* and the *Encyclopedia Britannica*, I regret to say, are generally wrong. Sufism, if I am to believe the writings of those who should know, the genuine Sufis of medieval and modern times, is not ascetic, quietistic, nor pantheistic.

Nor is it confined to Muslims. Nor has it been so heavily influenced by Christianity and Buddhism. On the contrary, the influence, the countercurrent, has been much more in the other direction.

And it is true that, though Sufism originated in Arabia, it existed before the birth of Mohammed. It was given an impetus and somewhat revised shape in Arabia during the first two centuries after Islamism was born. But it's chief shaping, and propagation, was done by the Moslemized Persians.

It is not ascetic. Though genuine Sufis practice moderation, they do not disdain tasty food. They may marry and often have and do. They can even have four wives. But they are wise, and I've not come across any record that a Sufi ever had more than one wife at a time.

They do not retire from the world to contemplate their navels or live in celibate monasteries. They may withdraw for periods. But they are usually out among them—to use an old Yankee phrase—working in and with people, dealing with life as it is, where it all hangs out. It is, in a sense, an autocratic discipline. This doesn't mean that its candidates are drawn only from the upper crust of society. Man or woman, peasant, fisherman, wealthy merchant or king, black, white, yellow, or brown, Christian, Jew, or Moslem, you can be a Sufi.

But its autocracy consists in this. No one can become a Sufi unless that person is accepted by a Master, one who has himself been the disciple of a Master. The way is long and hard—though not always. Many come to the Master—few are chosen. The Master separates the sheep from the goats, the potential Sufi from the nonpotential.

A Sufi may be a mystic—one who seeks for the ecstasy of direct apprehension of God—or of the True Reality. But this is neither the ultimate—nor even a necessary—goal.

I'm afraid that at this point I must eliminate much about Sufism which will be in the article. There just isn't time, and I may have stretched your patience already.

So—what is there to indicate that Sherlock Holmes went to Persia, Arabia, and Sudan because he was interested—perhaps intent on—learning about Sufism?

One clue. Holmes's final words in "A Case of Identity," which took place in 1887.

Holmes says, to Watson: "You may remember the old Persian saying, 'There is danger from him who taketh the tiger cub and danger also for whoso snatches a delusion from a woman.' There is as much sense in Hafiz as in Horace, and as much knowledge of the world."

Hafiz (or Shamsuddin Mohammed to give him his natal native) was not translated in its entirety into English prose until 1890.

Miss Madeline B. Stern (in her *Sherlock Holmes: Rare Book Collector*) suggests that "we must assume that Holmes's copy was either the 1800 Hindley edition of the *Persian Lyrics* printed in Persian and English with verse and prose paraphrases and a catalog of the Gazels, or of the fine 1875 edition containing a verse rendering of the principle poems by Bucknell."

This is fine and dandy, but what about the French and German translations? [I haven't tracked these down yet.] What about Holmes having read Hafiz, a great Sufi poet, in the original?

Holmes was an accomplished linguist in French, German, and Italian and probably was competent in Russian. And a man who can write a monograph on Chaldean roots in Cornish must know more than somewhat about Celtic and Semitic languages. Persian is not Semitic (though it uses Arabic writing) but is Indo-European, from the parent tongue of English, German, Sanskrit, Russian, etc. But Holmes may have been as well acquainted with Persian in the original as he was Latin. And as I'll demonstrate in the proposed article, he may have learned much from Sir Richard Francis Burton both about Persian and about Sufism. Burton claimed to be a Sufi, and he wrote a long Sufi poem, the *Kasidah of Haji Abdu el-Yezdi*, nine years before the publication of Fitzgerald's translation of *The Rubaiyat of Omar Khayyam*. Omar, by the way, was a Sufi, Khayyam, meaning Tentmaker, did not indicate that this distinguished mathematician and astronomer made tents. Khayyam had a hidden, or esoteric, Sufi meaning. And Fitzgerald's translation is inaccurate and almost totally misleading.

Holmes certainly did not go to the Mideast or Africa to learn about Moslemism per se. He would have visited Persia, and Mecca, and the Khalifa to learn about Sufism. He would have sought out, and talked with, Sufi masters in Persia and Arabia.

As for the Khalifa, I doubt he was a Sufi. He was a religious fanatic, bloody, violent, narrow-minded, a Wahhabi fundamentalist. But he would at least have had knowledge of local Sufis, and Holmes may have been directed to these by the Khalifa.

Also, this particular visit may have been partly inspired by Mycroft. Holmes's brother would have wanted to find out about the situation in the Sudan. Holmes, always an economist, could have combined a personal mission—a religious one—and a political mission.

Holmes was plainly a somewhat changed man after the Great Hiatus. We hear no more of his cocaine, or of excessive smoking, or of his drinking. And despite what Watson said, he is better tempered, has become more compassionate and tolerant. He even professes a faith in a personal God.

Some have attributed this to the influence of Buddhism during his Tibetan stay. I doubt it. I think that Holmes would have been repelled by the practice of Buddhism in Tibet. Just why I will detail in the proposed article.

I attribute the change in his temperament and attitude to his brief—but powerful—contact with the Sufi masters. Aided and abetted by his readings of Sufistic literature—however. He was not with the Masters long enough to have become a Sufi himself. Not nearly long enough.

But I do suggest here—and will maintain more specifically in the article—that he did suffer a partial strange sea change. And that it was because of Sufism.

The Problem of the Sore Bridge— Among Others

by Harry "Bunny" Manders

⁓ One ⁓

The Boer bullet that pierced my thigh in 1900 lamed me for the rest of my life, but I was quite able to cope with its effects. However, at the age of sixty-one, I suddenly find that a killer that has felled far more men than bullets has lodged within me. The doctor, my kinsman, gives me six months at the most, six months which he frankly says will be very painful. He knows of my crimes, of course, and it may be that he thinks that my suffering will be poetic justice. I'm not sure. But I'll swear that this is the meaning of the slight smile which accompanied his declaration of my doom.

Be that as it may, I have little time left. But I have determined to write down that adventure of which Raffles and I once swore we would never breathe a word. It happened; it really happened. But the world would not have believed it then. It would have been convinced that I was a liar or insane. I am writing this, neverthe-less, because fifty years from now the world may have progressed to the stage where such things as I tell of are credible. Man may even have landed on the moon by then, if he has perfected a propeller which works in the ether as well as in the air. Or if he discovers the same sort of drive that brought . . . well, I anticipate.

I must hope that the world of 1974 will believe this adventure. Then the world will know that, whatever crimes Raffles and I committed, we paid for them a thousandfold by what we did that week in the May of 1895. And, in fact, the world is and always will be immeasurably in our debt. Yes, my dear doctor, my scornful kinsman, who hopes that I will suffer pain as punishment, I long ago paid off my debt. I only wish that you could be alive to read these words. And, who knows, you may live to be a hundred and may read this account of what you owe me. I hope so.

☙ Two ☙

I was nodding in my chair in my room at Mount Street when the clanging of the lift gates in the yard startled me. A moment later, a familiar tattoo sounded on my door. I opened it to find, as I expected, A. J. Raffles himself. He slipped in, his bright blue eyes merry, and he removed his Sullivan from his lips to point it at my whisky and soda.

"Bored, Bunny?"

"Rather." I replied. "It's been almost a year since we stirred our stumps. The voyage around the world after the Levy affair was stimulating. But that ended four months ago. And since then . . ."

"Ennui and bile!" Raffles cried. "Well, Bunny, that's all over! Tonight we make the blood run hot and cold and burn up all green biliousness!"

"And the swag?" I said.

"Jewels, Bunny! To be exact, star sapphires, or blue corundum, cut *en cabochon*. That is, round with a flat underside. And large, Bunny, vulgarly large, almost the size of a hen's egg, if my inform-ant was not exaggerating. There's a mystery about them, Bunny, a mystery my fence has been whispering with his Cockney speech into my ear for some time. They're dispensed by a Mr. James Phillimore of Kensal Rise. But where he gets them, from whom he lifts them, no one knows. My fence has hinted that they may not come from manorial strongboxes or milady's throat but are smuggled from Southeast Asia or South Africa or Brazil, directly from the mine. In any event, we are going to do some reconnoitering tonight, and if the opportunity should arise . . ."

"Come now, A. J.," I said bitterly. "You *have* done all the needed reconnoitering. Be honest! Tonight we suddenly find that the moment is propitious, and we strike? Right?"

I had always been somewhat piqued that Raffles chose to do all the preliminary work, the casing, as the underworld says, himself. For some reason, he did not trust me to scout the layout.

Raffles blew a huge and perfect smoke ring from his Sullivan, and he clapped me on the shoulder. "You see through me, Bunny! Yes, I've examined the grounds and checked out Mr. Phillimore's schedule."

I was unable to say anything to the most masterful man I have ever met. I meekly donned dark clothes, downed the rest of the whisky, and left with Raffles. We strolled for some distance, making sure that no policemen were shadowing us, though we had no reason to believe they would be. We then took the last train to Willesden at 11:21. On the way I said, "Does Phillimore live near old Baird's house?"

I was referring to the money lender killed by Jack Rutter, the details of which case are written in *Wilful Murder*.

"As a matter of fact," Raffles said, watching me with his keen steel-grey eyes, "it's the *same* house. Phillimore took it when Baird's estate was finally settled and it became available to renters. It's a curious coincidence, Bunny, but then all coincidences are curious. To man, that is. Nature is indifferent."

(Yes, I know! stated before that his eyes were blue. And so they were. I've been criticized for saying in one story that his eyes were blue and in another that they were grey. But he has, as any idiot should have guessed, grey-blue eyes which are one color in one light and another in another.)

"That was in January, 1895," Raffles said. "We are in deep waters, Bunny. My investigations have unearthed no evidence that Mr. Phillimore existed before November, 1894. Until he took the lodgings in the East End, no one seems to have heard of or even seen him. He came out of nowhere, rented his third-story lodgings—a terrible place, Bunny—until January. Then he rented the house where bad old Baird gave up the ghost. Since then he's been living a quiet-enough life, excepting the visits he makes once a month to several East End fences. He has a cook and a house-keeper, but these do not live in with him."

At this late hour, the train went no farther than Willesden Junction. We walked from there toward Kensal Rise. Once more, I was dependent on Raffles to lead me through unfamiliar country. However, this time the moon was up, and the country was not quite as open as it had been the last time I was here. A number of cottages and small villas, some only partially built, occupied the empty fields I had passed through that fateful night. We walked down a footpath between a woods and a field, and we came out on the tarred woodblock road that had been laid only four years before. It now had the curb that had been lacking then, but there was still only one pale lamppost across the road from the house.

Before us rose the corner of a high wall with the moonlight shining on the broken glass on top of the wall. It also outlined the sharp spikes on top of the tall green gate. We slipped on our masks. As before, Raffles reached up and placed champagne corks on the spikes. He then put his covert-coat over the corks. We slipped over quietly, Raffles removed the corks, and we stood by the wall in a bed of laurels. I admit I felt apprehensive, even more so than the last time. Old Baird's ghost seemed to hover about the place. The shadows were thicker than they should have been.

I started toward the gravel path leading to the house, which was unlit. Raffles seized my coattails. "Quiet!" he said. "I see somebody—something, anyway—in the bushes at the far end of the garden. Down there, at the angle of the wall."

I could see nothing, but I trusted Raffles, whose eyesight was as keen as a Red Indian's. We moved slowly alongside the wall, stopping frequently to peer into the darkness of the bushes at the angle of the wall. About twenty yards from it, I saw something shapeless move in the shrubbery. I was all for clearing out then, but Raffles fiercely whispered that we could not permit a competitor to scare us away. After a quick conference, we moved in very slowly but surely, slightly more solid shadows in the shadow of the wall. And in a few very long and perspiration-drenched minutes, the stranger fell with one blow from Raffles' fist upon his jaw.

Raffles dragged the snoring man out from the bushes so we could get a look at him by moonlight. "What have we here, Bunny?" he said. "Those long curly locks, that high arching nose, the overly thick eyebrows, and the odor of expensive Parisian perfume? Don't you recognize him?"

I had to confess that I did not.

"What, that is the famous journalist and infamous duelist, Isadora Persano!" he said. "Now tell me you have never heard of him, or her, as the case may be?"

"Of course!" I said. "The reporter for the *Daily Telegraph*!"

"No more," Raffles said. "He's a free-lancer now. But what the devil is he doing here?"

"Do you suppose," I said slowly, "that he, too, is one thing by day and quite another at night?"

"Perhaps," Raffles said. "But he may be here in his capacity of journalist. He's also heard things about Mr. James Phillimore. The devil take it! If the press is here, you may be sure that the Yard is not far behind!"

Mr. Persano's features curiously combined a rugged masculinity with an offensive effeminacy. Yet the latter characteristic was not really his fault. His father, an Italian diplomat, had died before he was born. His English mother had longed for a girl, been bitterly disappointed when her only-born was a boy, and, unhindered by a husband or conscience, had named him Isadora and raised him as a girl. Until he entered a public school, he wore dresses. In school, his long hair and certain feminine actions made him the object of an especially vicious persecution by the boys. It was there that he developed his abilities to defend himself with his fists. When he became an adult, he lived on the continent for several years. During this time, he earned a reputation as a dangerous man to insult. It was said that he had wounded half a dozen men with sword or pistol.

From the little bag in which he carried the tools of the trade, Raffles brought a length of rope and a gag. After tying and gagging Persano, Raffles went through his pockets. The only object that aroused his curiosity was a very large matchbox in an inner pocket of his cloak. Opening this, he brought out something that shone in the moonlight.

"By all that's holy!" he said. "It's one of the sapphires!"

"Is Persano a rich man?" I said.

"He doesn't have to work for a living, Bunny. And since he hasn't been in the house yet, I assume he got this from a fence. I also assume that he put the sapphire in the matchbox because a pickpocket isn't likely to steal a box of matches. As it was, I was about to ignore it!"

"Let's get out of here," I said. But he crouched staring down at the journalist with an occasional glance at the jewel. This, by the way, was only about a quarter of the size of a hen's egg. Presently, Persano stirred, and he moaned under the gag. Raffles whispered into his ear, and he nodded. Raffles, saying to me, "Cosh him if he looks like he's going to yell," undid the gag.

Persano, as requested, kept his voice low. He confessed that he had heard rumors from his underworld contacts about the precious stones. Having tracked down our fence, he had contrived easily enough to buy one of Mr. Phillimore's jewels. In fact, he said, it was the first one that Mr. Phillimore had brought in to fence. Curious, wondering where the stones came from, since there were no reported thefts of these, he had come here to spy on Phillimore.

"There's a great story here," he said. "But just what, I haven't the foggiest. However, I must warn you that . . ."

His warning was not heeded. Both Raffles and I heard the low voices outside the gate and the scraping of shoes against gravel.

"Don't leave me tied up here, boys," Persano said. "I might have a little trouble explaining satisfactorily just what I'm doing here. And then there's the jewel. . ."

Raffles slipped the stone back into the matchbox and put it into Persano's pocket. If we were to be caught, we would not have the gem on us. He untied the journalist's wrists and ankles and said, "Good luck!"

A moment later, after throwing our coats over the broken glass, Raffles and I went over the rear rail. We ran crouching into a dense woods about twenty yards back of the house. At the other side at some distance was a newly built house and a newly laid road. A moment later, we saw Persano come over the wall. He ran by, not seeing us, and disappeared down the road, trailing a heavy cloud of perfume.

"We must visit him at his quarters," said Raffles. He put his hand on my shoulder to warn me, but there was no need. I too had seen the three men come around the corner of the wall. One took a position at the angle of the wall; the other two started toward our woods. We retreated as quietly as possible. Since there was no train available at this late hour, we walked to Maida Vale and took a hansom from there to home. Raffles went to his rooms at the Albany and I to mine on Mount Street.

☙ THREE ❧

When we saw the evening papers, we knew that the affair had taken on even more bizarre aspects. But we still had no inkling of the horrifying metamorphosis yet to come.

I doubt if there is a literate person in the West—or in the Orient, for that matter—who has not read about the strange case of Mr. James Phillimore. At eight in the morning, a hansom cab from Maida Vale pulled up before the gates of his estate. The house-keeper and the cook and Mr. Phillimore were the only occupants of the house. The area outside the walls was being surveilled by eight men from the Metropolitan Police Department. The cab driver rang the electrically operated bell at the gate. Mr. Phillimore walked out of the house and down the gravel path to the gate. Here he was observed by the cab driver, a policeman near the gate, and another in a tree. The latter could see clearly the entire front yard and house, and another man in a tree could clearly see the entire back yard and the back of the house.

Mr. Phillimore opened the gate but did not step through it. Commenting to the cabbie that it looked like rain, he added that he would return to the house to get his umbrella. The cabbie, the policemen, and the housekeeper saw him reenter the house. The housekeeper was at that moment in the room which occupied the front part of the ground floor of the house. She went into the kitchen as Mr. Phillimore entered the house. She did, however, hear his footsteps on the stairs from the hallway which led up to the first floor.

She was the last one to see Mr. Phillimore. He did not come back out of the house. After half an hour Mr. Mackenzie, the Scotland Yard inspector in charge, decided that Mr. Phillimore had somehow become aware that he was under surveillance. Mackenzie gave the signal, and he with three men entered the gate, another four retaining their positions outside. At no time was any part of the area outside the walls unobserved. Nor was the area inside the walls unscrutinized at any time.

The warrant duly shown to the housekeeper, the policemen entered the house and made a thorough search. To their astonishment, they could find no trace of Mr. Phillimore. The six-foot-six, twenty stone[1] gentleman had utterly disappeared.

For the next two days, the house—and the yard around it—was the subject of the most intense investigation. This established that the house contained no secret tunnels or hideaways. Every cubic inch was accounted for. It was impossible for him not to have left the house; yet he clearly had not done so.

"Another minute's delay, and we would have been cornered," Raffles said, taking another Sullivan from his silver cigarette case. "But, Lord, what's going on there, what mysterious forces are working there? Notice that no jewels were found in the house. At least, the police reported none. Now, did Phillimore actually go back to get his umbrella? Of course not. The umbrella was in the stand by the entrance; yet he went right by it and on upstairs. So,

[1] Two hundred and eighty pounds.

he observed the foxes outside the gate and bolted into his briar bush like the good little rabbit he was."

"And where is the briar bush?" I said.

"Ah! That's the question," Raffles breathed. "What kind of a rabbit is it which pulls the briar bush in after it? That is the sort of mystery which has attracted even the Great Detective himself. He has condescended to look into it."

"Then let us stay away from the whole affair!" I cried. "We have been singularly fortunate that none of our victims have called in your relative!"

Raffles was a third or fourth cousin to Holmes, though neither had, to my knowledge, even seen the other. I doubt that the sleuth had even gone to Lord's, or anywhere else, to see a cricket match.

"I wouldn't mind matching wits with him," Raffles said. "Perhaps he might then change his mind about who's the most dangerous man in London."

"We have more than enough money," I said. "Let's drop the whole business."

"It was only yesterday that you were complaining of boredom, Bunny," he said. "No, I think we should pay a visit to our journalist. He may know something that we, and possibly the police, don't know. However, if you prefer," he added contemptuously, "you may stay home."

That stung me, of course, and I insisted that I accompany him. A few minutes later, we got into a hansom, and Raffles told the driver to take us to Praed Street.

☙ Four ❧

Persano's apartment was at the end of two flights of Carrara marble steps and a carved mahogany banister. The porter conducted us to 10-C but left when Raffles tipped him handsomely. Raffles knocked on the door. After receiving no answer within a minute, he picked the lock. A moment later, we were inside a suite of extravagantly furnished rooms. A heavy odor of incense hung in the air.

I entered the bedroom and halted aghast. Persano, clad only in underwear, lay on the floor. The underwear, I regret to say, was the sheer black lace of the *demimondaine*. I suppose that if brassieres had existed at that time he would have been wearing one. I did not pay his dress much attention, however, because of his horrible expression. His face was cast into a mask of unutterable terror.

Near the tips of his outstretched fingers lay the large matchbox. It was open, and in it writhed something.

I drew back, but Raffles, after one soughing of intaken breath, felt the man's forehead and pulse and looked into the rigid eyes.

"Stark staring mad," he said. "Frozen with the horror that comes from the deepest of abysses."

Emboldened by his example, I drew near the box. Its contents looked somewhat like a worm, a thick tubular worm, with a dozen slim tentacles projecting from one end. This could be presumed to be its head, since the area just above the roots of the tentacles was ringed with small pale-blue eyes. These had pupils like a cat's. There was no nose or nasal openings or mouth.

"God!" I said shuddering. "What is it?"

"Only God knows," Raffles said. He lifted Persano's right hand and looked at the tips of the fingers. "Note the fleck of blood on each," he said. "They look as if pins have been stuck into them."

He bent over closer to the thing in the box and said. "The tips of the tentacles bear needlelike points, Bunny. Perhaps Persano is not so much paralyzed from horror as from venom."

"Don't get any closer, for Heaven's sake!" I said,

"Look, Bunny!" he said. "Doesn't that thing have a tiny shining object in one of its tentacles?"

Despite my nausea, I got down by him and looked straight at the monster.

"It seems to be a very thin and slightly curving piece of glass," I said. "What of it?"

Even as I spoke, the end of the tentacle which held the object opened, and the object disappeared within it.

"That *glass*," Raffles said, "is what's left of the *sapphire*. It's eaten it. That piece seems to have been the last of it."

"Eaten a sapphire?" I said, stunned. "Hard metal, blue corundum?"

"I think, Bunny," he said slowly, "the sapphire may only have looked like a sapphire. Perhaps it was not aluminum oxide but something hard enough to fool an expert. The interior may have been filled with something softer than the shell. Perhaps the shell held an embryo."

"What?" I said.

"I mean, Bunny, is it inconceivable, but nevertheless true, that that thing might have *hatched* from the jewel?"

☙ Five ❧

We left hurriedly a moment later. Raffles had decided against taking the monster—for which I was very grateful—because he wanted the police to have all the clues available.

"There's something very wrong here, Bunny," he said. "Very sinister." He lit a Sullivan and added in a drawl, "Very *alien!*"

"You mean un-British?" I said.

"I mean . . . un-Earthly."

A little later, we got out of the cab at St. James' Park and walked across it to the Albany. In Raffles' room, smoking cigars and drinking Scotch whiskey and soda, we discussed the significance of all we had seen but could come to no explanation, reasonable or otherwise. The next morning, reading the *Times*, the *Pall Mall Gazette*, and the *Daily Telegraph*, we learned how narrowly we had escaped. According to the papers, Inspectors Hopkins and Mackenzie and the private detective Holmes had entered Persano's rooms two minutes after we had left. Persano had died while on the way to the hospital.

"Not a word about the worm in the box," Raffles said. "The police are keeping it a secret. No doubt, they fear to alarm the public."

There would be, in fact, no official reference to the creature. Nor was it until 1922 that Dr. Watson made a passing reference to it in a published adventure of his colleague. I do not know what happened to the thing, but I suppose that it must have been placed in a jar of alcohol. There it must have quickly perished. No doubt the jar is collecting dust on some shelf in the backroom of some police museum. Whatever happened to it, it must have been disposed of. Otherwise, the world would not be what it is today.

"Strike me, there's only one thing to do, Bunny!" Raffles said, after he'd put the last paper down. "We must get into Phillimore's house and look for ourselves!"

I did not protest. I was more afraid of his scorn than of the police. However, we did not launch our little expedition that evening. Raffles went out to do some reconnoitering on his own, both among the East End fences and around the house in Kensal Rise. The evening of the second day, he appeared at my rooms. I had not been idle, however. I had gathered a supply of more corks for the gatetop spikes by drinking a number of bottles of champagne.

"The police guard has been withdrawn from the estate itself," he said. "I didn't see any men in the woods nearby. So, we break into the late Mr. Phillimore's house tonight. If he is late, that is," he added enigmatically.

As the midnight chimes struck, we went over the gate once more. A minute later, Raffles was taking out the pane from the glass door. This he did with his diamond, a pot of treacle, and a sheet of brown paper, as he had done the night we broke in and found our would-be blackmailer dead with his head crushed by a poker.

He inserted his hand through the opening, turned the key in the lock, and drew the bolt at the bottom of the door open. This had been shot by a policeman who had then left by the kitchen door, or so we presumed. We went through the door, closed it behind us, and made sure that all the drapes of the front room were pulled tight. Then Raffles, as he did that evil night long ago, lit a match and with it a gas light. The flaring illumination showed us a room little changed. Apparently, Mr. Phillimore had not been interested in redecorating. We went out into the hallway and upstairs, where three doors opened onto the first-floor hallway.

The first door led to the bedroom. It contained a huge canopied bed, a mid-century monster Baird had bought secondhand in some East End Shop, a cheap maple tallboy, a rocking chair, a thunder mug, and two large overstuffed leather armchairs.

"There was only one armchair the last time we were here," Raffles said.

The second room was unchanged, being as empty as the first time we'd seen it. The room at the rear was the bathroom, also unchanged.

We went downstairs and through the hallway to the kitchen, and then we descended into the coal cellar. This also contained a small wine pantry. As I expected, we had found nothing. After all, the men from the Yard were thorough, and what they might have missed, Holmes would have found. I was about to suggest to Raffles that we should admit failure and leave before somebody saw the lights in the house. But a sound from upstairs stopped me.

Raffles had heard it, too. Those ears missed little. He held up a hand for silence, though none was needed. He said, a moment later, "Softly, Bunny! It may be a policeman. But I think it is probably our quarry!"

We stole up the wooden steps, which insisted on creaking under our weight. Thence we crept into the kitchen and from there into the hallway and then into the front room. Seeing nobody, we went up the steps to the first floor once more and gingerly opened the door of each room and looked within.

While we were poking our heads into the bathroom, we heard a noise again. It came from somewhere in the front of the house, though whether it was upstairs or down we could not tell.

Raffles beckoned to me, and I followed, also on tiptoe, down the hall. He stopped at the door of the middle room, looked within, then led me to the door of the bedroom. On looking in (remember, we had not turned out the gaslights yet), he started. And he said, "Lord! One of the armchairs! It's gone!"

"But-but . . . who'd want to take a chair?" I said.

"Who, indeed!" he said, and ran down the steps with no attempt to keep quiet. I gathered my wits enough to order my feet to get moving. Just as I reached the door, I heard Raffles outside shouting, "There he goes!" I ran out onto the little tiled veranda.

Raffles was halfway down the gravel path, and a dim figure was plunging through the open gate. Whoever he was, he had had a key to the gate.

I remember thinking, irrelevantly, how cool the air had become in the short time we'd been in the house. Actually, it was not such an irrelevant thought since the advent of the cold air had caused a heavy mist. It hung over the road and coiled through the woods. And, of course, it helped the man we were chasing.

Raffles was as keen as a bill-collector chasing a debtor, and he kept his eyes on the vague figure until it plunged into a grove. When I came out its other side, breathing hard, I found Raffles standing on the edge of a narrow but rather deeply sunk brook. Nearby, half shrouded by the mist, was a short and narrow footbridge. Down the path that started from its other end was another of the half-built houses.

"He didn't cross that bridge," Raffles said. "I'd have heard him. If he went through the brook, he'd have done some splashing, and I'd have heard it. But he didn't have time to double back. Let's cross the bridge and see if he's left any footprints in the mud."

We walked Indian file across the very narrow bridge. It bent a little under our weight, giving us an uneasy feeling. Raffles said, "The contractor must be using as cheap materials as he can get away with. I hope he's putting better stuff into the houses. Otherwise, the first strong wind will blow them away."

"It does seem rather fragile," I said. "The builder must be a fly-by-night. But nobody builds anything as they used to do."

Raffles crouched down at the other end of the bridge, lit a match, and examined the ground on both sides of the path. "There are any number of prints," he said disgustedly. "They undoubtedly are those of the workmen, though the prints of the man we want could be among them. But I doubt it. They're all made by heavy workingmen's boots."

He sent me down the steep muddy bank to look for prints on the south side of the bridge. He went along the bank north of the bridge. Our matches flared and died while we called out the results of our inspections to each other. The only tracks we saw were ours.

We scrambled back up the bank and walked a little way onto the bridge. Side by side, we leaned over the excessively thin railing to stare down into the brook. Raffles lit a Sullivan, and the pleasant odor drove me to light one up too.

"There's something uncanny here, Bunny. Don't you feel it?"

I was about to reply when he put his hand on my shoulder. Softly, he said, "Did you hear a groan?"

"No," I replied, the hairs on the back of my neck rising like the dead from the grave.

Suddenly, he stamped the heel of his boot hard upon the plank. And then I heard a very low moan.

Before I could say anything to him, he was over the railing. He landed with a squish of mud on the bank. A match flared under the bridge, and for the first time I comprehended how thin the wood of the bridge was. I could see the flame through the planks.

Raffles yelled with horror. The match went out. I shouted, "What is it?" Suddenly, I was falling. I grabbed at the railing, felt it dwindle out of my grip, struck the cold water of the brook, felt the planks beneath me, felt them sliding away, and shouted once more. Raffles, who had been knocked down and buried for a minute by the collapsed bridge, rose unsteadily. Another match flared, and he cursed. I said, somewhat stupidly, "Where's the bridge?"

"Taken flight," he groaned. "Like the chair!"

He leaped past me and scrambled up the bank. At its top he stood for a minute, staring into the moonlight and the darkness beyond. I crawled shivering out of the brook, rose even more unsteadily, and clawed up the greasy cold mud of the steep bank. A minute later, breathing harshly, and feeling dizzy with unreality, I was standing by Raffles. He was breathing almost as hard as I.

"What is it?" I said.

"What is it, Bunny?" he said slowly. "It's something that can change its shape to resemble almost anything. As of now, however, it is not what it is but where it is that we must determine. We must find it and kill it, even if it should take the shape of a beautiful woman or a child."

"What are you talking about?" I cried.

"Bunny, as God is my witness, when I lit that match under the bridge, I saw one brown eye staring at me. It was embedded in a part of the planking that was thicker than the rest. And it was not far from what looked like a pair of lips and one malformed ear. Apparently, it had not had time to complete its transformation. Or, more likely, it retained organs of sight and hearing so that it would know what was happening in its neighborhood. If it sealed off all its organs of detection, it would not have the slightest idea when it would be safe to change shape again."

"Are you insane?" I said.

"Not unless you share my insanity, since you saw the same things I did. Bunny, that thing can somehow alter its flesh and bones. It has such control over its cells, its organs, its bones—which somehow can switch from rigidity to extreme flexibility—that it can look like other human beings. It can also metamorphose to look like objects. Such as the armchair in the bedroom, which looked exactly like the original. No wonder that Hopkins and Mackenzie and even the redoubtable Holmes failed to find Mr. James Phillimore. Perhaps they may even have sat on him while resting from the search. It's too bad that they did not rip into the chair with a knife in their quest for the jewels. I think that they would have been more than surprised.

"I wonder who the original Phillimore was? There is no record of anybody who could have been the model. But perhaps it based itself on somebody with a different name but took the name of James Phillimore from a tombstone or a newspaper account of an American. Whatever it did on that account, it was also the bridge that you and I crossed. A rather sensitive bridge, a sore bridge, which could not keep from groaning a little when our hard boots pained it."

I could not believe him. Yet I could not not believe him.

✵ Six ✵

Raffles predicted that the thing would be running or walking to Maida Vale. "And there it will take a cab to the nearest station and be on its way into the labyrinth of London. The devil of it is that we won't know what, or whom, to look for. It could be in the shape of a woman, or a small horse, for all I know. Or maybe a tree, though that's not a very mobile refuge.

"You know," he continued after some thought, "there must be definite limitations on what it can do. It has demonstrated that it can stretch its mass out to almost paper-thin length. But it is, after all, subject to the same physical laws we are subject to as far as its mass goes. It has only so much substance, and so it can get only so big. And I imagine that it can compress itself only so much. So, when I said that it might be the shape of a child. I could have been wrong. It can probably extend itself considerably but cannot contract much."

As it turned out, Raffles was right. But he was also wrong. The thing had means for becoming smaller, though at a price.

"Where could it have come from, A.J.?"

"That's a mystery that might better be laid in the lap of Holmes." he said. "Or perhaps in the hands of the astronomers. I would guess that the thing is not autochthonous. I would say that it arrived here recently, perhaps from Mars, perhaps from a more distant planet, during the month of October, 1894. Do you remember, Bunny, when all the papers were ablaze with accounts of the large falling star that fell into the Straits of Dover, not five miles from Dover itself? Could it have been some sort of ship which could carry a passenger through the ether? From some heavenly body where life exists, intelligent life, though not life as we Terrestrials know it? Could it perhaps have crashed, its propulsive power having failed it? Hence, the friction of its too-swift descent burned away part of the hull? Or were the flames merely the outward expression of its propulsion, which might be huge rockets?"

Even now, as I write this in 1924, I marvel at Raffles' superb imagination and deductive powers. That was 1895, three years before Mr. Wells' *War of the Worlds* was published. It was true that Mr. Verne had been writing his wonderful tales of scientific inventions and extraordinary voyages for many years. But in none of them had he proposed life on other planets or the possibility of infiltration or invasion by alien sapients from far-off planets. The concept was, to me, absolutely staggering. Yet Raffles plucked it from what to others would be a complex of complete irrelevancies. And I was supposed to be the writer of fiction in this partnership!

"I connect the events of the falling star and Mr. Phillimore because it was not too long after the star fell that Mr. Phillimore suddenly appeared from nowhere. In January of this year Mr. Phillimore sold his first jewel to a fence. Since then, once a month, Mr. Phillimore has sold a jewel, four in all. These look like star sapphires. But we may suppose that they are not such because of our experience with the monsterlet in Persano's matchbox. Those pseudo jewels, Bunny, are eggs!"

"Surely you do not mean that?" I said.

"My cousin has a maxim which has been rather widely quoted. He says that, after you've eliminated the impossible, whatever remains, however improbable, is the truth. Yes, Bunny, the race to which Mr. Phillimore belongs lays eggs. These are, in their initial form, anyway, something resembling star sapphires. The star shape inside them may be the first outlines of the embryo. I would guess that shortly before hatching, the embryo becomes opaque. The material inside, the yolk, is absorbed or eaten by the embryo. Then the shell is broken and the fragments are eaten by the little beast.

"And then, sometime after hatching, a short time, I'd say, the beastie must become mobile, it wriggles away, it takes refuge in a hole, a mouse hole, perhaps. And there it feeds upon cockroaches, mice, and, when it gets larger, rats. And then, Bunny? Dogs? Babies? And then?"

"Stop," I cried. "It's too horrible to contemplate!"

"Nothing is too horrible to contemplate, Bunny, if one can do something about the thing contemplated. In any event, if I am right, and I pray that I am, only one egg has so far hatched. This was the first one laid, the one that Persano somehow obtained. Within thirty days, another egg will hatch. And this time the thing might get away. We must track down all the eggs and destroy them. But first we must catch the thing that is laying the eggs.

"That won't be easy. It has an amazing intelligence and adaptability. Or, at least, it has amazing mimetic abilities. In one month it learned to speak English perfectly and to become well acquainted with British customs. That is no easy feat, Bunny. There are thousands of Frenchmen and Americans who have been here for some time who have not yet comprehended the British language, temperament, or customs. And these are human beings, though there are, of course, some Englishmen who are uncertain about this."

"Really, A.J.!" I said. "We're not all that snobbish!"

"Aren't we? It takes one to know one, my dear colleague, and I am unashamedly snobbish. After all, if one is an Englishman, it's no crime to be a snob, is it? Somebody has to be superior, and we know who that someone is, don't we?"

"You were speaking of the thing," I said testily.

"Yes. It must be in a panic. It knows it's been found out, and it must think that by now the entire human race will be howling for its blood. At least, I hope so. If it truly knows us, it will realize that we would be extremely reluctant to report it to the authorities. We would not want to be certified. Nor does it know that we cannot stand an investigation into our own lives.

"But it will, I hope, be ignorant of this and so will be trying to escape the country. To do so, it will take the closest and fastest means of transportation, and to do that it must buy a ticket to a definite destination. That destination, I guess, will be Dover. But perhaps not."

At the Maida Vale cab station, Raffles made inquiries of various drivers. We were lucky. One driver had observed another pick up a woman who might be the person—or thing—we were chasing. Encouraged by Raffles' pound note, the cabbie described her. She was a giantess, he said, she seemed to be about fifty years old, and, for some reason, she looked familiar. To his knowledge, he had never seen her before.

Raffles had him describe her face feature by feature. He said, "Thank you," and turned away with a wink at me. When we were alone, I asked him to explain the wink.

"She—it—had familiar features because they were Phillimore's own, though somewhat feminized." Raffles said. "We are on the right track."

On the way into London in our own cab, I said, "I don't understand how the thing gets rid of its clothes when it changes shape. And where did it get its woman's clothes and the purse? And its money to buy the ticket?"

"Its clothes must be part of its body. It must have superb control; it's a sentient chameleon, a superchameleon."

"But its money?" I said. "I understand that it has been selling its eggs in order to support itself. Also, I assume, to disseminate its young. But from where did the thing, when it became a woman, get the money with which to buy a ticket? And was the purse a part of its body before the metamorphosis? If it was, then it must be able to detach parts of its body."

"I rather imagine it has caches of money here and there," Raffles said.

We got out of the cab near St. James's Park, walked to Raffles' rooms at the Albany, quickly ate a breakfast brought in by the porter, donned false beards and plain-glass spectacles and fresh clothes, and then packed a Gladstone bag and rolled up a traveling rug. Raffles also put on a finger a very large ring. This concealed in its hollow interior a spring-operated knife, tiny but very sharp. Raffles had purchased it after his escape from the Camorra death-trap (described in *The Last Laugh*). He said that if he had had such a device then, he might have been able to cut himself loose instead of depending upon someone else to rescue him from Count Corbucci's devilish automatic executioner. And now a hunch told him to wear the ring during this particular exploit.

We boarded a hansom a few minutes later and soon were on the Charing Cross platform waiting for the train to Dover. And then we were off, comfortably ensconced in a private compartment, smoking cigars and sipping brandy from a flask carried by Raffles.

"I am leaving deduction and induction behind in favor of intuition, Bunny," Raffles said. "Though I could be wrong, intuition tells me that the thing is on the train ahead of us, headed for Dover."

"There are others who think as you do," I said, looking through the glass of the door. "But it must be inference, not intuition, that brings them here." Raffles glanced up in time to see the handsome aquiline features of his cousin and the beefy but genial features of his cousin's medical colleague go by. A moment later, Mackenzie's craggy features followed.

"Somehow," Raffles said, "that human bloodhound, my cousin, has sniffed out the thing's trail. Has he guessed any of the truth? If he has, he'll keep it to himself. The hardheads of the Yard would believe that he'd gone insane, if he imparted even a fraction of the reality behind the case."

ᴄ⁄ɔ SEVEN ᴄ⁄ɔ

Just before the train arrived at the Dover station, Raffles straightened up and snapped his fingers, a vulgar gesture I'd never known him to make before.

"Today's the day!" he cried. "Or it should be! Bunny, it's a matter of unofficial record that Phillimore came into the East End every thirty-first day to sell a jewel. Does this suggest that it lays an egg every thirty days? If so, then it lays another today! Does it do it as easily as the barnyard hen? Or does it experience some pain, some weakness, some tribulation and trouble analogous to that of human women? Is the passage of the egg a minor event, yet one which renders the layer prostrate for an hour or two? Can one lay a large and hard star sapphire with only a trivial difficulty, with only a pleased cackle?"

On getting off the train, he immediately began questioning porters and other train and station personnel. He was fortunate enough to discover a man who'd been on the train on which we suspected the thing had been. Yes, he had noticed something disturbing. A woman had occupied a compartment by herself, a very large woman, a Mrs. Brownstone. But when the train had pulled into the station, a huge man had left her compartment. She was nowhere to be seen. He had, however, been too busy to do anything about it even if there had been anything to do.

Raffles spoke to me afterward. "Could it have taken a hotel room so it could have the privacy needed to lay its egg?"

We ran out of the station and hired a cab to take us to the nearest hotel. As we pulled away, I saw Holmes and Watson talking to the very man we'd just been talking to.

The first hotel we visited was the Lord Warden, which was near the railway station and had a fine view of the harbor. We had no luck there, nor at the Burlington, which was on Liverpool Street, nor the Dover Castle, on Clearence Place. But at the King's Head, also on Clearence Place, we found that he—it—had recently been there. The desk clerk informed us that a man answering our description had checked in. He had left exactly five minutes ago. He had looked pale and shaky, as though he'd had too much to drink the night before.

As we left the hotel, Holmes, Watson, and Mackenzie entered. Holmes gave us a glance that poked chills through me. I was sure that he must have noted us in the train, at the station, and now at this hotel. Possibly, the clerks in the other hotels had told him that he had been preceded by two men asking questions about the same man.

Raffles hailed another cab and ordered the driver to take us along the waterfront, starting near Promenade Pier. As we rattled along, he said, "I may be wrong, Bunny, but I feel that Mr. Phillimore is going home."

"To Mars?" I said, startled. "Or wherever his home planet may be?"

"I rather think that his destination is no farther than the vessel that brought him here. It may still be under the waves, lying on the bottom of the straits, which is nowhere deeper than twenty-five fathoms. Since it must be airtight, it could be like Mr. Campbell's and Ash's all-electric submarine. Mr. Phillimore could be heading toward it, intending to hide out for some time. To lie low, literally, while affairs cool off in England."

"And how would he endure the pressure and the cold of twenty-five fathoms of sea water while on his way down to the vessel?" I said.

"Perhaps he turns into a fish," Raffles said irritatedly.

I pointed out the window. "Could that be he?"

"It might well be *it*," he replied. He shouted for the cabbie to slow down. The very tall, broad-shouldered, and huge-paunched man with the great rough face and the nose like a red pickle looked like the man described by the agent and the clerk. Moreover, he carried the purplish Gladstone bag which they had also described.

Our hansom swerved toward him; he looked at us; he turned pale; he began running. How had he recognized us? I do not know. We were still wearing the beards and spectacles, and he had seen us only briefly by moonlight and matchlight when we were wearing black masks. Perhaps he had a keen sense of odor, though how he could have picked up our scent from among the tar, spices, sweating men and horses, and the rotting garbage floating on the water, I do not know.

Whatever his means of detection, he recognized us. And the chase was on.

It did not last long on land. He ran down a pier for private craft, untied a rowboat, leaped into it, and began rowing as if he were training for the Henley Royal Regatta. I stood for a moment on the edge of the pier; I was stunned and horrified. His left foot was in contact with the Gladstone bag, and it was melting, flowing *into* his foot. In sixty seconds, it had disappeared except for a velvet bag it contained. This, I surmised, held the egg that the thing had laid in the hotel room.

A minute later, we were rowing after him in another boat while its owner shouted and shook an impotent fist at us. Presently, other shouts joined us. Looking back, I saw Mackenzie, Watson, and Holmes standing by the owner. But they did not talk long to him. They ran back to their cab and raced away.

Raffles said, "They'll be boarding a police boat, a steam-driven paddlewheeler or screwship. But I doubt that it can catch up with *that*, if there's a good wind and a fair head start."

That was Phillimore's destination, a small single-masted sailing ship riding at anchor about fifty yards out. Raffles said that she was a cutter. It was about thirty-five feet long, was fore-and-aft rigged, and carried a jib, forestaysail, and mainsail according to Raffles. I thanked him for the information, since I knew nothing and cared as much about anything that moves on water. Give me a good solid horse on good solid ground any time.

Phillimore was a good rower, as he should have been with that great body. But we gained slowly on him. By the time he was boarding the cutter *Alicia*, we were only a few yards behind him. He was just going over the railing when the bow of our boat crashed into the stern of his. Raffles and I went head over heels, oars flying. But we were up and swarming up the rope ladder within a few seconds. Raffles was first, and I fully expected him to be knocked in the head with a belaying pin or whatever it is that sailors use to knock people in the head. Later, he confessed that he expected to have his skull crushed in, too. But Phillimore was too busy recruiting a crew to bother with us at that moment.

When I say he was recruiting, I mean that he was splitting himself into three sailors. At that moment, he lay on the foredeck and was melting, clothes and all.

We should have charged him then and seized him while he was helpless. But we were too horrified. I, in fact, became nauseated, and I vomited over the railing. While I was engaged in this, Raffles got control of himself. He advanced swiftly toward the three-lobed monstrosity on the deck. He had gotten only a few feet, however, when a voice rang out.

"Put up yore dooks, you swells! Reach for the blue!"

Raffles froze. I raised my head and saw through teary eyes an old grizzled salt. He must have come from the cabin on the poopdeck, or whatever they call it, because he had not been visible when we came aboard. He was aiming a huge Colt revolver at us.

Meanwhile, the schizophrenic transformation was completed. Three little sailors, none higher than my waist, stood before us. They were identically featured, and they looked exactly like the old salt except for their size. They had beards and wore white-and-blue-striped stocking caps, large earrings in the left ear, red-and-black-striped jerseys, blue calf-length baggy pants, and they were barefooted. They began scurrying around, up came the anchor, the sails were set, and we were moving at a slant past the great Promenade Pier.

The old sailor had taken over the wheel after giving one of the midgets his pistol. Meanwhile, behind us, a small steamer, its smokestack belching black, tried vainly to catch up with us.

After about ten minutes, one of the tiny sailors took over the wheel. The old salt and one of his duplicates herded us into the cabin. The little fellow held the gun on us while the old sailor tied our wrists behind us and our legs to the upright pole of a bunk with a rope.

"You filthy traitor!" I snarled at the old sailor. "You are betraying the entire human race! Where is your common humanity?"

The old tar cackled and rubbed his gray wirelike whiskers.

"Me humanity? It's where the lords in Parliament and the fat bankers and the church-going factory owners of Manchester keep theirs, me fine young gentleman! In me pocket! Money talks louder than common humanity any day, as any of your landed lords or great cotton spinners will admit when they're drunk in the privacies of their mansion! What did common humanity ever do for me but give me parents the galloping consumption and make me sisters into drunken whores?"

I said nothing more. There was no reasoning with such a beastly wretch. He looked us over to make sure we were secure, and he and the tiny sailor left. Raffles said, "As long as Phillimore remains—like Gaul—in three parts, we have a chance. Surely, each of the trio's brain must have only a third of the intelligence of the original Phillimore I hope. And this little knife concealed in my ring will be the key to our liberty. I hope."

Fifteen minutes later, he had released himself and me. We went into the tiny galley, which was next to the cabin and part of the same structure. There we each took a large butcher knife and a large iron cooking pan. And when, after a long wait, one of the midgets came down into the cabin, Raffles hit him alongside the head with a pan before he could yell out. To my horror, Raffles then squeezed the thin throat between his two hands, and he did not let loose until the thing was dead.

"No time for niceties, Bunny," he said, grinning ghastily as he extracted the jewel-egg from the corpse's pocket. "Phillimore's a type of Boojum. If he succeeds in spawning many young, mankind will disappear softly and quietly, one by one. If it becomes necessary to blow up this ship and us with it, I'll not hesitate a moment. Still, we've reduced its forces by one-third. Now let's see if we can't make it one hundred percent."

He put the egg in his own pocket. A moment later, cautiously, we stuck our heads from the structure and looked out. We were in the forepart, facing the foredeck, and thus the old salt at the wheel couldn't see us. The other two midgets were working in the rigging at the orders of the steersman. I suppose that the thing actually knew little of sailsmanship and had to be instructed.

"Look at that, dead ahead," Raffles said. "This is a bright clear day, Bunny. Yet there's a patch of mist there that has no business being there. And we're sailing directly into it."

One of the midgets was holding a device which looked much like Raffles' silver cigarette case except that it had two rotatable knobs on it and a long thick wire sticking up from its top. Later, Raffles said that he thought that it was a machine which somehow sent vibrations through the ether to the spaceship on the bottom of the straits. These vibrations, coded, of course, signaled the automatic machinery on the ship to extend a tube to the surface. And an artificial fog was expelled from the tube.

His explanation was unbelievable, but it was the only one extant. Of course, at that time neither of us had heard of wireless, although some scientists knew of Hertz's experiments with oscillations. And Marconi was to patent the wireless telegraph the following year. But Phillimore's wireless must have been far advanced over anything we have in 1924.

"As soon as we're in the mist, we attack," Raffles said.

A few minutes later, wreaths of grey fell about us, and our faces felt cold and wet. We could barely see the two midgets working furiously to let down the sails. We crept out onto the deck and looked around the cabin's corner at the wheel. The old tar was no longer in sight. Nor was there any reason for him to be at the wheel. The ship was almost stopped. It obviously must be over the space vessel resting on the mud twenty fathoms below.

Raffles went back into the cabin after telling me to keep an eye on the two midgets. A few minutes later, just as I was beginning to feel panicky about his long absence, he popped out of the cabin.

"The old man was opening the petcocks," he said. "This ship will sink soon with all that water pouring in."

"Where is he?" I said.

"I hit him over the head with the pan," Raffles said. "I suppose he's drowning now."

At that moment, the two little sailors called out for the old sailor and the third member of the trio to come running. They were lowering the cutter's boat and apparently thought there wasn't much time before the ship went down. We ran out at them through the fog just as the boat struck the water. They squawked like chickens suddenly seeing a fox, and they leaped down into the boat. They didn't have far to go since the cutter's deck was now only about two feet above the waves. We jumped down into the boat and sprawled on our faces. Just as we scrambled up, the cutter rolled over, fortunately away from us, and bottom up. The lines attached to the davit had been loosed, and so our boat was not dragged down some minutes later when the ship sank.

A huge round form, like the back of a Brobdingnagian turtle, broke water beside us. Our boat rocked, and water shipped in, soaking us. Even as we advanced on the two tiny men, who jabbed at us with their knives, a port opened in the side of the great metal craft. Its lower part was below the surface of the sea, and suddenly water rushed into it, carrying our boat along with it. The ship was swallowing our boat and us along with it.

Then the port had closed behind us, but we were in a metallic and well-lit chamber. While the fight raged, with Raffles and me swinging our pans and thrusting our knives at the very agile and speedy midgets, the water was pumped out. As we were to find out, the vessel was sinking back to the mud of the bottom.

The two midgets finally leaped from the boat onto a metal

platform. One pressed a stud in the wall, and another port opened. We jumped after them, because we knew that if they got away and got their hands on their weapons, and these might be fearsome indeed, we'd be lost. Raffles knocked one off the platform with a swipe of the pan, and I slashed at the other with my knife.

The thing below the platform cried out in a strange language, and the other one jumped down beside him. He sprawled on top of his fellow, and within a few seconds they were melting together.

It was an act of sheer desperation. If they had had more than one-third of their normal intelligence, they probably would have taken a better course of action. Fusion took time, and this time we did not stand there paralyzed with horror. We leaped down and caught the thing halfway between its shape as two men and its normal, or natural, shape. Even so, tentacles with the poisoned claws on their ends sprouted, and the blue eyes began to form. It looked like a giant version of the thing in Persano's matchbox. But it was only two-thirds as large as it would have been if we'd not slain the detached part of it on the cutter. Its tentacles also were not as long as they would have been, but even so we could not get past them to its body. We danced around just outside their reach, cutting the tips with knives or batting them with the pans. The thing was bleeding, and two of its claws had been knocked off, but it was keeping us off while completing its metamorphosis. Once the thing was able to get to its feet, or I should say, its pseudopods, we'd be at an awful disadvantage.

Raffles yelled at me and ran toward the boat. I looked at him stupidly, and he said, "Help me, Bunny!"

I ran to him, and he said, "Slide the boat onto the thing, Bunny!"

"It's too heavy," I yelled, but I grabbed the side while he pushed on its stern; and somehow, though I felt my intestines would spurt out, we slid it over the watery floor. We did not go very fast, and the thing, seeing its peril, started to stand up. Raffles stopped pushing and threw his frying pan at it. It struck the thing at its head end, and down it went. It lay there a moment as if stunned, which I suppose it was.

Raffles came around to the side opposite mine, and when we

were almost upon the thing, but still out of reach of its vigorously waving tentacles, we lifted the bow of the boat. We didn't raise it very far, since it was very heavy. But when we let it fall, it crushed six of the tentacles beneath it. We had planned to drop it squarely on the middle of the thing's loathsome body, but the tentacles kept us from getting any closer.

Nevertheless, it was partially immobilized. We jumped into the boat and, using its sides as a bulwark, slashed at the tips of the tentacles that were still free. As the ends came over the side, we cut them off or smashed them with the pans. Then we climbed out, while it was screaming through the openings at the ends of the tentacles, and we stabbed it again and again. Greenish blood flowed from its wounds until the tentacles suddenly ceased writhing. The eyes became lightless; the greenish ichor turned black-red and congealed. A sickening odor, that of its death, rose from the wounds.

ఴ EIGHT ఴ

It took several days to study the controls on the panel in the vessel's bridge. Each was marked with a strange writing which we would never be able to decipher. But Raffles, the ever redoubtable Raffles, discovered the control that would move the vessel from the bottom to the surface, and he found out how to open the port to the outside. That was all we needed to know.

Meantime, we ate and drank from the ship's stores which had been laid in to feed the old tar. The other food looked nauseating, and even if it had been attractive, we'd not have dared to try it. Three days later, after rowing the boat out onto the sea—the mist was gone—we watched the vessel, its port still open, sink back under the waters. And it is still there on the bottom, for all I know.

We decided against telling the authorities about the thing and its ship. We had no desire to spend time in prison, no matter how patriotic we were. We might have been pardoned because of our great services. But then again we might, according to Raffles, be shut up for life because the authorities would want to keep the whole affair a secret.

Raffles also said that the vessel probably contained devices which, in Great Britain's hands, would ensure her supremacy. But she was already the most powerful nation on Earth, and who knew what Pandora's box we'd be opening?

We did not know, of course, that in twenty-three years the Great War would slaughter the majority of our best young men and would start our nation toward second-classdom.

Once ashore, we took passage back to London. There we launched the month's campaign that resulted in stealing and destroying every one of the sapphire-eggs. One had hatched, and the thing had taken refuge inside the walls, but Raffles burned the house down, though not until after rousing its human occupants. It broke our hearts to steal jewels worth in the neighborhood of a million pounds and then destroy them. But we did it, and so the world was saved.

Did Holmes guess some of the truth? Little escaped those grey hawk's eyes and the keen grey brain behind them. I suspect that he knew far more than he told even Watson. That is why Watson, in writing *The Problem of Thor Bridge*, stated that there were three cases in which Holmes had completely failed.

There was the case of James Phillimore, who returned into his house to get an umbrella and was never seen again. There was the case of Isadora Persano, who was found stark mad, staring at a worm in a match box, a worm unknown to science. And there was the case of the cutter *Alicia*, which sailed on a bright spring morning into a small patch of mist and never emerged, neither she nor her crew ever being seen again.

To the Wizard of Sci-Fi

I knew Forry Ackerman years before I met him.

Our first audiovisual contact was in 1953 at the World Science Fiction Convention hosted by the Philadelphia fans. But I had been very much aware of Forry Ackerman since 1929. That was the year I started to read science fiction magazines, in this case, Hugo Gernsback's *Air Wonder* and *Science Wonder*. It seemed to me then that every issue contained a letter from Forry in "The Reader Speaks" column. These were all signed quite formally: Forrest J. Ackerman.

Note the punctuation after the J. In those days Forry had periods.

Though I had not the slightest idea what he looked like, I envisioned a man about six feet six inches tall, very wide-shouldered, black-haired, and having a huge battleship-prow chin and piercing gray eyes. (All heroes had gray eyes in those days.) This image of a Tarzan-like superman was based on the extreme militance and excessive vigor of his letters. Never had I read such prose!

Of course, in these days, when we have become accustomed to such as Harlan Ellison, the language seems mild. But at that time it was considered not very nice.

Here's an example from an early *Amazing Stories*. This was, by the way, edited by T. O'Conor Sloane, Ph.D. Sloane was remarkable, or perhaps strange would be a better word, for two characteristics. One, he stated flatly that space travel was impossible. Two, he took so long to make up his mind about the stories submitted to him that many writers were convinced he went into hibernation in early November and did not emerge from his hole until late March. He took two years to decide on a novel submitted by Charlie Tanner, which provoked Charlie to write a letter of enquiry in which the editor was addressed as "To, Oh, Come On, Slow One!"

However, Sloane did print promptly the letters from his readers, and I reproduce a typical letter from Forry. This appeared in the Discussions section of the January 1932 issue of *Amazing Stories*. Forry's address at that time was 530 Staples Avenue, San Francisco, California. Here it is, verbatim and entire, so you may get some idea of the Forry Ackerman of that day, the Forry then generally considered the Demosthenes, the William Pitt, the J. J. Pierce, of SF letterhacks.

Preceding the letter, in big black letters, was the customary prefatory comment by T. O'Conor Sloane himself.

A CORRESPONDENT WHO SAYS WE DON'T KNOW OUR SHIRT FROM SHINOLA, BUT LIKES OUR STUFF ANYWAY.

Editor, *Amazing Stories*:

I beg of you to print this. You've been publishing stories lately containing brickbats so you surely should print this.

Where are the great illustrations and the great stories of yesteryear? Gone, gone with the (censored, Ed.)-ing snows. What's happened? Where did you go wrong? Good Heavens! I once thought you were the greatest, but I now think you're a (censored, Ed.)-head. You used to make me cream in my jeans once a month, make me swoon with ecstasy, when your rag hit the stands. But lately you've been feeding me and the long-suffering public a pile of (censored, Ed.).

Where are the incredible artists and the sense of

wonder of the *Amazing Stories* I once knew? Gone, gone down the (censored, Ed.)-ing drain. What happened to the incomparable Paul, Wesso, Morey? Where are the giants of purple prose: Ed Earl Repp, G. Peyton Wertenbaker, Captain S. P. Meek, Hendrik Dahl Juve, J. Lewis Burtt, B.SC., Miles J. Breuer, M.D., and Wood Jackson? These are all immortal names, destined to go down through the ages as classics, read as long as the English language lasts.

Your rivals, the twin magazines (censored, Ed.) have illustrations by these great artists and these great authors. So what's wrong with you, you (censored, Ed.) hole? Get these giants back and quit publishing tired old reprints of Verne and Wells and Rousseau, you cheap (censored, Ed.).

Otherwise, your rag isn't bad at all, and if it ceased publication I'd just die.

After Forry's letter, the editor added his usual comment. Or perhaps it wasn't so usual.

(Up yours, too, Forrest J. Ackerman. And in reply to your letter of October 20th, 1931, why should we pay you a cent a word for your letters? That's more than our authors get, when they get it.)

I hope I'm not shocking any of the thousands of Forry's admirers by exposing his youthful vitriolics or, as some might claim with some justification, lack of self-control. I quote this letter merely to show the contrast between the impetuous juvenile Jeremiah of the early 1930s and the Forry that we have known for so many years: the mild-mannered owner and occupant of stately Ackermansion. I was surprised when I first met Forry. I had expected a fiery stentorian-voiced eat-em-up-alive juggernaut. Instead, I found a pleasant gentle-voiced man of about my own age, one remarkably well-informed on SF and fantasy and movies. (I didn't know about his colossal collection then.) I was also to discover, through the years, that here was a man with about the biggest heart going, one without a trace of that vindictiveness and malice that most human beings have, whatever other good qualities they possess. Time and again, I've been amazed and touched at his generosity, his idealism, his gentleness, his constant kindnesses, and his thoughtfulnesses.

To keep from being accused of oversentimentality, I'll say here that Forry is not perfect. But then who is? And he has peccadilloes but no true sins.

One of the things about him that sticks in my mind, and there are many, is the yellow brick road he had in back of his house on Sherbourne Drive. Yes, Forry did have a yellow brick road in his backyard, hence the title of this encomium. I first saw it when I took my six-year-old granddaughter to show her the Ackermansion, its objets d'art, and its lord and master. Forry conducted her through every room, explaining what this and that was and where it came from. Then he led us out to the backyard, and we saw the yellow brick road. It started out just like the road in the movie, spiraled, and then, alas, disappeared. But my granddaughter Kim was delighted, entranced, I should say. She has never forgotten that, never will, I suppose. There really *is* a yellow brick road of Oz, and though she has her suspicions about the authenticity of Santa Claus, she doesn't have the slightest doubt about the existence of the yellow brick road.

Neither do I, and I suspect that Forry's faith is as deep as mine.

Forry, you see, is the man who built the yellow brick road. From fantasy, he constructed reality. And this is what he's been doing all his life. He fell in love with SF, and he took what was basically fantasy and built a real world out of it. He put together the fantastic Ackercollection in his Ackermansion, and he built his own life at the same time in accordance with the blueprints of SF. As SF grew, he grew, and vice versa.

So, Forrest J Ackerman, here's a *salud*, a toast, to you. I won't be at the Lunacon to lift a glass in your presence. But I'll be doing it here at home the night the attendees are honoring you. Here's to the Old Master Painter of Future Vistas, the Preserver and Advancer of Sci-fi, the Contractor Who Built the Yellow Brick Road.

A Fimbulwinter Introduction

I was born in the Fimbulwinter of January, 1918. At that time I little realized that, in addition to Baron von Richthofen and Mick Mannock and other great aces, G-8 and The Shadow were also aerial crusaders. Come to think of it, nobody else did either. I moved from my native town, North Terre Haute, Indiana before I was one, though with my parents' consent. At the age of six I came to live in Peoria, Illinois, where I've spent most of my life but by no means all.

Before I even knew pulp magazines, I was reading in the local library such authors as L. Frank Baum and Crump, and then, later, Doyle, London, Verrill, Hope, et al. At a very early age, however, I encountered Swift, Stevenson, Twain, and Homer. I believed then, and still believe, that Homer's *The Odyssey* is the greatest adventure story ever written. I fell under E.R. Burroughs' spell at the age of nine, and in 1929 additional fabulous worlds were opened for me when I purchased the first glorious copies of Gernsback's *Air Wonder Stories* and *Science Wonder Stories*. I determined at this time that I, too, would become a writer of stories of the far-off and the exotic.

This ambition wasn't realized until many many years later when I sold "The Lovers" to *Startling Stories* Magazine in 1952. I had sold one to *Adventure Magazine* (published in 1946), but this took place in Germany during World War II. Though a rather imaginative tale, it still was not science fiction.

My favorite pulp-magazine characters during my childhood and youth were Doc Savage, The Shadow, and heroes from the old *Argosy*: Singapore Sammy, Thibaut Corday, Bellow Bill Williams, Gillian Hazeltine, Peter the Brazen, Jimmie Cordie and his gang. *The Blue Book Magazine* provided some others, most notable of whom in my memory is Kioga.

This was during the Depression, however, and the dimes I had to spend on magazines were not many. So, when I had a choice to make between Doc Savage and The Shadow, I spent the dime on Doc. *The Shadow* and *Argosy* were begging, though I usually managed to borrow copies to read from my more affluent schoolmates.

College, in 1936, introduced me to classical literature. I had to quit in 1937 (because of the Depression) but I read the classics on my own. In 1939 I returned to college and in 1941 got married. My interest in Tarzan and the pulps waned for a long time; I was too busy working in a steel mill, being involved in the raising of two children, and in reading modern mainstream and the classics. I even lost interest in science fiction, though I still read *Astounding* and, occasionally, some of the other SF magazines.

In the meantime, I had returned to college, graduating in 1950. I regained my enthusiasm for SF, and by the time I'd sold "The Lovers," it was in full bloom again. The reprinting of the Doc Savage tales by Bantam Books rekindled an interest that I had thought died. Nostalgia never really perishes, however. The child in us may be deep, but it is ready to rise up if the lid is even momentarily lifted.

This time, on rereading the Savage tales and the long-ago-loved sagas from my collection, I had the advantage of knowing mainstream and classical literature. I began seeing certain valuable and significant elements in pulp fiction of which I had been entirely ignorant when I first read them. These elements will be described and amplified in my speech at the Classical Con.

From 1956 through part of 1969, I was an electromechanical

technical writer for the space-defense industry. A month before the first moon landing, I decided to go into full-time writing. Two years later I moved from Los Angeles to Peoria, and I've been here ever since. As of now, I've had published about thirty-three novels, two "biographies," and fifty-three short stories. My plans include doing biographies on Allan Quatermain, Arsène Lupin (the French equivalent of Raffles and Jimmy Dale), and the Wizard of Oz. I'll continue the Ancient Opar and the Lord Grandrith-Doc Caliban series, among others. And some day I hope to get permission to write *Escape from Loki*, the novel in which young Doc Savage meets the Fearsome Five in a German prison camp during World War I.

Osiris on Crutches

with Leo Queequeg Tincroder

S et, a god of the ancient land of Egypt, was the first critic.
Once he had been a creator, but the people ceased to believe
in his creativity. He then suffered a divinity block, which is similar
to a writer's block.

This is a sad fate for a deity. Odin and Thor, once cosmic
creators, became devils—that is, critics—in the new religion which
killed off their old religion. Satan, or Lucifer, was an archangel in
the Book of Job, but he became the chief of demons, the head-
honcho critic, in the New Testament. The Great Goddess of the
very ancient Mediterranean regions, named Cybele, Anana, Demeter,
depending on where she lived, became a demon, Lilith, for instance,
or, in one case, the Mother of God (and who criticizes more than
a mother?). But she had to do that via the back door, and most
people that pray to her don't know that she was not always called
Mary. Of course, there are scholars who deny this, just as there are
scholars who deny the existence of the Creator.

Those were the days. Gods walked the earth then. They weren't
invisible or absent as they are nowadays. A man or a woman could
speak directly to them. They might get only a divine fart in their

faces, but if the god felt like talking, the human had a once-in-a-lifetime experience.

Nowadays, you can only get into contact with a god by prayer. This is like sending a telegram which the messenger boy may or may not deliver. And there is seldom a reply by wire, letter, or phone.

In the dawn of mankind, the big gods in Egypt were Osiris, Isis, Nephthys, and Set. They were brothers and sisters, and Osiris was married to Isis and Set was married to Nephthys. Everybody then thought that incest was natural, especially if it took place among the gods.

In any event, no human was dumb enough to protest against the incest. If the gods missed you with their lightning or plagues, the priests got you with their sacrificial knives.

People had no trouble at all seeing the gods, though they might have to be quick about it. The peasants standing in mud mixed with ox manure and the pharaohs standing on their palace porches could see the four great gods, along with Osiris' vizier, Thoth, and Anubis, as they whizzed by. These traveled like the wind or the Roadrunner zooming through the Coyote's traps. Their figures were blurred with speed, dust was their trail, the screaming of split air their only sound.

From dawn to dusk they raced along, blessing the land and all on and in it.

However, the gods noticed a peculiar thing when they roared by a field just north of Abydos. A man always sat in the field, and his back was always turned to them. Sometimes they would speed around to look at his face. But when they did, they still found themselves looking at his back. And if one god went north and one south and one east and one west, four boxing the man in, all four could still see only his back.

"There is One greater than even us," they told each other. "Do you suppose that She, or He, as the case might be, put him there? Or perhaps that is even Him or Her?"

"You mean 'He or She,'" Set said. Even then he was potentially a critic.

Osiris on Crutches

After a while they quit staying up nights wondering who the man was and why they couldn't see his face and who put him there. But he was never entirely out of their minds at any time.

There is nothing that bugs an omniscient like not knowing something.

❧ Two ❧

Set stopped creating and became a nasty, nay-saying critic because the people stopped believing in him. Gods have vast powers and often use them with no consideration for the feelings or wishes of humans. But every god has a weakness against which he or she or it is helpless. If the humans decide he is an evil god, or a weak god, or a dying god, then he becomes evil or weak or dead. Too bad, Odin! Rotten luck, Zeus! Tough shit, Quetzalcoatl! Trail's end, Gitche Manitou!

But Set was a fighter. He was also treacherous, though he can't be blamed for that since the humans had decided that he was no good. He planned some unexpected events for Osiris at the big festival in Memphis honoring Osiris' return from a triumphant world tour, SRO. He planned to shortsheet his elder brother, Osiris, in a big way. From our viewpoint, our six-thousand-year perspective, Set may have had good reason. His sister-wife, Nephthys, was unable to conceive by him and, worse, she lusted after Osiris. Osiris resisted her, though not without getting red in the face and elsewhere.

This was not easy, since Osiris' flesh was green. Which has led some moderns to speculate that he may have come in a flying saucer from Mars. But his flesh was green because that's the color of living plants, and he was the god of agriculture. Among other things.

Nephthys overcame his moral scruples by getting him drunk. (This was the same method used by Lot's daughters many thousands of years later.) The result of this illicit rolling in the reeds was Anubis. Anubis, like a modern immortal, was a "funny-looking kid," and for much the same reason. He had the head of a jackal. This was because jackals ate the dead, and Anubis was the conductor, the ticket-puncher, for the souls who rode into the afterlife.

Bighearted Isis found the baby Anubis in the bulrushes, and she raised him as her own, though she knew very well who the parents were.

Osiris strode into Memphis. He was happy because he had just finished touring the world and teaching non-Egyptians all about peace and nonviolence. The world has never been in such good shape as then and, alas, never will be again. Set smiled widely and spread his arms to embrace Osiris. Osiris should have been wary. Set, as a babe, had torn himself prematurely and violently from his mother's womb, tearing her also. He was rough and wild, white-skinned and red-haired. He was a wild ass of a man.

Isis sat on her throne. She was radiant with happiness. Osiris had been gone for a long time, and she missed him. During his absence, Set had been sidling up to her and asking her if she wanted to get revenge on her husband for his adulterous fling with Nephthys. Isis had told him to beat it. But, truth to tell, she was wondering how long she could have held out. Gods and goddesses are hornier than mere humans, and *you* know how horny they are.

Isis, however, had to wait. Set gave a banquet that would have turned Cecil B. DeMille green with envy. When everyone ached from stuffing himself, and belches were exploding like rockets over Fort Henry, Set clapped his hands. Four large, but minor, gods staggered in. Among them they bore a marvelously worked coffer. They set it down, and Osiris said, "What is that exquisite *objet d'art,* brother?"

"It's a gift for whomever can fit himself into it exactly," Set said. Anybody else would have said "whoever," but Set was far more concerned with form than content.

To start things off, Set tried to get into the coffer. He was too tall, as he knew he'd be. His seventy-two accomplices in the conspiracy—Set was wicked but he was no piker—were too short. Isis didn't even try. Then Osiris, swaying a little from the gallons of wine he'd drunk, said, "If the coffer fits, wear it." Everybody laughed, and he climbed into the coffer and stretched out. The top of his head just touched the head of the coffer, and the soles of his feet just touched its foot.

Osiris smiled, though not for long. The conspirators slammed the lid down on his face and nailed it down, Set laughed; Isis screamed. The people ran away in panic. Paying no attention to the drumming on the lid from within the coffer, the accomplices rushed the coffer down to the Nile. There they threw it in, and the current carried it seaward.

❡❧ Three ❡❧

Some gods need air. Others are anaerobic. In those days, they all needed it, though they could live much longer without air than a human could. But it was a long journey down the Nile and across the sea to Byblos, Phoenicia. By the time it grounded on the beach there, Osiris was dead.

Set held Isis prisoner for some time. But Nephthys, who loathed Set now, joined Anubis and Thoth in freeing her. Isis journeyed to Byblos and brought the body back, probably by oxcart, since camels were not yet used. She hid the body in the swamps of a place called Buto. As evil luck would have it, Set was traveling through the swamp, and he fell over the coffer.

His face, when he saw his detested brother's corpse, went through the changes of wood on fire. It became black like wood before the match is applied, then red like flames, then pale like ashes. He tore the corpse into fourteen parts, and he scattered the pieces over the land. He was the destroyer, the spreader of perversity, the venomous nay-sayer.

Isis roamed Egypt looking for Osiris' parts. Tradition has it that she found everything but the phallus. This was supposed to have been eaten by a Nile crab, which is why Nile crabs are forever cursed. But this, like all myths, legends, and traditions, is based on oral material that is inevitably distorted through the ages.

The truth is the crab *had* eaten the genitals. But Isis forced it to disgorge. One testicle was gone, alas. But we know that the myth did not state the truth or at least not all of it. The myth also States that Isis became pregnant with a part of Osiris' body. It doesn't say what part, being vague for some reason. This reason is not delicacy. Ancient myths, in their unbowdlerized forms, were never delicate.

Isis used the phallus to conceive. Presently Horus was born. When he grew up he helped his mother in the search. This took a long time. But they found the head in a mud flat abounding in frogs, the heart on top of a tree, and the intestines being used as an ox whip by a peasant. It was a real mess.

Moreover, Osiris' brain was studded with frog eggs. Every once in a while a frog was hatched. This caused Osiris to have some peculiar thoughts, which led to peculiar behavior. However, if you are a god, or an Englishman, you can get away with eccentricity.

One of the thoughts kicked off by the hatching of a frog egg was the idea of the pyramid. Osiris told a pharaoh about it. The pharaoh asked him what it was good for. Osiris, always the poet, replied that it was a suppository for eternity.

This was true. But he forgot in his poet's enthusiasm his cold scientist's cold regard for cold facts. Eternity has body heat. Everything is slowly oxidizing. The earth and all on it are wrapped in flames if one only has eyes to see them. And so the pyramids, solid though they are, are burning away, falling to pieces. So much for the substantiality of stone.

Meanwhile, Isis and Horus found all of Osiris' body except for a leg and the nose. These seemed lost forever. So she did the best she could. She attached Osiris' phallus to his nose hole.

"After all," she said to Horus and Thoth, "he can wear a kilt to cover his lack of genitals. But he looks like hell without a nose of any kind."

Thoth, the god of writing, and hence also of the short memory, wasn't so sure. He had the head of an ibis, which was a bird with a very long beak. When Osiris was sexually aroused, he looked too much like Thoth. On the other hand, when Osiris wasn't aroused, he looked like an elephant. Usually, he was aroused. This was because the other gods left him in their dust while he hobbled along on his crutch. But Isis wasn't watching him, and so he dallied with the maidens, and some of the matrons, of the villages and cities along the Nile.

Humans being what they are, the priests soon had him on a schedule which combined the two great loves of mankind: money and sex. He would arrive at 11:45 A.M, at, say, Giza. At 12:00, after the tickets had been collected, he would become the central participant in a fertility rite. At 1:00 the high priest would blow the whistle. Osiris would pick up his crutch and hobble on to the next stop, which was, literally, a whistle stop. The maidens would pick themselves up off the ground and hobble home. Everybody else went back to work.

Osiris met a lot of girls this way, but he had trouble remembering their faces. Just as well. Humans age so fast. He never noticed that the crop of maidens of ten years ago had become careworn, workworn hags. Life was hard then. It was labor before dawn to past dusk, malaria, bilharzia, piles, too much starch and not enough meat and fruit, and, for the women, one pregnancy after another, teeth falling out, belly and breasts sagging, and varicose veins wrapping the legs and the buttocks like sucker vines.

Humans attributed all their ills, of course, to Set. He, they said, was a mean son of a bitch, and when he whirled by, accompanied by tornados, sandstorms, hyenas, and wild asses bearing leaky baskets of bullcrap, life got worse.

They prayed to Osiris and Isis and Horus to get rid of the primal critic, the basic despoiler. And it happened that Horus did kill him off.

Here's the funny thing about this. Though Set was dead, life for the humans did not get one whit better.

Four

After a few thousand years people caught on to this. They started to quit believing in the ancient Egyptian gods, and so these dwindled away. But the dwindling took time.

Female deities, for some reason, last longer than the males.

Isis was worshiped into the sixth century A.D., and when her last temple was closed down, she managed to slip into the Christian church under a pseudonym. Perhaps this is because men and women are very close to their mothers, and Isis was a really big mother.

Osiris, during his wanderings up and down along the Nile, noticed that humans had one method of defeating time. That was art. A man could fix a moment in time forever with a carving or a sculpture or a painting or a poem or a song. The individual passed, nations passed, races passed, but art survived. At least for a while. Nothing is eternal except eternity itself, and even the gods suddenly find that oxidation has burned them down to a crisp.

This is partly because religion is also an art form. And religion, like other art forms, changes with the times.

Osiris knew this, though he hated to admit it to himself. One day, early in the first century A.D., he saw once more the man whose back was always turned to him. This man had been sitting there for about six thousand years or perhaps for much longer. Maybe he was left over from the Old Stone Age.

Osiris decided he'd try once more. He hobbled around on his crutch, circling on the man's left. And then he got a strange burning feeling. The man's face was coming into view.

Straight ahead of the man was what the man's body had concealed. An oblong of blackness the size of a door in a small house lay flat on the earth's surface.

"This is the beginning of the end," Osiris whispered to himself. "I don't know why it is, but I can feel it."

"Greetings, first of the crippled gods, predecessor of Hephaestos and Wieland," the man said. "*Ave*, first of the gods to be torn apart and then put together again, predecessor of Frey and Lemminkäinen. Hail, first of the good gods to die, basic model for those to come, for Baldur and Jesus."

"You don't look like you belong here," Osiris said. "You look like you come from a different time."

"I'm from the twentieth century, which may be the next-to-last century for man or perhaps the last," the man said. "I know what you're thinking, that religion is a form of art. Well, life itself is an art, though most people are imitative artists when it comes to living, painters of the same old paintings over and over again. There are very few originators. Life is a mass art, or usually the art of the masses. And the art of the masses is, unfortunately, bad art. Though often entertaining," he added hastily, as if he feared that Osiris would think he was a snob.

"Who are you?" Osiris said.

"I am Leo Queequeg Tincrowdor," the man said. "Tincrowdor, like Rembrandt, puts himself in his paintings. Any artist worth his salt does. But since I am not worthy to hand Rembrandt a roll of toilet paper, I always paint my back to the viewer. When I become as good as the old Dutchman, I'll show my face in the mob scenes."

"Are you telling me that you have created me? And all this, too?" Osiris said. He waved a green hand at the blue river and the pale green and brown fields and the brown and red sands and rocks beyond the fields.

"Every human being knows he created the world when he somehow created himself into being," Tincrowdor said. "But only the artist recreates the world. Which is why you have had to go through so many millennia with a phallus for a nose and a crutch for a leg."

"I didn't mind the misplaced phallus," Osiris said. "I can't smell with it, you know, and that is a great benefit, a vast advantage. The world really *stinks,* Tincrowdor. But with this organ up here, I could no longer smell it. So thanks a lot."

"You're welcome," the man said. "However, you've been around long enough. People have caught on now to the fact that even gods can be crippled. And that crippled gods are symbols of humans and their plight. Humans, you know, are crippled in one way or another. All use crutches, physical or psychical."

"Tell me something new," Osiris said, sneering.

"It's an old observation that will always be new. It's always new because people just don't believe it until it's too late to throw the crutch away."

Osiris then noticed the paintings half buried in the khaki-, or kaka-, colored dust. He picked them up, blew off the dust, and looked at them. The deepest buried, and so obviously the earliest, looked very primitive. Not Paleolithic but Neolithic. They were stiff, geometrical, awkward, crude, and in garish unnatural colors. In them was Osiris himself and the other deities, two-dimensional, as massive and static as pyramids and hence solid, lacking interior space for interior life. The paintings also had no perspective.

"You didn't know that the world, and hence you, was two-dimensional then, did you?" Tincrowdor said. "Don't feel bad about that. Fish don't know they live in water just as humans don't know a state of grace surrounds them. The difference is, the fish are already in the water, whereas humans have to swim through nongrace to get to the grace."

Osiris looked at the next batch of paintings. Now he was three-dimensional, fluid, graceful, natural in form and color, no longer a stereotype but an individual. And the valley of the Nile had true perspective.

But in the next batch the perspective was lost and he was two-dimensional again. However, somehow, he seemed supported by and integrated with the universe, a feature lacking in the previous batch. But he had lost his individuality again. To compensate for the loss, a divine light shone through him like light through a stained-glass window.

The next set returned to perspective, to three dimensions, to warm natural colors, to individuality. But, quickly in a bewildering number and diversity, the Nile and he became an abstraction, a cube, a distorted wild beast, a nightmare, a countless number of points confined within a line, a moebius strip, a shower of fragments.

Osiris dropped them back into the dust, and he bent over to look into the oblong of blackness.

"What is that?" he said, though he knew.

"It is," Tincrowdor said, "the inevitable, though not necessarily desired, end of the evolution you saw portrayed in the paintings. It is my final painting. The achievement of pure and perfect harmony. It is nothingness."

Tincrowdor lifted a crutch from the dust which had concealed it all these thousands of years. He did not really need it, but he did not want to admit this to himself. Not yet, anyway—someday, maybe.

Using it as a pole up which to climb, he got to his feet. And, supporting himself on it, he booted the god in the rear. And Osiris fell down and through. Since nothingness is an incomplete equation, Osiris quickly became the other part of the equation—that is, nothing. He was glad. There is nothing worse than being an archetype, a symbol, and somebody else's creation. Unless it's being a cripple when you don't have to be.

Tincrowdor hobbled back to this century. Nobody noticed the crutch—except for some children and some very old people—just as nobody notices a telephone pole until he runs into it, Or a state of grace until it hits him.

As for his peculiarity of behavior and thought—call it eccentricity or originality—this was attributed by everybody to frog eggs hatching in his brain.

Phonemics

"Eny" for "any" is fine for Australia. But what about standard American, which generally pronounces "any" as "iny"?

I got interested in phonemic spelling when I was taking a graduate course in linguistics at Arizona State University. I like the idea of such, because an eight-year old child could be taught to spell properly in two weeks, maybe less.

However, dialectical differences cause some trouble. Englishmen would spell their words (many of them, anyway) somewhat differently than an Australian or a Scot or an American. I don't see that this presents any great difficulty, however. For instance, the adjustment of a Midwesterner to the spelling of a Texan would be slight.

But the big objection would be economic. All books worth reprinting would have to be issued with the new phonemic spelling. Also, after a new generation has grown up, it would be cut off from the old literature. Only scholars among the new generation could read the old stuff.

Also, the conservatives, who would in this case include most of the population of the US (and I imagine that of any English-speaking country) would oppose, perhaps violently, any such change. (Even if anyone could learn to read the phonemic alphabet in two weeks or less.)

Theodore Roosevelt tried to introduce some simplified spellings in government documents during his presidency. Such stuff as "thru" for "through." The reaction was so energetic and vociferous that he had to abandon the idea.

However, I'm all for it. Why don't you spell "any" as "eniy"? The "iy" stands for the diphthong.

hwat duw Θiŋk əv ðis aydiya? ay ləv it. meybiy səmdey itəl kætc on. bət ay daut it.

in phonemic spelling, capital letters can be discarded. you know when a new sentence begins because the previous one ends with a period or a question or exclamation mark or semicolon. izənt ðæt rayt, erik?

(erik: tuw bludiy rayt, fil. Or is "right" "rat" in Aussie dialect?)

but do you base the phonemic spelling on English as it is supposed to be spoken? or on rapid speech, which is slurred, contracting? what do you say = hwat duw yuw sey? = hwədyə sey?

Or, ay gat youw = ay gače?

Diacritical marks make writing slower, so č and š could be spelled ch and sh, though that isn't completely phonemic.

I'd like to see the very useful and natural *ain't* restored as standard English and to hell with the absurd pedantical prejudice against it. eynt ðæt rayt?

ay intend tuw rayt n artik'l n is s bjikt s m dey.

best, filip howzéy farm r

The Last Rise of Nick Adams

Nick Adams, Jr., science-fiction author, and his wife were having the same old argument.

"If you really loved me, you wouldn't be having so much trouble with it."

"There are many words for it," Nick said. "If you didn't have a dirty mind, you'd use them. Anyway, there are plenty of times when you can't complain about it."

"Yeah! About once every other month I can't!"

Ashlar was a tall scrawny ex-blonde who had been beautiful until the age of thirty-seven-and-a-half. Now she was fifty. A hard fifty, Nick thought. And here am I, a soft fifty.

"It does have a sort of sine-wave action," he said. "I mean, if you drew a graph."

"So now it's dependent on weather conditions. What're we supposed to do, consult the barometer when we make love? Why don't you make a graph of its rises and falls? Of course, you'd have to have some rises first . . ."

"I got to go to work," he said, "I'm months behind . . ."

"I'll say you are, though I don't mean in your writing! All right, hide behind the typewriter! Bang your keys; don't bang me!"

He rose from the chair and dutifully kissed her on her forehead. It was as cold and hard as a tombstone, incised with wrinkles that read *Here Lies Love, RIP.* She snarled silently. Shrugging, he walked up the steps toward his office. By the time he reached the third floor, he was sweating as if he were a rape suspect in a police lineup. His panting filled the house.

Fifty, out of breath, and low on virility. Still, it wasn't really his fault. She was such a cold bitch. Take last night, for instance. Ashlar's eyes had started rolling, and her face was falling apart underneath the makeup. He had said, "Did you feel something move, little rabbit?" (He was crazy about Hemingway.) And she had said, "Something's going to move. Get off. I got to go to the toilet."

Once it had all been good and true, and he had felt the universe move all the way to the Pole Star. Now he felt as if the hair had fallen off his chest.

He sat down before the typewriter and stroked the keys, the smooth and cool keys, and he pressed a few to tune up his fingers and warm up the writing spirit. He could feel the inspiration deep down within, shadow-boxing, rope-skipping, jogging, sweating, pores open, heart beating hard and true, ready to climb into the ring.

The only trouble was, the bell rang, and he couldn't even get out of his corner. He was stuck on the first word. The. The . . . what?

If only he could see some pattern in his sexual behavior. Maybe the silly bitch's sarcastic remark about making a graph wasn't so stupid. Maybe . . .

A bell rang, and he sprang up, shuffling, his left shoulder up, arm extended . . . what was he doing? That was the front doorbell, and it was probably announcing the delivery of the mail. Nick gave the mailman ten dollars a month to ring the doorbell. This was illegal, but who was going to know? Nick could not endure the idea that a hot check was cooling off in the mailbox.

He hurried downstairs, passing Ashlar, who wasn't going to get off her ass and bring the mail to him. Not her.

Since this was the first of the month, there were ten bills. But there was also a pile of fan mail and a letter from his agent.

Ah! His agent had sent a check, the initial advance on a new contract. Two thousand dollars. Minus his agent's ten percent commission. Minus fifty dollars for overseas market mailings. Minus twenty-five for the long-distance call his agent had made to him last month. Minus a thousand for the loan from his agent. Minus fifty for the interest on the loan. Minus ten dollars accounting charge.

Only six hundred and sixty-five dollars remained, but it was a feast after last month's famine. By the time he'd finished reading the fan letters, all raving about the goodness and truth of his works, he felt as if he was connected to a gas station air pump.

Suddenly, he knew that there was a pattern to the decline and fall of the Roman Empire he carried between his legs. In no way, however, was he going to take the edge off his horniness by explaining the revelation to Ashlar just now. He dropped his mail and his pants, and he hurried to the kitchen. Ashlar was bent over, putting dishes in the washer.

He flipped up her skirt, yanked down her panties, and said, "The dishes can wait, but it can't."

It would all have been good and true and the earth might have moved if Ashlar hadn't gotten her head caught between the wire racks of the washer.

"You're getting fat again, aren't you?" Ashlar said. "That's some spare tire you got. And you missed a patch on your cheek when you shaved. Listen. I know this isn't the time to talk about it, but my mother . . . what's the matter? Why are you stopping?"

Nick snarled and he said, "If you need an explanation, you're an imbecile. I'm pulling out like a train that stopped at the wrong station. I'm going back to my typewriter. A woman will always screw you up, but a typewriter's a typewriter, true and trustworthy, and it doesn't talk to you when you're making love to it."

Two minutes later, while Ashlar beat on the door with her fists and yelled at him, the typewriter keys jammed and he couldn't get them unstuck.

You couldn't even put faith in a simple machine. You could not trust anything. Everything that was supposed to be clean and good and true went to hell in this universe. Still, you had to stick with it, be a man with *conejos*. Or was it *cojones*? Never mind. Just tell yourself, "Tough shit," and "My head is bloody but unbowed. You have to die but you don't have to say Uncle."

That was fine, but the keys were still stuck, and Ashlar wouldn't quit beating on the door and screaming.

He got up, cursing and yanked the door open. Ashlar fell sobbing into his arms.

"I'm sorry, sorry, sorry! What a bitch I am! Here's the whole earth about ready to move all the way down to its core, and I pick on you!"

"Yes, you're truly a bitch," he said. "But I forgive you because I love you and you love me and no matter what happens we have something that is good. However . . ."

He wasn't going to say anything about his discovery of the pattern. Not now. He'd test his theory later.

An hour afterward, he said, panting, "Listen, Ashlar, let's take a vacation. We'll go to the World Science-Fiction Convention in Las Vegas. We'll have fun, and in between parties and shooting craps, we'll make love. The good true feeling will come back while we're there."

Or should he have said the true good feeling? What the hell was the correct order of adjectives in a phrase like that?

It didn't matter. What did was that Ashlar decided to go to the convention and didn't even complain that she had nothing to wear. Moreover, his theory had worked out. Up to a point, anyway, and that wasn't really his fault. The fans crowded around him, begging for his autograph, and he heard never an unkind word. As if this wasn't heady enough, not to mention the stimulation of his male hormones, three of the greatest science-fiction authors in the world invited him to dinner and paid him many compliments over the bourbons and steaks.

The first, Zeke Vermouth, Ph.D., the wealthiest writer in the field, didn't mention that they were going Dutch until after the meal was eaten. Even this didn't lessen Nick's pleasures. And then, glory of glories, Robin Hindbind, the dean of science-fiction authors, had him in for a private supper. Nick was happy as a man with a free lifetime pass to a massage parlor. It was fabulous to sit in the suite, which was as spacious as Nick's house, and eat with the creator of such classics as *Water Brother Among the Bathless*, *I Will Boll No Weevil* and the autobiographical *Time Enough For F**ing*, subtitled *Why Everybody Worships Me*.

Then, wonder of wonders, the grand old man, Preston de Tove himself, asked Nick to a very select party. De Tove was probably Nick's greatest hero, the man who had rocked the science-fiction world in the 40s with his smashing *Spam!* and *The World of Zilch A*.

De Tove, however, hadn't done much writing for thirty years. He'd been too busy practicing a science of mental health originated by another classic author, old B. M. Kachall himself. This was M.P. (Mnemonic Peristalsis) Therapy, a psychic discipline which claimed to enable a person to attain through its techniques an I.Q. of 500, perfect recall, Superman's or Wonder Woman's body, and immortality.

In essence, these techniques consisted in keeping your bowels one hundred percent open. To do this, though, you had to work back along your memory track until you encountered in all details, visual, tactile, auditory, olfactory, especially olfactory, your first bowel movement. This was called the P.U. or Primal Urge.

Kachall had promised his disciples that all goals could be reached within a year through M.P. Therapy. However, de Tove, like the majority of Kachall's followers, was, three decades later, still taking laxatives as a physical aid to the mental techniques. He had not lost faith, even if he did spend most of his time during the party in the bathroom.

De Tove had refused to go along with Kachall's S.P.L. Religion, a metaphysical extension of M.P. Therapy. Perhaps this was because de Tove had to wear a diaper at all times, and at- tendees at the S.P.L. services were forbidden to wear anything. In any event, the religion required that the worshipper send his C.E. (Colonic Ego) back to the first movement of the universe, the Big Bang. If the worshipper survived that, he was certified to be an

E.E. (End End), one who'd attained the Supreme Purgative Level. This meant that the E.E. radiated such a powerful aura that nobody would dare to mess around with him. Or even get near him for that matter.

Aside from having had to sit by an open window throughout the party, Nick was ecstatic. Nothing better could happen now. But he was wrong. The next day, two Englishmen, G. C. Alldrab and William Rubboys, invited him to a party for avant-garde writers. This twain had been lucky enough to be highly esteemed by some important mainstream critics and so now refused to be classified as mere SF authors. Nevertheless, when the convention committee offered to pay their airfare, hotel expenses, and booze if they'd be guests, they consented to associate, for three days at least, with the debased category.

Alldrab was chiefly famous for stories in which depressed, impotent, passive, and incompetent antiheroes passed through catastrophic landscapes over which floated various parts, usually sexual, of famous people. He was also hung up on traffic accidents, a symbol to him of the rottenness of Western civilization, especially the United States. He sneered at plots and storylines.

And so did his colleague. Rubboys was famous for both the unique content and technique of his fiction. It drew mostly on his experiences as a drug addict and peregrinating homosexual. Otherwise, he was a nice guy and not nearly as snobbish as Alldrab, though some were unkind enough to say that his camaraderie with young male fans wasn't entirely due to his democratic leanings.

Lately, he'd been getting a lot of flak from feminist critics, who loathed his vicious attitude towards all women, though he claimed it was purely literary. They couldn't be blamed. Try though they might to ignore his bias because of his high reputation as a writer, they'd gotten fed up with his numerous references to females as cunts, gashes, twats, slits, and hairy holes.

Rubboys' technique consisted of putting a manuscript through a shredder, then pasting the strips at random for the finished product.

Nick didn't care for either man's works, though he did admit that Alldrab's fiction made more sense than Rubboys'. But then whose didn't? However, to be their guest was an honor in some circles, and these were the critics with clout. Maybe they'd take some notice of him now—glory through association.

Nick was told that, even though he was middle-aged and wrote mostly square commercial stuff, he had been invited because of his experimental time travel story, *The Man Who Buggered Himself.* This was great stuff, obscure and unintelligible and quasi-poetic enough to satisfy the artiest of the arty.

Nick just grinned. Why should he tell them he had written the story while drinking muscatel and smoking opium?

The party was a success until midnight. Alldrab, pissy-assed drunk by then, tried to get his mistress to take Rubboys' rented car out and drive it at 100 mph into a lamppost. Thus he could witness a real crash and transpose it into sanguinary poetry in his next novel, *Smash!*, get to the root of the evilness in Occidental culture.

His mistress didn't care for this. In fact, she became hysterical. Rubboys wasn't too keen about it either.

Result: a stampede of pale tight-faced guests out of the door, Nick in the lead, while the girl-friend was dialing the police.

Ashlar was curious about why Nick had been so horny during the convention and for some weeks after that, then had quickly reverted to steerhood.

"What's the matter with you?" Ashlar said after one particular-ly distressing attempt. "Again?"

She dropped her cigarette ashes on his pubic hairs, causing him to delay his reply until he put out the fire.

"I'll tell you!" he roared. "You're always putting me down, literally and figuratively. Criticising me. You deflate my ego and hence my potency."

"The same thing happens when I get bad reviews or fan mail that knocks me or a rejection slip. But when fans and critics and authors praise me, which doesn't happen often, I'm inflated. There's no doubt about it. I've determined scientifically that my virility waxes and wanes in direct proportion to the quantity-cum (no pun intended) -quality of the praise or bumraps I receive."

"You can't be serious?"

"I drew a graph. It isn't exactly a bell-shaped curve. More like a limp cactus."

"You mean I got to say only nice things about you, keep my mouth shut when you bug me? Treat you like an idol of gold? You're not, you know. You have feet of clay—all the way up to your big bald spot."

"See, that's what I mean."

They quarreled violently for three hours. In the end, Ashlar wept and promised she'd quit pointing out his faults. Not only that, she'd praise him a lot.

But that wasn't honest, and so it didn't work out. He knew she was lying when she told him how handsome he was and what a great writer he was and how he was the most fantastic stud in the world.

To make things worse, his latest book was panned by one hundred percent of the reviewers.

"Thumbs down; everything's down," Nick said.

A week later, things got good again. Better than good. He was as happy as Aladdin when he first rubbed the bride given him by the magic lamp.

Dubbeldeel Publications came through with some unexpected royalties on a three-year-old book. The publisher offered to buy another on the basis of a two-page outline. Nick got word that a Ph.D. candidate at UCLA was writing a thesis on his works. The fan mail that week was unusually heavy and not one of its writers suggested that he wrote on toilet paper.

It did not matter now that he doubted Ashlar's sincerity. People with no ulterior motives were comparing him with the great Kilgore Trout.

He was so happy that he suggested to Ashlar that they take another vacation, attend a convention in Pekin, Illinois, which was only ten miles from their hometown, Peoria. Ashlar said that she'd go, even if she didn't like the creeps that crowded around him at the cons. She'd spend her time in the bar with the wives of the writers. She could relax with them, get away from shoptalk that wearied her so when the writers got together. The wives didn't care for science-fiction and seldom read even their husband's stuff. Especially their husband's stuff.

Nick wasn't superstitious. Even so he regarded it as a favorable omen when he saw the program book of the convention. In big bold letters on the cover was the name of the convention. It should have been Pekcon, fan slang for Pek(in) Con(vention). But it had come out Pekcor.

Later, Nick admitted that he'd interpreted the signs and portents wrongly. Had he ever!

At first, things went as well as anyone could ask for. The fans practically kissed his feet, and the regard of his peers was very evident. Some even paid for the drinks, instead of leaving him, as usual, to sweat while he settled a staggering bill.

Ashlar should have been happy. Instead, she complained that she couldn't spend the rest of her life attending conventions just to have a good sex life.

Nick got to talking with an eighteen-year-old fan with long blonde hair, a pixie face, huge adoring eyes, boobs that floated ahead of her like hot-air balloons, and legs like Marlene Dietrich's. Her last name was Barkis, she was willing, and he was overcome by temptation. They went to her room, and the sexual-Richter scale hit 8.6 and was on its way to record 9.6 when Ashlar began beating at the door and screaming at him to open it.

Later, he found out that a writer's wife had seen him and Barkis entering her room. She had raced around the hotel until she found Ashlar, who hadn't wasted any time getting the hotel dick and three wives as witnesses.

All the way to Peoria, Ashlar didn't stop yelling or crying. Once there, she swiftly packed and took a taxi to her mother's house. She didn't stay there long, since she had been so angry that she'd forgotten her mother had recently gone to a nursing home. Unfazed, she moved into an expensive hotel and sent her bills through her lawyer to Nick.

Each day he got a long letter from her—each deflating. Throwing them unread into the wastepaper basket didn't work. He was too curious, he had to open them and see what new invectives and unsavory descriptions she had come up with. So, after long thought, he sold the house and moved from Illinois to New Jersey. Only his agent had his forwarding address, and Nick told him to return all letters from his wife to her.

"Mark them: *Uninterested.*"

But he knew that she would find him some day.

Three months passed without a letter from her. Things went as well as could he expected in this world where hardly anybody really gave a damn how you were doing. He did find a young fan, "Moomah" Smith, who was eager to spend a night with him when he got good mail, good notices, and good royalties.

And then, one morning as he was drinking coffee just before tackling the typewriter, the phone rang. His agent's new secretary, one he didn't know, was calling. Her employer was in Europe (cavorting around on his ten percent, Nick thought), but she had good news for him. Sharper & Rake, really big hardcover publishers, had just bought an outline for a novel, *A Sanitary Brightly Illuminated Planet*, and they were going to give him a huge advance. Furthermore, Sharper & Rake intended to go all out in an advertising and publicity campaign.

Nick hung up. He was grinning, but he was also breathing hard. Definitely inflating, that news. His prick felt as long and as hard as the *Hindenburg*, and he only needed to moor it in Moomah for it to catch fire. He reached for the phone to call Moomah before she left for high school. The phone rang; he grabbed it; he heard a sexy female voice telling him how great he was. She was making a call from California (her parents didn't know about it but what the hell, she could handle them). She raved on about his work and how handsome he looked on the dust cover of a novel, and he saw no reason to stop her. Finally, when she hung up, he was in such a state that he had to get Moomah to the house.

He'd have to be tricky, lie a lot, since school security would check on the call. But he would do it. He must. By now his zipper was about to be torn loose from the fly.

The doorbell rang. On his way to answer it Nick opened the zipper and let air in and the peter out. He opened the door but stood behind it, looking around its side. For a moment he thought about grabbing the postwoman and pulling her in, but, fortunately, he had not lost all of his wits. Having signed the two special-delivery letter receipts, he closed the door.

The letters had been sent through his agent, and they were not, as he feared, from his wife's lawyers. They did send his blood pressure up, though in a healthy manner.

The first letter was from a member of the committee which handled the Pulsar Award. This was given once a year by SWOT, the Science-Fiction Writers of Terra. Nick belonged to this, although its chief benefit was that he could deduct the membership dues from his income tax. However, one of his stories, *Hot Nights on Venus*, had been nominated for the Pulsar. And now, and now— the monster felt as if it were the *Queen Mary* heading for port with a stiff wind behind it—he had won it!

"Under no circumstances must you tell anyone about this," the committee member had written, "The awards won't be given until two months from now. We're informing you of this to make sure that you'll be at the annual SWOT banquet in New York."

Nick read the second letter. It was from Lex Fiddler, the foremost American mainstream critic. Fiddler informed him that he had nominated Nick's Novel, *A Farewell to Mars*, for the highest honor for writing in the country. This was the MOOLA, the Michael Oberst Literary Award, established fifty years before by a St. Louis brewer. If Nick won it, he would get $50,000, he would be famous, his book would be a best seller, and an offer from Hollywood was a sure thing even if it didn't get the award.

Nick opened the third letter.

Whooping with joy, he whirled around and around, the end of his mighty walloper knocking over vases and flipping ash trays from tables. He stopped dancing then because he was so dizzy. Leaning on a table for support, gazing at the ever-expanding thing, he groaned, "I've got to get Moomah here. Only . . . I hope she doesn't faint when she sees it."

It was Nick who fainted, not Moomah. The blood spurted from his head, driving downward as his heart constricted in a final massive endeavor to supply what the ego demanded. His blood abandoned the upper part of his body as if the gargantuan paw of King Kong had squeezed it.

Had Nick been conscious, his terror would have halted the process, reversed it, and put the brobdingnagian member in its normal state, limp as an unbaked pizza. But his brain was emptied of blood, and he was aware of nothing as he toppled forward, was held for a moment from going over by the giant member, the end of which was rammed into the carpet, and then he pole-vaulted forward, his grayish slack face striking the floor.

He lay on his side while the pythonish member, driven by the unconscious, expanded. It swelled as a balloon swells while ascending into the ever-thinner atmosphere. But balloons have a pressure height, a point at which the force within the envelope is greater than its strength and the envelope ruptures violently.

The mailwoman was just climbing into her Jeep when she heard the blast. She whirled, and she screamed as she saw the flying glass and the smoke pouring out from the shattered windows.

The police found it easy to pinpoint the source of the explosion. The cause was beyond them. They shook their heads and said that this was just one of those mysteries of life.

The police did find out that the third letter, the one from the Swedish Embassy in Washington, D.C., was a fake. Whoever had sent it was unknown and likely to remain so. Why would anybody write Nick Adams, Jr., a science-fiction author, to inform him that he had won the Nobel Prize for Literature?

More investigation disclosed that the letters from the Pulsar Award committee and Lex Fiddler were also fakes. So was the call from his agent's secretary telling him that Sharper & Rake was giving him a huge advance. This was eventually traced to Mrs. Adams, but by then she was in Europe and there to stay. Besides, the police could not charge her with anything except a practical joke.

Ashlar is living in Spain today. Sometimes, for no reason that her friends can determine, she smiles in a strange way. Is it a smile of regret or triumph?

Did she write those letters and make that phone call because she knew what they'd do to her husband? Of course, she couldn't have known how much they would do to him: she underestimated the power of ego and the limits of flesh.

Or did she try to bolster his pride, make him feel good, because she still loved him and so was doing her best to make him inflated with happiness for at least a day?

It would be nice to think so.

The Freshman

The long-haired youth in front of Desmond wore sandals, ragged blue jeans, and a grimy T-shirt. A paperback, *The Collected Works of Robert Blake*, was half stuck into his rear pocket. When he turned around, he displayed in large letters on the T-shirt, M.U. His scrawny Fu Manchu mustache held some bread crumbs.

His yellow eyes—surely he suffered from jaundice—widened when he saw Desmond. He said, "This ain't the place to apply for the nursing home, Pops." He grinned, showing unusually long canines, and then turned to face the admissions desk.

Desmond felt his face turning red. Ever since he'd gotten into the line before a table marked *Toaahd Freshmen A-D*, he'd been aware of the sidelong glances, the snickers, the low-voiced comments. He stood out among these youths like a billboard in a flower garden, a corpse on a banquet table.

The line moved ahead by one person. The would-be students were talking, but their voices were subdued. For such young people, they were very restrained, excepting the smart aleck just ahead of him.

Perhaps it was the surroundings that repressed them. This gymnasium, built in the late nineteenth century, had not been repainted for years. The once-green paint was peeling. There were broken windows high on the walls; a shattered skylight had been covered with boards. The wooden floor bent and creaked, and the basketball goal rings (?) were rusty. Yet M.U. had been league champions in all fields of sports for many years. Though its enrollment was much less than that of its competitors, its teams somehow managed to win, often by large scores.

Desmond buttoned his jacket. Though it was a warm fall day, the air in the building was cold. If he hadn't known better, he would have thought that the wall of an iceberg was just behind him. Above him the great lights struggled to overcome the darkness that lowered like the underside of a dead whale sinking into sea depths.

He turned around. The girl just back of him smiled. She wore a flowing dashiki covered with astrological symbols. Her black hair was cut short; her features were petite and well-arranged but too pointed to be pretty.

Among all these youths there should have been a number of pretty girls and handsome men. He'd walked enough campuses to get an idea of the index of beauty of college students. But here . . . There was a girl, in the line to the right, whose face should have made her eligible to be a fashion model. Yet, there was something missing.

No, there was something added. A quality undefinable but . . . Repugnant? No, now it was gone. No, it was back again. It flitted on and off, like a bat swooping from darkness into a grayness and then up and out.

The kid in front of him had turned again. He was grinning like a fox who'd just seen a chicken.

"Some dish, heh, Pops? She likes older men. Maybe you two could get your shit together and make beautiful music."

The odor of unwashed body and clothes swirled around him like flies around a dead rat.

"I'm not interested in girls with Oedipus complexes," Desmond said coldly.

"At your age you can't be particular," the youth said, and turned away.

Desmond flushed, and he briefly fantasized knocking the kid down. It didn't help much.

The line moved ahead again. He looked at his wristwatch. In half an hour he was scheduled to phone his mother. He should have come here sooner. However, he had overslept while the alarm clock had run down, resuming its ticking as if it didn't care. Which it didn't, of course, though he felt that his possessions should, somehow, take an interest in him. This was irrational, but if he was a believer in the superiority of the rational, would he be here? Would any of these students?

The line moved jerkily ahead like a centipede halting now and then to make sure no one had stolen any of its legs. When he was ten minutes late for the phone call, he was at the head of the line. Behind the admissions table was a man far older than he. His face was a mass of wrinkles, gray dough that had been incised with finger-nails and then pressed into somewhat human shape. The nose was a cuttlefish's beak stuck into the dough. But the eyes beneath the white chaotic eyebrows where as alive as blood flowing from holes in the flesh.

The hand which took Desmond's papers and punched cards was not that of an old man's. It was big and swollen, white, smooth-skinned. The fingernails were dirty.

"The Roderick Desmond, I assume."

The voice was rasping, not at all an old man's cracked quavering.

"Ah, you know me?"

"Of you, yes. I've read some of your novels of the occult. And ten years ago I rejected your request for xeroxes of certain parts of *the* book."

The name tag on the worn tweed jacket said: R. Layamon, COTOAAHD. So this was the chairman of the Committee of the Occult Arts and History Department.

"Your paper on the non-Arabic origin of al-Hazred's name was a brilliant piece of linguistic research. I knew that it wasn't Arabic or even Semitic, but I confess that I didn't know the century in which the word was dropped from the Arabic language. Your exposition of how it was retained only in connection with the

Yemenite and that its original meaning was not *mad* but *one-who-sees-what-shouldn't-be-seen* was quite correct."

He paused, then said smiling, "Did your mother complain when she was forced to accompany you to Yemen?"

Desmond said, "No-n-n-o-body forced her."

He took a deep breath and said, "But how did you know she . . . ?"

"I've read some biographical accounts of you."

Layamon chuckled. It sounded like nails being shifted in a barrel. "Your paper on al-Hazred and the knowledge you display in your novels are the main reasons why you're being admitted to this department despite your sixty years."

He signed the forms and handed the card back to Desmond. "Take this to the cashier's office. Oh, yes, your family is a remarkably long-lived one, isn't it? Your father died accidentally, but his father lived to be one hundred and two. Your mother is eighty, but she should live to be over a hundred. And you, you could have forty more years of life *as you've known it.*"

Desmond was enraged, but not so much that he dared let himself show it. The gray air became black, and the old man's face shone in it. It floated toward him, expanded, and suddenly Desmond was inside the gray wrinkles. It was not a pleasant place.

The tiny figures on a dimly haloed horizon danced, then faded, and he fell through a bellowing blackness. The air was gray again, and he was leaning forward, clenching the edge of the table.

"Mr. Desmond, do you have these attacks often?"

Desmond released his grip and straightened. "Too much excitement, I suppose. No, I've never had an attack, not now or ever."

The old man chuckled. "Yes, it must be emotional stress. Perhaps you'll find the means for relieving that stress here."

Desmond turned and walked away. Until he left the building, he saw only blurred figures and signs. That ancient wizard . . . how had he known his thoughts so well? Was it simply because he had read the biographical accounts, made a few inquiries, and then surmised a complete picture? Or was there more to it than that?

The sun had gone behind thick sluggish clouds. Past the

campus, past many trees hiding the houses of the city, were the Tamsiqueg hills. According to the long-extinct Indians after whom they were named, they had once been evil giants who'd waged war with the hero Mikatoonis and his magic-making friend, Chegaspat. Chegaspat had been killed, but Mikatoonis had turned the giants into stone with a magical club.

But Cotoaahd, the chief giant, was able to free himself from the spell every few centuries. Sometimes, a sorcerer could loose him. Then Cotoaahd walked abroad for a while before returning to his rocky slumber. In 1724 a house and many trees on the edge of the town had been flattened one stormy night as if colossal feet had stepped upon them. And the broken trees formed a trail which led to the curiously shaped hill known as Cotoaahd.

There was nothing about these stories that couldn't be explained by the tendency of the Indians, and the superstitious eighteenth-century whites, to legendize natural phenomena. But was it entirely coincidence that the anagram of the committee headed by Layamon duplicated the giant's name?

Suddenly, he became aware that he was heading for a telephone booth. He looked at his watch and felt panicky. The phone in his dormitory room would be ringing. It would be better to call her from the booth and save the three minutes it would take to walk to the dormitory.

He stopped. No, if he called from the booth, he would only get a busy signal.

"Forty more years of life *as you've known it*," the chairman had said.

Desmond turned. His path was blocked by an enormous youth. He was a head taller than Desmond's six feet and so fat he looked like a smaller version of the Santa Claus balloon in Macy's Christmas-day parade. He wore a dingy sweatshirt on the front of which was the ubiquitous M.U., unpressed pants, and torn tennis shoes. In banana-sized fingers he held a salami sandwich which Gargantua would not have found too small.

Looking at him, Desmond suddenly realized that most of the students here were too thin or too fat.

"Mr. Desmond?"

"Right."

He shook hands. The fellow's skin was wet and cold, but the hand exerted a powerful pressure.

"I'm Wendell Trepan. With your knowledge, you've heard about my ancestors. The most famous, or infamous, of whom was the Cornish witch, Rachel Trepan."

"Yes. Rachel of the hamlet of Tredannick Wollas, near Poldhu Bay."

"I knew you'd know. I'm following the trade of my ancestors, though more cautiously, of course. Anyway, I'm a senior and the chairperson of the rushing committee for the Lam Kha Alif fraternity."

He paused to bite into the sandwich. Mayonnaise and salami and cheese oozing from his mouth, he said, "You're invited to the party we're holding at the house this afternoon."

The other hand reached into a pocket and brought out a card. Desmond looked at it briefly. "You want me to be a candidate for membership in your frat? I'm pretty old for that sort of thing. I'd feel out of place . . ."

"Nonsense, Mr. Desmond. We're a pretty serious bunch. In fact, none of the frats here are like any on other campuses. You should know that. We feel you'd provide stability and, I'll admit, prestige. You're pretty well known, you know. Layamon, by the way, is a Lam Kha Alif. He tends to favor students who belong to his frat. He'd deny it, of course, and I'll deny it if you repeat this. But it's true."

"Well, I don't know. Suppose I did pledge—if I'm invited to, that is—would I have to live in the frat house?"

"Yes. We make no exceptions. Of course, that's only when you're a pledge. You can live wherever you want to when you're an active."

Trepan smiled, showing the unswallowed bite. "You're not married, so there's no problem there."

"What do you mean by that?"

"Nothing, Mr. Desmond. It's just that we don't pledge married men unless they don't live with their wives. Married men lose some of their power, you know. Of course, no way do we insist on celibacy. We have some pretty good parties, too. Once a month we hold a big bust in a grove at the foot of Cotoaahd. Most of the women guests there belong to the Ba Ghay Sin sorority. Some of them really go for the older type, if you know what I mean."

Trepan stepped forward to place his face directly above Desmond's. "We don't just have beer, pot, hashish, and sisters. They're other attractions. Brothers, if you're so inclined. Some stuff that's made from a recipe by the Marquis Manuel de Dembron himself. But most of that is kid stuff. There'll be a goat there, too!"

"A goat? A *black* goat?"

Trepan nodded, and his triple-fold jowls swung. "Yeah. Old Layamon'll be there to supervise, though he'll be masked, of course. With him as coach nothing can go wrong. Last Halloween, though . . ."

He paused, then said, "Well, it was something to see."

Desmond licked his dry lips. His heart was thudding like the tom-toms that beat at the ritual of which he had only read but had envisioned many times.

Desmond put the card in his pocket. "At one o'clock?"

"You're coming? Very good! See you, Mr. Desmond. You won't regret it."

Desmond walked past the buildings of the university quadrangle, the most imposing of which was the museum. This was the oldest structure on the campus, the original college. Time had beaten and chipped away at the brick and stone of the others, but the museum seemed to have absorbed time and to be slowly radiating it back just as cement and stone and brick absorbed heat in the sunlight and then gave it back in the darkness. Also, whereas the other structures were covered with vines, perhaps too covered, the museum was naked of plant life. Vines which tried to crawl up its gray bone-colored stones withered and fell back.

Layamon's red-stone house was narrow, three stories high, and had a double-peaked roof. Its cover of vines was so thick that it seemed a wonder that the weight didn't bring it to the ground. The colors of the vines were subtly different from those on the other buildings. Seen at one angle, they looked cyanotic. From another, they were the exact green of the eyes of a Sumatran snake Desmond had seen in a colored plate in a book on herpetology.

It was this venomous reptile which was used by the sorcerers of the Yan tribes to transmit messages and sometimes to kill. The writer had not explained what he meant by "messages." Desmond had discovered the meaning in another book, which had required him to learn Malay, written in the Arabic script, before he could read it.

He hurried on past the house, which was not something a sightseer would care to look at long, and came to the dormitory. It had been built in 1888 on the site of another building and remodeled in 1938. Its gray paint was peeling. There were several broken windows, over the panes of which cardboard had been nailed. The porch floorboards bent and creaked as he passed over them. The main door was of oak, its paint long gone. The bronze head of a cat, a heavy bronze ring dangling from its mouth, served as a door knocker.

Desmond entered, passed through the main room over the worn carpet, and walked up two flights of bare-board steps. On the gray-white of a wall by the first landing someone had long ago written *Yog-Sothoth Sucks*. Many attempts had been made to wash it off, but it was evident that only paint could hide this insulting and dangerous sentiment. Yesterday a junior had told him that no one knew who had written it, but the night after it had appeared, a freshman had been found dead, hanging from a hook in a closet.

"The kid had mutilated himself terribly before he committed suicide," the junior had said. "I wasn't here then, but I understand that he was a mess. He'd done it with a razor *and* a hot iron. There was blood all over the place, his pecker and balls were on the table, arranged to form a T-cross, you know whose symbol that is, and he'd clawed out plaster on the wall, leaving a big bloody print. It didn't even look like a human hand had done it."

"I'm surprised he lived long enough to hang himself," Desmond had said. "All that loss of blood, you know."

The junior had guffawed. "You're kidding, of course!"

It was several seconds before Desmond understood what he meant. Then he'd paled. But later he wondered if the junior wasn't playing a traditional joke on the green freshman. He didn't think he'd ask anybody else about it, however. If he had been made a fool of, he wasn't going to let it happen more than once.

He heard the phone ringing at the end of the long hall. He sighed, and strode down it, passing closed doors. From behind one came a faint tittering. He unlocked his door and closed it behind him. For a long time he stood watching the phone, which went on and on, reminding him, he didn't know why, of the poem about the Australian swagman who went for a dip in a waterhole. The bunyip, that mysterious and sinister creature of down-under folklore, the dweller in the water, silently and smoothly took care of the swagman. And the tea kettle he'd put on the fire whistled and whistled with no one to hear.

And the phone rang on and on.

The bunyip was on the other end.

Guilt spread through him as quick as a blush.

He walked across the room glimpsing something out of the corner of his eye, something small, dark, and swift that dived under the sagging mildew-odorous bed-couch. He stopped at the small table, reached out to the receiver, touched it, felt its cold throbbing. He snatched his hand back. It was foolish, but it had seemed to him that she would detect his touch and know that he was there.

Snarling, he wheeled and started across the room. He noticed that the hole in the baseboard was open again. The Coke bottle whose butt end he'd jammed into the hole had been pushed out. He stopped and reinserted it and straightened up.

When he was at the foot of the staircase, he could still hear the ringing. But he wasn't sure that it wasn't just in his head.

After he'd paid his tuition and eaten at the cafeteria—the food was better than he'd thought it would be—he walked to the ROTC building. It was in better shape than the other structures, probably because the Army was in charge of it. Still, it wasn't in the condition an inspector would require. And those cannons on caissons in the rear. Were the students really supposed to train with Spanish-American War weapons? And since when was steel subject to verdigris?

The officer in charge was surprised when Desmond asked to be issued his uniform and manuals.

"I don't know. You realize ROTC is no longer required of freshmen and sophomores?"

Desmond insisted that he wanted to enroll. The officer rubbed his unshaven jaw and blew smoke from a Tijuana Gold panatela. "Hmm. Let me see."

He consulted a book whose edges seemed to have been nibbled by rats. "Well, what do you know? There's nothing in the regulations about age. Course, there's some pages missing. Must be an over-sight. Nobody near your age has ever been considered. But . . . well, if the regulations say nothing about it, then . . . what the hell! Won't hurt you, our boys don't have to go through obstacle courses or anything like that.

"But, jeeze, you're sixty! Why do you want to sign up?"

Desmond did not tell him that he had been deferred from service in World War II because he was the sole support of his sick mother. Ever since then, he'd felt guilty, but at least here he could do his bit—however minute—for his country.

The officer stood up, though not in a coordinated manner. "Okay, I'll see you get your issue. It's only fair to warn you, though, that these fuckups play some mighty strange tricks. You should see what they blow out of their cannons."

Fifteen minutes later, Desmond left, a pile of uniforms and manuals under one arm. Since he didn't want to return home with them, he checked them in at the university bookstore. The girl put them on a shelf alongside other belongings , some of them unidentifiable to the noncognoscenti. One of them was a small cage covered with a black cloth.

Desmond walked to Fraternity Row. All of the houses had Arabic names, except the House of Hastur. These were afflicted with the same general decrepitude and lack of care as the university structures. Desmond turned in at a cement walk, from the cracks of which spread dying dandelions and other weeds. On his left leaned a massive wooden pole fifteen feet high. The heads and symbols carved into it had caused the townspeople to refer to it as the totem pole. It wasn't, of course, since the tribe to which it had belonged was not Northwest Coast or Alaskan Indians. It and a fellow in the university museum were the last survivors of hundreds which had once stood in this area.

Desmond, passing it, put the end of his left thumb under his nose and the tip of his index finger in the center of his forehead, and he muttered the ancient phrase of obeisance, "*Shesh-cotoaahd-ting-ononwa-senk.*" According to various texts he'd read, this was required of every Tamsiqueg who walked by it during this phase of the moon. The phrase was unintelligible even to them, since it came from another tribe or perhaps from an antique stage of the language. But it indicated respect, and lack of its observance was likely to result in misfortune.

He felt a little silly doing it, but it couldn't hurt.

The unpainted wooden steps creaked as he stepped upon them. The porch was huge; the wires of the screen were rusty and useless in keeping insects out because of the many holes. The front door was open; from it came a blast of rock music, the loud chatter of many people, and the acrid odor of pot.

Desmond almost turned back. He suffered when he was in a crowd, and his consciousness of his age made him feel embarrassingly conspicuous. But the huge figure of Wendell Trepan was in the doorway, and he was seized by an enormous hand.

"Come on in!" Trepan bellowed. "I'll introduce you to the brothers!"

Desmond was pulled into a large room jammed with youths of both sexes. Trepan bulled through, halting now and then to slap somebody on the back and shout a greeting and once to pat a well-built young woman on the fanny. Then they were in a corner where Professor Layamon sat surrounded by people who looked older than most of the attendees. Desmond supposed that they were graduate students. He shook the fat swollen hand and said, "Pleased to meet you again," but he doubted that his words were heard.

Layamon pulled him down so he could be heard, and he said, "Have you made up your mind yet?"

The old man's breath was not unpleasant, but he had certainly been drinking something which Desmond had never smelled before. The red eyes seemed to hold a light, almost as if tiny candles were burning inside the eyeballs.

"About what?" Desmond shouted back.

The old man smiled and said, "You know."

He released his grip. Desmond straightened up. Suddenly, though the room was hot enough to make him sweat, he felt chilly. What was Layamon hinting at? It couldn't be that he really knew. Or could it be?

Trepan introduced him to the men and women around the chair and then took him into the crowd. Other introductions followed, most of those he met seeming to be members of Lam Kha Alif or of the sorority across the street. The only one he could indentify for sure as a candidacy for pledging was a black, a Gabonese. After they left him, Trepan said, "Bukawai comes from a long line of witch doctors. He's going to be a real treasure if he accepts our invitation, though the House of Hastur and Kaf Dhal Waw are hot to get him. The department is a little weak on Central African science. It used to have a great teacher, Janice Momaya, but she disappeared ten years ago while on a sabbatical in Sierra Leone. I wouldn't be surprised if Bukawai was offered an assistant professorship even is he is nominally a freshman. Man, the other night, he taught me part of a ritual you wouldn't believe. I . . . well, I won't go into it now. Some other time. Anyway, he has the greatest respect for Layamon, and since the old fart is head of the department, Bukawai is almost a cinch to join us."

Suddenly, his lips pulled back, his teeth clenched, his skin paled beneath the dirt, and he bent over and grabbed his huge paunch. Desmond said, "What's the matter?"

Trepan shook his head, gave a deep sigh, and straightened up.

"Man, that hurt!"

"What?" Desmond said.

"I shouldn't have called him an old fart. I didn't think he could hear me, but he isn't using sound to receive. Hell, there's nobody in the world has more respect for him than me. But sometimes my mouth runs off . . . well, never again."

"You mean?" Desmond said.

"Yeah. Who'd you think? Never mind. Come with me where we can hear ourselves think."

He pulled Desmond through a smaller room, one with many shelves of books, novels, school texts, and here and there some old leather-bound volumes.

"We got a hell of a good library here, the best any house can boast of. It's one of our stellar attractions. But it's the open one."

They entered a narrow door, passed into a short hall, and stopped while Trepan took a key from his pocket and unlocked another door. Beyond it was a narrow corkscrew staircase, the steps of which were dusty. A window high above gave a weak light through dirty panes. Trepan turned on a wall light, and they went up the stairs. At the top, which was on the third floor, Trepan unlocked another door with a different key. They stepped into a small room whose walls were covered by bookshelves from floor to ceiling. Trepan turned on a light. In a corner was a small table and a folding chair. The table had a lamp and a stone bust of the Marquis de Dembron on it.

Trepan, breathing heavily after the climb, said, "Usually, only seniors and graduates are allowed up here. But I'm making an exception in your case. I just wanted to show you one of the advantages of belonging to Lam Kha Alif. None of the other houses have a library like this."

Trepan was looking narrow-eyed at him. "Eyeball the books. But don't touch them. They, uh, absorb, if you know what I mean."

Desmond moved around, looking at the titles. When he was finished, he said, "I'm impressed, I thought some of these were to be found only in the university library. In locked rooms."

"That's what the public thinks. Listen, if you pledge us, you'll have access to these books. Only don't tell the other undergrads. They'd get jealous."

Trepan, still narrow-eyed, as if he were considering something that perhaps he shouldn't, said, "Would you mind turning your back and sticking your fingers in your ears?"

Desmond said, "What?"

Trepan smiled. "Oh, if you sign up with us, you'll be given the little recipe necessary to work in here. But until then I'd just as soon you don't see it."

Desmond, smiling with embarrassment, the cause of which he couldn't account for, and also feeling excited, turning his back, facing away from Trepan, and jammed his fingertips into his ears.

While he stood there in the very quiet room—was it sound-proofed with insulation or with something perhaps not material?—he counted the seconds. One thousand and one, one thousand and two . . .

A little more than a minute had passed when he felt Trepan's hand on his shoulder. He turned and removed his fingers. The fat youth was holding out to him a tall but very slim volume bound in a skin with many small dark protuberances. Desmond was surprised, since he was sure he had not seen it on the shelves.

"I deactivated this," Trepan said. "Here. Take it." He looked at his wristwatch. "It'll be okay for ten minutes."

There was no title or by-line on the cover. And, now that he looked at it closely and felt it, he did not think the skin was from an animal.

Trepan said, "It's the hide of old Atechironnon himself."

Desmond said, "Ah!" and he trembled. But he rallied. "He must have been covered with warts."

"Yeah. Go ahead, look at it. It's a shame you can't read it, though."

The first page was slightly yellowed, which wasn't surprising for paper four hundred years old. There was no printing but large handwritten letters.

"*Ye lesser Rituall of Ye Tahmmsiquegg Warlock Atechironunn,*" Desmond read. "*Reprodust from ye Picture-riting on ye Skin lefft unbrirnt by ye Godly.*

"*By his own Hand, Simon Conant. 1641.*

"Let him who speaks these Words of Pictures, first lissen."

Trepan chuckled and said, "Spelling wasn't his forte, was it?"

"Simon, the half-brother of Roger Conant," Desmond said. "He was the first white man to visit the Tamsiqueg and not leave with his severed thumb stuck up his ass. He was also with the settlers who raided the Tamsiqueg, but they didn't know who his sympathies were with. He fled with the badly wounded Atechironnon into the wilderness. Twenty years later, he appeared in Virginia with this book."

He slowly turned the five pages, fixing each pictograph in his photographic memory. There was one figure he didn't like to look at.

"Layamon's the only one who can read it," Trepan said.

Desmond did not tell him that he was conversant with the grammar and small dictionary of the Tamsiqueg language, written by William Cor Dunnes in 1624 and published in 1654. It contained an appendix translating the pictographs. It had cost him twenty years of searching and a thousand dollars just for a xerox copy. His mother had raised hell about the expenditure, but for once he had stood up to her. Not even the university had a copy.

Trepan looked at his watch. "One minute to go. Hey!"

He grabbed the book from Desmond's hands and said, harshly, "Turn your back and plug your ears!"

Trepan looked as if he were in a panic. He turned, and a minute later Trepan pulled one of Desmond's fingers away.

"Sorry to be so sudden, but the hold was beginning to break down. I can't figure it out. It's always been good for at least ten minutes."

Desmond had not felt anything, but that might be because Trepan, having been exposed to the influence, was more sensitive to it.

Trepan, obviously nervous, said, "Let's get out of here. It's got to cool off."

On the way down, he said, "You sure you can't read it?"

"Where would I have learned how?" Desmond said.

They plunged into a sea of noise and odors in the big room.

683

They did not stay long, since Trepan wanted to show him the rest of the house, except the basement.

"You can see it sometime this week. Just now it's not advisable to go down there."

Desmond didn't ask why.

When they entered a very small room on the second floor, Trepan said, "Ordinarily we don't let freshmen have a room to themselves. But for you . . . well, it's yours if you want it.

That pleased Desmond. He wouldn't have to put up with someone whose habits would irk him and whose chatter would anger him.

They descended to the first floor. The big room was not so crowded now. Old Layamon, just getting up from the chair, beckoned to him. Desmond approached him slowly. For some reason, he knew he was not going to like what Layamon would say to him. Or perhaps he wasn't sure whether he would like it or not.

"Trepan showed you the frat's more precious books," the chairman said. It wasn't a question but a statement. "Especially Conant's book."

Trepan said, "How did you . . . ?" He grinned. "You felt it."

"Of course," the rusty voice siad. "Well, Desmond, don't you think it's time to answer that phone?"

Trepan looked puzzled. Desmond look sick and cold.

Layamon was now almost nose to nose with Desmond. The many wrinkles of the doughy skin looked like hieroglyphics.

"You've made up your mind, but you aren't letting yourself know it," he said. "Listen. That was Conant's advice, wasn't it? Listen. From the moment you got onto the plane to Boston, you were committed. You could have backed out in the airport, but you didn't, even though, I imagine, your mother made a scene there. But you didn't. So there's no putting it off."

He chuckled. "That I am bothering to give you advice is a token of my esteem for you. I think you'll go far and fast. If you are able to eliminate certain defects of character. It takes strength and intelligence and great self-discipline and a vast dedication to get even a B.A. here, Desmond.

"There are too many who enroll here because they think they'll be taking snap courses. Getting great power, hobnobbing with things that are really not socially-minded, to say the least, seems to them to be as easy as rolling off a log. But they soon find out that the department's standards are higher than, say, those of MIT in engineering. And a hell of a lot more dangerous.

"And then there's the moral issue. That's declared just by enrolling here. But how many have the will to push on? How many decide that they are on the wrong side? They quit, not knowing that it's too late for any but a tiny fraction of them to return to the other side. They've declared themselves, have stood up and been counted forever, as it were."

He paused to light up a brown panatela. The smoke curled around Desmond, who did smell what he expected. The odor was not quite like that of a dead bat he had once used in an experiment.

"Every man or woman determines his or her own destiny. But I would make my decision swiftly, if I were you. I've got my eye on you, and your advancement here does depend upon my estimate of your character and potentiality.

"Good day, Desmond."

The old man walked out. Trepan said, "What was that all about?"

Desmond did not answer. He stood for a minute or so while Trepan fidgeted. Then he said good-by to the fat man and walked out slowly. Instead of going home, he wandered around the campus. Attracted by flashing red lights, he went over to see what was going on. A car with the markings of the campus police and an ambulance from the university hospital were in front of a two-story building. Its lower floor had once been a grocery store according to the letters on the dirty plate glass window. The paint inside and out was peeling, and plaster had fallen off the walls within, revealing the laths beneath. On the bare wooden floor were three bodies. One was the youth who had stood just in front of him in the line in the gymnasium. He lay on his back, his mouth open below the scraggly mustache.

Desmond asked one of the people pressed against the window what had happened. The gray-bearded man, probably a professor, said, "This happens every year at this time. Some kids get carried away and try something no one but an M.A. would even think of trying. It's strictly forbidden, but that doesn't stop those young fools."

The corpse with the mustache seemed to have a large round black object or perhaps a burn on his forehead. Desmond wanted to get a closer look, but the ambulance men put a blanket over the face before carrying the body out.

The gray-bearded man said, "The university police and the hospital will handle them." He laughed shortly. "The city police don't even want to come on the campus. The relatives will be notified they've OD'd from heroin."

"There's no trouble about that?"

"Sometimes. Private detectives have come here, but they don't stay long."

Desmond walked away swiftly. His mind was made up. The sight of those bodies had shaken him. He'd go home, make peace with his mother, sell all the books he'd spent so much time and money accumulating and studying, take up writing mystery novels. He'd seen the face of death, and if he did what he had thought about, only idly of course, fantasizing for psychic therapy, he would see her face. Dead. He couldn't do it.

When he entered his room in the boardinghouse, the phone was still ringing. He walked to it, reached out his hand, held it for an undeterminable time, then dropped it. As he walked toward the couch, he noticed that the Coca-Cola bottle had been shoved or pulled out of the hole in the baseboard. He knelt down and jammed it back into the hole. From behind the wall came a faint twittering.

He sat down on the sagging couch, took his notebook from his jacket pocket, and began to pencil in the pictographs he remembered so well on the sheets. It took him half an hour, since exactness of reproduction was vital. The phone did not stop ringing.

Someone knocked on the door and yelled, "I saw you go in! Answer the phone or take it off the hook! Or I'll put something on you!"

He did not reply or rise from the couch.

He had left out one of the drawings in the sequence. Now he poised the pencil an inch above the blank space. Sitting at the other end of the line would be a very fat, very old woman. She was old and ugly now, but she had borne him and for many years thereafter she had been beautiful. When his father had died, she had gone to work to keep their house and to support her son in the manner to which both were accustomed. She had worked hard to pay his tuition and other expenses while he went to college. She had continued to work until he had sold two novels. Then she had gotten sickly, though not until he began bringing women home to introduce as potential wives.

She loved him, but she wouldn't let loose of him, and that wasn't genuine love. He hadn't been able to tear loose, which meant that though he was resentful he had something in him which liked being caged. Then, one day, he had decided to take the big step toward freedom. It had been done secretly and swiftly. He had despised himself for his fear of her, but that was the way he was. If he stayed here, she would be coming here. He couldn't endure that. So, he would have to go home.

He looked at the phone, started to rise, sank back.

What to do? He could commit suicide. He'd be free, and she would know how angry he'd been with her. He gave a start as the phone stopped ringing. So, she had given up for a while. But she would return to it.

He looked at the baseboard. The bottle was moving out from the hole a little at a time. Something behind the wall was working away determinedly. How many times had it started to leave the hole and found that its passage was blocked? Far too many, the thing must think, if it had a mind. But it refused to give up, and someday it might occur to it to solve its problem by killing the one who was causing the problem.

If, however, it was daunted by the far greater size of the problem maker, if it lacked courage, then it would have to keep on pushing the bottle from the hole. And . . .

He looked at the notebook, and he shook. The blank space

had been filled in. There was the drawing of Cotoaahd, the thing which, now he looked at it, somehow resembled his mother.

Had he unconsciously penciled it in while he was thinking?

Or had the figure formed itself?

It didn't matter. In either case, he knew what he had to do.

While the eyes passed over each drawing, and he intoned the words of that long-dead language, he felt something move out from within his chest, crawl into his belly, his legs, his throat, his brain. They symbol of Cotoaahd seemed to burn on the sheet when he pronounced its name, his eye on the drawing.

The room grew dark as the final words were said. He rose and turned on the table lamp and went into the tiny dirty bathroom. The face in the mirror did not look like a murderer's; it was just that of a sixty-year-old man who had been through an ordeal and was not quite sure that it was over.

On the way out of the room, he saw the Coke bottle slide free of the baseboard hole. But whatever had pushed it was not yet ready to come out.

Hours later he returned reeling from the campus tavern. The phone was ringing again. But the call, as he had expected, was not from his mother, though it was from his native city in Illinois.

"Mr. Desmond, this is Sergeant Rourke of the Busiris Police Department. I'm afraid I have some bad news for you. Uh, ah, your mother died some hours ago from a heart attack."

Desmond did not have to act stunned. He was numb throughout. Even the hand holding the receiver felt as if it had turned to granite. Vaguely, he was aware that Rourke's voice seemed strange.

"Heart attack? Heart . . . ? Are you sure?"

He groaned. His mother had died naturally. He would not have had to recite the ancient words. And now he had committed himself for nothing and was forever trapped. Once the words were used while the eyes read, there was no turning back.

But . . . if the words have only been words, dying as sound usually does, no physical reaction resulting from words transmitted through that subcontinuum, then was he bound?

Wouldn't he be free, clear of debt? Able to walk out of this place without fear of retaliation?

"It was a terrible thing, Mr. Desmond. A freak accident. Your mother died while she was talking to a visiting neighbor, Mrs. Sammins. Sammins called the police and an ambulance. Some other neighbors went into the house, and then . . . then . . ."

Rourke's throat seemed to be clogging.

"I'd just got there and was on the front porch when it . . . it . . ."

Rourke coughed, and he said, "My brother was in the house, too."

Three neighbors, two ambulance attendants, and two policemen had been crushed to death when the house had unaccountably collapsed.

"It was like a giant foot stepped on it. If it'd fallen six seconds later, I'd have been caught, too."

Desmond thanked him and said he'd take the next plane out to Busiris.

He staggered to the window, and he raised it to breathe in the open air. Below, in the light of a streetlamp, hobbling along on his cane was Layamon. The gray face lifted. Teeth flashed whitely.

Desmond wept, but the tears were only for himself.

CREATING ARTIFICIAL WORLDS

Our subject is Creating Artificial Worlds. In the first place, that is a misnomer. Nobody creates anything; artists, in which I include writers, poets, sculptors, painters, and so forth, do not create; all they do is take the materials at hand and put it together. In other words, we are all "makers." There is only one original Creator and some people doubt whether He exists or not. He was the only one who ever took nothing and made something out of it. But all of us so-called artists only make things, we never create things.

Science fiction writers are known for constructing artificial worlds. When you say artificial worlds you immediately think of a science fiction writer. But the truth is that all writers in any genre, mainstream, historical, gothic or western, construct artificial worlds. A lot of mainstream writers like to think of themselves as being very realistic. But the truth is that even the most intensely realistic writer never matches reality one by one. Mainstream writers construct worlds that are entirely artificial.

All of us think that we see reality. Each of us—through this thing behind our eyes, these windows of perception—look out and we see certain items that we have agreed exist. But the truth is that none of us ever ever agree one hundred percent on just what this thing is, just how it exists, and how it operates. The only thing in which the science fiction writer differs from the other genres, is that he differs in degree, not in kind. But he does have a much harder job than the writer of mainstream or any of the other non-science fiction genres.

The mainstream writer, for instance, has all his materials at hand. He doesn't have to invent the world. He has a hard enough job as it is writing a story of a world that everybody knows about. Of course, the historical novelist has a harder job than a person who writes a contemporary novel because he has to do a tremendous amount of research. On the other hand, he is writing about the worlds that *did* exist. Whereas the science fiction writer writes about worlds that do not exist, that never existed, and that probably won't exist.

Now, I know some of you are thinking that there are a lot of writers who mostly deal with contemporary society. Like Harlan Ellison, for instance. But if you were to study Harlan carefully you would find that though he tends to operate mainly in the contemporary, the worlds that he constructs are not reality, one by one. There is a tremendous amount of fantasy in there and by the time he has gotten through the major part of the story, you are in a world that is as remote as Mars was supposed to be at one time . . . or as alien, I should say. I'm specifically thinking of Edgar Rice Burroughs' Barsoom or Heinlein's Mars. Harlan has taken the contemporary world, given you a background that many of you recognize, but by the time he is through—by the time he has looked at our world through his own particular doors of perception and then written a story—he has taken the material at hand and shaped them not into a mainstream novel—this might make him mad because he doesn't want to be known as a science fiction writer—he has taken his materials at hand and shaped them into a very alien world. Actually, his worlds are as strange and fascinating as any of Heinlein's. But whether you prefer Harlan or Heinlein is a matter of taste.

What I am trying to say is that all writers and all artists create artificial worlds, it doesn't matter what the genre. But then, as I said, it is a matter of degree, not of kind.

CREATING ARTIFICIAL WORLDS

As my subject is constructing artificial worlds, I will take as an example one of my lesser novels, titled *The Gate of Time*. This was put out by Belmont quite a few years ago, reprinted once, but I have a contract now to rewrite it with its original title. I called it *Two Hawks From Earth*, and Belmont for some reason retitled it *The Gate of Time*. I do not know why because it is not a time story, it is a parallel universe story. Belmont did a lot to the book. They cut out scenes here and there so that by the time I got it I didn't even recognize it. I imagine some other writers could tell you the same thing about some of their works.

A lot of people come up and ask me: "Where do you get your ideas from?" And I tell them, "I really don't know." I've gotten ideas from just hearing a phrase in an eavesdropped conversation; I've gotten them from reading poetry and prose; I've gotten them from dreams—a lot of ideas from dreams—I've gotten them from booze . . . By the way, while you *can* get ideas sometimes when you drink, don't ever try to write while you're drinking. It doesn't work. There used to be a lot of legends about Hemingway and some of the other boozers of his period. It was claimed that he would sit down at his typewriter with a full quart of whiskey and drink it all one day while he was writing. I don't believe that. Or, if he did, then he had to re-write the next day while he sobered up. Which probably didn't work either. Don't try to write while you're sobering up.

What happened was that I was reading a book on the evolution of horses some years ago and I came across several statements which said that the horse family originated in North America, as did the camel family. They originated here and eventually spread over to the Old World, and then they died out in 8000 B.C., or perhaps a little later. I had known this for years but it had just never occurred to me that it might be an idea for a story. So while I was reading this book I said, "Ahh!—you know, just like that, I didn't have to hit my head or anything—what if the North American and South American continents never rose from the sea?

There's your basic premise. We have already created an artificial world.

What this would mean, just to begin with, is that there are no horses or camels in the Old World. I suppose some of you are thinking, "So what?" Well, what this means is that transportation, communication, and warfare would have been considerably reduced. You see, without horses or camels trade goods, for instance, would have to be carried either on boats or on the backs of human beings.

Some of you are saying, "Well, what about oxen and elephants?" And I say that is a good point. Except that oxen are a very slow method of transportation. They are no good for anything like the horse for warfare. You can't get on the back of an ox and ride into battle . . . Elephants could be used a great deal more than they were in olden times, and that is something I overlooked when I wrote the first version of the book. But I'll change that. I would also like to point out that there is an old myth that African elephants can't be tamed, that only Indian elephants can. But that is not true at all. Hannibal of Carthage used African elephants to great effect in taking him up through Spain. I'm just throwing that in.

What are other important things that wouldn't exist if there are no Americas? There would be no potatoes, tomatoes, turkeys, syphilis, pumpkins, squash, rubber, quinine to treat malaria—malaria has taken a tremendous toll of human lives in history—tobacco, maize or Indian corn.

Another big thing is that the American Indian supposedly originated in Central Asia or up in Siberia. They were supposed to have been—according to the theory, not provable, just a theory—a blend of archaic Caucasian and Mongolian peoples. After all of these tribes were mixed up in Central Asia or Siberia, or both, the American Indian was formed. About 40,000 years ago, or maybe 100,000, the first Indian came across the Bering Bridge. But in an Americaless world there is no Bering Bridge. So what happens, according to my book, anyway, is that the Amerinds are frustrated. They go up to the Bering Strait, which is not a strait but part of the Atlantic ocean, look around and decide to come back. Instead of all being pushed out of Asia to America, where they developed their own culture, they turned inland. So my thesis is that they absorbed the Turkish-speaking peoples, became a very potent force, and so went back to the Old Stone Age.

Coming up to modern times in my parallel universe, they have drifted westward and they have also drifted southward. In the south they formed an empire in what we now call in our world, Earth I, northern China. Their push kept the people—I'm going to speak particularly of the Finnish-speaker—from drifting westward and going across the Aegean and then into Russia and eventually forming the dual nations of Finland and Estonia. Instead, they were shunted eastward and they got to the Japanese Islands before the Japanese did. The Japanese, according to the theory, were originally a Southeast Asian people who wandered on up and then went over to the Japanese Islands where they found the Ainu, who were an archaic Caucasian people. They just pushed them to the less-desirable areas and in time subjugated them. In Earth II, the Finnish speakers got to Japan first; the Japanese were thwarted, so they settled in Southeast Asia and what we call the Japanese Islands was called Saariset, which is Finnish for Islands.

What happened in Europe is that the Amerinds, by the time my story opens, occupy what we call Russia. These people speak a language that is related to Nahua, which is the same language the Aztecs and Toltecs spoke. They occupied most of Russia except for the extreme southern part.

The Iroquois, my favorite Indians, moved into what is now Bulgaria and Rumania, and formed a nation there. An Algonquin-speaking people which we call the Kinnikinuk, which is an actual Indian word, now quite distorted, the original meant "mixture," moved into what is Czechoslovakia. Now, all this is possible, given my premise.

By the time the story opens, which would be analogous to our 1944, because it starts out in World War II, there are no Slavs. They did not come out of their swamplands but were overrun by a group of Amerinds on one side and Lithuanians on the other side and absorbed. According to the theory, if I remember correctly, the

Slavs lived in a huge swampland in Poland. What happened was that a group of Mongolians came in and conquered and enslaved them all, brought them out, and sent them to various colonies. That is why they are called Slavs, coming from the Latin word for slaves. Then, in a couple hundred years, the slaves overthrew their conquerors and they started to expand into different parts of Europe. But in my world, Earth II, this didn't happen.

I hope you bear with me because I'm not working up to an entirely different world, but a world based on the premise that the two Americas did not exist. I'm trying to show you how to extrapolate.

The people who in our world are the Lithuanians, and the old Prussians (who were Baltic, not German), and the Latvians found a vacuum for a while and they expanded. As a matter of fact, back in the medieval period the Lithuanians at one time covered a tremendous stretch of country in Russia and Poland and so forth. The end result was that when the story starts, the Baltic speaking nation Perkunisha occupies the territory called Denmark, Germany, Poland, Holland and Austria in our world, Earth I. The reason I call this Perkunisha is that Perkunis was the original chief god of the old Prussians. Again, I stress that they were not German. Prussia is called Prussia today because when the Germans came in they conquered the Prussians and absorbed them and eventually their language died.

The Perkunishans of the Americaless world live in this huge heartland in Central Europe. They had actually absorbed all the people that gave rise to what we call modern Germany in Earth I. In lower Norway and Sweden, in Earth II, there were people who spoke a form of Scandinavian. In England and Ireland are people who spoke a form of English. I'm going to get to that in a moment because I want to show you that when you create a whole new world you have to deal with *every* aspect of it. I want to show you what it takes to do this.

So, we have Europe and Asia. The Indians go up to the Bering Strait, find out there is nothing but water out there, and they turn around and go down to Central Asia and China, and their presence there causes a bumping effect, a fall of dominoes. Now remember, this process took thousands of years, not all at once.

You have to remember that the Incans of our world would not be like the Incans of Earth II, for the simple reason that they are subject to entirely different influences. The Chinese of that period outnumbered them; even though they were conquered for a while, they absorbed the American Indians eventually. But Quechua was spoken in the upper part of China and Chinese in the lower.

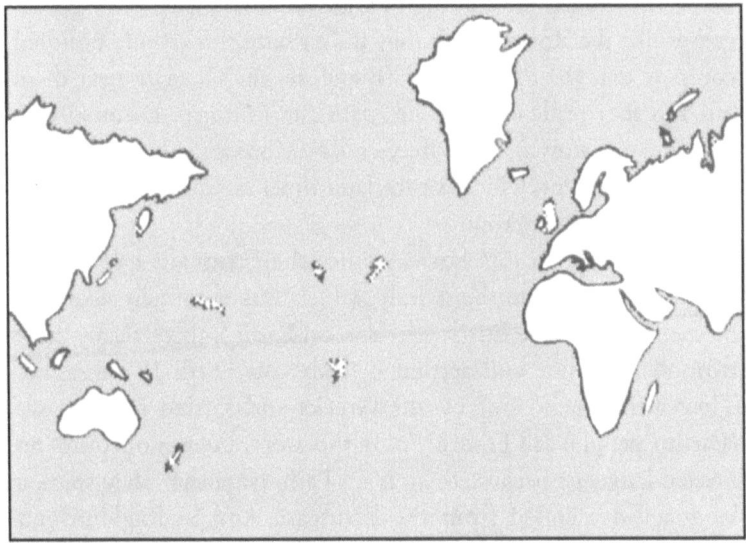

This is a map of Earth II, showing the lack of the North and South American Continents. In the center are (clockwise from 1:00) the Rockies, the Andes, and the Sierra Nevada mountain ranges.

The Amerindians come into here (pointing to a map drawn with chalk on the blackboard [reproduced above—Editor]) where our Aztecs and Toltecs settled. And as a result of all this westward bumping, the Greeks, who in our world originated in the Danube area, were bumped from this area into Italy. The Hittites, due to the vacuum created by the Greeks not being there, came over to the Hellenic peninsula and conquered the aborigines, and so Greece is called Hatti. The Greeks eventually conquered the whole Italic peninsula and absorbed the aborigines—either killed them off or intermarried—their language conquers and as a result there is no Latin, which means that there won't be any Roman Empire, and the languages relating to the Latin such as the French, Italian, Spanish, and so forth are all absorbed.

Originally, on Earth I, the Phoenicians, who lived north of Palestine, came and founded a colony in west North Africa called Carthage. Which, if I remember correctly, in Phoenician, means New City.

This time there is no Roman Empire for the Greeks to battle with. The Greeks are still highly individualistic; they can't get together like the Romans did; they didn't have this empire-building complex that the Romans did. Therefore, the Grecians beat them out and they settle in Iberia or Spain and Portugal. Eventually, at the time our story opens, Greece holds Morocco, Algeria, Tunisia Lybia, and Egypt, which was in later times conquered by Greece, so it was Greek-speaking.

On our Earth in Classical times the Etruscans had a great civilization up in northern Italy, which was eventually absorbed by the Romans. The Etruscans, who, on Earth I, theoretically came from Asia Minor and settled in Italy, on Earth II never did. They were chased out by the Greeks and settled in what we (Earth I people) call France. So, in this story, there is of course no French language because there is no Latin language. They speak a language descended from the Etruscan. And in England and Ireland we have a form of English, and in what is now Normandy and Brittany there is a Germanic-speaking country, and in France south of the Seine and also in Belgium. These are all called the Six Kingdoms.

The reason northern Europe is warm, even though it's so far north, is because of the Gulf Current. But since there is no Gulf of Mexico, there is no Gulf Current. Therefore, Europe is still in an Ice Age, or the end of an Ice Age, or something comparable to an Ice Age. Now this makes Scotland and Northern Ireland and the upper parts of the Scandinavian peninsula very cold. In fact, all of Western Europe has long winters and short summers. The winters are very cold, very harsh, and the summers are very short and not as warm as on Earth I.

That means that when Perkunisha, the Lithuanian (Old Prussian) speaking nation, had spread over a good part of Europe, it looked south for new conquests, especially North Africa. You see, back in 8,000 B.C. when the Ice Age was ending, the Sahara was a vast area, still green, very fertile, and with lots of rivers, elephants, hippos, antelopes—a happy hunting ground for the natives. It began to dry out slowly, but even in Classical times North Africa was still green enough to be the granary of the Roman Empire.

What I overlooked when I first wrote this book, and that was because I wrote too fast, was the North African countries with their vast agricultural regions. They would have been very important in the world of Earth II. In fact they would have been so powerful that Northern European nations would be comparably weak. Industry and technology hasn't kept up with these people.

The story takes place in 1944 and later but, due to the lack of camels and horses, which caused a delay in fast communications and trade, and due to some of the other factors I mentioned, the 1944 of Earth II is technologically behind the 1944 of Earth I. When our hero enters the story, Europe is going through the transition from steam to internal combustion engines and has discovered oil. You might say that their technology in some respects is about what ours was in 1912. But in others, comparable to that of 1880. What you don't want to do in a case like this is just say that these people are 100 to 150 years behind and then take the Earth of 50 or 80 years ago and transplant it. You have to sit down and think about what form of technology they would have; what forms of technology of 1880 and 1912 Earth I had that they lacked. You have to work out the whole thing.

Okay. We've got the geographical set-up, we've got the climatological set-up, we have the racial and the national set-up. Now, there are a lot of things that will be in the novel that I haven't told you about. There are a lot of things that I thought of that I wouldn't put in because I don't want to slow down the book too much.

I was talking about applying extrapolation not only to geography and geology and the vast migrations and so forth, but I'm also talking about language. My premise is that English developed much more slowly in Earth II than it did here, so it's an archaic and sort of creole language. You can do it easy, if you want to. You can go to an Old English text and read it and pick up a few phrases here and there and perhaps put a few phrases down and you'll look very wise and very learned. The only thing is, is that it wouldn't work that way. I mean, not in reality. You see, I'm assuming that there was an English language but in its later stages was subject to different influences than those of Earth I. Let's take as a base Wessex, which is one of the forms of Old English. Actually, standard English is much more influenced by Mercian, for instance, for which we don't have too many manuscripts. If you study Old English, you study Wessex because most of the manuscripts are preserved in Wessex. Well, that isn't going to stop me any because I'm assuming that Wessex was the basis of modern English of Earth II.

I'd like to give you one example of a conversation between Roger Two Hawks and Lady Ilmika Thorrsstein. Two Hawks kisses her hand—remember, she's a member of the nobility—and he says, "Ur Huskarleship," which means "Your Ladyship."

And she says, "Hu far't vi thi, lautni Tva Havoken?" which means, "How goes it with you, Freeman (or Mister) Two Hawks?"

Now, if you are an Old English expert, I bet you don't recognize that (lautni). That's because it is not English, it is Etruscan. It comes from an Etruscan word meaning "freeman."

And he replies, "Ik ar farn be'er," or "I am doing better." Then, "Ur Huskarleship ar mest hunlich aeksen min haelth of," which means, "Your Ladyship is most gracious in asking about my health."

What I did was to take Old English and figure the influences it had been subjected to on Earth II and try and work out the way it might have gone. What I'm trying to say is that if you want to make your world sound authentic and make it ring true, try and cover every aspect that you have in the story. Do some research.

If you want to make up your own language, you don't have to make up the whole grammar and syntax and so forth, but you should at least, in order to be authentic, figure out what sounds are in the language. That is, what sounds are rejected and what sounds are used; what sound clusters are there so that when you make up names for your characters you can given them a true ring. Be sure that the language has certain rules and that you do not use any sounds that just happen to come into your mind because all languages accept certain sounds and reject others, and also combinations of certain sounds. Be consistent.

So, in 1944 there was a big oilfield in Ploesti, Rumania, and the Ninth Air Force decides they are going to knock it out, little knowing that the Germans referred to it as Festung Ploesti, that is, Fortress Ploesti, and so they are in for a big shock.

Roger Two Hawks comes from around Syracuse and is part Onondaga Indian—I'm very fond of American Indians; I think they make great heroes, anyway—and he is in a B-24 bomber. The Germans are really rigged up—boy, are they ready for him. They've got haystacks all over the place with anti-aircraft machine guns behind them, behind every haystack and bush, every place, and a heavy concentration of fighter planes.

The bombers come up from Cyrenaica, North Africa, and Roger Two Hawks is the pilot. They come zooming in, and Roger notes that his leader has gone off in the wrong direction. He tries to call him, then he follows him a little bit, and then here comes a fighter plane. They collide, cutting each other's wings off. Roger Two Hawks and Pat O'Brien, his gunner, are the only two who survive. They don't know it, but the guy flying the German plane also survives.

They land—pretty hard, too—and the place pretty much looks like Rumania. It doesn't look like Ploesti, but they figure they have parachuted on the outskirts, and they are out in the country someplace. They skulk around and find some peasants. They are a lot darker than they should be, and they don't speak Rumanian or German and never heard of English. At least not the type that Roger speaks. Well, eventually, it dawns on Roger, who reads a lot—I like heroes who have read a lot because that enables them to explain things. I don't want him to be too dumb. Roger tells Pat that just before that German fighter hit them he had a strange, weird feeling of dissociation, but it only lasted two seconds. And he says what he thinks happened is that they went through a momentary gate or opening between Earth I and Earth II; they must be in a parallel universe. Pat O'Brien doesn't understand this, and he has a very hard time adapting to this world.

If people were transported to a parallel universe, some people would be able to adapt and others wouldn't. Eventually, Pat just dies; he just can't take it any more. He is a good gunner, but when he finds himself on Earth II surrounded by all these Indians . . . and no cigarettes or potatoes . . . he can't take it.

Remember that in this Earth II, except for a Celtic-speaking nation in Switzerland and our Iroquois nation of Hotinohsinoh, which means housebuilder, there are no democracies, they are all monarchies. Some good, some bad, as monarchies go. England is not called England, it is called Blodland, or Bloodland, because for a thousand years it was fought over by various invaders. English is not called English, it is called Inioinetalu. The word "Angle," or English, is originally supposed to come from one of the early Germanic gods, Ing, and probably originated in Denmark, or near there when the Anglos and Saxons lived there.

Well, we have our noble lady, Ilmika Thorrsstein, and though she is English, her first name is Greek and her second name is actually Old Norse. But her father was ambassador to what we call Hungary, but which is another Indian nation, and when the bad Perkunishans, who are an analog of the Nazis, invaded this land, and he got killed, our heroine fled and, naturally, she runs into Roger Two Hawks.

Here is another method of extrapolation. The Iroquoians, I'll call them that, can not believe Roger Two Hawks' story; they think he is either a spy or he is crazy. They decide that they will give him a break after they rough him up more than somewhat. They put him under the care of the Iroquoian equivalent of a psychiatrist. The ancient Iroquois of Earth I, our world, did have shamans who had a form of psychiatry in which they interpreted dreams. When the sick Iroquoian came in, the shaman would ask him to repeat his dreams. And he, quite often, would interpret the dreams just as they do nowadays. So they sent Roger Two Hawks and Pat O'Brien to this Iroquoian equivalent of a psychiatrist.

Again, you can not just pick up Freudian terms or Jungian and so forth and use them in Iroquoian psychiatry. You have to figure out how some other form of psychiatry used by the shamans developed in a modern nation. Because they do not live in tee-pees, and they no longer live in long houses, and they have had contact with the European nations and have been tremendously influenced by western culture. Therefore, you can not take the Iroquois tribes of 1780 of Earth I and transport them to Earth II without changes. You have to consider all the factors, everything that would influence the Hotinohsinoh: language, architecture, costumes, ways of raising children, everything.

Roger Two Hawks and Ilmika Thorrsstein flee Iroquoia when the Perkunishans invade. They work their way up to what we call Russia but Earth II calls Itskapintik, a Nahuath-speaking people. The two get to Tyrsland (Sweden) and, from thence, they take a boat and go to Blodland.

One good reason for having them escape and have all these adventures is it gives us a chance to go up here (indicates the map) and find out how the Nahuas developed. Then they get captured by the Perkunishans and find out how rotten they are. And when he is captured by the Perkunishans he runs into a guy named Horst Raske, who, it turns out, speaks German. He is the only German speaker in Earth II. And what happened was that he was piloting the German fighter plane that crashed; he went through the momentary opening between the two universes at the same time.

Anyway, Horst Raske is an engineer and he's given the Perkunishans a lot of advice on how to build faster airplanes that will enable them to shoot down the dirigibles and the primitive airplanes. Which will enable them to conquer Central Europe, sweep into Rasna, which is the Etruscan state, and eventually get down through Greece or as it is called Akhaivia.

Eventually—boy, I wish I could tell you that surprise ending.

It has to do with Raske and Roger Two Hawks . . . So, after many adventures, they have to flee to a string of islands way off past what we call the Atlantic—these are the tops of the Rockies. What has happened is that a group of Polynesians came from Hawaii or someplace else a long time ago and the tops of the Rockies are populated by Polynesians. And that is where the surprise ending comes.

THE 1980s

Announced as the fourth and final Riverworld novel, *The Magic Labyrinth,* came out in 1980 and the whole world noticed. It was a *New York Times* best seller. *Time Magazine* ran an article on the series. The ABC network started working on a TV series, although it never came to fruition.

Phil and Bette continued to attend many conventions and other events, beginning with an autograph party in Los Angeles for *The Magic Labyrinth*; the 38th WorldCon in Boston; a Special Program of Authors from Every Field at the San José Center of the Performing Arts; a book signing at Forbidden Planet in London; Aquacon in Anaheim; a One Day Conference at Southern Illinois University; InConJunction I in Indianapolis; the Fantasy Fair in both Dallas and Atlanta; the 40th WorldCon in Chicago; and the World Fantasy Convention in Chicago, 1983, where he published an excerpt from a forthcoming novel, "The Monster on Hold," in the convention program.

Two other excerpts came out in the early 1980s. An abridged version of *Jesus on Mars* was supposed to be serialized in *Asimov's Science Fiction* magazine, but the novel was released before *Asimov's* could print it. A long chapter with a battle scene had been cut from *The Magic Labyrinth*. Both of these works were published in a small press book, *Riverworld War: The Suppressed Fiction of Philip José Farmer.*

The early 1980s also saw the publication of the novel *The Unreasoning Mask*, as well as *A Barnstormer in Oz*, which fulfilled a lifelong dream Phil had of writing an Oz tale.

He only sold a couple of short stories in this period: "Spiders of the Purple Mage" to *Tales from the Vulgar Unicorn*; "The Making of Revelation, Part 1" to *After the Fall*; and "The Long Wet Dream of Rip Van Winkle" to the adult magazine *Puritan*.

Five new books were repackaged under the banner "Jim Baen Presents" for new publisher Tor: *Father to the Stars* collected all five John Carmody stories; *The Cache* included all the material from the 1962 Ace double *The Cache from Outer Space/The Celestial Blueprint*; *Stations of the Nightmare* collected all four stories published in the *Continuum* series, as well as the Farmer/Tincrowdor collaboration "Osiris on Crutches"; *Greatheart Silver* collected all three Greatheart stories published in *Weird Heroes*; and *The Purple Book* collected several short stories, including "Riders of the Purple Wage," "Spiders of the Purple Mage," and the retitled "Long Wet *Purple* Dream of Rip Van Winkle."

While *The Magic Labyrinth* was supposed to be the conclusion to the Riverworld series, Phil did leave himself a backdoor just in case. Pressure from fans and his publisher led to one of the biggest science fiction publishing events of the decade: *Gods of Riverworld*, the fifth novel in the series. Specialty publisher Phantasia Press scored quite a coup when they got the rights to print a signed limited edition of *Gods of Riverworld* that came out before Putnam's trade hardcover edition. Phantasia also published a limited edition of *River of Eternity*, one of the rewrites of the original novel *Owe for the Flesh* that had won the Shasta Prize Novel Contest back in 1953.

Revisiting the world he created in "The Sliced-Crosswise Only-on-Tuesday World," Phil expanded the idea greatly and launched his next big series with *Dayworld* in 1985, followed by *Dayworld Rebel* in 1987.

The mid-1980s also saw three important Farmer collections: *The Classic Philip José Farmer: 1952–1964*, *The Classic Philip José Farmer: 1964–1973*, and *The Grand Adventure*. The latter con-

This photo appeared in the PhilCon 89 program.

tained much informative writing about the works by Phil himself, as well as the story "The Adventure of the Three Madmen," which was a rewritten version of his short novel, *The Adventure of the Peerless Peer*, with Mowgli replacing Lord Greystoke as one of the main characters.

While Phil was mostly writing novels now, he did sell a few short stories: "UFO vs IRS" to *The Planets* and "St. Francis Kisses His Ass Goodbye" to *Semiotext(e)*. He also continued to write non-fiction: the entries for L. Frank Baum and Edgar Rice Burroughs in *20th Century Fiction*; "Memoir" in *Worlds of If: A Retrospective Anthology*; "Remembering Vern" in *Erbania;* and "The Journey" in *The New Encyclopedia of Science Fiction*.

Bantam brought out the first edition of *Venus on the Half-Shell* to have Philip José Farmer listed on the cover rather than Kilgore Trout. This edition also included an essay, "Why and How I Became Kilgore Trout."

Phil also embarked on editing the Dungeon series. These were books by different authors set in a world inspired by his works, but not directly related to any of them. He provided the introduction to each volume.

While the 1980s were very good to Phil, with many of his earlier novels and stories being reprinted in addition to all the new novels and collections being published, he did suffer another major setback. After the success of the film *Fantastic Voyage*, and the novelization of the movie written by Isaac Asimov, the film producers wanted to do a sequel. However, Asimov did not want to write the sequel and his agent, who was also Phil's agent, got Phil a contract to write the novel instead. He was to be paid over half a million dollars for the book. He took a mid-five figure advance and wrote the novel based on the screen treatment. Then a new editor on the project rejected the novel and asked for rewrites, and then rejected the rewrites. These were apparently a stalling tactic as they tried to get Asimov to change his mind, which he finally did, writing the novel after all. Phil was left with just his advance after nearly two years of working on the book.

Phil and Bette finished the decade the way they started, traveling around the country, and the world, as guests at many science fiction conventions: SeaCon in Brighton England; the Dallas Fantasy Fair in 1984 and 1986; Rusticon in Seattle; Magnus Opus Con 3 in Columbus, Georgia; Pulpcon in Dayton, Ohio; the Normal Beans 75th Anniversary of Tarzan of the Apes Dinner in Chicago; and the 53rd WorldCon in Philadelphia. They ended the decade on a particularly high note, the debut stage production of "Riders of the Purple Wage" by Chicago's City Lit Theater Company in November 1989.

The Making of Revelation, Part 1

G od said, "Bring me Cecil B. DeMille."
        "Dead or alive?" the angel Gabriel said.

"I want to make an offer he can't refuse. Can even *I* do this to a dead man?"

"I see," said Gabriel, who didn't. "It will be done."

And it was.

Cecil Blount DeMille, confused, stood in front of the desk. He didn't like it. He was used to sitting behind the desk while others stood. Considering the circumstances, he wasn't about to protest. The giant, divinely handsome, bearded, pipe-smoking man behind the desk was not one you'd screw around with. However, the gray eyes, though steely, weren't quite those of a Wall Street banker. They held a hint of compassion.

Unable to meet those eyes, DeMille looked at the angel by his side. He'd always thought angels had wings. This one didn't, though he could certainly fly. He'd carried DeMille in his arms up through the stratosphere to a city of gold somewhere between the Earth and the moon. Without a space suit, too.

God, like all great entities, came right to the point.

"This is 1980 A.D. In twenty years it'll be time for The Millennium. The Day of Judgment. The events as depicted in the Book of Revelation or the Apocalypse by St. John the Divine.

You know, the seven seals, the four horsemen, the moon dripping blood, Armageddon, and all that."

DeMille wished he'd be invited to sit down. Being dead for twenty-one years, during which he'd not moved a muscle, had tended to weaken him.

"Take a chair," God said. "Gabe, bring the man a brandy." He puffed on his pipe; tiny lightning crackled through the clouds of smoke.

"Here you are, Mr. DeMille," Gabriel said, handing him the liqueur in a cut quartz goblet. "Napoleon 1880."

DeMille knew there wasn't any such thing as a one-hundred-year-old brandy, but he didn't argue. Anyway, the stuff certainly tasted like it was. They really lived up here.

God sighed, and he said, "The main trouble is that not many people really believe in Me any more. So My powers are not what they once were. The old gods, Zeus, Odin, all that bunch, lost their strength and just faded away, like old soldiers, when their worshippers ceased to believe in them.

"So, I just can't handle the end of the world by Myself any more. I need someone with experience, know-how, connections, and a reputation. Somebody people know really existed. You. Unless you know of somebody who's made more Biblical epics than you have."

"That'll be the day," DeMille said. "But what about the unions? They really gave me a hard time, the commie bas . . . uh, so-and-so's. Are they as strong as ever?"

"You wouldn't believe their clout nowadays."

DeMille bit his lip, then said, "I want them dissolved. If I only got twenty years to produce this film, I can't be held up by a bunch of goldbrickers."

"No way," God said. "They'd all strike, and we can't afford any delays."

He looked at his big railroad watch. "We're going to be on a very tight schedule."

"Well, I don't know," DeMille said. "You can't get anything done with all their regulations, interunion jealousies, and the featherbedding. And the wages! It's no wonder it's so hard to show a profit. It's too much of a hassle!"

"I can always get D. W. Griffith."

DeMille's face turned red. "You want a grade-B production? No, no, that's all right! I'll do it, I'll do it!

God smiled and leaned back. "I thought so. By the way, you're not the producer, too; I am. My angels will be the executive producers: They haven't had much to do for several millennia, and the devil makes work for idle hands, you know. Haw, haw! You'll be the chief director, of course. But this is going to be quite a job. You'll have to have at least a hundred thousand assistant directors."

"But . . . that means training about 99,000 directors!"

"That's the least of our problems. Now you can see why I want to get things going immediately."

DeMille gripped the arms of the chair and said, weakly, "Who's going to finance this?"

God frowned. "That's another problem. My Antagonist has control of all the banks. If worse comes to worse, I could melt down the heavenly city and sell it. But the bottom of the gold market would drop all the way to hell. And I'd have to move to Beverly Hills. You wouldn't believe the smog there or the prices they're asking for houses.

"However, I think I can get the money. Leave that to Me."

The men who really owned the American banks sat at a long mahogany table in a huge room in a Manhattan skyscraper. The Chairman of the Board sat at the head. He didn't have the horns, tail, and hooves which legend gave him. Nor did he have an odor of brimstone. More like Brut. He was devilishly handsome and the biggest and best-built man in the room. He looked like he could have been the chief of the angels and in fact once had been. His eyes were evil but no more so than the others at the table, bar one.

The exception, Raphael, sat at the other end of the table. The only detractions from his angelic appearance were his bloodshot eyes. His apartment on the West Side had paper-thin walls, and the swingers' party next door had kept him awake most of the night. Despite his fatigue, he'd been quite effective in presenting the offer from above.

Don Francisco "The Fixer" Fica drank a sixth glass of wine to up his courage, made the sign of the cross, most offensive to the Chairman, gulped, and spoke.

"I'm sorry, Signor, but that's the way the vote went. One hundred percent. It's a purely business proposition, legal, too, and there's no way we won't make a huge profit from it. We're gonna finance the movie, come hell or high water!"

Satan reared up from his chair and slammed a huge but well-manicured fist onto the table. Glasses of vino crashed over; plates half-filled with pasta and spaghetti rattled. All but Raphael paled.

"Dio motarello! Lecaculi! Cacasotti! Non romperci i coglion! I'm the Chairman, and I say no, no, no!"

Fica looked at the other heads of the families. Mignotta, Fregna, Stronza, Loffa, Recchione, and Bocchino seemed scared, but each nodded the go-ahead at Fica.

"I'm indeed sorry that you don't see it our way," Fica said. "But I must ask for your resignation."

Only Raphael could meet The Big One's eyes, but business was business. Satan cursed and threatened. Nevertheless, he was stripped of all his shares of stock. He'd walked in the richest man in the world and he stormed out penniless and an ex-member of the Organization.

Raphael caught up with him as he strode mumbling up Park Avenue.

"You're the father of lies," Raphael said, "so you can easily be a great success as an actor or politician. There's money in both fields. Fame, too. I suggest acting. You've got more friends in Hollywood than anywhere else."

"Are you nuts?" Satan snarled.

"No. Listen. I'm authorized to sign you up for the film on the end of the world. You'll be a lead, get top billing. You'll have to share it with The Son, but we can guarantee you a bigger dressing room than His. You'll be playing yourself, so it ought to be easy work."

Satan laughed so loudly that he cleared the sidewalks for two blocks. The Empire State Building swayed more than it should have in the wind.

"You and your boss must think I'm pretty dumb! Without me the film's a flop. You're up a creek without a paddle. Why should I help you? If I do I end up at the bottom of a flaming pit forever. Bug off!"

Raphael shouted after him, "We can always get Roman Polanski!"

Raphael reported to God, who was taking His ease on His jasper and cornelian throne above which glowed a rainbow.

"He's right, Your Divinity. If he refuses to cooperate, the whole deal's off. No real Satan, no real Apocalypse."

God smiled. "We'll see."

Raphael wanted to ask Him what He had in mind. But an angel appeared with a request that God come to the special effects department. Its technicians were having trouble with the roll-up-the-sky-like- a-scroll machine.

"Schmucks!" God growled. "Do I have to do everything?"

Satan moved into a tenement on 121st Street and went on welfare. It wasn't a bad life, not for one who was used to Hell. But two months later, his checks quit coming. There was no unemployment any more. Anyone who was capable of working but wouldn't was out of luck. What had happened was that Central Casting had hired everybody in the world as production workers, stars, bit players, or extras.

Meanwhile, all the advertising agencies in the world had spread the word, good or bad depending upon the viewpoint, that the Bible was true. If you weren't a Christian, and, what was worse, a sincere Christian, you were doomed to perdition.

Raphael shot up to Heaven again.

"My God, You wouldn't believe what's happening! The Christians are repenting of their sins and promising to be good forever and ever, amen! The Jews, Moslems, Hindus, Buddhists, scientologists, animists, you name them, are lining up at the baptismal fonts! What a mess! The atheists have converted, too, and all the communist and Marxian socialist governments have been overthrown!"

"That's nice," God said. "But I'll really believe in the sincerity of the Christian nations when they kick out their present admin-istrations. Down to the local dogcatcher."

"They're doing it!" Raphael shouted. "But maybe You don't understand! This isn't the way things go in the *Book of Revelation*! We'll have to do some very extensive rewriting of the script! Unless You straighten things out!"

God seemed very calm. "The script? How's Ellison coming along with it?"

Of course, God knew everything that was happening, but He pretended sometimes that He didn't. It was His excuse for talking. Just issuing a command every once in a while made for long silences, sometimes lasting for centuries.

He had hired only science-fiction writers to work on the script since they were the only ones with imaginations big enough to handle the job. Besides, they weren't bothered by scientific impossibilities. God loved Ellison, the head writer, because he was the only human he'd met so far who wasn't afraid to argue with Him. Ellison was severely handicapped, however, because he wasn't allowed to use obscenities while in His presence.

"Ellison's going to have a hemorrhage when he finds out about the rewrites," Raphael said. "He gets screaming mad if anyone messes around with his scripts."

"I'll have him up for dinner," God said. "If he gets too obstreperous, I'll toss around a few lightning bolts. If he thinks he was burned before . . . Well!"

Raphael wanted to question God about the tampering with the book, but just then the head of Budgets came in. The angels beat it. God got very upset when He had to deal with money matters.

The head assistant director said, "We got a problem now, Mr. DeMille. We can't have any Armageddon. Israel's willing to rent the site to us, but where are we going to get the forces of Gog and

Magog to fight against the good guys? Everybody's converted. Nobody's willing to fight on the side of anti-Christ and Satan. That means we've got to change the script again. I don't want to be the one to tell Ellison."

"Do I have to think of everything?" DeMille said. "It's no problem: Just hire actors to play the villains."

"I already thought of that. But they want a bonus. They say they might be persecuted just for *playing* the guys in the black hats. They call it the social-stigma bonus. But the guilds and the unions won't go for it. Equal pay for all extras or no movie and that's that."

DeMille sighed. "It won't make any difference anyway as long as we can't get Satan to play himself."

The assistant nodded. So far, they'd been shooting around the devil's scenes. But they couldn't put it off much longer.

DeMille stood up. "I have to watch the auditions for The Great Whore of Babylon."

The field of 100,000 candidates for the role had been narrowed to a hundred, but from what he'd heard none of these could play the part.

They were all good Christians now, no matter what they'd been before, and they just didn't have their hearts in the role. DeMille had intended to cast his brand-new mistress, a starlet, a hot little number—if promises meant anything—one hundred percent right for the part. But just before they went to bed for the first time, he'd gotten a phone call.

"None of this hanky-panky, C.B.," God had said. "You're now a devout worshipper of Me, one of the lost sheep that's found its way back to the fold. So get with it. Otherwise, back to Forest Lawn for you, and I use Griffith."

"But . . . but I'm Cecil B. DeMille! The rules are O.K. for the common people, but . . ."

"Throw that scarlet woman out! Shape up or ship out! If you marry her, fine! But remember, there'll be no more divorces!"

DeMille was glum. Eternity was going to be like living forever next door to the Board of Censors.

The next day, his secretary, very excited, buzzed him.

"Mr. DeMille! Satan's here! I don't have him for an appointment, but he says he's always had a long-standing one with you!"

Demoniac laughter bellowed through the intercom.

"C.B., my boy! I've changed my mind! I tried out anonymously for the part, but your shithead assistant said I wasn't the type for the role! So I've come to you! I can start work as soon as we sign the contract!"

The contract, however, was not the one the great director had in mind. Satan, smoking a big cigar, chuckling, cavorting, read the terms.

"And don't worry about signing in your blood. It's unsanitary. Just ink in your John Henry, and all's well that ends in Hell."

"You get my soul," DeMille said weakly.

"It's not much of a bargain for me. But if you don't sign it, you won't get me. Without me, the movie's a bomb. Ask The Producer, He'll tell you how it is."

"I'll call Him now."

"No! Sign now, this very second, or I walk out forever!"

DeMille bowed his head, more in pain than in prayer.

"Now!"

DeMille wrote on the dotted line. There had never been any genuine indecision. After all, he was a film director.

After snickering Satan had left, DeMille punched a phone number. The circuits transmitted this to a station which beamed the pulses up to a satellite which transmitted these directly to the heavenly city. Somehow, he got a wrong number. He hung up quickly when Israfel, the angel of death, answered. The second attempt, he got through.

"Your Divinity, I suppose You know what I just did? It *was* the only way you could get him to play himself. You understand that, don't You?"

"Yes, but if you're thinking of breaking the contract or getting Me to do it for you, forget it. What kind of an image would I have if I did something unethical like that? But not to worry. He can't get his hooks into your soul until I say so."

Not to worry? DeMille thought. I'm the one who's going to Hell, not Him.

"Speaking of hooks, let Me remind you of a clause in your contract with The Studio. If you ever fall from grace, and I'm not talking about that little bimbo you were going to make your mistress, you'll die. The Mafia isn't the only one that puts out a contract. *Capice?*"

DeMille, sweating and cold, hung up. In a sense, he was already in Hell. All his life with no women except for one wife? It was bad enough to have no variety, but what if whoever he married cut him off, like one of his wives—what was her name?—had done?

Moreover, he couldn't get loaded out of his skull even to forget his marital woes. God, though not prohibiting booze in His Book, had said that moderation in strong liquor was required and no excuses. Well maybe he could drink beer, however disgustingly plebeian that was.

He wasn't even happy with his work now. He just didn't get the respect he had in the old days. When he chewed out the camera-people, the grips, the gaffers, the actors, they stormed back at him that he didn't have the proper Christian humility, he was too high and mighty, too arrogant. God would get him if he didn't watch his big fucking mouth.

This left him speechless and quivering. He'd always thought, and acted accordingly, that the director, not God, was God. He remembered telling Charlton Heston that when Heston, who after all was only Moses, had thrown a temper tantrum when he'd stepped in a pile of camel shit during the filming of *The Ten Commandments.*

Was there more to the making of the end-of-the-world than appeared on the surface? Had God seemingly forgiven everybody their sins and lack of faith but was subtly, even insidiously, making everybody pay by suffering? Had He forgiven but not forgotten? Or vice versa?

God marked even the fall of a sparrow, though why the sparrow, a notoriously obnoxious and dirty bird, should be significant in God's eye was beyond DeMille.

He had the uneasy feeling that everything wasn't as simple and as obvious as he'd thought when he'd been untimely ripped from the grave in a sort of Caesarean section and carried off like a nursing baby in Gabriel's arms to the office of The Ultimate Producer.

From the *Playboy* Interview feature, December, 1980.

Playboy: Mr. Satan, why did you decide to play yourself after all?

Satan: Damned if I know.

Playboy: The rumors are that you'll be required to wear clothes in the latter-day scenes but that you steadfastly refuse. Are these rumors true?

Satan: Yes indeed. Everybody knows I never wear clothes except when I want to appear among humans without attracting undue attention. If I wear clothes it'd be unrealistic. It'd be phoney, though God knows there are enough fake things in this movie. The Producer says this is going to be a PG picture, not an X-rated. That's why I walked off the set the other day. My lawyers are negotiating with The Studio about this, you can bet your ass that I won't go back unless things go my way, the right way. After all, I am an artist, and I have my integrity. Tell me, if you had a prong this size, would you hide it?

Playboy: The Chicago cops would arrest me before I got a block from my pad. I don't know, though, if they'd charge me with indecent exposure or being careless with a natural resource.

Satan: They wouldn't dare arrest me. I got too much on the city administration.

Playboy: That's some whopper. But I thought angels were sexless. You are a fallen angel, aren't you?

Satan: You jerk! What kind of researcher are you? Right there in the Bible, Genesis 6:2, it says that the sons of God, that is, the angels, took the daughters of men as wives and had children by them. You think the kids were test tube babies? Also, you dunce, I refer you to Jude 7 where it's said that the angels, like the Sodomites, committed fornications and followed unnatural lusts.

Playboy: Whew! That brimstone! There's no need getting so hot under the collar, Mr. Satan. I only converted a few years ago. I haven't had much chance to read the Bible.

Satan: I read the Bible every day. All of it. I'm a speedreader, you know.

Playboy: You read the Bible? (Pause.) Hee, hee! Do you read it for the same reason W. C. Fields did when he was dying?

Satan: What's that?

Playboy: Looking for loopholes.

DeMille was in a satellite and supervising the camerapeople while they shot the takes from ten miles up. He didn't like at all the terrific pressure he was working under. There was no chance to shoot every scene three or four times to get the best angle. Or to reshoot if the actors blew their lines. And, oh, sweet Jesus, they were blowing them all over the world!

He mopped his bald head. "I don't care what The Producer says! We have to retake at least a thousand scenes. And we've a million miles of film to go yet!"

They were getting close to the end of the breaking-of-the-seven-seals sequences. The Lamb, played by The Producer's Son, had just broken the sixth seal. The violent worldwide earthquake had gone well. The sun-turning-black-as-a-funeral-pall had been a breeze. But the moon-all-red-as-blood had had some color problems. The rushes looked more like Colonel Sanders' orange juice than hemoglobin. In DeMille's opinion the stars-falling-to-earth-like-figs-shaken-down-by-a-gale scenes had been excellent, visually speaking. But everybody knew that the stars were not little blazing stones set in the sky but were colossal balls of atomic fires each of which was many times bigger than Earth. Even one of them, a million miles from Earth, would destroy it. So where was the credibility factor?

"I don't understand you, boss," DeMille's assistant said. "You didn't worry about credibility when you made *The Ten Commandments*. When Heston, I mean, Moses, parted the Red Sea, it was the fakiest thing I ever saw. It must've made unbelievers out of millions of Christians. But the film was a box-office success."

"It was the dancing girls that brought off the whole thing!" DeMille screamed. "Who cares about all that other bullshit when they can see all those beautiful long-legged snatches twirling their veils!"

His secretary floated from her chair. "I quit, you male chauvinistic pig! So me and my sisters are just snatches to you, you baldheaded cunt?"

His hotline to the heavenly city rang. He picked up the phone.

"Watch your language!" The Producer thundered. "If you step out of line too many times, I'll send you back to the grave! And Satan gets you right then and there!"

Chastened but boiling near the danger point, DeMille got back to business, called Art in Hollywood. The sweep of the satellite around Earth included the sky-vanishing-as-a-scroll-is-rolled-up scenes, where every-mountain-and-island-is-removed-from-its-place. If the script had called for a literal removing, the tectonics problem would have been terrific and perhaps impossible. But in this case the special effects departments only had to simulate the scenes.

Even so, the budget was strained. However, The Producer, through his unique abilities, was able to carry these off. Whereas, in the original script, genuine displacements of Greenland, England, Ireland, Japan, and Madagascar had been called for, not to mention thousands of smaller islands, these were only faked.

"Your Divinity, I have some bad news," Raphael said.

The Producer was too busy to indulge in talking about something He already knew. Millions of the faithful had backslid and taken up their old sinful ways. They believed that since so many events of the Apocalypse were being faked, God must not be capable of making any really big catastrophes. So, they didn't have anything to worry about.

The Producer, however, had decided that it would not only be good to wipe out some of the wicked but it would strengthen the faithful if they saw that God still had some muscle.

"They'll get the real thing next time," He said. "But we have to give DeMille time to set up his cameras at the right places. And we'll have to have the script rewritten, of course."

Raphael groaned. "Couldn't somebody else tell Ellison? He'll carry on something awful."

"I'll tell him. You look pretty pooped, Rafe. You need a little R&R. Take two weeks off. But don't do it on Earth. Things are going to be very unsettling there for a while."

Raphael, who had a tender heart, said, "Thanks, Boss, I'd just as soon not be around to see it."

The seal was stamped on the foreheads of the faithful, marking them safe from the burning of a third of Earth, the turning of a third of the sea to blood along with the sinking of a third of the ships at sea (which also included the crashing of a third of the airplanes in the air, something St. John had overlooked), the turning of a third of all water to wormwood (a superfluous measure since a third was already thoroughly polluted), the failure of a third of daylight, the release of giant mutant locusts from the abyss, and the release of poison-gas-breathing mutant horses, which slew a third of mankind.

DeMille was delighted. Never had such terrifying scenes been filmed. And these were nothing to the plagues which followed. He had enough film from the cutting room to make a hundred documentaries after the movie was shown. And then he got a call from The Producer.

'It's back to the special effects, my boy."

"But why, Your Divinity? We still have to shoot The-Great-Whore-of-Babylon sequences, the two-Beasts-and-the-marking-of-the-wicked, the Mount-Zion-and-The-Lamb-with-His-one-hundred-and-forty-thousand-good-men-who-haven't-defiled-themselves-with-women, the . . ."

"Because there aren't any wicked left by now, you dolt! And not too many of the good, either!"

"That couldn't be helped," DeMille said. "Those gas-breathing,

Scorpion-tailed horses kind of got out of hand. But we just *have* to have the scenes where the rest of mankind that survives the plagues still doesn't abjure its worship of idols and doesn't repent of its murders, sorcery, fornications, and robberies."

"Rewrite the script."

"Ellison will quit for sure this time."

"That's all right, I already have some hack from Peoria lined up to take his place. And cheaper, too."

DeMille took his outfit, one hundred thousand strong, to the heavenly city. Here they shot the war between Satan and his demons and Michael and his angels. This was not in the chronological sequence as written by St. John, but the logistics were so tremendous that it was thought best to film these out of order.

Per the rewritten script, Satan and his host were defeated, but a lot of nonbelligerents were casualties, including DeMille's best cameraperson. Moreover, there was a delay in production when Satan insisted that a stuntperson do the part where he was hurled from Heaven to Earth.

"Or use a dummy!" he yelled. "Twenty thousand miles is a hell of a long way to fall! If I'm hurt badly I might not be able to finish the movie!"

The screaming match between the director and Satan took place on the edge of the city. The Producer, unnoticed, came up behind Satan and kicked him from the city for the second time in their relationship with utter ruin and furious combustion.

Shrieking, "I'll sue! I'll sue!" Satan fell towards the planet below. He made a fine spectacle in his blazing entrance into the atmosphere, but the people on Earth paid it little attention. They were used to fiery portents in the sky. In fact, they were getting fed up with them.

DeMille screamed and glanced around and jumped up and down. Only the presence of The Producer kept him from using foul and abusive language.

"We didn't get it on camera! Now we'll have to shoot it over!"

"His contract calls for only one fall," God said. "You'd better shoot the War-between-The-Faithful-and-True-Rider-against-the-beast-and-the-false-prophet while he recovers."

The Making of Revelation, Part 1

"What'll I do about the fall?" DeMille moaned.

"Fake it," The Producer said, and He went back to His office.

Per the script, an angel came down from Heaven and bound up the badly injured and burned and groaning Satan with a chain and threw him into the abyss, the Grand Canyon. Then he shut and sealed it over him (what a terrific sequence that was!) so that Satan might seduce the nations no more until a thousand years had passed.

A few years later the devil's writhings caused a volcano to form above him, and the Environmental Protection Agency filed suit against Celestial Productions, Inc. because of the resultant pollution of the atmosphere.

Then God, very powerful now that only believers existed on Earth, performed the first resurrection. In this, only the martyrs were raised. And Earth, which had had much elbow room because of the recent wars and plagues, was suddenly crowded again.

Part I was finished except for the reshooting of some scenes, the dubbing in of voice and background noise, and the synchronization of the music, which was done by the cherubim and seraphim (all now unionized).

The great night of the premiere in a newly built theater in Hollywood, six million capacity, arrived. DeMille got a standing ovation after it was over. But *Time* and *Newsweek* and *The Manchester Guardian* panned the movie.

"There are some people who may go to Hell after all," God growled.

DeMille didn't care about that. The film was a box-office success, grossing ten billion dollars in the first six months. And when he considered the reruns in theaters and the TV rights . . . well, had anyone ever done better?

He had a thousand more years to live. That seemed like a long time. Now. But . . . what would happen to him when Satan was released to seduce the nations again? According to John the Divine's book, there'd be another worldwide battle. Then Satan, defeated, would be cast into the lake of fire and sulphur in the abyss.

(He'd be allowed to keep his Oscar, however.)

Would God let Satan, per the contract DeMille had signed with the devil, take DeMille with him into the abyss? Or would He keep him safe long enough to finish directing Part II? After Satan was buried for good, there'd be a second resurrection and a judging of those raised from the dead. The goats, the bad guys, would be hurled into the pit to keep Satan company. DeMille should be with the saved, the sheep, because he had been born again. But there was that contract with The Tempter.

DeMille arranged a conference with The Producer. Ostensibly, it was about Part II, but DeMille managed to bring up the subject which really interested him.

"I can't break your contract with him," God said.

"But I only signed it so that You'd be sure to get Satan for the role. It was a self-sacrifice. Greater love hath no man and all that. Doesn't that count for anything?"

"Let's discuss the shooting of the new Heaven and the new Earth sequences."

At least I'm not going to be put into Hell until the movie is done, DeMille thought. But after that? He couldn't endure thinking about it, "It's going to be a terrible technical problem," God said, interrupting DeMille's gloomy thoughts. "When the second resurrection takes place, there won't be even Standing Room Only on Earth. That's why I'm dissolving the old Earth and making a new one. But I can't just duplicate the old Earth. The problem of Lebensraum would still remain. Now, what I'm contemplating is a Dyson sphere."

"What's that?"

"A scheme by a 20th-century mathematician to break up the giant planet Jupiter into large pieces and set them in orbit at the distance of Earth from the sun. The surfaces of the pieces would provide room for a population enormously larger than Earth's. It's a Godlike concept."

"What a documentary its filming would be!" DeMille said. "Of course, if we could write some love interest in it, we could make a he . . . pardon me, a heaven of a good story!"

God looked at his big railroad watch.

"I have another appointment, C.B. The conference is over."

DeMille said good-bye and walked dejectedly towards the door. He still hadn't gotten an answer about his ultimate fate. God was stringing him along. He felt that he wouldn't know until the last minute what was going to happen to him. He'd be suffering a thousand years of uncertainty, of mental torture. His life would be a cliffhanger. Will God relent? Or will He save the hero at the very last second?

"C.B.," God said.

DeMille spun around, his heart thudding, his knees turned to water. Was this it? The fatal finale? Had God, in His mysterious and subtle way, decided for some reason that there'd be no Continued In Next Chapter for him? It didn't seem likely, but then The Producer had never promised that He'd use him as the director of Part II nor had He signed a contract with him. Maybe, like so many temperamental producers, He'd suddenly concluded that DeMille wasn't the right one for the job. Which meant that He could arrange it so that his ex-director would be thrown now, right this minute, into the lake of fire.

God said, "I can't break your contract with Satan. So . . ."

"Yes?"

DeMille's voice sounded to him as if he were speaking very far away.

"Satan can't have your soul until you die."

"Yes?"

His voice was only a trickle of sound, a last few drops of water from a clogged drainpipe.

"So, if you don't die, and that, of course, depends upon your behavior, Satan can't ever have your soul."

God smiled and said, "See you in eternity."

Buddha Contemplates His Novel

When I was asked to title this lecture, I facetiously replied, "Buddha Contemplates His Novel."

But I am never more serious than when I'm facetious or fecetious.

What I had intended to do was to tell you how science-fiction takes in all fields of human thought and activity. I was going to demonstrate this by postulating a slightly different, or parallel-world, universe in which Gotama or Siddhartha or the Buddha was born in a time somewhat more technologically advanced than that we call "this universe."

In that other universe, Buddha lived and suffered and acted much as he did here. Except that he traveled by train or automobile, and he had a portable typewriter. And he was writing a novel.

The novel was pedagogic, basically educational, though Buddha was too good a writer to ignore a rather fast-moving plot, three-dimensional characterization, suspense, and all the elements that make for a readable if not perhaps a great novel. Of course, he would publish his philosophy in it, but more by implication, more through the actions and concise talk of his characters than through direct propagandistic lecturing.

"That," as they say in India, "is another story."

I won't tell you about it in detail, but I hope to write it some day.

Science-fiction is not just what you might think it is if you know it only through the movies. Nor is science-fiction prophetic. It doesn't, generally, try to tell you what the world will be in the future. No. Science-fiction is about the limitless world of imagination, and, like mainstream, mysteries, westerns, gothics, you name it, it contains stories ranging from very bad to very good and, sometimes, great.

Let me quote a small part of a review of my Riverworld series by Robert Anton Wilson. This review is in the current issue of "Heavy Metal" magazine, a periodical which deals much with science-fiction. Wilson was co-author of a series of books I highly recommend for those who like to be entertained at the same time they're educated and mentally and emotionally stimulated. I recommend the Illuminatus trilogy, *The Cosmic Trigger* (non-fiction, well, almost), *Masks of the Illuminati*, and the trilogy, *Schrodinger's Cat*.

Quote: The Riverworld novels of Philip José Farmer—*To Your Scattered Bodies Go, The Fabulous Riverboat, The Dark Design,* and *The Magic Labyrinth*—have a multitude of virtues. They boast as much smashing-and-bashing melodrama as ten years' worth of old *Doc Savage* magazines, they are full of odd and interesting bits of historical and anthropological knowledge, and they raise all the important questions of philosophy within the context of a hero's quest that is both exciting and metaphysical. Best of all, taken together, they weigh just enough to make an ideal bludgeon to batter the head of the next person who tells you that science-fiction is not serious literature. Unquote.

I've read this to demonstrate that science-fiction covers more than just space opera or monster movies or scenarios of the dismal future. The Riverworld series could be called theological-eschatological science-fiction.

Permit me to quote another section.

Quote: . . . but Farmer's greatest achievement, accomplished with brilliant understatement, is to make us gradually realize that our own situation here on Earth is just as mysterious as anything on Riverworld, or that the answer to the enigmas of the River-world might also be the explanation of the paradoxes of our own particular existence here and now. Once again . . . Farmer demonstrates my pet theory that sf is the only serious literature around these days, because it is the only literature that grapples with the ultimate questions of who or what we are and how we got here. Unquote.

While I don't agree in every detail with what Wilson says, I do agree with the essence.

In September, a new novel of mine, titled *The Unreasoning Mask*, comes out. I mention it because it is a philosophical-theological-eschatological science-fiction work. And because, during its writing, I found or discovered or flashed on or created what I believe to be an original concept in theology. To the best of my knowledge, it has never been voiced or printed. Even if it has, I've independently invented it.

What is this brand-new concept?

It's this. If God exists, He may be omniscient, but He is not omnipotent.

Why isn't He omnipotent, that is, all powerful?

Because he cannot *be* you. Or me.

No matter how powerful He is, He cannot be you, cannot become you. That is a deed beyond Him.

God could make a body exactly like yours in every detail, physically and mentally. He could then, I suppose, inhabit it. But He still would not *be* you. The gulf between you and your simulacrum is infinitely wide, and I do not use the word "infinitely" lightly.

Think about this concept. If you have arguments against, you may voice them during the question-and-answer period. Please stick to the statement I made, though, don't stray far afield; don't appeal to Scripture as an authority. Remain within the logic embodied in the statement: If God exists, then He may be omni-scient, but He is not omnipotent.

Which means, of course, that the definition of God needs restatement. You can't say that God is near-omnipotent. Either

God is omnipotent or He is not. Just as a woman is either pregnant or not, not just a little pregnant.

During the preparation of this lecture, I conjured up all the arguments I could think of to refute my concept. But I'm not going to state them now, as I did in the original draft of the lecture. That would take far too much time.

However, though I may be an amateur theologian, I am a professional writer of fiction. And it was almost inevitable that the concept I stated in *The Unreasoning Mask* should be percolating or circulating through my minds, my conscious, unconscious, and daemonic. And so I'll write a story which uses the concept as a springboard. Tentative title: *The Bronze Serpent*. It'll be a theological private-eye story.

One of the basic assumptions: That God decides for various reasons I won't go into here to become, for a while, the exact duplicate of an existing human being. To do this, He has to suppress completely His own knowledge that He's God inhabiting the body. So He compresses Himself, as it were, into the narrow compass of an individual's mind and body, and He also makes Himself unaware He is doing this. But, of course, when He is finally released from the body and becomes the expanded God again, He'll remember everything that took place when He was in the body and mind.

He also implants in the body's unconscious a command to free Himself of the duplicate body at a certain time, either in twenty years or at the death of the body, whichever comes first. While in fleshly bonds, He is as subject to the course of events as any other being, to accident and coincidence, or synchronicity, if you prefer that term. And He can't foresee what will happen. For story and philosophical purposes, I assume that God is not omniscient, that he can't see into the future, though He probably knows more about statistical probabilities than anyone else.

This is not a story about Jesus. Jesus has no relevancy to the story except through historical influence, and, indeed, the story will take place in near-future time.

An accident—or is it an accident?—destroys the preset command in his unconscious. And He has already been injected with the recently invented elixir which stops aging, as have all citizens of the United States. Barring accident, homicide, or suicide, He'll live forever. The story ends when the private eye turns the God-inhabited person over to the police, who then read Him His rights.

God will be sent to a prison for the criminally insane, and He won't be released until He's cured. But He won't be cured, though it's possible that science will some day discover how to cure such as He.

The Bronze Serpent is actually only in the stage where I'm making notes and abortive outlines for it. By the time the story is written, it may be, in form, plot, and character, somewhat different. But the basic assumption and logic will remain the same.

I don't want to get deeply into the argument advanced by C. S. Lewis, an amateur theologian/philosopher, and some professionals. That is, that God with one sweep of His eye can see past, present, and future because all events have already taken place, as far as God is concerned. But we humans are still caught up in the flow of time. Still going through our paces, as it were, still totally ignorant of what's ahead of us and not too knowledgeable, really, about what's behind us and more or less bewildered by the present.

As I said, this isn't the time or place to detail that theory. I'll just say that it won't wash, that it can be refuted logically. So, for the purposes of the story, *The Bronze Serpent*, I'll assume that God can't see the future though He probably knows more about statistical probabilities than anyone else.

Some of you are probably thinking, or should be thinking, "But what about Jesus? Wasn't He God in a human body?"

Let's assume, for the purpose of the story, that God was indeed Jesus in a human body. Let's dodge all the arguments and theories that come along with that, the unitarian, duotarian, trinitarian theories, the difference between the human and godly nature or their union, etc. That Jesus might or might not be such is of no interest to me or the reader. The point is that, if God did parthogenetically fertilize Mary's egg so that it produced a male baby, and if God somehow wholly or partially inhabited Jesus' body, God still was not attempting to be anybody dead, then living, or now living or potentially living.

Thus, the example of Jesus has no relevancy to the story.

What does is that, in the story, God decided to reincarnate once more. When he became reincarnate or inhabited Jesus' body, He went through the foetus and baby and childhood and adolescent stages of the body. And He was in an extraordinary situation, a prophet, a founder of a Jewish cult, and one who claimed, if we believe his chroniclers, to be destined to sit on the right hand of God.

But in the story God duplicates the body of a man who's just died, does away with the body, pretends to be resuscitated after being legally dead, and takes the place of the man, continues with his life, as it were. He does this because he wishes to empathize as fully as possible with the problems, wretchedness, meannesses, and also the victories, compassions, and glories, such as they are of a human being.

And, as I said, to be as nearly as possible like the man he's replaced, he buries deep in his unconscious mind the knowledge that he is God. Also buried is the preset command for the knowledge to come to the conscious mind after twenty years. Or at the death of the body, whichever comes first.

I won't go into detail about this story except to say that an accident—or is it an accident?—destroys the unconscious command. Also, scientists have found an elixir which stops aging and which, theoretically, will allow a person to live forever barring accident, suicide or homicide. The story ends when the private detective turns the God-inhabited character over to the police, who then read him his rights.

The intimation here is that God will be sent to a prison for the criminally insane and not released until he is cured. But he won't ever be cured and thus will be imprisoned forever or at least until the sun novas and destroys Earth . . .

The Bronze Serpent will be an example of theological s-f.

Let's go now to another example that is, the RW [Riverworld] series, though that is also more than just theological s-f.

This has many themes, basic conceptual threads running thru it. But the one I'd like to talk to most, though briefly, is this. One that's been explicit or implied in some other books or series of novels of mine. That is, that if God has not arranged matters so that all sapients, which includes Earthpeople, have immortality or salvation, then perhaps the sapients will do the job. These stories suggest that humankind has the potentiality for bestowing upon itself immortality and the means for making immortality worthwhile.

Perhaps that is evolution's goal as designed by God, if there is God and there is evolution. There's an overwhelming amount of evidence for the existence of both God and evolution, but the existence of neither has yet been proved in a truly scientific sense.

Re evolution, you should keep your mind open. Perhaps, some day, some genius will take a look at the Mt. Everest of evidence for evolution and say, "Hey! You've all been wrong! You've not looked at the evidence right. Both the creationists and the evolutionists are wrong!"

Keep an open mind. As Ouspensky said, "Think in other categories."

As for the existence of God, that can neither be proved nor disproved. Not thru scientific means, anyway. But there is more than one mode of knowledge, science is only one of them.

For those who may not have [read] the Riverworld series, it consists at the moment, of four novels and one novella. *To Your Scattered Bodies Go, The Fabulous Riverboat, The Dark Design, The Magic Labyrinth*, and the novella, "Riverworld."

The basic concept in these, along with other basic concepts, is that I spoke about a moment ago. That humankind, may be able to provide physical or spiritual immortality if it gets tired of waiting for God to provide it.

Every human being on Earth who's lived, between 150,000 B.C. and A.D. 1983 and who died after the age of five is resurrected at approximately the same time. If they died after the age of twenty-five, they're resurrected in rejuvenated bodies. Those they had or should have had at the age of twenty-five. Children above five are resurrected at the age they died and then grow normally until they reach maturity and then don't get older.

Apparently, the resurrection takes place on a planet which is Earthlike but not Earth. It's been remade by someone unknown into a ten million mile long river valley, and the resurrectees are scattered along it. People from different times and places find themselves mixed together in the various areas along The River.

The planet is mineral-poor, especially iron and copper poor. They're forced to live in a stone age.

There's not room enough for thirty-five or so billion resurrectees and land to grow crops. But they don't need the great acreage of soil to plant . . . Every Kilometer, on both sides of The River, is a metal-rock toadstool shaped structure which discharges vast quantities of electricity three times a day. The resurrectees have indestructible containers which, when placed upon the structures, called grails, holy buckets, etc. convert the energy into matter. That is, food, liquor, and other various goodies.

Most of these grails can only be opened by their original owners.

If a person is killed or dies, he or she is then resurrected at a distant place along with a new grail. Apparently, the place of the new resurrection is picked by some mysterious random method.

The human beings have no idea who has resurrected them or why. Much of the action and plot consists of several curious characters trying to find out.

In the end, explanations come, but they're too complicated for me to talk about them here. I suggest those who haven't read the series do so, reading them in chronological sequence, starting with TYSBG and ending with TML. RW, the novella, may be read at any time after reading the first of the series.

I've been told that many of the audience had read the series, and that some have questions. I'm ready to answer them as well as I can.

The Long Wet Dream of
Rip Van Winkle

Washington Irving did not know it. Rip did not dare tell it. Rip hadn't been asleep every day of those twenty years. At least, he didn't think he had. Sometimes he wondered if the reality had just been pleasant, indeed, ecstatic, dreams mixed with nightmares.

In A.D. 1772, Rip was thirty-five when he passed out from the booze snitched from the strange little men playing ninepins. When he awoke on the Kaatskill meadow, his whiskers were no longer than if a night had passed. The bowlers and his dog Wolf were gone. Wincing at every step because of his hangover, he reluctantly trudged over the hills, his hunting musket on his shoulder, headed for the Hudson River and home. And the hell his wife would give him.

Suddenly, he reeled, and he cried out. The world had become all flux. The leaves of the trees changed from green to many colors. Autumn fell like a dead bird and then snow dived after it. He was up to his waist in it, but he couldn't feel it. The snow melted. And snow fell again and again. The rains came; the land greened. The sun, the moon, and the stars raced across the sky.

Once a falling tree hurtled *through* him. Then it decayed and was gone while he yelled with terror and for mercy. He'd been bewitched by the little bowlers and justly so. He should've stayed home; repaired the fences and house, tilled and planted instead of lazing around, hunting, and thinking of forbidden cunt.

Suddenly, the moon slowed but soon resumed its normal pace. All was stable again. The hot summer night was noisy with insects and a great humming from the east. Trembling, he resumed his trip home. Presently, he stopped on a hill which looked down on the river, sparkling in the full moon. The narrow dirt road along the Hudson was now a broad highway of some kind of stone. It was brightly illuminated by lights at the tops of poles along it and by lamps in the fronts of . . . horseless carriages? The humming was the sound they made when heard from a distance, and they were going incredibly fast.

To his right, on top of an empty hill he'd passed yesterday, was a big house with many lights and people on the front porch and a very strange music emanating from it.

Rip went down the hill slowly and quietly. He was determined to get, somehow, through all these frightening witcheries to his village, where the holy presence of the church building would make them all disappear. But he stopped at the foot of the hill. Parked in a grove of trees was one of those scary vehicles, a topless one. Its lights were out. He crept forward until he saw by the moon that a woman was sitting in the back seat. She was smoking tobacco in a little white tube. He could hear an unfamiliar but stirring music, then someone shouting, "Hiyo, Silver! Away!"

Closer, he found that the sounds came from a box in the front part of the carriage.

He looked down past her right shoulder. Her skirt was up over her waist, and her hand was working up and down slowly inside some very thin lacy garments covering her loins. Her thighs gleamed whitely between the tops of her stockings—silk!—and the lacy garment. Her head was thrown back, the glowing tube sticking straight up, and she was moaning.

Rip was very embarrassed, but his tallywhacker was rising. Dame Van Winkle had cut him off after the birth of their eighth; it'd been a long time since he'd gone to bed with her. Or anyone.

Rip turned to retreat, and his musket stock banged against the metal door. The woman screamed. He started to run away, but his ankle turned, and he fell flat on his face. The next he knew, something cold and hard was pressed against his neck. He looked up at the woman. She was very pretty, big-busted, and enticing in that short shameless tight dress. The huge strange-looking pistol she held was not so alluring.

She spat out invective with a vigor matched only by Mrs. Van Winkle, who, however, would never have used such dirty words or blasphemous oaths. Then she let him get to his feet.

Eyes wide, she said, "What kind of crazy outfit is that? Are you a butler from that house?" Then, seeing the musket, she cried, "What in hell is that?"

He tried to explain. When she'd heard him out, she said, "Your name is *Rip Van Winkle?* Now I know you're a refugee from the funny farm."

"There's no farmer around here by that name," he said, "unless you mean Klaus van Fannij."

She looked at the tiny watch on her wrist. "Shit! Isn't he ever coming back? I get so goddam fed up waiting around for him while he's sneaking around spying on those big-shot crooks!"

She backed up to the car, reached behind to the rear seat, and brought up a silver flask. She unscrewed the cap of the flask with a thumb, and, still pointing the enormous weapon at him, drank deeply. He smelled gin.

"Here. Have a snort."

He took it gratefully. It *was* gin but terrible stuff. Still, it helped get rid of the shakes, and it warmed the cockles of his heart, not to mention those of his tallywhacker. She saw the expanding bulge; the barrel of her gun dropped as his barrel ascended.

She took the flask back, drained it, then looked at her time-piece again. "Well, why not? It'll serve him right," she said, her words slightly blurred. "Okay. Kneebritches. Off with them."

"My God!" she said as they climbed into the back seat. "It must be at least fourteen inches long!"

"Why, that's only normal," he said. "You should see Brom Dutcher's!"

She laughed and said, "Did you fall asleep and wake up in the twentieth century, Rip?"

He didn't know what she was talking about and didn't much care. After the second time, she offered him a tube which she called a Lucky Strike. He smoked it, but the paper came off on his lip and the tobacco tasted vile.

"I suppose," she said, "you think I'm promiscuous. You know, fucking a complete stranger."

He blushed. Such language from a woman!

"That looney son of a bitch runs around at night in his black hat and cloak, cackling, sneaking around, just itching to blast crooks with his two big .45 automatics. He's knocked off a lot of them, you know." (Rip didn't know.) "I suppose he does much good, socially speaking. But he sure doesn't do me any good. Won't give me a tumble though I practically rub his nose in it. He's not a fairy, so I figure he's either asexual or he thinks his profession, rubbing out gangsters, is holy, just like a priest's, and he's vowed to chastity, too.

"Cranston uses me to spy for him, but he won't let me go with him when he expects some real action. He says it's not women's work, the asshole!"

"Don't he know you're doing this behind his back?" Rip said as he started plugging again.

"He should. He claims to be the only one in the world who knows what evil lurks in the hearts of men. And of women, too. Oh, wow! Oh, God! Pour it in, Kneebritches!"

Maniacal laughter, shuddery and sinister, burst from the shadows. Rip sprang up, dived over the door, jetting, landed on the ground, got up, and began to pull his britches on. The woman, muttering curses, sat up and smoothed her skirt down. A tall man, lean, hawk-faced, with a huge curving nose and wild burning eyes, appeared out of the darkness. He was dressed in strange clothes and carried a bundle under one arm. Rip supposed that was the hat and cloak the woman had mentioned.

"Margo, what do we have here?" the man said. Suddenly, a gun like the woman's was in his long pale hand.

"Some nut who claims to be Rip Van Winkle, Lamont."

"I've stirred up a hornet's nest back there. They'll be on our necks in a minute. Let's go!"

Rip said, "Could you drop me off at my village? It's just down the road a mile or so."

The man waved the gun. "Get in the car. You're going to the city with us. I think you're a part of the plot, though I'll admit I don't exactly know how you fit in."

"Oh, Lamont!" the woman said. "Don't be so fucking paranoid! He's been to a masquerade party or he escaped from the puzzle factory or he *is* a time traveler!"

"You've been reading too much of that trashy science fiction. No. He's going with us. I'm getting to the bottom of this if it kills him."

Rip prayed as he held on to the side of the door and Margo's thigh. He was traveling at a speed the philosophers had said no human being could endure. The air rushing over the glass shield in front of him smote him. The lights of the oncoming traffic were blinding.

The nightmare voyage got worse every second. Then they were crossing a gigantic steel bridge over the Hudson. Manhattan was before him, but the island, which had been nothing but woods here, was packed with incredibly high buildings and more people in a mile's stretch than he'd seen in all his life before.

And then the flickering started again, the sun, moon, stars whirling, snowfall followed by rain by hot sunlight, flicker, flicker, flicker. When it stopped, he was sitting on the same street in bright day, his ass hurting where he'd fallen through the car, metal squealing, horns blasting, cursings, and the front of a car just touching his back. He had a vague impression he'd been there for a long time while countless hordes of cars had passed through his body. But these were solid, and if he didn't get to the sidewalk fast, he was going to be run over or badly beaten by the red-faced driver waving a fist at him.

When he got to the walk, he looked around. Some of the buildings he'd seen from the crazy man's car were gone, replaced by others even taller. At that moment a car pulled up to the curb near him. It was rusty and dirty with PEACE and LOVE in big letters painted on it. What Margo had called a "radio" during the mad journey to the city was blasting out some wild barbaric rhythms.

A young woman with a mass of frizzy yellow hair stuck her head out of its window. "Hey, man! Far out!"

The driver was a long-haired, bushy-bearded youth wearing fringed buckskin clothes and a leather headband. He looked like a frontiersman, an Indian fighter. The female and male in the back seat wore some kind of robes with many bright symbols woven on them. One wore on the chest a round metal object sporting the slogan: *McGovern in '72.* The slogan on the chest ornament of the other was: MAKE LOVE NOT WAR.

The driver said, "Hey, man, I dig those crazy threads. You going to the demonstration?"

Rip thought he might as well say he was. He needed some friendly people to guide him in his stay in this age. Oh, Lord, propelled two hundred years into the future without a return ticket!

Rip got into the front beside the girl, who introduced herself as Judy Gardenier. She asked him if he was going as the "Spirit of 1776." He said he didn't know what she was talking about. As the car headed east on a street that hadn't existed in his time, the three passed a burning tube around. It wasn't white like Margo's Lucky Strike but brown. Its smoke had a heavy acrid odor. Judy asked him if he'd like to try the joint, and he said, "Why not?" Watching him, she said, "Man, you from the sticks? You gotta draw it way down into your lungs and hold it as long as you can."

He did so, and after a few times he began to relax. Things didn't seem so bad now.

"You got any bread?" Judy said.

"Not a bite," Rip said, and the others howled with laughter. When he found out what she meant, he produced from his pocket his worldly wealth, two copper halfpence coins. Judy looked at the King George III heads and the dates, and said, "Wow, collector's items!"

Rip let Judy keep the coins. What the hell. The trip toward the "pad" in "Hell's Kitchen" was fascinating if sometimes shocking and always confusing. He was startled when he saw the first black and white couple walking along, the man feeling up the woman's ass. The attitude toward slaves certainly had changed. Or did the colonists now have white slaves, too? Whatever the situation was, the color barrier was down.

Women's skirts were, however, up, way up. After he got over his first shock at seeing so much leg, he reveled in it. Nobody else seemed to think such exposure was sinful, so why should he?

The "pad" was in a basement occupied by ten or twelve youths of two or three sexes. A very short stout man with a long red beard, Yosemite Sam, seemed to be the leader.

A girl whose thin blouse obviously had nothing under it, said, "You gotta be putting me on! Rip Van Winkle!"

"It's a fake name, of course," Judy said. "Rip, if you're on the run from the pigs, you're safe here. Unless there's a raid."

The four-room apartment was in bad shape, paint peeling, plaster falling, holes in the ceilings, and the furniture looked as if it had been second-hand before Noah's flood.

Everybody seemed to be having a good time, though there were some fierce cries about giving it to the fascist motherfuckers. He puffed a joint being passed around, and then an emaciated girl with huge glazed eyes asked him if he wanted some coke to snort. He said "Yes," but, when she gave him a slip of paper containing some white stuff, he sneezed, and the powder blew all over the girl. She yelled, "That'll be twenty dollars, Sneezy! The only thing I give away is my ass!"

Judy called the girl a freaking ripoff, and the next he knew Judy had thrown her out bodily. While this was going on, Rip told Yosemite Sam that he had to make water. Sam sent him to the place of convenience. But in which bowl was he supposed to urinate? The one on the floor was leaking from its base and had a big turd floating in it. Maybe it was reserved for crap only.

He retraced his steps to Sam and got him aside.

"You mean where you come from you don't have indoor plumbing? I'll bet you don't even have television!"

Rip confessed he'd never heard of either.

Mr. Sam bellowed, "Hey, everybody! Here's a dude so under-privileged you won't believe it! Gather around, folks, and hear him tell it like it is!"

Rip was very embarrassed. Besides, his bladder was hurting. "I'll be back," he muttered, and he tore loose from Sam's grip and pushed his way through to the bathroom. Still lacking instructions, he used the bowl with the pipes, one marked H, the other C. When he turned the handles, both gave cold water.

On the way back to the front room, he came to a stack of wooden crates holding books. Most had paper covers, something unfamiliar to him. The titles were strange: *The Story of O*, *Red Power*, *The World of Drugs*, *I Was a Black Panther for the FBI*, *The Mother Earth Catalog*, *The Annotated Fart*, *Lord of the Rings*, *Zen Archery*, *Love and Orgasm*.

A couple near him was arguing about UFOs, and he left the bookcase to get near enough to hear them clearly. But Judy Gardenier pulled him back to the cases, removed a volume, and showed it to him. *The Sketch Book of Geoffrey Crayon, Gent* by Washington Irving. She opened it to a story titled—amazing—"Rip Van Winkle."

"Here. Read about your namesake."

He sat down, his back against the wall, and he slowly lip-read through the tale.

When he was done, he gazed at the wall. He couldn't believe it, but it had to be true. Irving hadn't said anything about his time-traveling. Apparently, he knew nothing about it. Irving said that he'd slept for twenty years and woke up as an old long-bearded man.

Something that especially disturbed him was that his daughter Judith had married a man named Gardenier.

Judy staggered down the hall and sat down by him.

"Kinda makes you freak out, don't it?"

"You mean that you might be my I-don't-know-how-many-times-great-granddaughter?"

"You really like to put a person on, don't you? Nah. I mean

the coincidence, the names. Me Judy Gardenier and you Rip Van Winkle. He *was* a fictional character, wasn't he? Even if he was real, you couldn't be him. Could you?"

"Just now I don't know who I am."

"That's right. Be cool, baby. The fuzz really after you? No matter, never mind, as Mary Baker Eddy said. Meanwhile, we're all looking for an identity."

She wanted to take him back to the front room where he could tell how he'd been disadvantaged, downtrodden, oppressed, and persecuted. Rip agreed that he'd been all that. But he didn't tell her that it wasn't the capitalist-pig class that'd been doing it to him. It was his wife. And he really couldn't blame her for hen-pecking him. He *had* been a lazy shiftless good-for-nothing who only wanted to hunt and to lounge around in front of van Vedder's tavern.

He said, "Judy, I have to ease myself again. This beer . . . what's in it? . . . I used to be able to drink a gallon before I had to go behind a tree."

He went into the bathroom and pissed in the bowl with the two pipes, idly observing that four more turds had been added to the leaking bowl. He was wondering when the honey-dipper men would come to carry the crap away when the door opened and a woman came in.

He started to protest. She screamed and ran out of the room. A minute later, two men burst in as if they expected to find a wild Indian there. They looked at Rip and started laughing. Before he could make himself decent, they seized him and carried him down the hall to the front room.

"Hey, everybody, look at this!" one of the men shouted. "This is the club Annie thought he was going to hit her with!"

The two let Rip down, and he stuffed his pisseroo into his britches and buttoned his fly. He was both embarrassed and flattered by the raucous remarks of the crowd.

The party went on and on, far past midnight. Rip wasn't used to staying awake much after dusk, but excitement kept him going. Finally, after almost everybody else had left the pad or passed out, Rip found a place behind a sofa and hurtled into sleep.

Since he was as drunk as Davy's sow, his cock should have been snakeshit-limp. He awoke, however, with his maiden's delight as hard as a tax-collector's heart, rising heavenward like the Tower of Babel, expanding like the British Empire. In the dim light he saw Judy, naked, crouching by him, the end of his whacker engulfed in her mouth. She was moaning and sucking and tonguing while her head went up and down. She certainly wasn't bobbing for apples. Rip had always thought that dick-gobbling would disgust him, but he wasn't. Far from it.

Judy stopped blowing him, looked at the pulsing monolith in her hand, shrieked, and then crawled on top of him. His bumper slid into her greasy cunny as easily as a moneybag into a politician's pocket. She clamped her bunny muscle around his flailer, and they were off on the roller coaster, boxing the long compass, Eve riding Adam's tail. They came together, yelling as if the room was on fire.

Judy stood up then, his still stonelike thruster coming out with a wet plopping noise. His semen ran down her slim leg to her knee. She stared at it, licked a fingerdab of it, and said, "Rip, you're a phenomenon!"

After breakfast, Judy said, "The demonstration is this afternoon. This morning I'll start proceedings to get you on welfare."

She had to explain this. He was amazed. "You mean I get paid for not working?"

Judy, hearing this, laughed and said, "Rip, you're a natural-born hippie."

But his visions of paradise vanished when Judy found that he had no social security card, no ID of any kind.

"I don't know," Judy said. "Those clothes, the 1772 coins, your ignorance . . . you couldn't *really* be Rip Van Winkle, could you?"

"Would you believe me if I said I was?"

"Not unless I was on something. Never mind. I'll get you a card, and you can apply. Meanwhile, how about taking a shower with me? I sold your halfpence this morning and bought some pot with part of the bread, but I used the rest of it to pay a plumber to fix up the toilet and shower."

THE LONG WET DREAM OF RIP VAN WINKLE

Rip was agreeable since it seemed to him that there was more involved than just washing dirt off. He was right. This age was heaven, even if it was flawed. But then he was no perfectionist.

That afternoon he boarded a rusty old bus with about fifty others. It broke down a mile from where the parade started, and they walked the rest of the way. Rip carried a placard: DICK US NO DICKS. Judy carried: NO MORE BLOODSHED IN VIETNAM. He didn't know what the signs meant and didn't want to be ridiculed if he showed his ignorance. But it was all exciting. More had happened to him in one day than in all his life in his sleepy little village.

While he was marching along, the band playing, and he was shouting the slogans he heard the others cry out and giving the V sign, which he supposed meant, "Up yours," a beautiful redhead with huge conical tits grabbed his crotch.

"How're they, Pops? They say you're tops. You got a dong like King Kong; more jism than bishops have chrism."

Rip grinned. He felt as happy as a favorite nephew whose rich uncle has just died, as ecstatic as a stutterer who's just had a good vowel movement. So he usually didn't know what people were talking about or what was going on most of the time? Most of the people he'd met didn't know either, since they were stoned most of the time. And so the food and liquor tasted like someone had farted in them? He could acquire a taste for them.

Suddenly, there was a lot of yelling and screaming, whistles blowing, and he was running for no reason except that everybody else was, and he was laughing like a woodpecker that'd hammered its brains out drilling for bugs in a streetlamp post. Maybe he might get his head busted or get thrown into gaol, but it was worth it. Such fun!

He threw his placard down just before summer fell away like a politician's virtue at the first bribe offered. Snow he couldn't feel sifted through him. Nights and days blinked like a whore batting her eyes at him. The seasons whirled around like a brindled dog chasing its tail.

"Oh, no! Not again!"

As suddenly as it had started, the gallop of time ceased. He was on the same spot and in the blaze of summer. People elbowed and jostled and groped him, but they were not those he'd left in the 70s. However, something unusual was going on. A parade of some sort. Here came a band, followed by a float bearing a huge animal figure, a funny-looking elephant, and then a group of fat elderly men dressed like Algerian pirates. Fezes, baggy pants, fake scimitars. Their leader carried a sign:

SHRINERS FOR LEX N. ORDO
AGAINST ANTI-LIFE MURDERERS

At the rear was a man dressed like the Sultan of Turkey. His sign said:

ONE FAMILY, ONE HEAD, ONE VOTE

Behind him came marching women in white semi-military uniforms and wearing veils. Many carried infants in their arms or jerked along toddlers. Their leader's sign said:

CHURCH, CHOW, CHILDREN

A very pregnant young woman, wearing gloves despite the heat, bumped against Rip. She snarled at him; he backed away. He glimpsed the butt of a handgun in her open handbag.

Aimlessly, he made his way through the spectators thronged along the street. It seemed to him that he'd never seen so many knocked-up women in one place. All were gloved. Was there a new custom that pregnant females had to cover their hands when in public?

He approached a very young woman, big like so many nowadays, a head taller than he. Her size wasn't her only elephantine feature. Her belly looked like she'd been carrying the baby for eighteen months.

He mumbled, "I been kind of out of things for some time. What year is this?"

She stared at him, then laughed.

"You a wino? Or you been in the slammer? It's 1987, shithead. It's also the year of the greatest infamy in history! The blackest, the lowest, the most degrading, the Naziest! That self-righteous puritanical motherfucking male-pig-chauvinist tight-assed fascist Ordo!"

"What? Who?" Rip said, trying to back away but was stopped by the crowd.

"You must of been in solitary confinement! Or are you an acidhead? The President, you twit-brained prickface! That's who! He finally got the anti-abortion amendment passed! So . . . look at me! You can't even find a backroom butcher nowadays! They're scared they'll be sent up for life, and . . ."

"Here he comes!" someone shouted, and the cheering and clapping drowned out whatever else she was saying. The people were jumping up and down like barefooted sinners in hell and weeping tears bigger than horse apples. Nearby, a man, mouth frothing, eyes rolling, was down on the pavement trying to bite chunks out of the curbing. If no one else loved him, his dentist did.

First came six cars crowded with grim-faced men carrying rifles. Then a bunch of motorcycle cops. Then some armed toughs running ahead of a topless car. In its front seat were a driver and two men with set faces but nervous eyes and, in the back, a good-looking but aged woman and a man standing up and waving and grinning like an opium-smoker who'd just had a successful session in a comfort station.

The roar of the crowd pressed in on Rip like a bill-collector who's finally cornered his victim. It wasn't so loud, though, that it covered the almost simultaneous explosions of fifty—a hundred?—handguns. The big woman's pistol went off an inch from Rip's ear, causing him to crap in his pants. A second later, the gun flew high over him and landed in the street.

Rip whirled. Though deafened, he could read the woman's lips.

"There! Let the shitheads try to figure out who shot the asshole!"

Was it a conspiracy? Could a hundred women, or men, for that matter, keep a plot like that to themselves? Hell, no. A hundred pregnant women had just happened to come here with the same idea. Who knew how many more were further down the street, waiting for the chance they'd never get?

Now the guns were flying everywhere, like steel semen from a jacked-off robot. Their owners were getting rid of them and shucking their gloves, too. Their target was lying in the street, pumping blood from at least fifty holes. If he'd been an oil field, America could have told OPEC to fuck off.

Once more, Rip was running. The dead man's guards were firing everywhere, and innocent bystanders, some not so innocent, were dropping like fleas from a poisoned dog. Rip finally got clear of the massacre, though he was twice trampled, kicked in the balls once, and clawed so many times he lost most of his clothes and much of his skin. He was reminded of the one time he'd talleywhacked Brom Dutcher's wife. But now he wasn't getting any pleasure whatsoever.

He ran into a tavern. Panting, he stood by the window and watched the noisy turmoil outside. Then, hearing a small thunderous noise, he turned. Cold ran over him. The noise had been too much like that of the game of ninepins the little old men had played while he drank their Hollands gin, so excellent in taste but so surprising in its effects. He saw some bowling alleys, something new to him. But he paid them no attention. Facing him were two of the little old men. One was the commander, the stout old gentleman in the laced doublet, high-crowned hat, red stockings, and high-heeled shoes.

He spoke in a foreign accent. "It took us some time to track you through time, Rip. Too much of the elixir does more than put you into suspended animation. Anyway, let's go."

"No, no!" Rip said loudly, hoping the patrons would come to his rescue. "Please! This age isn't paradise, but . . ."

This wasn't old New York where everybody's business was yours. No one wanted to get involved now. While the patrons turned away or just watched, the other little man jabbed something into Rip's arm. Unconsciousness fell on him like a mugger.

Just as in the book he'd read, he awoke twenty years later in the same place where he'd fallen asleep. He had a backache ten times worse than all his hangovers put together. It wasn't from all the fucking he'd done. You couldn't lie on your back without moving for twenty years and not get a backache. Fortunately, the elixir had somehow kept him from freezing to death and had prevented bedsores.

Trudging down to the village, weeping for his lost if half-assed Eden, he thought about the little men. Contrary to what Washington Irving had written, Rip didn't think they were the spirits of Henry Hudson and his crew. They were men from outer space, maybe from one of those UFOs that couple had talked about. Or time travelers from the far future.

When Rip got to the village, he knew how to act. Hadn't the scenario been written for him, wouldn't it *be,* rather, by that hack Irving forty-seven years from now? But life wasn't too bad, as it turned out. He was an old man now, fifty-five, and nobody expected him to work for a living. Come to think of it, none but his now departed wife had ever expected it of him. His daughter's husband, a genial fellow, didn't mind supporting him, especially since Rip was now a living legend.

Rip sat often in front of Doolittle's Union Hotel, which had once been van Vedder's Tavern, and he told the story as Irving had, and he got so many free drinks he almost couldn't handle them.

Sometimes, late in the afternoon, loaded with more booze than a rum-runner's ship, he'd close his eyes and doze or seem to doze. The loafers and the tourists around him would see his face clench in fright. They figured he was having a nightmare, and they were right. He was thinking about the bad things in the 20th century, and those would give even the natives of that time nightmares.

Other times, he'd smile, his hips would rotate, and his beard would rise where it covered his fly. Chuckling, snorting, nudging each other's ribs with their elbows, they'd figure that old horny Rip was having a wet dream. They were right.

The Man Who Came for Christmas

R andall Garrett introduced himself to my wife Bette and me in Chicago in 1952 at the first science-fiction convention she and I attended. The tall handsome Robin Redbreastish fellow (who'd been published in *Astounding*!) overwhelmed us with his charm, anecdotes, jokes, puns, ribald ballads, limericks, parody-verses and Gilbert-and-Sullivan lyrics. We laughed until we wept.

After the con, Bette and I returned to Peoria; he, to Cincinnati. During his frequent and hours-long phone calls, he often sang the old classic, "How I Wish't I Was in Peoria!" When Bette found out he'd be alone on Christmas, she invited him to our house for the holidays.

Three years later, he left for New York.

Our children, all the neighborhood children, thought he was the best thing to come along since Santa Claus. Our daughter Kristen, 34 now, has very fond memories of "Uncle Randy." But Bette and I and our friends came to think of him as a combination of Falstaff and Henry Miller. In many ways, however, as time would reveal, he was then a sort of preconversion St. Augustine.

In 1953 we three went to an Ohio con with Beverly, his wife, who'd come from New Mexico for a final try at reconciliation.

The con hotel was Beatley's-at-the-Lake, which we called Beastley's. We shared a single large room to save money for such necessities as beer and booze. It was in this room that five-foot 90-pound Beverly floored six-foot 190-pound Randall with a single blow of her fist.

Why? Because he couldn't explain the lace panties sticking out from his coat pocket. He got up and reeled off, and, after he hadn't shown for several hours, I went out to find him. Wandering down Beastley's corridors, I heard a terrible commotion around the corner.

I turned it just as a young woman, naked, all her clothes under one arm, and screaming, ran past me. Then Randall, all his garments clutched to his chest, sped by me. Behind him came the manager's son and the hotel dick, their faces scarlet with rage. Randall was in trouble again.

When I got back to our room, I found him, now fully dressed except for one shoe, enduring a chewing out from Beverly and sporting a red eye that'd soon become black and blue. He finally confessed that he'd met an old flame in the bar, and, after many drinks, they'd gone to her room—they thought. But it was the room next to hers, which was unlocked, and Randall had bolted the door. Some time later, the legal occupant had tried to get in but was told by Randall to beat it.

The hotel dick and the manager's son were summoned. Randall told them to fuck off; he was busy fucking. They broke the door down, and in the ensuing argument the son hit Randall in the eye and chased the culprits down the hall but failed to catch them.

After not having seen him for more than twenty years, I ran into Randall at a party in Santa Maria, California. He was in clerical garb and informed me that he was an ordained minister. I thought it'd be indiscreet under the circumstances to mention any Beastley-like incidents. Or the time in Peoria when he was to join the church but failed to show up because he'd gotten drunk in a barber shop. However, he claimed to be cured of alcoholism, so I asked him why he was dipping so heavily into the rum-punch bowl. He said his psychiatrist had assured him that he was the only alcoholic in the world who could be allowed to drink. This remark was so typically Garrettian that I broke up.

"So," I said, "the Hound of Heaven finally caught you?"

"Yes. His bite is painful, but it hurts so good."

Though he continued to drink, he behaved like the very model of a priest. There were no loud burstings into Gilbert and Sullivan, no dirty jokes or limericks, no insults, no kissing and fondling of all women within reach, no passing out on the floor, no need for anyone to give him a shiner.

I was so impressed that I got loaded.

Plane Talking

AN EXCERPT FROM *A Barnstormer in Oz*

As the Jenny flew over Suthwarzha, Hank saw that Glinda's workers had really hustled while he was gone. They had built a larger hangar at the edge of a meadow on the east side of the castle. The meadow was, however, nearer the edge of the plateau than Hank liked.

The wind was coming from the southwest across the desert, bringing hot, dry, and gusty air. Just as he came in for the landing approach, he saw the windsocket turn to point into the northwest. He started to crab the Jenny, intending to turn her nose just enough so that, though the plane would be pointed one way, she would still move on a straight line. But the joystick moved without him, and the Jenny was at exactly the right attitude for the landing.

Hank felt cold run over his skin.

Though he was violating all his training and his pilot's reflexes, he took his hand from the stick and his feet from the rudder bar.

The Jenny straightened out just before her wheels touched, and she made a perfect three-point landing.

Hank swore softly.

He did not touch the throttle, but it moved, and the motor slowed. When the plane had slowed enough, she began turning slowly, and then she taxied into the hangar opening. Inside, with the rudder turned, the ailerons on the left wing lifted, the engine roared, and the Jenny turned to face outward. When that maneuver was completed, the ignition was turned off, and the engine stopped. Hank sat numbed until the propellor had quit whirling.

He got out of the cockpit and assisted his passengers to the floor. Lamblo greeted them and said she was to conduct them to Glinda.

Hank said, "I'll be along in a minute."

"Little Mother wants you now," Lamblo said.

Hank shrugged and said, "O.K."

But he went to the front of the Jenny and stared at the painted eyes, nose, mouth, and ears. The plane stared back.

"Please," Lamblo said. "She stressed that she wanted to see you as soon as possible. No delays."

"I'll catch up with you before you get to the big gate," he said.

Lamblo's eyebrows went up. She looked as if she would like to ask him why he wanted to stay behind, but she said, "You'd better." She and the honor guard marched the two kings out of the hangar. As soon as they were out of sight, Hank turned to the plane.

"Jenny? Are you there, Jenny?"

He felt ridiculous, but he had to say that.

"Jenny?" a Victrola-like voice roared. Though the red cupid's-bow mouth did not move, it was the source of the voice.

Hank was startled, though he had expected some such response. "Jenny? Is that my . . . name?"

She pronounced it as "Chenny." There was no "j" sound in any of the many dialects.

"Yes, your name is Jenny," he said. He whispered, "Jesus Christ!"

"Chiizuz Kraist?" the painted mouth said.

"I'll talk to you later," Hank said. "I have to go. Listen, stay here. Don't leave the hangar. Don't turn on the engine. Or can you do that?"

"Oh, yes, I can," Jenny said.

"How . . . ?"

He stopped. There just was not time for any interrogation.

He slapped her lightly on the propeller hub, and he said, "I'll be back." He ran off, though not without a backward glance. The airplane did not look alive. Or did she? Was there some faint light in those big blue long-lashed eyes?

And how would she know what he meant when he said "hangar" and "engine?"

As he trotted towards the castle, he muttered, "The big brass just won't believe this! I don't believe it!"

THE PEORIA-COLORED WRITER

As Hector pursued Patroclus around and around the walls of Troy, the great god Zeus weighed their fates in the scales of destiny, and Patroclus was found wanting. So, Patroclus died.

In any fight, unless there's a draw, someone has to lose.

The above event from Homer's *The Iliad* occurred to me when Byron Preiss asked me to write a general introduction to this collection. I was to evaluate in it my writing career. I was also to describe the times and places where I wrote my stories, how I felt then, what kind of a situation I was in then, what effect that had on my writing then, and so on.

What he requested was very difficult and perhaps near-impossible. To do it, I must split myself so that one of my half-personae could look objectively at the other. Or perhaps I should say that I was required to cut myself into three parts. One would be the god Zeus; one, the victorious Hector; one, the loser Patroclus.

The difficulty with this task is that it involves my self-image. Self-images are what we like to think we are. But, usually, the self-image corresponds very little to reality. If a person tries to look objectively at himself or herself, that person often fails to be critical or perceptive enough. A very few, like Jean-Jacques Rousseau in his *Confessions*, go to the other extreme and make themselves out to be worse than they are. Humankind, among other things, is *Homo self-fooling us*.

This introduction is not supposed to be a confessional or psychological self-analysis. It's to be an evaluation, a weighing of my career as a writer. If it is, then it has to have standards of comparison. Against what or whom? Dostoyevsky, Twain, Fielding, Balzac? Janet Dailey or Albert Payson Terhune? Or those in my field: Heinlein, Clarke, Ellison, Lem, Le Guin, Lin Carter, E. C. Tubbs? Or against the goals I set for myself, goals which had little to do with other writers? Well, that's not quite true. In my very early days, I was ambitious to be the American Dostoyevsky or twentieth-century Melville.

No. "Ambitious" is not the correct word. I had dreams, but I never worked to realize my dreams.

When I first told myself that I would be a writer someday, I meant that I'd be a mainstream writer. Though I'd been an ardent reader of science-fiction since the age of eight, I did not intend to be a science-fiction writer. I did think that I might write an occasional science-fiction work between mainstream short stories and novels. But being known as a science-fiction writer was not in my dreams.

Here I am, sixty-six years old, and my career as a mainstream writer seems to be a near-failure. I am not, however, grieving over it, nor have I given up. I regard this career as something that has just been long delayed in starting. Only now am I beginning it.

Until I've given birth to at least ten mainstream novels, I will not be able to say whether I've been a success, a failure, or an also-ran as a mainstreamer. I hope that I'll find out long before the tenth is completed. I'll be eighty then.

What I lacked in the early part of my writing career was the high-burning, all-consuming, and ever-driving flame. The flame that makes a writer write and write and to hell with the consequences or the circumstances. When this flame envelops you, it makes everything and everybody—family, friends, jobs—subordinate to the desire to write. If they have to suffer, too bad. The ambition comes first; all else is secondary.

This species of writer takes a job only when it's necessary to keep himself and his family from starving, and sometimes not then.

(There may be female counterparts of this type of writer, but I don't know any.)

The species of writer to which I belonged accepts his responsibilities as a writer and does his best—well, his near-best—to fulfill them.

I worked at mundane, boring, and physically exhausting jobs for many years. When I was on the second or third shift, I wrote in the mornings. When I was on days, I wrote in the evenings. And I tried to write as much as I could on the weekends when I was not working at the steel mill.

I also read a lot, and we had a social life that was not busy but still occupied a certain amount of time.

My wife complained because I did not spend enough time with her and the kids. She was justified in this, but, on the other hand, she knew when she married me that I wanted to be a writer. She just had no idea of what it was going to be like. Neither did I.

I tried to make a compromise on the time allotted for family demands and for my writing. Like many compromises, it satisfied no one. But, like most, it worked, though with a sixty percent efficiency.

That was not a bad rate when you consider that most human beings only operate at sixty percent or less of their potentiality. And that our cultures only develop about fifty percent of their citizens' potentialities. Or that our economic systems only work at about sixty percent of their potentiality.

If our automobiles operated at that low an efficiency, we would junk them.

I was not as hard-working as a writer or as a father and a husband as I should have been. I drifted. Instead of altering the course of events by a fierce determination to succeed and a willingness to sacrifice others, I let events carry me along. The years passed, and I had written a few mainstream short stories, all of which had been rejected, and a few science-fiction short stories, also rejected. I had written the first quarter of what was intended to be a mammoth mainstream novel. I had written the first fourth of a mystery novel. There were a few sonnets and triolets in the drawer, none of which had been sent out.

On January 26, 1952, I was thirty-four years old, had worked about ten years at Keystone Steel & Wire, and had sold one story, a 12,000-word novella, to a pulp-magazine, *Adventure*. "O'Brien and Obrenov" had gone first to the *Saturday Evening Post*, and the editor had said that he would buy it if I would cut out a drunk scene. I was tempted. The *Post* was a very prestigious publication, and it paid well. But I finally said no; I sent the story to *Argosy*. Its editor liked it very much but said that it was too long for *Argosy*. However, he did send it on to Ken White, the editor of *Adventure*. And he purchased it.

In 1952, I looked at the story, published in 1946, and wondered if this was not only my first but my last printed work. Should I quit the steel mill and try for a master's degree in English? In 1949, I had gone back to college. I had a year and a half of courses to complete having picked up a freshman year at the university of Missouri in 1936–1937 and a sophomore year and one semester of a junior year at Bradley College, Peoria. My wife, the driving force in our family, had said that she was tired of my drifting and was fed up with my wasting my brain and body at the steel mill. So I made arrangements to work a straight night shift, forty-eight hours a week, at Keystone, and I took seventeen semester hours at Bradley. My wife began to take classes designed to get her a medical technologist's degree.

Some of our expenses were paid for by the G. I. Bill, but there was not enough to cover the monthly house payments, food and clothing, etc. I had to work the night shift and study when I had the time and cut my sleep to five or six hours a day. In addition, we had a rousing social life, having met a group of G. I. Bill students who had formed a sort of pre-Beatnik community. In 1950, they were still called "bohemians."

I got my B.A. in English and Creative Writing in 1950 and then collapsed from physical exhaustion. Nevertheless, I took several courses on the master's level when the winter semester started. But I was no longer able to work a straight night shift; some of my fellow workers at Keystone wanted the night shift—I don't know why. I arranged for the two special tutoring courses available and took them. But from then on I'd have to take day courses at Bradley. To do that, I'd have to become a full-time student, and we just did not have the money. I had to work.

By then, I had decided that I really did not want to be a teacher. I'd talked to some teachers about their work, about faculty politics, about the low pay, and I said, "No. I don't want to be a teacher. I don't have the temperament. I'm a writer, and that's that."

There was, however, a vast gulf between being a writer—there are many of those—and being a successful writer, of whom there are few.

I looked at the career of Bob Bloch, author of hundreds of short stories and several novels. He had sold his first story to *Weird Tales* magazine when he was seventeen and had continued to sell steadily since. Yet he had not become a full-time writer; he had worked at several jobs and had written an abundance of stories in his spare time. *Why* had I not done this?

"Many are called but few are chosen."

Was I one of the multitude of called-but-rejected?

Or was it that I just had not tried hard enough?

The ancient Greek philosopher, Heraclitus, said "Character determines destiny."

Was my character that of a self-defeatist?

A psychologist, a student counselor at the University of Missouri, had told me that I was a self-defeater.

Well, I thought, what if that was true? That did not mean that I could not change my character. I have always believed in free will, even though I was heavily influenced by Mark Twain's determinism when I was young. I don't think that we're robots. What we *are* are semi-automatons who have free will. We can, in the psychical sense, lift ourselves by our bootstraps.

I do believe in genetic determinism, and the discoveries made in recent years have confirmed this belief. I also believe that environmental effects determine, to a certain extent, the direction the genetic drives will take. But there's a third factor, free will, that can override, to a certain extent, the integrated effects of genes and environment.

We are not robots.

Still, sometimes, when I'm depressed, I think that perhaps Twain and Vonnegut are right: We are automatons moved by events and the bad chemicals in our body. But I get over this and regain my unscientific near-religious belief that we do have free will. If many use their free will to choose not to use their free will that's their problem.

If people choose to believe that they are incapable of salvation, that they must rely on the coming of Christ or Mohammed or the Great Pumpkin to save them, then they have abandoned the free will that God or Nature or Whomever gave them.

It's up to the species *Homo sapiens* to save itself.

So far, we've done a bad job of that.

But science-fiction writers, the best of them, anyway, are concerned about the future and the welfare of humankind. They're idealists, the best of them, and they know what's gone wrong in the past and what's wrong now, and they hope that they can show how we can develop our potentiality to be human beings. The trouble in the past and now is that most of us have been people but not human beings. Here and there, now and then, a genuine human being comes along as an example to the rest of us. We can see what we could be, should be, if we realize the potentiality in us. Unfortunately, the real human beings are usually killed by the people. Or, if the examples and the teachings of the real human beings are taken up, then the people distort the teachings, corrupt them, and use them for their own purposes.

The semi-robots kill the human beings one way or another.

Good science-fiction writers try to show how we could become human beings. Or, if they don't do that, they show what has kept us from achieving the goal of evolution.

By that I mean that the main purpose of evolution is to get us to the stage where we, *Homo sapiens*, can see that this universe is not senseless. And, having seen, we can then use that perceived order and purpose for good ends.

So far, no one, not even the founders of the great religions or the great philosophers, has been able to prove that the universe is not senseless.

Science-fiction writers know that we must work the future as if it were dough. We must bake bread from that dough and cast the bread upon the waters of infinity-eternity. What comes back on the tide is usually ruined bread. But *Homo sapiens* is also *Homo optimus*, and we keep trying.

At the same time that we're optimists, we're also realists. We know that humankind is an imperfect animal and will never achieve Utopia. We don't think that utopia would be desirable because we then would have no goals to work for. But a near-Utopia would be a society in which every person would have open to him or her everything which could enable the realization of full potentiality.

Homo sapiens is also the only animal that's not perfect. All the others fit one hundred percent into their environments and flourish as long as the environment does not change. *Homo sapiens* operates more from rationality than from instinct—despite the fact that it's also irrational—and if the environment does not suit it, it changes the environment. But it, unlike other animals, makes mistakes because it is imperfect. At the same time, *Homo sapiens* can create civilizations and art and music and literature and new social institutions because it is an imperfect animal. Though it keeps screwing up, it has the potentiality to achieve near-perfection.

Homo sapiens is also the only irrational animal. But it has two types of irrationality. One is what I call the Bad Well of Irrationality, and the other the Good Well of Irrationality.

It's the waters from the Bad Well that make for such irrational things as tribalism, clanism, nationalism, sexism, racism, unrealistic ideologies, and self-righteous religionism.

At one time, these things had survival value. They kept the tribe or the nation from perishing because each tribe or nation was surrounded by other tribes or nations that wanted to destroy them.

But that time has long been gone. The only tribe or nation that should exist now is the tribe of Earth or the nation of Earth.

As you know, that state does not exist now, and the chances for its coming into existence are few.

The Bad Well spreads its waters everywhere.

The Good Well is that which makes for compassion, sympathy, and empathy. It also leads to religious impulses, to a high code of ethics, to a desire to make a society which will enable each person to develop his or her full potentiality as a human being. Some have more potentiality than others, but every one should have the chance to realize his or hers to the full.

I pause now. I consider and contemplate.

What I've been doing is retyping a 9500-word introduction.

But I've been veering away from the rough draft before me. I've been going off on tracks I had not considered traveling when I first wrote this.

So, I'm writing a new and much shorter introduction. I'm cutting this considerably. Eliminating thousands of words about what situation I was in when I wrote this or that story and how I felt then. I've already done that in the introductions to the stories herein. It's neither necessary nor desirable to describe how I felt when I wrote other stories or how I slowly gained experience in living and found out more and more about people, and then began selling my fiction and became, finally, a full-time writer in 1969 at the age of fifty-one. Nor is it necessary to describe how I became more or less successful and began to reap the rewards of my writing only when I had reached the age of sixty, a time when most people are seriously thinking of retiring.

That's all right. Better late than never. Anyway, I've always been a slow starter and a slow developer. I'm not a dasher; I'm a marathon racer. More of a tortoise than a hare.

Well, that's not quite true. It was the hare who took naps now and then, and I sure did that. So call me a tortoise-hare.

In my first draft of this introduction, I had written a lot of stuff that might be interesting. Such as revealing that Betty Friedan, the feminist pioneer, an organizer of NOW and the author of *The Feminine Mystique* and other influential books, was a sophomore at Peoria Central High school when I was a senior. I also described how, though I've been mainly concerned with the issues of future societies, infinity, eternity, and the purpose of the cosmos, my writings have reflected a certain provincialism. They've been streaked with my origins. Though I do write of things beyond the solar system, I am a Peoria-colored writer. No person escapes his origins.

But all this is not really important, and it should be reserved for a book-length autobiography. This introduction is too limited in space for all that I wanted to put in it.

I'll just list the things I've learned while writing and what the themes of my writing have been and have become. I think that I knew all this unconsciously when I started writing, but it took years of living to make these things known consciously to me.

1. Things are seldom what they seem.

2. Everybody has a self-image, and that usually does not correspond with reality.

3. For every advantage, there's a disadvantage and vice-versa.

4. Without personal immortality, this Universe is meaningless.

5. If we were not given immortal souls, then we must create our own. (That is one of the basic premises of my Riverworld series.)

6. We are not robots, nor are we, as Woody Allen says, "Monads with windows." We do have free will, but we don't use it very often.

7. *Homo sapiens* is both rational and irrational, and the Bad Well of Irrationality is what we usually drink from. But the Good Well is there to be used.

8. Some people think that there are many realities. There is, however, only one. We just do not know yet what that is.

9. Despite all I've said, it might be best if science-fiction writers forget they're prophets and philosophers and just stick to telling stories. They're as irrational as the other members of *Homo sapiens.*

R.I.P. If

A las! Poor *If* is dead!

I wish that I could also say, as Hamlet said of Yorick, that I knew him (it) well. But I did not know it well except during the late sixties. At least, that's what I thought when I started writing this. Then I read a short history of *If* in a science-fiction encyclopedia. And I found that the magazine started in 1952. I just don't remember its inauguration. I do, however, vividly remember picking up from a bookstand an *If* containing Blish's now classic "A Case of Conscience." I wanted to buy it but didn't because I was short of money. I preferred to invest what little I had in *Astounding* or *Galaxy* or the *Magazine of Fantasy & Science Fiction*.

This occurred, according to the history, in 1953. I made a mistake then. Blish's story was, as I discovered much later when I read it in the unabridged book, the best thing published in that year. Even though *If* was regarded as *Galaxy's* little sister and paid lesser rates than its big sister, it often had stories better than those in the more prestigious publications.

My first story to appear in *If* was "Heel" (May 1960 issue), a very minor tale. When it came out, I read it and the other stories in that issue, and that started me reading *If* more or less faithfully. Some of the stories were stimulating.

Then I took out of the "trunk" the manuscript of the original

Riverworld novel. *Owe for the River,* written in late 1952. It seemed to me that perhaps there might be a market for it. I decided to send it to Fred Pohl with the suggestion that if he liked it he could serialize it in *Galaxy.* (I bypassed John Campbell of *Astounding,* since he never liked *any* of my submissions.) Pohl wrote back that the concept of the Riverworld was too vast and had too many potentialities to be published even in a 150,000-word novel. He proposed that I should rewrite it as a series of novelettes. Thus, I could take my time and use all the space I'd need in developing the many ideas inherent in the concept. And I could also write as many of the story lines as I cared to

This seemed to be a good idea. It was one which I'd have proposed myself if I'd thought that there was any chance that an editor would accept it. As it turned out, owing to Fred's keen perception and his willingness to turn me loose, the Riverworld series was a far better story than the original.

Pohl also purchased a number of short stories from me for *If* during the later sixties. Some of these I've thought good enough to reprint in my 1971 collection, *Down in the Black Gang.* I became even more interested in *If* and so had the pleasure of reading such classics as Harlan Ellison's "I Have No Mouth, and I Must Scream" and Larry Niven's "Neutron Star."

However, Fred did not run the Riverworld series in *Galaxy.* He started it in another little sister, *Worlds of Tomorrow.* But when *WOT* folded, Fred transferred the series to *If.* I don't know if he'd have transferred the series to *Galaxy* when *If* was canceled. By then I'd decided not to write any more novelettes but to compose future Riverworld novels as complete books for issuance by book publishers.

Fred Pohl did a great job with *If,* and it wasn't his fault, but that of the shrinking market at that time, that the magazine was forced to fold. Though he couldn't pay the contributors to *If* as much as he paid contributors to *Galaxy,* his editorial thaumaturgy acquired Hugos for *If* as the best SF magazine for 1966, 1967, and 1968. On a shoestring and near-genius.

"Down in the Black Gang" was commissioned by Fred. He

wanted a story from me for a special issue of *If* containing only works by Hugo winners. At the time (late 1968 or early 1969), I was a technical writer for the space industry segment of McDonnell-Douglas. Shortly before I got Fred's invitation, I was standing near a group of engineers. One of them said, loudly, "What about the bleedoff?"

He was talking about rocket motors, of course, but that question, overheard by chance, sparked something in my mind. Relays began clicking. Lights blinked. My unconscious, whom I now image as a demon named Abysmas, plugged in hitherto unconnected circuits and, for all I know, grew some new circuits. The she-demon Abysmas, in partnership with my conscious, named Wabasso, developed the story.

The story is at least one-half autobiographical and wholly therapeutic. For me, anyway. The Bonder family (Bonder comes from the Old Norse and means the same thing as a farmer or peasant) is based on the Farmer family. We were living in a Beverly Hills apartment just like that described here. The people directly below us were as presented here; nothing about them is exaggerated. And I was the minor but pivotal character, Tom Bonder, caught in that cosmic human comedy which Tom unwittingly transformed into a tragedy and thus aided in providing more thrust for the universe, which is actually a spaceship driving towards some unknown port.

I don't know where we're going, but it's sure hell getting there. On the other hand, there are many joyous moments and some great rewards for some of us. Does that make the trip worthwhile? Only journey's end will tell us.

Why and How I Became Kilgore Trout

Not until I reread *Venus on the Half-Shell* in preparation for this foreword, and read the reviews and letters resulting from it, did I remember how much fun I had had with it.

When I sat down at the typewriter to begin it, I was Kilgore Trout, not Philip José Farmer. The ideas, characters, plot, and situations rushed in, crowding at my brain's front door. When they surged in, they swirled around, hand-in-hand, like super barn dancers or well-orchestrated members of the lobster quadrille. What a blast it was!

Six weeks later, the novel was done, but, all that while, the music was from Kant, Schopenhauer, and Voltaire. The caller was Epistemology, who looked a lot like Lewis Carroll. My wife knew I was having a good time because she could hear my laughter coming up the basement stairs to the kitchen.

I had been having a moderate writer's block with the then-currently scheduled novel. I was making slow and often halting progress. But, once I put that novel aside for the time being and adopted the persona of Kilgore Trout, sadsack science-fiction author, I wrote as if possessed by a degenerate angel. Which is what poor old Trout was, in fact.

The beginning of this project was in the early 1970's when I vastly admired and was wildly enthusiastic about the works of Kurt Vonnegut, Jr. I was especially intrigued by Kilgore Trout, who had appeared in Vonnegut's *God Bless You, Mr. Rosewater* and *Slaughterhouse-Five*. Trout was to appear in *Breakfast of Champions*, but that had not been published then.

While reading *Rosewater* (in 1972, I believe) for the fifth time, I came across the part where Fred Rosewater picks up one of Trout's books in the pornography section of a bookstore. It's a paperback (none of Trout's works ever made hardcovers) titled *Venus on the Half-Shell*. On the back cover is a photograph of the author, an old bearded man looking "like a frightened, aging Jesus" and below it is an abridged version of "a red-hot scene" in the book.

The section regarding *Venus* differs from others, which describe the plots of Trout's stories. Thus, Vonnegut via Trout, makes his satirical or ironic points about our Terrestrial society and the nature of the Universe. *Venus* has no descriptions of the plot, and the hero is known only as the Space Wanderer. Aside from the abridged text on the back cover, there is no inkling of what the book is about.

At that moment, rereading this part, a pitchfork rose from my subconscious and goosed my neural ganglia. In short, I was inspired. Lights went on; bells clanged.

"Hey!" I thought. "Vonnegut's readers think that Trout is only a fictional character! What if one of his books actually appeared on the stands? Wouldn't that blow the minds of Vonnegut's readers?"

Not to mention mine.

And I thought, who more fitted to write *Venus* than I, a sadsack science-fiction writer who's early career paralleled Trout's. I'd been ripped off by publishers, had to work at menial jobs to support myself and family while writing, had suffered from the misunderstanding of my works, and had had to endure the scorn of those who considered science-fiction to be a trashy genre without any literary merit. The main difference between Trout and me was that I had made a little money then, and none of my stories had been confined to sleazy pornographic magazines where they appeared, as in Trout's case, as fillers to accompany the photographs of naked or half-clad women. Although it is true then that the general public and the epicenous academics thought of science-fiction as only a cut above pornography.

My heart filled up like a nova, I wrote to David Harris, science-fiction editor of Dell (Vonnegut's publisher), proposing to write *Venus* as if by Kilgore Trout. He replied that he thought the idea was great, and he gave me Vonnegut's address so I could write him to ask for permission to carry out the project. I did not hesitate. After all, Venus would be my tribute to the esteemed Vonnegut. I sent him a letter outlining my proposal. Many months passed. No reply. I sent another letter, but many more months passed before I decided that I'd have to phone Vonnegut. David Harris gave me Vonnegut's number.

I had to nerve myself up to phone Vonnegut. He was a very big author, and I was a member of a group, science-fiction writers, for whom he had expressed a certain amount of disdain. But, when I did call him, he was very pleasant and not at all patronizing. He said that he did remember my letters, though he did not explain why he had not replied. I re-outlined my ideas, and, in arguing against his resistance to them, said that I strongly identified with Trout. He replied that he, too, identified with him. And he was afraid that people would think that the book was a hoax.

That flabbergasted me. Of course, it was a hoax, and people would know it. But I rallied, and I argued some more. Finally he relented and gave me permission to write *Venus* as Trout. I offered to split the royalties with him, but he magnanimously refused to except them. However, he did stress that no reference to his name or his works should appear in or on *Venus*.

I thanked him, and, elated, started to write. I was Kilgore Trout, in a sense, and I was writing the sort of book that I imagined Trout would write. But I tried to give the prose, characters, plot, and philosophy of *Venus* a Vonnegutian flavor. After all, Vonnegut had admitted that he was also, in a sense, Trout. I was only restricted in writing *Venus* by having to make the protagonist the Space Wanderer and by including my expansion of the abridged "red-hot scene" as described in *Rosewater*. I did not entirely emulate Vonnegut in the use of short words and a sort of See-Dick-See-Jane-See-Spot prose. But I did try to keep the text from becoming anything resembling William Faulkner's. Vonnegut wrote a very simple prose because he had a low opinion of the attention-span and general literacy and lexical knowledge of the 1970's college students, who formed a large percentage of his readers.

It's worth noting that such science-fiction writers as Isaac Asimov and Frank Herbert did not avoid complicated ideas and plots and long sentences and words, and they did very well among the college students and general reading public.

The protagonist of *Venus* was named Simon Wagstaff. *Simon* because he was a sort of Simple Simon of the nursery rhyme. And *Wagstaff* because he certainly "wagged" (and waved) his sexual "staff" around during various sexual encounters. I also, unlike Vonnegut, put in a lot of references to literature and fictional authors. It would not matter that the average reader would not understand these, and it would amuse the academics. Or so I thought. I was too obscure for even the supposedly overeducated academics.

How many knew that Silas T. Comberbacke, the baseball-fan spaceman was (sort of an Ancient Mariner) in *Venus* was the pseudonym of Samuel T. Coleridge, the great British poet, during his brief stay in the English army? Or that Bruga, Trout's favorite poet, was taken (with permission) from a novel by Ben Hecht, *Count Bruga*? And that Bruga, the wild Jewish Bukowski-like Chicago poet, was based on Hecht's friend Maxwell E. Bodenheim, the Greenwich Village poet and wino of the 1930's? Or that there are many similar references to other fictional writers? Who cared except me?

Most of the alien names in *Venus* were formed by transposing the letters of English or non-English words. Thus, Chworktap comes from *patchwork*. Dokal comes from *caudal*, which means having a tail. The planet Zelpst is a phonetic rendering of the German *selbst*, meaning *self*. The planet Raproshma is a rendering of the French *rapprochement*. The planet Clerun-Gowph derives from the German *Aufklärung*, enlightenment. And so on. Most readers sensibly do not concern themselves with such games, but I had fun with them. And I imagine that Trout, though he had only a high-school education, read widely, and he would have played the same game.

The philosophical basis of *Venus* dealt with free will and immortality. Trout, in *Breakfast of Champions*, longs to be young again. And predeterminism is certainly a theme that runs through many of Vonnegut's works.

Vonnegut is like Mark Twain in that he believes (or writes as if he believes) that everything is predetermined. Twain thought that all physical things and our thoughts and behavior were mechanically fixed from the moment the first atom in the beginning of this universe bumped into the second atom and the second atom into the third. And so on. Vonnegut apparently believes that our troubling and violent lives and irrational behavior are the result of "bad chemicals."

This interests me because I have been interested in the problem of free will versus determination for about fifty-eight years. But I believe that humans do have free will, though few, however, exercise that faculty. Perhaps I believe this because I am predetermined to do so. But, as Trout, I wrote as if Twain and Vonnegut were correct in their belief in predeterminism.

In any event, Vonnegut is a thorough predeterminist in that his works have no villains or heroes. No blame is put upon anybody for even the vilest deeds and most colossal selfishness, savagery, stupidity, and greed. That's the way things are, and they can be no other. Only God the Utterly Indifferent is responsible and perhaps not even He. Trout has the same attitude.

Just as Eliot Rosewater, the multimillionaire in *Rosewater, Slaughterhouse-Five*, and *Breakfast*, thinks that Trout is the greatest writer that ever lived, so Trout, in his *Venus*, has Simon Wagstaff, his hero, believe that Jonathon Swift Somers III is the greatest writer that ever existed. Wagstaff also has his favorite poet, Bruga. Some of Somers's stories are outlined, and some of Bruga's poems are printed in *Venus*.

Somers III is my creation, but he is the grandson of Judge

Somers and the son of Jonathon Swift Somers II. Those familiar with Edgar Lee Masters's *Spoon River Anthology* will recognize the latter two. (Mentioned with the permission of the Masters's Estate.)

One of Somers III's protagonists is Ralph von Wau Wau (Wau Wau is German for Bow! Wow!). He is a German Shepherd dog whose intelligence has been raised to human-genius level by a scientist. Ralph is also a writer, and I had planned to write a story as by him titled *Some Humans Don't Stink*. That story's main character would be Shorter Vondergut, a writer. (Shorter from *Kurt*, German for *short*, and Vondergut from the German *von der Gut*, meaning of the [River] Gut.) Thus, the cycle of fictional authors would be complete. In fact, I did write two stories under Somers's name about Ralph. These were published, but I doubt I'll ever write the whole cycle. I have passed through this particular phase. It was fun while it lasted.

The *Venus* manuscript went to Dell with some photographs of me as Trout (wearing a big false beard), a selected bibliography of Trout's works, and a biographical sketch of him. All done with tongue in cheek or wherever. The furor on its publication both amused and gratified me. There were even questions about the true identity of Trout in *The New York Times*. An article in *The National Enquirer* "proved" that Vonnegut wrote *Venus* because of its plots, characters, philosophy, and style.

Meanwhile, Mr. Vonnegut was neither amused nor gratified. He was, as I understand, flooded with letters asking if he had written *Venus*. Some of these said it was the worst book he had ever written; some, the best. The main cause of unhappiness, however, was that he misunderstood a remark made by Leslie Fiedler, the distinguished writer and literary critic, while Fiedler was a guest on William F. Buckley's TV show, "Firing Line." The subject was science-fiction and Vonnegut's name came up. Dr. Fiedler, who knew that I had written *Venus* but did not reveal its authorship, said that I had said that I was going to write *Venus* no matter what the obstacles, including Vonnegut. My memory is hazy on the exact wording. Vonnegut, however, apparently thought that Fiedler had said that I was going to write *Venus* without Vonnegut's permission. Something to that effect.

Whatever was said, Mr. Vonnegut became angry. Consequently, he forbade to write another Trout novel I'd planned, *The Son of Jimmy Valentine*. That would have been my last novel as by Trout, but it was not to be. Vonnegut had the right, of course, to refuse permission for me to write it.

Legally, I had the right to sell *Venus* to the movies. And, when a producer made a proposal to make an animated movie of it with The Grateful Dead providing the music, I was elated. But Mr. Vonnegut phoned me and expressed his regrets that his lawyer would sue the producer if a movie was made. Vonnegut told me he was sorry about this, but I was very prolific and so would not miss any money I might get from the deal. Again, he had the moral right to scotch this proposal. Also, I doubt that anything would have come from the proposal. I've had over forty of my works optioned for Hollywood, and nothing has come of any of these.

The fun continued. Many letters addressed to Trout were sent on by my agent or the publisher. One letter purported to be from another Vonnegut character, Harrison Bergeron. Trout was invited to be the artist-in-residence during the 1975 Bicentennial Literary Explosion in Frankfort, Kentucky. The editor of *Contemporary Authors* sent a letter inquiring about including Trout in the book for 1976. She complained that Trout was supposed to have written 117 novels, but she could find only a reference to *Venus on the Half-Shell*. "It would seem," she wrote "that Kilgore Trout is a pseudonym. Would your agent furnish the real name of the author?"

As Trout, I filled out the data-forms she had sent and mailed them to her through my agent. I explained that all my novels had been originally published by disreputable fly-by-night publishers who had not paid me any royalties and had not even paid a fee to register my books with the Library of Congress. I never checked the 1976 issue, but I doubt that the editor included the Trout item.

However, as time went on, I became worried about Vonnegut's displeasure at the idea that people might think he was the author of *Venus*. At the same time, it was beyond me why he should be displeased that people might think he wrote *Venus* and yet not be distressed because people knew he was the author of *Breakfast of Champions, Slapstick, Jailbird*, and *Deadeye Dick*.

To spread the word around that I, not Vonnegut, was the author of Venus, I revealed the truth at every chance to do so and did my best when I was speaking at conventions and conferences to bring up the subject. I did the same when I was being interviewed on radio and TV. Just how well the science-fiction grapevine has worked, I do not know. By now, it does not seem to matter. Time has cleared this problem away. In the past few years, when I spoke at universities and colleges, I found that only about four or five in audiences of 500 to 800 recognized the name of Trout or Vonnegut. And I was told by a fan who questioned Vonnegut about Venus after a lecture that Vonnegut had difficulty remembering anything about it, including my name. So, whatever he felt at the time regarding *Venus* has passed.

I wish to thank Mr. Vonnegut for his generosity in permitting me to publish *Venus* as by Trout. I am sorry that it may have caused him any perturbation. I am even sorrier that he could not understand that *Venus* was my tribute to him and my repayment for all the delight his pre-1975 works gave me.

For several years, I've been trying to get *Venus* published under my own name. Finally, it has come about.

But, for a brief though glorious period, I was Kilgore Trout.

St. Francis Kisses His Ass Goodbye

A great mission is made up of many small missions.

Francesco Bernardone, founder in A.D. 1210 of the Friars Minor, the Lesser Brothers, was thinking this as he walked down the steep and winding dirt path halfway up Alverno, a mountain given him by a wealthy admirer. Francesco had refused the gift as a gift; he would not own property, not even his brown woolen robe and the rope used as a belt. He had accepted the mountain as a short-term loan, no interest required.

Behind him ambled the heavily laden ass that was, at the moment, Francesco's small mission, part of a great one. Its nose touched the man in the back now and then, a beast's kiss of affection, though the man had not been near it until he had agreed to take it down to the village for Giovanni the charcoal-burner.

Perhaps the ass also needed to touch its brother, Francesco, for reassurance because the threatening summer storm made it nervous. The dark cloud that always hung near the tip of the peak, though usually brightly rimmed, had swelled like a cobra's hood. Lightning-shot, growling, it was sliding down the firry slopes like a black and fuzzy glacier. The wind was now a hand pushing against his back and snapping the hem of his robe. The storm, like a long-delayed rush of conscience, would soon overtake them; the ass would be terrified by the lightning. Francesco halted and put an arm around the beast's thick neck. Brown eyes looked into a brown eye. The ass's eye was clear with health and innocence; his eyes were clouded with sin and with the disease he had gotten when he had gone to Egypt to convince the Saracens that Jesus was not just one of the prophets, a forerunner, but was unique, the virgin-born son of God, the keeper of the keys to Heaven. He had come back to Italy after the disastrous siege by the Crusaders of Damietta with a great disappointment because his mission had failed, with the friendship of the Saracen king, Malik el-Kamil, and with the malady that blinded him a little more every year and always gave him pain. Brother Pain, who clung to him closer than a blood-brother. And, now that the oncoming clouds had dimmed the light, he could see even less.

He did not know what the ass perceived in his eyes, but he saw one of God's creatures—there were so many, far too many—who needed comfort. Whatever the ass saw, it quit trembling.

"Courage, my brother. If you are struck down, you will be free of your burdens."

Should that happen, he would have to carry the charcoal down the mountain because he had promised Giovanni to deliver the load to the house of Domenico Rivoli, the merchant, and to make sure that someone would bring the ass back up. It would carry food and wine and some money to the burner, his pregnant wife, and his five rib-gaunt children. Francesco could take the charcoal himself, no matter how many trips he had to make, but how could he recompense Giovanni for the animal?

Not one to dwell on possibilities, Francesco plunged on, gripping the ass's halter, and, then, the storm was upon them. He could not see at all. The wind seemed to be trying to tumble him on down the mountain. He was being jerked this way and that by the ass's efforts to tear loose from him. Lightning boomed around him, struck a tree, and dazzled and deafened him. For a moment, he seemed to be sheathed in a bolt, though he knew that he could not have been hit. If he had been, he would not be standing.

Suddenly, he could see. A light from above smote the darkness. It was no lightning. It was a blazing-white spherical mass in which even brighter ribbons turned and lashed out as the mass descended. The ass, braying, trembling again, stood as if transfixed while flame cracked out from its ears, nose, and tail. Sparks and tendrils of brightness shot from Francesco's own body; his fingernails spat fires from their ends.

His lips moving in silent prayer, his eyes shut, he thought that, surely, he was about to be burned alive. Then he opened his eyes. If he was to be burned by the Lord, then that was a martyrdom, and he should see it. Still, this was the first time that God had set one of His own faithful afire. Perhaps, this was like Elijah's being borne by God to Heaven in a fiery chariot. Or was that thought a sinful self-exaltation?

When he closed his eyes again despite telling himself to keep them open, he still saw the light. It seemed to fill his body to the end of his toes. The crash of thunder had ceased. Silence had come with the dazzle. At the same time, he felt a slight tugging—not from the halter—within his body. It was as if he was in the middle of a gigantic and hollow magnet, pulling him from every direction. The attraction was slightly more powerful on one side, but which side he did not know.

Then the halter was jerked from his grip. Though he was in terror—or was it ecstasy?—he leaped toward where he thought the beast was. He had promised to get it back to Giovanni, and his promises must be fulfilled even when God—or Satan?—had business with him. His hands flailing, one caught the halter. He grabbed the stiff short mane with the other, and, somehow, scrambled up the load until he was on top of it. He felt the pulling on one side of his body grow stronger. It seemed to him, though he could not see anything except the light, that he and the beast were rising. There flashed through his head—a dark thought in the white light filling his skull—that he was like Mahomet who ascended to Heaven on the winged ass, al-Boraq. That story had been told to him by Sultan Malik himself.

But now he was sitting above a cross, the T formed by the pale stripe across the ass's shoulders and down along its spine. In a sense, he was riding the cross that had ridden him most of life. A great burden he had rejoiced in bearing.

Despite the light, which had not lessened its intensity, he was catching sight of things, brief as lightning flashes but leaving dark, yet somehow burning, afterimages. There was a huge room with many men and women in strange clothes and white coats standing before boxes glowing with many lights and with words in an unknown language, and there were two towering machines in the background which whirled on their axes and shot lightning at each other. That vision was replaced by the dark, big-nosed face of a bearded man in a green turban—something familiar about it—the lips moving with unheard speech. That was gone. Now he saw a great city at night, pulsing with thousands of lights. It was far below him. Pure light banished it. Then it shot out again like a dark jeweled tongue from a mouth formed of light. Now he was closer to it; it was spreading out. Light again. And, once more, the city. He could see buildings with hundreds of well-lit windows, so tall that they would have soared above the Tower of Babel. Enormous machines with stiff unflapping wings flew over them.

He still had the sense of being tugged, though it had suddenly become weaker. He no longer felt airborne. The light was gone. He was in semidarkness. An illumination, feeble compared to that which had filled him, was coming from before him. When he turned his head, he saw a similar illumination behind him. He was in an alley formed by two buildings that went up and up toward a pale night-sky. Around him were a dozen or so figures in bulky clothes. They were staring at this man on the load on top of an ass as if they had appeared out of air, which must be what happened. He was in the middle of a circle formed by a layer of mud six feet across, weeds and bushes sticking at crazy angles out of the dirt which had been transported along with him. He was glad that the air was warm because his robe and he were soaked.

The silence of the journey was gone. The ass was braying loudly; men and women were yelling at him in a foreign language. Now he saw that there were other lights in the alley, flames from the tops of five or six metal barrels spaced out along and next to the two walls. The slight wind brought him odors of long-unwashed bodies and clothes, alcohol, old and fresh piss and shit, decaying teeth, and that stench that rose from the oozing pustules of hopelessness and festering rage.

He was surprised that he could smell all that. He had been immersed in it so long that he scarcely noticed it any more. Perhaps, somehow, his physical and spiritual nostrils had been cleansed during the transit.

Transit to where? This could not be Heaven. Purgatory? Or Hell? He shuddered, then smiled. If, for whatever reason, he had failed to be in God's grace, and there were many reasons why he might have, he could be in Purgatory or Hell. Come either place, he would have work to do.

His own salvation had never been his main concern, though it was a banked fire in his mind. He had stressed to his disciples that the salvation of others was their mission, that that must be brought about by their examples. If they were to be saved, they must not think about it. It must be done by tending to and taking care of others.

That thought was broken off, a branch snapping, when the dim figures swarmed around him, a mass swelled when others joined it from doorways and packing boxes. Before he could protest, he was hauled roughly from the load and cast painfully upon the pavement. The ass, braying, was pulled down on its side away from Francesco. Knives gleamed in the dull light. The beast tore the night with its death screams as the blades plunged into it. Yelling for them to stop, Francesco got to his feet and began pulling off, or trying to pull off the men around it. Giving up his efforts, he went to the animal, got down on his knees, and lifted the head, heavy as his heart. He kissed it on its nose, felt it quit shaking, and saw that the open eye was fixed.

The deed was done, and he was grieved, though he would have been glad to give these hungry men the beast to eat if it had been his to give. He had no time to dwell on that. Several men grabbed him and ran their hands over him, then shoved him away with angry exclamations. Apparently, they had been searching for money and valuables. A barefooted man who looked as if Famine and Plague were struggling to determine who would first overcome him, holding a big chunk of blood-dripping meat in one hand and a knife in the other, gestured savagely at him, speaking the tongue Francesco did not know. Hoping that he understood the man's signs, Francesco sat down on the pavement, removed the leather sandals, and handed them to the man.

"Take them with my blessings," Francesco said. He stood up. "If you need my robe, you may have that, too."

The man, scowling, talking to himself, had staggered off to one of the barrels by the side of a building. He threw the meat on a metal grillework on the open top, where it began smoking with the other pieces of meat laid there. The man sat down, wiped his bloodied hands on his coat, and fitted the sandals to his feet. By then, the load had been torn apart and most of it thrown by the barrels or added to the fuel in them. Francesco stood in the middle of the alley, nauseated not only by the too-swift events but by the feeling that he was hanging by the soles of his feet from an upside-down surface: The city itself seemed to him to have been turned over, and he was hanging like a fly on a ceiling. Yet, when he jumped slightly to reassure his confused senses that he was not kept from falling by a glue on the bottom of his feet, he came back to the pavement as quickly as he always had.

When he saw some monstrous white thing with two glowing eyes that shot beams of light ahead of it, speeding on the street at the end of the alley, he ignored his nausea and started toward the street. Before he got there, two more of the frightening things went by. But he saw the people within them and knew that they were some kind of self-propelled vehicle. He clung to the corner of the building while others shot by. Was he in a city of wizards and witches? If so, he must indeed be in Hell.

There was more to add to his bewilderment. The buildings along the street were fronted with gigantic panels on which icons of people and animals flashed and many words sprang into light and then disappeared. His mind swirling like the strange many-colored geometric patterns on some of the panels, he stepped back into the alley. He would speak to each of the people there and determine if any spoke Umbrian or Roman Italian or Latin or Provencal, or if any could understand the limited phrases he knew of Arabic, Berber, Aragonese, Catalan, Greek, Turkish, German or English.

He stopped, rigid at the sight of a black woman who was on her knees and holding with one hand the swollen penis of the white man standing above her while she moved her head back and forth along the shaft in her mouth. Her other hand supported a baby sucking at her nipple. In the man's hand was a piece of half-cooked meat. Her payment?

Before Francesco could recover, he heard a loud up-and-down wailing, and a huge vehicle screeched around the corner, making him dive to escape being struck. It stopped, its two beams making noon out of the twilight in the alley, blue and red lights on it flashing, the wailing it made dying down. The man pulled loose from the woman's mouth and ran toward a doorway. Some of the others fled from the barrels; some froze. Doors in the side and rear of the vehicle snapped out and down. Men and women in bright blue uniforms, wearing blue helmets, and holding what had to be weapons, though of a nature that Francesco did not know, sprang shouting from its interior. He, with the other alley people, was shoved with his face against the wall, his outstretched hands against the wall, his legs spread out. He looked around and was cuffed alongside his head with the barrel of a weapon.

But he looked again anyway, and he saw another huge machine, its front a great open mouth, lumber past the first vehicle. It stopped short of the carcass, waited while some uniforms pointed small flashing boxes at the dead ass, then scooped it up with a long broad metal tongue and drew it into the dark maw. The uniforms kicked over the barrels so that the fiery fuel and meat spilled onto the pavement. After this, the uniforms questioned the denizens of the alley but got very little response except some obvious cursing. Francesco could not answer his interrogator, but the uniform just laughed and passed on to the next man. Francesco turned around and, once more, was shocked, this time so much that he was unable for a moment to think coherently.

Three of the alley men were in a stage of activity at a point where they could or would not stop. A man buggering a tall and very skinny man whose lower garment was around his ankles. He had whiskers that radiated around his face, and in the center of the whiskers was the penis of a man standing before the whiskery man, sliding back and forth rapidly. The uniforms had not touched or questioned them. Evidently, they regarded the spectacle as comic because those standing around were laughing and jeering. But, just as two of the men were screaming with ecstasy, the round top of the second vehicle pointed a long metal tube at the trio, and water shot out of its end. The three were knocked down and rolled over and over until they collided violently with a wall.

The uniforms laughed, then became grim. After the alley people, Francesco among them, had been forced to set the barrels upright again, the hose on top of the machine washed the charcoal and the fuel and the pieces of meat and other trash down the alley until the mass was by an opening below the curb at the end of the alley. Many of the alley people were struck by the jet.

This distressed Francesco more than anything he had so far seen. It was a great sin to deny food to these hungry unfortunates.

Brother Sun arose a few minutes after the uniforms and their vehicles had left. Cold from the double-soaking despite the warm air, cold also from the transit and the aftermath, very bewildered, Francesco shivered. Not until day had worn on and the air had become hot did he stop quaking. By then, the alley people, looking even more tired, haggard, ugly, and hungry, had dispersed. Later, he would see several of them begging for money. He left the alley to walk on the sidewalk northward through the canyon street. The vehicles, scarce at first, soon became numerous. They jammed the streets as they crawled along, and their honking never stopped. By noon, when people swarmed on the sidewalks, an acrid odor which he had noticed about mid-morning became heavy, and his eyes burned. Then Brother Sun was covered up by his sister clouds. Despite this, the breeze became hotter.

Becoming ever more hungry, he tried vainly to stop some of the pedestrians to beg for bread. They were well-fed and luxuriously dressed, though the clothes of some of the women exposed so much that he was embarrassed. After a while, he got used to that. But his pleas for food were still ignored. He also encountered many crazed people, some beggars, some not, who talked to themselves or shouted loudly at others. These, however, had also populated his own world; he was used to them.

He passed a large building with many broad steps leading up to it and two large stone lions set halfway up the staircase. On the sidewalk near it he stopped by a cart from behind which a man sold food the like of which he had never seen before. Its odors made his mouth water. A man bought a paper sack full of some small puffy white balls and began scattering them for the pigeons abounding here. Francesco asked him for some of the white stuff, but the man turned his back on him.

Passing on, he saw glass-fronted restaurants crammed with customers stuffing themselves. He entered one and got the attention of a servant behind the counter by pointing to his open mouth and rubbing his stomach. A big man grabbed him by the back of his robe and forced him violently, though Francesco did not struggle or protest, back onto the sidewalk.

His belly rumbled. So did the thunder westward. The skies were now black, and the breeze had become a wind that rippled the hems of his robe. It was beginning to cool, though, and the stink that burned his eyes was lessening. The tugging inside him and the feeling of being upside down were still with him, present when he was not too absorbed in the strangeness. He turned to the west and walked until he came to a river. Though thirsty, he did not drink from it. He had often drunk from water that had a bad odor but this was too strong for him. He went north, then west, then south, then west again, and came to another river, equally malodorous. On both shores were elevated highways, jammed with the everhonking vehicles. The whole city was a din.

Now he did what many of the unfortunates were doing, opening garbage cans and searching therein. He found a half-eaten semicircle of a baked crust of dough with pieces of some strange red vegetable and of meat mixed with cheese. The box underneath it had printed words on it. One of them was PIZZA.

Derived from *picca*, meaning *pie*? He devoured that, though it was dry and hard, then dug up another half-eaten item made up of two slices of hard and moldy bread in the middle of which was meat beginning to stink. Nevertheless, he started to bite down on that when a stray dog stopped by him and looked pleadingly at him. Its mangy skin covered a body that seemed more skeleton than flesh. He tossed the bread and meat to the dog, who bolted it. Francesco petted the dog. After that, it followed him for a while but deserted him to investigate an overturned garbage can.

Despite not knowing any of the languages he overheard during his journey through the upside-down city, Francesco had made many interpretations by mid-noon. There were other languages than those issuing from mouths. For instance, the tongue of the city itself, the tongue composed of many tongues just as a great mission was composed of many small ones. Cities were the first machines built by man, social machines, true, but Francesco was especially adept at translating the unspoken languages of cities. The architecture, the artifacts, the art, the music, the traffic, the manners, the expressions of faces and voices, the subtle and the not-so-subtle body movements, the distribution of goods and food, the ways in which the keepers of the law and the breakers of the law (often they were the same) behaved toward each other and toward the citizens upon whom they preyed and who preyed on them, these all formed a great machine which was part organism and part mechanical.

God certainly knew, as did Francesco, that there were enough mechanical artifacts in this city to have provided all of the world that he knew with plenty of them. Aside from the vehicles, there were the blaring mechanical voices in every store and on every street corner and there were the moving and flashing icons that covered the fronts of buildings and were in unnumberable numbers inside the buildings. He did not know the purpose of most. But he understood that the flat cases people wore strapped to their wrists were used to talk at a distance with others and that the many booths on the sidewalks were used for the same purpose.

The whole city was, among other things, a message center.

But did these men and women understand the messages, the truth behind the words and images? Did they care if they understood correctly? Did the devices widen the doors for the entrance of the truth? Or did they widen the doors for more lies to enter? Or did they do both?

If both, then the result was that these people were more confused than those of his world. Too much information combined with the inability to separate truth from falsehood was as bad as ignorance. Especially when the disseminators of lies claimed that these were truths. Just as he concluded this, Francesco saw the gaunt man with the whiskery halo-fringe, the buggeree and sucker who had been interrupted in the alley by the uniforms. He was sitting on the sidewalk with his back against a building wall. Francesco could see the scabs, pustules, and blotches covering his face, arms, and the bony legs. He could also see that indefinable expression of the slowly dying. But it was changing into that of those who would soon be able to express nothing. Francesco had seen that too many times not to recognize it.

Now he knew that he was neither in Purgatory or Hell. Whatever else there was in those places, death was not there.

Francesco made his way through the throng, all of whom were ignoring the man, some of whom stepped over his bare legs. He knelt by the man and took his sore-covered hand. It was almost as fleshless as Brother Death's himself. Francesco, though he knew he would not be understood, asked what he could do for him? Did he need to be carried to a sickhouse? Was he hungry? His questions were intended to make the man comprehend that he was with someone who cared for him. There was really nothing that Francesco could do to stave off the irresistible.

The man leaned forward and mumbled something. Francesco took him in his arms and held him while the man's mouth moved against the robe. What was he trying to say? It sounded like *priest*. Suddenly, Francesco knew that the word was some kind of English, though certainly not what he had learned from Brother Haymo of Faversham, his English disciple.

"Prete! Prete!" Francesco said.

For the first time in his life, Francesco felt helpless. He had always been able to do something for those who needed help, but he could not make anyone understand what needed doing now, and he himself could do nothing.

The wind lashed out, even more cool now, and the thunder was closer. A few raindrops fell on his head. Lightning chainlinked the clouds. Then, the blackening clouds tipped over barrels of rain. He and the man were soaked, and the sidewalk was quickly emptied of all but himself and the man he held in his arms. That did not matter since they would not have helped him anyway.

He prayed, "O Lord, this man wishes to confess, to repent, and to be forgiven. Is not the intent good enough for You? What does it matter if no priest is here to hear him? I do not hate him, no matter what he has done. I love him. If I, a mere mortal, one of Your creatures, can love him, how much more must You!"

"He is gone," a deep melodious voice said. Francesco turned his head and looked up through the water blurring his already dimmed vision. As if there were a mirage before him—a dry desert phenomenon beneath the surface of the sea—he saw standing by him a tall man in a green robe and wearing a green turban. Francesco gently released the sagging corpse, wiped the rain from his eyes with his wet sleeve, and stood close to the man. He started. The face was that of the man whom he had glimpsed while in transit to this place. It was handsome and hawk-nosed, its eyebrows thick and dark, looking like transplanted pieces of a lion's mane. The leaf-green eyes in the almost black face were startling.

"It was not easy finding you," the man said. Francesco started. He had not realized until now that the man was speaking in Provinçal.

"Others are looking for you," the man said. "They are frantic to find you but they do not know what you look like and so will fail. In fact, they do not know if they have transported a man or a woman or an animal or some combination of these. But their indicators make them think that they have picked up at least one human being, possibly more. Unless someone else does for them what they cannot do, they will be responsible for an explosion which will considerably change the face of Earth and might kill all humans and much of the higher forms of animals. We have approximately three hours to prevent this event. If Allah wills . . ."

So, the man was a Muslim. That thought overrode for a moment the prediction of the cataclysm. Francesco started to ask a question, but the man continued.

"They did not know this would happen until immediately after they had transported you. Their . . ." He paused, then said, "You would not understand the word. Their . . . thinking machine . . . gave a false result because of a slight mathematical error put into the machine by the operator. Slight but reverberating greatly . . . swelling. To prevent an explosion of any degree, they must send you back. Not only you but all that came with you. That is impossible, but the effect may be considerably reduced if they send back not only you but a mass approximating that which was brought along with you. You will have to estimate that mass for them, describe what did come in with you."

The man stepped into the street and held a hand up. A black vehicle skidded to a stop a few inches before the man. He went to the front left-side window and spoke to the man seated there. A very angry-looking man and woman got out of the back seat a minute later. The green-turbaned man gestured to Francesco to come quickly. Francesco got into the back seat next to him. The vehicle's wheels screamed as it leaped like a rabbit that had just seen a fox. The man spoke a few short words of what had to be English into the small case strapped to his wrist. Numbers flashed on its top.

"There will be no more time travel experiments," the man said. "The data . . . the information . . . has been sent secretly to the government of this country and to those of all nations. The populaces will not be informed until after the explosion, if then. Notifying the people of this city would only cause a panic, and the city could not possibly be evacuated. Even if it could be, the people could not get far enough away unless they went in an airplane . . . a flying machine. And only a few could get away in time. The people in the project are staying. They will work until the explosion comes, and they hope that its effects, will be considerably reduced, as I said, by sending you back."

Francesco, clinging to a strap above the door, said, "Are you telling me that I have somehow been plucked by satanic powers from my time to a future time?"

"Yes, though the powers are not satanic. Their effect may be, though."

The man pointed out the window by Francesco at a building Francesco could see dimly. But he could make out a tall structure with many spires on the upper half of which was a gigantic panel. Its upper third flashed orange letters, one forming FRANCIS. The lower two-thirds displayed a bright and strange figure, a six-winged and crucified seraph surrounded by roiling light-purple clouds, which in turn were surrounded by swirling, fast-changing, and many-colored geometric figures. Then the vehicle was past it.

"A Catholic church, SAINT FRANCIS OF THE POOR. Attended mainly by the rich." The man chuckled, and he said, "Dedicated to you, Francesco Bernardone of Assisi."

Francesco, who had always felt at ease when events were going too swiftly for others to comprehend, was now numb.

"I was canonized?"

"Yes, but your order started to depart from your ideals, to decay, as it were, before your corpse was cold. Or so it was said."

Francesco bit his lower lip until the blood came, and he dug his fingernails into the palms of his hands until they felt like iron nails being driven in.

"I will *not* change."

"Because you know this? No, you will not."

"When did I die?"

"It would be wise for you not to know."

"But I am going back. Otherwise . . ."

"Obviously. But what happens here after you do . . . that is another matter. The force of the explosion caused by the interaction of matter and temporal energy will be proportional to the amount left here of the matter you brought with you. If, for example, you had held your breath during the transit, then expelled after arriving here, the amount of expelled air—if confined to a small area, and it won't be—would be enough to blow up that church and several blocks around it. What the project people need to know is just how much matter you did bring with you.

Francesco told him what had come in with him and what had happened to it.

"Your sandals, the urine you've pissed out, the dirt surrounding you, the plants and insects in the dirt, the body of the ass left after the butchering, the pieces of meat cooking on the barrels, the smoke from them, and the meat in the bodies of the men who ate it should go back with you. But, of course, they can't. You'll have to estimate an equivalent mass from your memory. The mass can't be exact, but if it's anything near that which was brought in, it will help cancel some of the effects of the mass-temporal energy explosion."

The man thought for a moment. He said, "After I deliver you, I will leave this area. Even I . . . no time for that now. The northeastern coast will be destroyed and much of the interior country. Many millions will die. But the world will go on."

Francesco said, "You seem to know so much. Why didn't you stop them? At least, warn them."

"I knew no more than they did what would happen. There is only One who is all-wise. I had nothing to do with the project, though I was well informed about it. I was not supposed to be, which is why they were so outraged and furious when I called in and told them I would search for you. They will try to arrest me when I bring you in, though that is stupid because I would be blown to bits along with them. They will not be able to hold me, and you will go back. The world knows when you died. So it is written that you return to your time."

"Not without the ass . . . an ass," Francesco said.

"What?"

Francesco told him of his promise to Giovanni, the charcoal-burner. "And there must be a load of charcoal, too."

The man spoke again to the case on his wrist, listened, spoke again, listened, then said. "They find it hard to believe that you would rather let the east coast blow up than go back without the donkey. I told them that I doubted that, but it would go easier and faster if they did what you want."

"Is it difficult to obtain an ass and charcoal?"

"No. The ass will come from a nearby zoo . . . a place where animals are kept. It should arrive soon even if it has to be air-lift . . . brought in a flying machine." He smiled and said, "I told them they should get the biggest ass possible. I suggested that they might substitute the head of the project if for some reason they couldn't get one at the zoo. He fits all your qualifications, aside from being bipedal and lacking long ears."

"Thank you. However, I do not like to go back without even knowing your name."

"Here I am called Kidder."

"Elsewhere . . . it's not Elijah?"

"I have many names. Some of them are appropriate." Francesco wondered why he had seen Kidder's face during the transit. The forces that had shot him from there to here must have been connected with some psychic—or supernatural—phenomena even if the people who were running the project did not know that. His question, however, was forgotten when the vehicle was caught in slow-moving traffic that did not speed up no matter how long and hard the driver blew the horn. The man talked into his wrist-case again, and, within two minutes, a flying machine appeared at a low altitude above them. It descended, pods on its sides burning at their lower end and emitting a frightening and deafening noise. It landed on a sidewalk, and Francesco and Kidder got into it and were whisked up and away. By then, Francesco was so frozen that he was not scared. The machine landed on top of a high building. He and Kidder got out and were ushered swiftly to an elevator that plunged downwards and stopped suddenly, and then they were hustled along by many white-coated men and women and some uniforms to a great room filled with many machines with flashing lights and fleeting icons and numbers.

Francesco was placed in the center of the room inside a circle marked on the floor. An ass with a burden of charcoal, a large handsome beast, so much better than the poor one that had come with him that he would have to tell Giovanni not to ask questions about it, just be grateful and thank God for it, was led in.

Francesco, his throat dry, said huskily, "*Signor* Kidder, satisfy my curiosity. What is today's date?"

"Seven hundred and eighty years after your birth," Kidder said. And he was gone, somehow removing himself from the crowd around him and the two uniforms who stood behind him. Francesco cried out to him that he remembered now where he had seen him before the transit. He had been in the camp of Sultan Malik, where Francesco had glimpsed him a few times but had not thought that he was more than one of the Sultan's court. Kidder probably had not heard him. Even if he had been in the crowd, he would not have caught Francesco's words. The uniforms were shouting too loudly as they tried to force their way through the crowd in search of Kidder.

Then bags of dirt were stacked alongside him and the ass in the center of the circle, and the workers withdrew. The crowd moved back to the walls of the room. They all looked haggard and frightened and white-faced. Francesco felt sorry for them because they knew that they were doomed no matter what happened to him. He blessed them and prayed for them and blessed them again.

The lights flickered; a terrible whining pierced his ears and skull. A great ball of swirling white light descended from a cone-like device in the ceiling. It surrounded him, and, though he cried out, he could not hear his own voice. The tugging sensation that had never left him became stronger. He was once more in that limbo in which he saw dimly, again, the men and women in the building and the turbaned head of Kidder.

Then he was in rain and thunder, and the ass was braying loudly beside him. Under his feet was a very thin section of the floor inside the circle. He no longer felt the tugging, and the world no longer seemed upside down.

It was not long after this that Francesco saw on Mount Alverno the vision of the six-winged and crucified seraph in the skies and that Francesco was blessed—or cursed—with the marks of the nails in his hands (which he tried to conceal as much as possible). And then, seemingly as swift as that transit of which he never spoke, the time came when he was dying. The brothers and sisters were gathered around him, speaking softly, church bells were ringing, and, outside the hut, the rich and the powerful and the poor were standing, praying for him. His blinded eyes were open as if he could see what the others could not, which indeed he could. He was wondering if the seraph he had seen on the panel on the church front during that wild ride had possibly influenced him, caused him to envision that awful, painful, yet ecstatic flying figure above the mountain.

Which had come first? His seeing the seraph on that panel in the far future or the splendor in the sky? He would never know. The mysteries of time were beyond him—at this moment.

He wondered about Kidder. Could he be that mysterious Green Man Francesco had heard about from some wise men of the East? He was supposed to have been the secret counsellor of Moses and of many others, and he showed up now and then, here and there, when the need for him was great. But that implied . . .

That thought faded as another Francesco, an almost transparent Francesco, rose like smoke from his body and stood there looking down at him. Its lips moved, but he could not hear its voice. It kneeled down by him and bent over. Now, he could read the lips.

"Goodbye, Brother Ass," he, the other, said. His body, that creature that he had treated so hard, driven so unmercifully, and to which he had apologized more than once for the burdens he had heaped on it, that was leaving him. No, he was leaving it. Now, he was looking down upon his own dead face. He leaned over and kissed its lips and stood up, happy as never before, and he had always been filled with joy even when hungry and wet and cold and longing vainly for others to have his happiness.

He was ready for whatever might come but hoped that he would have work to do.

Not like that on Earth.

The 1990s

E ver the jet-setters, Phil and Bette continued to attend a wide range of literary events through the beginning of the 1990s: the Conference on the Fantastic in the Arts in Fort Lauderdale in 1990 and 1992; Icon 15 in Coralville, Iowa; the World Fantasy Convention in Chicago, where the program printed his story, "Evil, Be My Good"; DragonCon in Atlanta; the 49th WorldCon in Chicago; Farmertacon in Tampere, Finland; Marcon 29 in Columbus, Ohio; Science Fiction Research Association Annual Conference in Arlington Heights, Illinois; and Tarzan, Oz and Mars: Myth Making in Illinois, back home in Peoria.

Just as in the 1980s, Phil only published a handful of stories: "One Down, One to Go" was his final story for *F&SF*, and he published three stories in a series of books about monsters: "Evil Be My Good" in *The Ultimate Frankenstein*; "Nobody's Perfect" in *The Ultimate Dracula*; and "Wolf, Iron, and Moth" in *The Ultimate Werewolf.* He also wrote the introduction to *The Ultimate Witch.*

The final two Dungeon books were published and he also edited two shared-world anthologies: *Tales of Riverworld,* and *Quest to Riverworld,* in which other writers got to play in his most famous world. Phil contributed four stories to the two volumes: "Up the Bright River," "Crossing the Dark River," "Coda," and "A Hole in Hell"; the latter was under the byline "Dane Helstrom."

Photo of Phil in his home used for a story in the *Peoria Journal Star*.

Phil, along with eleven other science fiction authors, was chosen to participate in a round-robin novel titled *Light Years*. Piers Anthony wrote the first chapter, and Phil wrote the second. But the project fell apart as later chapters tried to undo what had come before them. However, Anthony liked the first two chapters and decided to finish the novel with Phil; together, they wrote *The Caterpillar's Question*.

Phil published four long-awaited novels in the first half of the decade. Changing publishers mid-series, he published *Dayworld Breakup*, the third book in the series, with Tor. *Red Orc's Rage* was the first World of Tiers novel in fourteen years; based on real-world Tiersian therapy, it follows a teenage boy who roleplays in, or perhaps actually travels to, the World of Tiers. *More Than Fire*, published two years later, was the concluding novel in the World of Tiers series.

Another important novel of this period—one that was a life-long ambition of Phil's to write—was *Escape From Loki*, the story of how a young Doc Savage met his companions in a World War I POW camp. This novel was preceded by a DC comic that told the same story; the author of the comic had gotten the idea from Phil's biography, *Doc Savage: His Apocalyptic Life*, not realizing that this origin story was Phil's invention.

Approaching his seventies, Phil finally began to slow down in the mid-1990s. He didn't publish any short fiction, but he did write the first chapter of the round-robin novel, *Naked Came the Farmer*, along with twelve other Illinois authors.

The second half of the decade did see two milestones. He published his first mystery novel, the gritty noir tale, *Nothing Burns in Hell*, set in and around Peoria, IL. He had plans to write a sequel but did not complete it. After many decades of writing about Tarzan, and creating several Tarzan-like characters, he was granted permission to write an authorized Tarzan novel, *The Dark Heart of Time*. After fulfilling this lifelong dream, he retired from writing in 1999.

He also stayed close to home later in the decade, only attending two out-of-town conventions: Archon XIX in Collinsville, Illinois, and RiverCon XX in Louisville, Kentucky. He did give many speeches at various local clubs, churches, and libraries, including the "Philip José Farmer Odyssey: Five Decades of Science Fiction Innovation," a month-long exhibit at the Peoria Public Library in June 1998. This would be the first of many events held at local libraries in his honor. He also attended the book signing party for *Naked Came the Farmer*, where he assured everyone in attendance that he was not the Farmer in the title.

Evil, Be My Good

To Herr Professor Doktor Waldman,
University of Ingolstadt,
Grand Duchy of Bavaria

7 October, A.D. 1784

My Esteemed and Worthy Colleague:

This is indeed a letter from one whom you must long have believed dead and entombed. I, Herr Professor Doktor Krempe, your colleague for many years, am not as dead as you have thought. Bear with me. Do not reject this letter as the product of a crazed mind. Read it to its end, and consider well what is herein.

Though I am dictating this letter, the hands which are writing this letter are huge and clumsy, not my own small and artistic hands. Moreover, they are freezing, and so is the ink in the pot. The supply of writing materials is non-existent in this Godforsaken and icy desolation. The very limited amount available to me was brought from an icebound ship. Thus, I cannot give a detailed account of what happened to me since the time I was placed in my tomb.

Yes, this is, in a figurative sense, the voice of one everybody has assumed to be dead. It will be a shock, and it will seem to be an affront to both commonsense and logic. Only a professor of natural philosophy could possibly believe this narrative. I say "possibly" because even you, the most open-minded and liberal man I know, perhaps too much so, will find it difficult to put credence in it.

I repeat, please do not shred this letter because you believe that it is both fraudulent and written by a maniac. One item which will make you believe that this is an insane prank is the handwriting. You will compare it to the samples of my penmanship which are in your files, and you will readily see that the letter is not in my hand.

It is not. Yet, it is. Please keep reading. I will explain, though perhaps not to your satisfaction.

I am sending this by a native on skis from this utterly wretched outpost east of Archangel. I have great doubts that it will ever reach you. However, you are the only person who might think that my story could have some semblance of reality. I cannot send it to my wife. She would not understand anything in it; she would think it a cruel joke if it was explained to her.

Moreover, she has probably remarried. I must confess—a scandal no longer matters and you will keep it to yourself—that we did not, to put it mildly, care for each other.

To the breach, to my tale! Withhold your sense of disbelief until you have read the entire missive. Perhaps, then . . . but no, I doubt you will ever receive this.

The first stroke of lightning paralyzed me. That occurrence, as you know, was in September, 1780, on the grounds of our great university.

The second stroke of lightning, in November, of which you know nothing, freed me.

Yet, in many senses, the succeeding bolt put me in a prison far worse than the first. I could walk and talk after that stroke of hell's energy from the heavens. At the same time, I could not walk and talk. Another creature was walking and talking for me, though I did not want him to act as he acted.

(You are no doubt asking yourself, What second lightning stroke? Be patient. This and other matters will be explained soon.)

For many weeks after the first lightning bolt mummified me, as it were, I was faithfully attended by my wife, the nurses, and the best doctors in Ingolstadt. "Best" is only a relative ranking. All the physicians were quacks. They could have made some simple tests to ascertain if I was conscious and aware despite the fact that I could not move a muscle. But they assumed, in their ignorance and arrogance, that I was in a coma. And, to try to cure me, they bled me and, thus, assured that I did become unconscious from the loss of blood until my body restored the lost fluid!

May they all go to hell! And may that consist of being unable forever to move even their eyelids while they hear their wives, relatives, nurses, and attending quacks talk about them as if they were in their coffins! That condition, you stupid, lackwitted, and pompous practitioners of the unhealing arts, bringers of death to those whom Nature might have healed, would make you painfully aware of what your supposedly caring nurses and loving wives and servants really think of you!

I suffered more agonies than even the cruelest and most savage are doomed to endure forever. Murderers, mutilators, cannibals, blasphemers, freemasons, physicians, lawyers, bankers, and sodomists! You who have gone to hell and are destined to go! You will know little of real pain in that place! The tortures of the damned dead pale beside the tortures of the innocents who must live in the hell of the totally paralyzed!

I, Herr Professor Doktor Krempe, twice dead though not really dead, am back from two tombs, to write this! Yet, it is not my hand that moves the pen!

I owe all of my second hell to my student in natural philosophy, the ever-egregious, hubris-swollen, and morally unprincipled Victor Frankenstein. I knew what his private opinion of me was because another student reported it to me. Frankenstein, that smug, self-centered, self-righteous, utterly irresponsible, and totally spoiled infant in a man's body, that overbearing and utterly snotty student, said that I was short and squat and the repulsiveness of my hoarse voice was only exceeded by that of my face. Also, he told my informer that only the mercy of God kept my stupidity from being fatal to me. So enraged was I on hearing this from my informant on that dismal October evening that I ignored the cold and driving rain and the perils of the ravening night skies to venture forth on foot to confront the slanderous scoundrel in his own quarters. And I was struck down by a lightning bolt en route to Frankenstein's quarters to confront him. Is there Justice? Is there a God who believes in Justice?

Later, I was able to revenge myself upon him, though it was done through a very strange vicar, satisfyingly savage. What was not satisfying, I admit was my revenge. OUR revenge, I should say, and you will soon know what I mean by OUR! Nothing that could be done to Frankenstein on Earth or in hell would transform the fire in my bosom to sweetness and light, for which seemingly un-Christian statement I am fully justified.

Yet, according to the word of God as printed in the Holy Bible, I must forgive even my worst enemy. Otherwise, I go to hell, too. Is it worth it? I ponder this question often. My chief thoughts revolve around one possible solution to my dilemma. Did Frankenstein commit an unforgivable sin? The particular sin he committed is certainly not listed in the Holy Book. That unique offense against God, I suppose, would also make his sin an original sin. Thus, there are two more grave questions to concern the theologians, and God knows they have enough now that they cannot answer. Are there two unforgivable sins? Are there two original sins?

Unfortunately, or fortunately, they will not have to concern themselves with these matters. No one will ever know about the pair of double sins unless this account gets to a civilized nation. Or unless somebody else writes a book about the monstrous Frankenstein and his monstrous creation. That seems very unlikely. And it would, if it were written, probably be printed as a romantic novel, a fiction. Who among the unenlightened public, the ignorant masses, would believe it if it were presented as fact? For that matter, what learned man would put credence in it?

The day came that I died. That is, the purulent frauds attending me declared me dead. You can imagine, though the mental picture must be only a shadow of the real horror, how I felt! I strove to protest, to cry out aloud that I was still alive! I struggled so violently within myself, though in vain, that it was a wonder I did not have a genuine stroke! I was taken to the undertakers for the washing of my body, dressing me in my best suit, and obscene joking about the size of my genitals. I did manage, finally, to flutter my eyelids. Those drunken incompetents never noticed! Afterwards, while lying in state and listening to the comments about me from those hypocrites, my wife and relatives, I fought once more to blink. But, this time, I failed.

Fortunately for me, the practice among the English wealthy of embalming the body had not become as yet popular in Ingolstadt. Even if it had, my wife would not have permitted it because of the expense. As a result, I lived, though I can truly say that I wished it had been otherwise. I dehydrated, of course, while lying in state, two states, in fact. The other was the state of hell on Earth.

My dear colleague, put it in your will that a knife be driven into your heart before you are buried! Make sure that you are indeed dead before being buried!

The funeral was held—no doubt, you were there—and then the coffin was closed. Immediately thereafter, I was placed in the tomb. I expected to die quickly though horribly when the air in my coffin was used up. But my very shallow breathing made the oxygen last longer. Then, just as I was about to perish, the coffin lid was raised.

You must have already guessed, from my previous remarks, whose face I saw by the light of the torch in his hand. Young Victor Frankenstein, of course!

With him were two scroungy and scurvy fellows he had hired to assist him. They lifted me from the coffin and wrapped me in an oiled cloth enclosing ice chunks and put me in a wagon. In bright daylight! But my tomb was in a remote section of the cemetery, and he was in a desperate haste.

When the cloth was unrolled, I found myself in a filthy and cluttered room. His quarters off campus, I assumed. It looked like the typical degenerate student's room except for the great quantity of expensive scientific equipment. The usual stench of unwashed body and unemptied chamber pot was overridden by the odor of decaying flesh. I cannot go into detail about what followed because of the limited supply of paper and the increasingly wretched penmanship of the creature who is writing this. His hands are getting colder and colder, so I must not indulge myself any more. I must compress this incredible narrative as much as possible.

To be brief, Frankenstein dared to believe that he could make an artificial man out of dead bone and tissue and give the assemblage life! He would do a second time what God had done first! Man, the created, would become a creator! His creature was not visible since it was in a wooden box packed with ice and some preservative that he had discovered through his chemical researches.

I had believed and still believe that this scion of an aristocratic family was the acme of arrogance, stupidity, and selfishness. But God, for some unknown reason, had endowed this detestable being with the genius of Satan. The youth knew what he was doing or he blundered into success, probably the latter.

Yes, success!

He placed me in a box filled with ice, sprayed me with some substance I cannot identify, and then proceeded, though the cutting was not as painful as I had anticipated.

What happened when I began bleeding, I do not know. I can only surmise that he knew then that I was living. But, instead of making efforts to revive me, he continued his blasphemous and murderous work. I had known that he despised me, but I had not fathomed the depths of both his hatred of me and his relentless and conscienceless pursuit of a goal only a madman would desire or attempt to achieve.

I awoke late at night. The lightning stroke which he had drawn down from the storm clouds by means of a rod had revivified the body in which I found myself. Its body lived, and so did its brain.

However, the brain was mine!

How that fool of an inexperienced student had managed to connect the encephalic nerves to the others is beyond me. I would not have attempted it despite my deep knowledge of anatomy.

Though I am well known for my mastery of language, I do not have the words to describe the sensations of being only a brain installed in vitro in an alien body. And what a body! As I was to discover later, it was eight feet in stature and was a disparate assemblage of human and animal parts. As the workmen say, built from scratch.

Of course, I did not know at the moment of awakening that I was not in my own fleshly shell. But it did not take me long to realize the true state of location when the monster lifted my hands. MY hands! They were a giant's, yet they had to be mine! Slowly and clumsily, I rose from the huge table on which I—no, not I, he—had been placed before Frankenstein pulled down the blazing vital fluid from the sky. I was aware not only of my own sensations but of the creature's. This was very confusing and continued to be so for some time before I was able to adapt myself to the unnatural situation.

I said that his sensations were also mine. His thoughts, feeble and chaotic though they were in the beginning, were perceived by me. Integrated by me would be a better description. And, perhaps, I should not describe the thoughts as such. The monster had no language, thus, no words with which to think. He did have the power of using mental icons—I suppose even a dog has that—and his emotions were quite humanlike. But he had no store of images in his brain, which was a veritable *tabula rasa*. Everything that he first saw, smelled, touched, and heard was new to him and impossible for him to interpret. Even the first time he experienced bowel rumblings, he was astonished and frightened, and, if you will pardon the indelicacy, his morning erections disturbed him almost as much as they disturbed me.

How am I to express comprehensibly the relationship of his brain to mine? In the first place, why should his brain be a blank tablet when he was brought to life? (It was, in reality, my brain, but I shall henceforth refer to that portion of my brain used by him as being his own brain.) His own brain should, on revivification, have contained all that it possessed before I died. It did not. Something, shock or some unknown biological or even spiritual mechanism wiped it clean. Or pushed the contents so deep that the creature had no access to them.

If part of the brain was scoured clean, why did a part remain untouched? Why was my consciousness pushed into a corner or, as it were, under the cerebrumic rug? I have no explanation for this phenomenon. The process of creation should not have been like God creating Adam but like God bringing Adam back to life after his longevity of nine hundred and thirty years. Adam would have remembered the events of his stay on Earth.

Our mental connection was, however, a one-way route. I was aware of all he felt and thought. He was totally unaware that a part of him was not he. I could not communicate with him, strive though I did to send some sort of mental semaphore signal to him. I was a passenger in a carriage the driver of which knew nothing of horses or the road he was on or why he was holding the reins. Unlike the passenger in this example, who could at least jump out of the vehicle, I could do nothing about my plight. I was even more helpless and frustrated than when I had been paralyzed by the first stroke of lightning. I was also more frightened and despairing than when in that "coma." That was a natural and not unheard-of situation. This was unnatural and unique.

I saw through the monster's eyes. (These, by the way, were long-sighted. Frankenstein had botched the selection of the visual orbs just as he botched everything else, though he desired to make a perfect human being. Why, in the name of God and all His angels, did Frankenstein build an eight-foot high man? Was that his idea of a being who would not stand out in a crowd?)

As I said, I saw through the eyes of this blasphemy in flesh. Though they needed glasses for reading, their deficiencies were not responsible for the peculiarity of my visual acuity. I saw as if I were peering through the big end of a telescope. What the creature saw as normal-sized, I assume, I saw as if reduced in size. At the same time, the images I received were as if the large end of the telescope were dipped just below the surface of a pond of clear water. The intersection of instrument and fluid made for a peculiar and somewhat blurry picture.

This distortion extended to my hearing also. Thus, the construction of the eyes was not the cause of this irritating phenomenon.

It must have been the construction of the brain or, perhaps, a faulty connection between him and me that interfered with proper reception by me. Or perhaps that was the manner in which the creature saw and heard.

Great God! How I do run on! I know that both my time and the quantity of paper are limited. One may give out before the other does. Yet I, always noted for the clarity, conciseness, and absolute relevancy to the subject of my lectures to the benighted, apathetic, and thick-headed students of our university, am as silly and talkative as any one of the hundred passengers on Sebastian Brant's Ship of Fools. Forgive me. I have so many statements to make so that you will understand the story of Frankenstein, his monster, and myself.

Just now, the monster, despite my mental urgings, faltered in his copying of my mental dictation. It is not the cold in this shack which contributes to his weakness. It is the frigid finger of death touching him and, hence, me. I must hurry, must compress. However, as you must realize, you would not be reading this if I had not been successful in reactivating him into continuing the task I have set him without his knowing what he is doing or the reason for it.

He is falling apart, literally. It is my belief that he would have done so much sooner if Frankenstein, that unhappy combination of fool and genius, had not injected some chemical in him to prevent his organs, collected from different individuals and different species, from reacting poisonously upon each other. The chemicals used to effect this have, however, dissipated their strength.

Yesterday, his right ear fell off. The day before, his left leg swelled up and turned black. A week ago, he vomited all the polar bear meat and seal blubber that have been his—our—main ingredients of diet. He has been unable to keep much down since then. Most of his teeth are rotting.

Let us hope that I can keep pushing him until he hands over this letter to the messenger.

That hopelessly irresponsible Frankenstein was so horrified when his creation became alive that he ran away, leaving the monster, innocent as a baby and as full of potential good—and evil—as an infant, to his own devices.

I could do nothing but go along with the monster in his pathetic efforts to understand the world into which he had been involuntarily thrust. All of us, of course, had no say about our entering this harsh and indifferent universe. But most babies have someone to take care of their needs, to love them, and to educate them. This creature was, of all mankind, and it was human despite the doubts of itself and its maker, the most forlorn infant of all. Though I at first loathed him, I came to sympathize with him, indeed, to identify with him. Why not? Is not he myself, and is not myself he?

Onward more swiftly. As the end of his—our—lifespan approaches, so must the end of this letter be hastened.

No time for details, no matter how much they demand to be illuminated and explained.

The creature fled from Ingolstadt to the mountain forests near-by. He learned much about himself and the world and the people in this area. He longed for acceptance and love. He did not get either. He learned how to make and use fire. He approached a village in peace and was injured by the stones cast at him. He took refuge in an unused part of a cottage and spied upon the occupants, once-wealthy French aristocrats exiled and now living in poverty.

His eavesdropping enabled him to learn how to speak French. Part of that was my doing. I had by then managed to send him some messages of which he was not conscious. These were not commands which he obeyed or anything making him conscious of my presence, but the information stored in my brain, which included an excellent knowledge of French, oozed through to him.

(Incidentally, I discovered the most intimate details of the electrical, chemical, and neural constructions and functions of the human brain. Alas! No time to impart this stupendously vital information which would propel our knowledge of the brain to the high stage which I imagine the citizens of the twentieth century will enjoy. But I cannot resist informing you that the treelike organization of the nerves is a delight to the explorer. My travels up and down its trunks, branches, and twigs were the only joy I have had during my incarceration in the monster's body. I was, in a sense, a great ape swinging from branch to branch in the orderly jungle of the neural system, learning as I traveled. I discovered that the splanchnic nerve is actually three nerves and all control the visceral functions in various manners. I call them the Great, the Lesser, and the Least. I especially loved the Least Splanchnic Nerve, a modest, unassuming, and yet somewhat cheeky transmitter with unexpected after-effects, a rosy glow, in fact.)

The creature—it has never had a name, a lack which has greatly depressed its self-esteem but heightened its fury and its lust for revenge: you have no idea what being nameless does to a human being—finally revealed himself to the occupants of the cottage. He expected compassion; he got repulsion and horror. The occupants fled. He burned down the cottage and then wandered aimlessly around. He rescued a girl from drowning and was wounded by a gun for his heroic deed. This ingratitude intensified his hurt and rage, of course. Then he came to Geneva, Frankenstein's native city.

Here he murdered Victor's brother, the child William. While he was doing this, I screamed at him, if a voiceless being can be said to scream. No use. The monster's hands—my hands—choked the life out of the infant.

The man-made thing encountered his maker and got him to promise to make a female for him. Victor went to the Orkney Islands and did as promised. But, disgusted, suffering from Weltschmerz— with which the monster was also afflicted—Victor destroyed the female, which was as huge and ugly as her male counterpart.

Oh, the catalog of horrors! The ravening creature murdered Henry Clerval, Victor's best friend. He raped and murdered Victor's bride on their wedding night. After that hideous deed, he declared that evil would henceforth become his good. He was sincere when he said that. But the words were not his in origin even if they were his in spirit. They were a paraphrase of Satan's defiant statement in Milton's Paradise Lost. "Evil, be thou my good."

Yes, the monster had read that noble work. It contains, as you know, some of the greatest lines in poetry. However, there are boring passages which stretch their dryness to an intolerable length. The reader feels as if he were a parched traveler lost in a Sahara of iambic pentameter.

I was the unwilling actor in a tragedy which was real, not Miltonic. You cannot imagine the agony and the shame I experienced while the monster was performing his ritual of lust and murder upon Elizabeth, Frankenstein's bride. Yet, I must confess that I also shared the ecstasy of his orgasm; though, soon after I was transported, I loathed myself.

Frankenstein, after he was put in prison because he went temporarily mad—temporarily?—after his father's death, began to track down his creation in order to slay him. After much time and wanderings, both Frankenstein and his creature were in the Arctic, travelling on dogsleds. Victor became very sick but took refuge on an icebound ship. After telling his story to an Englishman aboard the vessel, he died.

Meanwhile, the ice pack broke up. The passage to warmer climes was open. But the monster came aboard just after his creator died. He had by then been stricken with the pangs of conscience, perhaps because he felt dimly my own reactions to his satanic deeds, though I was eager as he to slay Victor, and these, in a twisted way, caused the monster to repent.

I do not think that he had sufficient reason because of this to decide to kill himself. He was far more the injured of the two. What did Frankenstein expect? That the creature, like a true Christian, would turn the other cheek? He had not been instructed in Christianity and, anyway, how many of those so instructed would have forgiven such great evils done to them?

In fact, that the monster did have a conscience so tender and highly ethical trumpets forth his innate goodness.

But it may be that my mental urgings were by then influencing him, however small their voices. I had been trying to get him to kill himself, for his sake and, I have to admit, for my own. What a miserable life I had been leading! Starving and freezing with him, hurt with him, sick with fury and desire for revenge with him. I wanted our lives—actually, a single life—to end.

One of the unforgivable sins is suicide. But I was not killing myself through my direct action. The nameless and pitiful unnatural creature would be doing it. My hands were clean; his would be dirty. But he would not have to burn in hell for that deed. He had no soul. Nor would I burn. I had died once and should have gone to Heaven. Instead, Frankenstein, the foul incarnation of the archdemon, had brought me back to life. For that blasphemous crime, Frankenstein would exist forever after death as a shade on the plain of burning sands in the seventh circle of Hell. There, an eternal rain of fire would fall on him. There, according to the great Italian poet, Dante, are the blasphemers and the sodomites, the violent against God, which Frankenstein certainly was. There also are the usurers, that is, the violent against Art. Frankenstein belongs in their ranks. He violated God's Art by making the monster. Thrice accursed, thrice tortured!

His monster finally forgave him, but I cannot do that. Thus, the monster is more Christian than I. Theological and philosophical question for you, colleague. Does that indicate that God should or must endow the monster with a soul? If he does, to whom belongs the brain of that soul? What is my brain is his brain and always the twain shall be one. The implications are staggering. A whole college of St. Aquinases could consider that one question for aeons.

To resume. The creature—and myself—declared to the Englishman on the ship where Frankenstein died that he would build a funeral pyre and lie down upon it until his loathsome body was burned to ashes. Of course, you will find this ridiculous. Where, in this Arctic wasteland, could he find a single branch for fuel?

Then he boarded a large piece of ice and floated away. During the interval before the ice island came to land, I managed finally to communicate with the other part of my brain. It was a one-way form, that is, I could impart some of my mental suggestions or commands to him, though he was not aware of my presence or of the command. I do not know how I finally did it. I believe that it was his weakening state of health, his decaying flesh, that enabled me to overcome whatever obstacle had previously existed.

He—we—wandered over the snow-and-ice covered land until we came to this remote outpost inhabited by a few miserable natives. We were given food, disgusting fare but nutritious, and a shelter scarcely worthy of the name. Now, I could transmit my commands, though they became distorted in the passage as if they were flags manipulated by a drunken semaphorist. No doubt, this was because of the rapidly decaying state of the monster's neural system. Of course, that affected me, and my transmissions may also have been at fault.

The main problem is that, the weaker and more disorganized the creature's brain becomes, the easier it is for me to influence him but that very removal of mental obstacles decreases the monster's efficiency in carrying out my messages.

To put it in the colloquial, you pay for what you get. Also, the more progress you make in solving a problem, the more problems you encounter.

I really cannot see now how legible the handwriting is. The objects I observe through his eyes are getting smaller and smaller. And the watery veil now seems to have swirling particles in it. These are becoming more numerous. It may not belong bfore them coleisce to from a seemerly slodid well.

Ferwale . . . is end . . . Dog forgove . . . menster. Me too . . . evn fregiv his creatr . . . Farknesten . . . Dog . . . nodDog . . . min, God . . . God . . . furgiv . . . nodpar . . . pardin . . . pardon . . . fregiv . . . all . . . rweched . . . humn . . . beins . . . evn monste . . . humn too . . . iverbudy . . . for!gev . . . al . . . Gd . . . God . . . fregiv me

WOLF, IRON, AND MOTH

Less than Man, more than Wolf, he ran.
         More than Man, less than Wolf, he ran howling with ecstasy through the forest.

He had no memory of being Man any more than he would remember being Wolf when he again became Man.

Whenever the storm clouds were torn apart briefly by the howling wind, the full July moon was revealed. It seemed to him, though vaguely, that his howling worked the magic that rent the clouds. But he had no conception of magic. He lacked words and The Word.

Lightning as white as cow fat crashed. Thunder like the death cry of a bull bellowed. Being Wolf, he did not think of these comparisons. The tips of the trees danced under the whiplash of the winds and seemed to him to be alive. He sensed that the thunder and lightning were the orgasms of Earth Herself locked in frenzy with the moon, though this feeling had no link to human thought and image. Being Wolf, he had no words to voice such feelings. Words could never image forth Wolf feelings.

He ran, and he ran.

Where a man would have seen trees, bushes, and boulders, he saw beings that had no names and were not connected or grouped by word or thought.

They had in his mind no species or genus but were individuals.

The vegetation and the boulders he passed moved, changing shape slightly with each of his leaps, seeming to have their own life and mobility. Perhaps, they did. Wolf might know what Man could not know. Man knew what Wolf could not know. Though they occupied the same physical world, they lived in separate mental-emotional continuums.

A is A. Not-A is not-A. Therefore, never the twain shall meet. Not in the world of the mind. But werewolves . . . what are they? A plus not-A makes B?

He ran, and he ran.

Rain came from nowhere; he did not know that it was from above. Its nature changed when it dashed against the ground and splashed on his fur and into his eyes and on his nose. Raindrops had become something else, just wetness. He had no name for wetness. Wetness was a live being. It veiled his sight and his sense of smell. But the wind had carried the scent of lightning-frightened cattle to him before the rain absorbed the thousands of billions of scent molecules whistling by.

He floated over a wire fence and was among the cattle. He did bloody work there. The half-deaf farmer and his half-deaf wife and their stoned sons in the house a hundred feet away did not hear the loud cries of cattle-terror. The thunder, lightning, and booming TV censored the noise from the pasture. The wolf ate undisturbed.

"I've never seen a man gain weight so fast or lose it so fast," Sheriff Yeager said. "Seems to me it goes in a cycle too, regular as prune juice. You gain twenty or more pounds in a month. Then, come full moon, you seem to lose it overnight. How do you do it? Why?"

"If questions were food, you'd be fat," Doctor Varglik said.

Throughout the physical examination, the sheriff's pale-blue but lively eyes had fixed on the huge wolf skin stretched across the opposite wall of the room. It lacked the legs and the head, but its bushy tail had not been cut off.

"It doesn't seem natural," Yeager said.

"What? The wolf's skin? It's not artificial."

"No, I mean the incredibly rapid fluctuations in your weight. That's unnatural."

"Anything in Nature is natural."

The doctor removed the inflatable rubber cuff from Yeager's arm. "One twenty over eighty. Thirty-six years old, and you got a teenager's blood pressure. You can get off the table now. Drop your pants."

From a wall-dispenser, Varglik drew out a latex glove. The sheriff, unlike most men during this examination, did not groan, grimace, or complain. He was a stoic.

While he was bent over, he said, "Doctor, you still didn't answer my question."

The son of a bitch is getting suspicious, Varglik thought. Maybe he knows. But he must also think he's going bananas if he sincerely believes that what he's not so subtly hinting at is true.

He withdrew the finger. He said, "Everything checks out fine. Congratulations. The county'll be satisfied for another year."

"I don't want to be a nuisance or too nosey," Sheriff Yeager said. "Put it down to scientific curiosity. I asked you . . ."

"I don't know why I have such a phenomenally rapid weight loss and gain," Varglik said. "Never heard of a case like mine in a completely healthy man."

The wall mirror caught him and Yeager in its mercury light. Both were thirty-six, six feet two inches tall, lean, rangy, and weighed one hundred and eighty pounds. Both lived in Wagner (pop. 5000 except in tourist season), set along the south shore of Pristine Lake, Reynolds County, Arkansas. Yeager had an M.A. in Forest Rangery, but, after a few years, had become a policeman and then a sheriff. Varglik had an M.D. from Yale and a Ph.D. in biochemistry from Stanford. After a few years of practice in Manhattan, he had given up a brilliant and affluent career to come to this rural area.

Like most people who knew this, Yeager was wondering just why Varglik had left Park Avenue. The difference between Yeager and the others was that he would be checking out or had already checked out the doctor's past.

Despite their many similarities, they were worlds apart in one thing. Varglik was the hunted; Yeager, the hunter. Unless, Varglik thought, I can reverse the situation. But when did A and not-A ever exchange roles?

The doctor had removed the gloves and was washing his hands. The sheriff was standing in front of the wolf skin and looking intently at it.

"That's really something," he said. His expression was strange and undecipherable. "Where'd you shoot him?"

"I didn't," Varglik said. "It's a family heirloom, sort of. My Swedish grandfather passed it down. My mother, she's Finnish, wanted to get rid of it, I don't know why, but my father, he was born in Sweden but raised in upper New York, wouldn't let her."

"I'd've thought you'd've put it up on the wall above the fireplace mantel in your house."

"Not many people'd see it there. Here, my patients can see it while I'm examining them. Makes a good conversation piece."

The sheriff whistled softly. "He must've weighed at least a hundred and eighty. Hell of a big wolf!"

The doctor smiled. "About as big as the wolf that's terrorizing the county. But what would a wolf be doing in the Ozarks? Hasn't been one here for fifty years or more."

Yeager turned slowly. He was smiling rather smugly and without any reason to do so. Unless . . . Varglik's heart suddenly beat harder. He should not have been so bold. Why had he mentioned the wolf? Why steer the conversation to it? But, then, why not?

"It's a wolf, all right! I don't know how in hell it got here, but it's not a dog!"

"O.K." Varglik said. "But it had better be caught soon! The cattle, sheep, and dogs are bad enough! But those two kids!" He shuddered. "Eaten up!"

"We'll get him, though he's damn elusive so far!" the sheriff said. "Tomorrow morning, most of the county police, thirty state troopers, and two hundred civilian volunteers will be beating the bush. We're not stopping until we flush him out!"

Yeager paused, glanced sideways at the skin, then turned his head to face Varglik, "The hunt won't stop, day or night, until we get him!"

"Even the tourists are getting afraid," Varglik said. "Bad for business."

The sheriff turned to the pelt again. "Are you sure it's not artificial and you're not putting me on?"

"Why?"

"I don't know for sure. A minute ago, while I was looking at it, it suddenly seemed to glow. I thought my eyes were playing tricks on me. It had, still has, a light, very dim but a definite glow. I . . ."

"Aha!"

Yeager jumped a little. He said, "Aha?"

Varglik was smiling as if he were trying to conceal something behind it. His mirror image showed that too plainly. He uncreased his face.

"Sorry. I was thinking of the results of an experiment I made recently in my lab. I suddenly saw the answer to something that's been puzzling me. I apologize for not giving you my complete attention. It's rude."

Yeager raised his eyebrows. He was as aware as the doctor that the explanation was dragging one leg behind it. But he said nothing. He put on his Western hat and started toward the door. Hebe, Varglik's receptionist and nurse, appeared in the doorway.

"Phone call for you, Sheriff."

Yeager went into the front office. Varglik followed him to the office door and listened. Evidently, the wolf had gotten to Fred Benger's cattle last night and had killed four and crippled five. The Bengers had not heard anything, and the parents had not discovered the slaughter until they had returned from shopping in town. From Yeager's questions and his responses, Varglik deduced that the two sons were supposed to have put the cattle in the barn in the evening before milking them. But they had fallen asleep—passed out was closer to the truth—before the storm started. Old Man Benger's threats to kill his sons screamed from the phone.

But he, like everybody in the county, knew that they were on drugs and were not to be trusted.

"I'll be right out," the sheriff said. "But don't tramp around the pasture and mess up the tracks."

He hung up and charged out of the office.

"The bastard knows!" Varglik muttered. "Or he thinks he knows. But he must also be suffering great doubt. He's very rational, not the least bit superstitious. He's struggling as much as I once did to believe this."

For years, both in his Manhattan office suite and in his Ozark office, the wolf skin had hung where his patients could see it and he could observe their reactions. Yeager was the first to see its glow! The first to comment on it, anyway. Only one kind of person could see the light. His father would call the person *Kväällulf*. The Evening Wolf. His mother would name him *Ihmissusi*. Man-wolf.

He went into the reception room to tell Hebe that he was lunching in his office. Hebe was gone. At the stroke of twelve noon, she had fled, a daylight Cinderella running away from the ball, the answering machine turned on, waiting for her to come back at one. If he ate in, he was supposed to monitor incoming calls. Today, he would let the machine do the work.

In his private office, he sat down and opened a box containing three beef sandwiches, two orders of French fries, a monumental salad, three bottles of beer, and a jar of honey. A huge bite of sandwich in his mouth, he opened a brown-covered envelope that had come in today's mail. Hebe, following his orders, had set it aside unopened for him. She must be wondering, of course, what the envelope that came every four months contained. Probably thought it was a kinky sex magazine, *Hustler* or *Spicy Onanist Stories* or *The Necrophile Weekly* with an updated list of easily accessible mortuaries and a centerfold of this month's lovely female corpse.

The glossy-paper magazine he pulled out was *WAW*, a very limited-distribution publication. How had the editors of the Werewolf Association of the World known about him? His letter of enquiry to WAW had been answered with a cryptic note. *We have ways.* The magazine, though in English, was published and mailed from Helsinki, Finland. A small section was devoted to articles about the problems of Asiatic weretigers, African were-crocodiles, South American werejaguars, and Alaskan and Canadian werebears and mountain lions. One article on the extinction of the Japanese werefox concluded that overpopulation and pollution and the consequent loss of forest space had caused its demise. The last line of the article was grim. *The situation in Japan may soon be ours.*

Another writer, under the obviously false by-line of Lon Chaney III, gave the results of his survey-by-mail of werewolf sex habits. The sampling showed that 38.3 percent of male and female lycanthropes were unconsciously influenced by their lupine phases. When in their phase, they preferred that the female be on all fours and that the male use the rear approach. They also tended to howl and yell a lot. This had led to trauma in 26.8 percent of the nonlycanthrope partners.

One of the most interesting articles speculated that the genes for lycanthropy were recessive. Thus, a werewolf could be born only to parents each of whom had the recessive genes. But the son or daughter had to be bitten by a werewolf before the heritage was manifested. Or the offspring had to obtain a skin taken from a dead werewolf. Hence, the extreme scarcity of lycanthropes.

Having gobbled down all the solid food, his belly packed and yet still feeling hungry, Varglik spooned out the honey from the jar into his mouth while he read the Personals column.

WM, single, 39, handsome, vivacious, affluent coll. grad, loves Mozart, old movies, long walks in the evening, seeks young, lovely, coll. grad, polymorphous-perverse WF. Children no problem, won't eat them. Photo exch. Req. Write c/o WAW.

Jane, come home. I love you. All's forgiven. You may use the cat's litterbox. Ernst.

The magazine articles were serious scientific papers. But, surely, the WAW staff were making up most of the Personals column. Maybe to relieve the grimness of their lives. After all, being a lycanthrope was no fun. He should know.

Having read the magazine, he put it through the shredder. It hurt his bibliophile soul to do that, but the publisher's urgings to her subscribers to destroy their copies after reading them made good sense. On the other hand, the publisher might be keeping a small inventory of every issue hidden away, knowing that they could become quite valuable collector's items. His doubts about her intentions were probably unfounded. But being a lycanthrope, like being a dweller in the Big Apple, made one downright paranoiac. He had double reason to know that it was better to be suspicious than to be sorry.

It was also best to always play it safe. But the lycanthrope ejaculated all caution when the full moon was up. That had been yesterday. It did not matter. Two nights on either side of the full moon exerted almost as strong an influence. He was as helpless against the tug possessing him—soon to be a flashflood—as the moon was against the grip of its orbit.

Unable to fight the forces of change, not even knowing how to do it, he had once tried to cage himself during the metamorphosis. When its time was near, he had locked himself in a windowless room of his Westchester house with a side of beef as fuel for the re-transformation back into a man. Then he had pushed the key through the lock so that it fell on a paper in the hall just outside the door. As soon as he had felt the change beginning, a shudder running through him even more sweet and powerful than sexual arousal, he had smashed the furniture and bitten off the doorknob and howled so mightily that he would have awakened the entire neighborhood if his house had not been so isolated.

He had no memory of his agonies during his frenzied attempts to escape to freedom. But the wrecked room and the wounds in his arms, legs, and buttocks where he had bitten himself were just as good evidence as if he had taped the drama. When he regained consciousness as a man, he was so crippled and weak from loss of blood that he had almost not been able to pull back under the door the paper holding the key.

Somehow, he had gotten up, unlocked the door, put on his clothes, cut and torn, over the wounds, and phoned a physician friend to come to his house to attend his wounds. The doctor had obviously not believed his story about being attacked by a large dog while walking in the woods, but he had not said so.

Since the police could not find the dog, Varglik had had to take a series of painful rabies shots.

That was his first and last attempt to cage himself.

A diligent and experienced detective, the sheriff would have found out about the supposed attack. A few phone calls or letters to New York would be enough. He would also have learned about the dogs and horses slain in the area, though the scenes of the killings were twenty miles from Varglik's house. Yeager would have learned about the mutilation-murders of two hikers and two lovers in the woods. The police suspected that the killer was a man who had butchered the four so that they would appear to have been killed and partly eaten by wild dogs. Yeager would tend to believe that the killer was neither man nor dog.

"It must drive him nuts to have to believe that," Varglik muttered. "Welcome to the funny farm, Sheriff."

Whatever Yeager did or did not believe or intend to do, Varglik could do nothing about what was going to happen to his persona. He could only control where he would be when the inevitable happened.

At six P.M., he left his office. The wolf skin, rolled up, was in the attaché case he carried. He waited in his house, eating a huge supper and afterwards munching on potato chips, until 10:30 P.M. Then he drove his car through town, watching behind him, going in an indirect route, stopping now and then to check for possible shadowers. Within thirty minutes he was on a gravel country road deep within the county just north of Reynolds County. After ten minutes, he pulled into a sideroad and stopped the car in the darkness of an oak grove. The only sounds except for his accelerating breathing were the shrillness of locusts and the booming of frogs in a nearby marsh. Then, the whine of mosquitoes zeroing in on him.

Hastily, he opened the car trunk, removed the skin, doffed his clothes, and put them through the open window into the front seat. His breath sawed through his nose. He panted. His body seemed to be getting warm, and it was. The fever of metamorphosis was nearing its peak.

The wolf skin was draped over his shoulders when he stepped out from under the shade to stand in the full shower of moonlight. Though he was not holding the skin, it clung like a living thing to his back.

The moonlight beams, pale catalytic arrows, pierced him. His blood thumpthumped. The great artery of his neck jumped like a fox caught in a bag. He reeled, and he fell through a cloud of shining silvery smokepuffs. His head and neck hairs rose; the curly pubic hair straightened out. An exquisitely pleasureful sensation rippled through him. He swelled like the throat sac of a marsh bullfrog. His nose ran; the fluid oozed over his lips, which were puffing outward.

Without his will, his arms lifted and straightened. His legs expanded as if blood had poured through the skin. His bowels contracted and expelled his feces with the sound of an angry cat spitting. He emptied his bladder in a mighty arc. Then his penis became enormous and lifted toward the moon until it had almost touched his belly and seemed to his darkening senses to howl shrilly.

Howling deeply with his mouth, he fell hard backwards on the ground. The wolf skin was still fastened to him as if it were a giant bloodsucking bat. He felt forces shooting through the ground and then through him like saw-topped oscillograph waves, chaotic at first then organizing themselves into parallel but curving lines. They shook his body until he had to claw deep into the dirt with his outstretched hands to keep from falling off the planet.

He shot out his spermatic fluid, again and again, as if he were mating with Mother Earth Herself. His human spermatozoa were gone, and his glands were already pouring Wolf fluid into his ducts.

After that, he knew nothing as Man.

Only the moon saw his hair and skin melt until he looked like a mass of jelly that had been formed into the figure of a man. After a minute or so, the jelly quivered, and it kept on quivering for some time. It shone as pale and semisolid as lemon jello. Or as some primeval slug that had crawled out of the earth and was dying.

But it lived. The furious metabolic fires in that jelly had already devoured some of the fat that Varglik had accumulated so swiftly. The fires would eat up all of it and then attack some of the normal fat before the process was completed. In the dawn of Varglik's awareness of what he was heir to, he had tried to diet. He reasoned that if he lacked the fat, he would lack the energy needed to carry out the metamorphosis. But the sleeping Wolf in him defeated him. Varglik could no more stop eating great quantities of food than he could stop sweating.

The jelly darkened as it changed shape. The arms and legs shrank. The head became long and narrow, and newly formed teeth shone like steel spears. The buttocks dwindled, and from the incipient spine, now a dark line in the mass, a tentacle extruded. This would become the tail. Smooth at first, then hairy. Other darknesses appeared in his head, trunk, legs and arms. These were at first swirling, the cells shifting as they were reformed by the magnetic lines generated by the Wolf in him.

The Wolf did not become conscious until the change was completed. The wolf skin had become a living part of the living jelly and then of the metamorphosis. That completed, what had fallen as two-legs rose as four-legs. He shook himself as if he had just emerged from swimming. He sat down on his furry haunches and howled. Then he prowled around, sniffing at the feces and the fluids. He investigated the car despite its repulsive and over-powering stench of gasoline and oil.

A moment later, he was running through the woods. He ran and ran. He loped through a world that had no time. He saw the bushes and trees and rocks he passed as living beings which moved. He saw the moon as an orb that had not existed until then. He had no concept of a changeless moon rising from above the Earth in its orbit. It was a new thing. It had been born with him.

But the wolf knew what it wanted. Flesh and blood. And, being a werewolf, it desired human flesh above all flesh. Yet, like all creatures two-legged or four-legged, it ate what it could. Thus, he bounded over a fence and gripped the throat of a barking watchdog and carried it over the fence into the woods where he slew and ate it. That was not enough. He needed more prey to kill to thrill his nerves with ecstasy and to fill his belly for fuel for the change back into Man. He ran on until he came to a pasture on which horses grazed or slept. He killed a mare and disemboweled her and began tearing at the flesh until the aroused farmers came at him with flashlights and guns.

Then, in his wide circuit through the woods, he crossed a moonlight-filled meadow because sheep scent drifted across it to him. As he got close to the edge of the woods, he smelled, along with sheep, that flesh he most lusted for. A man stepped out from the darkness of the trees, the moon shining on the rifle barrel. He lifted it as Wolf leaped snarling at him.

Sheriff Yeager had not joined the hunting party just north of Benger's farm. Instead, outtricking his prey's every trick to detect a shadower, he had followed Varglik to the oak grove. He had sat in his car down the road until the wolf-howl had told him that what he had expected to happen had happened. After ten minutes, he had gotten out of the car and cautiously approached the grove. He was just in time to see the bushy tail disappearing into the dark woods.

Using his flashlight, he followed the pawprints in the wet earth. After a while, he heard distant shots. Guessing from which direction they came, he cut at an angle through the woods. Just before he got to the meadow, he saw the enormous wolf loping across it. He waited until the beast was almost ready to plunge into the forest, and he stepped out. His rifle cartridges contained no silver bullets. That was bullshit. A high velocity .30-caliber lead bullet would kill any animal, man included, weighing only one hundred and eighty pounds. The werewolf might seem to be of supernatural origin. But it was subject to the same laws of physics and chemistry as any other animal.

The bullet entered the gaping mouth, bounced off the roof of the mouth, tore down the throat, and angled into the liver. The wolf was dead and so was Varglik. Nor was there a change into the human body such as shown in many movies. The cells were dead, and the transformation principle could not act on the cells. The wolf remained Wolf.

Yeager did not want questions or publicity. He skinned the carcass and dug a grave and buried the wolf. In the process of remetamorphosis, the skin would have fallen off, he supposed, separating from the body and other parts of the skin. But it remained whole now, the process of change having been erased with the end of life.

Now, the pelt was stretched out against the stone of the fireplace in the sheriff's house. Every night, its light seemed to Yeager to be getting brighter. He considered destroying it. He knew or thought he knew what he would do soon if the skin stayed within his sight or within the reach of his hand. He had to burn it.

The hungry wolf will try to get at the meat even if it sees the trap. An iron filing does not will not to fly to the magnet. The moth does not extinguish the flame so that it will not be incinerated.

WHY DO I WRITE?

WRITER GUEST OF HONOR SPEECH GIVEN AT THE
1992 CONFERENCE FOR THE FANTASTIC IN THE ARTS

Members of the International Association for the Fantastic in Arts and honored guests, I'm pleased to be here as your professional-writer guest of honor. Like all of you, I love the "capital W" Word and make my living from words. Which is not to say that the members are wordy—though I suppose a few are. A few hundred.

The title of this speech is "Why Do I Write?" That derives from the title of the text of an entire publication issued in May of 1985. The title was "Why Do You Write?" Or, in the language in which it was published, "Pourquoi Écrivez-Vous?"

This was in a French super-size magazine with the overtitle of LIBERATION, edited by Daniel Rondeau and Jean-Francois Fogel. As far as I know, it was a single-shot publication. Subtitled: Des Grandes Signatures Venues de Monde Entier. That is, great signatures from all over the world. Subsubtitled: 400 Écrivains Repondent. That is, 400 authors respond.

Historically, the first time the question, Why Do You Write? was proposed by a French publication was in 1919. The replies from a hundred authors were printed in three issues of the revue *Littérature* starting in November 1919. That is, when I was a year and eleven months old. The authors who were asked the question,

Why Do You Write?, were all French except for the Italian poet, Giuseppe Ungaretti, and the Norwegian novelist, dramatist, poet, and winner of the Nobel Prize, Knut Hamsun.

In 1984, sixty-five years after the first inquiries, a French magazine, *Liberation*, sent the same question to authors. But, this time, it went to over 400 authors all over the world. Those who replied included a Samoan, two Zimbabweans, a Trinidadian, Palestinians, Israelis, and a Sudanese. Not included were authors from Greenland, Patagonia, Albania, and Lower Slobbovia.

Most of these I had never heard of before—or since. So much for my ignorance.

The Etats-Unis or U.S.A. section included such mainstream names as Mailer, Irving, Coover, Malamud, Barth, Carver, Highsmith, Oates, and Lurie. Five writers whom people think are science-fiction/fantasy writers were included. These were Asimov, Bradbury, Wm. Burroughs, Farmer, and Vonnegut. Burroughs and Vonnegut would object to being thus labelled. In fact, I object, but a lot of good it does me.

The shortest reply in the publication was from Charles Bukowski. He said, "If I knew why I write, I would surely no longer be able to write." Bravo for him!

To tell the truth, I didn't know why I wrote and I suspected that none of the 400 authors knew. But I was willing to try to figure out the why by writing an essay. So I did.

Under my name on page 52 was an editorial comment. "One of the fathers of science-fiction."

This is not true. I'm one of the children. I didn't originate any school of s-f unless, as my critics claim, it was the school of bad taste. Perhaps the editor meant that I'd fathered the school of erotic extrapolation in s-f.

The second editorial comment is "Born in 1918." This is true, if I am to believe my parents.

The third editorial comment is "A work to make libraries collapse." The verb is "plier," which means to fold or to bend or to yield. I translate it as "collapse." What the editor means here is that I've written a hell of a lot of books.

Follows the text. This was written in English by me and

translated by the editors into French. Unfortunately, I lost the original and could not, after so many years, reconstruct it in English. So, I had to translate the French back into English. Let's see how I've done though you must keep in mind that my original somewhat colloquial English has been slightly Frenchified, and, thus, spavined. I just couldn't help it. I've also shortened the text and I will add comments now and then.

The text begins: In the night of a wet space (my mother's womb) a spermatozoon was racing along with millions of others of his kind. During, this microcosmic marathon, all except one died. And the victor ceased to exist when it fused with the egg, both forming one: the other.

The spermatozoon landed upon the ovum as if it were an astronaut and the ovum was a distant planet. That day, Flash Gordon not only dropped in onto the unknown planet, the ovum, he fused with it.

From this fusion was created an Other (in the existential sense) named Philip José Farmer. Nine months later, this entity began his exploration of another unknown planet: the Earth. His story after crash-landing on Earth was a science-fictional one, in fact, every baby's story is science-fictional. And the newcomer fell into the hands of strangers who spoke an incomprehensible language and certainly did not think as he did.

His history is of a savage battle to survive on this planet while trying to become a complete human being, that which the Chinese call a "round man."

Aside: In one sense, I have certainly become a round man. I should weight 180 pounds. I do weigh 225.

But the entity which crash-landed, more or less human, a semi-robot, was doomed to labor all his life to become not-quite-human-enough. The realization of this would come at the end of his odyssey on this planet. Many have tried to become human. Few have succeeded, if, in fact, anybody has done so. And for all, apparently, the end is death.

Why then keep on trying to live? Perhaps because it's necessary to live a certain amount of time to develop one's self as fully as possible, to strive to become a round man, that is, a truly compassionate and empathetic person. And death is another forced landing, a crash-landing which also results in a fusion where we become an Other? Or where we combine with Some Thing to become Something Other? And if our free will doesn't overcome our semi-robot deterministic physical and mental mechanisms so that we can at least get close to being a real human being, a round man, will that prevent us from becoming an afterlife Other? Providing there is an afterlife, of course.

Human infants are semi-robots who possess, however, a limited though vigorous free will. Some of them become adults who use free will as much as possible. But the majority use their free will only once in their lives, that is, at the moment they unconsciously decide they won't ever use their free will.

I consider myself a born writer whose genetic drive to write was influenced by the environment. Since the age or eight or nine I've known that my main goal in life, aside from surviving, was to write fiction. This heritage influenced by the unique environment directed this semi robot toward the goal of being a writer and particularly toward the new genre of literature born of the industrial electronic era. That is, the genre of science-fiction. In the same way that the egg absorbed the spermatozoon, I absorbed the Bible, the *Iliad*, the *Odyssey*, Swift, Twain, fairy tales, the legends and myths of the ancient Mediterraneans, of the Medieval Norsemen, and of the native Americans. I absorbed also the boys' literature of the 1920's and 1930's. Also, the *Thousand and One Nights*, L. Frank Baum, Edgar Rice Burroughs, A. Conan Doyle, Robert Louis Stevenson, and some of Dickens' works. All these I read while in grade school.

In high school and college I absorbed too many classic, popular, and (so-called) subliterature works to list here. I thank God or Chance (one or the other) that my parents did not restrict my reading to the classics or works approved by the school authorities. A writer (or scholar) cannot truly know the literature of his nation unless he knows the popular literature also.

The books cited above (and many more) influenced me to a lesser or greater degree. And so did the silent films of my childhood and the talkies of my youth. Among a dozen or so films I saw while in grade school or before school, the most formative were the Black Pirate, the Thief of Baghdad, Robin Hood, The Lost World (which was based on Doyle's novel), and a week-end serial, The Green Archer. These made as much impression on me as any book I was to read. After all, I saw most of them more than once before I could really read. This influence of the movies demonstrates the power of environmental forces on genetic destiny. If I had existed in a time before movies existed, I would have been a somewhat different writer.

Also, whoever dealt me my genetic cards gave me a touch of earthiness, a dab of vulgarity. This streak of vulgarity, of earthiness, plus a horror of and yet fascination for the irrational behavior of *Homo sapiens*, led me to be particularly fond of the tales of the native American, who we called American Indian when I was younger, the tales about the great Tricksters. I was fascinated while still an elementary school student by the stories of Old Man Coyote of the Plains tribes and Wabosso or the Great White Rabbit of the midwestern tribes. Also, Tarzan is a classic trickster (in the books, not the films), and I read all of these available while still in grade school. The trickster theme has, as various critics have noted, been an oft recurring one in my fiction.

And Bugs Bunny, I feel, is a direct descendant of Wabosso and Coyote in this industrial-electronic era and also into this Age of Information.

The daily and Sunday comic strips of my childhood and youth also influenced me and shaped somewhat my literary mind. Among the many, perhaps the strongest, was George Herriman's KRAZY KAT. This was started in the Hearst newspapers in 1916, but I didn't become aware of it until about 1925.

Two demons sit on my shoulders while I write—and during other times, too. One is Bugs Bunny, the anarchist trickster, who crouches like Socrates' demon on my shoulder. He doesn't dictate what I should say or do, but he does make suggestions, and he counsels me. It was Bugs, not the wise men of the orient or the ancient Greek, Heraclitus, who revealed to me that anarchy and irrationality pulse and writhe and rage just beneath the surface of order and rationality, the skin of what we see as Reality.

Bugs sits on my left shoulder and asks me, "What's Up, Doc? Or down, as the case may be?"

The demon who sits on my right shoulder is Krazy Kat, who loves law and order but is also obsessed with love in the abstract and the particular. And Krazy Kat makes suggestions to me and counsels me. But, even when his voice (or her voice, since the strip never makes Kat's gender clear) happens to be stronger than Bugs' I keep envisioning the brick which the tricky Ignatz Mouse forever hurls at the back of Kat's head. I wince, and I feel as protective of Krazy Kat as Offissa Pupp was. And I think, Is that brick sometimes aimed at me?

It could be said that the tension created by the contradictory suggestions and counsels of these two demons makes me write.

Maybe, one day, their cries and their whispers will mix to make one voice, a unique voice. The sentence just spoken ended my essay in *Liberation*. However, I feel compelled to add to that. I must add: But my voice, like that of any writer's voice, is unique.

Thus, what I should say is that the two voices may mix to make not only a single voice, an Other's voice, but also a better voice.

This text was written in 1984 and published in French in 1985. I'm still waiting for the two voices to meld and make a single and thus better voice. I may be harsher in judgment on myself than others. I don't know. But, essentially I have to satisfy myself.

So, I've decided that the current fantasy novel I'm working on will be my last in that genre. I will keep on writing short stories in the science-fiction and fantasy field. My novels, however, will be mainstream or mystery. After all, when I began writing in the 1940's, my ambition was to be a mainstream writer despite my lifelong love of science-fiction. But things went awry; I became a science-fiction/fantasy writer. So, at the age of seventy-four, I'll start a new career. If that doesn't work out, I'll be eighty-four by the time that I find out.

Maybe I'll throw those two rascals from my shoulders and go shopping for brand new demons.

A Hole in Hell

by Dane Helstrom

His pen had hurled many into Hell. Now he, who should be in Heaven with his adored Beatrice, was in a pit such as he had depicted in *The Inferno*.

For years, he had searched along the River for the only woman he had ever deeply loved, the light of his life and his poetry. Now he was imprisoned by a man whom he deeply hated.

The eight-feet-square and twelve-feet-deep pit was on top of a foothill. Its sides were oak logs that slanted inward. (This whole world, he thought, slants inward and imprisons me.) The pit was in shadow except when the sun was directly overhead. Oh, blessed sun! Oh, swiftly moving sun! Stay in your course!

Ankle-deep in sewage, Dante Alighieri stood, his face turned upward. Dawn was an hour old. Soon, Dante's accursed enemy, Benedict Caetani, Pope Boniface VIII from 1294 to 1303, would come. Dante would know when Boniface was nearing because he would hear the barking and the howling of dogs. Yet there were no dogs in this place, which might be Purgatory or might be Hell.

A few minutes later, he stiffened. The yapping, barking, and howling sounded faintly. It was as if he had just detected the sounds erupting from the three heads of Cerberus, Satan's unnatural hound that guarded the entrance to Inferno. Presently, the noise became a clamor, and he saw the man who owned the dogs.

"Another God-given morning," Boniface said. "Time for my first piss. I baptize thee, Signor Alighieri, in the name of those whom you so hatefully consigned to Hell!"

His eyes shut, Dante endured the rain that did not come from the heavens. A minute later, he opened them. The pope had shed his robes and his wooden beehive-shaped tiara. The dogs—naked men and women on hands and knees or on hands and toes—prowled around the edges of the pits. Their fishskin collars were attached to leashes held by men and women of Boniface's court. The male dogs, by the edge of the pit and parallel with it, lifted legs to piss into it.

Boniface stuck his buttocks over the pit while two men held his hands to keep him from falling backward.

"In the name of those whom you wrongfully put in Hell in your vicious poem, I give you the bread and wine of the unblessed! Eat thereof, and glory in the transubstantiation of your fallen god, Lucifer!"

At the same time, a dozen dogs loosed their bowel contents. Only by standing in the center of the pit could he avoid being struck.

After a year of this, Dante thought, he should have been suffocated by the filth daily expelled into the hole. But the many excrement-eating earthworms kept the level of filth down to his ankles. Boniface had been pulled erect but again bent over as a series of slaves spat water between the pope's buttocks. Meanwhile, the dogs barked, howled, whined, and yipped.

Dante shouted, "May God force you for eternity to wear an iron tiara as white hot as His wrath!"

"Dante Alighieri never learns!" the pope screamed. "Does he get down on his knees, that stiff-necked Florentine, and beg forgiveness of those whom he has cruelly wronged? Not he! His mind is as the shit in which he lives!

"You committed blasphemy when you wrote of me in your Inferno as being in Hell while I was still living! Even God does not put sinners in Hell before they die!"

"You were and are evil!" Dante cried. "Would a godly man make dogs out of men, no matter what their offense?"

Boniface screamed, "Down on your knees, Guelf pig, and confess that you have wronged me and be truly contrite! Then you may continue your journey to find your beloved Beatrice! Though you should be seeking the Truth and God, not a slut such as she!"

"A fig upon you!" Dante screamed. And he bit his thumb and stabbed it at Boniface.

"Dante empits himself; he confesses his guilt and sin. Continue to suffer your rightful punishment!"

Then the pope, slaves, henchmen, and dog pack left. Four guards stayed behind to make sure that he did not find some means of killing himself.

Tonight, as every night, it would rain so hard that he could lie down in the water and drown himself. To do that would be to commit an unforgivable sin, one that automatically damned a soul. Would that be a sin in this world? Here, when a man died, he rose to life twenty-four hours later, though far away from where he had died. Was it then a sin to kill himself? Logic said that it was not. Yet he could not be sure. What God forbade on Earth should also be forbidden in this world. Or had the commandments been changed somewhat here to fit the situation?

Unheeding the soft squishy stuff under his feet, he paced back and forth. His mind went from the unanswerable question of suicide here to the conflicts raging during his lifetime. When he was calm and logical, which was not often, he told himself that the bloody quarrels between Ghibellines and Guelfs and between Black Guelfs and White Guelfs over politico-religious issues no longer mattered.

The huge majority of resurrectees had never heard of these conflicts and would yawn if they did. Only in this area, where Italians of his era lived, did the hatred burn fiercely. Yet it should be forgotten. Far more important things stalked the Rivervalley and should be dealt with. If they were not, salvation would be beyond their reach.

But he could neither forget nor forgive.

At high noon, the grailstones thundered. The echoes from the mountains had just ceased when he heard the dogs coming toward him. Presently, the barking and the howling, mixed with the crack of the dog-tenders' whips, were above and around him. Dante looked upward, shielding his eyes against the sun. He cried out and sank to his knees. He said then, "Beatrice!"

Boniface, standing naked by the edge of the pit, a leash in his hand, said, "Your long quest is over, sinner! Your beloved whore was brought in this morning by slave dealers! Here she is, a lovely bitch who must surely be in heat!"

Dante had averted his eyes, but he forced himself to look again. Once more, he cried out with horror.

She was naked and down on her hands and knees. She was weeping, her face so twisted that he should not have been able to recognize her. Something, some divine element, a sort of lightning flash between heaven and earth, had flashed from her to him. He had known instantly that she was Beatrice.

Boniface, grinning like a fox about to eat a chicken, pulled on her leash and kicked her, though not hard, in the ribs. She obeyed his orders to place herself parallel with the edge of the pit and very close to it. Then he gave the leash to a guard and got down on his hands and knees behind her.

"A bitch must be mounted from behind!" he shouted.

She cried out, "Dante!"

A whip wielded by another guard cut her across her shoulders. She cried out again.

"Do not speak!" Boniface said. "You are a soulless dog, and dogs do not speak!"

He eased himself forward over her. She screamed when he penetrated her.

Dante was leaping upward again and again and yelping like a dog. But he could not jump high enough to grab the edge.

"Look, look, sinner!" Boniface cried. "I am no dog, yet I am humping doglike the bitch you love so much!"

Dante wanted to close his eyes but could not.

And then Beatrice heaved upward and lifted Boniface with her. Though the guard jerked savagely on her leash, he could not stop her. She was at this moment as strong as if an avenging angel had poured his holy fierceness into her. She turned around and grabbed Boniface. Both screaming, they fell into the pit, the leash jerking loose from the guard's hand. She landed on top of the pope and knocked the wind out of him. Immediately, she began tearing at his nose with her teeth. She ceased biting when a spear cast by a guard from above plunged deep into her back.

She gasped, "Mother of . . . wish . . . die forever," and died.

The guards shouted at Dante to stay away from the pope. He had pushed the woman's corpse aside and was scrambling to his feet. Dante, crying out with grief and rage, jerked the spear from the beloved flesh and drove its point into the pope's belly. Then he yanked it out and started to turn.

A guard who had just dropped into the pit ran toward Dante, his spear held level. But his feet slipped in the filth, and he fell hard on his face.

Dante raised the spear to stab the guard. He hesitated. If he spared the guard, he, too, might be spared. But the pope's men would only do that to torture him and then, probably, cast him again into the pit.

As the guard, slipping in the filth, tried to get up, Dante cried out, "Beatrice! Wait for me!"

He rammed the spear butt against the log wall and pushed the blade into the pit of his stomach. Despite the agony, he kept on pushing until the blade was buried in him.

He was committing the sin of suicide. But it was the only way of escape. Someday, he would find out if it was unforgivable. If he eventually went to Hell because of his evil deed—if it was evil—he was willing to pay the full price.

Beatrice had been little more than an arm's length from him. Then, within two minutes, she was gone.

But she could be found again.

Though he might have to search for a hundred years, he would find her.

Surely, God understood his great love for her. He would not be jealous because his creature, Dante Alighieri, loved Beatrice more than he loved his Creator.

Dante's last thought dwindled into darkness. Forgive . . . didn't mean tha . . .

More Than Most

I first knew Robert Bloch, the writer, when I read in *Weird Tales* magazine his first published story. He was seventeen years old and a published writer. I was a little over a year younger and had never submitted any fiction. I was jealous of him, though not very much. If he could get started so young, so could I. Someday, I thought, someday soon, I, too, will be published. But that "someday soon" was a long way off.

I first met Bob Bloch, the man, when my wife, Bette, and I attended our first science fiction convention. This was the World Convention in Chicago in 1952. Like most people, we were both charmed and much amused by Bloch. His wide knowledge, his deep intelligence, and his photon-fast wit, ranging from the deep to the trivial, bowled us over. His wit was Voltairean rather than Rabelaisian (though he was not above making really corny puns).

But threaded with all this was a genuine warmth and caring. After forty-two years of knowing him, I can say that the warmth and caring are what I feel the most when I think of him, and that's often.

Bette and Bob Bloch resonated on the same frequency from the moment we met. They understood one another. They corresponded quite often and always managed to get together at conventions. When we moved to Los Angeles, we saw Bob Bloch and his wife,

Elly, frequently. Since Bob and Bette were both born on April 5, they always exchanged cards and, if possible, greetings by phone on that day. And Bette was the first person Bob told that he had cancer. That devastated her.

And recently, after a long-distance conversation, Bob signed off with, "Happy Birthday, Bette!" He knew he wouldn't be here next April 5.

As for me, I was numbed when I heard about the cancer. Bad news usually does that to me. It wasn't until Bob's death was absolutely certain that the long-suppressed tears broke out.

We've been fortunate in keeping many of his letters. Reading them over brings him back, and we can see the twinkle in his eyes, They're personal, but I think he'd give his permission for us to quote from some of them. For instance, here are some lines from a letter of June 9, 1990:

> I did a couple of TV sound bites (*Entertainment Today* and *Inside Edition*) but would have gotten a lot more exposure if I'd recorded a dirty rap album instead. Live and learn. If I were writing *Psycho* today, I'd put the motel in South Central Los Angeles and change Norman Bates' name to Bubba.

A postcard sent by Bob, dated September 26, 1992:

> Dear Phil:
> Let this be our secret. Don't tell anybody!

There was no secret. He tossed this off just for fun.

From a postcard, November 4, 1992:

> Dear Bette:
> . . . But hope you two survived the election. I voted for Harlan, but he didn't make it.

From a card to both of us:

> Hope you can get some rest and have a happy
> Easter. Elly just gave me a chocolate Jesus.

From a letter dated August 7 1/2, 1986, re Bette's dissatis-
faction with a doctor:

> Tell the orthopedist that if he wants to live cheap
> he should move to Peking and make his living
> repairing bone china.

There are so many quotable lines, but I'll not pursue them.
His conversation was even better, and his insight into society in
general and individuals in particular was very penetrating and
sometimes angry. Usually though, he tempered his criticisms with
a wry and witty comment. He was, however, not politically correct.
I'm glad, because I would have thought the less of him if he had
been. No writer worth his or her salt is politically correct. To be
that means that the writer is following the party line. But being
apolitically correct doesn't mean that the writer isn't compassionate
or understanding. It means that the writer makes his own judgments
based on the facts. That was the kind of writer Bob was.

Rereading the above, I see that it's almost hopeless to portray
him or, for that matter, anybody, unless you go to novelistic
lengths or compress him into a sonnet. All I can say, really, is that
Bob Bloch, the man, will always live in my memory and in Bette's.
He won't fade away in there. And we can say truly that we'll miss
him, There's nobody to replace him, never will be.

"All on a Golden Afternoon" is not the best short story Bob Bloch
wrote. I don't know what his best was, perhaps "Yours Truly, Jack
the Ripper." But "All on a Golden Afternoon" sticks most in my
memory, is my favorite, and the one I most reread.

One of the reasons is probably that I have loved Lewis Carroll's
Alice stories and *The Hunting of the Snark* since I first read them

when I was nine. But that wouldn't be enough for me unless Bob Bloch had incorporated the Carrollian spirit in the story. At the same time, he satirizes Hollywood types. Which was something he often did in his fiction and so is truly Blochian.

He also makes fun of the psychiatrists (licensed and would-be) who have tried so hard to psychoanalyze Carroll through the *Alice* books. They are sometimes very clever, but they haven't so far convinced me that their findings are valid. They're so grave, unlike fun-loving Carroll (and fun-loving Bloch). Yet, all their seriousness, gravity, and ludicrousness only make the perceptive reader laugh.

I suppose that, sometime in the future, the psychoanalytically inclined critic will tackle Bloch's works. He or she or they should have a field day. Will they conclude that Bloch was a psychopath who somehow sublimated his craving to kill and to mutilate through writing? Will they decide that Yog-Sothoth was a thinly disguised symbol for his mother? Do his Cthulhu Mythos stories reveal a deep fear of those dark, mysterious, and menacing forces which control us as if we were robots and to which no appeal is ever granted? Like the government in general, the Mafia, the IRS?

Bloch would enjoy analyses of himself, though he would poke fun at them.

So, enjoy this story. It's one of the very few Bloch stories in which good triumphs over evil. It sometimes does, you know, and that may be one more reason why this is my favorite story.

CASTING TURTLES

AN EXCERPT FROM *Nothing Burns in Hell*

E yes shut, my fingertips touching the mud now and then, I swam. Before I'd gone very far, my right hand struck a hard mound. I passed over it, then turned around and groped. The object might be a rock. Or it might be what its sloping surface suggested.

I needed air. Right now. But, if the object was what I thought it was, it could be used, and I couldn't leave it to go to the surface. I might not be able to find it again. Desperate, I wasn't going to ignore anything that could be a weapon. This thing, if used properly, could be that, and I knew how it could be.

My hands slid along the hard dome. But when I pressed a little on it, I felt a leathery substance. The turtle—I was certain now that it was a turtle—started paddling away. I seized one side of the rough shell with my left hand and gingerly used the other to feel its shell. There was a smaller plastron under the big shell. That, plus my contact with a long tail with a crested ridge and its ten-inch-long shell made me certain that it was a snapping turtle. I was glad that the head of this antediluvian reptile had been facing away from my hands.

I imagined its hideous naked head, its profile that of an aged and malignant senator voting to repeal the Child Labor Act.

I couldn't hold my breath any longer. I was no longer the youngster who could hold his breath underwater for almost four minutes, and I was weakened by fatigue, lack of food and water, and the fear of dying. Yet, I couldn't release the snapper. It'd move on; I'd never find it again.

My hands along the sides of the shells, I raised myself and brought my knees up against my chest. My feet sank into the toothless sucking mouth of the mud. I pushed upward by straightening my legs. My feet sank up to my calves in the mud. Nevertheless, my shove loosed them, and my head broke the surface. I breathed out and in twice. Some of the stinking water got down my throat, and I had a hell of a time to keep from coughing. Then I sank back until my mouth was just above the surface, and treaded water.

Now I saw Deak standing up in the boat, the beam of his flashlight probing into the darkness. A second later, a bolt not eighty feet away behind the boat illumined him. It also enabled him to see my head even through the dazzle.

He shouted, dropped the flashlight, and brought his rifle up to his shoulder. If he fired it, I didn't hear it. I let myself sink down under the surface, my knees bent. The turtle was still moving its flippers, trying to swim away from my grasp. I estimated its length at twelve inches and its weight at approximately thirty pounds.

Again I came up, standing on the mud, though slowly sinking. By another flash, I saw Deak seated and rowing the skiff toward me. He was looking over his shoulder and might have seen me. I drew in a deep breath and sank back down. I walked underwater toward the boat, I was leaning forward, my feet sinking deep in the slime.

I could only estimate very roughly the distance between me and the boat. If I misjudged, I might come up beneath the boat and bump my head against the bottom.

I counted one thousand one, one thousand two, one thousand three, one thousand four. At one thousand five, I bent my legs, then straightened them as I thrust upward. Suddenly, the water was only to my midriff. The turtle became heavy. Another flash, this one behind me, smote my ears. It must have momentarily blinded Deak.

He was standing not a foot away from me, bending over, looking down, his rifle pointed at a spot a few feet from me.

He yelled. The rifle boomed. Out of the side of my left eye, I saw the muzzle flash. I tossed the reptile at him with a strength that only an adrenaline surge could have given me.

The thrust drove me backward, and my feet were deep in the mud again, then I leaned backward, and my feet were free again.

As my head broke from the surface, another lightning streak, more distant than the previous one, showed Deak staggering backward. I could hear him screaming. My luck had held. I'd zeroed in on him. The ugly powerful beak was clamped around Deak's crotch. And he was falling over the side of the skiff. The boat rocked wildly but did not turn over. Another flash behind me, nearer this time, revealed an empty boat. The rifle, which he had dropped, had fallen upright, its butt on the bottom of the boat, its barrel leaning above the side.

Deak's screaming and thrashings came from beyond the other side of the boat.

I didn't have to climb back into the boat and chance completely turning it over. I was close enough to the shore that I could push it easily. Meanwhile, Deak's shrieks and his cries for help would have touched me deeply if the circumstances had been different and he was just another fellow human being who needed a Good Samaritan.

I looked again in his direction after I got the skiff moving. A flash showed that he was up to his waist in water. His face was twisted with agony, and the flapping tendrils around his lips made him look like some evil lake god who had tangled in mortal combat with an even more powerful lake monster

"Help me!" he screamed. "Oh, God, help me!"

I ignored him for the moment. Before I came near the shore, I looked for Milly Jane. Another lightning flash. She wasn't there. I hadn't thought she'd stand in the cold rain and wind until Deak came back.

After I'd dragged the skiff almost completely out of the water, I got the rifle, the knife, and the flashlight. By the beam of the latter, I looked at the M1 Garand. Four shots left in the eight-round clip. The other clips would be in the pockets of Deak's jacket.

Since I had no belt or sheath, I put the blade of the knife between my teeth. I turned the flashlight off and jammed it under my left armpit. I advanced, the rifle held in both hands. When I got to the storage shed, I cautiously looked around the side of the open doorway. The kerosene lamp was still on. Nobody there, though. I didn't go in. I wanted to find out if Deak's screams could be heard at this point. Yes, but very faintly, during the brief lapses of the lightning and the thunder.

Then I saw Deak by the glare of a bolt. Somehow, he had waded ashore with that heavy reptile hanging from his crotch like a Scotsman's sporran. Now, he was lying face-up on the shore mud, his feet in the water.

I couldn't have him behind me, though it seemed highly unlikely he'd be dangerous to me. I walked back to where he lay, his mouth working, his screams now sunk to moans, his eyes closed. I slammed the rifle butt against the side of his head. As an ex-LAPD officer, I knew the difference between a skull thumper and a skull breaker.

He quit groaning. The turtle still hung on. Folklore goes that it's impossible to break a snapper's grip. That isn't so. But it would take a surgeon to do the job.

I returned to the storage shack and carried out the big burlap bag containing the equipment Almond had taken from the trunk of my car. I put the flashlight, knife, and rifle on top of the bag. Then I went back inside and hurled the kerosene lamp against the wall. It shattered, and the flaming liquid spread over the wall and ran onto the floor. After putting the knife and the flashlight into the bag and then hoisting it over my shoulder, I left quickly. If Milly Jane saw the blaze, she'd be coming, and she wouldn't be unarmed.

When I got near to the shack, I heard the dog barking. The lamps shining through the window showed that the windowless door was shut. I stood partly behind a tree. Then the door seemed to explode wide open, Milly Jane, holding a double-barreled shotgun, charged through the doorway. I put a bullet into her left thigh. She fell heavily on her breasts. Her shotgun bellowed. I knew it had been accidentally fired because the pellets blew the dog apart.

I stepped out from behind the tree and shot but the bullet struck her shoulder. She grunted and rolled over. A moment later, she was screaming again.

I got quickly to her side and kicked the shotgun away. The butt of my rifle against her head silenced her. I picked up the shotgun with a finger through the trigger guard and threw it as far as I could. After which, I went to the side of the house and looked through its window. Almond was still lying on the floor, his mouth open, his eyes shut.

I didn't think he was playing possum, but I went into the shack ready to shoot if he did more than stir. Satisfied that he wasn't shamming, I knocked him deeper into unconsciousness and dragged him out into the rain alongside the woman.

It took a few minutes to tape over their mouths, to roll them over so I could tape their hands together behind them, and then tape their ankles together. It took longer to put my clothes and raincoat on my wet body, retrieve my keys, wallet, and other belongings from the table and stick them in my pockets, and scoop the money into the briefcase.

I took the briefcase and rifle outside before going back in and smashing both lamps against the wall. Then, I ran out before the flames reached the five-gallon kerosene containers I'd opened. Just as I did so, the kerosene containers in the storage shack exploded, and the fire billowed up above the tops of the trees.

I picked up the bag, briefcase, and rifle and headed for the end of the ridge. When I reached it, I heard the second explosion—Deak's shack. The night became day. However, the heavy rain would soon kill the flames.

My car was in a clearing off the road, the pickup close to it. I backed it over the weed-covered mud and drove down the dirt road. I hoped that I'd get out of Goofy Ridge before someone saw the fires. I didn't want the narrow passage blocked by people on foot or by cars.

I made it to the Mallard Club without seeing anybody, drove onto the paved road, then turned right. Instead of taking the same route back to Peoria, I'd decided to drive south on the county roads—very little traffic on them—until I got to Havana. Then I'd cross the bridge and go northward along the west side of the river. About two minutes later, I pulled off the road and turned off the motor. I was shaking like a dog passing worms. After a while, the reaction to the ordeal passed, and I resumed the journey homeward.

A little later, I passed close by a place where a tragical yet comical accident had happened. This was long ago, in 1866, during the latter part of a bright spring day. The sun was hanging above the top of the western bluffs when the *Minnehaha*, a sidewheeler steamboat, was tootling along northward in a stretch of river just wide enough for three boats abreast. Its flag whipping, smoke pouring from the tall black stack, steamwhistle shrieking and bells ringing, it would've gladdened any human being worthy of being called human.

Its owner and commander was Captain Augustus Minnie, a notorious drunkard, and it was carrying a cargo of pool balls and cue sticks from St. Louis to Peoria. Everything seemed fine. Then the boiler exploded with a roar that rang back from the hills and sped up and down the river. The boat was blown to pieces. There were no survivors.

Two duck hunters in a boat near the east bank of the river saw Captain Minnie soar from the wheelhouse high into the sky above the flames and the smoke. The westering sun silhouetted him, still upright, his plug hat on his head, a whiskey bottle tilted to his lips.

Before the hunters realized they were in danger from other than the flying fragments of the boat, the storm was upon them. One hunter was transfixed by a cue stick, fell into the river, and did not come back up alive. The other man, a shoulderbone smashed by a pool ball and an ear torn off by a cue stick, lived to tell his tale.

To this day, people sometimes find pool balls in the mixed sand and mud of the riverbanks along here. The wooden sticks, of course, decayed long ago.

THE 2000s

R etired from writing, Philip José Farmer only attended one event outside of Peoria in the 2000s, the 2001 Science Fiction Writers of America Nebula award ceremony, where he was named a Grand Master. The Peoria Public Library held their own celebration shortly afterward; thanks to publicity from his unofficial website, fans came from around the world to celebrate, including a group dinner that resulted in many fans visiting the Farmers' home.

Bette Farmer had so much fun, she wanted to do it again the next year. In 2002, the library held another event, celebrating the 50th anniversary of Phil's groundbreaking story, "The Lovers." Many of Phil's fellow science fiction writers sent in letters which were read to the audience. Once again, there was a group dinner and a visit to the Farmers' house.

After a few quiet years, things picked up in the mid-2000s when early material from Phil's files began to be published. In 2006, the giant collection of rarities, *Pearls from Peoria,* printed nearly every story and article by Phil that had not already been reprinted in one of his many short story collections. Additionally, it published, for the first time anywhere, the following stories: "Planet Pickers," "The Terminalization of J. G. Ballard," "Hunter's Moon," "The Rise Gotten," "Doc Savage and the Cult of the

Blue God," "The Princess of Terra," The Purple Distance," and "A Rough Knight for the Queen."

This was followed by *Farmerphile: The Magazine of Philip José Farmer*, a quarterly fanzine which ran fifteen issues and published articles about Phil and his work, as well as the following previously-unpublished material by him: "The Face that Launched a Thousand Eggs," "The Unnaturals," "That Great Spanish Author, Ernesto," "The Essence of the Poison," "The Doll Game," "Keep Your Mouth Shut," "The Frames," "The Light-Hog Incident," "A Spy in the U.S. of Gonococcia," "The Rebels Unthawed" "A Peoria Night," "The First Robot," "Duo Miaule," and "Getting Ready to Write" (with Paul Spiteri). *Farmerphile* also serialized the novel *Up from the Bottomless Pit* in the first ten issues, published several speeches and reprinted a few rare articles that were discovered after *Pearls from Peoria* was published.

After four years of no conventions or public appearances for Phil, Bette Farmer wanted another event in Peoria, similar to the two previously held at the Peoria Public Library, and FarmerCon was born. FarmerCon I was held in the summer of 2006 with fans coming from around the world to a formal event at the library, followed by a dinner that evening, then a picnic at the Farmer's house the following day. This pattern followed through 2009.

2005's *Myths for the Modern Age: Philip José Farmer's Wold Newton Universe* collected not only Phil's writings about the Wold Newton Family, but also articles written by other scholars about the wider Wold Newton Universe.

Specialty publisher Subterranean Press published several collections of Phil's work in the 2000s: *The Best of Philip José Farmer*, the aforementioned *Pearls from Peoria*, *Up from the Bottomless Pit and Other Stories*, (material from the first ten issues of *Farmerphile*), and *Venus on the Half-Shell and Others*, covering Phil's fictional author period.

Three unfinished novels by Phil were completed by other writers during the 2000s: Danny Adams completed the short novel, *The City Beyond Play*, which was published in 2007; Win Scott Eckert completed the novel *The Evil in Pemberley House*, published in 2009; and Christopher Paul Carey completed *The Song of Kwasin*,

From a photo taken sometime in the early 2000s.

published in 2012 in an omnibus along with *Hadon of Ancient Opar* and *Flight to Opar*. Both *Pemberley House* and *The Song of Kwasin* had been completed before Phil passed away on February 10th, 2009.

In 2010, Meteor House, the publisher of the book at hand, was launched with the goal of keeping Philip José Farmer in the public eye, by reprinting his works, publishing new collections, and even allowing authors to write licensed fiction set in the worlds he created. To date Meteor House has published: *The Worlds of Philip José Farmer* (volumes 1–4); an expanded version of the novel *Fight to Opar*, the first standalone edition of the novel *The Song of Kwasin*; the first trade edition of *The Evil in Pemberley House*; a deluxe hardcover edition of *Doc Savage: His Apocalyptic Life*; a fourth unfinished novel completed by another writer, *Dayworld: A Hole in Wednesday*, with Danny Adams; the collection *The Best of Farmerphile* and the first hardcover edition of *Tarzan and the Dark Heart of Time*. Meteor House has also published several novellas set in Phil's worlds written by other writers: *The Scarlet Jaguar* by Win Scott Eckert; *Exiles of Kho, Hadon, King of Opar*, and *Blood of Ancient Opar*, all by Christopher Paul Carey; *Phileas Fogg and the War of Shadows* and *Phileas Fogg and the Heart of Osra*, both by Josh Reynolds; and *Man of War: A Two Hawks Adventure* by Heidi Ruby Miller.

Meteor House has also continued to sponsor the annual FarmerCon gathering. Taking it on the road to Seattle, Washington, the 2010 FarmerCon was held in conjunction with the Locus Award and the Science Fiction and Fantasy Hall of Fame weekend. PulpFest became a more permanent home, first in Columbus, Ohio from 2011–2016, and then in Pittsburgh in 2017 and 2018.

Hopefully this *Centennial Collection* career retrospective, which makes its debut at FarmerCon 100 in celebration of Phil's 100th birthday, will not only thrill longtime fans, but also perhaps be a gateway for a new generation of readers.

THE FACE THAT LAUNCHED A THOUSAND EGGS

∾ ONE ∾

No Charlie," said Tim Howller, "I haven't a date for the political rally tonight. I'm going with Mark and some Phi Delts and Thetas who're going to try to steal the Black's banner."

Over the half-shield of an arm raised to permit smearing of deodorant on his right armpit, he looked at his mirror-self. It stared back, a Judas-pink on its forehead and cheeks.

Charlie Bluepress' eyes squinted sidewise from their trenches of fat while he forced lather and blue whiskers off his blade with running hot water.

He rumbled, "Is it true you'll be carrying the biggest torch at the rally?"

"Torch?" Tim said.

He lowered his arm and looked at Charlie.

"What biggest torch?"

Charlie slapped his enormous thigh.

"Haw!" he shouted. "I mean Francis Uquart's big torch!"

The bathroom rang with laughter.

Charlie's bellow subdued the rest.

"Look at him blush! Like a virgin—if there is such a thing. My gawd, kid, don't show all of your emotions. Toughen up. It's May 1937, you're nineteen, big enough, old enough to be a man. Be like me. Triple-bound in brass Charlie, they call me."

Tim quickly raised his left arm, ostensibly to rub on deodorant. His crooked elbow hid his nose and quivering mouth.

He said in a flat voice, "Triple-bound in brass Charlie? You mean hippo Charlie don't you? Two-ton Tony with the triple-tiered 'testines."

Laughter gurgled up from the cavern of Charlie's stomach and shook his breasts like thunder in a jelly bag.

He rumbled, "Got under your hide, haven't I? So you try to dig under mine by calling me Fatty. Won't go, Howller. I can look my belly in the face. But if you had my paunch, could you look it in the face? No. You can't look anything in the face. Why, you don't dare consider the fact that, though you've fallen for Uquart, you haven't the guts to ask her for a date."

"Sure," Keith Huston chimed in, "if I liked that luscious peach, I wouldn't stand back in the shadows, sucking my thumb."

"Looking like a dying calf," said Art Fey.

"Knees shaking," said Mark Hazar.

"Heart thumping," boomed Jack Phillips.

"Afraid to step up," sang Art Fey.

"Hot and cold . . . like running water . . . oh, my fevered brow! . . . writing poetry about her but afraid to show it to her . . . Byron himself . . . Dante and Beatrice . . . Petrarch and Laura . . . Ulysses and Helen . . ."

Charlie whacked his thigh.

"Red Helen!" he shouted.

"Yeah!" Keith barked. "That's right. Hey, Art, didn't you tell me that's Howller's most secret, most poetic name for Francis? Red Helen?"

Tim glared; Art paled.

"Wow!" chortled Keith. "I'm hot for Red Helen!"

"Listen, fellows," Charlie shouted, waving his hands and blowing his whiskey-breath in Tim's face. "Who is Francis Uquart, or, as this frightened poet who nests in our midst calls her, Red Helen?

"I'll tell you. A Junior in the University of Shomi, majoring in dramatics, social chairman of Kappa Kappa Gamma, fashion editor on the school paper, Queen of St. Patrick's Ball, Sweetheart of Beta Phi Theta, Homecoming Princess, and a string of etceteras as long as my arm.

"Moreover, this Titian-haired beauty, whom all of you have no doubt seen many times strutting her stuff—what stuff!—in the Workshop plays, has got a potful of dough. That is,"—Charlie leered—"she will have as soon as she finds some well-heeled sucker to marry her.

"And she almost did, for as *tout le monde* knows, not so long ago she wore the governor's son's frat pin. Think of it. Don Blairston, son of the governor of this glorious state.

"But, fortunately, Francie and Donnie quarreled, and she had to hand back the pin. And the potful of dough she might have had.

"But don't worry, gentlemen. She'll get another. A woman with her superb character is bound to win some great and rich man. Yes, she has a superb character, which I will now describe. It consists of a build that holds a candle to nobody's. Can a figure hold a candle? And it also consists of tresses, oh, so auburn they burn, or so burning they auburn.

"So, gentlemen, ta-ra, ta-ra, ta-ra, I give you the one and only— Red Helen!"

"Hooray!" shouted one of the boys.

"Wait, fellows," bellowed Charlie though no one had moved to leave. "We know Miss Uquart. But who is Tim Howller, this latter-day Ulysses, this would-be Paris? I'll tell you, though"— Charlie's voice quavered—"it's like tearing out my heart-strings. He's a freshman, a measly Lambda Lambda pledge who has no friends that amount to anything, no talents except for getting into trouble, no money, no nothing.

"So-o-o-o, brother Greeks, fellow Lambda, why blame the poor suffering guy? If you were this insignificant mote in the beam of Shomi campus life, would you ask Miss Uquart for a date? No. You wouldn't. So, why blame him?

"Bu-u-u-ut, he is in love. Capitals I-N-L-O-V-E. He's standing in the midst of a great blaze of passion as intense as any the martyrs burned in.

"And she"—Charlie raised a finger for emphasis—"she doesn't even know he exists!"

The bathroom stormed with laughter.

"Aw, that's a lot of hooey!" shouted Tim. "She does too know me!"

At Tim's first words, loud and hoarse, Charlie had stepped back and raised his hands in a half-warding gesture. But when Tim's voice trailed off weakly, Charlie stepped up. His hand slapped down on the youth's shoulder. A crimson five-petalled flower bloomed briefly on the white skin.

"Then," Charlie said in a tone half-paternal, half-condescending, "you've no excuse for worshipping her through binoculars. Ask her for a date."

"Yeah . . . yeah," chanted the others. "Date . . . date . . . boom-boomety-boom. Datity-date. Rate a date! Date a rate! Boom-boopity-date!"

Tim snarled, "You guys know where you can shove it."

He picked up his razor, deodorant, towel, brilliantine, tooth-brush, paste, and comb and walked out. Voices followed him down the hall.

"Red Helen . . . wow! . . . unrequited passion stalks the ivied halls of Shomi . . . Howller carries a mean torch . . . torch!"

As quickly as his fumbling fingers allowed he dressed. He flashed glances in the mirror. Was it true? Had their banter been merely a means to put across what they really believed? Was it true? No talents, no brains, no looks, no money, no guts. Especially no guts.

In a moment Art Fey came in. The light behind the smile and mockery he'd had in the bathroom was cut off: the upcurve of lips and squinting of eyes were caricatures of themselves.

Tim looked contempt at Art, scowled, and refused to look again. Inside, he was hurt. He had once, in a burst of over-whelming need to discharge some of the turmoil burning inside him, confided in Art. He had told how much he loved Francis

Uquart and how, whenever he thought of her, he called her his "Red Helen," because that was so intimate, exclusive, and poetical. That even she didn't know of it made it all the more valuable.

Having eased somewhat the tension, he had not thought it necessary to swear Art to silence. Like himself, Art was sensitive. Why should he think that Art would ever do such an unspeakably gutterish trick?

Art arranged his toilet-set on the bureau-top, all the while looking at his roommate out of the corner of his eyes and shifting weight from one leg to the other. After a silence unusual for Art, he broke out, "Look here, Tim, I don't want you to think I showed everybody that poem you wrote about Uquart. You know I wouldn't do a thing like that. I appreciated the fact that it was something intimate that you wanted only your best friends to see. I didn't betray your confidence. It's true I did show it to Mark Hazar, but he's one of your best friends, close-mouthed and sympathetic. If he mentioned it to anyone, I can't help that."

Tim grunted and finished buckling his belt.

Art bit his lip and said, "Well, I might have mentioned it to Traje Courke because he's one of your best friends, and I thought I could trust him. But outside of those two, and maybe Jack Littley, I—"

Lower lip sucked-in, two deep creases parenthesizing the inner ends of his brows, Tim walked out.

☙ Two ❧

Tim slammed the screen-door and walked out to the railing of the frat house's front porch. Mark Hazar followed him. Looking up at Tim he said, "What kept you from taking a poke at blubber?"

"He'd been drinking and wasn't too responsible. Anyway, nobody seemed to think he was out of order. I noticed you were in the chorus yourself."

"Sure," Mark said, "I feel Charlie is right when he said you shouldn't be afraid to ask her for a date. Still, I think he went too far."

"You know me, Mark. I have to be pushed hard before I'll fight."

"Charlie knows that," said Mark. "But for a moment he thought he'd pushed too hard. Did you see him get ready to take off? He ought to pick on somebody who can't beat the tar out of him."

"Why did he pick on me in the first place? I've done nothing to him."

"Cripes!" Mark exploded. "That's easy to see. After Francis Uquart split with Blairston, Charlie asked her for a date. She turned him down. He never said so, but I know he thinks it is because he is so fat and ugly. He's jealous of you because he knows you could get a date with her if you had the guts to ask her."

Tim turned quickly and put his hand on Mark's shoulder.

"Do you really think so?"

He was smiling.

"Cripes! I know it!"

Tim removed his hand and wrinkled his forehead.

"I don't think so. Charlie was right. She's got everything. I've got nothing."

"Nuts!" barked Mark. "You're a man, aren't you? Tim, you're too self-analyzing, too self-conscious . . ."

Mark cocked his head and said, "But then I'll have to admit this Uquart gal can get a guy muddled up. Look at the present political situation. It's partly her fault. You know the Betas were once in the Gold coalition, didn't you? That was when Zinter, the Sig prexy and Blairston were both rushing Uquart. When Blairston pinned her, Zinter got so nasty that Blairston lined up the Betas with the agricultural frats and talked Uquart's Kappa sisters into joining them. Now, even if Francis and Donnie are parted, the Black coalition still stands.

"Zinter and Charlie hate Blairston, and they're out to win the school government election, hook or crook. They've been whipping up such high feelings there's no telling what might happen. Both Blairston and Zinter have been popping off about having a show-down and beating hell out of each other.

"And if you and I, Tim, and those other guys that are going with us tonight, succeed in stealing the Black's banner, there'll be hell to pay. The last two years the Blacks have run us off, but in my freshman year I was with a gang that stole the banner. The Blacks found out where we were hiding, and they came after us. Cripes, what a brawl! Paddle-fights, fist-fights, rotten tomatoes thrown, a fire-hose dousing the crowd, and, finally, the police called. I got a bloody nose and my shirt was torn off, and I was soaked with tomatoes from head to foot. Cripes, what a brawl!"

Laughing, Mark walked out to his Model T, the Tin Centaur, parked by the curb.

He said, "I'm going to pick up our gang from frats here and there. Want to ride along?"

"No, thanks," Tim said, "I'll meet you in front of the Pi Phi's."

Tim Howller walked in the dusk towards the Pi Phi house, from which the Gold parade was scheduled to start. His scowling silence contrasted with the smiles and chatter and shouting and laughs of the crowds on the sidewalks and in the narrow streets. Boys and their girls walked along swinging their locked hands. Gangs of yelling boys charged through the crowd, stumbling and falling and knocking each other down. Clusters of girls giggled and screamed and yelled at the boys.

Many carried blazing torches which lit up white banners and signs on which broad black letters were painted.

Vote for Walker. Vote Gold. Walkaway With Walker. Yea Golds!

When Tim was walking past the Acacia house, he was stopped by a big man wearing a black sweater with a big gold S on its chest. Speaking loudly and officiously, the athlete tried to force a flaming torch on Tim.

Tim muttered, "No, thanks."

"Here, take it, bud. Get into the swing of things. You're not one of those damn Blacks are you?"

Tim swallowed and awkwardly took the torch. But when the athlete had gone, Tim threw it in the bushes. He didn't care whether or not the bush caught on fire. He walked on.

When Tim came opposite the Kappa House, which lay across

the street, he stopped, facing it, and his eyes raked the brick façade. Two lights glittered, one on the first floor in the front room and one upstairs. On the latter he fixed his eyes. While the crowd broke to flow around him, and while girls yelled at him to quit standing there gawking, and while boys accused him of window-peeping, he stood statue-like, seemingly unhearing.

Suddenly his rigidity disappeared in a spasm. Clutching at his back and giving a cry that was half-grunt, half-yell, he jumped a foot forward.

Behind him rose raucous, parrot-like laughter. That, plus the undignified and vulgar method of introduction, was enough to tell Tim that it was Trajan Courke.

Tall, lean Traje with the narrow skull, the sharp nose with a shallow pit on each side of its bridge as if thumbs had squeezed there while the bone was yet soft, and the yellowish-brown hair combed Mephisphelean into two horn-like waves.

The ever present cigarette jerked in the corner of thin lips. He chuckled. He said, "By God, Tim. Caught you again. I'll bet you were dreaming of your lovely Uquart doll, weren't you? I won't ask just which lovely portion you were mooning over."

"Darn it," said Tim. "Do you *have* to sneak up on a guy and do that?"

He made an upward stabbing with clenched fist and extended thumb.

"Best method in the world for recalling a guy to his present surroundings. Listen, Tim, what's the matter with you? Standing here in the midst of all this activity, teeming with possibilities for an enterprising young man, and conjuring up all sorts of scenes in which you are Antony and this Uquart doll is Cleopatra.

"Not history but herstory; the tale of a woman's attempt to become again a rib, warm and snug and well-fed and without worries. Yes, Tim, that's true. And I've nothing but a big sneer and profound contempt for these pantywaists who stand in awe of a skirt, who don't know that it's the slugger who gets in there and fights for her that she admires. It's action she adores, my boy . . ."

Tim said, "Yeah, I know."

He glanced with seeming desperation from side to side as if looking for an excuse to leave. When he saw the Tin Centaur rattling towards him, he grinned and heaved a sigh. The passengers, jammed into the topless car until they had to lean over the sides to make room, yelled, "Hey Howller, plenty of room. On the hood."

Tim blurted, "So long, Traje," and ran off.

Traje called out, "Don't forget, old buddy. It's action that gets the woman. Action. Action."

༄ Three ༄

While the election rally was breaking up in a tumult of cheering, whistling, and wild waving of torches, Mark Hazar yelled at Tim, "Come on. We're gonna go after the banner!"

But Tim shook his head and said, "I—I can't. I've got a—a date."

Mark shouted, "Huh? Since when?"

Tim reddened, hesitated, then said loudly, "I didn't quite tell you the whole truth, Mark. I do have a date, but it's not with a woman. It's—it's with action! Yeah, that's it! With action.

"You see, all the ribbing I took from Charlie and the boys, and the advice I got from Traje, have convinced me that maybe I am a dweller in shadows, a guy who lets others make off with the prizes and the girls. So—I got an idea. Instead of letting others make history, I'm going to make it. And I'm going to do it right now!"

He began to walk away before Mark could object.

Mark yelled after him, "I don't get it! Hey, Tim! You're missing out on a lot of fun!"

"Not on this date," said Tim.

Ten minutes later he walked into Campustown with his hands in his pockets and whistling with a merriness he didn't feel. A crowd was gathered on the sidewalk and street before the drugstore, grocery store, beer-joint, hamburger-joints, and jelly-joints huddled into one short block called Campustown. As the Black rally was over, most of the boys and girls milled around aimlessly. Many boys carried pine or oak or walnut paddles of the kind used in fraternities to thwack bent-over pledges. The paddle-swingers were mostly Agricultural students, for the Black coalition consisted of all the Ag frats, in addition to the Betas and three sororities.

Tim eyed the blue-jeaned men, half-apprehensive they would challenge him, even though common sense said they would have no way of telling a Black from a Gold. He stood around, hands in his pockets, listening, watching. Then he began drifting towards the banner strung high across the street between two iron power poles. In big black letters was: BARKER FOR PRESIDENT.

That banner was the challenge, and Tim, raking it from end to end with his eyes, felt like a spy in enemy country. He was conscious that he had a heart, for it beat furiously. He felt sweat trickling from under his armpits, despite the deodorant, and his belly was closing in on itself like a fist.

Calm down, he told himself. Nothing's happened. And from the looks of things nothing is going to happen. How in the world could I, alone, drag that banner down from those poles and make off with it through this crowd?

Obviously, he couldn't. But he could hang around until the Aggies took it down for him. And then, if he combined the serpent's cunning with the dove's speed, he might be able to catch them off guard and, who knows, run off with the banner as Jack did with the singing harp. The only difference between him and Jack was that he had no axe to cut down the route of pursuit. It was a big difference.

He decided to talk with one of the guards and find out when they planned to lower the banner and where they would carry it. But the guards suddenly shouted, "Look out!" and ran off in different directions.

Tim half-turned. He cried out in alarm. He flung up an arm, a useless, late gesture, for the blazing torch missed him by a foot. It slammed into the street-pavement and rolled over and over, bumping to a stop against the curbing, where it burned fiercely.

Three other torches described burning trajectories close to the path of the first.

Behind Tim, girls screamed.

One of the Ags, a big blond with a paddle in each hand, shouted, "Let's get those damn Golds!"

He ran off toward the dark, cupolaed James Hall, the university administration building. Three paddlers ran after him. Their destination was a group of boys standing under the bushes by the hall's big porch. Evidently, the torches had been flung by that bunch.

Tim, straining his eyes into the dark, thought he could make out Mark Hazar's short, broad figure.

Another Aggie called out, "Hold it, Jim. It's just a ruse to get us to leave the banner unguarded."

Jim stopped and came back. He said, "You're right, Bob. But those damn fools might've burned somebody bad."

Bob said, "Anything's likely to happen tonight."

He glanced at his wristwatch and then called to two other paddle-swingers. "Almost ten. We've given the Golds enough of a chance. Let's take the banner down."

"Yeah," said Jim. "They've got no guts."

Jim dropped his paddles, pushed aside a guard, and began climbing up the steps of one of the iron poles. Another boy ran across the street to the west pole.

Tim turned to see the women who had screamed. His heart had waxed and waned fast before; now it began the furious squeezing of blood, accompanied by a tightness in chest, that it always experienced at each fresh sight of Francis Uquart.

She was standing in a group of Kappas who had just come out of the Yellow Sable. Her large blue eyes locked with his; Tim opened his mouth to say hello, remembered that she might wonder what he, a Gold, was doing there, closed it, and half-turned to go as if he hadn't seen her.

But she said, "Hello, Tim Howller."

Her voice was curiously deep for a woman's, throaty, husky, vibrating, and hinting at the substratum of energy and emotion that would be well worth the effort a man would have to take to tap it.

Her voice reached out with strong, but delicate, fingers, and plucked at him. He felt the squeezing of blood and the tightness of chest, and he felt also something go *strum!* within him as her strong, delicate voice-fingers plucked a string.

"Hello, Francis," he said.

His voice sounded all right to him, just loud enough to sound confident and deep enough so she wouldn't guess how she shook him and friendly enough but not too friendly. He had never yet allowed it to betray him, but he could never be sure of himself until he had spoken.

He said, "Did one of those torches almost hit you?"

She laughed with a slight note of anger. She said, "Oh, yes. One of them just whizzed by my head. What's the matter with those nitwits? Don't they know they might seriously hurt somebody?"

"They're nitwits, all right," said Tim, despising himself for not thinking of something clever, something that would convulse her and the rest of the girls with laughter.

He stepped back to let big Jim off the pole. Jim had untied the east end of the banner, and it had fallen into upstretched hands below.

"O.K.," said Bob. "Fold it in two and roll it up tight. We'll put it in my car around the corner. Those yellowbelly Golds aren't going to try to steal it."

The banner consisted of a thin lath about ten feet long from which hung a rectangle of thin white cloth. The lath was broken in two and folded. The cloth was rolled around the lath into a tight stick about five feet long. Then the banner was picked up by two men who held opposite ends, even though one could carry it easily. Around it gathered six paddle carriers.

"Now," said Bob. "Honor-guard, forward! To the armored chariot. Ta-ra-ta-ra-ta-ra! Boom-boom-boom! If the Golds try any last minute raids, beat hell out of 'em!"

Tim had a vision of himself sinking in a sea of arms, each of which held a paddle thudding dust and pain from the seat of his pants.

His saliva dried, but sweat pebbled his forehead, soaked his armpits and the area between his shoulders.

Nevertheless, he began walking by the side of the guards, and he said, "Didn't the Golds make any real attempts to get the banner?"

"Yeah," one answered. "A bunch of guys in an old Model T drove down the street close to the banner, but we stood in front of it and scared them away by throwing our paddles at them."

He laughed. "I hit one right on the head. You should have seen him bleed."

Tim gulped. So Mark Hazar and those other guys had tried. And failed. The men of action had failed, and now it was up to Tim Howller, man of inertia, man who stood in the shadows and sucked his thumb, to carry out the rape of the banner.

He gulped again and ran his tongue over the dry stalactites of tension that seemed to hang from the roof of his mouth. Now or never. The banner had been carried around the corner to Bob's sedan. The backdoor was open, and the banner was about to be shoved in. Once that door was closed on it, he would have lost all chance to take it. And to ask the guards where they were driving it to on the off chance that he might be able to sneak it out of their hiding place, would be to expose himself to their suspicions.

He glanced over his shoulder to see if any paddlers were directly behind him. Lord! Francis was standing on the corner, and she was watching him! If he failed now! If he didn't have the guts! He'd lose forever his chance to distinguish himself enough to be able to ask her for a date.

Now or never.

The man holding the banner's front end was ready to shove it in the back seat. But his back was turned to Tim. And the man holding the rear end was laughing and looking away from Tim.

Now or never. Too many times now had slipped through bashful-fingers and never come home to roost.

He sucked in a deep breath, sucked in the now with the oxygen. Then, the now penetrating his blood, threaded with it so that it would not come out, he released his breath in a wild warwhoop. And at the same time that he gave that scream which he hoped would unnerve the guards, he leaped upon the banner.

His outstretched hands clutched it, felt the cloth and doubled lath, and tore it with the force of a hundred and eighty pounds of track-tempered physique and an immeasurable amount of determination and desperation from the slack grip of the carriers.

Around him the guards stood like men in a broken-down film, shock-suspended, bewilderment-frozen.

Then they were behind him, there was no one in front, and he was running down the middle of the street, the banner clenched in his right hand, whipping and swaying and vibrating like a white lance launched straight for the Lambda Lambda house.

Shouts and curses rose behind him. A hard-flung paddle spun by, narrowly missing his head. Another slammed into a tree-trunk on his left.

"Get him! Get him!"

Feet slapped the pavement behind him.

✂ Four ✂

Between 10:20 and 10:45 that night, telephones rang in the frats in the Gold coalition. Those answering were surprised to hear Charlie Bluepress' loud authoritative voice. He demanded that they round up all their available men, arm them with paddles and eggs, and get them down in front of Sigma Chi house as quickly as possible.

"What's the matter?" they asked.

The receivers bellowed: "What's the matter? Man, I was in a bull session with a bunch of politicos at the Sig Chi's, when Jack Littley phoned. He said there's three hundred Aggies and Betas in front of the Lambda house. They're bombarding it with eggs.

"Yeah . . . that's what I said . . . eggs . . . eggs . . . old rotten eggs they must've gotten down at the warehouse, or maybe from the Agricultural Labs . . . yeah . . . my gawd, Littley says the house-front is plastered . . . broken-in screens . . . cracked windows . . . smeared the hallway's walls and rugs . . . our housemother's in hysterics . . .

"Why? . . . haw! haw! . . . one of our pledges stole their

banner! . . . yeah, isn't that delicious? . . . I'll bet they're really frosted . . . snatched it right from their hands . . . ducked down alleys, ran like a stripe-tailed ape . . . outran them all the way to our house . . . then collapsed inside . . .

"Some of them trailed him, and now Litttley says there's a mob outside howling for their banner and the guy who stole it . . . they're threatening to come in and get him and shave his head and maybe tar and feather him and ride him around town on a rail . . .

"Naw . . . they won't do it . . . Littley and Weiss were in the house when the pledge got there . . . you know how big and tough they are . . . they'll clip the first guy that steps inside . . . but those Blacks are making a mess with the eggs . . ."

Charlie's voice switched off the bellowing joviality and became crisp and commanding.

"Enough of this blabber . . . hop in your cars and get over *tout de suite* . . . the touter the sweeter . . . and come with paddles and eggs . . ."

The receiver banged down.

ಬ Five ಬ

At 11:10 P.M. a loose phalanx of excited and determined students, numbering between four hundred and five hundred, left from in front of the Sig Chi's and marched down School Avenue towards the Lambda Lambda's, three long blocks eastwards.

These Greeks, however, unlike Agamemnon's or Achilles' warriors, were armed with pine paddles and paper sacks and wooden crates of eggs, referred to as pullets' pellets. Fortunately, the Aggies had not had the foresight, or the money, to buy out the entire stock, and the Golds had therefore caught the amazed operator of the downtown warehouse before he had closed up again. Putting off his questions about the sudden run on hen fruit with a multitude of witty and totally irrelevant answers, the Golds had seized his remaining stock, paid off, and taken off.

Now, heroically armed, they went into battle as so many heroes of the past had gone—with a song on their lips. It was a song that is, in one form or another, traditional on the campuses of the larger colleges. There at the University of Shomi it was entitled "Uncle Tom, What Makes the Grass Grow So High on the Beta Lawn?" and it was a song derived from the tradition that the Betas were one and all inclined to look down their noses at other frats. It is a song that is usually sung when non-Betas are tipsy or just feeling good, or, as on that night, looking for a fight. It is sung with the hope of enraging the Betas into retaliatory songs and imprecatory poems, or, even, into violence. It is usually a forlorn hope, for the Betas are too Olympian to reply by word or fist to mere mortals.

Though most versions of the song are earthier, it runs something like this:

> Oh, we'll all go over and do what the dogs do,
> > Do what the dogs do,
> > Do what the dogs do,
> > On the Beta lawn.
> Oh, we'll all go over and do what the dogs do, etc.
> We'll growl, growl, growl,
> > howl, howl, howl,
> > growl, growl, growl,
> > On the, on the, on the Beta lawn.

On this occasion, however, reflecting the high tension and bad feelings that had distinguished the election, and the fact that, inasmuch as Barker, the Black candidate for president of the student government, was a Beta, and that, therefore, the rape of the banner was a blow in their face, the Betas had come out of their ivory tower. They stood with the Aggies, facing the Golds.

Tim Howller, from the vantage point on the roof of the Lambda's porch, could see the whole situation. He was lying flat with his head raised and peering through the bars of the white-painted little railing that kept the boys from falling off when they sun-bathed or slept outside at night. Beside him was a sack of eggs that he had taken out of the kitchen refrigerator and which he was ready to drop on any Blacks who tried to invade the front door, three stories below.

Around him were the white broken shells and yellow yokes of unsuccessful attempts to pierce the third story windows beyond the porch-roof. None had hit Tim, for he had not come out of his retreat in the attic until Littley had reported seeing the Golds marching down the street. Now he watched. He saw Blairston, the governor's son, tip a bottle to his lips and then smash it against the pavement. He saw Barker going through the crowd trying to find out how many eggs were left. Unfortunately for the Aggies, they had launched most of them at the house and were now left with nothing but fists and paddles for defense. Evidently they felt naked, for an uneasy mutter ran through their ranks, and some loud voices counseled immediate flight.

Then the army of Golds marched to within ten yards of the Blacks. At a ringing command from Charlie Bluepress, they halted, after which they shifted uneasily, gripping eggs and watching the Blacks for sudden moves.

The Gold big shots stepped forward to confer with the enemy leaders. Zinter and Blairston put on a sideshow by arguing.

Tim watched them anxiously. He disliked both, for they had once dated Francis Uquart. Blairston had beat Zinter out by putting his fraternity pin on Francis. That was the beginning of the well-known feud between the two and the boasts of both that when it came to a showdown, each would kick hell out of the other.

Tonight, stimulated by the banner's rape, the damage done by the eggs, and the consequent excitement, not to mention a dozen beers and half a pint of whiskey, Zinter had decided to have it out.

Blairston stood with clenched fists and red face listening to the names Zinter was calling him. When he was accused of being a Judas because he had pulled the Betas out of the Gold coalition the preceding semester and lined them up with the Aggies, Blairston barked back angrily. Then everybody could see that the governor's son had also been hitting the bottle, for he mumbled and slurred and swayed.

Tim mentally hugged himself and hoped Zinter would swing. He'd like nothing better than to see the old stuff knocked out of Blairston. The guy deserved that and far more, for he had spread stories about Francis since their split-up that nobody but a liar and a degenerate and the tail-end of creation would permit to pass his lips. Especially when they were about Tim's Red Helen!

But shortly it became apparent that neither of the arguers had guts. Both were contenting themselves with calling each other names that should have aroused them to an instantaneous and blinding urge to kill. But they swayed and repeated each other's insults.

Nor was Charlie doing anything to urge his men on. He stood immobile, a huge fat Buddha, blinking and looking from side to side and talking in a very restrained way for him with Barker. Tim couldn't hear them above the drunkard's bickerings or the catcalls and insults passing back and forth between the main bodies. But he guessed by their gestures and the seriousness of their faces, revealed by the light of the arc-lamp above them, that they were discussing peace.

Disgusted, Tim rose to his feet.

"Ah, those lousy men-of-action!" he muttered. "They'll stand there talking forever and then slink home."

He picked an egg out of the sack, a nice extra-large one, balanced it in his hooked fingers, made a rapid estimate of the distance involved and force required, and sailed it out in the night.

The white oval rose, became black against the sky, suddenly dropped, and was white again.

Tim's eyes were focused on Blairston. He confidently expected the trajectory of the pullet's pellet to end in an explosion of yellow yolk against yellow hair.

Then he gasped. His aim was way off!

Charlie Bluepress let out a bellow of surprise and anger that drowned the shrill bickerers and dull mutter and hoarse jeering of the crowd. He wiped at his cheek and cursed. Then he plucked something from a paper sack in his left hand and cast it viciously.

Splop!

Even from his third-story height, Tim could hear it. And he could see a suddenly silent Blairston pawing at his dripping face.

Then Charlie shouted out an order and pulled out another egg and splop! And Barker was pawing at his face and cursing.

The Face That Launched a Thousand Eggs

There was a roar from the Golds. A cloud of white pellets sailed from them, broke and rained over the Blacks. There was another cloud—and another—and then a thunder of feet and a tumult and a shouting as the Golds rushed the Blacks.

Tim didn't see much after that, for he was struck with a laughter that seized him and pulled him to the roof and made him roll back and forth, shouting and holding his aching ribs. Then, when the convulsions lessened, and he could sit up and wipe his eyes and wheeze for breath, he noticed that he had rolled through the sack of eggs and that he was soaked with yolk. And that brought on other gusts of laughter that shook him until he was too weak to laugh anymore.

"Old Charlie got it! Big fat Charlie! Right in the kisser! Ha! Ha! Maybe that'll teach the overgrown hippo not to prate of action. Action! He wanted action, and he got an egg!"

He wiped his eyes.

He shouted, "Ha! Ha! I'm not sure now that my missing Blairston was unintentional. Ha! Ha! I'll bet that if Charlie could have seen what razzing me was going to lead to, he wouldn't have opened his big mouth."

And he laughed until he could laugh no more at the thought it was he, and he alone, supposedly inert, actionless, thumbsucking, shadowdwelling Tim Howller who had started the battle that was making clamorous and bitter and eggy the street in front of the white façade of Lambda Lambda.

And, of course, the shadowy card-player in the back of his mind had flipped out the inevitable Daliesque ace on which Tim-Paris sat on a topless tower of Ilium, leaning on his trusty lance, resting on his laurels, laughing at the thought that his desire for the most beautiful woman in the world, Red Helen, had started all this, and watching with Olympic aloofness the poor mortals of Greek and Trojan mix it.

✑ Six ✑

The next afternoon, Tim Howller, shaved, shampooed, showered, shined, and shining, dressed in new green-brown herringbone tweed pants cuffed at the ankles according to the vogue, a sport coat of gray-green herringbone tweed, a white shirt, and a green and red dotted bow tie, stood outside the jelly-joint. Grinning broadly, he looked like a very fresh and confident, almost brash, young man. Part of that effect came from the pseudo-spiritual feeling a clean body and clean clothes give; part, from an inner light.

The light was the glowing of a nimbus—a nimbus which soaked him through and through with a joy and an aggressiveness that had been largely lacking in that shy, moody youth. Much of the glow came from his previous night's exploit. That alone was enough to fill him with satisfaction and confidence. But much also fountained from the keen interest and joy displayed by his frat brothers—their urgings to tell and retell the story of the rape of the banner, how he snatched it from under the suspicious noses of the Blacks, how he outraced them, how he started the battle outside the Lambda's by accidentally striking Charlie. That brought roars of laughter from all, from Charlie most of all. He slapped Tim hard on the shoulder and bellowed that he'd make a politician and a big-man-on-the-campus out of Howller yet.

The only grey thread in the gold of the nimbus had been Tim's worry over the damage to the house, which he could not keep from blaming on himself. But that was dissolved, for Charlie said that the Ag leaders had agreed to pay for the damage. Their offer, said Charlie, wasn't as noble as it seemed, since Charlie had sworn to them that if they didn't cough up, the Golds would make similar raids on the Ag frats.

So it was that young Tim Howller rode in on a wave of glory much as young Lochinvar rode on his steed, rode into the Yellow Sable, jelly-joint par excellence.

The booths lining the walls were filled with couples or four-somes, or even sextets, who had dropped in for a jelly-date, local parlance for a cheap date during which one sipped on cokes, listened to the band, if there was one, and danced on the raised floor at the back of the joint, shouted at each other or whispered in soft, amorous tones, saw and were seen, and, in the dark corners, went through a series of facial contortions and nuzzlings known as smooching.

Though he was smiling buoyantly, Tim's heart was beating as fast at the idea of asking the hitherto unapproachable Francis for a date as it had when he was on the verge of stealing the banner. He had no such ideas as smooching. Not yet. It would take enough nerve to talk to her.

But he was determined to do it. After all, his name must be on everybody's lip, and she would be standing in reflected glory by being seen with him. The worst that could happen would be her refusal to date him.

He looked through the thick clouds of cigarette smoke. From long surveillance of her, he knew it was her habit to drop in there after her noon classes. He looked around and couldn't find her. For once, she had failed to come. He didn't know whether to feel disappointed or relieved. Then, as he walked around a counter, he saw her bright-red hair at a booth in one of the darker corners.

She was alone. He was lucky. It wasn't often that this girl was unattended. The chances were, she was waiting for her date, whoever he might be, to enter now.

Quickly, before he would lose his determination, and before some boy would come up and beat him to the draw, he walked up to her.

"Hello, Francis," he said, smiling at her.

"Hello, Tim," she said, smiling back.

"Mind if I sit down," said Tim, "I just happened to drop in and saw that this is one of the few spots unoccupied by a fanny. I'll buy you a coke."

"Of course, I don't mind," she said. "I always like company."

He didn't care for that. He didn't want to be considered just company.

"Is that a new dress?" he said. "It really is beautiful. That bright green with the yellow collar really goes good with your red—uh—auburn hair."

"Yes it's new. I'm glad you like it."

She smiled and patted her hair and said, "And you may call it red. It is. Auburn sounds so affected, don't you think?"

Tim said, "Yes. I think so."

The waiter came. Tim ordered a lime coke for Francis and a plain coke for himself. While they waited, he talked slowly and hesitantly, trying to keep the door shut on the bursting sea inside him. He wanted to ask her immediately if she would go this coming Saturday night with him to see Robert Taylor and Greta Garbo in "Camille."

But first, he had to know he was swimming in safe waters. He had to hear her words of praise and of wonder at his exploit and her breathless inquiry about what happened after he ran off with the banner. And he expected to send her into laugh after laugh with his comic account of the egging of Charlie Bluepress.

He waited, but she did not speak. Some of the nimbus chilled. Was it possible . . . ? Oh, no!

"Wasn't that an idiotic thing for those boys to do last night?" he burst out. "I mean, throwing the torches like that. They might have hurt somebody. They almost made me ashamed to be a Gold."

"Oh yes," she said. "One almost did strike me. But you know how boys are. Besides, they were anxious to get the banner."

He waited with beating heart. But she spoke of her part in the forthcoming Workshop play. At another time he would have blotted up every word, but now was no time to talk of the stage. Not unless he was on it.

"Listen," he said sharply in the middle of one of her sentences, "haven't you heard about the Black's banner being stolen last night?"

She raised eyebrows.

"You don't say? Well as I—"

"But, but," he said desperately, "it happened right after those torches were thrown. Surely you must have seen who ran off with the banner. You were standing right there watching!"

She looked around, saw someone she knew, waved. She spoke, her eyes roving, everywhere but on Tim. She spoke, and the nimbus chilled and turned to grey, and Tim knew that the now was flown and the never had come home to roost.

"Oh, no. Right after those torches were flung I decided it was too dangerous with those silly boys showing off, so I walked back to the Kappa House."

Keep Your Mouth Shut

Sometimes I think about Jimmy Maharg's murder, and I wonder how bad a time I might have had if Vogler or Rugford had not kept their mouths shut. For a long time afterwards I used to sweat about it, and every once in a while I'd wake up groaning from a nightmare in which Jimmy had been pointing his finger at me.

Only two months ago, over eleven years after Jimmy died, I dreamed I was working in the steel mill again. An open hearth door opened before me, and I saw Al Vogler and Barrett Rugford standing within it on top of the lake of white-hot molten steel, scooping out the stuff in a sieve while Jimmy stood behind them, spitting tobacco juice on them.

You might say I have a conscience, and I'm trying to work off my guilt by writing this story. I don't care. You're probably right, and nobody'll be hurt by what I'm telling. Vogler dropped over dead two years after Jimmy's skull was crushed. Two months ago Rugford fell or jumped off a boat while fishing in the Illinois' backwaters and wasn't found until a week later. Jimmy's wife was taken by cancer. And none of the three had any immediate relatives.

It all started for me the summer after Pearl Harbor. Medically discharged from the Navy, I returned to my native mid-Illinois city and applied for jobs at several industries. Within a week I reported for work at 7 A.M. as a laborer for Helsget Steel and Wire Company.

When the whistle blew, Moose Larkin, a foreman, opened a locker in our shanty and gave four of us shovels, picks, and rakes. We trailed after him across the smoky steelyard to the railroad tracks that ran around the east side of the open hearth building. There Moose put us to raking up the ashes between the rails that dropped from the yard locomotives like red hot puppies from an iron bitch. We shoveled the ashes into a wheelbarrow and dumped them against the foot of the levee about ten yards away.

This is easy, I thought. Where is that backbreaking labor they tell you you'll find in a steel mill?

At that moment, as I bent over my rake, I heard a voice that was loud, harsh, nasal, and hissing at the same time.

"S-s-say, Moose-s-s, I need a couple of boys for the furnaces-s-s."

I looked up.

Jimmy Maharg was a little old man about five feet four, and, as I later found out, close to seventy. Stoop-shouldered as a question mark, he looked as if he'd spent all his days hunkered down deep in the three feet high dust tunnels under the open hearth furnaces.

He wore a dirty high-crowned once-grey hat. Beneath its broad flappy brim his long white hairs bristled to form a shelf over his ears and the back of his frayed shirt collar. The chief thing you remembered about his long lipped Irish face were his eyebrows. Thick and woolly and black, they contrasted strangely with his white hair. Always in motion above his heavily lidded and pale blue eyes, they twitched and wriggled, rose and fell, writhed and squirmed, a pair of epileptic caterpillars. They seemed to be geared to his jaw, which chomped savagely upon a handful of Red Man.

Moose waved a huge and negligent hand and said, "O.K. We ain't got much to do. Take Vogler and that Alligator kid there."

"The name's Alliger," I said.

"Yeah," Moose boomed in a voice like a lion's with a sore throat at the bottom of a well. "Haw, haw! That's what I said! Alligator!"

I didn't mind Moose's laughter, because there was nothing mean in it, but I didn't care for Maharg's dry crackling laughter which sounded so much like radio static and had about as much real mirth in it. I said nothing, however. Putting my rake and shovel over my shoulder, I started after Maharg.

He spun around and shouted, "For cryin' out loud! Put them tools down! You won't need them where you're goin'!"

I was surprised and angered at such irritation, for my mistake was natural for a rookie. But I kept my face stony. Al Vogler, who'd leaned his rake against the side of the building, walked up, grinning.

He spoke in a high-pitched whining voice. "Stung you, didn't he, Alligator? But you did right, kid. Keep your mouth shut and stay out of trouble. Me, I talk all the time. I got to, else I'd blow up from here to Kingdom Come. But you keep your mouth shut and just laugh inside yourself at Jimmy. That's best, 'cause he hates college kids."

He spat and said, "He 'n I don't get along so well. Long time ago I worked here, and he fired me for nothing at all. If it hadn't been for him, I could a been a boss here by now, too. And had a lotta seniority and retirement pay coming up in ten years. As it is, I got nothing."

Vogler was tall and lean and as nervous as an old alley tom. He had a hooknose and a grin with long yellow-and-brown teeth. The grin seemed painted on because it was almost always there. Even when he ate, he'd be smiling at you, teeth and food and all.

"Why'd you come back here to work?" I asked.

"Oh, this is the third time in twenty-three years I worked at Helsget's, maybe it's because I hate Jimmy so much I hope he'll say something that'll make me mad enough to tie into him. Or maybe get something on him."

He paused to give me a peculiar look, his narrow head cocked slyly to one side. "You'll be hating his guts, too, before the day's over. He's easy to hate."

Another hesitation, then, casually, "Some day somebody'll drop a brick on Jimmy."

The next moment, we walked into some of the hardest work I'd ever done, and I forgot his words. For a while, that is.

Helsget's had three open hearth furnaces that ruminated on iron scrap and poured out molten steel, white and hot as Hell's own milk. These took a terrific punishment, and in time the bricks that bound the inferno within them weakened. Cracks formed and widened. Sections of the brick roofs fell in and had to be hastily and temporarily repaired. Parts of the walls collapsed. And after a while the heat was escaping so fast through the fissures and faults that it took too long to melt the scrap.

The furnaces ran six months before getting to the point where they just had to be rebuilt. They were shut down in order, one being torn down while the other two kept on operating. On the biblical principle that the last shall be first, we attacked No. 3 first. It had been cooling since Saturday morning, but by Monday morning the bricks still sizzled if you spat on them.

The furnaces were two stories high, towering stories. Jimmy's gang of six worked on the charging floor with several other gangs, wrecking the upper half. The thick grey insulation plaster on the outside of the furnace's walls was scraped off, put in large cardboard boxes, and carted away. Then a horde of demons, goggled, and masked in bandannas and respirators, charged the walls with bars and sledges and shovels. At the same time, other fiends pried apart the arching roof. Great clusters of bricks, mortared together like souls clinging desperately to each other in their fall into Hell, tumbled down into the big bowl of the furnace floor or into the slag pocket far below.

Heat like little pitchforks rose and stung the delicate linings of our nostrils. Hard driven, sharp edged bars and falling bricks clattering against each other knocked dust and chips into the air. Before long I was blinded by sweat filling my goggles. I was forced to stop every other minute, remove the goggles, and wipe them out. Then sweat mingled with the thick hot dust to form mud on the kerchief I used for cleaning. Soon, like the others, I left the goggles up on my forehead and took the chance of a chipped-off fragment hitting my eyes.

Vogler grinned at me, his face red as a steak just put on the pan.

"Just like tearing down the walls of Hell itself, ain't it? Matter a fact, this is a department of Hell. The whole world's Hell. Ever stop to think we already died some place else and came here to pay for our sins? And that religion's something the devils fixed up to keep us from blowing out our brains, so we'll go on living and suffering? Me, I don't believe in an afterlife, not really, but if there is one, I'll bet it's just as bad as this one. If that's possible."

Rugford, the big Negro, looked up from his sledge and said, "Vogler, you a flap-mouthed atheist. You don't wanna blaspheme that way, or you gonna catch it where it's *really* hot."

Vogler jerked a thumb at Rugford. "He used to be a preacher," he said.

Suddenly, Jimmy Maharg was standing behind us and shouting, "You won't tear down no furnaces with your mouths!"

We went back to our work, but Vogler whined, "This is Hell, and Maharg's one a the demons."

By mid-afternoon the walls of the upper half had been tumbled. Jimmy then took us downstairs to the open hearth pit, in front of the slag pocket. It was here that most of the bricks from the wall had fallen, burying the slag beneath it in a great pile. Jimmy ordered us to jump in and start clearing away the debris. To show us how to do it, the bent old man began picking up the bricks as fast as he could, using both hands. The broken ones he threw into the open end of a large iron pan outside the pocket; the good bricks he tossed onto a pile to one side.

When sweat had stained the armpits of the thick grey jacket he always wore, regardless of the heat, he straightened up and panted, "That's the way to do it, men."

His was a favorite trick of the foremen. Work fiendishly for five minutes and then tell the gang to keep up that pace for the rest of the day. Greenhorn though I was, I didn't fall for it any more than the old timers. I threw bricks until I was hot, then walked around the furnace to the other side, where I could get a salt pill and a drink of water. Moose Larkin hailed me and gave me a slip of yellow paper.

"That's a requisition for two new shovels for Jimmy's gang!"

he bellowed against the Niagaraish roar of the gas flaming in the nearby furnaces. "He'll sign it and probably send you after the shovels."

But when I returned, I couldn't find the old man. I walked around, searching, and finally located him in the narrow and murky canyon between No. 2 and No. 3 furnaces. I came up close to him from behind and shouted, "Hey, I got a requisition!"

He jumped and whirled, then struggled visibly to recover his dignity. I couldn't help grinning, for I knew he'd been spying on his gang to make sure they were working while he was gone.

He took the requisition in both hands and peered at it.

"You're holding it upside down," I said.

"Oh yeah? I know. I know."

Quickly, he turned it over and then ran his left hand over the breastpocket of his jacket.

"Must've left my glasses home. Besides, it's too dark here to read."

It wasn't so dark I couldn't read it. And earlier that day he'd bragged that his eyes were as good as when he was a young man.

"Who gave this-s-s to you?" he asked, angrily.

I told him what Moose had said, and he took out a pencil and printed a very neat but heavy J and M. Then he glared at me, his brows rising and falling like angry sea waves.

"What're you grinning at, Alliger? Just 'cause you went to college, you needn't think you're so smart."

I raised my own eyebrows, took the slip, and walked off to the storeroom. Later, I told Vogler of the incident.

He whinnied with laughter and said, "Yeah, he's illiterate, but he won't ever admit it to the men. The other foremen make out his time cards and slips for him, but they don't dare sign them. If they do, he blows his top, just like a ten inch firecracker."

Jimmy couldn't read or write, but there was nothing wrong with his lungs. All day long he raved at the top of his nasal and crackling voice, raging about this and that. One man didn't work fast enough; another took too long to get a drink; another, he swore, was goldbricking in the toilet; another didn't handle a shovel right; another threw too many good bricks into the dump pan.

I endured that rasping voice, but I never did get used to it. The point was, the heat that weakened and the dust that choked and the noise that deafened were enough to grind the skin off your nerves. But they were impersonal. Though heated, they were mechanical; they didn't radiate that different, human heat of passion. You could dislike them, bitch about them, but you didn't rage against them.

Jimmy Maharg had a devil of a whirling, snarling, grinding passion in him. And passion in a human being will strike off sparks in another—whether it's the passion of love or hate. I've found it possible to be indifferent sometimes to love but almost never to hate. I think this is true of most men.

"What's the matter with Jimmy?" I asked Vogler.

"Hell, he's always been that way. At eleven he ran away from his home in the Kentucky hills because his folks beat him and because they wouldn't give him an education. He's never been back, but he never went to school, either. He's a mean old bastard, and the only two times I ever saw him smile was when he got news his father died and the day after he came back to work from his first wife's funeral."

"Life must be hell for his second wife," I suggested.

"That's what you think. Jimmy's dumb, never learns. His first wife watched him like a hawk. Took his paycheck and gave him back enough to buy two sacks of Red Man. So what happens? Less'n nine months after she's died, he's hitched to a woman less'n half his age. And she pulls the same squeeze play on him. He never goes anyplace except to work, the store, or home, and he gets enough money for chewing tobacco. That's all."

Rugford said, "Maybe he'd drink all his money away if she didn't watch him."

"Ha-a-a, not him! He won't touch a drop. He's agin liquor just like he's agin everything."

When I came to work the next morning, I found the second and third shifts had cleared away the rest of the bricks and exposed the slag. It was a dull black mass about six and a half feet high, ten broad, and fifteen through. Our job was to blast and pry it apart so the new furnace would have a place to deposit its burden of impurities.

Jimmy showed Rugford and me how to drill a hole for a dynamite stick with an air-hammer in the lava-like stuff. While we pressed the yammering heavy tool downwards, we stood upon boards. Only a few inches below its surface, the slag was red hot. Imprisoned for six months, the heat now soaked through and over the boards, making ovens of our shoes. We endured it long enough to drill half a hole, then climbed down from the pocket to get a drink and cool our feet.

Rugford was a heavily built man about forty years old who looked like a black-skinned Jiggs. His blarney completed the resemblance, for he talked even more than Vogler.

Did I believe in the gospels, brother, in the savin' blood of the Lamb? Not in the way he did, huh? Well, he wouldn't argue. Not yet, anyway. But he went to church twice on Sundays, and I was welcome to come with him. We was all one color in the eyes of the Lord. He'd been a preacher himself, five years ago, but his lying deacons had run him out of town. Why? It didn't matter, brother, didn't matter. That was all past and forgiven, and the road to heaven looked straight and near to him.

He was by no means always serious. Usually, he was joking and laughing loudly, and when he was with Vogler it was a contest to see who could outtalk and outlie the other. Vogler had a slight advantage because he was an atheist and loved to dig Rugford's theological ribs. Rugford didn't mind a joke about God too much, but he was easily angered if anybody questioned His existence or Rugford's belief in Him. Then he'd argue loudly without a thought of backing down simply because Vogler was a white man. He was right, and he knew it, and his pride was based upon the unshakable authority of the Scriptures.

Moreover, despite his chatter and his frequent breaking into singing of hymns, he was as good a man as any and a harder worker than most. When the rest of us, weak and burning, stopped, he labored on. More than once he remained at the handles of the air-hammer while I went off for a drink, and when I came back he was outlasting another partner.

By lunch time, aided by Rugford's strong back and Jimmy's crackling unceasing voice, we'd blasted and carried away a quarter of the slag.

"No wonder," complained Vogler. "We're working our tails off. And Jimmy'd let you fall over before he'd tell you to take a break."

At twelve-thirty we returned to prying away at a huge wedge-shaped chunk that towered almost to the top of the pile. It would rock back and forth but stubbornly refused to be barred loose, remaining as tightly locked as if Jimmy's dynamite had driven it into the clifflike face of the pile instead of blasting it free.

There were three or four inches of sand between the brick flooring and the bottom of the slagpile, laid there as a cushion to prevent the hot slag from fusing with the bricks.

"Vogler," said Jimmy, pointing to the chunk, "dig that sand from under it. That'll make it easier to pry loose."

"Hell, no," said Vogler. "I ain't gonna stand right underneath that boulder. If it fell, I'd stand a fat chance of getting away."

Jimmy snarled, "For cryin' out loud, you afraid of that? Go ahead. Dig. That chunk couldn't fall over in a thousand years. Ain't we almost ruptured ourselves barring away at it? Go ahead.

"Damn it, don't then! Give me a shovel, somebody. I been working this slag for thirty years. Nobody knows more'n me about it. Here. Give me that shovel. I ain't afraid of that."

I started to hand him mine, but Vogler, red-faced, his grin gone, began taking the sand out with a long handled shovel. Jimmy at once picked up a bar, stuck it in the gap between the great poised boulder and the pile, and shoved.

Just as Vogler turned away to toss a scoopful of sand behind him, the chunk began to topple over.

I yelled, "Watch it, Vogler!"

He froze for a second, then jumped away. The black slab rushed out at him, fast, fast. He yelled and threw his hands up at the same time he was in the air. When he came down he touched the ground just before the black end of the chunk crashed. His right foot was caught, the metal of the shoe's safety toe pinned. And then he was screaming like a wounded horse, his face twisted, and his lips rolled back over his long yellow teeth in another painted grin, only a grin this time of agony.

"For chrissakes, get if off! My leg's burning up!"

He didn't have to tell me that. I'd smelled the same odor last December 7, and it did the same thing to me now that it had done then. I seemed to go crazy; nothing mattered except getting that man off to a place where he wouldn't have to stand being cooked alive and where he could quit that terrible screaming.

I leaped forward, and when Jimmy got in my way I shoved him aside so hard he fell over on his back. Then, along with three other men, I seized the chunk in my gloved hands and rolled it, somehow, off Vogler's foot. The odor of scorched cloth mingled with that of burning flesh, but it was over with quickly and we snatched off our gloves and threw them down on the floor.

Jimmy got up. "You knocked me down, Alliger."

"Shut your damned mouth," I snarled.

Shortly afterwards, the first aid men carried Vogler off in a stretcher to the company ambulance. We stood around and talked about the accident until Jimmy returned from the yard superintendent's office, where he'd been making his report.

"For cryin' out loud," he shouted, giving me a hard look, "he ain't killed. Get back to work. The rest of you ain't hurt. You think the company's paying you for standing around with your thumbs in your mouths?"

Rugford scowled and said, "It ain't paying you, Jimmy Maharg, to bar a chunk down on a man while he's digging out from under it, either."

The old man turned grey as his workjacket. He thrust his contorted face upwards towards Rugford, a rocket of sputtering incoherent rage, blowing out dark wet shreds of tobacco.

"You—nigger!" he screeched.

Rugford gave a roar and lifted his long handled shovel straight above him to bring the edge of the scoop down on Jimmy's head.

"I don't allow nobody to call me that! 'Specially trash like you that can't read or write!"

His pausing to tell Jimmy off before he killed him gave us time to act. Three of us fell on him at once. I grabbed the shovel and hung on, not because I cared if he split the old brute's skull but because I wanted to protect Rugford from himself.

"Don't do it!" I yelled in his ear. "He isn't worth going to the chair for!"

That did it. He stopped struggling and allowed his shovel to be taken away. Like a dog coming out of water, he shook himself free of his rage.

"You right, Alligator boy," he said huskily. "I ain't no blood-thirsty heathen. I almost spilled my brother's blood. *Vengeance is mine, saith the Lord.*"

For a moment he watched Jimmy walking away fast across the yard, then added, "But the Lord sometimes works through the hands of us human beings."

Maharg was not—as I'd hoped—fired. He did get a severe reprimand, but the company felt it had to back its foremen—especially its old timers. And it satisfied its conscience with a hundred dollars for Vogler.

During his time in the hospital, however, Vogler had no money coming in. Moose Larkin organized a collection to help him. Jimmy's name, in Moose's handwriting, was down on the list for a dollar. And that, I was sure, was all he ever contributed, for Vogler would have been sure to mention it if he had.

Meanwhile, Rugford and I refused to work for Maharg even if it meant being fired. Word had gotten out about our run-in with him after the accident, however, and somebody, Lemore the superintendent or Moose, figured that the old man had it coming to him. So we went to work for the other yard bosses during the rest of the furnace repair. When we met Jimmy, which was often, we stared through him, and he paid no more attention to us than we did to him. Finally, the hearths were rebuilt, and we all went back to our regular jobs. Once away from him, my intense dislike for him sank into a mere unpleasant memory.

Six more months. Furnace repair again. Production slowed, and those with low seniority were bumped back to the yard. There I saw Vogler. Except for a slight limp, he was his old self. I asked him why he was now working again on Jimmy's gang.

"Maybe I can get him in the same kind of spot he got me in," he replied through gritted teeth.

I considered that statement for a while, then I said, "I've been thinking what you said about dropping a brick on Jimmy. That is, purely as an academic problem, understand? But an interesting one. And I've been thinking it wouldn't work. If he was down in the pit, and you were on the second floor, you'd be too exposed to view."

His yellow painted grin was wider than ever. "You been getting a dream-revenge, too?"

"Don't get me wrong," I replied seriously. "I think murder is wrong. But I am a rabid detective story reader. I'm interested in the fine art of murder—technically speaking."

"Don't you think the world'd be better off without a stupid selfish sourpuss like him?" Vogler asked, still grinning.

"It might be, but I'm no judge. Let's consider this as a problem. For instance, what's the best place around here to kill a man? I'd say the tunnels beneath the furnaces are because he's always prowling around them, hoping to catch somebody loafing. You could finish him off there and make it look like an accident."

Rugford, who'd been listening, said, "Man, don't you know *thou shalt not kill*? 'Tain't good even to make jokes about such things."

"Jimmy's an old devil, isn't he?" I asked. "What if you killed a devil? That's different than killing a human, isn't it? And you wouldn't call Jimmy a human, would you?"

Rugford looked thoughtful. "I don't know. I confess I ain't never forgiven him for what he called me. And when I think of it, I get mad enough to bash his head in, even if it is a sin. But how would you do it 'thout getting caught?"

"Here's how," I said, getting interested in the technical aspects and caught up in the thrill every man, no matter how law abiding, gets when he thinks of pitting his wits against the police.

"You know that when you clean out the tunnels under the checker-pockets of No. 3 furnace you throw the dust and broken bricks into an enclosure between the two pockets. The enclosure is on the basement floor. The debris is put into two large buckets and hoisted out by the charging-floor crane, three stories up. It drops its hook through two square holes in the second and ground floors. The hole on the charging floor is usually covered by an iron plate. But the hole on the main floor is open, though it has a railing around it to keep a man from falling through to the basement.

"That hole is way back in the shadows; you can't see anybody back there unless you're there yourself or flash a light into it. And the plate that's supposed to be over the hole is usually left propped up against the railing.

"I'd wait until Jimmy went down there to examine the tunnels. Then I'd walk off the job under the pretence of going to get a bit to eat at the tool shanty, where we leave our lunch buckets. I'd get a sandwich, stick it in my pocket so I'd have an alibi, and run back to the hole.

"I'd crouch down behind the big propped-up plate. Jimmy'd only take a couple of minutes to complete his inspection. When he came out of the tunnel, I'd have a little bucket full of broken bricks poised above his head. Down it'd come. End of Jimmy. And even if you missed he couldn't see you because you'd be in the darkness and he'd have to look past that bright light in the enclosure. Either way, hit or miss, I'd hurry back to my job.

"I'd return through that little corridor that runs behind the checkers, and I'd walk out when nobody was around. When I went back to my job, I'd be eating my sandwich, which would explain my absence. If done properly, I could have it all over in five minutes of less."

"Where'd you get the bucket?" asked Vogler. "You can't have everybody see you lugging it around."

"While we were working on No. 2, I'd hide that bucket behind the propped-up plate, using my work gloves all the time, of course. It'd be there waiting for you."

"What about your footprints in the dust around the hole?" asked Rugford.

"As soon as Jimmy's body would be found, there'd be a commotion. If he was found on my shift, I'd go up to the hole and look around. There'd be some of your buddies tagging along, and they'd make so many prints that the police'd have nothing to go on. Anyway, there's always any number of tracks around there during a repair."

Vogler grunted but said nothing, which was unusual. Rugford muttered that the Lord had said an eye for an eye and a tooth for a tooth but that had been in the Old Testament.

Jimmy shuffled up, brows working, his pale blue eyes stabbing through Rugford and me as if we didn't exist. "Come on, Vogler, let's roll. You won't make no money standin' around like this-s-s."

A few days later we finished No. 2 and went on to 3. Most of the time I was unloading bricks from the freight cars for the masons, so I saw little of Maharg. But one morning Moose sent me back to Jimmy's gang because two of his men hadn't showed up for work. I didn't object. I figured I could get along with him for the little while left for furnace repair. I walked down to the electricians' shanty in the south end of the building and found his gang just leaving it, having finished their nine o'clock "sandwich" break. Jimmy, they told me, was inspecting the tunnels. On hearing this I didn't have any flash of premonition, but I did wonder where Vogler was.

"Went upstairs to get a coke," said one man.

I forgot about his absence until a few minutes later when we started down the spiralling iron stairway into the enclosure. It was then that the leading man yelled, "There's Jimmy! He's hurt!"

I wasn't nearly as surprised as I should have been. I'd pictured his hypothetical murder too vividly while describing it to Vogler and Rugford that I'd retained a still-scene in my mind, a prophecy of the real thing.

Jimmy lay between the big five-foot-high buckets, flat on his back, his face upturned to the harsh glare of the naked bulb on the wall, the top of his head crushed in, the blood still wet, though forming a dark red-grey mud, being mixed with the steel dust. Not far from him lay his hat and a large bucket on its side, broken bricks spilled out in a frozen stream from it.

I stood around for a while, getting sicker and more trembly all the time, then went up to the opening from which, presumably, the bucket had dropped for sixteen feet before striking Jimmy's skull. There I found Vogler and Rugford among the crowd around the railing. This, too, followed my outline for murder, for any footprints left by the killer were now mixed up with a dozen other pairs.

The two didn't see me, for they were standing shoulder to shoulder, their heads turned towards each other. On their faces was an intent look, one of tightened lips and of narrowed eyes, out of which they glared at each other.

Their expressions said, did *you* do it?

Then, as if by command, their heads swivelled, and they looked across the open well of the enclosure, across the body of Jimmy twenty feet below, straight at me. And under the shock and focus of their accusing stare, I cringed for just a second and gripped the iron bar of the railing. Then, I suddenly realized that I had upon my face exactly the same look.

We made a pretty picture for one who could read us—a triangle as eternal as the other kind and one whose ties were even more binding. One of us was guilty. I knew I wasn't, not legally, anyway, though I might be morally. But one of the other two was wondering which of us had done it, and one of them knew but he was pretending to be suspicious. And at the bottom of our hearts we'd all wanted Jimmy to be dead. He was now, and he no longer counted. What did matter was that we must keep our mouths shut.

If we didn't, we'd all be in for a bad time; I, because I'd proposed the plan and dreaded the publicity and scorn I'd get if it were known; the murderer, for obvious reasons; the other, because he wasn't really concerned with justice and because he was glad Jimmy was dead. There was a web in which we were caught, and in that three-cornered look we vibrated the strings so that each understood the unspoken vow of silence.

The police came and began their questioning. They got no place. Thirty men could have committed the murder, and there was scarcely anybody who'd worked for Jimmy who hadn't had one or more violent quarrels with him. Rugford was grilled about his attempt to hit Jimmy with a shovel, but they had nothing definite to pin on him. Everybody had had access to the enclosure; everybody had had a few minutes in which to do the deed.

I sweated for a while, and I suppose I looked guilty when I talked to the sergeant. But so did many other men.

Afterwards, the three of us avoided each other as if we were unclean or lepers. Only when our work demanded it did we speak and then as briefly as possible. And when our glances unavoidably clashed, each had that curious stony cast of features which hid his wonderings or his pretended wonderings.

Time went by, and after a while I managed to lock Jimmy in a compartment of my mind. After I quit Helsget's, I could forget him entirely. That lasted for years until Rugford's drowning seemed to have jarred loose that drawer in which I kept the body of the old man with the crushed skull. As I said in the beginning, I've been seeing him again in my dreams. I'm writing this in the hope that his ghost will be banished once and for all, and so I may get a good look at what happened. I want to decide if I, too, in a way, held that bucket above his head and then dropped it.

The Good of the Land

The doctor had gone, taking his instruments of detection and bottles of power with him.

The President's wife readjusted the pillow behind his back so he could sit more comfortably in the wheelchair.

"Don't worry," she said. "The people love you."

"Loved," he said.

His once deep and resolute voice quavered. He raised a thinly fleshed hand to brush to one side the flap of hair which fell over his forehead. It was a gesture which had characterized him and at the same time endeared him to the people as being down to earth. Now, the salt and pepper hair was white, and the eyes which had once glared in denunciation of enemies or shone with such charm towards friends lacked either light. The eyes were sunken in the shadows of bony ridges and blue-black craters.

"Loved," he repeated, almost sobbing.

"The people still love you," said the President's secretary. But his eyes behind their thick lenses shifted away from the President's.

"How can they love me?" whispered the President. "I am sick, dying . . ."

"Please don't say that," said his wife. "Please, you're sick, yes. Dying, not at all. The doctor . . ."

"The doctor," said the President. "Didn't you see the doctor's face as he left? He was smiling, not because he could tell me I was going to get well, but because he had good news for the people waiting out in the street, standing by the fence, looking towards the White House, waiting for him to appear, to go into the death dance. The people will see him and they will be happy."

"No, no," said his wife. "That's not it at all. He smiled because he could tell the people that you were going to get well."

"Then why didn't he tell me so?"

"He did. He said that things would be much better in a very short time."

Suddenly, the President's wife gasped, and she paled. The President smiled grimly.

"There you are. He could have meant one of two things. And you know and I know what he meant. No. The people will not groan and weep because I am so loved. Love me? When I'm so sick? And the land is cursed? When millions are jobless and hungry? When storms roar across the land, burying whole cities and towns in snow and floods, levelling houses and trees, making millions homeless, destroying entire crops? When this mutated polio rides like the Fourth Horseman across the face of the country? When our enemies are threatening war and we must eat humble pie because they have superior weapons? When gloom and fear lie like a heavy blanket, stifling the breath of the people? No, they don't love me. I am sick and taking too long a time to die. If only I would die, now, so my successor, a young and healthy man . . ."

He stopped because he felt his wife's nails digging into his shoulder. He looked up at her face, contorted with grief, and said: "They're coming now? So soon?"

"Don't be afraid," said his secretary. "It is for the good of the land."

"I am not afraid," said the President. He straightened up, and his voice took on some of the resonance it had so long ago lost. "This is right and just and it is the law. The health of the nation is the health of its leader, and . . ."

The doors of his bedroom swung open. In strode the Chief Justice, the Speaker of the House, the head of the FBI and many important men of the Capitol and the reporters and the TV men, pushing their equipment in on soundless rubber-tyred wheels. Those who had been wearing hats had taken them off, and all looked respectfully, but determinedly, at him. Some were weeping.

The group split into two. The doctor came forth, dressed in his ritual white surgical gown, reflector on his head and stethoscope dangling from his ears, the little black bag in his hands. Quickly, knowing what he would find, he made the ceremonial diagnosis.

After the doctor had disappeared into the crowd, the Congressional chaplain stepped forward and prayed.

Then the group parted once more. This time, the Vice-President walked towards his chief. The Vice-President was a tall, well-built man of forty-five, with hair red and bright as the morning sun and with a face sharp and fierce as a hawk's. He stopped in front of the President and lifted his hands so that all could see what he held in them.

The President looked at what he held. Then he smiled into the glare of the lights and the round eyes of the cameras and the tear-filled eyes of the men watching him. He smiled to show them that, come what might, he had not after all lost his courage or belief in the will of the people.

The eyes of the Vice-President were brimming; nevertheless he intoned loudly and firmly: "As it was in the old days, so it is now. In the old days, when the king was sick, the land was sick, too, and the people were afflicted with many plagues and troubles. Then, a young and healthy prince was chosen to do what he must to make the land well again."

The Vice-President paused. He raised the long thin cord with its three ritually correct strands of red, white and blue.

"For the good of the land!"

The First Robot

by Jeannette Rastignac

Trarg was beating the woman again, and her screams rolled the tribe from its sleeping-bags. Ansha, crouching by a fire, said, "It is bad for Trarg to strike her. What if he cripples their unborn child?"

Ganag said, "Trarg would never hurt her so much she couldn't work for him."

Ansha replied, "Why beat her? She works hard; she bears healthy children. What more does he want?"

Ganag stammered, "She . . . she lives in the cave with Trarg. Nobody else can live there unless he says so. He allows her to live there and gives her protection and food. She is . . . is . . ."

His hands waved, his fingers clutching as if he were kneading the air into new but known shapes. Almost, the word for property was born.

"She does all a good mate should do," Ansha answered. "Does she beat him?"

Ganag laughed. "Her? She is too small."

"Lusha is small, but she beats her mate."

"That is because he's a lazy hunter, and they often go hungry."

"He could beat Lusha in return."

"He knows he deserves her blows."

"But Trarg's woman deserves a caress, not a club." Ganag shrugged. "I don't understand."

"Neither do I, but I don't like it. What if all the men, well . . ."

They quit talking. Trarg had appeared in the narrow opening of his cave. He was a man who commanded silence, for he was tall and lean and had a thin nose curved like a sabertooth's claw and green eyes in which calculation burned coldly.

Without pausing for greetings, he walked into the forest, his flint-tipped spear in hand. He had a long day ahead; a man had to use all his strength and wit to bring in enough to fill today's mouths and store a little for tomorrow's. When winter came, the smoked strips of meat hanging from the cave-roof would be very much appreciated.

Trarg roamed until noon, empty-handed. Then he heard a low rumble which erected the hairs on the back of his neck— lightning rods spurting the lightning of fear. Nevertheless, he walked softly toward the noise. Meat wasn't caught by running away from it.

The scene he came upon thrilled his hunter's heart. A bear had stuck his head into a hole in a hollow tree and could not get it out. Trarg wondered why the shaggy eccentric hadn't scooped out the honey with his paw, but he didn't stop to do his thinking. Swiftly, he severed its spine with a spearthrust, then skinned it and hacked off a leg and cut out the heart, liver, and kidneys. While doing this, he paused. Why not watch this tree and catch other honey-stealers unawares? But a moment's reflection convinced him that nobody could be spared just to stand around and watch. And even if a child were posted, he'd need a man to guard him from the big cats and bears.

He resumed cutting. A minute later, he stopped again. Out of the clouds roiling in his brain had appeared a bright and solid picture. He'd once seen a pony run into a liana thicket and strangle itself to death. Now, if you were to fashion a noose . . . Thus . . . and set it on a game path so an animal's head entered the hidden ring, as the bear's had the hole in the tree, and if that noose could be set so that no matter how the creature struggled, the liana didn't come loose but tightened more and more . . .

On the way home, his green eyes swam, hot and moist as the drippings from the fat meat he envisioned. Not just one trap could be built. Many. Many. And they'd all be working for him like the woman in his cave while he was out hunting.

Head thrown back, chest swelling, he walked back to the cliff-side, dumped the load of meat wrapped in the bearskin on the floor, and told his woman to get to work. Busy washing her baby, she did not do at once what he ordered. He struck her. She snarled at him, and he hit her again.

Silently, she covered the baby with a fur and began working. He helped her. His hands did their required duties, but his mind was only partly connected with them.

A big rock or a heavy log could crush a bear or a lion. What if you balanced a boulder so delicately that just touching a small stick connected to its base would cause it to fall. The beast would bite down on meat tied to the stick; the rock would fall . . .

"Trarg!" said the woman.

"Shut up! I'm thinking!"

"But—"

He slapped her across the mouth, and she froze with terror, her lips bleeding.

"You must learn not to interrupt me," he said. "You're a woman; you're weaker; your place is obedience. I am the man, the planner, the strong. I will feed and protect you and our children, and you must do everything I say. Understand?"

"I'll go back to my parents," she muttered.

"They can not help you!" he blazed. "They are old and feeble!" And he struck her on the jaw but not hard enough to injure the child in her womb. She held her face and moaned, her eyes dull. Then, slowly, her shoulders sagging as if they'd never lift again, she picked up one end of the bearhide. Thereafter, she never spoke to him except to reply to direct questions. And when they lay down to sleep that night, she was a tongueless statue, her back turned, allowing him to talk without interruption.

He felt vaguely dissatisfied, but he didn't long think about it. He planned just how he'd build this thing that would work for him while he was not there to watch it. His heart beat faster at the vision; it did to him what his woman could not.

Next morning, he told her he'd be gone most of the day, and he gave her detailed instructions about the work she was to do. Though it was enough to keep two women running all day, she did not argue.

A little later, Trarg talked to Lusha's mate, the lazy one. That man then told Lusha he'd have no more of her backtalk and beatings. Afterwards, though he had to work himself into a screaming fury before he could do so, he struck her with his fists until she could not stand up.

Trarg grinned at her outcries and at the uneasy look in the women's eyes. They, like him, could see the beginnings of a new age. Then he strode into the forest and picked a spot on a game-path for his noose-trap. When dusk came, he was finished. Proud with what his male hand and brain had done, he picked up axe and knife and left the world's second robot behind him.

At home, inside the cave, moving efficiently but mechanically, operating upon preset instructions, devoid of the spark of love and hope, was the first.

THE PRINCESS OF TERRA

BY CHARLOTTE CORDAY-MARAT

Editor's note: The following is extracted from the book-review section of the Martian science-fiction and fact magazine, *Parallel*, formerly *Supersincere Science Stickler Stories* and still referred to by fandom as the Big S. The review was written by the prominent SF author and critic, Remlil Esspee, and was published in Vol. 69, dated (Martian style) *Day of the Devout Data Digger, Week of the Witching Wands, Month of the Muttering Mountebank, Year of the Yearning Yo-Yo, Cycle of the Psionic Seersucker.*

H ere we have a reprint of another book by a writer once regarded as a master of science-fiction, Erb of Anazrat. *The Princess of Terra* was the first of a series written about the third planet from the sun and needs no introduction for those who read the original when it appeared fifty-one years ago. But, for the third generation of readers, who may never have heard of Erb of Anazrat or may know him only through the movies based on his character Nazrat of Sepa, the story must be reviewed.

The novel begins over a hundred years ago, shortly after the end of The War Between The Estates. The hero, Noj Notrak, is an ex-officer of the gallant but defeated Short Stick Army. While prospecting for gold in the Great South and Sandy Wastes, he is forced to run for his life from a band of wild Painted Bottoms (pretty wild in those days but now mainly concerned with operating resort areas).

He takes refuge in a cave. There, he is put under a spell by an old witch of the Painted Bottoms. Through the spell or some means (Erb is vague about this), Noj Notrak, or his astral body, or something, is released from his corpse. He soars through space and lands on the surface of Terra, the native name for the planet we call Gongoos. Notrak has a very strong affinity for this world, the pagan god of war, and it is this affinity that attracts him like a nail to a magnet.

Presumably, on this principle, if Notrak had been a great lover instead of a great warrior, he would have gone to the second planet from the sun. Notrak, however, is rather shy with women and only feels at ease when impaling somebody on his trusty and never rusty blade (a phallic substitute?).

Why Erb chose this method of transporting his hero to Gongoos, or Terra, is a matter of speculation, if not of extreme wonder. Fifty-one years ago, it would have been scientifically valid to extrapolate interplanetary rockets. However, to be fair, rockets were not feasible in the period in which this story takes place. Perhaps, Erb was justified in using the unorthodox, even mystical, method of transportation. If it is considered as a form of teleportation, it even becomes credible. After all, many SF people, including the editor of this magazine, believe in this and other types of ESP.

Anyway, Erb wanted to get his hero quickly and without too much fuss to the third planet, and he certainly did that.

The reader who swallows the astral-corporeal method of space travel has only begun to choke. Erb paints a picture of a world based on the insufficient and sometimes incorrect data of his day. For one thing, though he correctly assumes a denser atmosphere for Gongoos than for that of our planet, he does not make the air as thick as scientists now know it to be. Actually, the gases are so heavy that beings with lungs just simply could not operate them efficiently enough to maintain life.

Erb also assumes vegetation, which probably does exist on

Gongoos, but his vegetation has an incredible variety and abundance. Given the known conditions of extreme humidity and heat, only a very primitive and hardy type of flora (such as our own ubiquitous ancient sea-bottom moss) could live. Fauna, if any, would be limited to the colder polar regions.

But Erb is only out to tell a rousing good tale and to exercise the imaginations of his readers. This he does, although the present generation, accustomed to the modern "staccato" school of writing founded by Yawgnimmeh, will find Erb's style rather old fashioned, and, indeed, bad. It is far inferior to the splendid literary offerings of the authors you read every month in *Parallel*. (Note especially the current serial, *Errand of Levity*, by Lah Tnemelk.)

Noj Notrak finds that he must move slowly and with some effort because of the great gravity of Terra. This is, however, no real handicap. Terran beings, though fast, are very lightly constructed and fragile. They have to be so in order to move at all against the gravity and heavy air. Attacked by a large beast of prey (four-legged!), the sturdy Notrak smashed it with his fist. The beast's porous muscles and hollow bones crumple at the first impact.

However, Notrak is taken prisoner by a tribe of black men with only two arms when they overcome him by sheer numbers. In an effort to be colorful, Erb ignored, or was ignorant of, the fact that beings with heavily pigmented skin just could not survive on Terra. The intensity of the sun would cause a very dark skin to absorb so much radiant energy that the internal temperature of a body would be raised to a fatal level.

Be that as it may, Noj Notrak is taken to the camp of the black nomads (who ride a beast called *nag*, also four-legged). There he finds a fellow prisoner, a beautiful woman called Siroth Hajed. She resembles us Martians, but she is pink-skinned and belongs to a species that bears its young alive. Despite her eggless method of reproduction (disgusting if you think about it long enough but only lightly touched on in Erb's narrative), she is soon loved by Notrak.

Siroth Hajed is a princess of Ingillan, a country entirely surrounded by water. (The astronomers of our planet designate Erb's Ingillan as Maraba, after the ancient stargazer who first saw it during one of those rare moments when its cloud cover dissipated.) She was captured by the blacks when the flying vehicle on which she was a passenger was forced to land because of engine trouble.

The vehicle does not use lighter-than-air gas. It depends on lift from extended surfaces and is driven forward by propellers turned by engines of great power. While it is true that the dense air of Gongoos, or Terra, would provide greater support than ours, it is also true that the energy required to force such a craft through the very dense air would make this method of flight mechanically and economically unfeasible.

Notrak and Hajed escape from the black men. Several chapters are then devoted to their ordeals on the surface of the vast expanse of waters on Terra's surface. Erb describes these as being of great depth. (Scientists have evidence that they cannot be more than neckdeep.) The waters swarm with huge ferocious creatures which not only live in but *breathe* the water. He does not bother to explain the biological mechanisms that would make this possible. Perhaps, this is for the better, since there is enough to strain the reader's sense of credulity without adding this.

There is, however, a very good scene (considering Erb's prose) about the terror that Notrak feels when he is suspended in a watercraft over this abyss of liquid. Every reader will respond as Erb intended, but Erb could hardly fail with such a horrible idea.

The two finally get to London. (Perhaps, Erb chose the name of a gas as the nomenclature of a city because the element London had just been discovered in his day and was being used in dirigibles.) It is interesting to note Erb's explanation for the large splotches of light seen by our astronomers on the third planet's night surface. Notrak finds that the cities are so large and so well illuminated that their light is visible even to us.

At one time, this was a popular speculation not easily refuted. However, in the past twenty years, we have developed instruments able to detect radioactivity at a distance of over 40 million miles. In view of the sporadically high radioactivity emanating from Gongoos (Terra), it is very likely that the many glows of light are heavy concentrations of radium or similar materials spilled out onto the surface by volcanic eruptions. This, in itself, would make a profusion of animal life very improbable.

Aside from the above objection, the proximity of cities such as London to so much water would overstimulate the growth of fungus and other vegetable life. The cities would be buried under the plants.

The Londoners have no such problem. Instead, they are on the verge of defeat in their war with the sinister Hoons of Jirmani. Led by Notrak, who slays the leader of the Hoons, the Kighzar, the Ingillaners defeat and invade Jirmani. Notrak then marries Siroth Hajed.

Suddenly, the air becomes too thick. People begin to die of oxygen richness. The whole planet is doomed. Notrak, however, during one of his adventures, found the secret entrance to the supposedly impregnable air-burning plant of Terra. This building has been built as a joint effort by all nations to oxidize part of the atmosphere. If it were not for this measure, the atmosphere would become fatally dense. Now the operator of the oxidizing plant has gone mad and turned off the equipment. Notrak gets into the building, kills the insane operator, and turns the air-burners back on.

Terra is saved, but it is too late for Noj Notrak. He dies and is hurled through space and finds himself in his original body (uncorrupted) in the cave on our planet. However, those who care to do so may read the sequels, *The Gods of Terra* and *The Warlord of Terra*, and discover how Notrak gets back to the third planet and wins his beauteous pink-skinned princess.

I fear that only those of my own generation who read Erb in their boyhood and want to experience a nostalgia, or those too young to have read much modern science-fiction or to know much of modern science, or the incurable romantics, will want to own these reprints.

That Great Spanish Author, Ernesto

The captain told me that the loading of the bananas would be finished in thirty minutes. I had time for several drinks and some more conversation with Sancho. Why waste it here? I left the ship and walked up *La Avenida del Conquistador Blanco*, a street which does not deserve its magnificent name at its waterfront end. Along both sides are mean adobe ranchos and bleached wooden huts on stilts and many black *zopilotes* with silver-tipped wings. As the big birds swing upwind from you, they radiate the stink of sun-rotten garbage.

Sancho's is a cleaner *posada* than you would expect from the neighborhood. There you can get cold drinks and entertainment by rubbing elbows and buttocks with tourists and representatives of every social stratum in Ticimarra, capital city of Huitzil.

Since it was mid-morning, there were only three in the place. Sancho, behind the bar, and two women at a corner table. Sancho smiled at me with a touching sincerity and joy. When he bobbed his head, his family of four chins, the two parents, the adolescent and the embryo, bobbed in unison.

"Buenos días, Sancho,"

"Don Felipe!" said Sancho in Huitzilian Spanish, the only

tongue he could speak well. "How goes it with the bananas and with you?"

That was our private joke. I replied, as always, "The bananas ripen. I ripen. Soon, we rot. Then, we stink. All goes well; all goes as it should."

For some reason, he always laughed.

One of the women left her table and walked towards me. I said to Sancho, "Still out of Scotch?"

He shook his chins. "Just out. I am always just out of Scotch. But if you can't make up your mind what else to drink, the simple thing to do is to take the next best thing, Mexican beer."

He talked much of the simple thing. Sancho himself is a simple. Simple does not have the meaning in the Central American nation of Huitzil that it has in the United States. In Huitzil, a simple is not an imbecile. He is one who looks at life with such simplicity that the complexities drop off like a leper's flesh, and the simple bones are seen. The simile, Sancho's, is gruesome, but it fits. Life walks on bones. Flesh is needed but not rotten flesh. Get rid of the rotten. Better yet, see the bones first, and then you will understand the flesh.

The philosophy of the simple takes some time to understand and more to practice. Most people find it too painful to pare away the rotten flesh.

The Mexican beer was too sweet and heavy, but it was cold, and that was what I wanted.

The woman, María, sat down on a stool by me.

"Buenos días, Don Felipe."

The title of don was mercenary flattery, but it pleased. It deserved a drink. Sancho set out her rum. And the other woman, a peroxide blonde also named María, walked over.

The dark María turned swiftly.

"Take thy greediness elsewhere."

The blonde María said, "Thy greediness! It was my turn!"

It seemed there was a violation of ethics.

"It was not thy turn. It was mine."

"Puta!"

"Ramera!"

"Aborticidia!"

"Onanista!"

They seemed ready to pull out the knives from their stockings. Sancho did not like that. Blood so early in the morning would upset his customers. He considered the simple thing to do. Either buy them a drink or throw them out. I thought it cheaper to throw them out. Sancho agreed. They knew better than to talk back; they got out.

I said, "For a moment, I thought I was going to see a scene à la Hemingway."

Sancho's heavy lids fluttered up like a window-shade.

"Hemingway? Ernesto Hemingway? The great Spanish author?"

I coughed up beer.

Sancho said, "Ah, Don Felipe, it is true that I read only the newspaper. But once a Yankee traveling book-salesman to whom I had given too much credit, may God forgive me for that, and who had run up a great liquor bill, parted with his private collection of Hemingway as payment for half of his bill. When he surrendered the books to me, he wept. It was true that he was given to weeping, especially late at night. But I thought that if this author could wring such tears, he must be worth reading. And, truly, he was."

"You mean the Ernesto who was born in Oak Park and who wrote stories based on his boyhood days in Michigan?"

"Michigan? I believe the foreword in that highly technical and philosophical book on bull-fighting—you have read it?— mentioned some such place. I thought it was a Basque town because his name sounds Basque or, perhaps, it was another spelling for the Mexican state of Michoacan. Which is it?"

"His name is not Basque. He was born in North America. Give me another beer."

"So, he is Mexican, even if he did love the country from which his ancestors came more than his native land. Ah, the next time I visit Mexico, I would like to make a pilgrimage to his native town. Is it remote?"

"It is remote."

"Too bad. Perhaps, some day, I will have the time and the means to go there. But this Ernesto is magnificent. You have read him in Spanish? No? In English, then. You should read him in the pure Castilian, a language not corrupted by Americanisms. I imagine he loses potency in translation. Spanish is the language for power and grace and beauty.

"Ah, Don Felipe, I loved all his books. The one of the technicalities and philosophy of bull-fighting. The novel of the drunken castrado. The tragedy of the Yankee who kissed war goodbye forever. The novel of the rum-runner. That great romance of the lovers and the bridge in the Spanish Civil War. And the one about the old fisherman and his big fish. All I loved and wept over.

"To me, they are almost faultless. Indeed, I have but one criticism. Too many of his characters are not Spanish, or of that descent, but are Yankees."

"That is the fault of many young writers," I ventured. "They love to idealize their heroes. And, since they know their countrymen too well to idealize them, they make their heroes foreigners."

"That is well said. I can see that now. And when Ernesto matured and rid himself of his youthful romanticism and became a realistic writer, he dropped the impossible foreign heroes. He wrote in his old age only of his great and glorious ancestors and of his ancestral country.

"I refer, of course, to that mighty work: *Don Quixote*."

I choked the grandfather of all chokes. Sancho shook his chins.

"The beer is not of the quality it used to be. Ah, yes, Don Felipe, when I read that of the old fisherman and the sea, I knew that Ernesto was destined to write what he should have been writing. But I did not think that he would ever surpass himself, that he had started too late. It seemed to me he must have poured out all the mighty juice of his life into those books. I thought the last would be a repetition of the others. And the others were so great it would be a—a—"

"Anti-climax?"

"Gracias. But I was wrong. The last was the best. *Don Quixote* was so magnificent, so truly Spanish, that the others seemed the work of an apprentice author."

"Pardon me. You said one of the books had a foreword about Ernesto. Did *Don Quixote* also have a foreword saying anything about the author?"

"There was none. The Yankee salesman had cheated me with a damaged copy. The cover, the back, the title page and the foreword were torn out. It is nothing. I am content."

A customer came in. Sancho served him and returned.

"Quixote's servant had my Christian name. A trifle flattering, no?"

I nodded.

He said, "Sancho Panza, like me, was a simple."

I said, "I thought Don Quixote was the simple."

Sancho's eyes twinkled.

"In the Yankee sense that he was somewhat of a fool, though like all Spaniards, fearless, yes. In the Huitzilian sense, no. Some day the word simple and the philosophy simple as we mean it, kindly and uncomplex and unselfish, will spread to the north. And then Huitzil will have the credit for civilizing North America, yes?"

I choked. Sympathetically, Sancho's chins shook. I recovered and looked at my wristwatch.

"The bananas will almost be loaded."

"Vaya con Dios," said Sancho. "I will see you on your next trip."

"If God wills."

I laid down four quarter-huitzils, three for drinks, one for Sancho's conversation, and walked off. Sancho followed me to the door.

He said, "I cannot recommend too much that you read *Don Quixote* again. This time, in Spanish, the tongue it was written in, the only tongue strong enough to bear up under Ernesto's power. And remember, when you read, that that great author has, I am sure, portrayed himself in the character of Sancho Panza. Panza is a simple. Ernesto, too, is a simple. You agree?"

"I understand that he has striven all his life for simplicity," I replied cautiously. "But I think that Ernesto was also Don

Quixote. He had a bravery that Panza lacked. But the good Don was also one of the brave ones."

"Perhaps you are right," said Sancho. "Yes, I know you are! What insight you have, Don Felipe! Ah, the great old knight!"

And tears flowed down his bulging cheeks.

I studied Sancho, wondering. Then, knowing he would hear, sooner or later, I said, "Ernesto is very ill. He had left Cuba and gone to Idaho."

"Aydajo? Where is that?"

"In the United States," I said. "He has a home there because it reminds him of Spain."

"That makes me sad," said Sancho. "But I am sure that he will face la muerte as fearlessly as all his heroes, especially Don Quixote, did."

"He will not shrink," I said. "He will do the simple thing."

For one second, I thought of presenting Sancho with his own moment of truth. Then, cowardly but perhaps wisely, I closed my lips. If he was happy, and he was, why should he not stay happy? Let the drunken joke of a drunken salesman live. I wanted to remain Sancho's friend. Not from me would come any shattering revelation.

I walked away, but before I had gone far, I turned for one more look back up the street. Sancho, standing in the doorway, waved. His family of chins waved. I waved and turned away and wondered if the twinkling in his eyes was his general good nature or something deeper. Also, I wondered which one of us was the simple.

In the Yankee sense, of course.

The Terminalization of J. G. Ballard

Considered as a Fall Off a Barstool
Or
Why I Want To Dick Dick

In and Out of the Last Chance Saloon

VECTOR PRODUCT: A vector c the length of which is the product of the lengths of two vectors a and b and the sine of their included angle, the direction of which is perpendicular to their plane and the sense of which is that of a right-handed screw with axis c when a is rotated into b. Ballard's sense was that of a left-handed screw, which accounted in the best scientific manner for his backward toppling from the barstool. Prior claims must be awarded, however, to the weight of the crumpled Cadillac radiator grille projecting from his anus. This tended to exert a simultaneous downward and counter-clockwise force which he vainly compensated for by a tight grasp on a bottle of beer.

SQUEEZING PSEUDOREALITY: Another tenuous hold on the world of angles, icons, and imaginary sexual perversions was the rectal face of U.S.A. President Dick flickering on the misshapen TV set over the bar. Explaining why. Everybody had been watching him intently, which was why Ballard came in unnoticed, limping, trailing the radiator grille and part of a licentious plate. Nor did they observe him extracting a spark plug from his ear.

A BIPSYCHO BUILT FOR DUE: Bartender/proprietor Al Jarry was a Frenchman. He wore a huge crucifix on a chain around his neck. On the mirror behind him was pasted a blowup of Jarry on a bicycle, leading the race uphill. He slid a beer down the counter to Ballard, giving him at the same time a peculiar isosceles look. Ballard read the coded glance as easily as if it had been a linear declaration of the intrapatellar distance of Minnie Schwartz, meter maid well known in this neighborhood. "Put it on the bill," Ballard murmured, looking at the Frenchman through the glass and its liquid contents, yellow like the sands of a final beach suspended in offshore water. The President's face opened in a smile as meaningless as an erased tape, as mechanical and joyless as the squeezing of a hand-operated rubber anus. Jarry rang up *No Sale* on the cash register.

THE TROPIC OF DESCENT: Thrown off balance by the removal of the glass, he began toppling backward and slightly to the left. Haven't I done this before? he asked himself. As usual, no reply, linear or curved. He felt a definite sense of inverse sexuality or perhaps it was obverse. Converse? Whatever the configurations of desire, the heavy grille was making him play Humpty Dumpty. In a corner an old man quit sipping his absinthe to cry a bon voyage. He was Hank Miller, whom Ballard owed more than any though hardly anyone knew it.

THE FREE LUNCH IS NAKED: "Happy landing!" shouted Bill Burroughs, looking up from the soft eggs hard-boiled in booze, potato salad mixed with mayonnaise of pederasty, pastrami sandwiches imported from nostalgia of old St. Louis (wouldn't you?), and morphine-sprinkled pretzels. Ballard had let old Bill stand for many a drink, but old Bill didn't care. Not as long as he could look at his right toe.

SIGN LANGUAGE FOR THE BLIND: His eyes were splintered, like smashed-in headlamps. The President's smile was a half-unzipped fly on an old pair of trousers. The open skylight showed him a balloon floating beneath a pale-ale moon, towing on a banner the gigantic face of Rosie Schmidt, down with terminal flatulence in the hospital around the corner.

WHY I WANT TO HUMP HUMP, TOO: Even in his rapid too-linear descent, during which he could not avoid the unavoidable images of Humpty Dumpty, Hubert Humphrey, and Humphry C. Earwicker, he had presence of mind enough to remove his pocket calculator. As his body arced back, he click-clicked estimates, castanets in the ears of science. The President's facial contortions were causing sexual-death wish fantasies among 86.2% of the tavern's patrons. Eleven percent of this regressive post-drip tendency was generated by visual reaction to the President's tiny yellow crooked teeth, incorrectly added digits in a sum of no-confidence. They had no business being there. Not even in the face of a used-car dealer or operator of a third-rate junkyard.

COLLISION OF SHADE AND LIGHT: The flickering from the TV set formed bizarre runes on the wall, notes in an unknown tongue voiced by mad syphilitic seers of a lost race, the shavings from a psychosomatic totempole. Others were fractured profiles of Janie Jones and Mary Brown, two friendly neighborhood whores. The lamppost under which they stood cut a line at exactly ninety degrees to the horizontal of the street surface. This line, in turn, went asymptotically around the earth, which is definitely pear-shaped at times. It all meant something, but the Roman letters of the code looked Arabic at this speed of descent.

THE CELTIC BULL, R.C. & W.C. SPECIALIST: "Go it, Sassenach!" Jim "Weak Eeyes" Joyce yelled. Ballard waved at him. He owed the defrocked priest (or was it prefrocked?) much, too. But his grief at not being able to repay him did not overcome his cool scientific detachment, which enabled him to estimate that 12% of the Irishman's death wish was the square root of the length of his (Ballard's) sideburns.

THE ACME PLUMBING COMPANY: The Spanish plumber, Sal Dali, and his Greek senior partner, Euclid, looked up from the disemboweled grandfather clock cum commode. Dali had pulled the works out of shape; Euclid was trying to straighten their corners. They'd bought many a drink for the English kid, and now it looked as if they'd never get paid back.

LOST IN THE CASTLE: Frankie Kafka woke up under a table. His head hurt as if a Rolls Royce had run over it. The throbbing of blood in his temples reminded him that quasars, too, pulsed in distant space. Where was he? Who was he? Why was he? Who had bought the last drink? He frowned. Ontogeny recapitulates a fill of gin, he . . . Ballard flashed by, the end of the crumpled grille dug into the wooden floor, acting like a vaulter's pole, Ballard being vaulted, and then the violent parting of man and grille sounding like the popping of a plumber's helper when lifted from the drain of a stopped-up sink. A man opened the door in time to let Ballard fly past him into the street. Frankie heard the screech of brakes and tyres, smelled the burning fiberglass, napalmed by friction, conceptualized the skidmarks as parallel lines which formed an absurd geometry with the spheres of the victim's buttocks, felt the smash and rumble, like a bowel movement, as vibrations ran through the earth and up the floor from the collision of light pole and car. Frankie shuddered and wished that he was a cockroach.

LOCUS TOCUS: Ballard staggered back in. He presented the optimum injury profile. Part of that profile was the bonnet ornament from a classic model 1932 Pontiac sticking out from between his buttocks. The patrons were later interviewed by psychometrists from General Motors. Asked to name their most unforgettable traffic accident, 95% unhesitatingly chose Ballard. "You can't drive out of the parking lot without running over him," old Hank Miller said, "He's definitely autopolymorphous perverse. We'll never see his like again."

THE BANALITY OF ANALITY: The only dissenter was Al Jarry. "The motorcar, it is for queers. Now you take the bicycle. That's a real man's weapon." Tests under extreme laboratory conditions proved that Jarry attained a proximal erection only at Golgotha. Case dismissed.

POST-IMPACT TRISTE: Ballard staggered in a stylized mode of *angst* towards the bar, causing 30.286% of the patrons to conceptualize blind cae(cums?)(ci?). The mouthparts of the President rearranged to form the breaking-apart of a jet-propelled Chevy composed of prepuces and vaginas. The third prepuce from the left remarkably resembled the face of Jerry Williams, janitor for the apartment building across the street and reformed Southern Baptist.

THE GEOMETRY OF ACCIDENCE: Not without pain which recalled the crash of tropical surf on brown beaches, the swift unrolling of toilet paper in the dead of night, the beauty of the sesquipedalian adjective *pseudoepiphenomenological*, Ballard clambered back onto the stool. The mirror behind the bar reflected his face, a pileup of angles at the entrance to the on-ramp of parturition.

ONE FOR THE ROAD: "Drink up, and get out," the bartender said. "Find some other place. And for God's sake find something else to amuse you besides traffic accidents." "Cancer?" Ballard said, but Jarry was giving good advice. If he didn't get out soon, he'd be trapped in the unyielding conjunctions of the terminal tavern with the dying and the dead. Going forever around and around in the Piccadilly Circus of stale repetition instead of speeding on the highway of the great open spaces where every road was a new one and there were no circles. "I'll go," he said, "but I want to make it clear that though I owe you all a great deal, I have acknowledged my debt. And I am my own model, not just a modification of last year. Right, fellows?" "Right," they said. "Good luck, kid." Satisfied, Ballard staggered out, the metallic head of Chief Pontiac wagging a final farewell to the habitues. He headed wrong way on a one-way street, ecstatic from the traffic noises, notes from that inevitable opera, *The Marriage of Ford and Freud.*

The Light-Hog Incident

An excerpt from an unpublished semi-autobiographical
novel titled *The Man Who Loved the Great Wizard*

H e hadn't been able to sleep. He lay there thinking while
Barbara snored gently, and soon he had an idea for a story.
It would be novelette length, say about 15,000 words, and he
could sell it to Stanley S. McDonald, the great editor of *Striking
Science-Fiction Stories Magazine*. McDonald paid three cents a
word, and at 15,000 words—hell, make it 20,000—that would be
six hundred dollars. McDonald should like the story very much,
provided he never caught onto the basic premise.

The story would be called "The Light-Hog Incident." Our
hero, Hilary Boone, is captain of a space liner which is attacked in
interstellar space by a horde of strange creatures, gigantic, barrel-
shaped, mouthless, noseless, earless, and eyeless. These beasts,
called light-hogs, actually inhabit outer space. They are adapted to
live, thrive, and move in the near-vacuum and near absolute zero
of the space between the stars. They don't breathe air or eat, of
course. They get all their energy by browsing on light as they
move over the three-dimensional meadows of space. They absorb
light—or any radiant energy—and the chemistry of their internal
organs converts the absorbed photons into hydrogen atoms. (He'd
have to work the chemistry out in a scientific, though not too

specific, detail. That would be a pleasing intellectual challenge. And it would please McDonald, too, who always liked his stories to be based on scientific fact.)

The herd of beasts would excrete the hydrogen atoms to get rid of them, both as refuse and as energy to propel themselves through space.

The herd of beasts would have been attracted by the spaceship's emission of energy from its atomic-powered jets, and the hogs would suck all the electrical and atomic power right out of the ship. Next, they'll suck the energy out of the crew and passengers, if they can get to them. But Hilary Boone saves the day, of course, and this gives the optimistic ending that McDonald insists on.

But the kicker was that Boone discovers that the light-hogs are in fact, responsible for the existence of galaxies or, indeed, for all matter in the universe. They take in light and excrete hydrogen atoms. And, as everybody knows—well, practically everybody—the continuous creation theory maintains that hydrogen atoms are, somehow, produced continuously in space from some unknown mechanism. These individual hydrogen atoms eventually fall together, form molecules, attract even more atoms, and after eons form cosmic clouds of dust or clouds of cosmic dust.

Out of these truly mind-staggering nebulae, suns and their planets and other phenomena form. The pressure of matter in objects of a large enough size cause fission and then fusion. Suns, stars, are born, and planets also form out of the accumulation of gases. The hydrogen atoms, the basic building blocks of the universe, begin to form complex elements, helium, iron, and so forth.

Half-asleep, he had chuckled so loudly that Barbara had jerked in her sleep and muttered something crossly.

The unstated premise of the story was that the universe was created from hog shit.

BIBLIOGRAPHY

COMPILED BY ZACHARIAS L.A. NUNINGA

The following bibliography lists first printings of books and first appearances of shorter works, plus any revised or expanded versions, in chronological order. Unless otherwise noted all entries are US editions.

NOVELS

The Green Odyssey, Ballantine Books, HC, 1957
Flesh, Beacon Books, PB, 1960; Doubleday, HC, 1968 (revised)
A Woman a Day, Beacon Books, PB, 1960; Lancer Books, PB,
    1968 (retitled **The Day of Timestop**); Lancer Books, PB,
    1970 (retitled **Timestop!**)
The Lovers, Ballantine Books, PB, 1961; Ballantine/Del Rey,
    HC, 1979 (revised)
Cache from Outer Space, Ace Books, PB, 1962
Fire and the Night, Regency Books, PB, 1962
Inside Outside, Ballantine Books, PB, 1964
Tongues of the Moon, Pyramid Books, PB, 1964
Dare, Ballantine Books, PB, 1965
The Maker of Universes, Ace Books, PB, 1965
Night of Light, Berkley Books, PB, 1966

The Gate of Time, Belmont Books, PB, 1966; Ace Books, PB, 1979 (revised/expanded as **Two Hawks from Earth**)

The Gates of Creation, Ace Books, PB, 1966

A Private Cosmos, Ace Books, PB, 1968

The Image of the Beast, Essex House, PB, 1968

A Feast Unknown, Essex House, PB, 1969

Blown, Essex House, PB, 1969

Lord Tyger, Doubleday, HC, 1970

Behind the Walls of Terra, Ace Books, PB, 1970

Lord of the Trees, Ace Books, PB, 1970

The Mad Goblin, Ace Books, PB, 1970

The Stone God Awakens, Ace Books, PB, 1970

Love Song, Brandon House, PB, 1970

To Your Scattered Bodies Go, Putnam, HC, 1971

The Fabulous Riverboat, Putnam, HC, 1971

The Wind Whales of Ishmael, Ace Books, PB, 1971

Time's Last Gift, Ballantine Books, PB, 1972; Ballantine Books, PB, 1977 (expanded)

The Other Log of Phileas Fogg, DAW Books, PB, 1973

Traitor to the Living, Ballantine Books, PB, 1973

Hadon of Ancient Opar, DAW Books, PB, 1974

The Adventure of the Peerless Peer, Aspen Press, HC, 1974

Venus on the Half-Shell (as by Kilgore Trout), Dell, PB, 1975

Ironcastle, (with J. H. Rosny), DAW Books, PB, 1976

Flight to Opar, DAW Books, PB, 1976; Meteor House, HC, 2015 (expanded)

The Dark Design, Berkley/Putnam, HC, 1977

The Lavalite World, Ace Books, PB, 1977

Jesus on Mars, Pinnacle Books, PB, 1979

Dark Is the Sun, Ballantine/Del Rey, HC, 1979

The Magic Labyrinth, Berkley/Putnam, HC, 1980

The Unreasoning Mask, Putnam, HC, 1981

Stations of the Nightmare, Tor Books, PB, 1982

Greatheart Silver, Tor Books, PB, 1982

A Barnstormer in Oz, Phantasia Press, HC, 1982

The Gods of Riverworld, Phantasia Press, HC, 1983

River of Eternity, Phantasia Press, HC, 1983
Dayworld, Putnam, HC, 1985
Dayworld Rebel, Ace/Putnam, HC, 1987
Dayworld Breakup, Tor Books, HC, 1990
Escape from Loki, Bantam Falcon, PB, 1991
Red Orc's Rage, Tor Books, HC, 1991
The Caterpillar's Question, (with Piers Anthony) Ace Books, HC, 1992
More than Fire, Tor Books, HC, 1993
Nothing Burns in Hell, Forge, HC, 1998
Naked Came the Farmer, (round robin with twelve other authors) Mayfly, TPB, 1998
The Dark Heart of Time, Ballantine/Del Rey, PB, 1999; Meteor House, 2018, HC (retitled Tarzan and the Dark Heart of Time)
Up from the Bottomless Pit, (Published in a collection, see under), Subterranean Press, HC, 2007
The City Beyond Play, (with Danny Adams) PS Publishing, HC, 2007
The Evil in Pemberley House, (with Win Scott Eckert) Subterranean Press, HC, 2009
The Song of Kwasin, (with Christopher Paul Carey) in Gods of Opar: Tales of Lost Khokarsa (omnibus), Subterranean Press, HC, 2012
Dayworld: A Hole in Wednesday (with Danny Adams) Meteor House, HC, 2016

BIOGRAPHIES

"The Obscure Life and Hard Times of Kilgore Trout," *Moebius Trip* (fanzine), 12/1971
Tarzan Alive, Doubleday, HC, 1972
Doc Savage: His Apocalyptic Life, Doubleday, HC, 1973; Bantam, PB, 1975 (revised); Meteor House, HC, 2013 (revised)
"Jonathan Swift Somers III: Cosmic Traveller in a Wheelchair," *Scintillation* (fanzine), 06/1977

COLLECTIONS

Strange Relations, Ballantine Books, PB, 1960
The Alley God, Ballantine Books, PB, 1962
The Celestial Blueprint, Ace Books, PB, 1962
Down in the Black Gang, Nelson Doubleday, HC, 1971
The Book of Philip José Farmer, DAW Books, PB, 1973
Riverworld and Other Stories, Berkley Books, PB, 1979
Riverworld War, The Ellis Press, TPB, 1980
Father to the Stars, Pinnacle/Tor Books, PB, 1981
The Cache, Pinnacle/Tor Books, PB, 1981
The Purple Book, Tor Books, PB, 1982
The Classic Philip José Farmer 1952–1964, Crown Publishers, HC, 1984
The Classic Philip José Farmer 1964–1973, Crown Publishers, HC, 1984
The Grand Adventure, Berkley Books, TPB, 1984
Riders of the Purple Wage, Tor Books, PB, 1992
The Best of Philip José Farmer, Subterranean Press, HC, 2006
Pearls from Peoria, Subterranean Press, HC, 2006
Up from the Bottomless Pit and Other Stories, Subterranean Press, HC, 2007
Venus on the Half-Shell and Others, Subterranean Press, HC, 2008
Up the Bright River, Subterranean Press, HC, 2011
Tales of the Wold Newton Universe, Titan Books, TPB, 2013

ANTHOLOGIES—Edited by Philip José Farmer.

Mother Was a Lovely Beast, Chilton Book Company, HC, 1974
Tales of Riverworld, Warner Books, PB, 1992
Quest to Riverworld, Warner Books, PB, 1993

SHORT FICTION—The list includes his stories, poems, serials, extracts, fictional biographies, and outlines. Some stories were written much earlier than published, because of their later discovery.

"O'Brien and Obrenov," *Adventure*, 03/1946

"Imagination," (poem), *America Sings*, 1949

"Good But Not Good Enough," (poem), *Bradley Quarterly*, 08/1949

"The Lovers," *Startling Stories*, 08/1952

"Sail On! Sail On!" *Startling Stories,* 12/1952

"The Pterodactyl," (poem), *Sky Hook* (fanzine), Winter 1952–1953

"Sestina of the Space Rocket," (poem), *Startling Stories,* 02/1953

"The Biological Revolt," *Science-Fiction Plus*, 03/1953

"Mother," *Thrilling Wonder Stories*, 04/1953

"Moth and Rust," *Startling Stories*, 06/1953

"Beauty in this Iron Age," (poem), *Starlanes* (fanzine), Fall 1953

"Attitudes," *Fantasy and Science Fiction*, 10/1953

"Strange Compulsion," *Science-Fiction* plus, 10/1953

"They Twinkled Like Jewels," *Fantastic Universe*, 01/1954

"Daughter," *Thrilling Wonder Stories*, Winter 1954

"Queen of the Deep," (aka "Son"), *Argosy*, 03/1954

"The God Business," *Beyond Fantasy Fiction*, 03/1954

"In Common," (poem), *Starlanes* (fanzine), 04/1954

"Rastignac the Devil," *Fantastic Universe*, 05/1954

"The Celestial Blueprint," *Fantastic Universe*, 07/1954

"The Wounded," *Fantastic Universe*, 10/1954

"Totem and Taboo," *Fantasy and Science Fiction*, 12/1954

"Black Squirrel on Cottonwood Limb's Tip," (poem), *Sky Hook* (fanzine), Winter 1954–1955

"Father," *Fantasy and Science Fiction*, 07/1955

"The Night of Light," *Fantasy and Science Fiction*, 06/1957

"The Alley Man," *Fantasy and Science Fiction*, 06/1959

"Heel," *If,* 05/1960

"Open to Me, My Sister," (aka "My Sister's Brother"), *Fantasy and Science Fiction*, 05/1960

"A Few Miles," *Fantasy and Science Fiction*, 10/1960

"Prometheus," *Fantasy and Science Fiction*, 03/1961

"Job's Leviathan," (poem), *First Fandom Magazine* (fanzine), 06/1961

"Tongues of the Moon," *Amazing Stories*, 09/1961

"Uproar in Acheron," *The Saint Mystery Magazine* (UK), 11/1961

"How Deep the Grooves," *Amazing Stories*, 02/1963

"Some Fabulous Yonder," *Fantastic*, 04/1963

"The Blasphemers," *Galaxy*, 04/1964

"The King of the Beasts," *Galaxy*, 06/1964

"Day of the Great Shout," *Worlds of Tomorrow*, 01/1965

"The Many Dooms of Harold Hall," (as by Charlotte Corday-Marat; attributed to Philip José Farmer), *Bizarre! Mystery Magazine*, 11/1965

"Riverworld," *Worlds of Tomorrow*, 01/1966

"The Suicide Express," *Worlds of Tomorrow*, 03/1966

"The Blind Rowers," *Knight*, 03/1967

"The Felled Star (part 1)," *If*, 07/1967

"The Felled Star (part 2)," *If*, 08/1967

"A Bowl Bigger than Earth," *If*, 09/1967

"Riders of the Purple Wage," **Dangerous Visions**, Doubleday, 1967

"The Shadow of Space," *If*, 11/1967

"Don't Wash the Carats," **Orbit 3**, Putnam, 1968

"The Jungle Rot Kid on the Nod," *Broadside*, 1968

"Down in the Black Gang," *If*, 03/1969

"The Oögenesis of Bird City," *Amazing Science Fiction Stories*, 09/1970

"The Voice of the Sonar in my Vermiform Appendix," **Quark/2**, Paperback Library, 1971

"The Fabulous Riverboat (part 1)," *If*, 06/1971

"The Fabulous Riverboat (part 2)," *If*, 08/1971

"Brass and Gold," **Quark/4**, Paperback Library, 1971

"The Sliced-Crosswise Only-on-Tuesday World," **New Dimensions 1**, Doubleday, 1971

"Only Who Can Make a Tree?" *Fantasy and Science Fiction*, 11/1971

"Tarzan Lives," (aka "An Exclusive Interview with Lord Greystoke") *Esquire*, 04/1972

"Seventy Years of Decpop," *Galaxy*, 07–08/1972

"The Sumerian Oath," **Nova 2**, Walker, 1972

"Skinburn," *Fantasy and Science Fiction*, 10/1972

"Father's in the Basement," **Orbit 11**, Putnam, 1972

"Towards the Beloved City," **Signs and Wonders**, Revell, 1972

"Mother Earth Wants You," **And Walk Now Gently Through the Fire**, Chilton, 1972

"Sketches Among the Ruins of My Mind," **Nova 3**, Walker, 1973

"Monolog," **Demon Kind**, Avon, 1973

"After King Kong Fell," **Omega**, Walker, 1973

"Opening the Door," **Children of Infinity**, Watts, 1973

"The Two-Edged Gift," **Continuum 1**, Putnam, 1974

"The Startouched," **Continuum 2**, Berkley/Putnam, 1974

"Extracts from the Memoirs of 'Lord Greystoke,'" **Mother Was a Lovely Beast**, Chilton, 1974

"The Evolution of Paul Eyre," **Continuum 3**, Berkley/Putnam, 1974

"Venus on the Half-Shell (Part 1)," (as by Kilgore Trout) *Fantasy and Science Fiction*, 12/1974

"Venus on the Half-Shell (Part 2)," (as by Kilgore Trout) *Fantasy and Science Fiction*, 01/1975

"A Scarletin Study," (as by Jonathan Swift Somers III) *Fantasy and Science Fiction*, 03/1975

"Passing On," **Continuum 4**, Berkley/Putnam, 1975

"The Problem of the Sore Bridge—Among Others," (as by Harry Manders) *Fantasy and Science Fiction*, 09/1975

"Greatheart Silver in Showdown at Shootout," **Weird Heroes, Volume 1**, Pyramid, 1975

"The Return of Greatheart Silver," **Weird Heroes, Volume 2**, Pyramid, 1975

"The Volcano," (as by Paul Chapin) *Fantasy and Science Fiction*, 02/1976

"Osiris on Crutches," (with Leo Queequeg Tincrowdor) **New Dimensions 6**, Harper & Row, 1976

"The Doge Whose Barque Was Worse Than His Bight," (as by Jonathan Swift Somers III) *Fantasy and Science Fiction*, 11/1976

"Fundamental Issue," *Amazing Science Fiction*, 12/1976

"Greatheart Silver in the First Command," **Weird Heroes, Volume 6**, Pyramid, 1977

"The Impotency of Bad Karma," (aka "The Last Rise of Nick Adams") (as by Cordwainer Bird) *Popular Culture*, 06/1977

"Savage Shadow," (as by Maxwell Grant) **Weird Heroes, Volume 8**, Jove/HBJ, 1977

"The Henry Miller Dawn Patrol," *Playboy*, 12/1977

"It's the Queen of Darkness, Pal," (aka "The Phantom of the Sewers") (as by Rod Keen) *Fantasy and Science Fiction*, 08/1978

"The Freshman," *Fantasy and Science Fiction*, 05/1979

"The Leaser of Two Evils," *Playboy*, 07/1979

"J. C. on the Dude Ranch," **Riverworld and Other Stories**, Berkley, 1979

"Jesus on Mars," **Riverworld War**, The Ellis Press, 1980

"Riverworld War," **Riverworld War**, The Ellis Press, 1980

"The Making of Revelation, Part 1," **After the Fall**, Ace, 1980

"Spiders of the Purple Mage," **Tales from the Vulgar Unicorn**, Ace, 1980

"Rip Van Winkle's Long Wet Dream," (aka "The Long Wet Purple Dream of Rip Van Winkle") *Puritan*, 1981

"The Monster on Hold," (excerpt from unfinished novel) **World Fantasy Convention 1983**, 1983

"The Adventure of the Three Madmen," **The Grand Adventure**, Berkley, 1984

"Uranus or UFO Versus IRS," **The Planets**, Bantam, 1985

"St. Francis Kisses His Ass Goodbye," **Semiotext[e] SF**, AK Press, 1989

"One Down, One to Go," *Fantasy & Science Fiction*, 10/1990

"Evil, Be My Good," **World Fantasy Convention 1990**, 1990

"Nobody's Perfect," **The Ultimate Dracula**, Dell, 1991

"Wolf, Iron, and Moth," **The Ultimate Werewolf**, Dell, 1991

"Crossing the Dark River," **Tales of Riverworld**, Warner, 1992

"A Hole in Hell," (as by Dane Helstrom) **Tales of Riverworld**, Warner, 1992

"Up the Bright River," **Quest to Riverworld**, Warner, 1993

"Coda," **Quest to Riverworld**, Warner, 1993

"Naked Came the Farmer," *Accent*, 01/1998

"The Good of the Land," *RG Magazine* (Bermuda), 10–11/2002

"The Face That Launched a Thousand Eggs," *Farmerphile* #1 (fanzine), 07/2005

"Up from the Bottomless Pit (Part 1)," *Farmerphile* #1 (fanzine), 07/2005

"The Unnaturals," *Farmerphile* #2 (fanzine), 10/2005

"Up from the Bottomless Pit (Part 2)," *Farmerphile* #2 (fanzine), 10/2005

"That Great Spanish Author, Ernesto," *Farmerphile* #3 (fanzine), 01/2006

"Up from the Bottomless Pit (Part 3)," *Farmerphile* #3 (fanzine), 01/2006

"The Essence of the Poison," *Farmerphile* #4 (fanzine), 04/2006

"Up from the Bottomless Pit (Part 4)," *Farmerphile* #4 (fanzine), 04/2006

"The Doll Game," *Farmerphile* #5 (fanzine), 07/2006

"Up from the Bottomless Pit (Part 5)," *Farmerphile* #5 (fanzine), 07/2006

"Doc Savage and the Cult of the Blue God," **Pearls from Peoria**, Subterranean Press, 2006

"Hunter's Moon," **Pearls from Peoria**, Subterranean Press, 2006

"Planet Pickers," **Pearls from Peoria**, Subterranean Press, 2006

"The Princess of Terra," (as by Charlotte Corday-Marat) **Pearls from Peoria**, Subterranean Press, 2006

"The Rise Gotten," **Pearls from Peoria**, Subterranean Press, 2006

"The Terminalization of J. G. Ballard," **Pearls from Peoria**, Subterranean Press, 2006

"Keep Your Mouth Shut," *Farmerphile* #6 (fanzine), 10/2006

"Up from the Bottomless Pit (Part 6)," *Farmerphile* #6 (fanzine), 10/2006

"The Frames," *Farmerphile* #7 (fanzine), 01/2007

"The Light-Hog Incident," *Farmerphile* #7 (fanzine), 01/2007

"Up from the Bottomless Pit (Part 7)," *Farmerphile* #7 (fanzine), 01/2007

"A Spy in the U.S. of Gonococcia," *Farmerphile* #8 (fanzine), 04/2007

"Up from the Bottomless Pit (Part 8)," *Farmerphile* #8 (fanzine), 04/2007

"Up from the Bottomless Pit (Part 9)," *Farmerphile* #9 (fanzine), 07/2007

"The Rebels Unthawed," **Up from the Bottomless Pit and Other Stories**, Subterranean Press, 2007

"A Peoria Night," **Up from the Bottomless Pit and Other Stories**, Subterranean Press, 2007

"Up from the Bottomless Pit (Part 10)," *Farmerphile* #10 (fanzine), 10/2007

"The First Robot," *Farmerphile* #11 (fanzine), 01/2008

"Duo Miaule," *Farmerphile* #11 (fanzine), 01/2008

"Down to Earth's Centre," *Farmerphile* #12 (fanzine), 04/2008

"Getting Ready to Write," (with Paul Spiteri) *Farmerphile* #13 (fanzine), 07/2008

"Cougar by the Tail," (excerpt from unfinished novel) *Farmerphile* #15 (fanzine), 01/2009

"Newly Born, Newly Dead," **The Worlds of Philip José Farmer: Protean Dimensions**, Meteor House, 2010

"My Summer Husband," **The Worlds of Philip José Farmer: Protean Dimensions**, Meteor House, 2010

"What I Thought I Heard," **The Worlds of Philip José Farmer: Of Dust and Soul**, Meteor House, 2011

"Strangers & Brothers: Francis Uquart," **The Worlds of Philip José Farmer: Of Dust and Soul**, Meteor House, 2011

"Kwasin and the Bear God," (with Christopher Paul Carey) **The Worlds of Philip José Farmer: Of Dust and Soul**, Meteor House, 2011

NON-FICTION—The list includes articles, essays, reviews, autobiographies, and published speeches. It does not include the many introductions, forewords, afterwords, etc. written for both his and other author's works, nor published letters.

"Introduction," (autobiography) *Adventure*, 03/1946

"Lovers and Otherwise," *Fantastic Worlds 3* (fanzine), Spring 1953

"The Tin Woodman Slams the Door," *Destiny 10* (fanzine), Summer 1954

"White Whales, Raintrees, Flying Saucers . . ." *Fantastic Universe*, 07/1954

"Parables are Pablum: A Reply to Mr. Farmer, a Letter to Mr. Campbell," *Sky Hook* (fanzine), Winter 1954–1955

"The Golden Age and the Brass," *The Burroughs Bulletin* #12 (fanzine), 1956

"Like Some Opinions: Philip José Farmer," *SaFari Annual* #1 (fanzine), 04/1960

"On a Mountain Upside Down," *JD Argassy* #55 (fanzine), 1960

"Blueprint for Free Beer," *Knight*, Volume 6, No. 1, 07/1967

"Reap," *Science Fiction Review* #28 (fanzine), 11/1968

"Oft Have I Travelled," *The Pontine Dossier* Vol. 2 No. 2 (fanzine), 04/1969

"Reply to Questionnaire," **The Double:Bill Symposium**, D:B Press, 1969

"Report," *Luna* 6 (fanzine), 1969

"Introduction (Memoir)," **Special Wonder**, Random House, 03/1970

"Book Reviews," *Science Fiction Review* #39 (fanzine), 08/1970

"The Arms of Tarzan," *The Burroughs Bulletin* #22 (fanzine), Summer 1971

"Tarzan's Coat of Arms," *ERB-dom* #52 (fanzine), 11/1971

"A Reply to 'The Red Herring,'" *Erbania* #28 (fanzine), 12/1971

"The Two Lord Ruftons," *The Baker Street Journal* Vol. 21 No. 4 (fanzine), 12/1971

"The Great Korak-Time Discrepancy," *ERB-dom* #57 (fanzine), 04/1972

"The Lord Mountford Mystery," *ERB-dom* #65 (fanzine), 12/1972

"Writing the Biography of Doc Savage," *Pulp* #5½ (fanzine), 07/1973

"From ERB to Ygg (Part 1)," *ERBivore* #6–7 (fanzine), 08/1973

"Getting A-Long with Heinlein," *Moebius Trip Library S.F. Echo* #19 (fanzine), 01/1974

"Charles R. Tanner," *Locus* #155, 02/1974

"A Language for Opar," *ERB-dom* #75 (fanzine), 02/1974

"To the Wizard of Sci-Fi," **Lunacon '74** (program), 04/1974

"The Feral Human in Mythology and Fiction," **Mother Was A Lovely Beast**, Chilton, 1974

"Some Comments," (aka "The Source of the River") *Moebius Trip Library's S.F. Echo* #22 (fanzine), 04/1975

"Philip José Farmer Sez . . ." (aka "A Fimbulwinter Introduction") *Apart* #3 (fanzine), 08/1976

"Phonemics," *Gegenschein* #27 (fanzine), 1976

"How Dinosaurs Did It," *Citadel* (fanzine), 1976

"Religion and Myths," **The Visual Encyclopedia of Science Fiction**, Pan Books, 1977

"Farmer's Lupoff Week," *Algol* #31 (fanzine), Spring 1978

"The Remarkable Adventure," **Science Fiction: Contemporary Mythology**, Harper & Row, 06/1978

"The Affair of Logical Lunatics," *Farmerage* Vol. 1 No. 3 (fanzine), 02/1979

"Creating Artificial Worlds," *Pulsar* (fanzine), Summer 1979

"Farmer Writes," **Science Fiction and Fantasy Literature (Vol. 2)**, Gale Research, 1979

"Philip José Farmer," **World Authors** (1970–1975), The H.W. Wilson Company, 1980

"Maps and Spasms," **Fantastic Lives**, Southern Illinois University Press, 01/1981

"Farmer on Wilson," (aka "God's Hat") *Heavy Metal* #54, 09/1981

"The Man Who Came for Christmas," **The Best of Randall Garrett**, Timescape, 01/1982

"Pornograms and Supercomputers," *New York Times Book Review*, 09/1984

"Edgar Rice Burroughs," (aka "An Appreciation of Edgar Rice Burroughs") **20th Century Fiction**, Gale/St. James, 1985

"L. Frank Baum," (aka "Witches and Gnomes and Talking Animals, Oh My") **20th Century Fiction**, Gale/St. James, 1985

"Memoir," (aka "R.I.P. *If*) **Worlds of If**, Bluejay, 1986

"Remembering Vern," *Erbania* #57 (fanzine), 09/1987

"The Journey," (aka "The Journey as the Revelation of the Unknown") **The New Encyclopedia of Science Fiction**, Viking, 1988

"Hayy ibn Yaqzam, by Abu ibn Tufayl: An Arabic Mowgli," *Journal of the Fantastic in the Arts* Vol. 3 No. 3, 1991

"Special Review by Philip José Farmer," (aka "Review of *How the Wizard Came to Oz*") *Locus* #380, 09/1992

"An Appreciation (Robert Bloch)," *Locus* #406, 11/1994

"More Than Most," **Robert Bloch: Appreciations of the Master**, Tor, 1995

"A Letter from Philip José Farmer on His Hadon of Opar Books" **Heritage of the Flaming God**, Waziri Publications, 1999

"Dede Weil: An Appreciation," *Locus* #479, 12/2000

"Acceptance Speech," **Nebula Awards Showcase 2002**, Roc, 2002

"I Still Live!" *Farmerphile* #3 (fanzine), 01/2006

"Why Do I Write?" *Farmerphile* #4 (fanzine), 04/2006

"The Purple Distance," **Pearls from Peoria**, Subterranean Press, 2006

"A Rough Knight for the Queen," **Pearls from Peoria**, Subterranean Press, 2006

"The Brueckel/Harwood Letter," *Farmerphile* #9 (fanzine), 07/2007

"Jongor in the Wold Newton Family," *Farmerphile* #12 (fanzine), 04/2008

"Sherlock Holmes and Sufism—and Related Subjects," *Farmerphile* #12 (fanzine), 04/2008

"Three Metafictional Proposals," *Farmerphile* #12 (fanzine), 04/2008

"Uncle Sam's Mad Tea Party," *Farmerphile* #12 (fanzine), 04/2008

"Polytropical Paramyths," *Farmerphile* #13, 07/2008

"The Wild Weird Clime," *Farmerphile* #13, 07/2008

"Doc Wildman's Coat of Arms," *Farmerphile* #14, 10/2008

"Greatheart Silver Notes," *Farmerphile* #14, 10/2008

"Buddha Contemplates His Novel," *Farmerphile* #15, 01/2009

"Myadzian Journal," *Farmerphile* #15, 01/2009

"Riverworld Dawn Notes," *Farmerphile* #15, 01/2009

"Time Has Its Mirages," *Farmerphile* #15, 01/2009

"The Legend of Mishiwapo," **The Worlds of Philip José Farmer: Protean Dimensions**, Meteor House, 2010

"A Writer's Prayer," **The Worlds of Philip José Farmer: Protean Dimensions**, Meteor House, 2010

"Philip José Farmer on Roger Zelazny," **FarmerCon V** (program), 2010

"Faith in 2097," **The Worlds of Philip José Farmer: Of Dust and Soul**, Meteor House, 2011

"Mark Twain and Kurt Vonnegut Versus Free Will," **The Worlds of Philip José Farmer: Of Dust and Soul**, Meteor House, 2011

"A Slender Tribute to a Big Man," **The Worlds of Philip José Farmer: Of Dust and Soul**, Meteor House, 2011

"Strangers & Brothers: Pitch to Publishers," **The Worlds of Philip José Farmer: Of Dust and Soul**, Meteor House, 2011

"Over All, After All," **The Worlds of Philip José Farmer: Portraits of a Trickster**, Meteor House, 2012

"Pecon 2 Guest of Honor Speech," **The Worlds of Philip José Farmer: Voyages to Strange Days**, Meteor House, 2014

Compiling a high-level bibliography of Philip José Farmer's works isn't as straightforward as one might expect. Such an extensive and varied publishing history inevitably throws up many challenges when trying to sort and categorize his work. The approach taken here is logical and as consistent as possible. Hopefully a smile or two will cross your lips as you read over the titles of Phil's extensive oeuvre.

For a far more complete bibliography, including all known reprints of novels, stories, and nonfiction, as well as an exhaustive list of foreign editions, please visit Zacharias L.A. Nuninga's outstanding Philip José Farmer International Bibliography website at www.philipjosefarmer.com.

METEOR HOUSE TITLES

THE WORLDS OF PHILIP JOSÉ FARMER
Anthology Series edited by Michael Croteau
Volume 1: Protean Dimensions
Volume 2: Of Dust and Soul
Volume 3: Portraits of a Trickster
Volume 4: Voyages to Strange Days

The Best of Farmerphile edited by Michael Croteau

WOLD NEWTON SERIES
Doc Savage: His Apocalyptic Life by Philip José Farmer
Tarzan and the Dark Heart of Time by Philip José Farmer

THE KHOKARSA SERIES
Exiles of Kho by Christopher Paul Carey
Flight to Opar (Restored Edition) by Philip José Farmer
The Song of Kwasin by Philip José Farmer and Christopher Paul Carey
Hadon, King of Opar by Christopher Paul Carey
Blood of Ancient Opar by Christopher Paul Carey

THE PAT WILDMAN SERIES
The Evil in Pemberley House by Philip José Farmer and Win Scott Eckert
The Scarlet Jaguar by Win Scott Eckert

THE PHILEAS FOGG SERIES
Phileas Fogg and the War of Shadows by Josh Reynolds
Phileas Fogg and the Heart of Osra by Josh Reynolds

Visit us at meteorhousepress.com